MIRANDA;

OR,

THE HEIRESS OF THE GRANGE.

A ROMANCE,

BY THE AUTHOR OF "ADA THE BETRAYED," "JANE BRIGHTWELL,"
&c., &c., &c.

LONDON

PREFACE.

The judicial records of this country afford us, unfortunately, too many instances of the danger of forming a judgment upon merely circumstantial evidence, even when that evidence appears most clear and condemnatory of the accused. Men have been tried, convicted and executed, protesting their innocence to the last ; but the stain of crime has remained upon their memory for years, till perhaps the chance revelation of some despairing sinner on his death-bed, has declared the really guilty, and amidst unavailing regrets it has been confessed that an innocent man had suffered through a judge and jury's confidence in circumstantial evidence.

It was partly to illustrate this fact that the following tale was written ; and it will not have been penned in vain if any one should by its perusal be led to suspend his judgment on his fellow man, and even when appearances are blackest, to " lean to mercy's side.'

The aim of the novelist should be to pourtray nature in all its aspects ; but while he thus holds up the mirror he should not forget that he wields an instrument powerful for good or for evil, and in his transcripts from humanity he should endeavour, as the author trusts he has done in the present work, to elevate virtue and nobleness—to show how the pure, and the truthful, and the innocent, achieve, even in their sufferings, a higher triumph than can ever be attained amid the turbulence of vice.

London, September, 1848.

MIRANDA.

A Romance.

CHAPTER I.

THE DUEL.

"On the twentieth day of November, 1767, two men were executed at York, for a murder unequalled in its atrocity and remarkable for the mode in which it was perpetrated."

The above brief announcement of the conclusion of a domestic tragedy, which in its coarser features only met the eyes of the world, has awakened dormant recollections, and aroused from the slumbering cells of memory, scenes and events which together with their actors have passed away, but which still, according to their various phases of joy or sorrow, produce tears or smiles upon the face of those who with a reverential love look back upon the dreary past.

* * * * *

The season was autumn, and although the latter end of October

No. 1.

wa s fast approaching, nature st I looked beautiful in the maturity of her charms The trees wore a thousand different magical tints, and the morerich and lovely of the summer flowers were yet lingering in their dazzling beauty, as if loath to leave the world to the chill and cheerless dominion of the coming winter. The keen northern blast was, however, rapidly stripping the trees of the hardy leaves which had long outlived their fellows, and the sunshine, although bright and beautiful, was could and white, presenting but a faint mockery of the genial glow of the vernal season.

On a morning such as this, at the early hour of six, when but a dim and uncertain light gleamed from the awakening east, two figures stood in a shallow valley, some half a mile from an irregular but picturesque building, situated about five miles from York, and called from time immemorial "The Grange."

The two figures were those of men, but as dissimilar in personal appearance as any two human beings could be. One was a man apparently past the meridian, of life, tall and fair, with that irresolute and undecided expression of countenance, denoted by the half open mouth, ever shifting eye, and general want of firm purpose in all his movements.

The other was shorter, and his dark brilliant eyes were well contrasted with a deep olive complexion and a firm compressed mouth, which showed that for good or for evil he would hold his purpose. At the first glance this man might have been thought handsome, but although a more minute investigation of his features, might not entirely do away with the first impression, it would modify it in a peculiar manner, and that was, there did not appear one kindly feeling in the expression of the physiognomy, and people would shrink from Bernard Varley instinctively and they knew not why.

The air was loaded with a damp mist in the low ground where they stood, and its excessive coldness brought a shiver to the limbs of the tallest and the finest of the two men, as he remarked to his companion, in his usual irresolute tone and manner,—

"Varley, the air is keen. You will look to my girl, should anything befal me. My poor fond Miranda—you will miss your father. You solemnly promise me, Varley, to uphold her interest—to watch over her ?"

"Could I," rejoined the other, " be so unhappy as to lose so good a friend as yourself, I should have but one consolation, and that would be that the fair Miranda would allow me to fulfil a father's place."

"You—you would marry her ?"

"Even now—twice rejected I would."

As he said the words, twice rejected, an expression of a perfectly demoniac character crossed his face, and the fire of smothered feeling flashed for a moment from his eye.

" The affections are not our own," said the other sadly, " we cannot make them dependant upon the will."

" No, Sir George Rankley, but——"

He paused, and silently pointed in the direction of the rising sun, as he laid his other hand lightly upon the shoulder of Sir George Rankley, who was his companion.

" They are coming," he said.

Two dim figures by the uncertain light that prevailed, were seen slowly approaching, and as they neared Sir George and Varley, some clock far off chimed the quarter-past six.

"Now, Varley," said Rankley, "as Heaven is my judge, let the issue of this contest be what it may, I have been forced into it."

"Forced ? said Varley, his cheek reddening. "Yes, forced by insult past endurance. Yes—yes, most true—most true. You have been hardly used. Think again of those injuries, and nerve yourself to expiate your wrongs upon the head of him who has inflicted them."

" The issue of such contests as these, Varley," said Sir George, " is in the hands Heaven."

" Is it ?" muttered Varley to himself.

" It is for my—Miranda—my child, that I feel now pangs more exquisite than even death can inflict upon me."

" Should your worst fears be accomplished," remarked Varley, with a scarcely perceptible sneer, " you leave behind you Bernard Varley, a warm friend."

Sir George shuddered, and the other immediately added,—

" You view the matter too seriously. The Squire of Larkswood may fall."

" Crime upon crime!" muttered or rather groaned Sir George Rankley, " murder, for such it is, added to——"

" Hush!" cried Varley ; " let not that word pass your lips ! No more. no w The time has come for action !"

" It has indeed. I feel it has," said Sir George Rankley. " I am prepared."

The approaching parties now paused, and at the moment there came a straggling beam of sunlight from the distant horizon, which for some minutes previous had been obscured by clouds, which, falling on the side of the gentle declivity, at the base of which the four men now stood, imparted to the scene a rich and varied beauty it could not before pretend to.

" You must remain where you are," said Varley to his principal, " while I settle the necessary preliminaries."

With these words he advanced towards the new arrivals, and bowing with much courtesy, although it seemed a little overstrained, he said,—

" Does the Squire of Larkswood offer a humble apology?"

" No, sir, he does not," replied one of the new-comers, a gentlemanly-looking man. " The Squire of Larkswood never yet did or said what he was ashamed of. It is for your principal to humbly apologise, if he has so much grace left him."

" Then, sir, we proceed," said Varley, " as we can accept nothing but the most humble and submissive apology."

There was about his tone a sneering air of insincerity as he spoke, which, coupled with the words themselves, evidently produced an effect that by his lurking smile he looked for and wished to see.

" This is really quite irregular," suggested he who had not yet spoken. " I believe I have the—the honour to address Mr. Bernard Varley?"

" My name is Varley, sir ; and in this business I act as second to Sir George Rankley. You, I presume, perform the same friendly office to the Squire of Larkswood?"

The squire himself fell back several paces, while the seconds advanced together.

He was a fine specimen of an English gentleman, and he glanced towards Sir George Rankley with a look of painful regret, while the latter's eyes were fixed upon the gable-ends of the old Grange, which could just be seen above its shield of trees, glancing in the morning light, and its ancient rugged outlines made beautiful by the sunlight that was momentarily increasing now in brilliancy. The thoughts were evidently of a painful nature that were passing through his mind ; for tears slowly filled his eyes, and prevented him, after a few brief moments, from seeing anything clearly ; so he turned away his head, and with one long-drawn sigh appeared to have taken a last farewell of his home. But what was that home to him, endeared as it was by a thousand associations, compared with the enthusiastic love he bore to one within its ancient walls, who slept the calm sleep of innocence and youth, while he, her father, was from home on such an unholy errand as his present one. Yes ; his child, his dear, beautiful Miranda, the last of her race, slept on in peace, while such a storm was hovering over her young head as she, in the wildest moment of her fancy, could not have pictured to herself, or had she done so, would have smiled at the dreamy improbability of the imaginary circumstances.

" My child—my dear Miranda," thought Sir George,—" am I never to see you more, my own beautiful child? Heaven knows that by some fell agency I have been hurried into this act, I know not how. May——"

" Twelve paces, and I have won for you the light," whispered, at this moment, Varley in the ear of Sir George. " Are you ready ?"

" Quite—quite."

In a few more moments the combatants were placed in their proper stations, and then Bernard Varley raising his voice, said,—

" Gentlemen, your signal for firing will be my dropping this glove. Are you quite ready ?"

" One moment yet, Squire of Larkswood," said Sir George Rankley. " As Heaven is my judge, I come to this extremity with you most reluctantly. We are both fathers—both love our children——"

His voice faltered, and he could not proceed ; which his opponent perceiving, he in his turn spoke, saying mildly, but firmly,—

" Sir George Rankley, time was when there was not a hand in all Yorkshire I could have grasped with more honest fervour than yours ; but the insults you have heaped upon me—the contumely which you have so wantonly——"

" Gentlemen," interposed Bernard Varley, " shall I retire along with the friend of the squire, while with mutual civil regrets you terminate this business between you ? I am a peace-maker as you both know, and have laboured to avert this meeting ; even now it appears to me, that any humble apology on each side may avert hostilities."

" Sir George, I fear you have been ill-advised," said the squire ; " why did you write to me in the terms you did ?"

" I did but retort," said Sir George. " You know, Varley, how unwilling I was."

" Enough—enough," said the squire, " we have gone too far to retreat."

" Not so, gentleman," said Varley, " you can each of you go comfortably to your houses, setting a peaceful example to the whole country. Some people may certainly smile at the Christian forbearance of Sir George Rankley and the great squire of Larkswood, who after defying each other to mortal conflict, made up matters on the battle field ; but what of that, gentlemen—you will have the approbation of all lovers of peace, all men of sound discretion."

The Squire of Larkswood turned and gazed full upon the eyes of Varley as he said slowly and distinctly :—

" I have received from Sir George Rankley insults which the usages of society compel me to resent ; but as for you, sir, I hold you as a villain."

A deadly paleness spread over the face of Varley as he replied,—

" There may come a time, sir, when your too candid avowal of your opinions may cost you dear."

The second of the Squire of Larkswood was a mild, inoffensive looking man, who seemed too timid to venture any opinion of his own, and during the whole of the foregoing dialogue, he had looked from one speaker to the other in a nervous state of mind, not knowing very well what to say or do. It was a relief to him when Varley now hastily added,—

" Sir George, are you quite ready ?" and at the same moment held his glove at arm's length. Not a word now was spoken—the glove fell—one sharp ringing report awakened echoes far and near—an execration burst from the lips of Varley, as he saw that both the combatants were standing apparently quite uninjured.

It was but for a moment, though, that they thus stood, and then, with a shudder, Sir George Rankley placed his hand upon his breast, and turning round upon his heels, he made several desperate plunges to keep his feet, after which, with a gasp, he fell heavily upon the green sward.

CHAPTER II.

THE MEETING.

The Squire of Larkswood was the first to fly towards the fallen man, and, kneeling by his side, he said feelingly,—

"Rankley, Rankley, speak to me. Oh, what a madman I have been to do this deed! Rankley, my friend, my old companion, speak to me—speak to me."

"He is not much hurt," said the squire's second, as he tore open the coat and waistcoat of Sir George, and showed that the wound was high in the shoulder; "he has only fainted from the shock the system has received. Come, we have some water."

"There is a spring not a hundred yards along the valley," said the squire; "take my hat—quick—quick."

Varley stood with his arms folded across his breast, gazing upon the prostrate man, but taking no part in the proceedings for his recovery. Such conduct, however, seemed rather the result of want of thought at the moment than a determination to be a mere spectator of the scene, for he suddenly roused himself, like one awakening from a sleep, and affected a degree of officiousness about Sir George Rankley that was strongly at variance with his former indifference.

The water was brought in the squire's hat, and, upon dashing some of it in the face of Sir George, he gave a convulsive shudder, and opened his eyes.

"Rankley, you are not much hurt," cried the squire; "all will be well again."

"What has happened?" said the wounded man.

"A mere scratch," continued the squire; "come, come, think nothing of it."

"We had better," said Varley, "get Sir George home as quickly as possible. This may not turn out such a mere scratch as you may suppose."

"I want none of your ill-omened croaking," cried the squire, "peace, sir. From my soul something strikes me that by some hellish means you have produced all this unhappiness. There's a lurking devil in every line of your countenance. By Heavens, I was mad to be made your tool! A film appears now to have fallen from my eyes. Bernard Varley, you are a villain."

There was a tempest of passion evidently labouring in the breast of Varley, but by a strong effort he repressed its exhibition, and merely replied,—

"You do well, sir, after placing the life of him you call your old friend in such great jeopardy, to turn upon me. I say you do well, sir. Should you find your way to the York assizes for the murder of Sir George Rankley, I presume your line of defence will be in character with your present conduct. Perhaps, too, you can find some excuse for provoking this quarrel you have brought to so successful a termination in your dislike to Bernard Varley."

The Squire of Larkswood was about to make some angry reply, when a scream smote his ears with such terrible distinctness, that he involuntarily clasped his hands in horror, and was afraid to turn his eyes in the direction from whence it came.

"Miranda is coming," said Varley; "she has recognised, from the brow of yon eminence, who it is who lies so bloody and still at your feet. Squire of Larkswood, she is coming—shall I or you explain this little tragedy?"

"Father—father," cried a young and beautiful girl, attired in a morning dress, and her long and glossy auburn ringlets serving as her only head dress, as she threw herself on her knees by the side of the wounded baronet. "Father—oh, what has happened? There is blood upon you; oh, Heaven help me! Why do you look upon me, gentlemen, with such pitying eyes? Can none of you tell me what is the meaning of all this? Father, father, speak to me. It is your child—your Miranda, who calls you. Help, help! he does not speak; he does not move. Who killed my father? who spilt his blood? Show me the man. Squire of Larkswood, you look pale and wan—speak, oh speak!"

The squire turned his face away, and uttered no sound, but Varley stooped to the ear of the beautiful girl, and whispered,—

"Miranda!"

She immediately sprang to her feet, and, as she stood by the again insensible form of her father, she pointed with both hands at Varley, and in a voice of awful solemnity, she said,—

"It—it is all true—you are here to confirm the vision sent by Heaven, to warn me of this deed of blood. Bernard Varley, since you, by some mysterious means, ensnared my poor father's soul, the shadow of some terrible catastrophe has been hanging like a funeral pall upon my mind—and—and now it is consummated. All is revealed—I know you—I know you."

For a moment, but no more, Varley stood the fixed gaze of that fair young creature, and then as she continued speaking, he cowered before her, and shrunk back, although he seemed unable to withdraw his eye from hers. He trembled in every limb, and the big drops of perspiration stood upon his brow as he muttered,—

"Miranda Rankley, what mean you? I am your father's friend. You are raving."

"What brought me here?" she said.

"I know not."

"I have had a dream, Bernard Varley—an awful dream. Shall I relate it to you? I—I——"

She cast her eyes upon her father at this moment, and her excitement gave way in a moment. She sunk upon his bleeding form, and wept with a bitterness of anguish that was terrible to hear.

Varley drew a long breath and gave a sickly smile, as he said,—

"Well, well, I—suppose I am to be the butt of everybody's wild fancies. But here comes help."

There now approached the group a strange, grotesque figure. It was that of a young man, scarcely past the age of twenty, but habited in the most singular and opposite articles of costume that can be imagined. He wore a cast-off faded military coat, and dependent from a paper cap, that was placed jauntily upon one side of his head, was an immense bunch of various coloured ribbons. The rest of his person was dotted here and there by bows and long streaming ends of ribbon. He came forward with a wild bounding kind of step, that looked like an imitation of some wild animal, and, as he neared the party, he shouted,—

"Whoop, whoop—more sport. Where's the foremost dog? The hawk has had strange dreams."

"'Tis the poor idiot, Martin," said the squire, "but he can carry a message. Martin come hither."

The idiot either did not hear or did not heed the call of the squire, for he paused opposite to Varley, and, with a loud laugh, cried,—

"I dreamt of you last night. A famous dream."

"Indeed!"

"Yes, all night long. I've laughed ever since, and I've come on purpose to tell it to you. It's rather a secret though yet."

"Martin, run to the Grange," cried the squire, and bring some of the servants directly. Sir George is wounded."

"Wait a bit—wait a bit," said the idiot. "I must tell Bernard Varley my dream first."

"Nay, you need not go at all," said the squire, "for I see some of the household hurrying hither."

The idiot beckoned Varley, and placing his mouth close to his ear, he shouted,—

"I dreamt I saw you hanged at York!"

Varley changed colour, as he said,—

"Fool! how dare you!"

"Ha, ha, ha " roared the idiot, "I saw the crowd round the scaffold, so I pushed in among them, and some said, 'Let him see it—he knows the man.' Then I came quite close, but I didn't know you then, for a cap was over your face, but the corner of it was lifted up by some one, and then I knew you. Ha, ha, ha, Bernard Varley, I saw you hanged at York."

Varley sprung upon the idiot, and grasped him by the throat, as he cried,—

" I will stop your vile croaking, or know the reason why."

" Hands off," cried the squire ; " leave him whom God afflicted alone."

Varley released the poor creature, who said,—

" Well done, squire—well done, Bernard Varley will be hanged at York."

Four of the male domestics from the Grange now arrived upon the spot, and, with an air of malicious gratification, Varley cried,—

" Your master has been shot by his old friend, Mr. Percy, the Squire of Larkswood. Remove him gently home."

The men looked at each other perfectly bewildered for a moment, and nothing was said till the idiot shouted,—

" That may be all true, but Bernard Varley will be hanged at York."

The squire said not a word, but with the care of a father, he lifted the insensible form of Miranda, for she had fainted, from her father's breast, and motioning to the servants to lift their master, he set off for the Grange, scarcely feeling the light weight of the delicately lovely girl he carried.

The men carried their master among them, and followed the squire, with wonder, alarm, and grief depicted on their countenances. Varley tarried a few moments until they had got in advance of him. Then he raised his clenched hand and shook it menacingly as he muttered,—

" Sir George Rankley will never recover from that wound. An insurmountable barrier is raised between Miranda and the son of the Squire of Larkswood. I shall be master of the whole Grange ; Miranda will be dependant upon my bounty."

" And Bernard Varley will be hung at York," screamed the idiot, as he scoured off across the fields.

CHAPTER III.

THE MURDER.

At the hour of twelve that night there sat in a small antique room in the Grange, two men, upon whose pale and ghastly features the flickering light of a small lamp shone with an unsteady lustre. No one could have looked into the countenances of those men without a conviction that they had perpetrated, or were about to perpetrate, some awful crime, at which humanity might shudder. Even then they were suffering some of the pangs which would haunt them to their graves, and open for them an hereafter without hope. They were standing on the brink of that awful precipice of guilt, down which the murderer plunges, never—never to re-ascend to the height he had so madly dashed himself from. The minutes they were now passing were those horrible ones between the conception and the execution of the crime alike denounced by God and man—murder! and now that years had elapsed into months, months into weeks, weeks to days, until the actual hour had come for which they had plotted, longed, and toiled, they shrunk from themselves and from each other, aghast and trembling.

One of these men was Bernard Varley ; the other, a person of mean dimensions and crafty sinister aspect, who as he sat in his chair trembled so excessively, that he was fain to clutch the carved arms of it to give himself the least appearance of steadiness.

There was wine before them, and Varley now filled a brimming glass for each, and pushed in silence one over to his companion.

With cold and clammy fingers they clutched their glasses, and drained them off; but they might as well have drunk of the coldest spring, for all the reviving effect the generous liquid had upon them.   They remained cold and trembling as before.

"What is the time?" asked Bernard Varley.

"Some minutes after twelve," replied his companion.   "That wine is—is very cold."

"And the fire," added Varley, "gives no heat."

They both shivered as they spoke, and glanced uneasily at each other, after which another long pause ensued, which was at length broken by Varley, who said,

"You heard what the surgeon said."

"Yes, yes—I did. He said there was no danger whatever—none, none."

Varley turned his eyes upon the other, as he remarked, in a hollow voice,—

"But we know better. There is great danger—sudden and immediate danger."

"Yes, yes—there is. Shall we persevere, Varley, or—or now draw back?"

"Draw back! Are you mad? What have I striven for, for two years, and you for one? No, we will not draw back. Recollect your reward. The revenue of the Grange estates is about three thousand pounds per annum—you have one."

"Yes, that is understood."

"But Sir George must not recover. You have a great stake in this business, but I have a far greater. Rouse yourself—the time is near at hand."

"My strength will fail me, Varley; you had better depend upon yourself, and leave me here. I should, perhaps, mar everything—I am of weak nerves."

"Leave—you—here! And pray of what earthly use would your testimony be, if you are left here?"

"I—I will swear."

"I know you would, but your oaths want corroboration. Come you must—come you shall. The nurse is prepared for our visit; yes, I told her I would relieve her watch for an hour after midnight."

"Good. We have no time to lose. Drink—drink."

"The wine goes through my veins like ice. I will drink no more. 'Tis very strange how the mind will thus conquer the body, and change its very nature, so that fire will not warm—wine will not intoxicate."

"Pshaw," said Varley, trembling, as he nervously rubbed his hands together. "These are the feelings that ever wait on great actions before their execution. Come, we must go."

Varley rose as he spoke, and stood holding by the back of his chair, while with nervous haste his companion left his seat.

"It will be over soon," he added. "A moment's pang, and it is done. Then we begin, indeed, to reap a golden harvest."

Varley took up the lamp, and moved to the door, and the other tremblingly followed him; but before they left the room, he laid both his hands upon Varley's arm, and in a husky whisper, he said;—

"Shall—we—think—again?"

"No, we have now to act upon former thoughts."

"But—but, Varley. Consider."

The lamp shook in Varley's hand as his companion in guilt kept a trembling clutch of his arm, and continued to mutter,—

"But, Varley, if he should resist. You know one cry, and we are lost—lost for ever."

"Fool!" said Varley. "Do you see me tremble thus?"

"Your hand shakes, Varley."

"Let go my arm, and you will find it steady."

"A clammy moisture is upon your brow, and your lips are pale as ashes."

"The last meal not well digested will cause all these symptoms," said Varley, with so ghastly an imitation of a smile, that the other let go his arm, and recoiled from him in sudden fright.

"What now?" said Varley. "You are full of fancies."

"You looked dreadful, Varley. Do not try to smile again. 'Tis too horrible."

Varley bent his brows upon the man with anger, as he said, slowly and sternly,—

"Follow me at once. You have gone with me thus far, and I will not now allow you to pause. Come on. You are strangely timid of a wounded and enfeebled man."

"Oh, if the pistol of the squire had but been aimed at his heart, Varley, what would it not have spared us."

"I would it had; but such regrets are useless. The wound, which is not mortal, must be made so. A safer, easier mode than this, of—of——."

"Murdering!" said his trembling comrade.

"Have it so, if the term please you," continued Varley; "I say a safer mode could not be devised. Suspicion cannot be awakened; we shall be quite secure."

As Varley spoke, a pang came across him, for the words of the idiot seemed to be ringing in his ears, and he could almost—such was the power of imagination—have sworn he heard a voice say, "Bernard Varley shall be hanged at York."

He said no more, but, seizing the other by the arm, he led him from the room on to a landing, from whence a staircase led to the upper part of the house.

The lamp shed but a dim light as they in silence ascended the staircase, followed by their flickering shadows, which danced upon the walls and balustrades assuming many forms and strange shapes, grotesquing humanity.

How awful in the state between the conception and the perpetration of some crime at which humanity shudders, and which, even after its commission, leaves upon the shrinking soul a damned spot, which may not in this world, or that which is to come, ever cease to eat like molten lead into its inmost core.

But there are human passions which will turn men from humanity; there are dark feelings lying, like hideous coiled snakes, at the bottom of some men's hearts, which have but to be aroused from their lethargic state, and they will rise in all their glittering and lustrous deformity, carrying death and destruction to all.

Revenge and avarice will stir some minds to awful deeds. Ambition will induce some to stoop from the high pinnacle of innocence on which Heaven has placed them, and grovel in crime and iniquity, in order to seem great to those whose opinions they affect to despise and hold in utter contempt.

In these two men, who now crept shivering up the ancient staircase, might have been noted the two grand phases of action, which, however they might lead to a similar result, were widely different in themselves.

Bernard Varley's lips were compressed until all colour had forsaken them, and his features wore a livid paleness that made him resemble one newly arisen from the grave to commit some dreadful purpose that had been stayed by the hand of death. He moved, breathed, and spoke, not like a living man.

His companion, on the other hand, exhibited but one feeling, and that one was, cowardice. He had the will to have a deed of blood done by which he might reap advantage, but his courage failed him at the time of action.

Now, as he crawled after Varley, his knees shook under him, his teeth chattered, and he grasped the banisters of the stairs with a nervous energy that made his fingers crack again, and forced the blood from their joints, leaving them cold and stark, like the hands of some galvanised corpse.

Varley, when they had reached the landing of the first flight of stairs, turned to his companion, and in a low voice, which sounded hollow as if from some sepulchre, he said,—

"You tremble. It is too late now to shrink."

The other twined his arm in the banisters to support himself, as he replied with a ghastly attempt at a smile,—

"No—no—I—am firm—my nerves may be weak, but the object is a great one—a—very great one."

"It is, and if possible more advantageous to you than to me."

"I—I don't see that. The Lady Miranda is very beautiful."

No. 2.

" Pshaw ! what have you to do with beauty? Come on—each moment now is precious."

Varley now proceeded up the stairs, and the other cautiously followed him until they came to a door that was partially open, and through the crevice of which streamed a faint ray of light from a night lamp that burned in the chamber of the wounded man.

Varley turned and laid his fingers on his lips, and then slowly pushed open the door wide enough to allow him to pass into the chamber.

His companion followed him, and as they came fairly into the room a low, muttering voice came upon their ears.

" No—no—a mad thought—a mad thought—Varley save me—save me," murmured the wounded man, in the partial delirium occasioned by the shock his system had received.

The nurse, who was in the room, rose and curtseyed to Varley, who said in a low tone, pointing to the bed, around which the curtains were very carefully drawn,—

" Alas, he raves."

" Ah, poor soul," said the nurse, in a whisper, "he has been going on about something that I can't make out a bit. He keeps talking about a cheque and some money."

" Indeed!"

" Yes, sir. Don't you think he'd better have the quieting draught?"

" Yes, I intend to give him a quieting draught. We will relieve you now in your watch while you get an hour's repose."

" Thank you, sir—you are very good. Ah, poor gentleman, I'm afraid he's very bad."

" I'm afraid he's in great danger," said Varley, in a hollow voice.

" 'Tis the next crime to murder," muttered the wounded man.

Varley started, and his companion dropped into a seat with a heavy groan.

" Ah, poor soul," said the nurse, "that's the way he goes on."

" An hour's rest will refresh you," said Varley.

" Thank you, sir. If you should want me, I'm only up stairs. I'm very wakeful, dear heart. Ah, poor gentleman, he'll have a hard time of it, I know."

Shaking her head, and muttering to herself, the old woman left the room.

Then a sickness came over even Bernard Varley as he stood by the side of the bed, and listened to the heavy breathing of the man he had come deliberately to murder.

Neither spoke for some minutes. Then Varley beckoned with his finger to his comrade, and said,—

" Come."

The other slid from the chair on his knees, and in faltering accents, while he wrung his hands, he said,—

" Oh, spare him—spare him. Have mercy upon me, and upon him. Oh, Mr. Varley—I cannot—cannot. God help me, I cannot."

Varley ground his teeth together with passion, and raising his clenched hand, he struck the kneeling man in the face, which was in a moment covered with blood.

" Mercy—mercy," he groaned.

" Mercy," echoed the wounded man from the bed.

Varley leaned his head down until his mouth was level with the ear of his companion, and then he said,—

" If you dare to shrink now from performing what you have undertaken, I will do the deed myself, and by all the powers of hell, I will seize you, and alarming the house, accuse you of it to your face, declaring I was too late to save him whom you have murdered."

" Oh, no, no—mercy !"

" You will do your part?"

" I—must."

"True, you must. No power on earth can save you now. Remember, you are in my power, in consequence of the large quantity of plate you have from time to time stolen from this house. You are now on your road to independence."

"You have the will?"

"I have."

"I will consent to a reduction of my share if you will do all yourself—I am weak."

"Idiot! coward!" ground Varley, between his closed teeth. "You shall do your part, or rue the consequences. Now—now!"

Varley approached the bed, followed by his trembling companion.

They both started—for when they drew the curtains partially on one side, it seemed as if he who lay wounded on that bed was glaring full at them. The eyes were wide open, although he slept; and, with a low moaning noise, he continued to mutter disjointed sentences.

"He sleeps," said Varley.

"His look is horrible," said the other. "Oh, God, save me from being haunted by that look."

"Miranda," muttered the wounded man; "Miranda, my beautiful child—my darling—my own dear child. Kiss me, dear, dear Miranda; so—so like your mother. Ah—ah! will they not pay the cheque? No, no, no. Who forged it then—who, I say? Five thousand pounds—yes, yes, my child—God bless you. Bernard Varley is a villain! You are my own beautiful girl—my Miranda—joy of your poor father's heart. So I—I nearly robbed you of all. Hence, he comes, he comes, he comes. The—the executioner. Oh, God! oh, God!"

"Lean off the bed," said Varley; "you shake it by your trembling."

"His words are very strange," remarked the other. "To what does he allude?"

"No matter. His allusions will soon cease," said Varley.

"My child—God bless you," murmured the still sleeping man. "May you and him you love be happy, bless you both—both.

"Curses!" muttered Varley, "on the wish. Now I am nerved. There wanted but this."

"The door, the door," faltered his companion.

"Bolt it," said Varley, in a husky whisper; "bolt it, and then come here and hold him."

"God! no—I—I cannot."

"You must. Hold him, I say, while I stop his breath for ever."

"He will struggle. Good God, Varley, come away now. I have heard of men having the strength of giants in their dying struggle. I am weak; oh, spare me, spare me!"

The light from the lamp fell across the demoniac features of Bernard Varley, as he turned his face to his supplicating comrade, and he might well have been taken for the spirit of all evil, in his own proper person, so awfully devilish was the expression upon his face.

"Once for all, hear me," he said. "I love Miranda—the only human being I ever did love. She has scorned me for one who this night's act will place for ever away from her. I love money, because with it comes power. I love power because I can exercise it upon my fellow men, whom I hate—hate with a hatred so bitter, so intense, that I have no pleasure but in their pain—no pain but in their pleasure. You have your ample share of this night's deed. Immunity for the past, and riches for the future. A rent charge of five hundred pounds per annum is secured to you in the will."

The other made no reply, but he rubbed his cold clammy hands together, and looked at Varley with an expression of terror that was perfectly frightful.

"Miranda, Miranda," murmured the victim; "Miranda, my darling, speak again to me."

He tossed his arms wildly about, and betrayed evident symptoms of increasing fever and delirium.

"We waste time," said Varley. "Hold him, I say, hold him. Upon the next five moments hangs your fortune."

The scene that now ensued was a dreadful one. Varley drew the pillow from under the head of the sleeper, and holding it for a moment in his hand, he then placed it across the face, pressing upon it with all his strength.

The wounded man awakened with a stifled cry, and drawing up his feet convulsively, he nearly succeeded in freeing his mouth from the pillow. Varley then threw himself upon the bed, while his companion made futile efforts to grasp the arms of the struggling man.

The contest was brief, but terrible. Once only did the wounded man succeed in getting his breath, and then he shrieked—a shriek so horrible, that even Varley bit his nether lip through in the excitement of the moment.

"Hold him, hold him," he cried.

A few more plunges and struggles ensued, and then all was still. Varley still held the pillow tightly over the face of the now dead man; and his companion lay in a fainting fit at the foot of the bed.

At that moment a sharp knocking sounded at the door, and Varley, with a gasp of apprehension, removed the pillow from the face of the corpse.

CHAPTER IV.

THE BEAUTIFUL MIRANDA AND HER SOLITARY WATCH BY THE DEAD.—THE MURDERED KEEPER.

THE knocking at the door of the chamber of death continued, and Varley hastily arranging the disordered clothing of the bed, and composing the limbs of the murdered man, proceeded to open the door, while his whole frame was convulsed with fear.

When the bolt was removed, and Varley held the half open door in his hand, his first exclamation was one of surprise, for before him stood Miranda, now an orphan, and little dreaming that she faced her father's murderer.

"Miranda!" exclaimed Varley, "this—this time of night, and you up?"

"I could not sleep," said she, with a shudder, rather as if addressing herself than Varley. "I could not sleep till I had seen my father."

She tried to pass into the room, but Varley stood in her way.

"He sleeps," he said, "his slumber is most critical, as you know."

"As I know?"

"Ay, have they not told you that if he die not in the first sound sleep after his wound, that his hopes of recovery will be much greater?"

"Hopes?" echoed Miranda, while the light tinge of colour that had still lingered on her cheeks deserted them. "Hopes? they told me no danger was to be apprehended, but I fancied I heard a cry of help, and I could not sleep till I had seen my father."

"Miranda, retire—you must not ——"

"Sir?" said the girl, fixing her eyes upon the cold pale man who tried to stop her, with an inquiring look.

"I tell you he sleeps," said Varley, avoiding her gaze.

"Let me pass, sir; a daughter's footstep is far less likely to disturb a dear father's slumbers than that of a hired ——"

"Hired, Miranda; I am your father's guest."

"Be anything, but let me pass."

"Consider, Miranda, because you have had a dream, are you to force yourself into a sick chamber?"

" Mr. Varley," said the beautiful girl, with a firmness that gave him a pang, because it argued future disturbance to his schemes and projects, " Mr. Varley, you call yourself a guest here. If you be such, do not assume the right of a master. Remember that one word ———"

" Ah, you threaten ?"

" I do, Barnard Varley—I say to you beware. Let me pass, sir, to my father."

" This is unmaidenly, at such an hour."

Indignation flashed from the eyes of Miranda as she said—

" Villain, I know that my father lies upon a bed of sickness, you think that you can triumph in this house, but whatever may be the horrible secret, which you say gives you a hold upon my poor father's life, you shall not use it as an instrument of torture. I will pass this door, Barnard Varley ; my mind misgives me that some monstrous villany has been———"

" Hush, hush !" said Varley, trembling excessively, " you will wake him."

A loud crash at this moment from a distant part of the building, so alarmed Varley that he involuntarily stepped back, and Miranda glided into the room.

She proceeded towards the bed, and gently withdrawing the curtains, she looked as well as the very dim light that burned in the chamber would permit her, upon her father's face, which was partially covered by the bed clothes. He appeared to her to be soundly sleeping. The horrible truth did not for an instant glance across her mind, and with a murmured prayer to Heaven for his recovery, she sat down in the nurse's chair by the bed side, resolved to wait there until he should awaken.

" Alas ! he slept the sleep that knows no waking."

Bernard Varley's companion had recovered from his partial swoon, during the discourse between Varley and Miranda, and with what he thought a felicitous idea, he crept underneath the bed, supposing that she would be gone in a moment.

His position, however, now was rather an uncomfortable one, for he cou'd scarcely make his presence known, without drawing down upon him much suspicion from Miranda.

Varley stood by the open door with his hands clenched, and his face working with diabolical passions. Alarmed, as he had been by the noise in another part of the mansion, he was still more alarmed, as each moment he expected the burst of grief from Miranda, which should proclaim her knowledge that her father was no more.

" She may faint," he thought, " and then all may—all must be well."

But moment after moment passed and all was still, to the surprise of Varley, who now advanced towards the bed, and whispered,—

" Miranda ?"

She rose and pointed to the still form on the bed, as she said,—

" I will await his wakening."

" Be it so," said Varley, while a smile of ill-concealed triumph flitted across his features. He walked to the door, and then, like a flash of lightning, it came across his mind that his comrade in guilt was still somewhere in the room.

With his clenched hands above his head he cursed him in his heart, silently, as he foresaw that now the greatest danger consisted in Twitter having hidden somewhere in the room, and being discovered when Miranda should give an alarm that her father was dead, a fact which each moment increased the probability of her immediately discovering. Then what could save him from a strong suspicion of being accessory to the death of the baronet, but his denunciation of him, Bernard Varley ; which Varley knew sufficiently of the disposition of the other, to feel certain he would do.

While these thoughts were rapidly passing through Varley's mind, Miranda was silenty weeping by the bedside, for being dispirited and weakened by her fears for her father, she could not stand with her usual firmness her altercation with Varley, and now in silence, not allowing even one faint sob to escape her, she wept by her dead father, not knowing that he was so, and controlling every sigh, lest she should disturb him, who we will hope was with his God.

A half-suppressed cry suddenly burst from Varley's lips, as he saw something moving along close to his feet, and although one moment's reflection convinced him that it was his companion moving from the room, his heart beat so violently, that he could hardly speak to Miranda, who looked through the curtains in alarm.

"What means that cry?" she whispered.

"I know not," said Varley, stepping between her and the crawling form of his companion. "The house to-night seems full of strange cries."

"It does—it does," shuddered Miranda, as she again seated herself by her father.

The curtains of the bed fell around her once more, and the trembling comrade of Bernard Varley stood safe at the door.

Varley then beckoned him from the room, and they both crossed the threshold. Then Varley turned and shook his hand in the direction of the bed, as he muttered,—

"Miranda, you are mine! Never in this world did the subtlest devil that ever inhabited it, ever contrive so rare a plot. I have not a passion unavenged. I am master of the Old Grange."

"And—and—I—I——" suggested his companion.

"You," sneered Varley; "wretch, what share of my triumphs do you deserve? but we will not quarrel. Your evidence will be wanted—come now—we will sit up somewhere until we hear—Ha! who comes?"

A gleam of light now flashed along the corridor in which they stood, and presently a man came gliding along cautiously and noiselessly.

Varley, who wanted not for mere moral courage, but was far deficient in moral attributes, would have rushed forward, but his companion grasped him by the arm, saying in a whisper,—

"Look—look. Do you see that dress?"

"Dress? Yes."

"It's the spectre of the murdered keeper!"

"The what?" said Varley, as the word spectre came upon his ears, moving back a pace.

As Twitter spoke, the figure appeared slowly to recede through a wall, and to disappear, as the light it carried became dimmer and dimmer.

"What mummery is this?" said Varley.

"The servants say," replied Twitter, "that about fifty years ago, one Tom Renshaw was killed by accident in the town—he was shot in a mistake, at night —and ever after that his spirit walks the Old Grange."

"Pshaw!—absurd," said Varley, although his rapidly shifting eye, and deathly paleness, betokened how ill at ease he was. "Come to the room we left," he continued. "There is a fire there. The night is very cold."

Trembling as they went, and starting at their own shadows, these men, with a weight of guilt upon their souls, which never—never—could be pushed off— repaired to the room they had so recently left, and in the table on which lay the wine they had left.

The fire upon the hearth was dim, and Varley threw on a log of wood to replenish it, as he said, without looking to his companion,—

"Twitterall has succeeded. You may remain here at the Grange, or go elsewhere, as it may suit your fancy."

"I—I cannot speak—it is so cold."

"Well, as you please. I tell you, Twitter, that I would sell my soul for that girl. Did you see her—pale even as she was to-night, how beautiful she looked. She must be mine—dependent upon me entirely, she surely will give way at last. Twitter, I adore that girl."

"Hush—what was that?"

"Nothing. I heard nothing."

"We—we—shall hear something, Bernard Varley, soon. Do you not know that the moment must come when Miranda will find who and what she is keeping her solitary watch beside."

"What care I now. She might faint—she might scream, but I would rather the former, were I there to snach a dozen kisses from her lips. By G—! I——"

Twitter buried his face in his hands, and Varley breathed with difficulty, as a scream so loud, so shrill, so awful, that it seemed to linger an indefinite time upon the air, burst upon their bewildered senses.

"There—there," cried Twitter, "now she—she knows he's dead: oh, that horrible scream! It will haunt me till I die. Varley, you look like stone—oh, God!"

Varley snached up the light and strode to the door; then turning, he said, in a deep hasty voice,—

"She has discovered a corpse, where she thought lay a sleeping man. Be careful of every word you now say. Upon your evidence and mine agreeing everything now depends. Recollect when we left him he was breathing very hard and short."

"Yes—yes."

"But he was alive."

"I—I will swear, of course, all we agreed upon, for my rent charge."

"Now remain where you are, and leave me to manage the remainder of this business."

"Not in the dark; I—I cannot stay in the dark a moment," said Twitter.

"Fool—you have the fire-light."

A trampling of feet now resounded through the house, and cries of help came plainly upon their ears.

Twitter had risen from his chair, and was trying to take the light from Varley, when the door of the room was flung open, and a crowd of servants appeared in the entrance.

CHAPTER V.

A DAUGHTER'S GRIEF.—THE ROBBERY.—A HOUSE OF WOE.

CONSTERNATION sat upon every countenance of the many that crowded the doorway of the room which Barnard Varley had been upon the point of leaving, and as the unanimity of feeling among the domestics was sufficient to induce them all to speak at once, the confusion of tongues was, for a moment, contrasted with the stillness that had reigned before throughout the mansion, perfectly confounding.

"The keeper's ghost!" cried some.

"Thieves!" shouted others.

"Sir George murdered!" was the cry of four or five at once.

"Peace!" cried Varley, "what is the cause of all this uproar? If you wish to be heard, certainly speak at once. If understood, take it by turns. How dare you, when your master now is dangerously ill, to make such an uproar, thus in the dead hour of the night?"

"Hold! Bernard Varley," cried Miranda, suddenly bursting through the throng. "Be you the last to speak."

She held her finger pointedly at him, as she stood pale and still as a marble statue at the door, and Varley visibly writhed and shrunk under her gaze.

The sudden appearance of Miranda struck every one dumb for a few moments, and a more singular group could scarcely be conceived, than was presented by the various persons assembled in and about the doorway of that small apartment.

By a great effort Varley then spoke.

"Miranda," he said, "are you mad?"

"No—Heaven has yet spared my reason, that I may tell you all there—you, who are all attached servants of my father—you, who have known him years—that he is murdered."

"Murdered?" echoed every voice.

"Yes, murdered. You have no master; I—I have no father. I am not mad—'tis Heaven's mercy that I am not. For one whole year now—a year which has seemed an eternity of time—that man (pointing to Varley), he who now comes before my gaze—he who you see, shrinks aghast from the daughter of his victim—that man has persecuted me : and I have loathed him more and more, as his black heart became known to me."

"Remove her to her chamber," cried Varley; "her wits wander."

"No—no—no," cried Miranda,—"hear me all. Bernard Varley has murdered my father."

"Beware!" cried Varley,—" I say beware!"

"That word," cried Miranda,—"that frown has no terror now. He is gone—gone. Fiend—monster, you have done your worst."

"You see she is mad; you hear her," said Varley, clasping his hands together to endeavour to stop their agitated trembling.

Miranda wrung her hands bitterly.

"Follow me—follow me," she said, with a sudden dropping of her voice from passionate earnestness to the deepest pathos. "My poor fond father is dead. They have killed him—his blood is upon their heads. Bernard Varley must have this deed to answer for. I was watching by his bedside, thinking that he slept : then I tried to hear him breathe, but could not: and my own heart almost ceased to beat, as I placed my hand upon his. It was cold—cold. My father is dead. I shall never see him smile again—never hear his voice—never—never—nev——"

She was caught by some of the servants near to her, as her feelings overcame her, and she relapsed into a happy state of insensibility.

"Grief for her father's wounded state," said Varley, "has turned the girl's head, or she has had some dream."

The servants seemed perfectly bewildered, and looked on each other's faces like men suddenly aroused to some new state of existence.

Varley poured himself out a bumper of the wine that stood upon the table ; and drinking it off at a draught, he held on by the back of a chair, while he said,—

"Go to your master's chamber, all of you, and see if it be really true that he is no more, or only the coinage of this girl's disturbed brain."

Miranda still continued insensible, and they placed her in an easy chair which was in the room ; he who had caught her, and saved her from falling, saying,—

"I'll go and call up some of the women. Poor thing, she seems nearly dead."

"A little wine will restore her," said Varley. "Go—go all of you to your master's chamber. I will attend to Miranda until some of the female servants are up. Twitter, go you and see to your master."

A violent ringing of a bell now sounded in the house, and one immediately exclaimed,—

"That is Sir George's chamber-bell."

"The—the nurse is ringing," stammered Twitter.

"For shame, men—are you afraid?" cried Varley. "Away with you."

The servants hurried now towards the staircase leading to their master's chamber, Twitter slowly following, the last of all.

Varley listened for a moment ; and when the last footsteps on the staircase began to be indistinct, he turned his eyes upon the pallid face of the young thing who reclined in the large chair by the fireside.

"If I have lost heaven," he muttered. "I have gained an angel. Oh, how I have panted for such an opportunity as this, to imprint unrebuked one burning kiss as no damned soul has ever tasted, and they will not obliterate this moment! Miranda—Miranda, you are mine. I have bartered my soul's salvation fo you and I will have my reward."

He trembled as he took her unresisting hand and pressed it to his lips. He raised her drooping head. Once he pressed his mouth to hers—her long, silken hair fell upon his breast—her brow, her cheeks, her lips, he kissed with maddening fervour.

"Miranda, Miranda," he cried; "who shall step between me and my prize? I triumph—I triumph. God of heaven, this is joy, to hold her thus pillowed on my breast—to rain kisses of fire upon her pouting lips."

A light flashed across Varley's eyes at this moment from the half-shut door. The same figure he had seen disappear from the corridor stood before him—a stunning blow fell upon his head. It seemed to him for a moment as if he was surrounded by a million dazzling lights, and then all was a blank—the villain fell stunned to the floor.

* * * * * * *

In confusion and dismay the servants reached the chamber of their master. The nurse was pulling again the bell-rope as they entered, and with a "thank God! you're all come," she told them that Sir George was no more.

"He must have gone very sudden," she added. "I never knew the like; the first I heard of it was Miss Miranda screaming terrible like. I was just waking and thinking to myself that it was time for me to go and let Mr. Varley and Mr. Twitter go, when I heard her, poor dear thing, and when I came here she bolted past me like a shot, crying out that her papa was dead, and there sure enough he was."

The nurse then drew aside the curtains, and there lay the still corpse as if sleeping. The features were calm and serene, and the only sign of the least disturbance was a long scratch across the face, and some blood which had oozed from the wound, some of the dressings of which had given way in the struggle between the victim and his murderers.

"Ah, poor soul," continued the nurse, "it's very sudden, a very sudden call indeed."

The servants looked on with blanched faces, and then one said,—

"Who's gone for the doctor?"

"You—you see he's dead," said Twitter; "what's the use of a doctor now. My poor master is a murdered man, and the Squire of Larkswood must suffer for it."

"Henry Lee has gone for the doctor; I heard him say he would," remarked one.

"And here he is, here he is," cried several who were nearest the door.

The medical man now made his appearance, having been much surprised at being called to Sir George in the night, for he really considered in his own mind the wound to be trifling, if proper care was taken. To hear therefore that his patient had slipped through his fingers so suddenly, very much amazed and surprised him indeed.

"How is Sir George?" he said. "I suppose he has fainted, or something of the sort."

"He is dead, sir," said four or five at once.

"Hush, hush," cried the surgeon. "I don't at all believe it."

He took the cold hand of the corpse in his—there was no pulsation at the wrist. He laid his ear flat against the heart—all was still.

"My good friends, it was very little use sending for me," he then said, "Sir George has been dead for some time. We must have an inquest of course. My opinion is that a sudden shock to the nervous system, such as a shot wound, has occasioned the unexpected decease. It's very disagreeable—rather odd—and I may add provoking. Who was with him when he died?"

"His daughter, sir."

No. 3.

"Well, I'm sorry, very sorry—it can't be helped—I should like very much to hear her account of it, if she is up and well enough to speak to me."

" Can nothing be done, sir ?" said the nurse.

" Certainly not, my good woman.   While a spark of life remains one can sometimes fan it up into a blaze, but when vitality has fairly ceased, why—ahem."

" Ah, well, he was a kind soul, though a bit nervous and fidgetty like. He's gone quite like a lamb."

" How did he get that scratch ?   I did not see it when I dressed his wound."

" Lor, sir, I don't know.   Well I never, that is a long scratch to be sure."

" Indeed it is.   It's curious how he could have come by it—people may scratch themselves accidentally, but they never begin under the eye and go on to the chin."

The surgeon continued for some moments in deep thought, then he said,—

" Has he had anybody to see him ?"

" No, sir—not one."

" Well—the body must not be touched.   There will be an inquest I dare say to-morrow or the next day at furthest, and in the meantime just leave everything as it is.   In fact, the door had better be locked."

The servants now made a general rush from the door, as pale—tottering—and her hair dishevelled, Miranda came into the room.   She had recovered without assistance from her servant, and as quickly as she could ascended to the chamber where lay her father.   The first person she saw was the medical man, and him she clung to with frantic eagerness, crying,—

" Oh, save him—save him—save my poor father, sir.   He is not dead."

" My dear young lady, compose yourself," said the surgeon.   "Come now, sit down—you must bear these things with fortitude."

" Oh, God!   Oh, God !   What will become of me ?   Rowland, where are you now—dear Rowland."

" Who does she mean ?" said the surgeon.

" She means young Mr. Percy, sir."

" Oh, my dear young lady, he is not here."

" Not here ?   He should be here.   Rowland—father.   He was here. I dreamed he kissed me.   My poor father is murdered—and—our last words were not so kind as they had been.   Let me see him—let me see him !"

" No, no—indeed you must not—take her to her own room—take her away."

A simultaneous cry of surprise now burst from several of the servants, and one and all pointed towards he door, where rapidly walking away, was the figure in the green hunting-dress, that Twitter had declared to be the spectre of the murdered keeper.

CHAPTER VI.

THE SPECTRE OF THE KEEPER.—THE CHASE.—THE CAPTIVE.—AN ACCUSATION.

For the space of a moment, every one who looked on the strange figure seemed paralysed, and it was only the voice of the medical man calling loudly,

" That's no ghost, lads—seize him.   It's much more likely a thief," that roused them from their lethargy, and then a simultaneous rush was made in the direction the figure had taken.

There were two staircases opening and descending from the corridor, and the supposed ghost chose the one farthest from the door of the chamber, descending with great rapidity.   The foremost among the servants just saw which direction the figure turned in, when it reached the foot of the stairs, and then they pursued it with good speed ; the excitement of the chase going far to dissipate the fear with which they had first beheld the phantom.

The Grange was one of those old irregular buildings which contain so many intricacies and hiding places, that any one well acquainted with its topography might for a long time puzzle others not possessing so much knowledge ; and in the present case, it appeared that none of the servants were half so well informed with regard to all the ins and outs of the Grange as the spectre, for it found two or three doors in the old wainscoting, of which they were not at all aware, and darted up and down staircases and disappeared in various situations where there appeared no outlet, and altogether led its pursuers so troublesome a chase that they finally all assembled in the great dining-room to consult, after quite losing all trace of the object of their active but useless pursuit.

Miranda, when first the pursuit had began, started from the arms of the surgeon, and would have flown after the servants, but he gently though forcibly detained her, saying,—

"Now, be calm—you will make yourself ill. Let me persuade you to go to your chamber. This person is most probably either one of the servants playing off a prank—and if so, he might have waited for a more seasonable time—or some thief who having heard of the legend concerning the ghost of the keeper haunting the house, has taken advantage of it to steal the plate."

" Or it may be real," said Miranda, with a shudder.

" Pho—pho—nonsense. Here, nurse, I will remain here while you see the young lady to her room. Pray let me persuade you to go to bed, my dear young lady. Your grief, of course is quite natural, but you should, nevertheless, control it, as well as you can."

" I cannot sleep—let me remain here," sobbed Miranda.

" Well, if you will not go, just sit down by me here a little while and compose yourself."

" Oh, this frightful day! and now for frightful night!" said Miranda. " If I could but awaken and find it all a dream. First, my father fighting a duel with his best and oldest friend. Then being in his own house murdered."

" Murdered ?"

" Yes—I know it."

" My good girl, how can you say so ? Tell me all that happened while you kept watch by your father."

" Alas!—I know not—my mind is all confusion—but my heart tells me he has been murdered—murdered!"

" Who do you suspect ?"

" Bernard Varley."

" Your father's intimate friend ?"

" His worst—his most deadly foe."

" Indeed!"

" Yes—Bernard Varley is in possession of some terrible secret, which gave him a real or fancied power over my poor father."

" Oh, she's wandering in her mind," thought the surgeon ; " she don't know what she's saying."

" All was happiness," continued Miranda, " till he came here. Then, as you may have seen some—some fair summer sky overclouded never to be bright again —all became dark—drear—and desolate."

She clasped her small white hands over her face and wept bitterly.

"That will do her good," thought the surgeon ; " she'll be ten times more rational now."

" Yes," continued Miranda, " from the moment that Bernard Varley came to the Grange, all was changed. My father and the squire have quarrelled about I know not what. Rowland, who I am sure my father loved, has been harshly forbidden to enter our doors, and the end of all is death—death."

" Humph. Where is Mr. Varley, nurse ?"

" Here !" said Varley, staggering into the room, covered with blood.

Miranda started to her feet, and the medical man regarded him with amazement.

"I am here," continued Varley ; " I have been the victim of an attack from some one who is in this house, for no good purpose. I was struck down by a man in a green dress."

"Attired like a forester?"

"The same."

"Then," cried the surgeon, "it is quite clear that this supposed ghost is flesh and blood. My life on it, if your father, Miranda, has come by his death unfairly, it is from the hand of the person now so closely pursued by your servants—this supposed spectre."

Varley was silent for a moment, then he suddenly exclaimed,—

"Good Heavens! a new light breaks in upon me. Sir George has been murdered."

"You know it!" said Miranda.

"I."

"Yes, Bernard Varley, I accuse you."

"This is midsummer madness," said Varley. "You see, sir, that I am badly wounded in endeavouring to secure a man, who—whoever he may be, we may all fairly suspect; and lo, I am myself accused by this young lady in consequence of some fancied offence I have given her. I am nearly fainting from loss of blood."

The surgeon now looked to Varley's wound, which, although merely a scalp one, was by no means slight.

"I think when you see that Mr. Varley is himself injured, young lady, you will be inclined to acquit him of any share in your suspicions of persons who may have injured your father."

"We've got him! we've got him!" cried several voices from the staircase now. The surgeon ran to the door.

"He's in the dining-room, sir, tied hand and foot."

Miranda, before they could prevent her, rushed down the staircase, and burst through the throng of persons in the dining-room, who were surrounding a tall young man, dressed in a green hunting-dress.

"Miranda!" he said.

"Rowland Percy," shrieked Miranda.

"The same. Why do you look aghast, all of you? You know me now, though you have not seen me for some little time. Oh! I forgot my wig. Ah! Miranda you have penetrated my disguise. Now, before you all here, I proclaim Bernard Varley a villain. I believe you will find him lying on the floor in his own room. I know I am in this house unwelcome and unbidden. I assumed this disguise unknown to all, with the hope that I might encounter Miranda, as she took her usual early morning's walk in the conservatory. Pardon me if I have caused an alarm in the house. I suppose I—what—what makes you all so silent? Is your father up, Miranda?"

"My father?"

"Yes, I have not been two hours in this neighbourhood. What is the reason of your alarmed looks?"

"Rowland—Rowland," cried Miranda, "Tell me. Swear to me you know nothing of——"

"Of what, Miranda?"

"My father's death."

The young man started back, as he exclaimed,—

"His death? You—you jest."

"No, Rowland, my father is no more."

"Good God! I—I came here with the hope of healing the unhappy differences between him and my father. Absence was insupportable to me, and in this disguise I hoped ——"

"Hold, young sir—hold," said Varley, walking through the throng of persons; the less you now say the better."

"The less I say? Bernard Varley, you are a scoundrel. I bless my happy stars that I was here this night to rescue from your polluting touch innocence and virtue. Villain, I have not yet done with you."

" Nor I with you, unhappy young man."

" Unhappy?"

" Ay, be cautious, sir, in your speech. Sir George has been murdered!"

" Murdered?"

" You start, sir. 'Tis well acted. I repeat Sir George is murdered."

" Then, if so," cried Rowland Percy, " he who I rescued the daughter from I suspect has been the murderer of the father."

" Beware, misguided, unhappy young man ; I forgive you freely your desperate attack upon my own life, for my soul is shocked at your situation."

" Explain yourself, villain, or I will pluck your meaning from your heart."

Varley turned to the assembled throng of persons, and in an affected voice of deep grief and compassion, he said,—

" Friends, all here assembled, I will make a long tale brief. Some time since your poor master, now lying dead, discovered a clandestine correspondence between this young man—this Rowland Percy—and his daughter here. The consequence was a quarrel, and this young man was forbidden the house—his father took up his quarrel, and after much aggravation, a duel was the result. Sir George is slightly wounded ; but is—I say it advisedly, for there are appearances upon the corpse to warrant me,—murdered in his bed."

A thrill of excitement and horror ran through the assemblage.

" I repeat, murdered in his bed. Who did the deed ? Who had a motive—who a quarrel? who is found skulking about the house, and only secured after much toil and difficulty—who made an attack upon me, and fancied he left me for dead? Who have we now a prisoner? Rowland Percy—Rowland Percy, who upon circumstantial evidence, I here accuse of stealing into this house to night, and taking some opportunity of murdering Sir George."

" Liar!" shouted Rowland.

" Hear me," cried Varley, as he fixed his eyes upon the trembling and utterly confounded Twitter. " Myself and Sir George's valet left him, as we considered, asleep for about five minutes ; during that time the deed must have been done. My own opinion, by the look of the body is, that he has been smothered in his bed."

" Seize the murderer," cried several voices.

" Hold !" said Miranda, rushing forward and clasping the hands of Rowland. " Hear me all here present. I know not if I am mad or sane, for my brain whirls, and my temples throb with the awful events of this night, but if this be not all some horrible dream, I here proclaim my faith in the innocence of Rowland Percy to be equal to my faith in Heaven."

" My Miranda !" cried Percy.

" Hush—hush, Rowland ; hear me out. You all knew and loved my father. Would I take the hand of his murderer ? look in this face and look in that."

She pointed from Rowland to Bernard Varley, and the difference was indeed most striking between the open, candid countenance of the young man, and the villanous physiognomy of Varley.

" See," continued Miranda, " he shrinks aghast from the words of truth—he has described the mode of my poor father's death, and he, and none but he, could describe it."

" Seize the murderer," cried Varley, pointing to Percy. " This girl raves, poor thing. The Percys are a ruined race, and Sir George alone stood in the way of patching up their broken fortune by a marriage with the heiress of the Grange. Secure him, and let the law, upon such evidence as can be produced, pronounce him innocent or guilty."

The servants made a rush towards the young man, for there was something so terrible in the charge made against him, that they forgot all their predilections in his favour in their horror at his supposed crime.

Rowland drew himself up proudly, as he said,—

"The man who attempts to lay a hand upon me had better look to his safety. I know not how far I may be entangled in the meshes of some plot woven by that villain (pointing to Varney); but I have faith in my own innocence, and far from avoiding, I claim investigation."

"Fetch me officers," said Varley.

"No—no," cried Miranda; "he is innocent—he is. I have no friend now in the wide world but him—I am the last of my race—an orphan. Rowland let me cling to you."

"Miranda," said the young man mournfully, "Heaven knows how dear you are to me! but a chasm so deep, that its far down descent is lost in its own gloom, is now opened between us. Proof of my innocence must fill it up, and then we may meet again as we have met.—Leap it, and all is lost!"

Miranda shuddered, but still she clung to Percy; she spoke in a strange tone,—

"Rowland," she said, "some fiends are at work about us—we are deserted of Heaven. Some terrible machinations against us have succeeded for a time—we are lost."

"No—Miranda; innocence will, like an angel, burst its way through bars and bolts, through water, earth, and fire, and wing its flight unto its own blue Heaven, with not a pinion ruffled—all will yet be well."

"Well—well?" she muttered, and with a shudder, fainted in her lover's arms.

CHAPTER VII.

THE EARLY DAWN.—IS IT A DREAM?—MIRANDA'S DESPAIR.—THE REALITY OF WOE.

LIKE a storm upon a fair smiling summer's day, had ruin and destruction fallen upon the house of Sir George Rankley, the once much envied possessor of the Grange, one of the most magnificent estates in Yorkshire. But one year previous to the melancholy occurrences it has been our duty to relate, everything wore a smiling aspect in and about the superb mansion which Sir George had purchased as a place of rest for himself and his child, the beautiful and accomplished Miranda.

Wearied with the bustle and excitement of a commercial life—for Sir George had accumulated his large fortune as the principal of a banking house of great reputation—he had given a sum exceeding three hundred thousand pounds for the Grange, and thither retired to endeavour to forget one cankering core, that like a plague-spot eat into his heart. What the mystery was, the thought of which would occasionally blanch the cheek of Sir George Rankley with terror, and produce a tremour of many minutes' duration, even in his hours of gayest converse, no one could divine. All that was known of his history was, that he had entered the banking establishment, of which he ultimately became the head as a junior partner, with but a very small share of the profits of the business. From that day, however, his career of prosperity appeared to date itself, for he rapidly became a rich man; and, finally, in an epoch of commercial pressure, he, to the surprise of his partners, offered to throw a very large sum into the concern, provided they would make him a partner on equal terms with themselves. His offer was gladly accepted, and he, in a very few years, from his energy and promptitude, became the head of the concern which he had entered as the lowest partner.

How all these things came about was a mystery to his partners, who were much older men than himself; but there was one circumstance which caused them the greatest uneasiness, and that consisted in a series of frightfully extensive forgeries on the bank, which nearly threatened the dissolution of the business.

Rankley, on these occasions, always came forward to the assistance of his partners, but invariably that he did so, had fresh articles of partnership entered into which gave him an increased interest in, and ascendancy over the business.

This state of things continued for some years, when the senior partner dropped into the grave, leaving Rankley at the head of the concern, not nominally but really.

An accommodation then to a noble duke of the blood royal to the tune of some forty thousand pounds, led to the baronetcy he retired with, and Sir George Rankley had arrived at the summit of his desires and ambition.

So far the personal history of the baronet was well known, but behind the curtain there were fearful secrets which would, if divulged at any moment, have torn that man from his splendid home, and consigned him to a gallows.

It would seem in the history of human nature that there is ever a retributive justice going on, and that the higher bold villany shall succeed in soaring, the more certain, rapid, and awful shall be its fall, and that the most subtle and high working mind that ever gave impulse to human actions, was ever doomed in some manner to commit itself among its own intricacies, and fall a victim to its own wild ambitions.

The veriest wretch that ever solicited alms from door to door was happier than Sir George Rankley ; and he would have given worlds, had he possessed them, to obliterate twenty-five years of his life, and to again commence his mercantile existence as the junior partner in the house he had so completely made his own. But, alas ! time may not be recalled, or how many who have been allured by the glittering *ignis fatuus* would bargain to be stripped of all the worldly dross they have collected about them, and sent into the public streets to beg their bread, provided they could obliterate some years of feverish vice, and blot out for ever the deep record of their hideous crimes.

The Larkswood estates joined to that of the Grange, and an intimacy had sprung up between the families—an intimacy which, in the case of Miranda and young Rowland Percy, had ripened into one of those soul-clinging affections which but few natures were capable of appreciating.

Thus was a love illimitable, unchangeable, full of the sweet confidence, the firmness, the enduring gentleness of a passion that knows no doubts, no fears, but glides in the deep consciousness of its own strength and purity, without a ripple.

But how true it is that—

" The course of true love never yet ran smooth !"

A cloud was hovering in the horizon of their joy ; and at a time when they fondly hoped that the sun of their happiness was climbing to the meridian of its glory, it was sinking, alas ! in gloom and storm, leaving behind it but the traces of its God-like presence in their glowing hearts.

Alas ! that it should be so—that ever the first dear feelings of the heart—that one inheritance from Heaven, which some pitying angel begged might yet be left to man—love ! Oh, that love in all its purity, in all its devotion, its self-sacrificing beauty and sublimity, should ever be wrecked on the sands of suspicion, or sacrificed on the altar of mammon ! But so it is ever. The first grand feeling of life is to love ; the second, a fruitless effort to forget.

The sunshine which had appeared in its intensity to be shining for ever upon the path of the lovers was suddenly and awfully withdrawn, and left behind a mass of horrors and darkness which no eye could pierce.

The early morning was dawning, and the birds were singing blithely among the tall trees that surrounded on three sides the Grange : the low of the cattle in the distance, the bark of dogs, the hum of many insect things, all bespoke and hailed the coming day ; and there had been a time, and that, too, but a few short sunrises since, when Miranda had delighted in all those sounds of life, animation, and joy—a time when she had sprung from her dreamless couch to snatch the early rose that to the first beam of sunshine had opened its odorous breast—a time when the wild notes of the forest birds were to her ear sweet melody—but now—now how was all changed ! It is the heart that makes or mars its own malady and now all that had been so fair and so beautiful—so lovely, so delightful—

sounded harsh and discordant to the ears that were no longer attuned to listen to them with pleasure.

Miranda slept, indeed, but she had not retired to rest. She lay upon the outside of her couch, in an uneasy morning slumber, after a night of tears, agony, and watching. Her sleep was now so light that all the sounds of coming morning made themselves cognizant to her senses; but they brought no pleasure—no beaming smile acknowledged the lark's sweet melody. Tears coursed each other down her pale cheeks, and in her sleep she muttered words of suffering and pain.

"Rowland, Rowland," she sobbed, "he is innocent, he is; unhand him. Think you I—I would screen the murderer of my own father? Oh, no—no—no —he is innocent."

Deep sobs now burst from her labouring breast, and she covered her face with one white exquisitely rounded arm, as a ray of sunlight came dancing like a stream of molten gold in at her window, and fell across her face both borrowing and giving beauty.

The light slumber was broken—Miranda started—pressed her hands across her eyes for a moment, and then looked wildly about her. Each well-remembered object met her eyes—her vases filled with flowers—the trailing crimson roses that dappled with radiant beauty her window—her drawing implements—the gold fish swimming in their everlasting restlessness around their glassy prison—her piano— all the little cherished remembrances of youthful friendships and affections which she set so much store by—her eye wandered rapidly from one to the other as if in bewildered surprise. Then she raised a cry of joy—of such ecstacy as the heart feels when some load of grief is by one word lifted from it.

Miranda clasped her hands, and a flush of colour rushed to her cheeks as she said,—

"A dream, a dream—oh God, a dream—it was but a dream. Thank Heaven! I—I—oh, thank Heaven, it is not real—'tis all a dream—an awful dream."

She sunk into a chair and burst into an hysterical passion of laughter mingled with tears. This convulsion of feeling gradually subsided, and she said, with more calmness,—

"Foolish Miranda, to be so affected by a vision. Yet what an awful one. A dream so like reality, that even now I shudder. Yet—how is this, not undressed —the bed untouched—what could have possessed me? Oh, Heaven, am I mad? No, no; I must have come to my room wearied and thrown myself on the bed, and then fallen into the uneasy sleep that brought me such torturing visions. What is to-day? I surely have slept long."

She flew to a small French time-piece which had been a gift from Rowland Percy. It was silent, and the hands pointed to half-past four. She pressed her hands to her brow, as she said,—

"What could have made me forget to wind up my pretty clock? A dream—a dream; yes, it—it must be all a dream. Can I put together its absurd creations? Let me consider; my father murdered by Rowland—Rowland, my Rowland, who will return and claim me for his own. Yes, it surely was a dream."

A knock at her chamber door now startled her, and she cried,—

"Who is there?"

"It's me, miss," said a female voice.

"Oh, it's you, Annie; come in and help me to dress. I declare—I—I—what, in tears?"

The girl's eyes were red with weeping, and she stood staring at her young mistress's smiling face in consternation, and as much surprised as if she had seen a spectre.

"Well Annie," said Miranda, "what is the matter? Have you, too, had a dream?"

"A dream, Miss Miranda?"

"Yes; I—have had a terrible one."

"Lor', miss, I don't wonder at it, considering."

"Considering what, Annie?"

"All that's happened. I shall never—no, never, as long as I live forget——"

Miranda staggered to her seat, as she said,—

"Forget what, Annie?"

"Oh, miss, I haven't your fortitude, and I was so afraid you would be quite ill."

"Fortitude! fortitude! I have had a dream—I dreamt my father was—dead."

"Dreamt, miss; why, goodness gracious! so he is."

A scream burst from Miranda, and she clasped her hands together, crying,—

"No, no, no—it cannot, cannot be."

"Oh dear! oh dear, miss—it is all true, and

young Mr. Rowland—sweet young man as he is——"

"Girl!" cried Miranda, clutching her tightly by the arm, "you—you are hatching some hideous tale to drive me mad!"

"Murder! murder!" cried the girl.

"Hush—hush, Annie—hush; I—will hear all. Oh, God! is it real? is it real—you spoke of Rowland."

"Ye—ye—yes, miss—they—they have taken him to York."

"For what?"

"The murder."

"Save me, Heaven!" cried Miranda.

She dropped on her knees, and muttering—"It is real—it is real!" she prayed

No. 4.

for strength, and that she might not go mad, but preserve her senses to proclaim the innocence of Rowland Percy. The big tears rolled down her cheeks as she prayed, and then a passionate burst of weeping succeeded.

It was well that her highly wrought feelings found such timely vent, or her fine brain might not have endured the awful shock it had sustained ; she rose calmer and firmer—Heaven was in its mercy reserving her for other purposes. The storm of grief and horror was over, and Miranda was now prepared to take her part in the great drama of domestic life that was awaiting her.

CHAPTER VIII.

THE INTERVIEW.—AN AWFUL DISCLOSURE.—A VILLAIN'S PROPOSAL.

It was well for Miranda that the excess of her agonised feelings had subsided, for she had scarcely changed her apparel and refreshed herself by dashing cold spring water over her eyes, than a message was brought to her with Mr. Varley's compliments, and a request for an interview.

"He request an interview from me ?" said Miranda. "Go, Annie, and tell him I will not see him. What will become of me—yet stay, send some one to Mr. Percy directly—tell him to come to me."

"Lor miss—Mr. Percy is gone away."

"Gone away !"

"Yes, miss—after the duel."

"I am distracted," said Miranda, "even now all is confusion in my brain—tell me, Annie, briefly what occurred."

"Why, miss, as far as I know, your father fought a duel with old Mr. Percy, the squire, and was shot somehow. Then they do say as young Mr. Percy came in the night and murdered your father in his sleep."

"That is what you are told," said Miranda, forcing herself by a great effort to be calm. "I—begin now to recollect all. There has been some fearful—some horrible machinations—alas! where can I turn for succour—have I a friend now in the wide world ?"

"I am sure, miss, there's one," sobbed Annie.

Miranda shuddered, and sat pale and motionless for some moments—then she rose, and throwing a shawl over her shoulders she said,—

"I will see this man—this Bernard Varley—yes, I will see him—my heart tells me he is the author of all this misery. From his hand has been launched the bolt which has fallen with such destructive vengeance upon our house. I will see him !"

"He is in the breakfast-room," sobbed Annie, "they say—shall I tell him, Miss Miranda, that you are coming ?"

"No ; I will go and meet my father's murderer alone."

"Lor, miss, you don't think——"

"I do, Annie—I care not who hears me say so. My firm impression is, that Bernard Varley is my father's murderer—his very accusation of Rowland Percy is sufficient."

"Well, you knows best, miss, and you be now mistress of the Grange."

"Mistress of the Grange, Annie ?"

"Yes, miss, as poor dear master is dead and gone, why, in course, they says among all the servants that you be mistress now, and all belongs to you outright."

"I—I had not thought of that," said Miranda. "My poor father's remains shall no longer be insulted by the presence of his murderer—Bernard Varley shall leave this house."

" Well, miss, I am glad of that, because—beeause——"

" Because what, Annie ?"

" Thomas says as he'll knock him down, and then Thomas might get into trouble, as you see, Miss Miranda, Mr. Varley is alway teasing me so."

" He, or I, leave this house to-day," said Miranda. " By some means this man had acquired a power or ascendancy over my poor father—an ascendancy so great, that even an insult to me dared not be resented ; but that is over now—alas! how fearfully! and, if I have the power to call this house my own, he shall now leave it."

Miranda now paused a moment, then she said to the wondering girl,—

" Annie, send one of the men servants immediately to York, and tell him to bring back with him, if possible, one of the ablest lawyers he can find. I have duties now to perform which my private griefs must not interfere with. I—I must weep in secret, but be firm in the cause of innocence, and in punishing the really guilty. Another shawl, Annie, I am very cold."

" You are all of a shiver, miss."

" Yes—yes—I am cold."

" You had better breakfast, miss, afore you see Mr. Varley."

" No—no—I am better now—Heaven will grant me strength. If it were not, Annie, I should drop down at your feet—nay, don't look so much alarmed. You see I am calm—quite calm now. I will see this demon in human form—this Bernard Varley, who has made me an orphan. May Heaven forgive him, but I— now that my heart is bleeding with the fresh wounds he has inflicted upon it—I cannot—no—I—I cannot yet—yet I will see him."

There was a calmness about Miranda, but it was the calmness of overwrought feeling, mingled with despair. It was well too that the gentle and affectionate girl was not thrown altogether upon her griefs, but that indignation and resentment claimed some portion of her attention, and contributed to keep her mind in a more healthy state than it otherwise would have been, had it been resigned to one set of feelings only.

Of Rowland Percy's innocence she was convinced, and the feeling that it probably lay with her, and her only, to save him from the dreadful suspicion which Bernard Varley strove to attach to him, nerved her to exertion.

" I have heard of young, feeble, tender-hearted women," she said to herself, as she descended from her chamber, " daring more than the mightiest and strongest men for a cause they threw their whole hearts into, and shall I shrink from saving Rowland from this most calumnious charge? Oh, spirit of my father! if from heaven you can look down upon your child, and direct her in the right path to save the innocent—guide me now, and let the guilty alone tremble. Be still, my heart now—I must go through this trying interview with nerve. Be still, my heart —be still."

Villain as he was, and unscrupulous in the ways by which he strove to accomplish his unholy purpose, Bernard Varley could not, with the confident air he would have wished, meet the daughter of his murdered victim.

The interview he had sought with Miranda, he knew was a necessary one, and he did not wish to avoid it; but still he shrunk from it with an abject trembling fear, such as conscious guilt ever feels in the presence of bright intelligence, of purity and virtue.

He was pacing the breakfast parlour with rapid strides, when the door opened, and Miranda, pale as any spectre, stood upon the threshold.

Varley started at the great change in her appearance, which the day and night of exquisite misery and suffering had inflicted upon her. She was not less beautiful ; there was the same beautiful contour of face and form : there were the same lustrous beaming eyes, the same delicately modelled mouth ; but it was the expression which was new.

But four-and-twenty hours since, a look of cloudless joy had mantled on her cheeks ; for, although she had in her heart some cause for woe, in the misunderstanding between her father and her lover, she believed it to be but slight, and tha a very short time would make all friends again. In fact, some might have objected to the beauty of Miranda as being too infantine, for a lurking smile, like that upon a cherub's face, was ever ready to burst into a laugh of ringing melody; her fair countenance was ever ready,

> "Like a sweet lake, which the breeze is upon,
> To break into dimples, and laugh in the sun."

But now, as she stood upon the threshold of that well-remembered room, in which she had passed so many happy hours, it seemed as if the hand of time had gently touched the varied beauties of the young girl, but in all its stern reality swept across her mind, leaving behind it the trace of its presence in the expression of deep thought, and contemplative sadness, which sat upon her marble brow.

She held her hands tightly pressed upon her heart as she entered the room, and, declining Varley's offer of a chair, she said in a tone of forced and painful calmness,— .

"I understand you have something to say to me; I am here, Bernard Varley."

"Lamenting, as I do," commenced Varley, "the most painful events——"

"Hush," said Miranda, "leave me to lament. All sorrow must sink beside mine. The mockery of woe is—horrible."

"Mockery, Miranda!"

"Sir?"

Miranda drew her slight figure up proudly as she added,—

"When you address me, sir, I am the Lady Miranda Rankley."

"So proud," muttered Varley; "we shall see." Then he said aloud,—

"With all due deference to the Lady Miranda Rankley, I have something to communicate to her, which may so far alter our respective situations as to make it not so stupendous an act of assurance for me to address her without her title."

"Perhaps, sir, you still consider yourself a welcome guest here," said Miranda, "if ever you were really one."

"A welcome guest!"

"Ay, sir, a guest. I am waiting to know what Mr. Varley may have to say to me in my house before he leaves it, never again to cross its threshold."

Varley looked astonished at the tone and manner of the young girl, whom he had ever looked upon as a child in simplicity, and from whom he never could have expected, in his wildest dreams, any such exhibition of moral courage. The spectacle, however, added fuel to the unholy passion which was consuming him; and as he regarded her now, in all her beauty, all her pride of virtue, loathing him and treating him with the bitterness of lofty contempt and horror, such as he might well quail before, his love for her became the master passion of his soul, and, in the depths of his black heart, he swore an oath, terrible in its denunciations, that she should be his, or he would perish, body and soul.

He spoke to her in a low tone of suppressed passion, and his words seemed to sink like liquid fire into her brain.

"'Tis well, Miranda," he said, "for those who have power to use it; 'tis well for the haughty to make much of their pride; 'tis well for the great and the rich to command; but 'tis better far, before they assume so much, to be quite certain their power rests on a more solid foundation than their own surmises."

"Surmises!"

"Yes. Do you understand me?"

"I am no reader of riddles," said Miranda. "I have, perhaps, foolishly and unadvisedly, accorded you an interview. Say on, sir, and say explicitly, what you have to communicate."

"I will be most explicit. I am no guest here."

"No guest! True—true I understand you. You are, indeed, no guest, Bernard Varley. He who, from some cause I know not of, was compelled to tolerate your presence, is now past your malice—he is now gone. Bernard Varley, leave this house."

"Indeed!"

" Ay, sir ; your presence is a contamination—an insult to the dead."

" What if I refuse ?"

" You dare not."

" I dare."

" Then the servants shall force you from the door. Let the first act, oh, Heaven ! of my sad possession of this once happy home be to free it from the insidious monster who has banished peace from its fireside, and brought death and despair across its threshold."

" Hold !" cried Varley, as Miranda moved towards the door.

" Wherefore shall I pause ?"

" For his sake who lies above in the cold embrace of death."

Miranda shuddered.

" For his sake," continued Varley, " who now inhabits the cell of a felon."

Miranda clasped her hands and uttered the name of Rowland Percy.

" For your own sake," added Varley, " dependent as you are upon me."

" Upon you ?"

" Yes."

" I ? The daughter of as good and kind a father as ever drew the breath of life, dependent upon you, Bernard Varley ?"

" 'Tis even so. You state the case most fairly."

Miranda for a moment felt as if her senses would desert her, and she sunk into a chair.

CHAPTER IX.

THE INTERVIEW.—THE PROPOSAL.

VARLEY gazed upon his victim with the gloating eyes of passion, and then in a low tone, which he adopted rather as an excuse for bending his head towards her until his hot breath almost fanned her cheek, than for any other reason, he said,—

" Miranda, I am master here."

" No, no !" cried Miranda, starting to her feet , " this is some horrible delusion —such things cannot be. Bernard Varley, I was once a week irresolute girl, but that time has passed away, and now I have the courage and the strength to act."

" Act as far as you have power."

" I have power in my own house—my father's house, now mine. I have power, and I will use it to drive you hence—you, who from the bottom of my heart, I believe to be the cause of all the misery which has fallen, like a bolt from Heaven, upon so many persons. Once more I say, Bernard Varley, no longer pollute this once happy home with your presence."

" Pause yet a moment, beautiful Miranda—more beautiful to me in your wrath, when the fire of indignation is flashing from your eyes, than in your more melting moments. Hear me, and I swear, by whatever you may deem most sacred, that I have power, which you will do well to mollify and not defy."

" You, power ?"

" Ay, power over you."

" Over me ?"

" And Rowland Percy—aye, even the dead have I power over, for they leave behind them as their most imperishable legacy, their reputation. Miranda, one word from me would brand your father's memory with infamy."

" No—no—no—oh, God, no."

" That word shall never pass my lips while Miranda is willing to keep them sealed."

Miranda dropped her head upon the table and wept, while Varley proceeeded :—

"I can save Rowland Percy from an ignominious death, or I can, by the evidence 'tis easy to produce, conduct him to the scaffold."

"You know he is innocent."

"The admission costs me nothing," said Varley. "Agreed, he is innocent, but yet shall he suffer, if I, Bernard Varley, say he shall."

"Monster."

"Nay, that is not all. By a will which your father has left behind him, properly signed and witnessed, all his wealth is left to me—the Grange, the meadows, all."

"Impossible!"

"Tis true—in trust—in trust, mark me, for you, always provided, you wed —me!"

"You!" shrieked Miranda, springing from her seat and holding her hands extended before her, as if to keep off some loathsome object. "You, Bernard Varley?"

"Even so—I love you."

"You love? But—but 'tis impossible. It is not true—a more unfounded, base fabrication could not be—absurd. My father make such a will? No—no—he could not—he did not. Bernard Varley, still I do defy you."

"You do?"

"As I reverence Heaven, I do abhor you."

"Beware, Miranda, I will paint you two pictures—pictures of the imagination, if you please. You shall examine both minutely, and then make your choice."

"I will not hear you."

"But you shall."

"Shall?"

"That was my word."

Miranda flew to the bell, but Varley caught her wrist, and in a hissing w   sr he said—

"To the first person who enters this room from your summons, I proclaim your father a felon, and brand his memory for ever with a stigma of guilt which never can be effaced. Tempt me not, Miranda, or I can raise a cry against even the cold remains of your father that shall reach your heart, although it may pass over his."

Miranda released her hold of the bell-rope, as she gasped,—

"What—what crime?"

"Forgery," said Varley. "Your father made his fortune by forging checks on the bank he was himself a partner in, and others."

"No—no—he did not."

"I have proof."

"His sense of honour—his integrity."

"Ha—ha—ha! his sense of honour! I tell you I have proof, Miranda. You know now my power—use or abuse your knowledge as you may."

"Still do I defy you."

"You do?"

"I do. The innocent will not fall, though the guilty be powerful.'

"Look on this parchment," said Varley, drawing a small packet from his pocket. "Do you recognise that name?"

He turned down a corner of the parchment, and Miranda saw her father's signature.

"This parchment," continued Varley, "invests me with full power over you, and all that belongs to you. If you wed not with me or with my consent, you become a beggar; your inheritance becomes mine, and I turn you on the world to starve."

"Then," said Miranda, clasping her hands, "if this be true, I commend my-self to Heaven,, and if it be its will that I should starve, that I should lie me down and die of famine in some lonely spot, let Heaven's will be done."

"Reflect, Miranda. In wedding me, you wed wealth—you remain mis   of your ancient home—your wildest caprices shall all be indulged—I swear by Heaven !"

"Hold—hold! Take not the name of Heaven in vain for the most unholy purposes—you and your offers I alike despise and abhor. I will see closely to your right to exercise the power you talk of, and if it really be that my poor father was compelled to make you the depository of all that was his, and to attach to my very means of existence so terrible a condition, I shall lament the more for him, not love his memory less."

"You have no relations."

"None."

"No friends."

"Save Heaven."

"Pshaw? Bethink you what you lose—station, wealth, luxury !"

"Peace—peace ! nor profane my ears with such base reasoning. I will leave you, if I must, to the quiet possession of what you have wrung from him who is now no more. Welcome poverty, welcome woe, want, death, in preference to breathing the same air with Bernard Varley, the murderer."

"Murderer ?"

"Yes, murderer ! Bernard Varley, you know well that to accomplish your own dark and evil purposes you have contrived all the misery which now afflicts my throbbing brain."

"Miranda, you rave. From any one but you such language would excite my warmest indignation—you rave, girl, you rave."

"No, Bernard Varley, 'tis you who rave, when you fancy that the intricate path of guilt you have chosen will lead to aught but destruction. Heaven is not so unmindful of its creatures as to leave them at the mercy of the machinations of such men as you. Tremble, for a day will surely come when all your fine-drawn schemes will be overwhelmed in one common ruin. Oh, madman—madman ! to fancy that treachery, deceit, and crime would bring you other results than despair and death ! You rave, Bernard Varley, you rave !"

"Peace, I say," cried Varley ; "shall I be bearded here, where I alone have power? Girl, your wits desert you when you dare—but, but, no matter—let it pass ; your wondrous beauty is excuse for much—your voice, even in anger, is sweet music. Miranda, I love you with a love as exceeding the cold passion, called by such a name, as do the mighty Alps a gentle bank of earth. I love you with a fiery, fierce, undying love that in its intensity absorbs all other feelings. Where, oh where, can you find one who will, as I do, prefer you even to heaven ?"

"Such love," said Miranda, shuddering, "is a wild and unholy passion. Bernard Varley, I almost doubt if you be human. You have in this brief interview revealed enough to make its mere recital on my part most dangerous to you."

"Indeed. Add to it then that Bernard Varley showed you this which he picked up on the floor by the bedside of your father."

As he spoke, he produced a small set of ivory tablets, which Miranda had often seen in the possession of Rowland Percy.

"This conclusive evidence, coupled the other facts, will seal the fate of Rowland Percy," said Varley. "You alone can save him."

"Monster !"

"Call me what you will, but save your father's memory from shame—Rowland Percy from death on a public scaffold—yourself from a depth of poverty you cannot understand, and all those dependent upon you from deep woe, by giving me your hand."

"Never !"

"You have made your election ?"

"I have—I swear——"

"Hold ! you may repent your oath."

"There needs no oath," said Miranda.

"And yet I make one that you shall be my wife."

Miranda walked to the door.

"Bethink you well of how you act," said Varley, following her. "You stand upon a precipice, down which you may rashly precipitate ourself, or you may step back in time."

"You are far down the slippery descent," said Miranda; "there is no stepping back for you."

"I wish not. My blood dances through my veins like tongues of flame!—my love for you is——"

"Peace—peace!"

"Nay, hear me!"

He rushed between her and the door

"Beautiful being!" he cried, "beautiful in your pride—beautiful in your hate! I would barter kingdoms for one kind look—for one smile—I would give a hundred lives such as Rowland Percy's for a kiss!"

Miranda flew to the bell and rang it violently.

Varley withdrew from the door, and with a bitter smile, he said,—

"Pass out, Heiress of the Grange. You are but as a bird held by a brace—you are in my power, go where you will. I am your good or evil genious, as you make me."

CHAPTER X.

THE RIDE TO YORK.—A MEETING WITH THE SQUIRE OF LARKSWOOD.—THE ATTEMPTED EXPLANATION.—A DAUGHTER'S LOVE.

WHEN Miranda left Varley, she proceeded immediately to her own room, and sinking into a chair, she burst into tears and commenced such a paroxysm of weeping that the young girl who attended her, was alarmed beyond description. She threw herself at the feet of her young mistress, crying,—

"Oh, Miss Miranda, do pray leave off crying so. It's dreadful to hear you— it is indeed. You will break my heart—you that was always so light-hearted, and so happy, that you made everybody happy around you——"

"Hush—hush," said Miranda, dashing the tears from her eyes; "I am better now, and I hope this is the last time I shall give way to such weakness—I am much better now."

"Oh, miss, you don't know how much pleasure it gives me to hear you say so."

Miranda rose, and dashed cold water plentifully on her face to desrroy the trace of tears. Then turning to the girl, she said—

"I know not what may happen in the next few days—but believe nothing —heed nothing that you hear from that dreadful man."

"Mr. Varley, miss!"

"Yes, Bernard Varley; he is a fiend in human shape. Let him say what he will—swear what he will, always do you, and all the servants in the house, remember that Rowland Percy is innocent. He would not have harmed a hair of my poor father's head. Heaven knows he is innocent."

"Yes, miss. I'm quite sure such a nice young man as Mr. Rowland Percy could'nt be no other than a lamb; in pint o' innocence, I means, Miss Mirnda."

"Yes—he is innocent," repeated Miranda.

"Oh, miss! don't you take on so," said the girl. "If I could only see you a little calmer, and more patient like."

"I am calm and patient," said Miranda.

"But your hands are so cold."

"My heart is cold too, now but I shall soon be much better. I am quite calm. Surely you and all will believe me calm when I can speak of—of my father, whom I loved next to Heaven."

"Oh! don't speak of poor, dear master, miss."

"Yes. I am calm enough now. My father has been murdered. He who loved me, Rowland Percy, is accused of the awful crime. That is all I have to contend against now. My heart is nearly turned to stone, and I am very calm. Duty must henceforward take the place of feeling. I must see the innocent righted."

She sat down, and held her head with her hands for some moments, then she said,—

"I sent some one to York."

"For a lawyer, miss?"

"Yes—yes—I recollect now. Has he come?"

"No, miss."

"Then let my horse be got ready; I must be in York within the hour. This is a time for personal action."

"What! your dear little Jessy, miss, that—"

"Hush—hush! I mean Jessy, of course. You know it was a gift from my father on—on my birthday. The patient, gentle creature will speed me on my journey. Give orders to have it ready as soon as possible. Quick—quick—and fetch together what things are mine by gift of my father in these rooms. Collect them all together; for as Heaven is my judge, I know not but the very doors of my father's house may, by some machination of that man, be closed against me soon."

"Lor, miss! Why, old Mathew, the steward, was but half an hour ago telling of all the servants, as you, and you only now, was missus and master of the old Grange."

"It may be so, or it may not," said Miranda, with a shudder. "But go—go at once, and do as I bid you. I must go to York."

"But, miss, don't you think as it won't look quite well for—for—— "

"For what?"

"For you to be riding to York so very soon?"

"I understand you. You mean so soon after my father's death. No. It looks far from well. But there are duties that defy the world's opinion, and which in their performance must throw us for succour alone upon our consciences and the judgment of Heaven. All forms—all ceremonies—must give place to what I have to do."

"Lor, miss, you quite frighten me."

"Go—go. Delay no longer. Go!"

The girl left her, and Miranda stood by the table, pale as a marble statue.

"I have to rescue Rowland Percy,' she said, in a faint tone. "Yes—I have to rescue Rowland Percy, and if the faith of a heart that knows but venial errors, can nerve the mind to such exertions as may be necessary for that object, I will do it, and he shall be saved. Oh, what a tangled web of villany has not Bernard Varley woven? How can I—how can Rowland escape its meshes? Yet, surely there may—there must be men accustomed to all kinds of guile, who will, with their clear judgments, see a clue to the plot which baffles my judgment. My trust is in Heaven; it will not desert the right. If my poor father be murdered, as I fear must prove too true, then Barnard Varley is the murderer, and seeks to screen himself by bringing the innocent Rowland to the scaffold."

A shudder passed over Miranda's frame as she pronounced the horrible word scaffold, and in her mind's eye, she saw the throng crowding around to witness the awful preparations for the ignominious death of the noble, the gifted, and the innocent Rowland Percy.

"Oh, Heaven! preserve my senses," she exclaimed, as with clasped hands, she dropped upon her knees, and tried to pray.

The door gently opened, and the tearful voice of the girl said,—

"Please, miss, Mr. Varley says as no horse shall leave the stables."

Miranda sprung to her feet, and a flash of resentment came from her eyes, as she cried,—

"Bernard Varley says so?"

"Yes, miss."

"How dare—but no—I will be calm—my riding-habit, girl—quick—my hat—. my hat—there, that will do—now—now I am ready—we shall see if Bernard Varley can prevent me in my father's house from using that which is mine own. Oh! this is most surprising insolence, and yet I thank Heaven it is so, for, were I left to no feeling but grief—were all around me kind and mild and dutiful, I think I could lie down and die; but there is a slumbering spirit of resistance to insult and oppression in my heart, that a touch—a whisper, will awaken into life and energy—I will have my horse—I will ride to York within this hour."

The girl looked at Miranda, terrified, for her small beautiful figure seemed to dilate into dignity as she spoke, and the eloquent blood mantled in her cheeks, as it was wont to do in happier days.

"My horse, my horse," she added, and walked with a firm step from the room followed by the trembling girl, who could not understand the feelings of her young mistress, and thought she must be going mad.

Without a tremour, now that her gentle spirit was fairly roused, Miranda descended the marble staircase of the ancient mansion, and reached the hall without meeting with any one. Then she entered a small room which was used as a waiting-room for strangers, and rung the bell therein.

The summons was answered by an old, grey-headed domestic, who started with surprise when he saw Miranda attired for riding.

"Mathew," she said, calmly, "I want my little nag, I say, directly."

"Yes—yes—yes—Miss Miranda ; I will go and see."

"Go and see, Mathew?"

"Yes, miss, there's Master Varley has been to the stables and locked 'em up."

"Indeed !"

"Yes, miss, and he swears you sha'n't have no horse to-day, miss."

"We shall see, Mathew ; it is time the servants should know who is to command here, and who is to obey—come with me."

Miranda walked from the room, followed by the old man, and crossing the hall, she descended a flight of steps, which terminated in a door leading to the stables. Passing onwards, she paused not until she came to the stabling, when she t rne to Mathew and said,— d

"Summon hither all the servants."

"All, miss ?"

"Yes—without exception."

"This will do it, miss," said the old man, and he took hold a rope which communicated with an alarm bell, and gave it so lusty a pull, that the whole place echoed again with the deep sonorous sounds.

In a moment servants came running from all directions, and the old man, with a smile of self-complacency, said,—

"That will do, I think, Miss Miranda."

When the throng of servants saw their young mistress, they fell back to a respectful distance ; but Miranda beckoned to them to approach, and said, in her usual voice,—

"I want my nag, Jessy."

There was a pause for a moment, and then a groom stepped forward and said,—

"Please, miss—that d——d—I beg your pardon, miss, but Master Varley has locked the stable, and had the d——d—a—hem—impudence to take away the key.

There was a dead silence for the space of nearly a minute, then Miranda spoke,—

"My father," she said, "is now no more. I am his only child."

"And, in course, our young missus," said the groom, with a triumphant look at his fellow servants, who all nodded their approbation.

"How many of you are there ?" said Miranda, " men, I mean."

"There's eleven on us, Miss Miran'a," said Mathew.

"Eleven men servants, have I ?"

"Yes, miss—yes," cried several voices.

"And one man keeps the key of my stable, and detains my horse !"

The groom began slowly turning up his cuffs, and when he had accomplished that process, he turned to Miranda, and said,—

"Please, missus, I'm going to get the key."

"Do so," said Miranda.

"What is the meaning of all this ?" cried Varley, suddenly appearing from behind the throng. "How dare you all congregate here, you lazy hounds ? Back to your several occupations this moment !"

"I want the key of my stable," said Miranda, to the groom, and not even looking at Varley.

"And you shall have it too, miss," said the sturdy fellow, as he steeped up to Varley, and shouted in far from a courteous tone,—

"The key !"

"Scoundrel !" cried Varley.

"Vagabond !" said the groom. "I wants the key."

Varley turned as white as a sheet, and stepping back a pace, he cried,—

"Here, all you gaping there, turn this fellow out of the house."

No one moved, and the groom said,—

"I aint a going. Give us the key !"

"You are drunk, sir," cried Varley. "I am master of this house, and I will be obeyed."

The groom looked at Miranda, who still preserving the same calmness of emeanour, said,—

"I want the key of my stables." He then seized Varley by the cravat, and held him in a grasp of iron, as he said,—

"It'll save you trouble and me too, now, if you gives up the key."

Varley thrust his right arm into his breast, and drew a pistol, but the groom was too quick for him, and with his disengaged hand he snatched the weapon from him, and threw it singing through the air to a considerable distance over a wall.

"You cowardly vagabond !" he cried. "So you can't fight like a man, eh ?"

Varley now put forth all his strength in an endeavour to shake off his antagonist, but the other stood the struggle, as firmly as a rock, and when Varley relaxed his exertions, the groom said,—

"Now it's my turn," and immediately threw him on his back, with a heaviness that quite confused his faculties for a few moments, during which the key was taken from his coat-pocket.

CHAPTER XI.

THE PUMPING.—THE RIDE TO YORK.—MIRANDA'S REFLECTIONS.—LOVE IN A
COTTAGE.

A GENERAL hurrah from the assembled servants proclaimed their joy at the defeat of Varley, who was detested by the whole establishment, but Miranda held up her hand, and said,—

"Peace, peace ! Remember this is the house of mourning now. Saddle me my horse—I must ride to York. I will be back early. But, before I go, remember, all of you, that Rowland Percy is innocent."

Varley had by the time Miranda's little palfrey was ready, and she had been assisted to mount, risen to his feet. He was perfectly livid from passion, and with clenched hands, he stamped on the earth, crying,—

"They shall all repent of this, Miranda Rankley, as surely as the sun will rise to-morrow ! You shall most bitterly repent ! I will have vengeance against you more terrible than you are aware of. You have raised a devil you will in vain attempt to quell again ! And you—you base hinds, I will have every one of you in York Castle for an assault.

"Friends," said Miranda, as she turned her horse's head in the direction of the gate, which several of the servants had opened for her, "I leave you to accept of what insolence your English notions may enable you to put up with from this man."

"We won't put up with nothing," cried one.

The groom who had gained such a victory over Varley, now appeared at the stable-door, leading a horse ready for mounting.

"How dare you bring that horse out ?" shrieked Varley. "Take it back, sir."

"I'm a going to ride arter my missus, if you please, sir, and have no objection," said the groom with mock civility, as he sprung into the saddle.

"Will none of you side with me ?" cried Varley. "Five pounds to the man who pulls yon scoundrel off his horse."

" It's dangerous work," said the groom, " for I bite, and the horse kicks Perhaps you'd like to try to earn so much yourself."

The groom then commenced backing his steed towards Varley, who turned and ran towards the house, to the great amusement of all the domestics.

" Oh, you won't," said the groom ; " very good ; and now, my boys, it's my opinion as our young missus don't by any means want Mr. Varley to stay to dinner. Good-bye to you."

He then galloped after Miranda, who had got some distance by this time from the house.

The servants looked now at each other in some degree of doubt. They evidently wanted a leader, now the groom was gone, and it is doubtful whether Bernard Varley would have fallen into the mishap that soon befel him had he not himself committed an act that at once induced a spirit of indignation against him among even the most irresolute of the servants.

It was this; the young girl who attended upon Miranda attempted to pass him in the door-way, whither he had flown for shelter from the heels of the groom's horse. She just touched his elbow accidentally, when he turned, and boiling with rage against everybody, he struck her a severe blow.

The girl screamed, and at once half a dozen of the men servants rushed forward and secured Varley before he could take refuge in the house, which he attempted to do, for he saw at a glance his danger.

He was dragged into the stable-yard in a moment, and then there was a pause for an instant, to know what to do with him, when a stable boy, who had received at different times several hard knocks from Varley's riding whip, for not being so quick in saddling for him a horse when he required one, as he, Varley, thought, in his overbearing violence, he should have been, called out,—

" Pump on him."

The suggestion was adopted in a moment ; and amid an universal shout of—

" To the pump—to the pump !"

Bernard Varley was dragged across the stable-yard towards an ancient and venerable pump that had stood there for a hundred years or more.

For a moment or two he seemed paralyzed at the turn affairs had taken, and scarcely made any resistance. Then, however, he commenced kicking and fighting with desperation, but all was in vain—his enemies were too numerous, and four of the stoutest among them carried him along easily by his arms and legs, notwithstanding all his exertions.

" You'll all be hung !" he shouted. " You dare not—you cowards—villains ! I'll ruin you all. You shall suffer for this the longest day you have to live !"

They now reached the pump, and the malicious stable-boy planted himself at the handle, saying in a voice of great exultation,—

" I know how to work the old pump better than any one. Pop him under, and shan't he have it—oh, no—not at all !"

" A hundred pounds among you to let me go !" screamed Varley, as they worked the pump. " You don't mean it ? You can't mean it ? I'll forgive you all up to now."

His assailants were inexorable, and he was held under the spout of the pump in such a position that the first deluge of the cold water came full upon his face, and well did the stable-boy redeem his pledge of making the old pump work well, for there came from the old fashioned lion's head, that formed the spout, such a stream of cold water that, for a moment, Bernard Varley was nearly suffocated, and could neither speak nor move, being just turned about at the pleasure of his tormentors.

There was scarcely a servant in the establishment who had not some grudge to pay off against Bernard Varley, who had since his residence at the Grange, been conspicuous for his petty tyranny; so that it was full five minutes before he was removed from under the spout of the pump, and set upon his feet completely saturated with water, and as cold and miserable as he could possibly be.

" Now be off with you," cried one, " while you have a whole skin."

Varley looked around him, from one to the other, but he said not a word. His passion lay too deep for expression. Revenge engrossed all his faculties, and he had now but one immediate object, which was to reach York, and procure warrants against the various servants who had treated him so roughly.

There was, however, one difficulty which came across his mind; and that was, he did not know some of their names. He turned round as he walked towards the gate; and in a voice thick with rage, he said,—

"Who will come with me to York to earn fifty pounds, and be made steward of the Grange within a week?"

A general laugh was his only answer; and shaking his clenched hand in the air, he dashed out at the gate, in the direction of the city.

In the meantime Miranda had gone on her journey at a smart canter, after waiting a moment to allow the groom to overtake her, whom she would not send back, although she had contemplated riding alone.

The road wound through a richly cultivated country; but Miranda's thoughts were too much concentrated in the perils, and dangers, and treacheries that surrounded her, to know a smiling corn-field from the most desolate waste.

The course she meant to adopt, and it was certainly the most rational one she could think of, was to proceed at once to a solicitor in York, who she knew had been employed occasionally by her father, and whose name she knew, although not his address.

Before him she meant to lay the whole circumstances, without reservation, and beseech him to take up her cause against the villain who was endeavouring not only to possess himself of all that she had been taught to consider her own, but to destroy the only being now in existence to whom her young heart yearned with affection.

As she rode along the beautifully diversified road, she strove to recollect and arrange all that had passed within the eventful four-and-twenty hours, which had not only made her an orphan, but produced more extraordinary circumstances than could be crowded probably into the whole space of her future existence.

More particularly did Miranda strive to call to mind every word uttered by Bernard Varley in his interview with her of that morning, and she found, when she came to consider all that had passed, so much to engender suspicion against Varley, and so little against Rowland Percy, that her heart felt lighter, and she thought that the right would triumph.

But Miranda little knew the desperate subtlety of the man she had to deal with; nor was she so well aware as he was of the peculiar course of legal evidence which made her conversation with him of but little avail without other corroborative evidence tending to prove the truth of his own partial admissions.

"Rowland must be free!" she cried; "and if this man—this dreadful Varley—even should succeed in retaining possession of the dear home to which I am so much attached, surely we can be happy elsewhere, however humbly. We need no wealth to make us happy. The humblest roof will shelter us as well as the lordly Grange. He may wrest from us all but our innocence, our integrity, and our love. Those are dear possessions bestowed by Heaven, and no mortal power can tear them from fond trusting hearts." Comforted by these thoughts, Miranda urged her steed to quicker progress, and entered a narrow lane which ran along for some distance by the road side, and then left it abruptly, cutting off a considerable part of the distance between the Grange and the city of York.

The lane was enveloped in deep shadow, for the tall trees on either side of it were amply sufficient to hide even a noontide sun from the narrow bridle-path which wound among them.

The delicious odours of a thousand wild flowers here greeted Miranda, and when she reached the middle of the lane, she involuntarily allowed her steed to relapse into a gentle walk, and to nibble some of the soft, rich green herbage from the sloping banks.

It was a scene such as would have delighted the soul of some painter fond of shadow and deep massive colouring. Miranda gazed around her with pleasure—

the first pleasure that had ever dawned upon her mind since the calamitous events had occurred which had given rise to her present journey.

The groom was some distance in the rear, and Miranda was little dreaming that any one was near her, when, from a gap in the hedge, there suddenly came forth a man, who, at the first glance, Miranda knew to be Mr. Percy, the Squire of Larkswood.

She reined in her steed on the instant ; and the squire, shading his eyes with his hand, looked in her beautiful face before he spoke. Then in a voice of deep emotion he said,—

" Miranda, friends we cannot be ; but are we enemies ?"

" Enemies, sir ?" said Miranda. " Heaven knows I am no man's enemy, but——"

" But what ? You hesitate."

" I do ; for there is a circumstance too painful for me to refer to further, which must make us strangers, Mr. Percy."

" There is, Miranda," said the squire, with a deep sigh. " A circumstance that that will embitter the remainder of my existence. Oh, Miranda ! to you I have to explain how and why it was I came to lift my hand against your father."

" Hold, sir," said Miranda, " I wish to hear no more. The deed was done. Let me know nothing or what led to it. It is done, and the cause is with Heaven."

" But, Miranda, you know that your father was my friend."

" Did you know it when you met him in deadly strife ? Oh, Mr. Percy, you have made hearts bleed with anguish by that one act, which would have resisted, with a stern command of feeling, misery from any other hand. Say no more, sir. There is an insuperable bar between even our acquaintance."

" But hear me, Miranda."

" What needs it that I should be told by you that the dread of the world's opinion made you sacrifice your own and attempt my father's life ? Mr. Percy, had an angel from heaven come to tell me that from your hand would have come such a blow, I should have thought I dreamed."

" I have sought you, Miranda," said Mr. Percy, laying a trembling hand upon her bridle. " I have sought you to say some words which now stick in my throat."

" Say them briefly, sir."

" They are brief. But—but—you do not look at me, Miranda."

" I cannot, sir. The well-remembered face of a friend looks so different when estranged by the infliction of an act which I, as well as you, must ever dread to think of."

CHAPTER XII.

THE EXPLANATION.—THE PROMISE.—MIRANDA'S GRIEFS INCREASE.—THE FATHER'S ANGUISH.

THERE was a pause of some moments, and Mr. Percy turned away his head. Miranda thought he was weeping, and her heart smote her for the apparent harshness of what she had said to him. Her gentle nature could not brook the idea of inflicting pain on any one, and it was with a softened tone and manner that she said,—

" Mr. Percy, I am bound to York, upon an errand that concerns you as nearly as it does me. Time may be precious. Will you say now to me what you have to say, and let me go on my way?"

He turned his face towards her. It was deathly pale, and then, in a voice of deep emotion, he said, " Miranda, you do not, you cannot know what forced this fatal quarrel on me. An insult past all bearing."

"Hold, Mr. Percy, I cannot listen to such a mode of justification. As Heaven is my judge, I do believe my father was incapable of wantonly insulting any one, and much less you, of all living men. Oh, sir, you have stood before him with a weapon aimed at his life, and I have heard him speak of you in terms of brotherly love; he valued you next to the one being who now speaks to you, the only one who can claim his name, and yet——"

"Yet I fought a duel with him, Miranda."

"You did, and——"

"Hear me once more; and oh, suspend your judgment for a while, while I disclose to you the causes that led to this most fatal awful encounter. Miranda, you see before you a ruined man. My fortune has long been tottering, and now it has fallen, never again to rise."

"Ruined, Mr. Percy?"

"Yes, I am a beggar. I have scarce a home now in which to lie my weary frame. The once wealthy Squire of Larkswood is, I repeat, a ruined man."

"Much, sir, as I grieve at misfortune," said Miranda, "I cannot see that that was cause to make you my father's enemy?"

"It was remotely so, Miranda, as you shall hear. For more than twelve months now has ruin, most absolute and irretrievable, been hanging over me. The fact was known but to myself and one other, far, very far from hence, as I thought, but by some means it must have come to your father's knowledge."

"You are mistaken, Mr. Percy—on my life he knew it not."

"I have evidence, Miranda. My dear son, Rowland, was actually forbidden the Grange."

"But not on such grounds. Setting aside, sir, all false delicacy, and the natural dislike I have to converse on such a theme, I aver that the recommendation —for it was, at first, no more—of my father to Rowland, not to visit at the Grange, arose from a prudent doubt of the stability of the affection of one so young, and of such little knowledge of the great world."

Mr. Percy shook his head.

"Nay, on my soul's best hopes," said Miranda, "it was so; Rowland then reasoned intemperately—my father became angry, and they did part in one of those quarrels which compromise neither party, but which may, with mutual honour, be made up again."

"Miranda," said Mr. Percy, "will you read this letter?"

He handed her a note, as he spoke, and after a moment's hesitation, Miranda took it, and looking at the superscription, saw it was addressed to Mr. Percy.

"Read that," he said, "and then judge of my wounded feelings."

Miranda opened it, and then read as follows:—

"SIR,—I am desired by Sir George Rankley to express to you his indignation at your presuming to allow your son to visit at the Grange, when you must know that both of you are on the verge of ruin. Your unsuccessful speculations are known to Sir George, and he desires me to say that he drops all communication with one who maintains, or endeavours to maintain, an appearance in the county, so much at variance with his real means.

"I am, sir, yours, &c.,

"BERNARD VARLEY."

"Is not that proof?" said Mr. Percy, when he saw that Miranda had finished the epistle.

"No," cried Miranda boldly.

The squire looked astonished at her prompt negative, and then added,—

"It is as strong proof as man can well conceive."

"This letter was never dictated by my father," said Miranda. "Oh, Mr. Percy, you have allowed yourself to be made the tool of a man so base, so crafty, that I sometimes doubt if he be really human."

Mr. Percy drew his breath hard, as he said,—

"Have you proof of what you say?"

"I have belief."

"But you may be mistaken—you must be. Oh, Miranda, well I know that poverty perverts the understanding more than riches. It makes us see slights which, not otherwise suspecting, would pass us like the idle wind. It makes us fancy disrespect where none is meant; but here is surely proof that I have been led away by no absurd fancy. I was despised because I was poor, and my boy's trusting, honest heart was thought no longer worthy of meeting with the heiress of the Grange, because his father was unfortunate. Is not that the true reading?"

"No" said Miranda; "no—you are wrong, Mr. Percy, and, like myself, you are envelopen in a mist of circumstances most strangely contradictory, created by the villain, Bernard Varley. Time may explain what now to me is manifest as a whole, but obscure in its details. That letter never received the sanction of my father."

"You think it Varley's own act?"

"I do!"

No. 6.

"No, no—it cannot be. Miranda, I answered this letter. Mildly and temperately I answered it, for I knew that my poor boy's happiness was at stake, and I suppressed my feelings. I admitted the distress of my circumstances, but I pleaded that although I had lost all else, I had preserved my honour, and could leave my son an unsullied name."

"What followed, then?" said Miranda, with much emotion.

"I received another note. It is here, and then a third. Read them."

Miranda, with a beating heart and her eyes swimming with tears, took the two notes. The first one ran thus:—

"Sir,—Your contemptible conduct, in endeavouring to bolster up your own fallen fortunes by an union between the Lady Miranda and your son, has induced Sir George Rankley to command me to inform you that he will expose your conduct on every opportunity, and bring down upon you the well-merited disgrace which he will take care to see heaped upon your head. Sir George would, did he not deem it quite derogatory to his character to meet you, insist upon satisfaction in the field for your vile conduct; but he trusts you will spare him the necessity of adopting some means of chastising your insolence, by instantly forwarding to me, for him, a humble apology.   "I am, sir,

                    "By order of Sir George Rankley,
                         "Yours, &c.,
                              "Bernard Varley."

Miranda made no remark, but opened the other epistle. It contained only these words;—

"Sir,—I am desired by Sir George Rankley to request you will name a friend for the purpose of arranging a hostile meeting.

                    "I am, sir, yours, &c.,
                              "Bernard Varley."

The last epistle dropped from Miranda's hands, and she looked on the pale suffering countenance of Mr. Percy with inexpressible anguish, as she said,—

"And during all this correspondence you never saw my father?"

"Never."

"Oh, Heaven!"

She resigned the bridle of her horse, and had not Mr. Percy supported her, she must have fallen to the earth.

"Speak, Miranda—speak," he said. "For the love of mercy, speak! You hint at some frightful mystery—your words freeze my very heart. Tell me, though the news blast me, that I have been duped—deceived."

"You have—you have," gasped Miranda. "A light gleams through my brain. I begin to see the hellish plot that has been laid for the destruction of us all. My father murdered—you deceived, and a store of remorse laid up that must last even unto the grave's brink. My poor, poor, devoted Rowland, innocent, yet accused of what may take his life, and I desolate—oh, God, most desolate!"

Miranda burst into such an hysterical passion of weeping, that Mr. Percy was fain to help her from the horse, and lay her upon the verdant bank, where for some moments her deep grief knew no remission.

She felt that Bernard Varley had done all that she had enumerated, and while she sickened at the extent of his wickedness, she trembled for the future, when she thought of the success of his frightful machinations.

CHAPTER XIII.

THE RECONCILIATION.—THE ARREST.—THE DESOLATION OF MIRANDA.

MR. PERCY himself was deeply affected at the inconsolable grief of Miranda, and he exclaimed,—

"Oh, Heaven, what have we all done that we should be visited by such calamities?"

"Oh, how could you believe," sobbed Miranda, "that those letters came from my father? They are the fabrications of Varley. 'Tis he, and he only, who has caused all this dreadful suffering. Mr. Percy—you—you should have seen my father."

Mr. Percy clasped his hands as he said,—

"Reproach me, Miranda, as you will. I am a broken-hearted man."

"Forgive me," said Miranda; "forgive me, sir, I knew not what I said. You have been, as doubtless was my poor father himself, the dupe of a villain's arts. I do not blame you. Forgive my heedless words."

She held out her hand to him, and he took it between his, as he replied,—

"Mirianda, you can never look upon me with friendly eyes. It is scarcely in human nature that you should, and I will not vex you by my presence or company. I have but one hope on earth now, and that is, that my poor innocent boy, Rowland, should be spared to me, and that you will forget his father, and still be happy with him, poor as he is, for he at least is in no way connected with these most melancholy occurrences. He was far away, and his return was as unexpected by me as by any one else. Forget me, Miranda, and I will live the remainder of the life that Heaven spares me, in some solitude away from you."

"No, no," said Miranda, through her tears, "Heaven judges motives, not acts. Let me, with my weak human wisdom, do so likewise. The world may look strangely on me, and point the finger of scorn at me for clinging to you, but as I have hopes of joy hereafter, I do believe thyt you have been the victim of the same plot that has made us all unhappy. Together we will endeavour to effect the liberation of Rowland, and be you, Mr. Percy, my second father."

"Can you think and act thus generously?"

"Call it not by such a name. It is no more than simple justice."

"And yet, Miranda, dear to my heart as is your generous confidence, I should be base indeed to take advantage of it. You shall not hear one cold remark—be subjected no one cold look for companionship with me. Had I the means of offering you all that I could once have offered, I might hesitate; but go, heiress of the Grange, and its wide possessions—shun the poor as you would shun mortal contagion. For your words of peace to me, accept the heartfelt thanks of one who not long will linger behind your father; and should we meet in that blessed abode where sorrow never comes, and there be such feelings, grown purer with their heavenly intercourse, as on this earth bind in the chains of dear love kindred hearts, I will tell him that his dear child—his much-loved Miranda, has forgiven me, and blotted out the word of my transgression with a tear, as pure as any shed by a bright angel for the sins of mortals. Farewell, Miranda; life is before you like a sunny landscape. Ah! that there may be no more shadow than will serve to make the light more beautiful. Save my boy—and then the old and sorrow-stricken man will lay him down in peace to die. Farewell—farewell."

"Stay—stay," cried Miranda.

Mr. Percy moved slowly away.

"Oh, stay with me," she cried—"where have I another I can call a friend?"

He paused.

have that, Miranda, which will surround you with hosts," he cried—"you

possess the glittering lore that will throng your halls with anxious men, each striving hard with each to do you service."

"No—no—you mistake."

"Mistake?"

"Ay. Even that is denied."

"You are heiress of the Grange."

"Bernard Varley claims all."

"Impossible!"

"He does. He taunts me with being dependent upon him. That I cannot be;
but he claims all. The—old forest trees—all—all this arch fiend claims as his
own, and I—I—Miranda, know not if I dare claim the meanest trifle that in
fondness my poor father bestowed upon me."

"This passes all belief," said Mr. Percy. "Am I awake, or is this some dream
of such frightful circumstantial reality that it appears all true?"

"It is no vision," said Miranda. "Shun me not that you are poor   I know
not but I am destitute."

"Then, Miranda, no power on earth shall tear me from you! I will beg for
you, Miranda, but you shall know no want. May Heaven accept as some atonement for my sin in raising my arm in unholy strife, against a fellow creature, this
vow I now make—never to desert you, Miranda, if what you say should prove
true; my fading strength shall all be expended in your service. I have done you
grievous wrong—and my future life shall be one of atonement."

At this moment a crackling among the dry branches of the hedge, which
was immediately opposite to where the Squire of Larkswood and Miranda
were conversing, announced the approach of some one, and the next instant
the singular face of Martin the idiot protruded itself forward from among the
leaves.

"Aha!" he cried, "I'm here. Bold Hawk's my name, and I'm bold hawk by
nature? They are coming! Do you hear me, squire? They are coming! I have
skimmed along the meadows like a bird—over hedge, ditch, and brier, have come
to tell you. Down by the old preserve I came with a whoop, and a hilloa, and a
cry, and I heard the hares whispering together, "Look at Bold Hawk! There he
treads like the wind! See, how he flies! Ha! ha! ha! a southern blast tried to
follow me, but it could not! No—no—Bold Hawk cannot be overtaken! They
are coming, squire! They are coming! Give the poor Hawk a silver piece; 'tis
but to charm away pains and aches."

The poor fellow looked appealingly at Miranda, and held out his hand in which
she placed sixpence, as she said,—

"Who are coming, Martin?"

"Ah, you don't call me by my proper name. I was Martin once, but that was
before my nature changed. I am Bold Hawk, and I tell you, squire, they are
coming."

"Whom do you mean?"

"I have come from York—I heard them say they would have the squire."

"What can he mean?" said Miranda.

The groom now rode up, and touching his hat, said,—

"It's, may be, no business of mine, but there's two officers gone into the home-
stead by your house, squire."

"Officers?"

"Yes—I have seen them in York."

"It is I they seek,' said Mr. Percy. "A warrant, I was told, was issued
against me, at the instance of some one, for murder."

"Murder!" echoed Miranda.

"Yes, murder; the murder, they say, of your father. They will have it that my
poor boy is guilty, and that I knew of his intention. Heaven above knows we are
both innocent!"

"And will you, too, be snached from me?" cried Miranda. "It is doomed
against me, surely, that I must be friendless."

"They are coming this way now," said the groom, as he raised himself in his saddle, and looked in the direction of the Larkswood grounds.

"I told you they were coming," cried Bold Hawk. "I came from York before them—like the wind came poor Bold Hawk."

"Fly, oh, fly," cried Miranda, laying her hand upon Mr. Percy's arm.

"No, no," he said, "that were to encourage a presumption of my guilt. Let them sacrifice me, if they will—I am prepared."

"You are right—you are right," said Miranda; "'twas from an impulse, not reflection, that I spoke; but I have learned to dread the power of Bernard Varley."

"The triumph of the wicked shall be but for a season," said the squire.

Even as he spoke, two men appeared in the lane, and the foremost one immediately pointed out to his companion the squire, who stood by the side of Miranda, pale, but firm.

"Shoot them—shoot them, squire," said Bold Hawk; "they put me in prison once. That's strange, though, of them taking you. Have you been begging? Look, they are soon scared. Away—away with you."

As he spoke, the poor fellow took from his pocket a small piece of wood, and presented it at the officers as if it had been a pistol, whereupon they immediately halted in great consternation, and one called out,—

"Hilloa, hilloa! no violence; we come in the king's name."

"Aha," cried Bold Hawk, "you are brave men—mighty brave men; you dare not face Bold Hawk, though."

"Keep off, fellow—keep off," cried one of the men, who was the parish constable of a little place about midway between the Grange and the ancient city of York. "I discharges you to resist me, in the king's name."

Bold Hawk made a rush towards the men, and they immediately both turned, and sought safety in flight, till one of them happened to perceive the harmless nature of the weapon which the poor fellow presented at them, and then, with a degree of courage quite remarkable, they returned, and one of them, shaking his fist at Martin, cried,—

"Very well—very well, you mislisted us in our duty. We'll make you smart for this."

"Nay, nay," said the squire, "leave the poor fellow alone. He can scarcely be answerable for his harmless eccentricities."

"We've got a warrant agin you, squire," cried the constable from York. "You are my prisoner."

"I shall not resist your warrant," said Mr. Percy. "On what charge am I arrested?"

"For murder."

"I am innocent."

"That may be, and it mayden't be," said the parish constable. "Don't be insolent, and it'll be all the better for you. Come quietly, and you may come as fast as you like, or more slowerer."

"Hold yet a moment," said Miranda; "I am the daughter of Sir George Rankley."

"Why, it's for his murder as we reprehends Mr. Percy," cried the constable.

"Then, hear me declare my belief in the innocence of Mr. Percy. Surely if I am satisfied, who shall call him guilty?"

"Why, you see, miss, he's considered as what we in the law calls successory afore the fact."

"'Tis useless, Miranda, to speak for me," said Mr. Percy. "These men must do their duty, and have no discretion whatever."

"Ellow—ellow!" cried the constable; "do you hear that? He says we have no discretion; why, he might as well call us fools at once. Isn't that abuse in the discharge of our duty?"

"If you don't hold your fool's tongue," said the officer from York, "I'll cram my staff down your throat. Be off with you."

"Be—off—with—me?"

"Yes.   I only brought you to identify the prisoner."

"Me ? do you mean me—parish constable, bell-ringer, sexton, and post-master of the village of Beagles?   Me—me?"

"Yes, you, you blockhead.   Mr. Percy, you are my prisoner."

"Gracious! I'm topsy-turvy, or turvy-topsy ; I am all of an immense heap. Is we on our heads or our *eels ?*"

"Who'll go to the hanging?" screamed Bold Hawk, in a startling voice.

"What hanging?" cried the officers.

"Bernard Varley's—Bernard Varley's."

Miranda sprung towards her horse, as she said, "I will be at York within half an hour, Mr. Percy.   Fear not, all may yet be well.   Let us put our trust in Heaven."

"I do—I do, Miranda," cried Mr. Percy ; "farewell for a time.   As Heaven s my judge, let all hear me declare my innocence."

"You hear that," cried Bold Hawk; "he is innocent—he says he is—I know it.   My dreams all come true, and I'll tell you why.   My name was Martin ; I was a poor fellow then, but something changed me, and I am as you see me now. They say I'm mad, and so I am by daylight, for the sunshine makes me blink, and I don't quite understand all I see or hear ; but God gives poor Bold Hawk dreams at night, to make up to him for the scoffs and the gibes of those that ought to know better than he; so I tell you, Bernard Varley will be hanged at York. There will be a rare crowd, the like was never seen.   Hurrah—hurrah— rri!"

He clapped his hands vehemently, and then bounded along the gr een lhanahe a hunted hare."

CHAPTER XIV.

TWITTER AT THE GRANGE.—THE APPOINTMENT IN THE SHRUBBERY.—A BOLD
HIGHWAYMAN.

WHILE these occurrences were taking place in the green lane between the Grange and York, the greatest confusion prevailed within the former abode. The servants were in a state of excitement from the scene which they had witnessed between her whom they considered their young mistress and Bernard Varley, which totally incapacitated them from following their ordinary occupations, and they retired to the hall, in which they usually sat in the evening, in a state of mind which could only be allayed by talking, and which admitted of no other exercise.

There was but one out of the whole household who, throughout the scene which had taken place, had never made his appearance, and that was Twitter, the valet of the murdered baronet. He sat in his own small-room—the same which had witnessed several memorable scenes in our history. His face was the colour of a corpse, and he drew his breath short and thick, as he heard the various sounds of strife issuing from the part of the premises where Bernard Varley was undergoing so just a punishment for his brutality.

"They are murdering him," thought Twitter, "and then what shall I do? I— I need his support. I—I don't at this moment recollect one word of what I w to swear to. When I am examined on the inquest, I shall be lost, utterly lost, without him.   He is bold and resolute, fertile in schemes, while I am rather nervous. They shout dreadfully—it's all about that horse, too ; he had better let her have it, and go in peace. If I show myself, he will call on me for assistance, and—and never like to assist anybody."

Twitter trembled, and rubbed his hands nervously together, as he spoke, looking he mos t abject picture of terror.

In a few moments he crept to the door of the room, muttering to himself,—

"I—I can peep into the stable-yard from the low window of the laundry; there I can see without being seen. If they kill Varley, I can be evidence against them all, and then rob the house."

Creeping along as if he feared his own shadow, Twitter made his way to the window he had mentioned, and which commanded a view of the whole of the proceedings in the stable-yard.

There was a low malignancy about Twitter which made him enjoy the punishment Varley was then receiving at the hands of the enraged servants ; and something like a smile crossed his pallid face as he saw him dragged to the pump.

"Indeed," he muttered, "they are going to pump upon him. Well—well, I cannot help it ; and, if I could, I——"

Twitter glanced behind him before he ventured on saying, "I wouldn't," and then he smiled again, as he saw all Varley's frantic efforts to relieve himself entirely overcome, and his head placed under the pump.

"He—he often taunts me about many things," muttered Twitter, "and he has often struck me, too. I don't forget, although I'm not often in the humour to resent it ; besides, he's stronger than I am. On my soul, I am glad to see him so mauled—ha, ha, ha ! Eh, what was that ?"

The echo of his own laugh had put him in a fright, which made his heart beat for several minutes.

"'Twas nothing—nothing. So, Master Varley, you are overcome. How your proud, revengeful soul must be maddened now. I am glad, very glad, and when next you taunt me, Master Varley, with stealing the plate, I'll mention the pump in the stable-yard, and make you fume again with passion. There now they've left him—by Heaven he's half dead already. Ha ! he leaves the place— now he turns—he will come back—no—he is gone, and I am at liberty to keep my appointment, for doubtless Bernard Varley is off to York to concoct the means of vengeance. Well, well, I would fain see the Grange cleared of some of them. They already look with suspicious eyes upon me—I would that they were all gone."

He took his watch from his pocket as he spoke, and then exclaiming,—

"So near my time ?" he hurried from the room he was in, and making his way to a smaller apartment, in which were kept many valuable articles, he unlocked a plate-chest, and proceeded to fill a bag with numerous massive silver articles of great value.

"There is no one now," he muttered, "of whom I need be afraid. If Bernard Varley succeed in claiming the Grange, and all its possessions as his own, he dare not complain of me for taking the plate as I have done for these six months past. If Miranda becomes mistress here by any accident, why beyond a few articles she has seen in daily use, she knows not what plate her father possesses, and he is dead—yes, dead ! Plate can be of no further use to him, so I will take it freely."

He nearly filled the bag with valuable articles, and then lifting it with some difficulty, for the weight was considerable, he passed out of the little room, and then taking his way by a private staircase towards the gardens, which were on the southern side of the mansion, he paused not until he reached a spot of considerable extent, nearly hemmed in by gigantic trees, and on one side of which was a low thick wall, fronting the road to London in one direction, and to York on the other.

"He's sure to come," muttered Twitter, as he placed the bag among the tangled roots of a tree which had stood for ages in the generous soil . "He is quite sure to come. Highwayman as he is, I know I can trust him to send me my fair share of the price the plate fetches in London. He boasts of being a man of his word, and pretends to keep a conscience—a highwayman's conscience! I may as well say as much—why I am no worse than he. I did not murder Sir George—no, no —not I. It was Bernard Varley's doing, so that I did not even see it done—no— I am glad it was not I."

He tremblingly approached the low wall, and taking from his pocket a whistle, he blew one note upon it, which was immediately answered from the other side, and the hands of a man appeared on the top of the wall, and in a few moments he drew himself up, and leaped down on the side nearest to the Grange.

" You are punctual, Ned Witlet," said Twitter; " you are a man of your word."

" I know it," said the stranger, who was a tall wiry-looking man, past the prime of life, and slightly bald. " I know I'm punctual—Ned Witlet never breaks his word. But be quick, for I must be in London as soon as possible, and it's a long ride down here. "

" But you do a little business on the road ?"

" Certainly I do. Do you think I'd travel over a hundred miles, and stop nobody ? Ha ! ha ! There was a fat grazier trotting on a Suffolk punch some fifty miles nearer London—I stopped him—" your money or your ears," said I. The fellow roared for mercy. He thought I meant to do it, so he gave up a leather bag that was as greasy as his own mutton, with a hundred and sixty pounds in it."

" A famous booty," muttered Twitter.

" Yes—a windfall that seldom now comes in a professional gentleman's way, but for that very reason I must be off to London at once. There will be a hue and cry all over the country side. I cannot take heavy plate with me this time, for I may have to ride for my neck."

" I have nothing but plate."

" Well, then, you must keep it till some other time—I must be off. You can write to me at the post-office as usual, and I will drop you a note to let you know when I can come down here again."

" Then you will take nothing ?"

" Nothing. By-the-bye I heard of a countryman, as I came down the lane, some story about Sir George being killed."

" He—he is dead !"

" How ?"

" He was shot in a duel, but some seem to think he was murdered afterwards !"

" Then I'm d—d if I don't suspect you did it ! It's just a job in your line !"

" I—I—upon my oath I did not."

" Very well—very well. I suppose there will be some changes down here now."

" There may, and should they occur before we meet again, I will be careful to send you word of the nature of them."

" Do so. We have been dealing on the square now for some months, and, of course, I know it couldn't last for ever. You wrote to me to offer half the proceeds of the plate if I would fetch it, and take the trouble to convert it into cash in London. There couldn't be a more straight-forward business-like transaction."

" Of coarse not. You take a right view of the case, Ned Witlet ; but I hope we may still do business together, for if I remain here, my opportunities may be as great as ever."

" A young girl comes to the property, don't she ?"

" Yes—a—yes."

" What do you mean by that ? You say yes, as if you meant no ; but as I suppose I aint left a legacy, I needn't trouble my head about it ; so good-day to you."

" Cannot you manage to take something with you ?" said Twitter, who could not bear the idea of returning the plate again to the place from whence he had abstracted it.

" No ; something tells me that I shall have a hard run for it. I may be wrong, but I think I shall be hard pressed between here and London. I have come this last fifty miles just to keep my word, not to encumber myself."

" You have your horse with you ?"

" Yes, just over the wall."

" He would not feel the weight."

" Feel it, or not feel it, I take nothing to-day. He is tired enough as it is. So now good-day to you, once more ; I'm off."

The highwayman scrambled over the wall, and mounting his steed, which was quietly plucking the short herbage that grew by the road-side, he set off at a smart trot towards London.

Twitter, with a bitter curse, took up the bag of plate, and peering about him in great terror of being seen, he re-entered the house, and deposited it in the closet from whence he had brought it so short a time before.

"Lost! clearly lost!" he muttered. "Varley may make an inventory of these things. Yet, let him—let him. He is more in my power than I am in his; for he did the deed, and there can be no mercy shown to him! Why should I fear Bernard Varley, and allow him to make conditions, and have all things his own way, when 'tis I who should dictate to him? We shall see—we shall see, Master Varley."

He was silent for a few moments, and then a new and agreeable thought seemed suddenly to strike him, and he said,—

"Miranda has valuable trinkets, and in Sir George's bed-room are some articles of personal jewellery, of considerable price. Now is my time. Such an opportunity of secreting such things for my own purposes at any future time may never occur again. Miranda and Bernard Varley both away, and Sir George dead. Yes—yes—I will make a rare morning's work of this, although Witlet has disappointed

me; and now for the trinkets of Miranda. Methinks I have seen her wear some costly gems."

The absence of Twitter from the servants' hall occasioned no remark, for since his first coming to the Grange, he had never mingled with them, but had shut himself up so constantly and invariably, when not wanted by Sir George, in his private room, that the other servants would now have been much more surprised at his appearance than they could possibly be at his absence.

Hence, he felt that there was every probability of his reaching Miranda's chamber without interruption, and with a sickly smile upon his face, which was the very

No. 7.

antipodes of all mirth, he crept up the principal staircase, towards the corridor, from whence opened the different bed-chambers.

From his constant habit of peering and prying about, Twitter was well acquainted with the topography of the Grange, and there was not a corner in it that had escaped his inquisitive investigation. He proceeded direct to the room in which the beautiful Miranda always slept, and adjoining to which he knew was a smaller apartment, in which she kept her wardrobe, and such books, shells, and other matters as she most valued, either from their own intrinsic worth, or as being gifts at different times from her father.

The door of the bed-chamber was open, and Twitter entered, with the stealthy step of a cat.

"Humph!" he muttered, "all in confusion here—I must be quick, or some of the officious servants will be coming in to put the room in order, and this is about the only one in the house that I should find it no easy task to account for being in."

As he spoke, he crossed to the small inner room, and then began hastily to put in his pockets various little valuable gems which lay upon a table. He next forced the lid of a small writing desk, which was locked, and his gloating eyes fastened upon a set of brilliants which had been presented to Miranda by her father, on the occasion of her last birthday.

"Ha! here are indeed sparkling gems," he cried, as he eagerly tore them from their case, and crammed them into a pocket in his vest.

With a nervous eagerness, he tumbled over the papers in the desk, in order to be sure that no other article of value had escaped his search; but he could see nothing that he thought worth the taking, saving a seal, which, although not of much value, he took, rather than miss anything.

As he was rummaging among the papers, one fell over the edge of the desk, on to the floor, and upon picking it up, he was struck by the name of Rowland Percy, written on it. Upon examination of it, his face assumed an expression of contempt. On the paper were some verses addressed by young Rowland to Miranda, and that she had placed them in the only locked depository she kept, showed the store she set upon them.

"Ah," said Twitter, "love verses—I never loved anybody. Miranda is beautiful, and if ever I had felt such a sensation for any one, I might for her; and then I should take some pains to place this Rowland Percy perhaps in a worse situation than he is—but I love money—I love the power that money gives to its possessor—I love the cringing lip-service that the rich ever receive—I love, too, to play the tyrant over the poor."

He started, as a slight noise in a distant part of the mansion met his ears, and so strong a fear of detection came over him, that he sunk into a chair, unable to move hand or foot.

CHAPTER XV.

THE SERVANTS OF THE GRANGE.—THE COPY OF VERSES.—A FRIGHT.

TWITTER's alarm was greatly increased, as he heard a footstep in the outer room. The necessity of adopting some immediate means of concealment came upon his mind with sufficient intensity, even to overcome the paralysis occasioned by his fears, and rising, he softly crept to a corner of the room where there were several boxes and other large articles, among which he crouched down, so as to be tolerably well concealed from any one who might enter the room casually.

The step still sounded in the outer room, and as there was no mode of exit from the one he was in but through it, Twitter was fain to wait in an agony of impatience until whoever it was should have accomplished their errand and leave.

From the movement of the various articles in the room, he now became convinced that it was one of the female servants who had come to arrange the chamber, and with a sigh, he calculated upon at least an hour more of durance.

"Curses on her!" he muttered, "had she but come five minutes later, all would have been well ; but now each moment teems with danger to me. What can I do? If I could alarm her in any way, so that she would fly from the room, and so give me an opportunity of escaping, all would be well. I must try.

It required all the exertion of Twitter to enable him to make this resolution, and when he did, and was upon the point of carrying it into execution, he was as much startled at the sudden sound of the girl's voice, who was in the outer room, as he intended she should be at his.

"Ah! well," she said, "I wonder what will happen next? there is nothing but trouble now come over the old Grange. Master killed—poor dear young missus never so unhappy—and young Mr. Rowland, who, I'm sure, is quite a nice young man, and never came here but he said—'How do you do, Nancy? I see you are as pretty as ever,'—is sent to prison. Ah, me! Now if they had hanged Mr. Varley, and that unsociable wretch, Twitter, there would have been nothing at all to grieve at."

"Indeed!" muttered Twitter.

"It's always the way," continued the girl; "misfortunes, they never comes single, they don't—and in the middle of all this, · my sweetheart, Tom, he goes and has the banns put up atween him and the nursery-maid—a forward, disagreeable chit, that, I'm sure, only come here to stare at the men with her great eyes—oh, the wretch!"

Nancy having satisfactorily summed up the character of the nursery maid, set to work making the bed, with all that vigour that is imparted to any one's proceedings by considerable mental irritation.

"I could almost cry," muttered Nancy, as she threw the pillow into its place with a dash; "but I won't—no, I won't cry for nobody. There's Miss Miranda's watch-pocket has come undone—well, I must sew it on again, I suppose, and there will be a trot down stairs for needle and thread!"

"Thank Heaven!" said Twitter.

"No, there won't though," hastily added Nancy; "Miss Miranda always leaves her work-box open, and there's some there in course."

So saying, the girl walked hastily into the small room in which Twitter was concealed.

A cold perspiration broke out upon the cowardly ruffian, as he heard the light footstep of this young person cross the floor, and he calculated with fearful accuracy the consequences of discovery should he be arrested with Miranda's property in his possession, and consigned to a gaol at the time when he was looking forward to reaping the profits of his most unscrupulous villany.

A thought flashed across his mind of murdering the girl; but then he had not nerve for such an act, and he knew it—moreover, who among all the household was more likely to be at once suspected of the deed than himself, in bad odour as he was with all the servants, and with a former character which he knew would not stand any very close examination.

In the midst of his reflections, Nancy cried—"Well, I never did know Miranda to leave her writing-desk open before—poor thing, she must have been flurried indeed. I dare say now there's some sweet letters from Mr. Rowland Percy. Oh dear me, nobody writes me sweet letters. Tom might have done so, but he can't write ; to be sure I always send myself a valentine just to show the servants in the hall, but that's nothing. Oh, here's some verses, I declare."

Nancy picked up the verses addressed to Miranda by Rowland Percy, and then a fear came over her that she was not doing what was exactly right in thus prying into her young mistress's private affairs, and she hesitated a moment before she could muster courage to read any of the writing.

"Oh, dear," she said, "I do wish Miss Miranda had not left her desk open. She never did before, and I never thought anything of it. It's quite a temptation now, I declare. Here's letters and verses, and oh, such loads of secrets, I dare say, and I am so fond of secrets. There's nobody up stairs at all. The house is quiet. It can't be much harm only to read a little. I won't take anything. I wouldn't for worlds do such a thing."

Nancy carefully unfolded the copy of verses, and then exclaimed—

"Ah! this is something like verses, and not like them as the gardener sent me in my last place, as begun,—

> " Oh, lovely, uncommonly pretty Nancy,
> You strikes a great blow at my fancy,
> And I hopes of my boldness you will be a pardoner,
> And without more ado marry the gardener."

" Them was very good, but these verses is lines I can see. I wonder if Miss Miranda will mis 'em if I was to take 'em away to read over afore I goes to bed of a night. I am sure I should dream then as some gentleman's gentleman offered me his hand and his heart, and vowed to make a lady of me, and open a house in the eating line. No, I mustn't take 'em. That would be very hard, for Miss Miranda, poor thing, might want to read 'em herself, so I'll just take a look at 'em here, and try to recollect 'em. Oh, dear; they is most lovely. What a good job it is I can read.

"TO MIRANDA.

> " Listen! listen! dearest maiden,
>   To thy lover's gentle vow,
> And ever, dearest maiden,
>   He'll love as loves he now.
>
> " Fond hearts are often broken,
>   By vows too rashly made,
> But what thy love has spoken,
>   Ne'er can be unsaid.
>
> " Then listen, dearest maiden,
>   To thy lover's earnest vow,
> And ever, dearest maiden,
>   He'll love as loves he now.
>
> " Though years may leave their furrows
>   On thy brow so fair,
> And wintry time may steal the hue
>   From out thy raven hair :
>
> " Yet still thy own true lover,
>   Heeding not time's flight,
> Will see thy cheek as fair,
>   Thy eye as sparkling bright.
>
> " Then listen, dearest maiden,
>   To thy love's soul felt vow,
> And ever, dearest maiden,
>   He'll love as he loves now.

"Well, in all my life, I never. Oh, they is as tender as a house lamb, they is," exclaimed Nancy, when she had finished Rowland's verses. "He is a uncommon nice young man."

"I'll frighten her, if possible," thought Twitter, "or she will stay here another hour."

He then uttered a low groan.

For an instant, Nancy was struck dumb and motionless with fright, and then she rushed from the room with a scream that made Twitter tremble in every limb, and put him into such a sudden tremor, that he could not avail himself of the opportunity he had for flight.

With difficulty he rose from among the boxes, and rushed from the room. He crossed the bed-chamber in a moment, and reaching the gallery, he darted along it with the speed of lightning, nor paused until he reached his own chamber, where he scrambled into bed, and covered himself to the chin with the clothes, so that if any inquiry were made for him, he might be able to say that feeling unwell he had retired to rest.

Nancy continued her screams until she reached the servant's hall, where she was immediately surrounded by a crowd of anxious faces, and such a confusion of tongues ensued as would have quite astonished the builders of the Tower of Babel.

"What's the matter? What have you seen? Who was it?—a ghost?— a thief?—the keeper's spirit?—master's ghost?—where?—how?—when?"

Some even, in their impatience, went so far as to shake Nancy, to get sooner from her lips an account of her cause of alarm. One dashed a quantity of cold water in her face. Another poked a burnt feather to her nose, but Nancy was not going to faint, and her first intelligible words were the explanatory ones of,—

"Oh dear."

"Hush—hush—hush," cried everybody. "She's going to tell us."

"Oh dear," said Nancy again.

"What have you seen?"

"I don't know."

"Then what did you scream for, you idle, slutterly thing?" cried the housekeeper, bustling through the throng.

"Because, Mrs. Morgan, I saw a groan."

"You saw a groan?"

"Yes. Oh dear! oh dear I was a making missus's bed—no, I wasn't. I was a mending a watch-pocket—no, I wasn't."

"What do you mean?" said the indignant housekeeper, "and what is that you have in your hand?"

"My hand," said Nancy, and looking down she saw that she still clutched the copy of verses.

"Oh, ma'am!" cried the poor girl, "I brought this away by mistake. I did indeed."

"And pray what is that?"

"Some verses."

"Verses! Some nonsense, I suppose."

"Yes—yes—yes. I was a reading 'em when there came a groan, such as never was."

"Ah!" said the housekeeper, with a vibration of her head, implying superior wisdom. "'The devil always finds some work for idle hands to do,' while, on the contrary, 'How does the little busy bee keep shining every hour.' Go to your work, you wretched girl. Go—go and study the Reverend Elias Jonas M'Swoddlenus's pious work on the mortification of the flesh. Is my luncheon ready?"

CHAPTER XVI.

MIRANDA AT YORK.—THE HUMANE LAWYER.—THE EVIDENCE AND THE WILL.

MIRANDA made great speed to York after her most distressing but in some respects satisfactory meeting with Mr. Percy. She entertained no doubt whatever in her own mind but that Varley had been the prime mover in, and suggester of, the quarrel between her father and the squire. Nay, it was more than probabale that the letters purporting to come from even the squire to her father, if such there were to be found, of a quarrelsome character, were written by Varley himself. Miranda could easily imagine how two persons sufficiently estranged from each other as not to be on speaking terms, except in the phrases of ordinary civility, might by the artifices of such a man as Bernard Varley, be made to inflict insults upon each other that nothing could efface. Each moment of reflection seemed to bring the whole affair clearer; and by the time she reached York, she had as good a notion of the conduct of Varley as it was possible to gather merely from conjecture and circumstantial evidence, and in ignorance of the real facts in the order of their occurrence.

Miranda knew the names of her father's solicitors in York, but she knew not their exact place of abode. A very few moments inquiry, however, enabled her to discover them, and upon alighting she was received by one of the partners with all the courtesy which distinguishes those lawyers, who are likewise, by a felicitous combination, gentlemen.

"You have heard," said Miranda, when she was seated in the private room of Mr. Anderson,—

"Spare yourself, my dear young lady, any painful explanations. I believe I am cognisant of all the unhappy circumstances of the last four-and-twenty hours. The unhappy criminal ——"

"What criminal, sir?"

"Young Rowland Percy."

"Have you then, sir, adopted a belief in his guilt? Oh! Mr. Anderson, you may have heard much, and yet know but little of the circumstances which have made me an orphan; and first, let me at once declare to you before Heaven my entire belief in the innocence of Rowland Percy."

"His innocence?"

"Ay,—sir,—his innocence. I came to you to ask you not only to believe him innocent, but to use every energy with which you are gifted to save him from a most unjust persecution. If, sir, you are, however, so prepossessed with an opinion of his guilt that you cannot rid yourself of it, I will carry my griefs and my supplications elsewhere."

"God forbid, my dear young lady," said Mr. Anderson earnestly, "that I should be prepossessed against any one. It gives me much more pleasure to hear you express your confidence in the innocence of the accused than had you brought me undeniable proof of his suspected guilt."

"Then you will aid me, sir?"

"With all my heart will I."

Miranda could only look her thanks; and then she was silent for some moments, from excess of emotion. Hers was one of those pure spirits that a few kind words easily overcome, but which rise always in proportion to the pressure to which they are subjected, ever being most bold in most danger—most timid and tearful in confidence and peace.

"You will, Mr. Anderson," she said, "undertake to do all that is possible for Rowland?"

"I shall consider myself from this moment as not only his attorney, but his friend. Your opinion of his innocence, unless the evidence against him should be undeniable, will have great weight with every one."

"Then there is hope?"

"Great hope. From all that I have hitherto heard, I expected to find in you an accuser of this young man instead of a warm defender."

"I loved my father," said Miranda, "with a love that cannot be spoken There is a grief now at my heart, which I sometimes think must break it, but the cause of the innocent is so sacred in the eyes of Heaven, that I must struggle to support my weight of private woe in order to avert this dreadful wrong that is sought to be perpetrated. Rowland Percy is innocent, but a subtile dangerous villain is his foe, and accuser."

"Do you mean Mr. Varley?"

"I do."

"It does not become me, in ignorance of facts, to give any opinion of Mr. Varley's conduct, but believe me all shall be done that can be done for the purpose of arriving at the truth."

"Save him, Mr. Anderson, and you will have the heartfelt gratitude of a bereaved heart. I am now an orphan—my poor father has been mercilessly snatched from me—but, oh! what an aggravation of my sorrow would it be to feel that the innocent had suffered for the guilty."

"Doubtless it would," said the lawyer, "but not by your conduct. It is very rare, indeed, that the laws, and particularly the criminal ones of England, are badly administered. There shall be the most searching examination instituted into this affair, and now let me request you to tax your memory to relate to me every little incident fully, which you think can in any way near or remote bear upon this most painful subject."

Miranda then entered into a narrative of everything that had occurred from the moment she was first alarmed by hearing that her father was fighting a duel in the immediate neighbourhood, when she rushed from the Grange, and was horrified at the sight of his bleeding form, to the last meeting with Mr. Percy.

Mr. Anderson listened to her with the profoundest attention, and her account of her interview with Bernard Varley, wherein he had more than hinted at the innocence of Rowland Percy, seemed to make a strange impression upon him, and to fill him with surprise.

"There is strange presumptive evidence," he said, "of an awful plot concocted by this man Varley, but there is very little legal evidence which can be brought to bear against him."

"Oh! sir, bring him to justice," said Miranda, "for as I live, I do believe that he is the murderer of my father."

"Control your feelings till after the inquest," said Mr. Anderson. "It will take place to-morrow, and from the medical and other evidence there produced, you will be better able to judge of what grounds of accusation you may be able to discover against this man. There is, however, one matter which should be instantly seen to, and which very nearly, indeed, concerns yourself. That is with regard to this will which Varley pretends your father has left."

"I had forgotten it."

"But it must be seen to immediately. I cannot believe it possible that such can be the case. Your father ever entertained not only the sincerest affection for you, but the justest possible notions with regard to his property. I have heard him frequently state that you and he were quite alone in the world, or if you had any relations, they were in India, and very distant both as to family connexion and geographical position, so that were I to die—he has gone on to say—Miranda, as heir at-law, must inherit all I possess. When he has spoken thus, I have ever tried to reason with him, and persuade him to leave behind him a will, which he has as often refused."

"Yet Bernard Varley says he has one."

"It may be forged?"

"It must be."

"If it contain such provisions as he mentioned to you, I should say it surely was. But that is a subject that shall be most fully investigated, and if it be a forged will, Bernard Varley may have caught himself in his own snare; for the knowledge of that fact would invalidate any untrue testimony he might give against Mr. Rowland Percy. For my present view of the case, as regards the accused young man, is, that he has far more to fear from the perjury of Bernard Varley than from the curious coincidence of circumstances that brought him to the Grange on that most fatal evening."

"True,—true," said Miranda, "and I dread the power of Varley. I do believe him, from my heart, so subtle and crafty a villain that, like the dreaded tiger of the wilderness, he will calculate well his chances ere he make a spring upon his hopeless victim."

"Do not despond. The craftiest, subtlest villain that ever lived, will generally leave some point open through which he may be attacked, and the more deeply conceived and complicated the scheme he is engaged in, the more probable is i that he will not be armed at all points. Be of good cheer, then, and hope for th best."

"I will not give way to sorrow while action is required of me," said Miranda. "But I must see Rowland."

"That will be difficult."

"Difficult to see an accused man? Surely 'tis misfortune sufficient to be wrongfully accused; and the needless cruelty of depriving him of all consolation in his unhappiness surely will not be added."

"Nothing but an order from a magistrate will enable you to see him, and no other magistrate but he who has already seen and remanded Mr. Rowland Percy need be applied to, for from delicacy to him who heard an outline of the case they will not interfere, and with him I think you have small hopes. Indeed, under all the circumstances, I should advise you not to see him just at present. I, as his solicitor, shall have free access to him at all reasonable times, and be assured that whatever comfort he can experience from knowing your noble confidence in his innocence shall not be denied him."

"Be it so then, for the present," said Miranda, rising. "But concerning Mr. Percy, Rowland's father?"

"There can be nothing to implicate him. The inquest, and the evidence of the surgeon, will, in all probability, free him; for if it be sworn that the wound your father received from Mr. Percy was not mortal, or in any way dangerous to life, he cannot be detained on a charge of murder, and Bernard Varley can say nothing about the duel because he himself was one of the actors in it, and equally criminal with all denounced. You may depend upon it that the arrest of Mr. Percy is of no consequence, and you need give yourself no uneasiness whatever about it."

"Thank Heaven, then, all is not so bad as I supposed," said Miranda.

"All may be well; but I will go with you to the Grange, for I am most anxious concerning this will."

Miranda shuddered at the mention of going back to the Grange, but what other home had she?

"I shall be thankful to you, sir," she said. "So little as I value riches, I would not willingly allow such a man as Bernard Varley to wrest me from my birthright."

Miranda thought likewise of what Mr. Percy had told her of the sad condition of his fortunes, and she shuddered as the reflection came across her that destitution might be staring her in the face in addition to her other grievous trials.

CHAPTER XVII.

BERNARD VARLEY'S REVENGE.—THE CHANCE MEETING.—MORE MACHINATIONS.

WHAT tempest in its utmost intensity was equal to the rage which swelled in the bosom of Bernard Varley, as he took his way to York, after being so very summarily ejected from the Grange? He flew, rather than ran, and taking a short cut across the fields, he was soon in advance of Miranda mounted as she was; and her long interview with Mr. Percy in the green lane, enabled Varley to reach York considerably before her.

As he entered the suburbs of the city he felt not pain or fatigue, for the tumult in his mind had swallowed up every other consideration.

But one passion filled his mind, and that was an insatiable desire of revenge—bitter and wild revenge upon Miranda, and all at the Grange who had been in any way instrumental in his disgrace.

Once or twice he paused to debate with himself if he should really appeal to the law, or take some private means of achieving a much more exemplary revenge than it would allow him.

"What laws can satisfy a hate like mine?" he cried. "What cold proceeding that they call justice, will do for me when I am burning to take lives—to reek with human gore—to kill—to kill! And she, Miranda too—who, in spite of all, I love—who the more she contemns me, the more I adore her—she knows that I have been disgraced, bearded by a common herd of lacqueys and kitchen wenches. I, Bernard Varley, who, in my ambition have defied Heaven itself! but I will have vengence on them all! I must have my revenge!"

His hasty walking had done much to dry his saturated garments, and by the time

he walked to York he was getting into that most uncomfortable of all states
after a wetting, namely, a half feverish, half moist kind of heat, which makes the
skin dry and hard, while the steamy garments come against it with an unwholesome
touch, marking it with a semblance of moisture only to leave it more feverish than
before.   His lips were parched and dry—his hair hung about his face in wiry
masses, and his whole appearance was so disordered and strange, that many a
chance possenger stopped to look after him, and wondered where he could have
been to get in so strange a state.

Varley, however, did not notice that he was an object of attraction, for there
was something about his compressed lips—dilated nostrils, and corrugated brow
which induced people to let him pass on before they indulged their curiosity by a
long stare at him.

He proceeded direcely to a house in a small, narrow street, leading from a
handsome and commodious thoroughfare in the immediate vicinity of the Minster.
A brass plate, not more brazen than was the countenance of the man whose name
it bore, was on the door, bearing the words, " Mr. Querral, solicitor."   A dark
smile came over Bernerd Varley's face as he knocked at the door and muttered—

" Here is the man who, for a consideration, will do anything.   A most
useful member of your profession are you, Mr. Quarrel.   I would not lose
you for a thousand pounds."

The door was quickly opened, and the question if Mr. Querrel was at home
being answered in the affirmative, Varley was hushered into a little, mean room ;
the only furniture of which consisted of one stool, a desk with writings, and an old
blue bag.   In fact, Mr. Querral's waiting-room was coldly severe, and not at all
calculated to induce people to wait long.

Bernard Varley's patience, however, was not much taxed ; for in a few moments
a big, burly man made his appearance, and with an air of candour and sincerity
quite astounding said—

" My dear sir, how do you do ?   Ah ! you are not looking well.   You know
me—the soul of sincerity and candour—I say what I think, and think what I say.
Some people call me blunt, but I cannot temporize with my feelings, and therefore
I unhesitatingly tell you to your face, M. Varley, that I never saw you look so
strange in my life.   Upon my word, of course its ridiculous, but do you know
Mr. Varley, I never saw any one look like you but once."

" Indeed, sir ?"

" No—upon my word ;   you know my sincerity, candour.   There was a man
who looked just as you do now ; he had been pumped upon—he had indeed."

Varley's face assumed the scowl of a demon as he said in a voice of concentrated passion—

" Mr. Querral, I do not come here to listen to your absurd remarks, but to
employ you professionally.   You are aware probably that Sir George Rankley
is dead ?"

" Yes, and I beg to congratulate you, sir, upon the important trust left to you,
for I cannot forget being so very recently honoured by drawing up the poor
gentleman"s will, in which he bequeathes to you everything he possesses in trust
for his daughter, if she marries you, or with your consent, and absolutely to you,
should she not do so."

" You are right, sir," said Varley—" most admirably have you stated the conditions of the will.   By-the-by, did you preserve the letter sir George wrote to
you containing his instructions ?"

" I did."

" Then it may be useful ;   for this girl, Miranda, already shows symptoms of a
wilful disposition, and may dispute the will."

" She cannot, my dear sir.   I am the soul of candour, and I have no hesitation
in saying, that when I draw up a will it cannot very easily be disputed."

" Very well.   You will be in readiness if sent for by me, and as you have had
some trouble, Mr. Querral, and may have more, pray charge accordingly."

" I shall do myself that pleasure, Mr. Varley, always in moderation.   Being the soul of candour and sincerity, I shall make my little bill most unobjectionable."

"Well, then, Mr. Querral, you must accompany me to a magistrate, for I am about to take out warrants against several parties for assaults, and I shall place them in your hands for due execution."

"An assault, my dear sir? Then you have been pum—pum—pumped?"

"Sir?" said Varley.

"Eh? oh, dear, nothing—I only thought——"

"Mr. Querral, if it is any satisfaction to you to know that overpowered by numbers, I was pumped upon, you know it now."

"My dear sir, think nothing of it."

"I think a great deal of it, but you or any one might have been subjected to the same thing under such circumstances."

"Certainly, certainly, I have," added Mr. Querral to himself, "I have been pumped upon twice."

"Come, sir," said Varley, rising. "We will go for the warrants."

The first object that presented itself to Varley when they reached the Highstreet, was Miranda leaning upon the arm of Mr. Anderson. He started, and would have avoided her, but he saw that Mr. Anderson's eye was upon him, and putting a bold face upon the matter, he confronted them, saying—

"It strikes me that Miranda Rankley would look better in the eyes of the world were she to keep her home under present circumstances."

"When the hawk's abroad, sir," said Mr. Anderson, pointedly, "the bereaved dove may wander from its nest."

"Indeed, sir you are metaphorical,"

"And yet I would fain use plainer language. We are on our route to procure a conveyance to the Grange."

"And may I ask," said Varley, "What procures me the honour of Mr. Anderson's company at the Grange?"

"Mr. Anderson is my visitor," said Miranda.

"Oh, indeed. Then as the guardian of this young lady, sir, I cannot at present approve of her seeing company."

"Then," said Mr. Anderson, "I believe this young lady declines the further honour of your stay at the Grange."

"And yet I shall stay," said Varley, with a perfectly unmoved countenance "I have a will of Sir George Rankley's, which makes my stay there a matter of right."

"That will, I presume, you have no objection to show me at once, as the professional adviser of this lady, Miranda?"

"It will be publicly read after the inquest," said Varley, as he walked away with a smile of triumph upon his face.

"Miranda," said Mr. Anderson, "you may depend this villain has taken his measures well, and has strong grounds to go upon, or he would never treat us thus superciliously."

"Alas! alas!" said Miranda, "my heart tells me that all is lost. Surely Varley must be some demon, permitted for a time to wear the human form, to bring ruin upon the innocent."

"Do not despair. My now going with you to the Grange would be useless; but to-morrow I will be with you on the melancholy occasion it will bring forth."

"Ah! the inquest, shuddered Miranda. "Well, I must nerve myself even for that. When, oh, when, will all these dreadful trials cease? I must see Rowland Percy. Ah! Mr. Anderson take me to see him. If my agony be great, what must his be. I have head it said that the consciousness of innocence was a support to the falsely accused, but it ever appeared to me that injustice was the hardest lot of all to bear. What can the felon feel when accused of his guilt, in comparison with the honest heart that knows no guile, and scorns deceit? The one may be angry at the discovery of his iniquity, but the other's heart must surely be near the breaking at the unjust charge. I must see him. I must, sir, see Rowland Percy."

" We will, at least, make the attempt," said Mr. Anderson.

CHAPTER XVIII.

THE INTERVIEW BETWEEN ROWLAND PERCY AND MIRANDA.

THE attempt to see Rowland Percy was made, and made successfully, for within half an hour Miranda was with Mr. Anderson at the gloomy door of the building in which the accused was confined. Rowland Percy was sitting alone in a small cell, whither, at his own earnest request, he had been placed, as he preferred solitude to the company of the vicious persons who inhabited that wretched home. The coarse jest of the felon was to him a terrible infliction, and he infinitely preferred the company of his own thoughts, sad and mournful as they were, to such companionship.

The whole proceedings had been so strange, and his transition from liberty and hope to the gloom of a prison so rapid, that it was some hours after his incarceration before he could sufficiently arrange his ideas to come to a clear understanding of his situation.

The fatigue both of mind and body he had undergone, did not at all assist him in his endeavour to clear up the mysteries by which he was surrounded ; and more than once, so glaringly improbable did the whole circumstances appear, he was inclined to believe himself the victim of some mental delusion. He paced the narrow confines of his room with rapid and unequal 'strides, repeating to himself in a tone of surprise, which the familiarity of the idea by no means decreased,

" I am accused of the murder of Sir George Rankley, the father of Miranda— and to whom his death at all was a piece of news that came upon me like a thunderbolt. How can I unravel all this mystery—how connect the chain of circumstances, link by link, which has placed me in this awful situation ? My brain is racked with thought, and I have but two ideas to ring the changes upon. Firstly I am accused of murder ; and, secondly, Miranda believes me innocent. Oh, that is a thought that will indeed, sustain my sinking spirits. Though the whole world should with one voice swelling into thunder proclaim me guilty, let but that one pure and sinless heart believe me innocent, and I will find a consolation in my wrongs—a triumph in my sufferings. Oh, Miranda, Miranda—my own much-loved Miranda—will you still resist the voice of calumny and believe in my innocence ? Will you believe that the heart that cherishes your image as its fondest, dearest treasure, would have risked its own annihilation rather than your father should have come to harm ! Even in the face of condemnation, should it be my awful fate to suffer wrongfully, can you still cling to the holy belief in the innocence of him who loves you ?"

Rowland Percy threw himself into the only chair which the apartment afforded, and covering his face with his hands, he gave himself up for some moments to the saddest, gloomiest thoughts.

The unhappy young man heard not the opening of the door of the room, so absorbed was he in his own painful reflections. He heard not the footsteps of those who entered. But a voice—a voice which even then he was dreaming of, though it spoke in low and gentle accents, such as scarcely reached his ear, aroused him from his lethargy, with more certainty than would the sound of a trumpet. It was the voice of his Miranda—the voice of the one cherished idol of his heart—and he sprung to his feet with a cry of pleasure and an animation of countenance, that brought a flush of radiant colour to the pale cheeks of Miranda as she allowed him to clasp her hand in his.

For a moment neither spoke, and Mr. Anderson beckoned the 'gaoler from the door, and closed it upon the lovers.

"Miranda! Miranda!—my Miranda!" was all he could say for several minutes, and the gentle girl herself—she who had carried so high a spirit to Bernard Varley, and heartily repelled sorrow in the presence of those who sympathised not with her griefs, now burst into tears, and sobbed convulsively upon her lover's breast.

Not a sound disturbed the solemn stillness of that room, but the deep sobs of the beautiful being who had thus sought him who was accused of her father's murder. Rowland could not speak—his heart was too full, and it was not until Miranda's passionate grief had somewhat subsided that he could master his feelings sufficiently to say—

"Miranda—you still believe me innocent ?"

"As I believe in Heaven's mercy!" she replied.

Rowland Percy lifted up his eyes and exclaimed—

"Then I am prepared'for all. Let evil fortune do her worst. Let them take my life. Let them brand me with a felon's name. Let them give me a felon's grave —I will still thank Heaven, for you believe me innocent."

"I do—I do. Rowland—you did not—you could not be my father's murderer. I will plead for you—pray for you. You are innocent, Rowland—you are innocent."

The young man's face kindled with enthusiasm as he exclaimed in a voice of rapture—

"Bless you, Miranda, for these words. I am free, free in spirit—free in imagination—nor bolts nor bars can now confine me. The mind—that pure subtle essence that defies all oppression in its own integrity, will leap the prison walls, and coming though the rich domains of thought, will cheat the dungeon of its terrors. Oh! Miranda, you know not how happy you have made me by your words. I am innocent—Heaven knows I am, and the pure faith we both avow teaches us to expect assistance from above. The time will come, my Miranda, when the guilty shall be confounded, and although your poor Rowland's ashes may be mingled with the dust, and the stigma of a false charge may be affixed to his name—Phœnix-like will he rise from his ashes, and the memory of his wrongs will live in the hearts of men, when he and all he loved, are mingled with the elements of nature. The innocent may be sacrificed—villany may triumph, but a day of retribution will as surely come as to-morrow's sun will shine upon the world.

"But Rowland," sobbed Miranda, " you shall not fall a victim to that man. I will plead for you. They cannot say you did the deed."

"They will say so," he replied, " Hear, me, Miranda, and I will tell you how I came so inopportunely to the Grange. When dissension commenced between your father and mine, from what cause I know not, I was compelled to absent myself, but still my heart lingered around the well-known home of all its affection. Though absent, I was ever near to you. There was no joy for me but in the recollection of your voice, your latest words, and every fond word of our trusting, faithful hearts. Then memory from a blessing, became a curse, for it pictured to me scenes of happiness which I longed with such a yearning as we are told the Swiss exiles yearn for home, to look upon you once again. The wish grew into an impulse—I could think of nothing—dream of nothing but of the means of seeing you, and learning from your own lips that you still thought of your poor Rowland Percy, as one who with unshaken faith had loved you long, and as one who from no fault was banished from your side. I longed to hear your voice, to note if it were as kindly tuned as of yore. The impulse grew to a wild passion—I should have died, my Miranda, if I had not been enabled to come to you."

"Oh, Rowland—Rowland," sobbed Miranda, " at what an unhappy hour did you come !"

"As it chanced, Miranda, I did come at a most unhappy hour. For many days

I bethought me of some plan by which I could meet you, until at length, the scheme which I put in practice, wild, as it was, grew into hope in my fevered brain. I knew that the servants at the Grange were all firm believers in the old legend of the murdered keeper haunting the estate. Upon this superstition I founded my plan, and attiring myself in the dress the apparition was supposed to wear, I thought to obtain, from my intimate knowledge of the localities of the house, easy access, when I trusted to good fortune to meet you, and enjoy the interview I so much panted for. As evil fortune would have it, I put my scheme in execution at an inauspicious time, and am accused of murder at the moment when I hoped to heal a difference which had arisen between our parents from causes which still to me are involved in mystery."

"You did, Rowland, come at an inauspicious time," said Miranda. "The villain Varley had sown the seeds of dissension between your father and mine, until they brought forth the bitter fruits of personal strife. They met in most unholy and deadly conflict."

"I have heard as much, but could not give credence to the tale."

"It is true. Some false sentiment of honour on both sides urged them on to a duel. My father fell."

Rowland clasped his hands with a deep sigh, and Miranda continued in a tearful voice, interrupted by frequent sobs.

"On the morning of that dreadful day my poor father met his death, how I know not, but something tells me it was by the hands of Bernard Varley, who seeks to throw his guilt on you."

"I see it now," cried Rowland. "My presence at that time, and in disguise, furnished him with an excuse for my arrest; but that will not suffice to condemn me of what I am innocent of. Fear not, my Miranda. They cannot call me a murderer on such scanty grounds of accusation."

Miranda shuddered as she replied—

"You know not Bernard Varley. I have learned to fear him. His machinations are awful. Heaven, which looks into all hearts, can only tell what means he has prepared for your destruction."

The door was now opened by the gaoler, who uttered the one word.

"Time."

Miranda started, and then clung to the arm of Rowland.

"Must I leave you?" she sobbed.

"Yes," he sighed; "but I am not alone. The memory of this visit will people my cell with images of the past. Oh, Miranda, you have made a palace of my prison."

Miranda could not speak, but she clung to Rowland. and sobbed aloud.

"Farewell," said the prisoner. "Be of good cheer. We have Heaven with us."

Mr Anderson advanced, and gently put Miranda's arm with in his.

She could but wave her hand, and the door closed upon him she loved.

CHAPTER XIX.

THE INQUEST.——THE EVIDENCE.——THE VERDICT AND MIRANDA'S DESPAIR.

THE news of the extraordinary occurrences at the Grange had spread far and wide through the surrounding country, producing much excitement in the city of York in particular, where all the parties connected with the melancholy transaction were known.

Exaggerated as were the various rumours upon the subject, none came near the truth as regarded the real atrocity of the crime, or the magnitude of its results. It was simply in popular estimation an extraordinary murder, for the medical man who had attended Sir George Rankley, had made but little secret of his opinion, that he had come by his death from other causes than the wound received in the duel with Mr. Percy.

A post mortem examination of the body was to be made a few hours before the inquest commenced, by order of the coroner, and as twelve o'clock approached, all was bustle and expectation at the Grange. Many professional gentlemen from York, both legal and medical, attended the proceedings, as well as a vast concourse of persons who could not get admittance to the mansion, but remained anxiously awaiting the results in the vicinity.

But what were the feelings and the anxiety of all these in comparison with the mental agony endured by Miranda?

Accompanied by her father's attorney, she reached the Grange at an early hour, and sat in solitary anguish in her own room, looking like some beautifully chiselled statue of purity and grief. There was something terrible to Miranda in the very preparations for the judicial examination into her father's decease, and she clasped her hands with convulsive energy, as she exclaimed through her tears,—

"Oh, would that this dreadful day were over. Who, a few days since, could have imagined this happy house to be in so short a time changed from its bright aspect of joy and sunshine, to one of desolation and gloom? there were but two spots upon the sunshine of my joy, the one was Bernard Varley and the other the unhappy difference between my father and Mr. Percy—now those spots have become one hideous mass of blackness, and Bernard Varley alone stands before my affrighted imagination, as the mighty colossus-like fiend, who is predestined to be the shadow of my existence, and the evil genius of the innocent. Oh, Heaven! save thy creatures who love and reverence Thee, from the machinations of that man."

A low knock at the chamber door now startled Miranda from her reverie.

"Come in," she said, in so strange and altered a tone, that the young girl who entered, could hardly believe it was her mistress who answered her.

"Well, Annie," said Miranda, "am I wanted?"

"Oh, dear no, miss, not yet; but Mr. Varley has just come, and I thought I would tell you—he has brought with him three such odd-looking men, Miss Miranda."

"It matters not—it matters not," said Miranda. "To day must settle all."

"Yes, miss, so they do say so. The coroner gentleman hasn't come though, yet."

"What is the time?"

"It wants nearly twenty minutes to twelve, miss—James forgot to wind up your pretty French clock."

"I shall never touch it again," said Miranda; "let it be, Annie—I—I have not the heart to do anything—a brighter sun must shine upon my heart than does at present ere I can attend to those things which formerly made up my days of happiness; my heart is now absorbed in one object."

"Oh, miss, we must all die sometimes you know, and you shouldn't grieve so much."

"You mistake me," said Miranda. "Even grief for my poor father is swallowed up in other feelings. He is free from the busy evils of mortal strife. He is with his God, but the living are still entangled in the meshes of the world's cares. The innocent may suffer because human judgment is fallible. My father will have justice at the bar of Heaven, but Rowland Percy may, though innocent, be sacrificed to the machinations of his enemies. It is for him I feel, because there is doubt and anxiety over his fate; of my father there can be none—all is over."

Miranda shuddered as she spoke, and then, as if human nature mocked the philosophy of the brain, she leant her head upon her breast and sobbed bitterly.

The girl wept from sympathy, and for a few moments not a word was spoken.

Then the sound of carriage wheels on the gravel drive which swept round the lawn, came upon Miranda's ears, and she started as she exclaimed—

" Who is that, Annie ?"

The girl rose and left the room. As she did so, the ancient clock of the Grange struck twelve.

" The time has come," muttered Miranda. " Rowland's fate must soon be decided, I am told that the evidence produced on the inquest to-day will be decisive of his fate one way or the other. Ah, they cannot, dare not sacrifice him."

" The coroner, miss, has come," said the girl, as she re-entered the room ; "and there's quite a room full of gentlemen in the dining room."

" Yes—yes," gasped Miranda ; " in a short time they will want me. Some cold water, Annie. Let me bathe away the traces of these tears. I should be firm— not weak and tearful. I must speak for him, for Rowland, the falsely accused, or his enemies may overpower him. I must raise my voice for him. You know, Annie, he is innocent."

" Yes,'miss—I'm sure such a nice young man couldn't do nothing wrong."

" He is innocent—quite innocent," continued Miranda. " Let me think. By an unfortunate coincidence he came here on the night of my father's death—but he is innocent—as innocent as I am. Why does Bernard Varley not accuse me ? He might just as well—Hark ! what noise is that ? Go, Annie, go and bring me word what noise is that. I hear a tramping of many feet. Why are they coming here ? Hark, hark !"

The girl left the room, and then in a moment returned and said—

" It's the gentlemen, going—going—

" I know what you would say," interrupted Miranda, making a strong effort to speak. " They are going to view my father's poor remains. Yes—yes ; it is proper—most proper."

So awful a paleness came over the face of Miranda that the girl in alarm rung the bell before her mistress could prevent her.

" Hush, hush, Annie—I am better now," said Miranda. " Give me your Cologne water. There—I am better now—a sudden faintness. Hark ! they are returning—how awful in the house of death sounds the tramp of those men—they have seen him."

The sound of the feet of the jury as they returned from viewing the body which lay in a chamber on the same floor that Miranda's room was on, died slowly away and then all was as still as the grave, for the dining-room was far distant. For a moment or two Miranda stood as still as a statue, then suddenly turning to the girl, she said,—

" A scarf, Annie—give me a scarf. Quick, girl, quick !"

' Oh, Miss Miranda, where are you going ?" said the alarmed girl.

" The dining-room, you say," muttered Miranda, as she hastily arrayed herself in a large black mantle. " The dining room ?"

" The gentlemen are there, miss."

" And there I am going."

" Oh, dear, Miss Miranda, you had better stay away, indeed you had."

" No," said Miranda, firmly, " who knows what may be said of the innocent, and no one there to contradict. It is my duty—it is my duty."

" Then you must let me go with you, miss ?"

" No—do you remain here. Should I want you I will send for you. Bernard Varley must not think me weak. See, I am firm and calm ; my hand trembles not. I do not look nor speak like one who has lost a dear father, but I will look and I will speak like one who would protect the innocent from the guilty. The dining room—yes—the dining-room."

She glided from the room as she spoke, looking more like a spectre than the living, breathing, beautiful girl she really was. Her lips were firmly compressed, and there was a cold sternness upon her brow as if she had summoned every feeling of resistance in her nature to carry her through the scene which she felt was near at hand.

" I will raise my voice for him—for Rowland. They may call it unmaidenly but what is justice in the eyes of Heaven, should be right on earth. He shall not perish undefended."

She rapidly descended the marble staircase, which was one of the finest ornaments of the house, and crossing the hall, she paused a moment as the murmuring sound of voices from the large dining-room in which the inquest was held, met her attentive ears.

For an instant the hall, and each well known object it contained, swam before her eyes, and Miranda thought she should have fainted; but by a strong mental effort she sustained herself, and whispering to her heart, courage! courage! she turned the handle of the lock and entered the spacious room.

Her sudden and unexpected appearance attracted universal attention, and there was a dead silence of a moment or more, when the coroner said—

No. 9.

" Gentlemen, we must proceed. Will the lady be seated, or retire again?"

" Miranda Rankley," said Varley, " is a heroine when she pleases—her nerves are strong—she will doubtless remain."

It was well for Miranda that Bernard Varley spoke, and better still that he spoke so mockingly, for all her sinking spirits revived at the insult, and in an instant she was calm, collected, and had perfect command of herself.

" Yes," she said, and her clear voice sounded through the room like the vibration of a silver bell. " Yes, Miranda Rankley will remain. Gentlemen, I am the daughter of him whose mortal remains you have but now looked upon. He loved me past the power of telling. My lightest wish found ever a ready echo in his heart; I am his only child. His heart was large enough to love many, but its concentrated tenderness all fell upon me ; and with even his thoughts of Heaven he mingled his dear love for his darling child. Such was my father, nor was I insensible to such affection. Heaven knows, and many on earth can bear witness to how I returned that affection. I will not speak upon that head, but you must judge that some motive, strong and overwhelming in its power, has effaced all traces of grief—that grief which I should feel for such a father, must have nerved me to this act of coming with a calm and steady mien—an eye in which no tear is visible, among you. Oh, judge me not harshly ; say not to your hearts that I am callous to a father's fate; rather look for some high feeling which has wrought upon me to whisper to my grief, ' Be still awhile that I may do my duty.' "

Miranda raised her arm, and pointing at Varley, who shrunk back immediately, continued,—

" Look on that man. Mark him well! See even now how he shrinks before me, not from what I have said, but from a dread of what I may say. Twelve months since this roof covered as happy and united hearts as ever beat in human breasts, but Bernard Varley came, and gloom and discord came with him. I denounce him as morally guilty, if I cannot prove him legally so. Mark him well, and when you see another like to him proclaim him a murderer!"

All rose from their seats as Miranda spoke, and a general feeling of amazement pervaded every breast, and shone fully from every countenance. Miranda still pointed at Varley, who, with his arms stretched before him as if he feared she would approach nearer, stood pale as ashes, and trembling in every limb.

CHAPTER XX

THE EVIDENCE OF THE MURDERERS.—THE IVORY TABLETS MEMORANDUM.

IT was, however, but for a minute that Bernard Varley lost the power of action, for rousing himself from the state of alarm into which the words of Miranda had thrown him, he cried in a voice of harsh vehemence—

" Is this fair? Is this the mode of proceeding at a judical inquiry   Am I to be insulted by a girl who is crack-brained, because there is good reason to believe her lover has committed a murder?"

" 'Tis false," cried Miranda, " false as thy own heart, and you know it."

" I claim protection from you, sir," cried Varley to the coroner. " Is this insane girl to remain here to the detriment of justice ?"

" Remain here, I will," cried Miranda. " If any human being has more right than another to remain here, it is I. If this awful inquiry concerns any one more than another, surely—ah, surely, that one is myself. For the excitement of my feelings, which has led me to be rude of speech, I apologise to all but to that man. Too well he knows that no language can depict what he is."

"Let me recommend you to retire," said the coroner to Miranda; "your grief will but find fresh food in the details we must necessarily enter into."

"No, no—I am calm," said Miranda in an altered tone; "but I have heard that at the trial of a murderer the very stones have risen up in judgment—I have heard that fresh blood has flowed from the stiffened corpse—I have heard that sighs have been breathed from breasts cold in death, and that Heaven has permitted strange things of preternatural import, when it has pleased it, to visit upon the head of the murderer human vengeance for his crimes. Wonder not, then, that I, a timid maiden should raise my voice when taunted by that dreadful, fearful man."

"This is midsummer madness," cried Varley, stamping violently, and flinging his arms about in wild passion. "The evidence—the evidence. I claim to be heard against these charges."

"Silence all," cried the coroner. "Lady, if you persist in staying here, a resolution, which I hope you will change, you must let justice take its even course.

"I am still—I am still," said Miranda, as she sunk into a chair, and leaned her face upon her hands.

"Bring in the prisoner," said the coroner.

Rowland Percy, who was brought from York Castle in custody, was led into the room.

His lightning glance fell upon Miranda, and in a tone of sadness, he ejaculated her name. She sprung from her seat, and dashing the hair from her face, which had fallen in wild disorder, she stretched out her hand, as she said,—

"Here, Rowland Percy, before all these persons as I would before the world, I take your hand, and proclaim it guiltless of shedding blood. You are innocent. God knows it, and one other."

"One other, lady," cried the coroner.

"Yes!" cried Miranda. "You may see him there."

She pointed at Varley, who gnashed his teeth in impotent rage.

"Let the witnesses be sworn," cried the coroner.

The first witness examined, was the medical man. He gave his evidence clearly and distinctly. Sir George Rankley's wound was found upon dissection to be very slight, and could not have produced death.

"What was the cause of death?" said the coroner.

"From the appearance both internal and external of the body, Sir George Rankley was suffocated."

A thrill of horror pervaded the assemblage, which was now increased by all the servants of the household.

"Of that you are sure?" said the coroner.

"My brother medical man and myself both agree on one point. It is our decided opinion."

"That is all you have to say?"

"It is."

"Bernard Varley," said the coroner, and the villain, with an assumption of confidence that sat but ill upon his ghastly countenance, stepped forward, crying—

"Here."

"State what you know of this transaction."

"Sir George Rankley," commenced Varley, "after some differences with Mr. Percy, fought a duel with him, in which, after much persuasion, I acted as second. He received a wound; a slight one, as I was led to believe, but it confined him to his bed. I felt the greatest anxiety concerning him, for he had been to me a kind patron, and I agreed with the nurse who was attending on him, that I and Twitter, his valet, would relieve her at night, and sit some time with the wounded man while she took repose. We kept our words, but on our passage to the chamber of the baronet, we hough we saw a figure glide past us on the stairs, and we pursued it, but in vain. Believing, then, that our imaginations must have deceived us we went to the chamber."

"You found Sir George alive?"

"We did."

Miranda listened with painful interest to what would follow, and in a hollow voie, Varley continued—

We had not been many minutes by the bedside, when the light being nearly expiring, I left Twitter in the room while I went down to the apartment we had left, to procure a fresh light. When I returned, I found him lying in a swoon at the foot of the bed, and Sir George Rankley was murdered."

Here Varley paused, and reaching a glass of water which stood near him, he moistened his parched lips, while a silence as of the grave pervaded the deeply interested assembly.

"Go on, sir," said the coroner.

"Before I could think what to do, for the occurrence confounded me, this young lady, Miranda Rankley, came into the room, to my great surprise, dressed as if she expected some one. In vain I tried to keep her from the bed-side, for I was afraid the shock would be terrible to her, of finding her father dead. She persisted, and I left her there until I hurried from the room to procure assistance. As I crossed from my own room, then, to the servant's hall, a figure rushed upon me, attired in a green hunting-dress. By the hall-lamp I saw his face.

"Who was it?"

"Rowland Percy."

"You will swear that?"

"I will. He struck me on the head ere I was aware of it, and I lay for some time insensible, when I recovered, I cried for help, and immediately went to the chamber of the murdered Sir George, and on the floor I found these tablets."

The ivory tablets were handed to the jury.

"You will find the name of Rowland Percy written in ink upon the first one," said Varley, "and you will likewise find a memorandum on another page, I grieved to see.

"'Tis false," cried Rowland. "Those tablets were never written on by me."

'Silence," said the coroner, "you shall be heard. Gentlemen, I will read you the memorandum. It runs thus:—'An account of the Grange property, which would descend to M. R. in case of G. R.'s sudden death, without a will. Five farms, two tenements in York, seven hundred acres of cultivated land, the Deen forest, the Grange—estimated value twelve thousand per annum. Mem. To be at Grange by seven o'clock—after duel—if not fatal—a good exchange by wedding simple M. R. from difficulties to splendour.'"

"That is the memorandum, gentlemen," said the coroner.

"I deny it before the God of Heaven," cried Rowland Percy. "As I hope for mercy hereafter, I never wrote one word of it."

"You hear," said Miranda, "he denies it. The villain Varley wrote it to destroy him. 'Tis forged—'tis forged. You hear, gentlemen, Rowland Percy did not write it."

"We are not trying the prisoner," said the coroner; "and all I can do is to seal up those tablets, and send them to the magistrate who committed the prisoner. What more have you to add, sir?"

"Nothing," said Varley, "with the exception that Sir George, before his death, expressed his firm conviction that Rowland Percy sought a marriage with his child to better his condition."

"Have you any questions to ask him?" said the coroner to Rowland.

"No," said Percy, "to ask him questions were, indeed, a vain task. He is a perjured villain. That I was in the house I will not deny, but——"

"You had better reserve your own statement," said the attorney, whom Miranda had retained for him, "until you have heard all the evidence."

"I bow to your decision," said Rowland.

"Although you all mark that he is innocent," cried Miranda,

Samuel Twitter was summoned next, and pale, trembling, and awful looking, the guilty valet crept forward to the end of the large table, at which the jury sat. He licked his parched lips with a ghastly vehemence, and he clutched the edge of the table to endeavour to stop the nervous twitching of his hands. His state of mind seemed a most pitiable one, and as he gazed around him upon the many anxious and excited faces, all bent towards him, he could have sunk upon his knees from abject fear, and confessed all, but that his weak mind was enthralled by the dark spirit of Bernard Varley, and he dreaded him more than he dreaded the vengeance of Heaven, because the one was near at hand, and the other, in his ignorance, he considered remote, as if Heaven's mercy, and Heaven's justice were not ever present at all times, and at all seasons.

He took the oath, and then stood breathing hard, and with hysterical vehemence, as the coroner, with a firm, solemn voice, said—

" State now, Samuel Twitter, what you know of this melancholy affair."

" Yes, yes," he said ; " I am—I was the valet of Sir George Rankley. On the morning of the duel, Mr. Varley came to my room, and asked me to sit up with him a few hours, while we kept watch in the sick chamber of Sir George. On our route thither, we saw a figure glide by us dressed in green."

" What made you and Mr. Varley not alarm the house at sight of this figure ?" said one of the jury.

" There is a superstition among the servants," said Twitter, " that the spirit of a murdered gamekeeper walks about the passages and staircases, and particularly when any inhabitant of the Grange is about to die."

" And did you suppose such to be the case ?"

" The hour was midnight; and all men are, under certain circumstances, more or less superstitious ; when we reached the chamber, Sir George was alive."

" You are certain of that ?"

" I am."

" Pray go on."

" The truth," said Miranda.

Twitter's knees trembled, and he evidently could not speak for some moments.

" Wherefore do you feel so much emotion," said the coroner.

' I—I am a nervous man," he gasped, " and my master's death has quite un-manned me. He was very kind to me. We had not watched long when Mr. Varley went for a light, leaving me alone with Sir George, who was moaning in his sleep. I was standing at the foot of the bed, and scarcely had Mr. Varley been gone two minutes, when by the dim and nearly expiring candle that was in the room, I saw a figure enter the apartment."

" Can you describe it ?"

" I can. It was dressed in green—it approached the bed—I was paralysed with fear. Then a sudden brightness from the candle, which will frequently occur when they are near expiring, showed me his face."

Every ear was now bent forward and every heart beat with feverish excitement as after a slight pause, Twitter continued—

" It was Mr. Rowland Percy !"

A deep sigh seemed to come from the depths of every heart, as Twitter swore to this conclusive evidence against Rowland, and the young man himself clasped is hands as he exclaimed—

" Is this a dream, or do I really hear these men perjure themselves before high Heaven ! Oh, Miranda—Miranda ! it is false— it is false !"

" I know it is false," said Miranda. " Heaven yet will right the innocent. Be patient, Rowland, be patient."

" You will swear to what you say, distinctly and without reservation ?" said the coroner.

" I will," replied Twitter, with a groan.

" What happened next ?"

" He took the pillow from under the head of Sir George and placed it over his face."

A thrill of horror pervaded the assembly, and several who were near to the unhappy Rowland shrunk back from him as if he had been afflicted with the plague.

" I know not well what happened next;" said Twitter, " my brain swam round —whether he struck me down, or I fainted, I cannot tell, but it was long before I became sensible again, and then I was told my master was dead."

" Villain !" cried Rowland Percy. " I pity you from my soul ; for as surely as you now stand there a false accuser in the sight of Heaven, there will come a day of such dreadful—of such fearful retribution, that your shrieking soul will howl in its despair, and ask in vain for that mercy you can never expect. On your death-bed this scene will rise before you in horror. Oh, man—man ! repent you, while yet you may."

CHAPTER XXI.

THE VERDICT.—MIRANDA'S NOBLE CONDUCT.—THE READING OF THE WILL.

Twitter fainted, and fell on the floor heavily.

The greatest sensation was produced in the room; and while some raised the terror-stricken man, others opened the windows to let in air. Such a scene of confusion as ensued for a few moments was rarely ever seen on such a solemn occasion.

" Gentlemen," said the coroner, " let me beg of you to keep your seats. The witness will be no doubt recovered sufficiently to resume his examination."

" We have heard enough," said one of the jury, " unless the prisoner wishes to ask him questions?"

" No, I will ask none," cried Rowland. " I am innocent, so help me, Heaven ! and those two men are perjured. God forgive them this deep sin !"

A whispered consultation now ensued between the jury and the coroner, and then the coroner said—

" Miranda Rankley, the jury wish to put to you some questions."

" I am ready." said Miranda.

" Did you expect the accused to come to the Grange on the particular evening to which this inquiry refers ?"

" I did not."

" Can you speak with certainty as regards your father being alive or dead when, as stated in evidence, you took your station by his bed-side ?"

" I cannot. I thought once I heard him breathe, but that might have been a delusion."

" The jury will not trouble your further."

" Then hear me," said Rowland.

" In courtesy," said the coroner, " we will hear you make what statement you please, but the evidence distinctly sworn to makes it quite impossible for us to return any other verdict than one of wilful murder."

" Then," said Mr. Anderson, " I strongly advise you, Mr. Percy, to say nothing, beyond a declaration of your innocence. No statement from you can be of the least benefit here ; for under the circumstances the jury have no sort of discretion. Nothing but a weight of contradictory evidence can have any effect."

" I thank you, sir," said Rowland, " for your kind advice ; yet I feel strongly at every stage of these unhappy proceedings I ought to speak. I cannot vary in my tale because it is the truth. It is for those who hatch falsehoods to be careful what they say, and when they say it. I hear from you, sir, that you must return a verdict against me upon the oath of these deeply-perjured men. Be it so ; and yet I am innocent, and yet will I speak. Some time since, from whatever cause I knew not, my father told me to forget Miranda Rankley, for that he, as we as I had received deep insults by letter from Sir George, and at the same time he hinted to me that his circumstances were not flourishing. I entreated him to explain to me more fully what he meant; but he shrunk from so doing, and without an interview with this lady, I was compelled to depart some distance from this place. What was then occurring in my absence I had no means of knowing. I wrote once to Sir George himself, begging for some explanation, but I received no answer. Then, stung by the torments of absence from all I held dear, tortured by suspense, and unhappy beyond expression, I formed the perhaps foolishly romantic notion of obtaining an interview with Miranda, under cover of a disguise which I knew would leave me unquestioned by the household. It was my cruel fortune, gentlemen, to arrive on that fatal night which has wrung so many tears from gentle hearts, and the issues of which are in the hands of Heaven.

"The Grange and its grounds have been familiar to me from earliest childhood. I believe, indeed, I know more of its intricacies than any dweller now within its walls. Favoured, then, by such knowledge, I easily gained admission to the house, and in crossing a corridor, I saw that man Varley and Twitter crawling like men of guilt towards the chamber-door of Sir George. They were trembling with fear, and their faces were ghastly. In my endeavours to avoid them, they saw me, but I escaped, and hid for some time in the small oratory which had been for years in disuse. From thence, after a time, hearing much confusion in the house, and not knowing its purport, I advanced towards the suite of rooms on the ground-floor, one of which is an apartment usually occupied by that man, Varley. Through the half open doorway of that room, I saw a sight that made the hot blood dash through my veins like liquid fire. The lady had fainted, and yon villain, Varley, was about to take that opportunity to press his lips upon her cheek. I dashed into the room, and with one blow felled him to the ground. After that all was confusion. My object was to leave the house and ascertain from some one out of the establishment what had occurred, for even then I was quite ignorant of the death of Sir George. I was pursued, and allowed myself to be taken, believing that my utmost penalty would be the anger of Sir George Rankley; and likewise I longed to denounce the villain, Varley, whose base conduct I had been a witness to. I never for a moment was in Sir George's chamber. The tablets are mine, but I never wrote one word in them—except my name. I am innocent—I swear it by my hopes hereafter—by the life to come—by the Majesty of Heaven—to which I now appeal—I declare to you my innocence."

For a few moments after Rowland Percy had done speaking, there was a dead silence, and Twitter, who had recovered partially from his insensibility, was seated, gazing at him with a face as pale as that of some resuscitated corpse.

"Your declaration can do you no harm," said the coroner "but our verdict must be in accordance with facts sworn before us. Gentlemen, what say you?"

The jury whispered together for a moment or two, and then said—

"Wilful murder against Rowland Percy."

"Oh—no—no," sobbed Miranda; "oh, think again. Can you believe those men?" Look at them! Perjury is written by the hand of Heaven upon their brows. See how they shrink—see—they have already received some of the wages of guilt. They are miserable men, for they have not the truth in them. Oh! spare him—he is innocent. He is innocent—innocent!"

"Our duty, lady, is a painful one," said the coroner, "but we must do it. The verdict is recorded—gentlemen, you are relieved from your duties."

Miranda sunk back on a chair, and covering her face with her hands, she sobbed convulsively for a moment; then suddenly rising she walked to Rowland, and while the tears still glistened in her eyes, she said—

"Rowland, when you were prosperous and happy, and life lay before you like a summer-garden, I could not say to you what I say now, and care not who hears me; you, and you only have my heart's love, Rowland. My poor father is gon —a mother's care I never knew, for fate snatched her from me, ere I had breathed a few days in this world of sorrow. Relations, friends, I have none. You, and you only, are the link that now binds me to a world which I never could have believed so bad as it seems now to be. In sickness or in sorrow, in grief or in joy, persecuted, or acquitted, Rowland Percy, I am yours."

"Then let fate do its worst," cried Rowland, "I defy it. Innocence, my Miranda, ever comes brighter out of the fire of suspicion. My name may for a time, be dimmed by the odium of the crime laid to my charge ; but the day will come, when it will survive its detractors, and I may be pitied, although not saved. If it be the will of Heaven that the wicked triumph, I will not repine."

"You shall be saved, Rowland," said Miranda ; "there are still warm feeling hearts that will, for your own sake, as well as for mine, crowd round you. You will see no more tears from me—my mind is made up now to cast all weakness from me, and to be intent but upon one object, namely, your freedom. My voice shall be heard loudly proclaiming your innocence, wherever the smallest whisper to your prejudice has reached. Rowland, be comforted."

"No angel's voice could bring such joy to my heart as yours," whispered Rowland.

"Come," said the officers, touching Percy on the arm, "we must go."

"Yet a moment," said Miranda. "Rowland, dear Rowland, I will visit you in your prison—you shall not be deserted."

"Nay, nay, Miranda think of yourself more than of me. Though all the world should condemn me, I have a shield now over my heart which will resist all attacks —it is your dear love which will keep me from a wound."

"I cannot wait s aid the officer.

"One moment more," said Miranda. "Rowland, I will send you books— letters—I will come often."

"Farewell !" said Percy, in choking accents, for the generous devotion of Miranda touched him severely. "Farewell ! hope for the best ! "

"Now," said the officer.

"Farewell, Rowland ! To-morrow I will see you ! Do not despair. There is Heaven above us, and all will yet be well. Treat him gently, sir," to the officer ; "he is innocent—indeed he is !"

"I don't know anything about that," said the officer ; "all I know is that I must take him to York."

"Once more farewell, Rowland, till to-morrow," said Miranda, as she slowly released her hold of Rowland's arm.

He could not speak, but taking her trembling hand, he pressed it to his lips. Then a faintness came over Miranda, but she struggled against it, and overcame it. "I—must be firm," she thought. "He shall not leave me as he thinks. in sorrow ; I—I will smile upon him even now !"

She slowly turned to the door—Rowland was passing through it, and his eyes were fixed on Miranda. She waved her hand, and tried to smile, but the effort was too much for her. With difficulty she restrained her tears—Rowland was gone. The jury were leaving the room, and she sat down, unconscious for a few moments of anything. She muttered to herself abstractedly the words—"Wilful murder ! wilful murder !" Then with a shudder she said—

"No—no—I will not go mad ! I will be calm and save him yet.

"Miranda," said Mr. Anderson.

She heard him not ; her thoughts were with her lover, and she still muttered the awful words—"Wilful murder !"

"Miranda," repeated Mr. Anderson, "calm yourself ; there is still much to do. Your father's will."

She started as she exclaimed—

"Bernard Varley claims all, but I can beg from door to door for Rowland Percy Yes, Bernard Varley kills the father and robs the child."

"Hush, hush," said Mr. Anderson, "come with me, and we will insist upon having the will read."

Miranda rose, and leaning heavily upon his arm, walked with him to the principal drawing-room of the mansion. It was empty, and when they reached it, Mr. Anderson said,—

"Be seated now, Miranda, and endeavour to command your feelings, while I insist upon seeing the will which this man says he has."

"I will be calm," said Miranda, "and yet, oh, Heaven, what is to become of me? Wealth, I never envied, but now the means of successfully defending Rowland may be wrested from me, and at the moment when I might do so much, I am about to be deprived of the means of doing anything but starve; —starve—oh, horrible—just Heaven, what have I done?"

"Hush, hush," said Mr. Anderson; "do not, I charge you, impugn the justice of Heaven's decrees."

"I know not what I say," gasped Miranda. "Heaven will forgive the few words of impatience wrung from a suffering heart."

"Do not abandon hope, Miranda; I will now summon this man here, and demand to know on what pretence he remains in this house?"

Mr. Anderson rung the bell,

and when a servant appeared, he said,—

No. 10.

"Is Mr. Varley within ?"

"Yes, sir," was the reply.

"Then tell him that Miss Rankley's solicitor wishes to see him immediately on business of importance.   I will await him here."

"Now, Miranda," added Mr. Anderson, turning to her, "Varley must produce the will he speaks of, or leave the house ; and if he even produce it, and I have my suspicions that it is not genuine, I will take upon myself in your name, to have him turned out of the Grange."

"Alas," said Miranda, "we have to deal with one who, I fear, is more than a match for honesty and determination.   I dread the power of Varley.   A man who is quite unscrupulous is to be feared."

"Hush—leave all to me.   He comes—say not a word unless I ask you a question."

"I will be mute," said Miranda.

The door of the room was flung open, and Varley with an insolent swagger walked in.

CHAPTER XXII.

THE FATAL CLAUSE IN THE WILL.—THE ATTEMTED ASSASSINATION.

WELL did Bernard Varley seem to know that much depended upon the interview he was about to have with Mr. Anderson, for although he strove to assume an air of perfect assurance and self-command,   yet there was an evident anxious expression on his face, which did not escape the keen eyes of the attorney, who purposely remained silent for some moments, in order that Varley should not recover from his anxiety by his immediately speaking.

"Well, sir?" said Varley, when saw that Mr. Anderson did not immediately open the conference, " I am here in obedience to your wishes."

"Very well, Mr. Varley : you will understand that I speak in the name of Sir George Rankley's daughter now present, when I ask you when it will suit you to leave the Grange !"

"Suit me to leave the Grange, sir ?" cried Varley, his face at once reddening with passion.   "The Grange sir, is mine—my own !"

"Yours, Mr. Varley."

"Yes—I have it devised to me by Sir George Rankley—I told you so. You shall see the will."

"It is very strange, Mr. Varley, that Sir George Rankley, loving his daughter, as all who were of his acquaintance knew he did, should disinherit her in favour of you."

"I said not disinherit," said Varley, "Miranda may still be mistress of the Grange ; but I will read you the will, sir, from courtesy."

"I beg your pardon there, Mr. Varley," said the attorney; "you read it to me from necessity, for this young lady, as heir at law, claims the property, and it is for you to make out your title by proving the will you speak of."

"Very well, sir," said Varley, drawing from his pocket a folded parchment,— "here is the will.   You shall hear it, whether from courtesy or necessity I care not."

"You have no objection, I presume, to let me read it myself?"

"None whatever," said Varley, as he handed the document to the attorney, and at the same time, kept a wary eye upon it.

Mr. Anderson opened the document, and after a few moments' careful examination he said,—

"Miranda, here is an enumeration, carefully made, of your father's property after which the will consists of but one clause, which I will read to you."

Miranda said nothing, but fixed her eyes upon Mr. Anderson's face, while in a clear audible tone he read as follows :—

"I hereby give and bequeath the whole of the above-mentioned property, together with whatever personal effects I may die possessed of, to Bernard Varley, my sincere friend, to have and to hold in trust for my beloved daughter, Miranda; and it is my wish that she marry Bernard Varley; if she refuse to marry him, the whole of my property above-mentioned is to become his absolutely and without reservation, excepting such allowance as he shall please to grant to her, unless she marry some one with the said Bernard Varley's full consent, in which case she shall be entitled to the whole of my property, with the reservation of an annuity of one thousand pounds per annum, to be paid from my estate to Bernard Varley.

"This is my last will and testament,

"Witnesses— "GEORGE RANKLEY."

"FRANCIS HEARN,
"HENRY REEVES."

"This will is dated on the morning of the day which closed the mortal career of your father, Miranda," said Mr. Anderson, in a sad tone. "Will you look carefully at this signature, and say it is your father's?"

Mr. Anderson handed Miranda the parchment, who took it into her trembling hands. For a moment a film seemed to come across her eyes, and then it cleared away, and the name George Rankley stood before her in terrible distinctness. Once or twice she essayed to speak, but the words died away ere they reached her lips.

"If, Miranda," said Mr. Anderson, "you were on your solemn oath in a court of justice, to say yes or no to the question of, 'Is that your father's signature?' what would be your answer?"

Miranda let go the will, and it fell with a rustling sound to the floor, as she said,——

"Yes !"

Mr. Anderson clasped his hands, and Bernard Varley advancing, pointed to the will, while a smile of triumph lit up his demoniac face.

"Miranda! Miranda!" cried Mr. Anderson. "Are you sure—have you no doubt ?"

"None—none," said Miranda. "All is over. There is no hope—poor—poor Rowland! Who will help you now?"

"Ha—ha—ha!" laughed Varley, as he took up the will. "Poor Rowland needs help now, I think."

"Peace! scoffer of the pure feelings you cannot understand," cried Miranda. "Peace, I say. If you must exult in villany, do so where none can hear you; but do not insult your victims."

"Harsh words, Miranda Rankley," said Varley. Exceeding harsh words, considering who and what I am now!"

"All the power which Heaven ever gave to mortal man—all the wealth which ever the bowels of the earth yielded to the miner's toil—could not make you other than you are," said Miranda,—" a most consummate villain!"

"Hush, hush, Miranda," said Mr. Anderson. "Remember your promise to me."

"I had forgotten," said Miranda. "I was goaded to speak—pardon me, Mr. Anderson."

"You have ample excuse," said Mr. Anderson; "and now tell me, sir, what may be your intention, supposing for a moment, we admit the genuineness of this document ?"

"You shall—you must admit it," said Varley. "There is my evidence!"

He pointed to Miranda, exultingly, as he spoke.

" Enough of this," said the attorney. " Supposing, then, that this will is established, what do you intend to do ?"

" Conform to the intentions of it," said Varley. " I hold the wishes of Sir George Rankley as commands. I here offer freely my hand and heart to Miranda Rankley, and every shilling of her father's estates shall be settled on herself"

" That is absurd," said Mr. Anderson. " You must feel that such an union can never take place."

" It was the wish of Sir George," sneered Varley, " and so pious and loving a daughter as this young lady will surely look upon the will as a command. It is as if her father spoke to her from the grave."

" Hold, impious man," cried Miranda. " Nay, Mr. Anderson, I must speak. Each moment I feel more and more convinced there is some juggle in this business. That signature, on my conscience, I could swear to be my father's; but on my solemn oath likewise, I could swear he never dictated that will. I am placed most awfully—I know in my own heart two things I cannot prove—Rowland Percy's innocence, and the falsity of that will. You talk of a voice from the grave, Bernard Varley, and I say to you, beware, for one even now seems to ring in my ears, to tell me that the time will come when your villany will be confounded. When you will cry—not as I do now for justice and find none, but for mercy and find none. You may well tremble, for your name shall become a by-word and a reproach. Your memory shall be accursed. God has given me for this minute the favour of prophecy—and I proclaim that you, Bernard Varley, will suffer more pangs than ever you in your height of iniquitious power can inflict. You may turn me a beggar from my own home. You may bring to death him whom I love, but still do I in my inmost heart pity thee, for thy fate will be torment without end, while our tears shall be fleeting as an April shower, our misery short as a winter's day."

" Ha! ha! ha!" shrieked a voice in wild laughter, at the window which opened upon a lawn. " There is Bernard Varley, who is to be hanged at York. Look at him now. The dead man's sweat is upon his brow—hanged at York. Hanged at York, and poor Bold Hawk there to see it. Ha! ha! ha!"

For a minute or more, Varley seemed quite overwhelmed; and then snatching a loaded pistol from his pocket, he fired at the window where the poor idiot was stationed.

Mr. Anderson rushed from his seat and seized Varley's arm, but too late to prevent the shot from going.

Miranda screamed, and flew to the window.

" God bless you, Miss Miranda, and your bright eyes," cried Bold Hawk. " He cannot shoot me. I am not what I was. Once swords would hack me, bullets pierce my skin—fire burn, and water drown me; but I am changed—changed and Bernard Varley will be hung at York."

With a wild cry, the poor creature bounded across the lawn, and was in a moment or two lost to sight in the thick plantations that bordered its northern side.

" Mr. Varley," cried the attorney, " you should take shame to yourself for this act."

" Why did he taunt me," growled Varley, who had bitterly repented of the shot the moment he had fired it. " Why does he taunt me with his ill-omened croaking ? Am I to be for ever the subject of such gibes? He has been taught to say what he is continually shrieking in my ears by some enemy."

" He is bereft of sense, and you should not heed him."

" There's no harm done—the pistol had no bullet in it. 'Twas only powder."

" Bernard Varley lies again," cried Miranda, as she pointed to a round hole in one of the large squares of glass.

" 'Tis false," cried Varley.

" Swear it," cried Miranda, " and you will add another record to the book kept by the Eternal against the perjurer and the murderer."

" For Heaven's sake," said Mr. Anderson, " let us come to some better understanding. I again ask you, Mr. Varley, what are your intentions ?"

"Will you read the will again?" said Varley.

"No—but what are your intentions upon it?"

"I love, as such a nature as mine only can love, this haughty lady. I will wed her, though she should rave at me morning, noon, and night, if she will go to church with me. I like her wild, untamed, haughty spirit; it jumps well with my own. As her legal and, I presume, friendly adviser, you will do well, sir, to advise her to marry me."

"You jest, sir, most untimely," said Mr. Anderson.

"Nay, I adore her," said Varley. "If she will this moment pledge her word to be my wife, I will destroy this will before her face."

"Never, never, never," cried Miranda. "Were on one side the most horrible death that man could devise to await me, and on the other life with you, I would embrace torments rather than ——"

"Hush—enough," said Varley, "you are sealing your own fate. I shall act upon the will, unless you marry me. And if you do, I will save Rowland," he added, in a whisper close to the ear of Miranda.

"Fiend!" cried Miranda, starting back, "away—approach me not; your touch is pollution."

"Mr. Varley, stand back," cried Mr. Anderson; "I will not see this young lady insulted by you."

"Then take her away," said Varley; "she is in my house. You are interlopers here. Away with you—you are no guests of mine."

"Sir," said Mr. Anderson, "I will take the highest legal advice, with regard to that most extraordinary will; and if Miranda were other than a young and unprotected female, I should advise possession to be held of these estates until, by proper legal means, you succeed in establishing your ownership. As it is, though, I advise her to take possession of what personal property she herself possesses and leave this place, although it would be far more decent for you to leave it until Sir George Rankley's remains were laid in the grave."

"You appeal to me for consideration?" sneered Varley; "to me, upon whose head this lady has heaped every epithet of scorn she could think of? No; she or I shall be in power here. She may remain; but if she does, she remains at my kind clemency, and eats my bread at my table."

"Welcome death first!" said Miranda. "I will leave this place now, and if it be the will of Heaven, for ever. On the day which sees my poor father's mortal remains hidden in the tomb, no power shall keep me from there; but until then I will find a shelter where I may, for I will not sleep beneath the same roof with Bernard Varley, the perjured murderer."

"By hell, if you insult me by such names, I will take measures to make you repent it!" cried Varley.

"Perjured murderer!" shouted Miranda. "Can you really feel, perjured murderer—assassin—false witness?"

Varley rushed forward to strike her, but Mr. Anderson held his arm, crying,—

"Help—help here! Servants, protect your mistress."

CHAPTER XXXIII.

THE REMOVAL FROM THE GRANGE.—MIRANDA'S DESTITUTE STATE.—THE PRISON.

SEVERAL servants hearing Mr. Anderson's cries, at once hurried into the room, but before any one could speak, or adopt any course of action, Miranda cried, in a firm voice,—

"I am prepared to go. Those who are my friends will respect the sanctity of this house now, for it contains the remains of one so dear to me in life, that even in death affection clings to the casket from which the bright jewel has fled. I will go now, Mr. Anderson. Let there be no strife. I am ready. Such few fond records of my poor father's love, as, of right, I can lay claim to, I will take with me. I ask for nothing more."

"Miranda," said Varley, "this is your home."

"I have no home," said Miranda, with a shudder. "'Tis loving hearts that make a home, and where I free to choose now, I should call the prison-house of Rowland Percy the home to which I should go."

"You will repent this precipitancy," muttered Varley. "Miranda Rankley, I pledge you my word that by staying here you shall experience no annoyance from me."

"Peace—peace," cried Miranda. "You are master here. Enjoy, sir, your dominion. How acquired, ask your own conscience and read the answer there in letters of blood. I am going—but first I will to my chamber, and collect those trivial things which surely are mine own."

"Mr. Varley," said Mr. Anderson, "surely you contemplate making some immediate and suitable provision for the daughter of Sir George Rankley?"

"Here is the will," said Varley. "Does it say so much? Can you torture one of its phrases into such an intention? There are certain conditions named, and by them must I abide. If this young lady will remove herself from my protection, I cannot help it. The doors of this house shall ever be open to her, but I cannot force her to enter them."

"Nevertheless you surely will not—cannot allow her to go forth destitute, because she does not please to reside in the same house with you, or permit herself to remain under your protection?"

"Here is the will," said Varley, speaking with evident difficulty, and his very lips assuming an ashy paleness. "Let Miranda decide. I offer wealth—a home—unbounded freedom."

"All of which I reject from you," said Miranda. "Say no more, Mr. Anderson. Welcome, poverty—welcome, woe and distress, rather than one crumb of bread from Bernard Varley. If it be that the law will permit him thus to wrest from me my inheritance, I must suffer so much wrong, and happier shall I be, perchance, in the humble state to which I am reduced, than Bernard Varley, with the never-ceasing small voice of conscience, whispering despair to his heart."

Miranda left the room, and hastening to her own apartment, she, with a rigid calmness, that had something more awful in its manifestation than the wildest grief, proceeded to pack into a small compass, such few things as she prized, and would fain carry with her even to the grave. Then she lit a taper, and destroyed many letters and papers, which, under happier auspices, she would have kept, but now all minor feelings were merged in the tremendous excitement which her mind had undergone, and was still undergoing. Her own jewels—gifts from her father, she secured about her, and then, with eyes in which there were no tears, for her feelings lay too deep for such relief, she glanced around her on each well-remembered object in the room, which, perchance she was never more to see.

"Farewell!" she said, sadly; "farewell! I have been too happy, and Heaven is now pleased to reverse the picture, and show me the dark and gloomy side of human nature. I—must bear with it as I may; farewell! farewell!"

She tottered to the door, and then she turned to look again. Not an object in that room which met her gaze but was endeared to her by some dear remembrance. Either from love to the giver, or the occasion of the giving, each little cherished ornament of her chamber had an interest in the eyes of Miranda, and it was like parting with a troop of dear and valued friends to tear herself away. Once—twice—thrice she tried to leave the room, and as often turned back to glance again upon the roses as they trailed in at the open window, filling the air with a delicious perfume, and dappling the casements with rare beauty.

"If I could weep now," said Miranda—"if I could weep as many do on leaving much-loved objects, I think my heart would not feel quite so heavy, but I think I have no more tears—I shall never weep again. The grief that finds a vent by the eyes is weak and fleeting compared to mine! Oh! what a catalogue of miseries have I not to contend with! my father murdered—he who loves me, a prisoner—myself destitute—Fortune has done her worst. What other arrow half so venomous can she have in her quiver to launch at poor Miranda Rankley?"

Miranda plucked one of the roses, and placed it in her breast.

"I will keep this," she said; "it will remind me of my once happy home, and when its leaves become withered, and its fragrance gone, it will be a fit companion for me. We both shall have come from one home where we were happy, and we both are withered to the heart, but mine the most—mine the most."

She opened the door, and as she did so, some one turned the handle on the other side; Miranda started—a scream was upon her lips, but she repressed it, and summoning all her courage to support her, she confronted Bernard Varley.

For the space of several moments, there was a dead silence, and Miranda had time to note the appearance of her enemy. Varley trembled in every limb, and his face was the picture of agonised anxiety—the state of his mind was evidently awful. He spoke with choking accents, and his words were wild and fearful.

"Miranda, Miranda," he said, "have mercy upon me; you in your well-schooled heart cannot dream of the awful whirlwind of passion that rests in a breast like mine. Have mercy on me, and gaze not thus like a marble statue on one who, for your sake, has forfeited even the faintest hope of Heaven's mercy—oh, think what must have been the love which has driven me to war even with my God, to curse my soul—to foredoom myself to everlasting torment—mercy—mercy—Miranda Rankley, have mercy upon me."

These words were rather shrieked than spoken, and Miranda shrunk back, appalled at the awful vehemence of the wild confession.

"You shrink from me," he cried, "you loathe me—you abhor me—oh! girl—girl—drive me not quite mad—there is a raging fire in my brain—my blood no longer flows in healthful currents—I am a desperate man—I could now wage war with Heaven itself—and all—oh! God, 'tis all for love of thee, Miranda!"

"Love," said Miranda, "call you that love?"

"Yes, wild, passionate love—the love that consumes the heart—that knows no bounds—that feeds upon the very soul—that begins in agony, and ends in madness. Hear me, Miranda—when first I came to the house and saw you, I thought you some rare and wondrous work of nature, born but to be worshipped from afar off. I had no thought of breathing my idolatry—I would as soon have dreamt of speaking vows of adoration to a statue—but then came on a mortal breathing man like myself; and he approached the shrine, which, to me, was holy ground. He spoke to you of love, and you heard him with a smile. From that time, my bursting heart knew but two passions—love and hate."

"I will hear no more," cried Miranda, as she passed him into the corridor. "Bernard Varley, I will hold no converse with you."

"Miranda, Miranda," he cried, "yet a moment hear me, ere you leave me to despair—I will restore all—I will save him—ay, even him will I save who stands between me and hope."

"If," said Miranda, "even you do repent of your great wickedness, Bernard Varley, and will save the innocent, I will pray for you."

"No—no—no prayers! I am past prayers. Heaven's gates are shut to me for ever. No—no—no prayers! but if you would save him yourself, and all who in your fall must fall too, in one common ruin, give me but the smallest room to hope—say but one word to turn the current of my dark despair!"

"Never!" said Miranda.

"Think. Oh, think again!"

"I have thought until reflection has dried up even the natural resources of grief. I have no tears even for my father's memory. Bernard Varley, you have been the evil spirit of me and mine. May Heaven have mercy upon you!"

"Miranda, Miranda!" he shrieked. "Are you an angel or a devil in the shape of one, that you torment me thus? Why are you beautiful, but that men may love you?"

He sunk on his knees at her feet, and when she strove to leave him, he clutched her dress, and in accents of grovelling despair besought her to hear him.

"One word—one little word, to tell me that you will not always hate me—one word to let me know that you pity the wild fancies which could make me the wretch I am."

"Bernard Varley," said Miranda, "release me, or I will call for help. Kneel to offended Heaven—not to me."

"You are my Heaven!" he cried. "I worship none else. I will be your slave. Love me but a day, an hour, and then kill me if you will.'

"Detain me another moment, and I alarm the house!" cried Miranda.

"See, I kneel—pray to you!" he shrieked. "Where will you find such love as this? You see I am abject. Miranda—Miranda—save me—save me!"

Miranda tried to leave him; but with sighs, tears, and groans, he crawled after her.

"I am going mad!" he cried. "Miranda, you will drive me mad!"

"Help! help!" cried Miranda, who began to get seriously alarmed at his vehemence.

A servant near at hand heard her cries, and suddenly appeared. Varley sprung to his feet. He pressed his hands upon his head for a moment, then in a low voice he said,—

"'Tis done—'tis done—the die is cast—rack—ruin—blood—blood blood!"

He dashed down the corridor, and disappeared in his own sleeping chamber, leaving Miranda in a state of mind bordering upon despair; for now she knew there was the very worst to fear from the terrible passions of Varley, roused, as they seemed to be, to absolute frenzy.

"Just Heaven!" she thought, "protect me from this man. What an awful scene have I passed through! May reason yet conquer the storm within his breast, and make him penitent! Oh, Rowland, what an enemy you have!"

"Did you call, Miss Miranda?" said the servant.

"I did," said Miranda; "but 'tis no matter now. I am leaving here, it may be for ever. Do you, when I am gone, tell all in the house that I wish them happiness; and though doomed to leave this house——"

Miranda paused—she could say no more, and waving her hand to the astonished domestic, she walked quickly down the staircase to the room in which she had left Mr. Anderson.

She found him anxiously waiting her return; and when she appeared, he said,—

"Miranda, may I ask a favour of you?"

"Alas, sir! I have no power to confer one," she replied. "You forget who and what I am."

"It is," continued Mr. Anderson, "that you will become my guest as long as it shall be agreeable to yourself."

"Till to-morrow," said Miranda, "I will accept your kind offer, sir; but do not be offended with me when I tell you that I am resolved, since it has pleased Heaven to throw me on my own resources, to submit to the decree withou more murmuring than human nature in its weakness cannot but give] utterance to· I cannot eat the bread of dependence."

"Not when accompanied by as sincere a welcome, Miss Rankley, as man can give to it?"

"No, Mr. Anderson. Such accomplishments as my poor father's' love as given me must now be turned to usefulness. I must work; but yet I have matured no plan. I scarcely know what I say. Forgive me till to-morrow; yes, to-morrow," said Miranda. "Let us leave this place now. I cannot breathe freely here. Come, Mr. Anderson, and as we go, I will tell you of a scene I have just passed through, which I can never forget."

She took Mr. Anderson's arm, and they together passed out of the room into the hall. Miranda started back, and a cry of grief escaped her as she saw there assembled all the servants of the household, with sorrowing countenance.

"Friends," faltered Miranda, in vain endeavouring to command her voice, "what—what are you all assembled here for?"

"God bless you, Miss Miranda," cried one, "we heard you were going away, and as we couldn't believe it, we all came here to ask you yourself."

"I am going," said Miranda.

The servants looked at each other in amazement, and then the spokesman said—

"We all understood you were our young mistress."

"It has turned out an error," said Miranda—"God bless you all—farewell."

She tried to move towards the door, but the domestics, not one of whom but had received some kindness at her hands, pressed around her, some tearfully and some clamorously beseeching her to stay.

"Dear Miss Miranda," cried one; "what are we all to do when you are gone?

No 11.

—Do stay with us—we are all willing to work night and day for you.   What have we done, Miss Miranda, to offend you?"

" Nothing—nothing," said Miranda.   " Bernard Varley claims the Grange ; so you see, my good friends, I am compelled to go.   We shall meet once more at— at my father's funeral—farewell."

Miranda leaned heavily on Mr. Anderson's arm, and hid her face as she passed through the throng that opened to let her go.   Some wept aloud, and then Miranda wrung her hands, saying—

" Tears are denied to me.—Why cannot I weep ?"

Many cried " God bless you !" as she crossed the threshold.

She could but wave her hand, and then with one deep sigh, she left her once happy home.

CHAPTER XXIV.

THE VISIT TO THE CHAMBER.—THE DIAMOND RING.—THE ROBBERY.

BERNARD VARLEY remained for more than an hour in his own room—and what were his thoughts, and what the mental agony he indured during that hour, was only known to Heaven and to himself.   When he emerged, he looked some years older than when he had entered, but to all outward appearance he was perfectly calm.   He walked with a slow and steady step to the drawing-room, and then ringing the bell, he ordered Twitter to be sent to him, and in a few minutes the wretched terror-stricken valet made his appearance.

Even he, Twitter, absorbed as he was in his own hopes and fears, glared at Varley as if he had been an apparition, so remarkable was the change his countenance had undergone within an hour.

" Wherefore do you fix your eyes on me with such surprise ?" said Varley.

" You are much altered," said Twitter.   " Good Heavens, Varley, I should scarce have known you."

" Not know me ?—what folly is this ?"

" Your face is quite changed—I am sure there are hollows and wrinkles in it that were not there before, and your eyes are much more deeply sunk."

Varley's lips quivered as he said—

" Pshaw, I did not send for you to criticise my personal appearance, but to consult upon our ulterior operations.   I have thought it safest to leave your name out of the will, Twitter."

" Leave my name out ?" gasped Twitter.   " Then—then am I to have nothing ?"

" You shall have more than was promised you, and to set your mind at rest I will give you now my note of hand for five hundred pounds payable at the bankers where I believe lies a large sum, whenever the necessary legal steps have been taken to prove the will."

" But I was to have so much each year, said Twitter.

" And so you shall have—ay, and twice as much if you please, provided I succeed in my purposes.   I have solemnly sworn that Miranda Rankley shall be goaded to despair by poverty—want and distress shall assail her wherever she may fly, and Rowland Percy shall be hanged, if I rake hell itself for evidence against him."

" You are strangely passionate."

"No, I am calm, quite calm.   Passion is all past now.   My next intense feelings will be when I have had my revenge."

" Well, so long as in your revenge you do not lose the Grange estates, it matters not to me."

"Certainly not, but I have sent for you to know if you can identify any of the servants who assaulted me in the stable-yard ?"

"That I cannot."

"Very well. I must be content to have those only I can myself name apprehended. I have brought the officers with me for the purpose. No one, high or low shall escape my vengeance if once they give me cause. Now, Twitter, I think you had better remain here nominally in the same capacity you are now in, but actually as my friend."

"Yes—yes," said Twitter, eagerly, "I will remain, Bernard Varley, who knows but you may die some day, and leave the Grange to me."

"When I do I will," said Varley; "but something strikes me that I shall outlive you, Twitter. You are looking far from well."

"Who, I?" cried Twitter, much alarmed; "I am very well, and you are some years my elder."

"Well, well, we will not discuss that. I am now going to York upon several errands. I must appear against these servants for assaulting me, have the will forwarded to London, and give directions for Sir George's funeral. During my absence do you always see any one who may come to the Grange."

"I will; but tell me, Varley, does not the verdict of the jury virtually acquit the 'Squire of Larkwood ?"

"It does, and he will, no doubt, be immediately set at liberty."

"Is he not to be feared ?"

"No; he is a ruined man, and I am certain that he scarcely knows now where to lay his head when he shall be released from prison. I have them all at my mercy. Miranda is entirely dependant upon me. Rowland Percy must suffer, for the very means of defending him will not be found, and the squire himself must skulk about in hourly fear of arrest for debt."

"You have managed well, Varley."

"No, Twitter; but for some fortunate accident, we should have been in great difficulties. Had not young Percy chanced to come here on that eventful night, I know not what might have occurred, I should most probably have had you to thank for a speedy transition to the gallows."

"Me, Varley !"

"Aye, even you. But this is idle talk now. Your very blunders through fear have, as chance has decreed, worked well for my purposes. I am now for York, and remember caution is the word should any one call here during my absence."

To the consternation and anger of the whole household, Varley walked into the servant's hall, accompanied by the two constables he had well feed to come with him from York, and pointing out those he was able to name as being foremost in pumping on him, they were taken into custody, and hauled off without further ceremony. Casting then a glance of contempt and defiance upon the remainder of the domestics, Varley turned upon his heel, and left the house, muttering to himself as he mounted his horse—

"There shall not so much as a scullion of Sir George's household remain on these premises three days ; I will have servants who will more freely obey me as a master than these will ever be taught to do."

He then clapped spurs to his horse, and at a hard canter proceeded to York, whither he was followed by the prisoners in a cart.

When he was gone, Twitter glanced around him in his quiet suspicious way, and then muttered—

"So I am left out of the will, and dependent upon the generosity of Varley for my reward. Humph ! By the assistance of Ned Witlet, my highwayman friend, I think I can manage to increase the five hundred per annum. Master Varley may graciously condescend to give me something more, and who knows but chance may place it in my power to play him yet as good a trick as he has played Sir George Rankley. If I had but nerve, which I have not, and a little courage, which I confess I have not, I might do something better than continually robbing the Grange of all its plate and valuable articles, which is all that I can see my way clearly to do at present. It's—it's very strange they none of them have said anything about the diamond ring Sir George had upon his finger when he died. I saw it glittering as his hand lay upon the bed. Bernard Varley has forgotten it. 'Tis worth a hundred pounds. I may as well possess myself of it."

The struggle in Twitter's mind between avarice and fear was great. The dread he had of entering the chamber of the man he had passively helped to murder, brought such fear and trembling to his heart, that it was long before the tempting prize could induce him to seek the much dreaded room. What, however, will not the love of gold stimulate those men to, in whose hearts the feeling has become a passion? He lingered long, but at last consented to inflict upon himself an amount of suffering by which he was dearly purchasing the diamond he hoped to take from the dead man's finger.

Slowly, and afraid even of his own shadow, Twitter crept up the stairs till he came to the corridor, from which the sleeping apartments opened. There was no sound to disturb him. Everything seemed as still as the grave. It would appear as if the corpse had spread around it the mysterious and awful silence of its own inanimation.

"'Tis nothing," whispered Twitter to himself. "Why do I tremble? he is nothing but a senseless clod. I must arouse myself from this state of nervousness or it will surely kill me."

Striving hard to shake off the deadly fear that was at his craven heart, he paused at the door of the chamber containing the body, for some moments before he could find courage to turn the key which was in the lock, and open it. When he had done so, he paused again, and it was only by great efforts sthat he could induce himself to enter the chamber of death.

The shutters were all closed, save one from which streamed a broad ray of light upon the corpse, which was entirely covered by a sheet, giving it a much more ghastly and dreadful appearance than even were the face exposed; for when we know there is something of a fearful nature, the more of it there is left to the imagination's picturing, the more fearful it will ever become.

Twitter stood by the bedside for full five minutes, and neither spoke nor moved. His clammy cold face was fixed and rigid, and he drew even his breath with difficulty as he thought—" How am I to get his hand out, and see if he still has the ring?" After much mental agony, he lifted one side of the sheet, and there was the long, shrunk, cold hand of Sir George, with the ring which, strange to say, had been forgotten by every one, glittering in very mockery of the dead hand it adorned.

"Yes, yes—I am right, it is there," gasped Twitter, " it is there."

But to remove it was now the fearful task, and to him it was, indeed, a most fearful one. To take in his the hand of a dead man, was 'at any time a horrible proposition to the cowardly valet, but when that man was one whom he had known in life, and from whom he had received many kindnesses—one, too, who by the joint machinations of him and Varley, had been jostled, as it were, from existence and made the fearful object he was—that was terrible. The ring glittered, and appeared each moment to be sending forth brighter scintillations of light. Time was travelling fast, and the danger of interruption each moment increasing. Something must be done, and done quickly. He touched the hand—the cold seemed to thrill to his very heart. He by a desperate effort closed his fingers over the wrist, and then with the other hand strove to drag the ring from the finger but the joints appeared to have swollen, and a moisture had come upon the skin' which made it difficult for him to succeed in his object of robbing the dead.

Scarcely less pallid than the corpse itself, Twitter tried hard to possess himself of the ring. He turned it round and round upon the finger, but off it would not come. His hands shook so much that he was nearly powerless; but despite of all, his intense desire to possess the costly jewel increased each moment, although his dread of the corpse was far from decreasing in the same ratio.

Now he made one desperate effort, and the skin upon the finger broke as he dragged the ring over the joint which had hitherto impeded him. It came off the finger then so suddenly that Twitter's hand jerked the sheet from the face of the corpse, a fact that he was unconscious of until he looked up and saw the pallid ghastly countenance of the murdered man with a long scratch, to which the surgeon had made allusion, painfully visible.

"I have it—I have it," muttered Twitter, as he nervously wiped the glittering bauble. Then his eyes fell on Sir George's face, and with a cry of terror he started back to the door.

"Mercy! mercy!" he shrieked; for he thought, in his fright, that the corpse actually moved.

With his hands stretched out before him, and his eyes rivetted upon the face from whence he had not the power to withdraw them, he stood now for some moments immoveable. Then, as he felt assured that all was still, he began to breathe a little more freely.

"Some accident uncovered the face, surely," he said, "It must be covered again—so pale—so ghastly! What expression is that which sits upon his countenance! I did not kill him. Heaven knows I did not do the deed. I know not but something might even have moved me to prevent it had I not fainted at the time. Yes! This is Bernard Varley's murder—not mine."

He crept slowly towards the bed, and taking the corner of the sheet in his trembling hands, he placed it again over the face of the corpse with a shudder; then he sorted the covering as it was before his robbery, and faint and sick at heart, he turned to leave the room, when the door was slowly opened from without, and while terror rooted him to the spot, he saw Miranda enter the room.

After leaving the Grange, and seeing Varley pass by a bridle road rapidly towards York, she had returned with Mr. Anderson by a back entrance to the house, in order to take one last look upon the face of her father ere she left the home of her love and happiness, perhaps for ever.

A cry of surprise came from Miranda's lips, and it was echoed by another from Twitter, who thus caught in his guilt, was utterly confounded, and knew not what to say.

CHAPTER XXV.

THE LAST ADIEU—AN ADVENTURE ON THE ROAD TO YORK.

MIRANDA first spoke. "What do you here," she said, "with my father, Perjured man—false witness—what awful errand brings you to invade the sanctuary of this chamber?"

Twitter could do nothing but glare from her to the corpse, and from the corpse to her, in speechless terror for some time, and Miranda had repeated her question ere he found words to say—

"I—I—merely came to see that my poor lost master was not disturbed—I was his attendant in life, and I thought it my duty to visit even his remains."

"Base man," said Miranda, "are your nerves so hardened, is your conscience so callous, that with the weight of sin you have upon your soul, you can venture into the presence of him who, from my heart, I believe you destroyed, or assisted to destroy?"

"No—no," cried Twitter, "I am innocent—I am innocent."

"Peace," cried Miranda, "the pages of heaven's record are blotted with guilt—protest not to me your innocence, or if you must add to your already jured soul, new guilt, place even now your hand upon the heart of th wear—"

"No—no—" interrupted Twitter, darting to the door, "I will not give way to such superstitions—I will leave you, Miss Miranda—I am innocent—I am innocent!"

He crawled out of the room as he spoke, and encountering outside the door Mr. Anderson, he bowed humbly to him, hoping he was well; but the humane attorney shrunk back from the wretch, and merely shook his head indicative of his determination to have no conversation with him.

Clutching then the ring, still in his hand, Twitter walked down the corridor, and when he had reached his own room, he sat down, and drawing a long breath, smiled after his disgraceful fashion, and muttered to himself—

"I have the ring—I have the ring—'twas worth the trouble—and yet how dreadful did that dead face look to me, and she came too, when least expected. What evil fortune brought her back at such a juncture; but I have the ring—yes—yes—I have secured the ring—and so far have outwitted even Bernard Varley."

Miranda stood for some moments alone in the room, gazing on the lifeless remains of her father, and as she did so, her heart swelled with grief, and a thousand traits of his kindness to her, crowded to her recollection.

She slowly approached the bed, and removed the sheet from the face of the corpse. A chill came over her heart as she gazed upon the immovable features, and she would have given the world then to have wept.

"Father—dear father," she whispered, "you are now, perhaps, from Heaven looking down upon your child, and if it be that mortal vows ever reach the fine sensibilities of immortal spirits, hear me, now, in presence of your cold remains, swear to relax in no energy—to spare no toil until justice has overtaken those who robbed you of life."

She paused, and as she looked on the face of the dead, she fancied that a change came over it—it might have been her fancy, or it might have been some one of those sudden changes which occur, during the rapid progress of decomposition; but, be it what it might, Miranda shuddered as she noted it, and replacing the covering over the face, she said—

"Farewell—farewell—until we meet again in the world which is without end—farewell."

Her heart beat tumultuously as she turned from the sad spectacle, and she could not help telling herself how saddened with other thoughts and considerations her heart must be, to make her to look upon such a sight so calmly as she had, when the mere thought of a similar scene, but a few days before, would have brought gushing tears to her eyes, and plunged her into exquisite grief.

Mr. Anderson gave her his arm when she left the room, and without a remark, for he felt how sacred were a child's feelings towards a departed parent, he led her slowly down the corridor. They descended a back staircase, which led them to the gardens behind the Grange, and were soon in the open air. Then Miranda spoke in a calm tone, but still one which had in it the cadence of deep melancholy.

"I will remain with you until to-morrow only, Mr Anderson," she said, "and I have now a request to make to you, which I hope you will pardon—I have some jewels—gems that were much valued, and more for the giver than the gifts—will you take them, and as far as they will go in providing the necessary means, use them in the defence of Rowland Percy!"

"Miss Rankley," said Mr. Anderson, "you must grant me a favour, if you please. Now, although you have already refused me the one upon which I had set my mind—namely your acceptance of the hospitality of my roof, but now let me, as a friend, request that you will allow me to undertake Mr. Percy's defence, unaided by any one. I have a solemn and firm conviction of his innocence, and let me implore you to keep the jewels you mention, either for happier days or for a contingency that may arise which shall make them of importance."

She was silent for a moment; then she said in a tone of emotion—

"ot to refuse another's offer to befriend Rowland. Your kindness, Mr.

Anderson, shall never be forgotten ; and if you save the innocent from an unjust persecution, your own conscience will bestow upon you a far higher reward than any which the applauding breath of thousands can bestow upon you."

"Say no more of it, Miranda. All that man can do shall be done to save Mr. Rowland Percy from the snare which is spread for his destruction, and you must recollect that what to any one else would be seriously expensive, is not so to a professional man ; so, if I am entitled to any praise for generosity, let me not be offered more than my due."

Mr. Anderson assisted Miranda into the chaise, and in a few minutes they were rapidly leaving the old Grange far behind them.

They had not, however, proceeded far when they observed, coming rapidly in the opposite direction, a mounted horseman. He was coming up at a smart trot, and in appearance bore a strong resemblance to some fox-hunting 'squire going to, or returning from, the chase—not that he was altogether attired in sporting costume, but still the fashion of his garments, and the long boots he wore, shewed an animus that way. His horse was a splendid animal, and evidently of great value, although from the foam that hung about his mouth, and his general appearance, he was much tired.

It was more than probable that the horseman would have passed Miranda and Mr. Anderson with merely such a passing glance at them as they cast upon him, had it not been that his horse, when within a dozen paces of the chaise, stumbled, and after making several ineffectual efforts to rise, fell over on his side, entangling the rider so much in his stirrups, that without some assistance it was more than probable he could not have disengaged himself. In fact, he seemed to be injured ; for he lay perfectly still, while the animal made some desperate efforts to recover its feet.

Mr. Anderson, with the promptitude of humanity, immediately drew up, and saying to Miranda,—

"Hold the reins, for Heaven's sake !" he leaped from the chaise, and flew to the assistance of the fallen horseman. To disengage his foot from the stirrup was a work of some trouble, but by great efforts Mr. Anderson accomplished it, and then taking him by the shoulders drew him away from the horse, who now after rolling over once or twice, rose trembling, and evidently much frightened, to his feet.

"Is he hurt ?" said Miranda.

"I fear he is," said Mr. Anderson. "He must have struck his head against the ground, for he seems stunned."

"Will the horse stand quietly, Mr. Anderson ?"

"Yes. He is used to waiting for me."

Miranda immediately sprang from the chaise, and for the moment forgetting her own troubles and intense anxieties, she approached the wounded man.

"Pray Heaven he be not killed," she exclaimed. "Place him in the chaise Mr. Anderson, and I will walk."

"He is only stunned by the sudden fall. The ground is soft and could not do him much injury. If we had some water now to give him."

"Nay," said Miranda, to whom the neighbourhood was familiar, "there is a spring close by. I will fetch some in a moment."

"Here take his hat, Miranda," said Mr. Anderson. "You are a noble-hearted girl, oppressed as you are by troubles enough to appal the stoutest heart, you still feel for the misfortune of others."

Miranda did not stay to hear Mr. Anderson's praise, but hastened down a narrow turning to where she knew a clear cold spring bubbled from its gravelly bed. With some difficulty she got some into the hat by lifting it up with her hand, and hastening back to where she had left the injured man, she knelt by his side, and dashed the cold, refreshing water in his face and on his hands.

"See, he is recovering," said Mr. Anderson. "He will soon be all right again."

As Mr. Anderson spoke, the wounded stranger slowly opened his eyes and fixed them in unmingled surprise upon the lovely face of Miranda. For several moments his whole returning powers of perception seemed absorbed in gazing upon her, while she, all unconscious that it was her rare beauty bursting so suddenly upon his sight, that gave rise to the surprised expression of his face, said anxiously as she bent over him—

"Are you better now?"

"What—what's happened?" he murmured—"who did it?"

"You have had a fall from your horse," said Mr. Anderson, "and we fortunately were near you."

"A fall from my horse?" he muttered, "then I have fallen into heaven and this is an angel!"

Miranda drew back, and a faint tinge of colour came to her cheek, as she said,—

"He raves, Mr. Anderson."

"Pardon me, lady," said the stranger, "I would not offend you for worlds. God bless you for feeling compassion for a poor fellow who might have died on the road-side. I recollect now my horse stumbling, and I must have had an infernal rap on the head, for it is now beating like a hundred blacksmiths' hammers."

"Drink some water," said Mr. Anderson; "it will refresh you."

Miranda still held the hat, and she now advanced and handed it to the stranger, who with his eyes still rivetted upon her face, dashed the remainder of the cold spring water upon his head at once.

Then he drew a long breath as he said,—

"I am better now—where's my horse?"

"He is quietly grazing there by the road-side," said Mr. Anderson.

"Poor Starlight," said the man, "its not his fault. I had over ridden to-day —Ho! Starlight, boy,—ho! ho!"

The horse pricked up his ears and cantered up to his master, who narrowly examined him before he spoke again, and then with a satisfied air he rose to his feet saying gaily,—

"Well, I don't think there's much harm done this bout, at all events."

"I am glad you are not hurt," said Mr. Anderson.

"Thank you, sir, and you, young lady. Now, tell me, did you really get some water from the spring, or did I dream it?"

"She did," said the attorney, "and with a prompt humanity which ever distinguishes her."

"I can only thank you, miss," said the man as he mounted his horse, "and if you will tell me your name, I shall be proud always to remember it with gratitude."

"This lady's name is Rankley—Miranda Rankley," said Mr. Anderson.

"Of the Old Grange?" cried the man.

"The same!"

"God bless you then, miss. It may be in my power to do you more good than you know of, or myself either just now; but you shall never want a friend while Ned Witlet ives."

"Witlet—Witlet," repeated Mr. Anderson. "You don't reside about here sir?"

"I reside nowhere," replied the highwayman; "all the world's my home, but when any one wants me particularly they put an advertisement in the York Herald and say Ned's wanted at such a place, by such an one, naming the initials, and then I'm sure to come, if I'm above ground. I've heard that there has been strange work at the Grange, Miss Rankley, but your kindness to me to-day I will——but never mind. That's as much as I can say now, so good day to you. Thank you, sir, and God bless you both."

So saying he gave the rein to his horse, and without waiting for a reply to his singular address, he rode rapidly off in the direction of the Grange.

"Who can that be?" remarked Mr. Anderson. "Amid the general coarseness of his manners there peep out occasionally the traces of better breeding. His name I never heard of in York or its neighbourhood."

"It matters not," said Miranda, sadly; "we have done but our duty in succouring a fellow creature in distress, Mr. Anderson."

"True; but, Miranda, may not this be one of the mysterious ways by which Providence works out its ends? This accidental encounter may, trivial as it appears, be really fraught with great results. Something seems to whisper to me that this man will be in some manner woven up with your fate."

"'Tis strange," said Miranda; "but when I first saw him, before he fell from his horse a similar feeling came over my mind, though subsequent events quite obliterated it. It seemed to me as if I could have stopped him and said—'Tell me, how are you mixed up in the events which it is the will of Heaven I shall go through?'"

"I have often," replied Mr. Anderson, "experienced such feelings, and it may be that Providence adapts the minds of its creatures to circumstances which are to surround them by permitting them such faint glimpses of the future.

CHAPTER XXVI.

THE VISIT OF MR. QUERRAL TO ROWLAND.—NEW VEXATION.

Poor Rowland Percy left the Grange with a heavy heart. He had, as we knew in the preence of Miranda, striven, and striven most successfully, to put on an appearance of confidence, of hope, and of fortitude, which his heart was far from sharing in. A noble spirit can struggle against misfortune in almost any shape. Pain—want—misery may we bear, and the pure spirit may rise triumphant over a concatenation of circumstances of the most depressing character; but of all the hard trials for the mind—of all the maddening things to bear—false accusations are the very worst.

To find himself surrounded by men ready with every circumstantial detail to perjure themselves before Heaven for the sake of ensuring his destruction, raised a tumult of passion in his breast, which only the presence and the sufferings of Miranda at all enabled him partially to subdue and prevent from bursting forth, in indignation which would have known no restraint.

The thought of Miranda, however, was his strength— in the same manner that the fine sense of duty Miranda felt to rescue him, if possible, from his enemies, fortified her gentle nature to bear with misfortune, under which in ordinary circumstances she must have sunk.

"She thinks me innocent," was the only solace Rowland could lay to his heart and when he was left alone in his dreary cell, he could calm the effervescence of his mind by continually repeating to himself that assurance, which like a ray of light, amid an unusual gloom, lit up with hope his heart, which would otherwise have sunk into the abyss of despair.

"I a murderer!" he cried, aloud. "Oh! could all this have been foretold me but a few days since, how I should have scouted the prophet! I accused of the murder of the father of Miranda! Oh! monstrous! What can these two men mean? What can they hope to gain which shall repay them for their perjury before high Heaven?"

While Rowland was busy with these reflections, his door was opened by one of the turnkeys of the prison, who, in a rough voice said,—

"Here's a lawyer come to see you."

In a moment a man, who was an utter stranger to Rowland, entered his room, and with an affectation of great politeness, bade him good morning.

"Rowland eyed his visitor earnestly for a moment, and then being quite sure that he did not know him, he said,—

"Sir, you make some mistake, for I have not the honour of your acquaintance.'

"No mistake, Mr. Percy," said the visitor, who was no other than Mr. Querral the very questionable man of business of Bernard Varley, and who, with unblushing effrontery, had claimed and obtained admittance to Rowland, by representing himself as sent for by him to arrange his defence. "No sort of mistake, sir at all, I am a blunt man—plain, and straight-forward. In fact, I often injure myself by my unwelcome candour. You know, Mr. Percy. people don't like the truth to be spoken to them at all times."

"Will you oblige me, sir, by stating at once, your business with me?" said Rowland, who by no means liked his visitor's manners.

"Why, then, sir, in one word I came to serve you.'

"I am obliged for any offer of service," said Rowland; "but you will excuse me, when I state that my knowledge of human nature has been so different within these few days to what it was before, that I have grown suspicious." •

"Ah!" said Mr. Querral, with a deep sigh, and moving his hands up and down like the fins of a turtle, "human nature does not improve upon acquaintance. Nevertheless, Mr. Percy, there are exceptions."

"To the point, sir."

"Well, then, my young friend, I am a solicitor, and as such, I have no hesitation in saying, that you stand in very perilous circumstances."

"That I know, sir," said Rowland. "The most perilous state a man can be is to be falsely accused by villains who scruple at no wickedness i carrying out their machinations."

"Ah, very true! Very true, Mr, Percy; but safety, I take it must be just in your principal object?"

"What do you mean, sir?"

"Why, sir, I have no objection on earth to being explicit indeed. I have seen Mr. Varley this morning."

"What!" exclaimed Rowland. "You dare to come to me when you have been in communication with that fiend in human shape?"

"Hush, hush? my dear sir, do not get into a passion now, but hear me out. I repeat, I have seen Mr. Varley, and I can, in my blunt and candid way, assure you that no person feels greater regret at this prosecution than he does."

"Villain!" cried Rowland, "how dare you presume thus to insult me in my persecution?"

"Now, be calm—be calm," said Mr. Querral, "I have a proposition to make. Hear me out. What I mean to say is this:—that, from consideration of your youth, Mr. Varley will, as he can, so tamper with the evidence on your trial, as to insure a verdict of acquittal."

Rowland's indignation was so great that he allowed Mr. Querral to go on for some time, merely because he could not decide in his own mind, what species of punishment he should inflict upon him.

A verdict of acquittal!" repeated Querral, always provided you give up all claim to the hand of Miranda Rankley, and advise her to fulfil the wishes expressed in her father's will—you understand me, I hope, perfectly Mr. Percy?"

"I do sir," said Percy, "and your reward shall be an exposure of your villany. You said you came to do me service, and unconsciously you have done so, for after this, who can believe a word that comes from the lips of such a man as Bernard Varley?"

"He—he—he!" laughed Mr. Querral, with a sort of disagreeable laugh; "we are one to many for you there, Mr. Percy. If you repeat any words that I have said who will believe you. Where's your witnesses?—he—he—he!"

For a moment Rowland was confounded by the cool impertinence of the scoundrel; and then, surmising what he said was perfectly true, namely, that in his, Rowland's situation, such a tale, coming from his lips, and contradicted by the attorney, would meet no belief, he determined that his tormentor should not escape scot-free for his unblushing assurance, and, suddenly clutching him by the collar, Rowland gave him such a shaking, that he had not breath to call for help, and it was not until the exasperated young man let him go that he could scream—

"Murder—murder!" at the top of his lungs.

Mr. Querral's cries soon brought several officers of the prison to his assistance.

"What's the matter now?" cried a man in a gruff voice, with a bunch of keys in his hand.

"He wanted to murder me," said Querral. "The scoundrel wanted to commit another murder, because I refused to go to Mr. Varley and persuade him to tamper with his conscience in giving evidence on the trial."

"Hilloa, my gaol bird," said the turnkey to Rowland, "you are a nice article, surely."

"What that man says is false," cried Rowland. "He came here from his rascally employer to make such a proposition to me, because they know well my innocence of the crime laid to my charge."

"Oh," cried the turnkey, with a laugh, "everybody is innocent as comes here. Bill did we ever have any one who was guilty yet?"

"No," replied his companion, "I should think not."

Rowland turned in disgust from the man, and resolved to waste no mo e words in attempting to deny what he was accused of.

"He assaulted me," cried Querral, with malice—"he assaulted me like a ruffian as he is Oh, my spark, this will mend your case nicely, I think—I am a blunt man an uncommonly candid man, and I assure you, my fine young gentleman, that you will be hanged. Do you hear that? hanged like a dog."

"Come, come, none of this," said the turnkey. "If you can't agree, Mr. Lawyer with your client, just come away with you at once."

'I his client?" cried Rowland, goaded to speak, despite his resolution to be silent. "I never saw this man's face before to-day, and knew not of his existence."

"Oh, oh, oh," said Querral, lifting up his hand. "Gentlemen," appealing to the turnkeys, "I have a note from him at home, commencing with 'honoured sir,' and ending with 'your unfortunate, but humble servant, Rowland Percy.'"

"Liar," said Rowland.

"There, that'll do," said the turnkeys, "we shall have the governor about our ears if we don't mind. Come on, I say."

They then hustled Mr. Querral out of the cell leaving Rowland in a state of vexation beyond description.

He paced his solitary place of confinement to and fro, like some melancholy caged denizen of the forest, and impatience getting the better of him, he exclaimed against the cruel fortune which had loaded him with such a weight of ills.

Not for long, however, was Rowland left to his own reflections. The door of his prison-house was opened, and a visitor of a much more welcome character than the former one, was announced to him. It was his father.

Rowland was as surprised as he was delighted with so very unexpected a visitor, for he had been informed that his father was in custody on account of the duel.

"Father, dear father," he cried, "what merciful chance permits you to come and visit me?"

"Alas, my Rowland," said Mr. Percy, "call it not a merciful chance. The magistrates have only discharged me, because it is believed there is ample evidence to destroy you. Oh, my poor Rowland, what dreadful train of circumstances has brought you to this sad strait?"

"I can scarcely tell you," said Rowland, "but, on my conscience, I believe we are both, in this most unhappy business, the victims of some awful conspiracy, which Heaven may, in its mercy to us, some day bring to light, but which at present I can but guess at."

"I am myself," said the elder Percy, "quite bewildered by the rapid events of the last few days. I was goaded to fight with Sir George Rankley, but now that my judgment is calmer I do most deeply regret that a false sense of honour, and a too senstiive dread of the world's opinion, drove me into the field. Oh, Rowland, the grave hides many failings, and when those we have once loved, and been on terms of dear companionship with, have left us for ever, and gone to that bourne from whence no traveller returns, we sigh for the past, which we cannot recall, and passion sinks in its own ashes, a prey to never-dying regret."

"But, father," said Rowland, as he saw how much oppressed was his parent's spirit with Sir George's death, "you did not kill Sir George."

"No, thank Heaven!" cried Mr. Percy; "but I gave myself too readily, Rowland, as an instrument in the hands of villains. From my heart I do distrust that man, Varley. Something seems to whisper to me that he is the arch-fiend who has contrived all this load of misery, which has made so many weep tears of blood, and the issues of which are still in the hands of Heaven."

Rowland Percy was silent for some moments; then he said, in a tone of deep emotion,—

"Father, Miranda is now an orphan. Do you be a father to her, and make up in loving kindness to the child any want of discretion as regarded the father. I am confident she will see this most unhappy duel between you and her father in its proper light, and forgive you for being the victim of the same dark scheme which in its horrible success has been the ruin of us all. Take her to your heart, father, as if she were a daughter of your own; and, should it then be the will of Heaven that I suffer innocently, love and cherish her for my memory, and her virtues."

"Alas! alas!" cried Mr. Percy, "Rowland, you forget, or you know not that I have no longer a house—that all I had is swept away from me. I am a ruined man."

"All, father?"

" Yes, Rowland, all ! With the exception of some trifles which may support me for a few days—I am destitute."

Rowland was silent for a few moments, then, lifting up his hands, he cried,—

" Oh, Heaven ! why do these accumulated miseries occur when I am thus helpless ? Give me liberty, and I would toil while nature would sustain me, for those I love ? But here—here, I must nurse my despair, and feed upon the bitter thoughts that rend my heart."

" Do not despair, my Rowland," said Mr. Percy, although his trembling voice belied the tenour of his words. " Do not despair—you are innocent—Miranda believes so ; and even me, after an explanation which I have given her, she exculpates from further blame than that which arises from the frailty of human nature in being misled too easily."

" Did I dream it ?" said Rowland, " or is true that the villain, Varley, claims all that Sir George possessed ?"

" It is true, and even as we are ourselves nearly destitute, is the much envied Miranda."

" When will all this have an end ?" cried Rowland. " Have we already, father, felt the worst blows of fate, or are we yet to expect some crowning misery to transcend all that have gone before ?"

" We must be patient—patient," said Mr. Percy, as the tears slowly rolled down his cheeks, and he thought that the crowning misery of all might be the conviction of his innocent and noble-minded son. " We must be patient, my Rowland. Trust in Heaven—its mercy may come, even at the eleventh hour.—We will not despair."

The door of the cell was opened and the turnkey holding it in his hand, said,—

" Time's up, sir, Besides, here's a gentleman with an order to see the prisoner."

" Must I leave ?" said Mr. Percy.

" Yes, sir, time's up. You can come any time between eleven and two, but we can't let you stay long."

" Father, farewell," said Rowland, " and remember what I have said to you of Miranda. You can be near and protect her, though you cannot offer her a home."

" I will, Rowland, I will. Heaven bless her. In poverty or woe she shall never want one to stand between her and every ill while I live. Farewell, Rowland, we shall meet again to-morrow."

" Farewell."

Young Percy turned away his face to hide a tear, as his father wrung his hand, and then followed the turnkey from the gloomy room.

Misery, of however short duration, works strange changes in the physical structure ; and in the midst of all his own engrossing distress, it was with an exquisite pang of grief that Rowland marked how much the last few days had altered his sorrowing father. His form was bent, and deep lines had appeared in his cheeks, while his voice had undergone as great a change as might have been expected in ten years.

Rowland, however, had scarcely time to heave a sigh over these melancholy reflections, when Mr. Anderson was introduced to him, and, advancing towards the prisoner, he took his hand, saying,—

" Well, Mr. Percy, I hope my visit is not an unwelcome one ?"

" Unwelcome, sir, it cannot be," said Rowland. " The unfortunate may well feel gratified for any kind attention."

" You will fully understand, Mr. Percy, that I come here as your legal adviser, with a full and complete assurance of your innocence.'

The colour came to the cheek of Rowland, as he said,—

" Mr. Anderson, for your generous confidence in my innocence, I thank you from my heart ! but with such poor eloquence as God has given me, must I plead my own cause, for at this juncture it so happens that I have no means of adequately repaying you for undertaking my defence."

"Oh, that is all settled," said Mr. Anderson ; "Miranda has arranged all that with me ; so you will give me leave, I hope to consider myself as empowered by you to take whatever steps I consider necessary in my endeavours to unmask the villany of which, I feel confident, you are a victim."

"Miranda ?" exclaimed Rowland. "Am I indeed indebted to this suffering angel for so much ? Oh, Mr. Anderson, could you believe that there would exist a villain bad enough to wrong her ?"

"Gold, my dear sir," said Mr. Anderson," is a bait that will lure thousands to the greatest iniquities. But my visit to you now must be a brief one. It was quite necessary that you should know that I am professionally engaged for you, but to-morrow we must have a long consultation which I cannot now spare time for, as I wish to retain counsel this day, who, if I be not active, may fall into the hands of your enemies."

Mr. Anderson then shook hands warmly and cordially with Rowland, and hurried from the prison.

CHAPTER XXVII.

THE ROBBERY.—THE ALARM OF GUILT

THE sun had sunk upon the broad lands comprising the Grange estate, and the sighing wind was sweeping across field, orchard, and lake, closing the leaves of the wild flowers as it took its devious course, and gently rustling the corn, which with an undulating motion like the sea, bowed before it, when Twitter crept from the Grange by the garden entrance, with an open note in his hand, which had been given to him about an hour previously by a servant, who had received it from a country lad. He paused when he got a short distance from the house, and holding the note so as to catch the faint light that still lingered in the west, as if loath to leave the world, he read it slowly and distinctly. It was as follows.—

"Meet me one hour after sunset at the old place."   "N. W."

"One hour after sunset," muttered Twitter. " 'Tis that time now, and he will be there. Witlet is an important man—a most important man. I am glad he has come, for it might be dangerous to keep this ring about me, and he can take it to London, where it will fetch its price. 'Tis monstrous though to give him half—most monstrous. I must again represent that to him. He ought to be content with much less—very much less—and yet I scarcely think he will. One hour after sunset at the old place. By Heavens, Master Varley, since you have left me out of the will, I will help myself, and likewise protect myself. I must ask Witlet to bring me some arms, for the thought keeps ever coming uppermost in my mind that Varley may, in order to make his safety doubly sure, destroy me some day. He would think nothing of taking my life. I must protect myself. Now, if I could trust Witlet, it would be a brave scheme to serve Varley, even as he has served Sir George. Why should not I, as well as he, be master of the Grange? Heavens ! how I would lord it over them all. They should feel my power, by its never wearying exercise. I would make up for years of abject submission, by showing my might. Oh, it would be glorious for me to be master of the Grange."

Pleasing himself with these thoughts, Twitter slunk onwards towards his place of rendezvous with Ned Witlet, the highwayman, which, upon reaching, he cautiously scrutinised before he gave the signal. The moment he had done so, it was answered by the whistle of Witlet, who commenced climbing over the paling.

"Well, Twitter," he said, "what news to-night?"

"No news, Witlet," replied Twitter, "at least, none in particular. I am glad you have come, very glad."

"Have you more plate?"

"No, not packed just now, although, if you could wait, I think I could get you some; but I have a diamond here, set in a ring, which is valuable."

"Humph" said Witlet, as he turned the sparkling gem about. "'Tis a rare one."

"Yes, Witlet, it is, and I am thinking you ought to let me have more than half the proceeds of such an article. The trouble of conveying it is nothing, and, with your facilities of disposing of such things in London, I cannot but think you drive too hard a bargain with me."

"I tell you what, Master Twitter," said Ned, "I'll keep this ring altogether if you say any more in that strain, and that will be a woeful lesson to you for the future."

"Gracious—no!" cried Twitter. "Give me the ring—Witlet, you surely would not rob me?"

"I don't know why I shouldn't," said the highwayman, with a laugh; "I rob everybody else, and why the devil should you escape?"

"Honour among thieves," said Twitter, with a bitterness of tone, that produced no other effect upon Witlet than a hearty laugh, and a ——

"Well said—well said, Twitter, most apt. Now for that you shall have your share of the ring, so that's settled; but don't talk to me about driving hard bargains. It's d——d ungentlemanly that it is."

"Well, well," said Twitter, "I suppose I must submit. When can you come again, Witlet?"

"Why, I've some idea of staying in the neighbourhood a little while," replied the highwayman. "By-the-bye, you have had a death here, and an inquest, and so on."

"Yes. Sir George Rankley is dead, and Bernard Varley, of whom I have spoken to you, is master of the Grange."

"Does that make any difference in your favour?"

"None, Witlet, none. What put that in your head?"

"Nothing; I only asked because you always used to pay a great many compliments to this Mr. Varley's talents as a mighty great rogue, and as I knew you dabbled in the same sort of business, I thought you might have made something by the sudden change of proprietors."

"No. I merely continue in my situation."

"What's become of the daughter of Sir George?"

"The—the—daughter? Miranda?"

"Aye, Miranda."

"Why, she has left the Grange; but she is nothing to us, Witlet. Sir George left all his property to Varley, on condition that he should marry Miranda; and he is quite willing, but she is not, so he keeps the property himself."

"Oh, indeed! Now, between you and I, Twitter, what an infernally unlikely will that was for a father to make."

"Unlikely; Oh—I—I don't know."

"Curse me if I don't think it's a lie from beginning to end."

"What do you mean, Witlet."

"Why, I mean it's as likely as that twenty shillings make a pound, there's some swindling in the whole affair."

It was too dark for Witlet to observe the colour in Twitter's countenance as he spoke, or his hinted suspicions would have been more than strengthened. As it was, several minutes elapsed before the guilty man could reply. Then it was in a faint low voice that he said,—

"I have no opinion upon the subject. I have nothing to do with Mr. Varley's private affairs. I know nothing about the will or the estate."

"Oh! very well. I only asked out of curiosity. Then I suppose the girl is not very well off?"

"Miranda do you mean?"

"Yes—to be sure."

"No—that is, I dare say she is not. You must know she actually takes part with him who is upon clear evidence committed to prison for the murder of her father."

"That looks uncommonly queer again," said Witlet; "why no child would or could do that, Twitter. You may depend upon it he didn't do the murder, or else she never could take his part."

"It—it is supposed," faltered Twitter, "that he murdered Sir George with the hope then of becoming possessed of the Grange estates by marrying the daughter. He came here in disguise on the night of the murder, and everything points to him as the perpetrator of the deed."

"And yet she takes his part."

"She does—is it not strange?—and—and very wicked?"

"I don't know; but, however, as you say, it's no business of ours. I'll see you again in this place, at the same hour, the evening after next."

"Do so, and I will have a packet of plate ready for you."

"Very well. You think you can carry on the old trade, do you? I saw this Varley once, and he seemed a keen hand."

"I will try," said Twitter; "where did you see him?"

"At York once, and I shall never forget his confounded leer as long as I live. Why, he's just the sort of fellow to do a sneaking thing, and as for stopping any one on the highway, why he wouldn't be equal to it on any account. Good morning to you."

Witlet got over the wall, where stood his horse patiently waiting for him, and with some expressions of kindness, which the creature seemed fully to comprehend, he mounted him and galloped down the lane which led into the bridle-road to York, by luxuriant corn-fields, rich orchards, and pasture land.

One of the most singular anomalies in human nature, and yet one far from rare is the facility with which persons engaged in notoriously evil courses will separate their particular branch of iniquity from every other, and find some, as they think, redeeming features in it, which do not belong to any species of crime.

Thus the highwayman who stops you on the highway with a pistol at your head, demanding your money or your life, will speak with contempt of the man who, by the aid of skeleton keys, &c., creeps into your house at midnight, and plunders you while you sleep in unconscious security of your plate and money.

The housebreaker in his turn despises the highwayman, and as the notorious Ned Riches, who was executed in the early part of George the Third's reign, remarked on his route to Tyburn, "he thanked Heaven he was a cracksman, and had never stooped to the vulgarity of a highway-robbery."

Our friend Witlet was a notable example of this obliquity of intellect, for as he trotted along the bridle path, he felt great indignation at the mere supposition that Bernard Varley had forged a will, and wondered if he wanted money, he didn't act like a gentleman, and take the road at once.

"But," added Witlet to himself, "there is no accounting for tastes, and some people will go sneaking through the world when they might do quite different."

Ned went cantering on as these observations passed through his conscience, nor did he cease declaiming now and then against the supposed villany of Varley, until he heard a horse cantering towads him, in the direction from York.

"Hilloa," muttered Witlet, as he reduced his pace to a quiet walk. "Here may be a chance. There ain't a prettier spot than this in the whole country for stopping a greasy farmer, or lightening the pocket of a rich squire. There's not a public-house within a mile, or a private one within two. He's coming a good rate whoever he is. Well that's not much matter—there aint a great deal of room to spare in this bridle-path when two horsemen pass each other, and we must try to make that littlle less.

The advancing horseman was within some hundred paces of him now, and Witlet raising his voice, cried,—

"Hilloa, friend, not so fast ; there's an obstruction here that you may have an ugly fall over,—

The horseman drew his rein immediately, and answered roughly,—

"What's the matter, and be d—d to you ?"

"Thank you for nothing," said Witlet, "an oath breaks no bones, but there's a sink here."

"A sink ?"

"Yes, nothing but gold runs into it hou h; so, my fine fellow, who-ever you are, I'll trouble you to hand me over your purse, or I'll pop a par of leaden arguments in your brain, that will sharpen its faculties a little."

Their eyes met, and then Witlet exclaimed—

"So it's you, Mr. Varley, is it. Well this is a lucky chance—you've just come i to some property, and I don t see why I shouldn' ave a slice of it."

Varley's cy s flashed with rage, as he said,—

"Who are you that wants to swing on the gallows tree ?"

"I'm thinking you stand as a good chance as I do, Master Varley," said Witlet ; "but we won't ar e that point now Your money and watch if you h d one."

A moment's reflection convinced Varley that submission was inevitable, unless he chose to throw away his life for the sake of retaining for a few moment's longer, a sum of upwards of a hundred pounds which he had in his pockets. Besides, he was completely unarmed, and any attempt at resistance would have been perfect madness.

"An unarmed man," he muttered, "is no match for one with fire-arms. There is my purse."

"You may look as hard at me, to know me again, as you like," said Witle "but if ever you venture to injure me, it will be the worst day's work you ever did in your   e."

"What do you mean?"

"Remember the will," said Witlet, looking as closely as he could by the dim light, into the countenance of Varley, to note the impression his words made on him ; nor was he disappointed, for Varley trembled, and turning ghastly pale, said,—

"Come with me to the Grange and tell me who you are, and I will treble the amount I have now handed to you."

"To the Grange?" said Ned.

"Yes—I will make it worth your while to explain to me how and where——"

Varley paused, for the thought struck him that after all he might be speaking too fast, and blinded by his apprehension, say something to do himself an irreparable injury.

"Oh, you can go on," said Witlet, "I know everything. So you may as well make a clear breast of it."

"Clear breast of what?" said Varley, who had now recovered from his first surprise, and became cautious.

"Just as you like—just as you like.   I'll trouble you for your watch."

"I have none."

"You have," said Witlet, as he pressed the pistol closer to the cheek of Varley.

"Take it then," said Varley, bitterly. "Now, I suppose, I can pass on?"

"Wait a moment, if you please.   What put it into your head ever to suppose Miranda Rankley would marry such a gaol bird as you look? Why, Varley, you are enough to frighten a horse with your black brows and your cream cheese of a complexion. You must have been mad, man."

"In the name of hell, who are you?" said Varley.

"I'll tell you directly," replied Witlet. "But, between you and I, that will business is rather too bad."

Varley drew his breath sharp and thick as he gasped,—

"Man or devil, I implore you to tell me who you are.   I will make it worth your while.   Come home with me now, and you shall not repent it."

"Oh, yes, I should," said Witlet. "I only want to give you a little friendly caution, and as I never give anything for nothing, you see I take the means to pay myself.   Look out, Bernard Varley, you have done things that would place your neck in a disagreeable predicament, and I warn you now not to know me ever, unless I speak to you.   You understand me?"

"I do," faintly replied Varley. "I do.   But now tell me who you are."

"Incline your ear."

Varley leant forward, and Witlet placing his mouth close to his ear, whispered solemnly,—

"The devil!"

He then instantly set spurs to his horse and galloped down the bridle-path, leaving Varley perfectly bewildered, and in a clammy perspiration from intense fear.

The wind howled past him, and now a muttered roar of thunder far off betokened a coming storm, while a vivid flash of lightning, preceding a louder clap, lighted up with its wild awful brilliancy the landscape for one fleeting moment, and then left it in tenfold darkness.

Varley, with a cry of terror, plunged the spurs rowel deep into the horse's flanks. The animal reared for a moment, and then with a terrific plunge, darted off at a tremendous gallop.

CHAPTER XXVIII.

THE STORM.—THE SPECTRE OF THE MURDERED KEEPER.

VARLEY's steed continued its mad career, until he mechanically checked it, as he neared the Grange. The storm was each moment increasing in violence—vivid flashes of forked lightning increased the terror of the horse almost to madness, and the rumbling thunder sounded to the guilty mind of Varley like the denunciations of Heaven upon his blood-stained conscience.

When he reached the stone steps of the hall, he, with difficulty, reined in the plunging steed, and calling loudly for some one to hold his horse, he flung himself from the saddle, and with a face of unearthly paleness stood upon the first step leading to the hall door, holding the bridle in his hand.

With a wild laugh then some one bounded from among the shrubbery of the lawn, and coming close to Varley, screamed in his ear,—

"Ha—ha—hanged at York—Bernard Varley will be hanged at York—rare sport—there will be a frightful mob when Bernard Varley is hanged at York."

"Fiend !" cried Varley, as the mocking face of the idiot, Bold Hawk, leered upon him; "are you tired of life, that you thus mock a desperate man ?"

"Ha ! ha !" laughed the strange being, clapping his hands, "the fire won't burn—the water won't drown—the lightning won't scorch Bernard Varley, because, how could he then be hanged at York?"

Varley let go the bridle of his horse, and strove to grapple with the demented creature ; but Bold Hawk skipped away from him, and with shrieks and yells, fled over the lawn, while the affrighted horse, with the stirrups goading him to fury, tore off at a tremendous gallop, and was quickly lost both to sight and hearing.

Varley lifted his clenched hand to Heaven, and was upon the point of uttering an awful imprecation, when the sky seemed to open and a glance of electric light suddenly flashed across the whole extent of space. Varley covered his eyes with his hands, and trembling with fear, slowly ascended the hall steps. He rang the ponderous bell, whose echoes seemed to fall upon his heart like a death knell, and just as an awful peal of thunder appeared to strike the Grange to its foundation, the door was opened, and Varley faint, weary, and alarmed, staggered ito the hall.

He sunk into the first seat that presented itself, and while the servant who had admitted him, gazed with surprise and terror upon his ghastly face, he breathed heavily, and glared around him as if he expected his eyes to be blasted by some fearful spectacle.

"Are you not well, sir ?" the servant ventured at length to say.

"Why came you not to the door when I called?" gasped Varley. "Is this a night to keep me waiting ?"

"Indeed, sir, we did not hear you ring but once. The storm must have drowned your voice. There's the thunder again. It's quite impossible to hear anything outside. The servants are all terrified, for they say there have been strange noises in the Grange."

"Noises ! What—what noises ?"

"I haven't heard anything myself, sir ; but they say that from the long corridor there have been heard moans and groans enough to frighten any one."

"'Tis untrue," cried Varley. "How dare they say such things ? Am I to have my home made frightful by such superstitions? How dare they say so ? Mark me, whoever sees or hears anything of such a character in the Grange leaves it that hour. You understand me. I am free myself—quite free from superstition, but I will not have such tales circulated. You hear me, sir ?"

"Yes, sir."

"Let me have lights, then, and tell Twitter I would speak with him. The lights first—the lights first."

" In which room will you please to have the lights, sir ?"

" The small parlour. Quick—quick. Will the storm never abate? What an awful night is this! Who could that have been who seems to know so much? His dark hints were to me appalling! Could they be accidental, or are they really based upon a knowledge of things which I thought at least were confined to the breasts of three persons—myself, Twitter, and Querral. Surely I am not betrayed ? No—no, what could they gain by my destruction ?"

Varley would not leave the hall till the lights were brought him, and then he followed a servant, who carried them, into the small room he had indicated. In a few moments Twitter made his appearance, quite as glad of company on that night of storm as Varley could possibly be, and closing the door, the two guilty men glared at each other with pale, ghastly faces, trembling at each peal of thunder, and shrinking as now and then a vivid flash of lightning would make itself be seen, despite the lights which were in the room.

" Twitter," said Varley, after a long pause, " this night on my return from York, I met one who seemed to know too much for your safety and mine. He was an armed man, and I could not resist him, so he robbed me ; but that was little compared to the frightful hints he threw out concerning his knowledge of things which you and I thought could not possibly stray beyond the precincts of our own breasts."

Twitter felt sure in a moment that it must be Ned Witlet to whom Varley alluded, and he replied,—

" Indeed ! What manner of man was he ?"

" A stout, tall man, mounted on a black horse. He spoke of the will, aye, as confidently as if he had been at our elbows when it was made."

" Your elbow," corrected Twitter, faintly. " You know I never saw the will. You and your friend Querral performed it. Your elbow you mean, Varley."

" Pshaw ! why quibble about words," cried Varley. " There must be imminent danger somewhere. How on earth could yon stranger, if he be a mortal man, ever come to the knowledge of that which he seemed to know so well ?"

" I know not," said Twitter. " 'Tis very strange ! Would he not tell you who he was ?"

" No; that question he turned to a jest, although at the moment it startled me."

" What jest ?"

" He said he was——"

They both instinctively covered their eyes as a blazing flash of lightning seemed for an instant quite to extinguish the lights in the room, and to linger between earth and heaven an unusual time. Then succeeded such a peal of thunder that in its echoes it seemed endless, and Twitter involuntarily grasped the chair on which he sat, as with a voice of intense alarm, he said,—

" Oh, Varley! Varley! what will become of us ? Is this storm doomed to be our destruction? Heaven, have mercy! I did not do the deed! You know, Varley, it was you ! You know it was—I could not prevent you ! Have mercy, Heaven ! Oh, have mercy !"

" Wretch !" cried Varley, as he rose and seized Twitter by the collar, "make the night more hideous than it is by your vile croaking, and I will rid myself of you at once, by taking your worthless life !"

Twitter could not speak, but he slid upon his knees, and looked beseechingly in the face of Varley, which was working with diabolical passion. What might have been the result of the fury which was raging in Varley's heart at that moment it is impossible to say, for ere another minute elapsed, the door of the room was flung open, and there stood in the entrance, a figure, the exact counterpart of that which Rowland Percy had assumed in order to gain admittance to the Grange. The form was dressed in the faded green dress of a gamekeeper, and as it stood in the dim light cast by the candles through the door-way, it seemed of herculean size.

Varley's eyes were facing the door, but Twitter's were not, and the latter could only suppose that some sight of terror had met his companion's gaze, by seeing the cold perspiration break out upon his brow, and the fixed horrible stare of his eyes.

"What do you see?" gasped Twitter. "Varley—Varley, why do you glare thus on vacancy? What is it?"

"Off—off—off," said Varley, in choking accents, as he let go his hold of Twitter, and retreated backwards to the further end of the room.

The valet then as he still knelt, turned his head, and saw the object of Varley's alarm with a terror that at once deprived him of all power of speech or action.

The supernatural-looking figure then slowly stepped backwards, fading away in the darkness of the hall. The door was slammed to violently, and Twitter with a deep groan fell on the floor, while Varley stood with his lips apart, and his arms stretched out before him, as if he feared the strange appearance would approach close to him, and drive him to madness by its hideous contact.

It was many minutes before either of the affrighted men could speak, and then it was Varley who broke the silence, by pronouncing the name of Twitter.

He was answered only by a groan.

"Twitter—Twitter," he again said, and then the valet looked up in his face, and whispered,—

"Is it gone?"

"Yes—yes," said Varley; "it is gone! Tell me, Twitter—good Twitter, tell me what think you of this visitation? Speak, Twitter, speak."

"This was no idle superstition," said Twitter. "We have seen the spirit of the murdered keeper! Oh, Varley, this will be a terrible home. We dare not stay here; if the spirit of one murdered man, and that too one whose generation had passed away, be permitted to wander through this place, why ay not a t the lifeless remains of which even now are buried!"

"Hush! hush!" said Varley, "why utter so horrible a suggestion? Are you mad, Twitter, that you speak, thus? Peace! peace!"

"What shall we do? What shall we do?"

Varley remained for some minutes silent, then he said in a low voice, as if he feared to be overheard by the beings of another world,—

"Twitter, I cannot live here. The rents from the Grange estate will provide an ample revenue, and I will reside in York. I dare not sleep in this house now!"

"Nor I—nor I," said Twitter. "You will allow me money, Varley? Remember your promise. You will allow we money?"

"I will keep my word; to-morrow shall see me bid adieu to this place. I can reside at York in as much splendour as I wish. Constant fears would torment me in this house! We—we will sit up to-night, Twitter."

"Yes," faltered Twitter; "I would not be alone, Varley, for worlds."

"You are superstitious," said Varley, while his teeth chattered with fear. "Yon supposed figure that we saw could but be the coinage of our fancy. Do not be superstitious, Twitter. I will not think it real."

Twitter shook his head as he said,—

"No—no, Varley; it was no fancy. How could the door open and shut so mysteriously?"

"That must have been the wind," said Varley, who would fain have reasoned himself out of his rooted belief that he had really seen a supernatural visitant. "I tell you that must have been the wind, Twitter; and yet I will not remain in the house, because the imagination would be ever active in playing the judgment such tricks."

"We will both live at York," remarked Twitter, "and we need never visit this place again. It will ever be frightful to us!"

"Ever—ever," said Varley.

"Let us have wine here, Varley, and then fasten the door. We will remain until the morning, and the light of day will then assure us that we may take some rest. I never heard of these frightful visitations when the sun was shining."

"Yes—wine—wine," said Varley, catching at the suggestion. "We will say nothing of what we have seen, but to-morrow I will take measures to break up the establishment here."

As Varley spoke, loud cries, mingled with piercing and appalling screams proceeded from the servants' hall, which was in the immediate vicinity of the small parlour in which he and Twitter were sitting.

They both immediately started to their feet, and glanced in terror towards the door which in another moment was opened, and presented in the hall a crowd of the domestics, some of whom were bearing lights and all pointing with frantic gestures in the direction of a conservatory, which led towards the gardens, and the inner door of which was at the top of three steps from the end of the hall.

The door was open, and Varley could see the same figure which had alarmed him and Twitter slowly pacing down the centre of the conservatory.

"The keeper's ghost! the keeper's ghost!" said a dozen in a breath, and then the figure disappeared in the gloom to which it was walking.

CHAPTER XXIX.

THE MORNING OF THE FUNERAL.—VARLEY'S MISERIES INCREASE.

THE sun was shining, and the blythe birds were merrily singing from bough to bough of the tall chesnuts that graced the avenue to the Grange, ere Twitter and Bernard Varley ventured to steal to their respective chambers, to snatch some brief repose ere the business of the day should commence. It was the one fixed for the funeral of Sir George Rankley, a measure which Varley had hurried on with almost indecent haste, because his anxiety to get the corpse of his victim out of the house had been intense; but now that the Grange had grown hateful to him, and he dreaded spending another night under its roof, such anxiety had ceased in a great measure, although he felt a sense of satisfaction that the grave would soon hide the mute witness of his crime.

Sleep, however, would not visit the weary and terror-stricken man and, after an hour's feverish tossing in bed, he again rose, and determined to proceed to York, to consult with his prime councillor Querral, about the measures to be adopted for mmediately giving up the establishment at the Grange; he by no means intended to let the lawyer know the reason of his sudden resolve.

The funeral was not to take place until one o'clock, so that Varley had ample time to ride to York and be back again in time for the ceremony. The church-yard of a humble village, within a mile of the Grange, was to receive the remains of Sir George, and as Varley in his capacity of sub-executor and trustee for the deceased had give all the necessary directions, he left word at the Grange that he would be back in good time to join the melancholy procession, and that if Miranda should make her appearance, she was to be allowed to assume whatever station she thought proper as regarded the funeral.

With his courage somewhat strengthened now that the dim and dusky shadow of night had given way to the clear sunshine of a glorious day, Bernard Varley then mounted his horse, (which had been found in the early morning quietly grazing on the lawn) and cantered towards York. He paused not until he reached the office of the man of law, and was soon closeted with the unscrupulous villian who for money would engage in any iniquitous enterprise, and without whose legal assistance Varley would have found some trouble in carrying out his wicked and nefarious designs.

It must not be imagined that Varley had wholly made a confidant of the awyer, although the latter more than suspected all that Varley could have told him, had he sat down with an intention of concealing nothing from him. The only circumstances of which Querral was fully aware, consisted in the preparation of the will which was to supersede one that was being likewise prepared by Mr. proved the signature of Sir George to the one prepared under his own instruction Anderson. Having thus the two documents in his possession, Varley had adroitly by Querral, and which that wily practitioner had taken care should be an unexceptionable legal document.

Mr. Querral looked curiously and scrutinisingly at the pale face of his client, and certain misgivings as to a sum of a thousand pounds, which he was to receive upon the will being proved, passed though his mind as he eagerly inquired if anything of an unfavourable character had occurred.

"Nothing, nothing" said Varley, "but I have a fancy to live in York, instead of the Grange, and I have merely come to you to consult you on the matter."

"Oh, you don't like the Grange?"

"No—it's too—too quiet for me—much too quiet. I shall see more life in York —I never was particulary fond of the country."

"That you unquestionably will, Mr. Varley ; but may I ask what you intend to do with the Grange?"

"I would fain let the house and the immediate surrounding land," repl ed Varley 'although the income from the general estate is quite ample for my purposes.

"The recent events connected with the death of Sir George," said Querral, "will deter many people from renting the house ; but we can try."

"Certainly—that is all I wish ; and now tell me what progress you are making in the prosecution of this young man, the murderer of Sir George."

"Read that," said Querral, handing him a note, which Varley took and read as follows :—

"Sir,—Understanding you have the conducting of the prosecution against Mr. Rowland Percy for the murder of Sir George Rankley, I beg to inform you in professional courtesy, that I have the honour to be retained for that innocent and falsely accused gentleman's defence.

"I am, sir, yours, &c.,
"Stephen Anderson."

"You see, Mr. Varley, the enemy is active," remarked Querral with a smile. "And what is more, I have had money refused by some of the principal men in the circuit, on the plea that they had just been retained, on the other side."

"Let them work their utmost," cried Varley, " I can bring proofs of guilt that will confound them, and yet I would save that young man on one consideration."

"And that is——"

"Miranda's compliance with the provisions of the will. If she would become my wife, I would have Twitter removed, and so modify my own evidence as to ensure an acquittal."

"That might be done as regards Twitter, but your own evidence cannot now very well be altered."

"There will not now be occasion to attempt it," said Varley, gloomily ; "Miranda, with a haughty scorn, repels all my advances, and leaves me to the barren enjoyment of the estate, all of which I would barter for one smile from her."

"Well, Mr. Varley," said Querral, shrugging his shoulders, "give me leave to say that for a man of your very great enterprising spirit, your extraordinary feelings as regards this girl are to me most incomprehensible."

"I love her—I adore her," said Varley, with a groan.

Mr. Querral again shrugged his shoulders, and wondered what loving and adoring meant. Then he added,—

"Well, Mr. Varley, that's your own private business, and as it is altogether out of my line, I can give you neither advice nor assistance in it."

"Poverty," said Varley, "may unbend the sternness of her nature ; I must reduce her to abject want, and then make another effort to procure a welcome from her—but I must leave you now. The funeral takes place to-day, and I shall be for a brief time blessed with a sight of her, although she may treat me with scorn. Querral, you know not what it is to have a passion such as mine, filling your heart until you fancy it must burst. I have struggled with my infatuation for Miranda Rankley, until I have nearly destroyed my reason,—but 'tis all in vain—a fierce passion for her fills my soul. To make her mine, I would forego all that used to make up the ambition of my life—I would even take the place of Rowland Percy in his dungeon, if Miranda would but come to me, and bless me with her smiles and words of consolation."

Mr. Querral took up a pen, and began very busily mending it in order to occupy his mind, while Varley was what he called raving.

The other then rose, and with a saddened air, walked to the door, saying,—

"You cannot understand these feelings—gold was once my idol as it is now yours. The love of wealth held undisputed sway in my breast, until this new and more fearful passion took possession of me. I pray you search in York for a habitation that I may reside in. Let it be rich and gorgeous—I would fain still hope, that when Miranda has felt the chilling influence of poverty and want, she may listen to my suit."

"I shall do as you wish," said Querral, "and touching that trifle of a thousand pounds?"

"You shall have it," said Varley, "and more, for we shall have yet more business to do—I will never lose sight of this girl—I will haunt her like her evil genius, and there shall be no depth of poverty and woe, but I will sink her to a lower, until the grave closes over her or she smiles upon my suit—I have sworn it by all the powers of Heaven and hell, and I will keep my oath. Yes, I will keep my oath."

"That man must be a little mad," remarked Querral to himself, when Varley had left him. "However, it's nothing to me, as long as I get tolerably well paid. A thousand pounds to begin with is not so much amiss, and I do not exactly see how Mr. Varley can refuse to lend me a few hundreds now and then, when I may choose to want them, which shall be just as often as I think I can get them, without coming to an open rupture with him."

When Varley stepped into the street from Mr. Querral's house, he started back, and an exclamation of surprise escaped his lips, as the first object that presented itself to him, was the highwayman of the preceding evening standing with all the cool indifference in the world close to the doorway.

He turned his eyes full upon Varley, and with a familiar nod, said,—

"Good morning. You are early in York."

"Shall I denounce this man?" thought Varley, "and risk all, or shall I temporise with him, in dread of his knowledge?"

It would seem as if Ned Witlet, by the glance which Varley cast around him, was aware of what was passing in his mind, for he said,—

"Beware, Bernard Varley—beware."

"Of what?" said Varley. "Tell me, man, in the open face of day, who you really are."

"I have told you once," said Witlet. "By-the-bye, I suppose you were rather alarmed last night at the ghost of the murdered keeper?"

Varley looked astonished, as he said,—

"How know you of that? Are you an inhabitant of this world, or a fiend sent to tempt me on until I sink for ever where there is no hope?"

"Hope!" laughed Witlet; "you don't mean to pretend that you have any hope? Good evening, your soul would be a dear purchase at half a farthing."

"Stop," cried Varley. "Tell me whence you got that ring. I know it well —it belongs to——"

"Sir George Rankley," said Witlet, calmly. "He gave it me himself this morning just before cock crow."

So saying, the highwayman walked leisurely away, quite sure that Varley's superstitious fears would never allow him to denounce him as a robber.

For a few moments, Varley stood looking after him with intense surprise, and a cold chill at his heart acknowledged the dreadful fear that he began to have of the stranger, who seemed by some mysterious means acquainted with every circumstance, as it seemed, in connection with him.

"Am I," he muttered, "the victim of some unearthly influence? Can it be possible, that the agents of another world are environing me? Have I indeed

gone so far in crime as to be obnoxious to the influence of beings not mortal? Who can this mysterious man be? if he be mortal,—and from whence can he derive his strange information? That ring too— never thought of it till this day, when I saw it glittering on his finger, was the property of Sir George—nay he wore it at the duel—it must have been on his finger when he died—how could this stranger become possessed of it? Bernard Varley, are you awake, or is all this some confused vision of slumber?"

The lad who was holding his horse, looked at him with surprise as he glanced after Witlet, and muttered, in disjointed words, the reflections of his tortured soul.

"Shall I walk him up and down, sir?" said the boy, with a view of attracting the attention of Varley.

He startled, and crying harshly,—"No, no," mounted his steed. Then throwing a small silver coin to the boy, he said, as he pointed to the retreating form of Witlet.

"Boy, do you know yon man?"

The boy shook his head.

"No, sir— never seed him afore."

Varley put spurs to his horse, and galloped away with despair at his heart, and his teeth set close with passion, that he should be the victim of so much doubt and apprehension, at the very time when he had imagined that by the removal of Sir George, all would be plain and easy before him, as regarded the amplitude of his means, and the contemplated possession of the Grange estates.

"The funeral—the funeral," he muttered, "I shall be easier when that is over."

CHAPTER XXX.

THE FUNERAL OF SIR GEORGE.—MIRANDA'S GRIEF.—THE WILD OFFERS OF BERNARD VARLEY.

MIRANDA rose with a heavy heart on the morning which was to see her father consigned to his last sad home. Her rest had been disturbed by frightful images, which, had she been inclined to believe that in dreams was shadowed forth dimly the future fate of the vexed sleeper, would have exercised an additional depressing weight upon her mind, already burthened as it was with many sorrows.

She had resolved that she would no longer trespass upon the hospitality of Mr. Anderson, but that by her own industry, if need should arise, she would not only endeavour to earn for herself an honourable subsistence, but assist the persecuted Rowland, whose destinies seemed yet darker than her own.

Mr. Anderson could not but mark the deep dejection that sat upon the countenance of Miranda, as she sparingly partook of the morning meal, and he strove by such attentions, and such topics of conversation as presented themselves to his mind, to wean her from the sad thoughts that occupied her sinking heart.

What human consolation, however, could withdraw Miranda from a contemplation of the solemn ceremony which was that day to take place. To leave in the tomb even the poor remains of her father, seemed like again losing him, for it was severing the last tie that still bound the senseless clay to the breast of the living. It was passing that great barrier between life and death where there is no return.

The funeral was to take place at mid-day, and Sir George was to be placed in a vault he had purchased beneath a humble but picturesque church, within one mile of the Grange. He was the first of his race that would occupy that dreary abode, and by the complexion of the present circumstances, it would seem as if he would be the last, for his dearly beloved child, his Miranda, was doomed to wander from the home which, in the fondness of the father's heart, he believed he had provided for her, and become an alien from the scenes endeared to her by every blissful association, by every endearing tie that had previously made her life like a sweet walk in a sunny garden, where she had but to stretch forth her hand to pluck the fair flowers that bloomed in beauty around her.

But now how awfully was all changed—what a moral tempest had arisen to sweep before it all the traces of her happiness, and like our erring parents when the gates of Eden closed on them, for ever shutting them from the glory, the sunshine, and the bliss in which Heaven had placed them, Miranda felt cold to the very heart's core, as her mental vision looked to her future life, and the long weary pilgrimage she might have to endure.

It was hard for one so young to nerve her mind to meet so great a storm of sorrow. It was hard for one so nurtured in luxury, ever surrounded with loving hearts, ready to do her bidding, and anticipate the half-formed wishes of her soul, to meet the cold charities of a heartless world, and struggle against the waves of a destiny which might well have appalled the bravest.

These, and a thousand such gloomy thoughts, chased each other through the mind of Miranda, as with a face pale as monumental marble, she put on the dismal mourning apparel, which Mr. Anderson had provided for her.

"'Tis well," she said, "I should mourn, but how weakly do these sad trappings pourtray the real grief of a wounded heart!—oh! what a mockery is this mourning apparel! when the heart really suffers, when the brain throbs, and all the faculties of the soul are absorbed in some great sorrow, this affected outward manifestation of the feelings, is as futile as it is to the mourner an additional source of aggravation."

The hour of eleven was now at hand, and Mr. Anderson sent to Miranda to tell her that it was nearly time that they should go upon their melancholy errand Miranda was ready, and obeying the summons, she glided down the stair-case looking more herself like one risen from the dead than a mourner at another's obsequie

Her mental sufferings had robbed her cheek of all its healthful bloom, and the sombre garments she now wore gave a thinness to the form, and showed a striking contrast to the delicate whiteness of her complexion. In the words of the poet,—

> " She looked more beautiful than death,
> Though just as sad to gaze upon."

Mr. Anderson, when she entered the parlour in which he was awaiting her coming strove to speak cheerfully to her, but he saw that her heart was too full to answer him, and he desisted from the fruitless attempt to win her from her sorrows.

In silence then he handed her into his chaise, and they were soon on the road to the Grange. The birds were gaily singing from every bough as they passed along the tract of richly cultivated country lying between York and the estate of Sir George. Thousands sof busy insect things were humming songs of joy in the sunny air—all nature appeared rejoicing—and it was a painful, and heart-striking contrast to glance from the face of nature to that of the beautiful young girl, who sat by Mr. Anderson, looking as pale as monumental marble, and so deeply immersed in the sad feelings of her own wounded spirit, that sights and sounds of joy and gladness which, under happier auspices, would have responsive feelings in her heart, passed by her quite unheeded, or were converted by the mind's subtle alchemy into, wailing and sorrow.

"Miranda," said Mr. Anderson, as they came in sight of the old gable ends of the Grange, "let me hope that you will change your determination and stay with us as our much honoured guest."

"No—no," said Miranda sorrowfully, "believe me I am not unheedful of the kindness of the offer, but as Heaven hath appointed me to feel the hand of woe heavily, I will abide my destiny ; I am young, Mr. Anderson, and why should I be a burthen to any one while I have strength or health to toil ?"

"Toil, Miranda? Heaven forbid. I am not without a hope that I may wrest from Bernard Varley some portion of his ill-gotten wealth. Remain with me at least until the experiment is tried."

" I cannot, I cannot," said Miranda, "but I will ever look upon you as my best friend and councillor. In poverty or in comfort I will make bold to consult you, but I cannot become a burthen upon you, although your generous heart would fain make me so."

Mr. Anderson saw that any attempt to shake Miranda's fixed determination would be futile, and he wisely abstained from pursuing the subject, consoling himself with the conviction that he should always be able to come to her assistance, and by keeping strict watch upon her, prevent any very serious misery from assailing her.

As they now neared the Grange, all subjects, save the mournful one, that called her there, faded from the mind of Miranda, and her whole thoughts became concentrated on the approaching ceremony.

Over the principal entrance to the house was a hatchment which struck a chill to the heart of Miranda as she saw it; but she made no remark, allowing Mr. Anderson in silence to hand her from his chaise, and place her arm within his own as they ascended the hall steps. The news of the arrival of her, whom they still considered as their young mistress, soon spread among the few domestics of Sir George, who still remained at the Grange, and she was greeted with affectionate sympathy by those humble hearts which felt for her the sincerest interest, and not one of whom but would have run any danger, or incurred any sacrifice for her service.

Miranda strove to call a smile to her wan cheeks as she timidly thanked them, but the effort was too much for human nature, and with a deep sigh she passed onwards, clinging to Mr. Anderson's arm.

"Go some of you," said the attorney, "and tell Mr. Varley that I and Miranda are here."

"You will remain close to me," whispered Miranda, "for I wish not to have converse with that man."

"He shall not annoy you in any manner," said Mr. Anderson. "He will not attempt it, and should he be so lost to every sense of common decency upon such an occasion as this, there are plenty of persons here, as well as myself, who will protect you."

In a few moments a servant came to tell Mr. Anderson that Varley desired to see him in his study.

"His study," thought the attorney. "The insolence of this fellow grows daily, Miranda, will you permit me to leave you for a short time?"

"Go, ' said Miranda, "you had better see him, and tell him that the daughter of his victim only comes to see her poor father's remains laid in their last home, and then she will leave him to enjoy, if Heaven will permit him, the fruits of as deep a villany as ever human brains conceived, or mortal hands executed."

Mr. Anderson followed the servant from the room in silence, and was ushered presently into a small but richly furnished apartment, where sat Bernard Varley and his man of business, the veracious Mr. Querral.

"Oh, Mr. Anderson," said Mr. Querral, "I hope I have the pleasure of seeing you perfectly well."

"Sir," said Mr. Anderson, "I have not your acquaintance."

"Oh, indeed! He! he! he!" answered Querral, with a short disagreeable laugh. "You see, Mr. Varley, two of a trade never agree—the old maxim verified?"

"You sent for me, sir," said Mr. Anderson, looking full at Varley, who wavered beneath his gaze.

"I did," said Varley; "but it was for your satisfaction, sir—not mine. Mr. Querral, my professional adviser, will prove to you that I have taken ev ry necessary measure for substantiating the will of Sir George Rankley; and it remains for you, if you be so ill advised, to do what you please in the way of attempting to resist that strictly legal document."

"What may be my intentions, or what advice I may give to Miss Rankley, remains with me alone," said Mr. Anderson. "My present visit here has sole reference to the funeral of Sir George; and his daughter, as a matter of course, claims the right of attending the ceremony."

"I wish," said Varley, his eye shifting as he spoke, "to say a few words to—to Miranda."

"She positively refuses to hold any communication with you," said Mr. Anderson, coldly.

"Positively refuses?"

"Yes. Those were my words."

"And by your advice, I presume?"

"No, Mr. Varley; although, had she asked my advice, it would have been given in confirmation of her own expressed disinclination to have any communication with you on any subject whatever."

"We understand each other," said Varley, setting his teeth, and looking with a savage scowl upon Mr. Anderson.

"I trust we do," was the other's reply.

"You might," added Varley, "have made me your friend, and the friendship of the owner of the Grange estates to a professional man is not to be despised; but you have chosen to make an enemy who never forgets an insult, nor forgives an injury."

"Your friendship I hold as lightly as your enmity," said Mr. Anderson. "Despising alike both, I leave you to your own choice."

"Dare you brave me in my own house?"

"Were it twenty times your own house I would," replied Mr. Anderson. "Robber of the orphan—despoiler of the virtuous and innocent, I do brave you here, on the spot where you have established yourself like a pestilence upon the ruins of all that is good, and great, and virtuous."

Varley would in his passion, have rushed forward to strike Mr. Anderson, but he was restrained by Querral, who, holding him forcibly, said,—

"My dear sir— bring an action against him—he called you a robber—that is clearly an actionable word—it will make a pretty suit—action for defamation— Varley v. Anderson."

Mr. Anderson slowly left the room, leaving Varley and his adviser to digest, as best they might, his frankness and his scorn.

CHAPTER XXXI.

THE FUNERAL.—AN INTERRUPTION.—AN UNEXPECTED GUEST.—VARLEY'S DESPAIR.

WHEN Mr. Anderson reached again the room in which he had left Miranda, the time for the departure of the melancholy train was near at hand, and saying nothing to her of the angry scene which had passed between him and Varley, he rung the bell, and desired the servant who answered the summons to let him know when the funeral cortege was ready to start.

The sounds of many footsteps now came distinctly upon Miranda's ears, accompanied by a strange lumbering noise, which her heart too well told her was the moving of the leaden coffin, in which the remains of her father had been early that morning encased, and which was being carried from the chamber in which he had died down into the hall. Mr. Anderson, too, heard and understood the cause of the noise, but he said nothing to Miranda, being greatly in hopes that she did not comprehend what was going forward.

The sounds then suddenly ceased, and all was still as the grave for some moments, until the door of the room was gently opened, and a servant appearing said, in a low voice,—

"All is ready, sir."

Mr. Anderson offered his arm to Miranda, who started to her feet, saying in an abstracted manner—

"Yes—yes—ready—quite ready for the grave. Oh! father, would that I was with you in your long, long sleep,—that would be happiness."

"Live for others—" whispered Mr. Anderson—"what hope has Rowland Percy, but in you?"

"Thank you—thank you for that thought," said Miranda, "I have my duty to do—I have the innocent to rescue from death—thank you—thank you."

She leaned heavily upon the arm of Mr. Anderson, as she walked by his side, towards the hall. It was thronged with persons, who made a path for the pale beautiful girl, and remained silent while she slowly moved on, in involuntary respect for her deep sorrow. Then the steps were descended, and there was the funeral coach which was to follow first in the melancholy train. Mr. Anderson assisted Miranda into the vehicle, and then followed himself, and the door was closed. Neither spoke, for at the moment the kind attorney felt that the ordinary topics of conversation would be impertinent, and he had none other to offer, while Miranda felt the greatest possible relief, by being spared the necessity of maintaining a conversation with any one, which, to her, would have been a grievous effort just then.

A few moments then elapsed, ere the funeral train got into motion, and when it did, the pace was so slow, and so solemn, that the movement was, to Miranda scarcely perceptible. It was a long and tedious journey, that one mile only, to Sir George Rankley's tomb, but it was at length accomplished; and as the clock of the little suburban church struck two, the cortege drew up at its entrance.

The deep tone of the solemn funeral bell struck upon Miranda's ear, as it seemed in its melancholy tolling, to find a voice, and peal forth to the world, that a human soul had gone to its account, and had passed away like a dream from among the living, to mingle with the spirits of the past, and form an item of that world which is eternal.

Mr. Anderson resolved within himself that should he see the spirits of Miranda much overcome, he would try again the potent spell of her lover's name, which had already had so happy an effect in weaning her from an indulgence in too great an abandonment of grief for the dead by bringing to her recollection her self-imposed duties to the living.

How sad to the afflicted heart, are the details of such a scene as that Miranda was now going through—how "stale, flat, and unprofitable," appear all the various little familiarities which the mere hirelings on such occasions take such pains to surround death with. Miranda, with a kind of stupor, arising from the intensity of her feelings, listened to the prayers within the church, and then leaning still upon the arm of Mr. Anderson she approached the low door which led into the gloomy vault.

The attendants on the dead made room for her, and then the coffin was carried to the top of the steps. The necessity of sloping it, in order to carry it to its final resting place, caused the pall to slip from it, and Miranda saw the plate on which was the name of her father.

A convulsive spasm shook her frame for a moment, and then she was still again.

One of the bystanders whispered to another, that the daughter of Sir George didn't seem much to care, for he had watched her, and she had not shed a tear yet! That man was happy, for he had yet to experience that grief which lies too deep for tears.

As the coffin now slowly disappeared from before the eyes of Miranda, in its descent down the staircase, she became aware of the presence of a person directly opposite to her—one glance told her it was Bernard Varley—he was ghastly pale—his lips were quivering, and he was scarcely able to stand, as her eyes fell upon him.

"Miranda," he said, in a deep hollow tone.

Miranda clung closer to Mr. Anderson, who said—

"Beware, sir—at such a moment as this, at least, be silent."

Miranda now made a movement to descend the narrow dark staircase, leading to the vault, but Mr. Anderson gently restrained her, saying—

"You will not surely descend, Miranda—let me prevail on you to come away now."

"No—no," she replied faintly—"I will stay till the last—till the last.

Mr. Anderson made no further opposition, but accompanied her into the vault

It was some moments before Miranda's eyes became accustomed to the dim light of that place of sepulchre, and when they did, she looked round her with fearful interest, such as only that place could have awakened in her mind, associated as she felt it would henceforward be with her most dismal and distressing reminiscences.

The clergyman had now taken his place at the head of the corpse, and commenced in a low solemn voice, reading the service of the dead. His tones echoed in the gloomy vault, and the promise of the resurrection and eternal life which was to come, seemed to find a responsive sound in the moaning air that filled that abode of death.

All were hushed as so many statues, until the last words of that solemn and affecting ritual were spoken, and then with slow steps the clergyman left the vault, after pronouncing a benediction upon all present.

Miranda gazed upon her father's coffin, and at that moment it seemed to her as if her heart was breaking. Mr. Anderson saw the terrible struggle of feeling which was going on in her breast, and touching her gently on the arm, he whispered,—

"Miranda—remember Rowland Percy."

She started and said,—

"Yes—yes—I do—Heaven knows I do—father, father—farewell, farewell."

These words were spoke with such exquisite agony, that Mr. Anderson involuntarily trembled as he stood by her side, and his own voice was full of deep emotion as he said,—

"Come, come, Miranda. Let us now leave this place—all is over—oh! come away."

"Leave—me—here, alone," said, or rather gasped Miranda, as she clasped her hands, and still kept her eyes fixed upon her father's coffin.

"No, Miranda, no," said the compassionate attorney, "I beg that you will leave with me. Do not injure your mental and bodily enegies by indulging in such exquisite grief. I implore you now to come away."

"Command me," said Miranda, faintly, "in all else, but let the child remain a brief space to breathe one prayer with no ear but that of Heaven to listen to it, by her father's corpse."

This was unanswerable, and Mr. Anderson felt he had no resource but to comply. He glanced round the vault, and saw that all had left it but himself and Miranda. Then inclining his mouth to her ear, he said,—

"For your own sake as well as for the sake of those who love you, Miranda, be brief. I will wait for you at the entrance of the vault. Call to me when you wish to ascend the stairs, and I will come to assist you."

He waited not for a reply, but hastily left the gloomy place, and Miranda fancied she was alone with the dead.

She lifted up her hands, and in a voice of thrilling emotion she said.—

"Oh! God, grant me tears of sorrow for my poor father. Let the gushing drops that coming from the eyes relieve the bursting heart, bedew my cheeks. It seems, oh! Heaven, that while I cannot weep, there must yet be in store for the unhappy Miranda some exquisite agony, some wild grief yet greater than that which now rends her heart for her father. Oh! Heaven, grant me tears—tears."

She sunk on her knees by the coffin, and a look came over her countenance expressive of the utmost despair. Her brain throbbed—the blood bounded through each artery of her frame like a bubbling torrent. She clasped her head with her hands, and cried,—

" Save me, Heaven—save me from madness."

Suddenly then she started. A human voice breathed her name. Was it a delusion conjured up by her racked imagination? No—it was real. Some one in a tone of agony as exquisite as her own, said, "Miranda."

" Who—who speaks?" she cried ; " who calls on the wretched Miranda ?"

" I—I—," cried a voice, and from a gloomy niche in the vault Bernard Varley crawled to her feet.

It was strange to see those two living persons in the presence of the dead, regarding each other with singular feelings. Bernard Varley looked up in the face of Miranda like some devil which had wandered from its allotted home, after warring with Heaven, and having met some brighter, purer spirit, was employing its intercession with the offended majesty of Heaven. While Miranda with lips slightly apart—her slender, delicate figure drawn back to evade his contaminating touch, and a look of abhorrence, mingling with the painful feelings that were depicted in her countenance, looked, indeed, the pure seraph of heaven, recoiling from the touch of the being cast out from the realms of joy for its deep sinfulness.

" Once more—once more, Miranda," he said, as he grovelled at her feet—" once more I pray to you—I who never prayed before for mercy. Oh ! you know me not.—Miranda—Miranda, take the Grange—take all back again ; but if you would save a mortal soul from the agony of despair—if you would light with joy the chambers of a brain which is nearly maddened, you will look with pity on me, Bernard Varley."

" Monster !" shuddered Miranda.

" I love you—I love you !" he cried, as he beat his breast in his bitterness of feeling. " I love you with such a love as man never yet felt for woman.—You lie enshrined in my heart deeper than ever devotee enshrined the saint he oked to for salvation. Bid me murder—bid me deny Heaven—anything, so that you give me hope that in the fulness of time the day may come when you will not scorn me, Miranda ; but with a gentle voice tell me that you pity me, that you will try to love—"

" God of Heaven !" cried Miranda, " has thy judgment fallen already upon this man, and made him what he is, filling his soul with this strange infatuation ?"

" It is—it is an infatuation," said Varley. " There never in the wildest, dreamiest pages of romance, was a love pourtrayed like mine. It is to me life, light, joy, breath, hope, the world that is, and that which is to come. Oh, Miranda, where can you hope to find a heart so bound to you as mine? I know that women are capricious, and like slaves—make one of me. Smile upon me one moment, and frown the next—the memory of the smile shall charm the perception of all harshness. Say that you will think kindly of me—do not loathe me—and then ask of me what you will it shall be granted. Am I not abject, Miranda?— Miranda, I love—adore—I worship——"

" Appeal to Heaven," said Miranda, who began to be alarmed at his wild frantic distress. " Appeal to Heaven, and not to one of Heaven's humblest creatures. What mercy can I show you, wretched man ?"

" I am—I am," he cried, " wretched—most wretched. The world will envy me, because they will fancy me rich, and that to be rich is to be happy; but do you, Miranda, take all, so that you smile upon the wretched Bernard Varley, who will then be a prince in happiness, a Crœsus in the wealth which knows no diminishing—that wealth which is coined in the heart and passess current in the teeming brain. Miranda—Miranda, say that you will be mine—feed me with hope—a word, a look will suffice to make me happy."

" Let me pass," said Miranda, " or I will call for help."

" Oh, leave me not to despair," he said. " Hear me, Miranda—I will save Rowland Percy—I, I will give him wealth which he can spend in some foreign land—I will—I will——"

"Peace—peace," cried Miranda. "Bernard Varley, I here swear by yon mute form, which lies so cold and still there, and the pure spirit of which may even now be listening to my words, never to

"No—no, kill me not with such an oath."

"Ne'er to relax in my endeavouring to convict you of his murder until justice has overtaken you. An invisible voice even now seems to assure me you did the deed!"

"Miranda," said Varley, in choking accents, "you—you are destroying two persons—one whom you love, and one whom you hate. Rowland Percy shall die, and I will die; but when at the judgment seat of the eternal I am challenged for aught done in my mortal life, I will shriek your name, Miranda, and I will urge that you are less merciful than the wildest savage, who refused one word to save my soul from deep damnation."

"I will not hear this profanation," cried Miranda. "Help—help—oh—help!"

Varley sprang to his feet—he darted towards Miranda, and with a strength that her feeble efforts could not resist, he clasped her in his arms—he pressed his burning lips to hers.

CHAPTER XXXII.

THE RESCUE FROM THE VAULT.—THE DIAMOND RING.

MIRANDA uttered shriek after shriek as she found herself clasped in the embrace of the loathed Bernard Varley, until the vault re-echoed again with her frantic screams. A wild demoniac spirit seemed to possess the ruffian, and he laughed aloud as he struggled with the beautiful and horror-stricken girl, whose strength was decreasing each moment, when Varley was suddenly siezed from behind by a powerful grasp, and hurled with such vehemence to the farther end of the vault, that he lay quite stunned with his fall.

"Save me, save me," cried Miranda, as she clung to the arm of her deliverer, without looking to see who it was that had rendered her so timely a service.

"You are a pretty scoundrel I think," exclaimed he who had so unceremoniously worsted Varley, who was no other than Ned Witlet. "So you are at your old tricks, are you, and didn't think I was so near at hand."

Varley sat on the damp rotten floor of the vault looking bewildered, first at Miranda and then at Witlet, who he really began to believe must be his evil genius. What with the wildest excitement he had worked himself up to in his interview with Miranda, and the heavy concussion with which he had encountered the wall of the vault, he was in a state of mental confusion which prevented him from speaking for some moments, and it was not until Witlet again spoke that he recovered sufficiently to understand fully where he was or what had happened to him.

"Mark me, Master Varley," said Witlet; "I will be always near you and if you attempt any more of your villanies, I say beware."

"Fearful man," cried Varley, struggling to his feet; "tell me now, though the information should kill me, tell me who and what you are?   Why haunt you me? Why dodge me from place to place?   In the name of Heaven, or by a more fearful adjuration, I charge you, tell me who you are?"

"I've told you once," said Witlet, who was much amused at the accidental train of circumstances which had enabled him to exercise so strange and so unexpected a control over the mind of Bernard Varley. "I've told you once—don't seek to know more till the time comes."

Varley groaned and struck his breast as he exclaimed—

"Am I to be haunted—am I to be haunted?"

"Of course you are," said Witlet. "It serves you right and you know it. Allow me, miss, to see you safe to your friends. They are just above here I believe."

"To whom am I indebted for this rescue?" said Miranda.

"Never mind me or who I am," replied Witlet, "I am your friend, let that suffice.   In other respects you might not like me half so well."

The dim light of the vault was not sufficient to enable Miranda to get a clear view of the face of her deliverer, or it is probable she might have recollected the circumstance of her first encounter with him when proceeding from the Grange to York with Mr. Anderson; she, however, clung to his arm with confidence, and without another glance at Bernard Varley, ascended the staircase leading from the vault.

The discomfited villain was, however, by no means inclined to be left alone in that receptacle of the dead, and he no sooner observed Miranda and Witlet half way up the staircase, than with a cry of terror he rushed after them, for an impression had, on the moment, seized his mind that the strange man who had thwarted him, might have both the will and the power to close up the entrance of the vault, and leave him a living prisoner in the loathsome tomb.

So firmly had this sudden thought flashed across his mind, that in a moment it appeared to him as if he had actually been threatened with such a punishment, and as he rushed up the staircase after Miranda and Witlet, he cried—

"No—no—mercy—not that. Let me out. Air—air—fresh air. Oh, Heaven, leave me not with the dead. Mercy—have mercy upon me."

"You deserve to be left where you are," said Witlet, "except that it would be a pity to cheat the gallows, which surely will some day come into its reversionary interest in you. Pass on, cowardly hound. Pass on, your time has not come yet."

Miranda and Witlet stood on one side, and allowed the trembling Varley to pass them on the narrow staircase, which he did with a frantic trembling eagerness that showed to what a height his apprehension had reached of being detained. When he reached the mouth of the vault, and merged into daylight, he bounded across the church-yard with the speed of a hunted hare. His ghastly pale face, quivering limbs, and set teeth, gave him, to those who were standing near the entrance of the vault, more the appearance of some resuscitated corpse, embracing that opportunity to rush from the embraces of the grave, than a living man. They fell back and made way for him in silent horror, and when another glance at the narrow opening of the tomb showed them more forms advancing, one and all, of the idle villagers, whom curiosity had brought to the spot, fled in wild dismay. Then the guilty Varley fancied that they must be in pursuit of him, and he flew rather than ran, in the direction of the Grange, where he hoped to find shelter. His agony of mind became excessive; he bit his lips through in his intense agitation, and although one glance behind him would have assured him he was not pursued, even in appearance, beyond the precincts of the church-yard, he paused not until faint, weary, and exhausted, he rushed up the marble staircase, leading from the hall, nor paused in his frantic career, until he had locked and double locked himself in his own room, and snatched from a bureau some loaded fire-arms, with which he stood in an attitude of defence for a few moments, until exhausted nature would support him no longer, and he sunk trembling into a chair.

While Varley was thus in terror and mental agony, in some measure expiating his crimes, Miranda reached, along with Witlet, the mouth of the vault, where she looked in vain for Mr. Anderson, who had promised to be within call, but who was now nowhere to be seen.

Miranda then turned to her companion, and by the light of day she at once recognised him, which he perceived by her glance.

"You know me now, Miss Rankley," he said; "that is, you know as much of me as I wish you, and as I hope you ever will. You have been kind to me, and as you are about the only person that ever was so, I ought to make much of it. Now, if you will recollect that you have a friend in me always, I shall be very much obliged to you, for though some folks think me no better than I should be, I am not ungrateful."

"I have cause to be grateful to you," said Miranda, "for you rescued me from yon ruffian when all my other friends seemed to have deserted me."

"Mine was a return of a favour," said Witlet. "Your kindness to me when my nag threw me, was quite another thing; and now, Miss Rankley, I have a favour to ask of you."

"A favour?"

"Yes, will you, without asking any questions, about how I came by it, accept a present from me?"

Miranda paused a moment before she replied. Then she said,—

"It is I who ought to make some return to you for your services; but I have not now the means."

"Never mindd that. Will you accept my present?"

Miranda was perplexed extremely. She knew not what to say, but when she thought of how she had been rescued from Varley by him who was now addressing her, she no longer hesitated ; but replied,—

" If it be such a present as I shall, upon knowing what it is, feel inclined to keep. I answer you yes ; but I must reserve my right to return it to you should I think proper."

" As you please," said Witlet. " Take this ring."

As he spoke he took from his own finger the diamond ring which the avarice of Twitter had induced him to wrench from the dead hand of Sir George Rankley. The trinket was well known to Miranda, and as she took it from Witlet she exclaimed,—

"Good heavens ! my father's ring. How could this come into your possession?'

" Remember your promise," said Witlet. " No questions as to how I came by it. Will you keep it or return it, to me?"

" I will keep it," said Miranda, " as a memento of him who is gone. You know I shall prize this glittering bauble. It will remind me of happier days, and when I see it glistening in all its beauty and brightness, it will make me think, that although the hand of misfortune may press heavily upon me, still the bright jewel of the soul—integrity, may never lose its lustre."

" Humph," said Witlet. There are some people, Miss Rankley, who may have let that sort of lustre grow a little tarnished now and then, but who still possess a few good qualities that will peep out like bright spots among the rust; but that's neither here nor there, and if I mistake not, here come some friends of your's, so good by, and God bless you, for a kind-hearted girl and a credit to your sex."

" With this, the highwayman walked briskly away, and advancing from among the tombs, Miranda saw Mr. Anderson and the elder Mr. Percy.

"I have to apologise to you, Miranda, for leaving you," said Mr. Anderson, " but I was called away by Mr. Percy here, and trust you suffered no inconvenience."

" It is no matter," said Miranda, who thought a recital of the insult she had been subjected to by Bernard Varley, could not possibly do any good.

Mr. Percy advanced, and there was a tear in his eye as he took Miranda's hand, and said,—

" Miranda, I have been trying to prevail upon Mr. Anderson to concur with me in a proposition which I would fain you should consider kindly."

" What proposition?" said Miranda. " Name it, Mr. Percy, and if it be within my poor ability it shall be done."

" It is," continued Mr. Percy, " that you would look upon me in some measure as a substitute for him who is gone. That as, if Heaven had so willed it, you would have been the wife of my dear boy—you will look upon me now, in your orphan state, as a second father. Together we can consult and contrive much for lightening the weary hours of Rowland's most unjust persecution. We can speak comfort to each other's hearts, and should my dear boy be returned to his father's arms, which I trust, in the justice of heaven he will, we may once more, casting over the past the veil of resignation, be happy. Oh, Miranda ! consent to an old man's prayer. The sufferings of the last seven days have added many years to those I had already numbered. I am alone now in the wide world and with but one object next my heart for which I would fain still preserve the embers of an existence that else I would most gladly render up to him who gave it me. That object is the liberation of my poor boy, Rowland,"

The father paused. He could have said more, but tears choked his utterance, and after a vain attempt to suppress his deep emotion, he sobbed audibly.

Miranda was deeply affected, as she replied,—

" This is no time to fence the feelings of the heart round with cold formalities. I here declare it, and I would do so before the world—that let his fate be what it may, Rowland Percy is my affianced husband. "

"Bless you, for those words! Bless you," said Mr. Percy.

"As such," continued Miranda, falteringly, "you his father, I, in my orphan state, will cling to as a second parent, and oh! may it yet be in the designs of Providence, that he, our joint hope and care, may be restored to us,"

"Miranda—my dear child!" said Mr. Percy; "together we will talk of Rowland, and we shall never weary of the theme."

"Never," said Miranda, "I accept your offer, Mr. Percy, and such duty as a child should give a parent, will I give to you."

"I cannot," said Mr. Anderson, "object to such an arrangement as you are now making. My house and means, as Miranda knows, were freely offered to her, so long as she chose, as a cherished friend and honoured guest, to dwell beneath my roof. But, let it be as you propose, and, although Miranda refuses my hospitality, I trust she does not my friendship."

"Can you think me ungrateful to you, sir?" said Miranda. "You, who have sustained me, through the weary week which has now passed. I were indeed ungrateful could I ever forget how much I owe to your disinterested friendship."

"Then, let me add," said Mr. Anderson, "that I'm not without a hope in the midst of all the gloom which has surrounded us, of finding one ray of light, however small. It consists in my belief that I shall be able to rescue some of Mr. Percy's property from the general ruin. It may be a very small portion, but when weighed against nothing, it becomes important."

"Heaven grant you success," said Mr. Percy. "My poor Rowland will require means."

"Put your mind at rest upon that point," said Mr. Anderson. "I believe I may say that I and Miranda have quite arranged all that. Nothing shall be spared in the conducting of his defence, which I have undertaken to prepare and see properly brought forward."

Miranda could only look her gratitude to Mr. Anderson, and the little party of attached friends declining to accompany the funeral cortege back to the Grange walked on till they reached the stables, where was Mr. Anderson's chaise, after which they proceeded to York—Miranda being in a calmer and happier frame of mind than she had yet experienced since the full tide of troubles had set in upon the haven of her joy.

CHAPTER XXXIII.

VARLEY'S HATRED TO THE GRANGE.—THE DEPARTURE.—TWITTER OUTWITTED.

It was more than an hour before Bernard Varley recovered from the state of agitation into which he had been thrown by the proceedings in the vault, and even then when he became a little more composed, and could assure himself that his fears of being followed from the churchyard were groundless, he was lost in conjectures of the most painful nature as to who and what the mysterious man could be who seemed ever at hand to thwart him, Varley, in his designs, and to know things which he had believed locked up in the recesses of his own breast.

A more striking example of the terrors which beset a guilty conscience could scarcely be found than in the horror with which Varley had come to regard the highwayman, whose real knowledge of Varley and his proceedings was so very small, but whom Varley's fears converted into a being who had obtained a key to the most hidden secrets of his heart. Thus it is ever with the o'erburthened conscience of the guilty—facts and circumstances, which to the pure of purpose and innocent of heart, could produce no disquietude, are to them sources of dread and alarm, as the thief

"Sees in each bush an officer."

Then Varley had another source of deep disquietude, and that consisted in his superstitious fears, which had been all awakened by the strange and mysterious appearance of the spirit of the murdered keeper to him—a visitation which he could not otherwise account for than by supposing it to be purely supernatural. Thus he thought, and the drops of perspiration, engendered by fear, stood upon his brow, as he made the reflection—"Why may not one disembodied spirit as well as another revisit in the likeness of its mortal form the spots familiar to it? And if such be the latter case, how am I to know but the day may come when, in the solitude of some chamber, remote from human aid, where my cries would be unheard, I may meet the spirit of Sir George Rankley, which might drive me to madness with horror."

Varley trembled with apprehension as these horrible reflections passed through his brain, and he became each moment more and more strengthened in his determination to remove from the Grange, every room of which was now to him replete with disagreeable associations, and residence in which could not but be exceedingly tormenting and agonizing to his guilty soul.

"Yes," he muttered, "I will remove from here. This is no longer a fit abode for me. I will dwell ever near Miranda, with the hope but of sometimes seeing her, and treading in her footsteps as she walks abroad. I think even now I could confess all, and suffer all the penalties of such confession, would she but smile upon me for one fleeting moment. Heaven help me! what can be the meaning of this world of passion that possesses my soul for this young maiden? Long since, 'tis true, I loved her, but it was with a feeling that my better judgment could controul, and not with the wild fervour of my present feelings, that know no bounds, but seem ever on the point of driving me to some act of madness, ending in destruction."

Bernard Varley groaned aloud as he made these remarks, and at one time he would pace his room with unequal steps, then throwing himself into a chair, he would assume a serious attitude, in the vain hope that by bodily ease and luxury, he should be able to calm the excitement of his mind.

A low, timid knock at his door suddenly aroused him, and before he could shape a reply to the summons, Twitter slowly entered the apartment.

Hating—detesting—despising Twitter as Varley did, even his presence was a relief at that moment of mental prostration, and it was almost in a tone of kindness and welcome that he said,—

"Ah! Twitter, is that you? Come in. I have something to say to you, and was wishing for your presence."

"Is—the funeral over?" said Twitter, glancing furtively around him, as if he each moment expected to see some sight which would blast his faculties and unnerve him.

"The funeral is over," replied Varley, "but it is not of that I would speak to you. The time has come, as I always thought it would, when the Grange has become hateful to me."

"The Grange hateful?" said Twitter.

"Yes," added Varley, "and were you, which you may be, as full of—of—I will not call it apprehension, but of conviction, that this house was the abode of beings of another world, as I am, you would be equally anxious to quit it."

"You—you have no grounds," said Twitter, nervously, "for supposing that any being of another world is calculated to be a sight of terror to us."

"Hush—hush," said Varley. "Let it suffice that I have ample reason for quitting the Grange, and quit it I must and will."

Twitter's face assumed a sallow hue, as he struck his hand feebly upon the table, in order to affect an energy he did not feel, and said,—

"Then—then, how am I to be paid if you leave the Grange—where am I to find you? Recollect our bargain—I was to have an annuity."

"And so you shall," replied Varley. "I shall still require your assistance; for, know, Twitter, that what I have already succeeded in accomplishing, is but as nothing compared to that I have still to do."

" Indeed !"

" Yes ; think you it is as easy a task to bend the stubborn will of a girl, as it is to work upon the weak mind of a man, and so contrive that he shall go from mortal life as Sir George Rankley has done, so soon as all is accomplished that I wished, and that instead of a great assistance and a source of ample means, he became an encumbrance in the steep path of my ambition."

" You still, then," said Twitter, " intend to persevere in your hopeless pursuit of Miranda ?"

" I do," said Varley, with vehemence ; " but call it not hopeless. That it can never be, until she or I have sunk to the grave—I will hope on, in the face of scorn, contempt, derision, hate—nothing but death shall turn me from my purpose. I love her with one of those wild headlong passions rare in our northern clime, but which resemble a mountain torrent in fierce impetuosity and freedom—I love her with a love goaded to madness by opposition. Each glance of hatred —each word of scorn, that I receive from her, but adds fuel to the flame that already seems consuming my heart—I love her, I love her !"

" He's mad," thought Twitter, " he's mad. I never particularly loved anybody but myself."

" Listen to my plan of operations," continued Varley. " You may, or may not continue with me to assist as you please—my non-residence on the Grange estate can make no difference in its rental, nay, it may rather increase it, for this mansion may be let. I shall remove at once to York, and near to where Miranda lives, there will I take up my abode. Night and day I will watch her. She shall not stir abroad but I will be upon her path—she shall feel that I am as a shadow, ever closely following her for good or for evil, as she may herself make me. This lover of hers, if she will not save him by becoming mine, shall assuredly die on the scaffold the death of a murderer—she herself shall be plunged into a poverty, a destitution, she, the child of luxury, cannot even picture to herself."

" But," interrupted Twitter, cautiously, for he was half afraid of contradicting Varley, his manner was so violent. " Don't you think that it is possible there may be some who will step between you and your victim, and by assisting Miranda, place her far above the state to which you would reduce her ?"

" Yes," cried Varley, dashing his fist upon the table with a violence that made Twitter start and tremble. " Yes, there are such ; but who shall dare to stand between me and my plans—my hopes and expectations ? Let them beware who do ! I have commenced a career, which beginning in blood, may as well go on in the same ensanguined hue."

" You—you don't mean to say that you'd murder them ?" faltered Twitter.

" Let them beware ! Let them beware !" said Varley. " I am a desperate man ! I have ample resources, and I am devoured by a passion which knows no bounds—has no scruples ! I say, then, let those beware who cross me !"

Twitter groaned, for in perspective he could fancy he saw the absolute ruin which Varley must bring upon them both, by his indulgence in a passion which set reason at defiance, and which if he pursued in the strain he was laying down, must end in his destruction. " And then what is to become of me ?" thought Twitter, with a groan.

" Surely—surely," continued Varley in an under tone, as if rather reasoning with himself, than addressing Twitter, " hunger and wretchedness must have their effect even upon such a mind as Miranda's. When she feels the acute pangs of absolute want, she may be glad of relief even from my hands ; when benumbed by the winter's cold, she may forget some of the stern pride of her heart, and give a smile to me for bringing her to warmth and comfort. One by one I will remove every prop she has in this world. I will follow her like the embodied spirit of an evil destiny, until she becomes mine ! irrevocably mine !"

" You will bring trouble and destruction on us both," groaned Twitter. " I see nothing but ruin in what you propose to do. Why can't you enjoy yourself now that you have ample means of doing so ?"

" Peace—peace," said Varley. " You cannot turn me from my purpose. Peace, I say. Let it suffice for you that I will fulfil my agreement with you. Remain with me or not, you shall have the sum I promised to you."

" If, I remain with him," thought Twitter, " I shall be in a constant fright; but then I shall know when I am in danger, and when I am not, whereas if I live away from him, I shall never know a moment's peace from constant apprehension that he is committing some wild extravagance for love of Miranda, that may place both his and my own neck in the haltar.'

" Have you decided?" said Varley.

" I tell you what I'll do," replied Twitter, a sudden thought breaking in upon him, which he imagined might extricate him from his difficulties. " Give me ten years amount of the sum I am to receive yearly, and I will release you from all further charge"

" Six thousand pounds?"

" Yes—yes. Then you know, Varley, you will be rid of me altogether, and might pursue this girl whenever you chose you know."

" No," said Varley. " There are several reasons why I shall not do so; but one will suffice. I will not allow you to enjoy without risk, the benefit in full of that which you lent so tardy and inefficient a hand in performing. You shall not escape, Twitter, if I fall! You understand me? While I hold the Grange estates, and escape all suspicion of the crime for which Rowland Percy is now in prison, you shall with me enjoy the proceeds."

" Then I implore you," said Twitter, who saw by the manner of Varley that he was inexorable on the point. " I implore you to give up this mad pursuit of Miranda, which can only end in our mutual ruin."

" 'Tis in vain to talk to me," said Varley. " I have now but one object in life, and that is Miranda Rankley. Come death—come destruction, I will pursue her to the last."

" Lost, lost," said Twitter.

Varley rose and paced the room for some minutes, then turning to Twitter, he said,—

" Once more I ask you, do you go with me or not?"

" I—I will go with you, said Twitter, " with the hopes of in some measure protecting you from the consequences of your rashness."

" 'Tis well—'tis well," said Varley. " Now for York. Leave here some trustworthy person in charge of the mansion and its contents, I will sleep in York to-night."

" There—there is one thing," said Twitter, " which I am sure is so very reasonable, you will consent to it at once, Varley."

" What is it?"

" Only that in case of any accident to you, you see, you will make a will in my favour."

Twitter turned away his eyes from the face of Varley, as he said these words, but Varley with two strides came close to him, and laying his hand heavily upon his shoulder, he said,—

" Twitter, it may be, that in my wild passion for Miranda Rankley, I want the sober judgment which you know can usually guide my actions, but in all other respects I am the same Bernard Varley as ever I was. Your shallow scheme is as evident to me as if you had proclaimed it openly.'

" My—my scheme?" stammered Twitter.

" Yes—you would get me to make a will, leaving you my successor to the Grange estates."

" Only in case of—of accident, you know, Varley. Human life is—very uncertain."

" It is," said Varley. " Life is very uncertain. It is one of those things we cannot command; but, Twitter, death is very certain. '

" Death?"

"Yes! Now, tell me in sober sincerity, how long it would be after I had made the will you suggest, before the accident, which it is to provide you against, happened to me? Eh, Twitter?"

"You suspect me?" said Twitter.

"No," whispered Varley in his ear, with a hissing sound, like the noise of a snake. "I do not suspect you, Twitter, but I know you."

"You will not make the will?"

"I will not. But I will do this much for you, Twitter. Be assured, that as we are now living men, should ever anything arise to bring me to de-

struction,—should any of those trifling accidents, which will sometimes overturn the best-laid schemes, and like the abstraction of some supporting beam from a huge building, bring the whole fabric of our ambition upon our heads—you shall not escape. We have plotted—planned together—murdered together—taken the price of blood together—and be most amply assured, Twitter, that if there shall be a day of retribution, we will suffer together."

Twitter trembled as Varley spoke, and when he had ceased, with a faint voice, he replied—

"Enough Varley, enough. We will speak no more upon this subject. Let us, as you propose, go to York."

"You understand me thoroughly," said Varley.

"Too well—too well," shuddered Twitter.

"Then to York—to York."

CHAPTER XXXIV.

THE EVENING BEFORE ROWLAND'S TRIAL.—A PRISON SCENE.—MIRANDA'S ASSUMED SPIRITS.

It wanted but an hour to sunset, on the evening preceding the day on which the innocent Rowland Percy was to take his trial for the murder of Sir George Rankley, when two persons paused at the massive gates of the gloomy prison in which the unfortunate young man was confined. These persons were, Miranda and Mr. Percy.

Although but a short time had elapsed since last we presented the once rich and happy Squire of Larkswood to the reader, any one would have imagined from his bent form and trembling steps that years must have passed over his head, leaving behind them the traces of their onward march in the physical prostration of the prematurely aged man.

Oh, how lightly time touches the happy—how gentle it glides past them—how tenderly it marks the wrinkles of the once blooming face—by what inperceptible and gentle touches does it turn the raven locks to silver grey, until the mild autumn of life looks almost as healthful and as beautiful as the sweet spring tide of existence. But when misfortune—the heart's agony—the throbbing brain and the fevered pulse mark the progress of the fell destroyer—how quickly are the hale and strong prostrated to a state of trembling decrepitude—a single night will plant furrows in the cheek, and bend the stoutest form. So was it with Mr. Percy. The time which had elapsed since his duel with Sir George Rankley, and the whirl of terrible events which had surrounded it so closely, could only be measured by weeks. But, oh! how changed was he in that brief time—scarcely any one who feasted at his board, one little month before, would have imagined in the trembling, weak, infirm, old-looking man, who paused with the beautiful girl resting on his arm, the hearty, jovial Squire of Larkswood, on whose cheek glowed the healthy tint of temperance, and whose clear eye and open brow proclaimed a mind serene and quite at ease.

And Miranda, too—had no change marked the heart's painful throbbing on her gentle brow? Had suffering failed to rob her of the charms her beauty wore? Yes; it had failed to do that, but it had converted her from the youthful Hebe she once was, to a living representation of melancholy.

The roses no longer bloomed upon her cheek. Her charming eyes were no longer lit up with the radiance of the happy heart; but, pale and sad, although with a look of holy resignation on her face that made her resemble more some sorrowing angel than a thing of earth, she looked up at the heavy gates which shut her lover from her sight.

"Miranda, my child," said Mr. Percy, for he loved to talk to her like a father. "You wrote to my dear boy that we should be here this night?"

"Yes," said Miranda—"Hark! The Minster clock strikes eight. That was the hour I mentioned."

As she spoke, the solemn-toned bell of the magnificent cathedral boomed forth the hour of eight. The two sorrowing friends paused involuntarily until the last stroke had died away, then the old man said, with a faltering voice,—

"Let us now seek admittance, Miranda. He will expect us. Do you knock. Rowland will think we are late in coming."

Miranda timidly knocked at the small wicket, which was as a minor door let into the massive gate, and in a few moments a coarse red face peered at her through a grating, while a not very harmonious voice cried,—

"Well, what now?"

"We have an order to see Mr. Percy," said Miranda.

"Oh! have you!" said the turnkey, "Come in, then, I suppose you know," he added, as Miranda and Mr. Percy entered the stone vestibule, "that he is to be tried to-morrow?"

"Yes—yes!" said Mr. Percy. "Heaven protect him!"

"Oh! as to that, it 'll all depend on the evidence, old gentleman," said the man. "To-morrow's Friday, that's why he's to be tried to-morrow. It gives him longer time, you see, miss, in case it goes hard with him."

Miranda shuddered, but made no answer. She knew too well to what the man alluded and as she passed onwards through the narrow vaulted passages, she breathed silently a fervent prayer to Heaven to spare the innocent, even if the guilty should not be brought to judgment.

They were conducted into a small room, where the order of admission they had procured from a magistrate was duly inspected, and being pronounced genuine, they were given in charge to one of the under turnkeys, with direction to conduct them to the prisoner.

In a few minutes Rowland was in his father's arms. Then he clasped Miranda to his breast, as he whispered to her with a forced smile, that sat but badly upon his wan, pale face,—

"Courage, my Miranda, courage; all will be well; we shall be happy yet."

Miranda could not speak, but she looked earnestly in his face to see if indeed he felt the hope his tongue gave utterance to; then turning away her eyes, she shook her head, saying,—

"Heaven help you, Rowland,—it alone can save you."

"And it will, Miranda," he said; "never doubt it. I am innocent—there is my strength. Indulge in no gloomy anticipations, dear Miranda. If I could see you smile and look cheerful and full of hope, I could almost be happy here."

"You smile, Rowland," said Miranda, "but——"

A rising sob choked her utterance, and Rowland said in a voice that slightly shook,—

"You would say my smile is not one of joy, my Miranda; but it is one of hope, over doubt. Ought I despair when I have such a heart as yours to feel for me. Here have I the two beings in the whole world who possess my warmest love—yourself and my father, to comfort me. There is such a heavenly majesty—such a glorious light from above around the truth, that it must triumph. I have great faith that to-morrow will be to us a day of great rejoicing—and then, Miranda, we shall be the happier for the trials we have gone through. The sunny joy of our remaining life will look the brighter that it has been preceded by such storms. Cheer up, dear Miranda, and let me, to-morrow, when I hold up my hand, and, in the face of Heaven, declare my innocence—not feel weighed down by fancying you in grief. Oh, if I could see you now hopeful and serene, it would give me new life."

"Forgive me, Rowland," said Miranda, "I should come here to cheer you, not depress you. I will hope for the best. You ar innocent, Rowland, and surely you will be protected by Heaven."

"Doubt it not, Miranda," he replied. "Moreover the judges of the land are keen of discernment and knowledge of human nature. They look on things dispassionately, and the well concerted tale of the villains, Varley and Twitter, may lack some connecting link, which to the practised judgments of such, may invalidate the whole. It is the frequent fate of deep laid plots to fail through some mere accidental omission, that the judgment of a child would have supplied, but which, through the interposition of Providence, escapes the acute perception of the most artful and designing villains that ever conspired against the life of the innocent."

"I will hope all that, Rowland," said Miranda. "Do not to-morrow think of me as tearful and despairing, but as one calmly waiting for the consummation of a dear hope, that even now glows in my breast. Should you meet me to-morrow, Rowland, you shall see me smile—you shall, Rowland—I—I promise."

Mr. Percy had sat down on a small bench near the iron-barred window of the room, and leaning his head upon his hands, he seemed to have given himself up to the bitterest reflection.

"It is I—it is I," he said, "who am most guilty. I have caused all this misery. Can you, Miranda—can you, my own Rowland, ever forgive your erring father?"

"Talk not thus, father," said Rowland, "unless you would quite unnerve me for the morrow. You, as well as Miranda and myself, are the victims of the machinations of the villain Varley. I have no moral doubt whatever that he committed the crime of which I stand accused; and be assured the day will come, however distant, when the truth will be apparent, for never yet was 'man's blood by man shed' but in Heaven's good time the awful deed came to light."

"I believe it," said Mr. Perey, "and yet am I most guilty, for by my weakness I gave our enemies strengeh."

"Say no more, father, on that head. Let us now look to the future, and pray it may be happier than has been the past. Mr. Anderson told me he would call you both as witnesses upon the trial."

"And we will appear," said Miranda. "Surely those upon whose judgments you depend, Rowland, will listen to me. Who can doubt that I loved my father? Who can say I could commit, in the sight of Heaven, so hideous a sin as to perjure myself to screen his murderer? The truth must be apparent."

"It will, Miranda—it will," said Rowland, who was pleased to see her in so hopeful a state of mind. "To-morrow will be a day of rejoicing to us."

"Oh, grant it may," said Miranda. "I will tell them how I have been persecuted by this Bernard Varley—how with his fulsome addresses he has knelt to me, ever saying that he would save your life if I would be his."

"And tell them likewise, Miranda," said Rowland, "how you spurned the villain—how you scorned his cringing offers. Rather would I die ten thousand deaths than purchase a degraded life, for such it would be at such a sacrifice."

"Here's Mr. Anderson," said the turnkey, as he opened the door, and the humane lawyer entered.

"Welcome, my dear sir," said Rowland. "You have come in time to confirm the hopes I am giving to Miranda, that all will be well to-morrow."

As he spoke Rowland looked significantly at the attorney, who understood him and said,—

"Yes; the innocent should be ever full of hope. All will be well, no doubt."

"You really do think so, Mr. Anderson?" said Miranda, fixing her eyes with such a painful interest upon his face that he could scarcely say,—

"Yes—yes—certainly. Rowland and I must certainly have another consultation to-night about some serious matters, and by this time to-morrow evening I hope to see him a free man."

Miranda breathed more freely, for she had a great reliance upon the judgment of Mr. Anderson, and to hear him speak such words of confidence, gave her more comfort than she had felt from anything Rowland could say.

Mr. Percy rose to go, and again he embraced his son; his feelings would not allow him to speak, and wringing his hands in silence, he tottered to the door.

Miranda tried to smile, as Rowland took both her hands in his, and said,—

"Farewell, dear Miranda, till to-morrow."

"Farewell!" was all she could say, and then placing her arm within Mr. Percy's she went some steps from the door. She could not refrain then from turning again, and her eye fell upon Rowland's face—it was sad looking and depressed.

"Rowland, dear Rowland," she cried, as she sprang to him, "you do not feel the hope you would fain light up in my heart."

"Yes, Miranda—yes—I do—I never can despair while I have your love to light up with joy the gloomiest chambers of my brain. Believe me, I am hopeful—most hopeful. Once more farewell, dear Miranda, farewell."

Miranda took a long earnest look in his face, and then turned away, saying—

"To-morrow—to-morrow. We shall meet again to-morrow."

A shudder passed across her frame as the door closed between her and her lover, and she thought to herself as she paced the gloomy passages to the outer gate.

" Heaven help me if I have more to suffer—preserve my reason—I—I think I shall go mad if Rowland be not saved."

CHAPTER XXXV.

NED WITLET'S WARNING.—VARLEY'S WILD PASSION FOR MIRANDA.—THE FEARS OF TWITTER.

WHEN Miranda and his father had left him, Rowland Percy turned to Mr. Anderson, and with a voice of deep emotion, he said,—

" Mr. Anderson, let the issue of to-morrow be what it may, you shall ever carry with you the prayers and blessings of those you have been so kind to. I need not ask you when I am gone,—if it should be my unhappy fate to fall beneath this persecution,—to comfort my poor father, and she, who, in my happiest dreams of life, I have pictured to my fancy as the dear companion with whom I should pass through existence serene and happy."

" Be assured," said Mr. Anderson, " that my own sympathies are too much enlisted for Miranda, ever to permit me to lose sight of her; but I pray you not to contemplate so gloomy a prospect. Sufficient for the day is the evil thereof. We might, by conversing on such themes now, be exhausting your energies and weakening your resolution for no purpose. Think of the bright side of your destiny, and let to-morrow speak for itself."

" I am content it should be so," said Rowland ; " but there is one favour I would ask of you."

" Name it, and it shall be done."

" I have a young friend, by name Charles Trevor, to whom you have already forwarded one note ; what I now beg of you is to forward to him this other one the moment the verdict to-morrow is pronounced, should it be an unfavourable one. If favourable, let me have the note back again."

" It shall be done," said Mr. Anderson, as he placed the note carefully in his pocket.

" Then I am easy," said Rowland.

" There was something so peculiar in the manner in which this was said, that Mr. Anderson was half tempted to ask an explanation of it ; but he forbore, as he thought, that, perhaps, he had better not know, peculiarly situated as he was, than be made a confidant of in a matter that he might be forced to condemn.

In about an hour, Mr. Anderson left the prison, promising to see Rowland very early on the following morning. The morning being miserably cold, he walked rapidly towards his own home ; but he had not proceeded the length of three streets, when he became conscious of some one following him with rapid steps ; and, upon turning to see who it could be, he was accosted by a tall man, with a hat very much slouched over his eyes, and a thick handkerchief concealing nearly all the lower part of his face.

" Your name is Anderson ?"

" It is," said the attorney.

" You are the solicitor for Mr. Percy, who is to be tried to-morrow for the murder of Sir George Rankey ?"

" I am—what then ?"

" Why, then, if you won't be inquisitive to know who I am, I can suggest to you a question or two, to ask Bernard Varley and his associate, Twitter, when they appear as witnesses against the prisoner."

" Indeed," said Mr. Anderson, "I am not much in the habit of trusting to friends without names."

" As you please," said the stranger ; "you may, or may not, as it pleases you, accept of my proferred services. I do not pretend to say that what I have to suggest to you is of great importance, but it may have the effect of throwing Varley off his guard, which is no smaller matter with such a man as he."

Mr. Anderson had the interest of Rowland and Miranda so much at heart, that he was loth to throw away the chance of obtaining any hint that might be serviceable in the approaching trial let it come in whatever suipicious way it might, and he said—

" Whoever you are, you must be fully aware that any good you can do to the innocent Rowland Percy must be much more effectual if done openly, and without concealment. I beg of you to make yourself known to me, and pledge my word not to reveal to any one who you are, if you do not wish it."

" I do not wish it, " said the stranger ; " so there can be no good in telling you."

" Then I must listen to you," said Mr. Anderson, "and use my own judgment with regard to what you may suggest."

" What I have to suggest, as I said before, aint much, but it may flurry Varley, and you may make good use of that flurry. Ask him upon his oath to detail what passed between him and the horseman he met at night in the bridle path from York to the Grange."

" What passed ?" said Mr. Anderson.

" Nothing of any real importance ; but the sudden question will confuse him, and the remainder of his examination may be more satisfactory to you as interested for the prisoner."

" This is very strange," said Mr. Anderson, "won't you tell me what passed?"

" It would do you no service to know ; but I have no more doubt that Bernard Varley, by some underhand means, procured that will to be made, upon which he claims the Grange estates, than that I am, at this present moment, talking to you."

" Have you any evidence?" said Mr. Anderson, eagerly.

" Not a tittle," replied the stranger, in whom our readers will readily recognise Ned Witlet, "but Varley thinks I have, which is sufficient to torment him. I will, however, promise you, that should I come by any positive information, you shall know it ; and I am rather in the way of getting it than not."

" The question you propose, I will undertake, at all events, shall be put to Varley," said Mr. Anderson ; " but I should certainly prefer your telling me, in strict confidence, who you are."

" No," said Ned ; " it might be as awkward for you as for me. I have, by telling you what I have, done you and your client all the good I can ; so now good night, and good luck for young Rowland Percy to-morrow."

So saying, he turned from Mr. Anderson, and walking very quickly away, and was soon lost to sight. For some moments the attorney stood in deep thought. "Is this the commencement of some deep piece of villany on the part of Varley ?" he thought, " or has this man some knowledge which the mere hint of, will have an effect upon the nerves of Varley ? Surely it is worth the trying. The question is a very simple one, and can do the defence no possible harm. I will have it put at all risks."

While this scene was passing between Mr. Anderson and Ned Witlet, two other personages, whose proceedings and actions are important to the course of our narrative, were slowly and cautiously following from the prison gate the slow footsteps of Rowland Percy and Miranda. Those persons were Bernard Varley and Twitter. Varley was a pace or two in advance of his companion, and never for one moment took his eyes off the beautiful form of Miranda, who looked more strikingly lovely by the side of the form of Mr. Percy.

" You don't mean to speak to them," faltered Twitter, as he touched Varley on the arm ; " surely you don't mean to speak to them ?"

"Hush, hush," said Varley, in a hollow voice; "I must know what spot she blesses with her presence—I must follow her—oh, is she not beautiful, and she scorns me—hates me, while my love for her increases like a raging conflagration until all objects, near or remote, are tinctured by its livid glare. I must follow her—I must follow her, though she should lead me to death."

Twitter lifted up his eyes and hands, as with a groan he muttered,—

"Who would have guessed this? He is infatuated—each hour he becomes worse and worse—he has gone mad for love of this girl, and we shall both be ruined. Varley, Varley, think of your situation; reflect upon your own danger, if you will not upon mine. Varley, Varley, oh, think of what you are about."

"Hush, hush," said Varley, "trouble me not. She is beautiful as an angel—I cannot choose but love her. The passion has grown upon me hourly, until now it has absorbed all other feelings. Miranda, Miranda, Miranda! oh, if you would smile upon me, I would give all back again to you, and you would surely be happy with one who would make you the idol of his fondest idolatry."

"Mad, mad—quite mad," groaned Twitter.

"There, there," said Varley suddenly, as Miranda and Mr. Percy paused at the door of a small house, where they had taken temporary lodging until the trial of Rowland should be over; "you see, Twitter, she pauses—saw you ever such wondrous grace? Is there a sunshine around her—the halo of her beauty?"

"I wish she was dead," said Twitter.

"Dead!" echoed Varley. "No, such beauty surely is immortal—she cannot die. There, she blesses that house with her presence—now shall I know where to wander, and please myself with the idea that I am near her—that I am breathing the same air with her, and that, although she scorns me, I am watching over her. Now, now she is gone; Twitter, we will see if we cannot live opposite."

"Good God, no," said Twitter; "you will not surely be so mad."

"I must, I must," said Varley; "an invisible hand seems to drag me onwards in my chase of her. My destiny commands me, Twitter, and resistance is useless. Henceforward, I live but for her—I will haunt her footsteps—I will hang upon her path, and for evil, or for good, as she may frown or smile upon me, shall she ever find me hovering over her, constant as her shadow."

"We shall be lost, ruined, undone," moaned Twitter; "oh, that I should be so besotted as to league myself with a madman!"

"Come, come," said Varley, as he crossed to the opposite side of the way from that where he had seen Miranda enter. "We will inquire if we can have accommodation here."

"But we have one lodging already," urged Twitter; "what on earth can yo want with another?"

Varley turned to him, and with flashing eyes, and an expression of countenance that made Twitter start back several paces in alarm, he said,—

"Twitter, once for all, hear me, and mark well my words. What I determine upon, I will do, though all hell, with its hideous rabble rout, were to bar my progress. Shall I be turned aside, then, by such a worm as thou art? Shall I forsake the fixed purpose of my soul, because you tremble and are afraid? No—'twere easier to stride onwards over your corpse. You understand me, Twitter? Do not tempt me."

Twitter trembled, and turned of an ashy hue, as he said, in a whining, faltering tone,—

"It was for your own good I presumed to advise you, Varley, you know."

"Then presume no more," said Varley; "you are in my power. Remember that, and do not tempt your fate."

Twitter wrung his hands as he silently followed Varley, with but too strong a conviction that he was indeed in his power. "Oh, if I had but insisted upon my name being in the will," he thought, "all would have been well, and I could have made my escape to the continent with a large sum. Then Berrard Varley might have brought his neck to the halter as soon as he liked, for mine would have been safe; but now ——"

A disagreeable, sympathetic, choking sensation came over Twitter, and he gasped again with terror as he muttered,—

"We—we shall all be hanged some day; I feel sure we shall."

Varley strode up to the door of the house, which was immediately opposite to the one in which Miranda and Mr. Percy resided, and without hesitation knocked at the door, which was opened by a homely-looking woman.

"I want to hire some rooms in your house," said Varley.

"Rooms, sir! Lor, we never lets none."

"But you can, and will, if you get a high price."

"Please to walk in, sir," said the woman, "and I'll ask my husband. To be sure we doesn't let lodgings; but then, as you please to say, as price aint an object, sir, why it may be as we may——"

"Exactly," said Varley. "Name your own price for one of your front rooms."

The woman looked surprised at Twitter, as he uttered a groan, upon following Varley into the house.

"Please, sir, are you ill?" she said.

"No, no—quite hearty," replied Twitter, "only, nothing—nothing!"

"My friend," said Varley, "has just run the risk of his life, and is a little nervous—that's all."

"Yes—ye—yes," stammered Twitter.

"Oh, dear me!" said the woman, "I don't wonder at it, really. I should be all of a shake myself, I declare; won't you take a seat, sir?"

"I thank you," said Twitter, in a despairing tone.

The woman then bustled from the room to report to her husband that any price would be given for one of their front rooms, which so worked upon the love of money inherent in human nature, that he at once consented to receive so rare and desirable a lodger.

While she was gone, Varley turned to Twitter, and said,—

"These people will accept my offer, and I shall remain here to-night, while you can sleep at our other lodgings. We shall meet to-morrow, and remember well what has to be done before another sunset."

"You—you will not be persuaded?" said Twitter.

"Beware!" said Varley, and again his eyes assumed the strange demoniacal glare which so much terrified his weak companion in guilt.

The woman soon returned with the intelligence that a room on the first floor was quite at the "gentleman's service." She only asked about three times its value, and when Varley said, "Very well," an exquisite pang of self-reproach shot across her breast. At her own extortion? No; but because she had not put on a few shillings more.

"Good night!" said Twitter, with something between a sigh and a groan. "Shall I call for you in the morning?"

"Yes—do," said Varley.

In a few moments Twitter was gone, and Bernard Varley was in the room that commanded a view of the opposite house, upon which he fixed his eyes, and never removed them for hours; while his brain became nearly maddened from intense thought, and the agony of his hopeless passion—a passion which Heaven had surely tortured him with as a punishment for his crimes.

CHAPTER XXXVI.

THE TRIAL.—POPULAR EXCITEMENT.—MIRANDA'S SPIRIT AND ENERGY.— TWITTER'S DESPAIR.

THE morning's dawn still found Varley at the window of the room he had hired. The hope of catching a glimpse, however transient, of Miranda had fixed him to the spot, and in bitterness and anguish, such as the guilty alone can know,—for even in the greatest misfortunes of the innocent there is a consoling power in the pure heart—he had scarcely moved from the position he had first occupied.

Sleep he felt that he could not, or even if by chance slumber had closed his eye-lids, how was he to ensure himself upon that eve of Rowland Percy's trial, against some awful visitation to his disturbed fancy, that might drive his soul to madness, or, at all events, unnerve him for that which he was to go through on the morrow?

Gently and softly, like a smile upon the cheek of a babe, did the morning's light steal over the face of nature. The first streak of glowing, beautiful sunlight fell upon the ancient minster, gild-ing with rare beauty the fretted architec-ture, and making the worn edges of the old stones look like rich chasing worked by a skilful hand.

The busy hum of life began to arise throughout the city. The artizan sought the place of labour for the day—the idler was unwontedly early, for the coming trial possessed an absorbing in-terest to all classes of society, and was amply sufficient to cause sloth to rise from its slumber, and walk abroad in the first resplendent glory and beauty of the morning.

Soon as the sun climbed the eastern sky, floods of light streamed upon the house-tops. Each instant the sounds of animation became more and more distinct, until the unceasing war of sounds which the dwellers in cities, from long habit, do not notice, but which, to a chance visiter, from the silence of the woods, or the valleys, is so apparent, filled the teeming air.

But what to Bernard Varley were the hopes, the fears, the joys, sorrows, the

No. 17.

wishes, or the anticipations of the thousands of warm, bearing hearts by which he was surrounded ? What a lone man was he in this world, teeming with life and animation ! What communion had he with his fellow-men ! He felt like a wanderer on earth's surface, who had been cast out from the ranks of his species—one alike denounced by man, and accursed by Heaven.

But one all-engrossing subject filled his mind—but one anticipation—but one hope, if it could be called one, filled his heart—the love of Miranda, the passion that made now the whole sum of his existence. Oh, how strangely had the heart of that man of crime become filled with a wild and unholy love for the daughter of his victim !—a love which seemed implanted in his heart by Heaven as a punishment, because it was so utterly hopeless a passion.

The sufferings of Rowland Percy in his prison—the anxiety he endured—the bitterness of his heart at the false accusation under which he was groaning, were as nothing compared to what was endured by his persecutor, Bernard Varley, who, had Rowland been upon the scaffold, would have changed places with him, provided by so doing he could tell himself that he possessed as much of the heart of Miranda as did the lonely prisoner in his cell.

Miranda had not slept that night, for her thoughts were too active for repose. She passed many of the weary hours before the morning's light beamed in at her casement window, in prayers to Heaven for the innocent, and if ever prayers from a pure and unsoiled heart ascended gratefully to Heaven's throne, surely those of the beautiful and good Miranda found a welcome where such spirits as her own dwell in bliss unspeakable.

But Providence works in its own way, and the glorious issues of mortal life are worked out in mystery. Twitter suffered as much during that night, if not indeed more, than his associate in crime, Bernard Varley ; for he had a superadded terror of the result of Varley's infatuation for Miranda, which the other was free from. When he reached the lodgings they jointly occupied, after leaving his companion in the house opposite to where Miranda dwelt, Twitter sat down with a deep groan, and a feeling of such despair and terror came over him, that he could scarcely be said to possess the common use of his mental faculties for a time.

"What will become of me? what will become of me?" he moaned. "I am lost—I am lost. Bernard Varley is going mad, and soon he will commit himself in some manner that will bring destruction upon us both. What shall I do—oh, what shall I do?"

With clasped hands, and a face so ghastly pale, and so distorted by fear, that it would have alarmed any one to look upon it, he now sat for more than an hour like a statue of grim despair. Then, in a low moaning voice, he spoke again, saying,—

"He, too, Bernard Varley, of all men, to take so strange and wonderful a fancy —he who ever affected to despise all human weaknesses, and to hold himself aloof from anything but the love of gold and power—he to fall a victim to a hopeless passion for a girl, and to drag me, as he will, into the abyss of destruction he is rapidly himself approaching. I cannot fly from him—I am quite dependent upon him for means. Beyond an inconsiderable sum I have realised by the robberies I have from time to time committed at the Grange, I am destitute ;—oh, fool—fool— I have committed myself in this business for nothing, and every day shall run the most frightful risk of detection. Then, to-morrow—aye, to-morrow—what a day will that be to me. How I shall be tortured—cross-examined—my every look watched—the tone in which I speak commented upon—oh, how I dread to-morrow !"

He then rose, and shuffled, rather than walked, up and down the room, occasionally wringing his hands and groaning as his perilous and miserable situation presented itself to him in different shapes.

"I dare not denounce him," said Twitter ; "I could turn evidence against him and tell all. I could do so, and have the barren satisfaction of saving my life, while, with the execration of all, I retired to misery and want. If I had much money, I would do it, but now I dare not. I dare not—I must run no risk ; but should suspicion light upon me, and gather sufficient strength to be dangerous, I will tell all, and Bernard Varley shall ascend the scaffold alone—yes, I will denounce him. They may point at me the finger of scorn—they may hoot me, but I will have my revenge against Bernard Varley—yes, he shall be hung while I escape ; but what damning miseries shall I not, in the meantime, endure? Then there is to-morrow—to-morrow—to-morrow."

He again sunk into a chair, and was seized with such an attack of nervous trepidation that he thought he was upon the point of death, and cried aloud for help to the great alarm of the people of the house, who rushed into his room to know what was the matter with him.

The report of Rowland's trial coming on that day at the York assizes, had brought many persons from all parts of the country to witness the proceedings, which had acquired great interest from the situation in life of all the parties concerned, as well as the very singular circumstances connected with the whole transaction ; many strange statements and reports concerning which had been, from time to time, published in the metropolitan and county newspapers.

Altogether, so much popular excitement had seldom, if ever, been witnessed regarding a criminal proceeding ; and never, perhaps, was popular opinion so much divided upon any subject.

Numbers of persons believed Percy to be innocent, for they could not conceive the possibility of his guilt under the circumstances of his attachment to Miranda, and her subsequent conduct towards him ; while there were others who found in those very circumstances a deep aggravation of his presumed guilt, and openly expressed their abhorrence of the unnatural daughter who could cling with such constancy of affection to her father's murderer.

The inns of York were crammed with visitors, and scarcely a bed could be procured at any of those establishments. At an early hour the streets were thronged with pedestrians, and the excitement among all classes of the towns-people seemed, each moment, to be greatly increased by the influx of strangers, who, from mere report, appeared to have got up so lively an interest in a matter concerning which they could hardly be expected to feel so much as those who were acquainted with the parties, and in possession of many minute particulars which strangers could not have an opportunity of acquiring a knowledge of merely from printed statements.

Before ten o'clock every avenue to the court was crowded to excess, and there was as much clamour and anxiety for admittance within its precincts as exists in a metropolitan theatre on the evening of some unprecedented attraction. Each passing moment, too, added to the arrivals, and when at about twenty minutes before ten the judge who was to preside in the criminal court, arrived near the scene, it was with the greatest difficulty, and only by the exertions of a powerful body of constables, that his carriage could get at all near to the entrance of the building.

The excitement of the multitude then became intense, and those in the rear made a rush forward with the hope of inducing so much temporary confusion as to give them a chance of getting more forward in the throng.

Cries, oaths, and shouts rent the air, and many persons were much hurt in endeavouring to escape from the dense pressure of the multitude. The counsel who were to take part in the trial, as well as many others who attended the court as spectators merely, became almost inextricably mingled with the crowd, and by ten minutes to ten o'clock a scene of confusion was proceeding, which presented but a slender chance of the business of the court commencing at the accustomed hour.

Some one now cried out—

"Open the door—we are being crushed to death !" and immediately a thousand voices echoed the cry of " open the doors—open the doors."

The judges became apprehensive of some serious disasters, and collecting all the available constabulary force, they directed the doors of the court-house to be opened, but no more persons to be admitted than it would conveniently hold.

When the order for opening the doors was complied with, the rush was so tremendous that in five minutes time the officers became completely mingled with the throng, being borne into the court, and totally unable to keep in a body so as to act at all effectually. The consequence of this was, that the court became crammed to suffocation, while a large concourse of persons were still struggling and striving for an entrance. Those who had been so fortunate as to get in, soon found that if they expected to remain in with the smallest notion of comfort they must defend the vantage ground they had obtained, and accordingly a fierce struggle ensued between those within the court and those without—one party determining that no man should pass in, and the other as resolved to make good an entrance if possible.

This was a state of things which, of course, could not be permitted to last, and the judges determined upon having some of the most foremost of those who were pressing at the doors for admittance, taken into custody, as an example to the others. The constables succeeded in struggling to the doors, and the crowd within upon being informed by the crier of the court, that a movement was about to be made, to prevent the annoyance they were then suffering from the pressure without, assisted as much as possible the efforts of the constables to collect in force at the door.

The result of this was, that one by one, the foremost of the rioters were seized upon, dragged into the court, and thence through a lane made by the spectators, through a door-way at the back, communicating with a place of confinement.

By the time some dozen or more had been secured this way, the crowd began to see the propriety of making a backward movement, and after much yelling and hooting, as great a rush was made from the doors, as had been made to them, leaving the officers masters of the field of battle.

Comparative quiet was now restored, and by half-past ten o'clock, the judge took his seat upon the bench, along with some of the authorities of the city.

Those of the counsel who had come in carriages, had been fortunate enough to gain admittance to the building, and among them were the counsel for and against Rowland Percy; but their more unfortunate brethren, who had come on foot, were still absent, whereupon an application was made to the judge to swear in a body of special constables to assist the jurors, witnesses, and counsel into court.

The application was complied with, but it took some time to carry it into effect; and it was eleven o'clock, before Miranda, and old Mr. Percy, to whom all eyes were directed, entered the court.

What were Miranda's emotions upon the occasion, could not be gathered from her face, for that was covered by a veil of white lace, which effectually hid her countenance from the prying eyes of the multitude, many of whom had travelled miles to catch a sight of her reported beauty.

There was a murmur of sympathy from many upon her appearance, and from some a subdued hiss, but the judge immediately said,—

"Officers, seize any one who gives expression to approbation or disapprobation in the court, and I will commit him."

This threat had the effect of silencing both parties, and Miranda was suffered to take a seat in silence. None saw the wan pale face—none saw the look of deep emotion upon her face; but there was one heart that bled for her, and could guess the feelings that agitated her gentle breast. That heart was Mr. Anderson's. With a deep sigh, he whispered something to the counsel he had engaged for Rowland, who shook his head, and looked distressed.

That something was, that Miranda would never be able to go through her evidence.

CHAPTER XXXVII.

THE PRISONER.—STRANGE INTERRUPTIONS.—THE TRIAL.

SCARCELY had Miranda and Mr. Percy taken their seats, and the excitement caused by their arrival somewhat subsided, when Bernard Varley, pale and haggard and wearied looking, was led into the court, closely followed by Twitter. The villain had remained at the window, where we last left him, until he saw Miranda come forth with Mr. Percy. He had then followed her, but in the throng outside the court, he had lost sight of her; and now his first glance around him was discover if she was there.

The white veil caught his eye, and he said to the officers in a suppressed tone,—

"I—will sit there—there by Miranda Rankley."

The officer conducted him to the same bench, but Mr. Percy saw him advancing, and said something to Miranda, who immediately rose, and throwing aside her veil, confronted the man of blood.

Varley recoiled before the face of Miranda, which was as pale as monumental marble. A great sensation was produced in the court, and all eagerly pressed forward, to get as close a look as possible at that beautiful face, which, even divested as it was of all colour, was most lovely.

What a contrast was presented by these two persons as they stood, for the space of nearly a minute opposite to each other in silence. Varley's lips were white and dry, but his face was flushed with an unnatural colour, and his eyes were blood-shot, while he drew his breath with a hissing sound, as if to respire was a great labour to him, and so it was at that moment.

Miranda fixed her eyes upon him, and he could not advance. There was something in the mournfully beautiful gaze that deprived him of all power, and without a word being spoken, he felt that he dared not pursue his intention of sitting near Miranda. He stepped back, slowly whispering,—

"Somewhere else—somewhere else."

Miranda again covered her face with her veil, and sat down by Mr. Percy. A deep sigh, that seemed to come from the very depths of her heart, was the only sound she uttered, and then all was still again.

Bernard Varley was in the meantime conducted to a seat on the other side of the court, where, closely followed by the trembling Twitter, he walked like one possessed, and sat down with a hollow groan.

This incident, trifling as it was, caused a deep sensation in the minds of the spectators. Varley's agitation—his look of horror as he shrunk from the gaze of Miranda—and the expression of awful villany that lurked in his knit brows—prepossessed all against him; while the noble purity, the heavenly innocence, depicted on the face of Miranda, looked perfectly incompatible with a bad cause.

The jury were rapidly sworn, and then a breathless silence ensued. The very breathing of the spectators seemed to be suppressed. The judge was conversing in a low whisper with the mayor of York; then he glanced to the dock, and slightly waved his head—all eyes were directed to the bar. There was a slight movement among the officials, and in another instant Rowland Percy stood forward.

He was pale, but perfectly calm. Not a nerve shrunk, his eye quailed not, and the lofty glance of calm integrity that he cast around the court, astonished all who marked it; and many whispered to themselves,—

"Can this man be a murderer?"

The effect his appearance had was evidently highly favourable. His youth—the candour that was in his face—the gentle expression that pervaded every feature, and the intellect that was marked by the commanding brow—all pointed him out as, of all men there assembled, the least likely to commit a crime of the character he stood charged with.

Rowland's sudden appearance in the crowded court, from the solitude of his confinement, prevented him for a moment or two from being able sufficiently to individualise the persons he saw around, to name any one in particular; but, after a second glance around him, he eye fell on his father, whose tearful gaze was settled on him.

The crowded auditory followed the direction of the prisoner's eyes with theirs, and when Mr. Percy saw that he was seen by his son, he clasped his hands, and, while the tears coursed each other down his cheeks, he said,—

"God bless you, my dear boy; God bless you!"

The "hush" of the crier was very faint, for he, as well as all present, was affected by the scene. The judge affected not to hear the father's blessing upon his son, and bent his head low over his note-book.

There was one who heard it, however, with an emotion that kindled every feeling of her mind. That one was Miranda; and by an impulse that she paused not to question or resist, she rose, and throwing back her veil, said,—

"The blessing let me echo. God bless you, my innocent, affianced husband!"

"Miranda!" cried Rowland, and he stretched out his arms, while his face kindled with pleasure.

The scene overpowered all the court, and, forgetting all prudence or caution, many of the spectators clapped their hands, crying,—

"He is innocent—he is innocent!"

In the midst of this, Bernard Varley rose, and cried,—

"Air—air—air!"

Some windows were broken then by those who were nearest to them, and a scene of confusion ensued for some moments which completely baffled the attempts f the judge to quell it.

A rush of cold air from the broken windows was felt most gratefully by all, for the crowded state of the court rendered the ordinary ventilation totally ineffectual. Then the judge's voice was heard, saying,—

"I must have the court cleared, if this sort of interruption continues. I am willing to believe that it has arisen from the suffering occasioned by the extreme heat of the atmosphere."

This was a kind construction for the judge to put upon the interruption which had occurred, and every one felt it to be such; so that, in a few moments, the same breathless silence subsisted which had reigned throughout the densely crowded court, previous to Rowland Percy being placed at the bar.

The clerk of the arraigns now read the indictment, which charged Rowland Percy with the wilful murder of George Rankley, commonly called Sir George Rankley, by means of some deadly drug or weapon, or by suffocation. The indictment went on to a great length, in the usual verbose manner of such instruments, until it was finished, when the prisoner was asked to plead guilty, or not guilty.

Upon this, Rowland lifted up his hand to Heaven, and in a voice that, although not loud, went with the force of conviction to almost every heart,—

"Not guilty, as I hope for Heaven's mercy!"

The names of the jury were then called over, after which there was a slight bustle, as every one in the crowded court assumed the position he thought would best enable him to catch the speech of the counsel for the prosecution.

Before, however, any further progress could be made in the case, a loud voice cried from a distant part of the court—

"Bernard Varley will be hanged at York!"

The voice was something between a scream and a shout, and electrified the nerves of all who heard it, particularly as it was succeeded by such a wild frantic scream of laughter, that every echo far and near was awakened.

"Good God!" cried the judge, in the excitement of the moment, "what is that?"

The officers made a rush in the direction from where the sounds proceeded, and dragged to the front of the bench the poor idiot Bold Hawk, who, then pointing the fore-fingers of each hand at Varley, shrieked,—

"Hanged at York—Bernard Varley will be hanged at York—ha! ha! ha! —ha! ha! ha!"

Varley immediately rose, and while his eyes flashed with rage, and his whole countenance was distorted with passion, he cried,—

"He is mad—remove him—he is mad, I say. Am I to be insulted thus? Remove him—imprison the madman!"

"See, see," cried Bold Hawk, "he trembles—he turns pale. He knows the rope that is to hang him is already twisted, and he can't shoot me, though he has tried hard to do so."

"Remove him," said the judge; "he is surely mad."

Mr. Anderson whispered something to the counsel for Rowland, who nodded, and then immediately said to the judge,—

"My lord, I am informed that this person is a poor lunatic who is perfectly harmless; the only words of truth he has uttered being his assertion concerning Bernard Varley's attempt to shoot——"

"I really, my lord, submit that this is most irregular and monstrous," interrupted the counsel for the prosecution, in a loud voice.

"It is quite irregular," cried the judge. "Let that poor maniac be removed."

Bold Hawk was immediately dragged from the court by two officers, but for some minutes his wild shrieking voice could still be heard shouting loudly,—

"Bernard Varley will be hanged at York—ha! ha! ha! Bernard Varley is proof against steel and bullet—water will not drown him, for he is a doomed man, and will be hanged at York."

This event proved a disturbance of a more lasting character than any that had preceded it, and it was many minutes before the excitement into which the vast audience assembled has been thrown, could be sufficiently allayed for the transaction of business.

When, however, comparative quiet was restored, the counsel for the prosecution rose; and while every eye was fixed upon him he commenced,—

"My lord, and gentlemen of the jury—" but before another word could pass his lips, the counsel for the prisoner rose and said,—

"My learned friend will pardon my interruption, but I have an application to make to the court on behalf of the defence, which I am quite sure my learned friend will pardon me for urging just now, before, with his usual perspicuity and eloquence, he proceeds to open the case."

The counsel for the prosecution looked very much vexed as he replied,—

"I apprehend my learned friend is extremely irregular in interrupting me in he p sent stage of the proceedings in this case."

"No," said the other, "certainly not. The case after the pleading of the prisoner, is fairly in court."

"I apprehend that is the fact," said the judge; "but there should be extreme delicacy."

"My lord, we have too important interests at stake to be delicate," said Rowland's counsel. "When the happiness, the life, of an innocent man are on the issue, God forbid that I should be deterred by false delicacy from doing my duty."

These words were pronounced with such a fearless tone of confidence and candour, that they had a visible effect upon the jury; and some of the counsel, who were sitting under the judge, smiled at each other in a very meaning manner. The counsel for the prosecution, however, was too vexed to admire the other's tact, and feeling a little partizanship, as all counsel do, more or less, in the cause they are retained in, he said to the judge rather warmly,—

"I beg to submit to your lordship that the time has not yet arrived for my learned friend to endeavour, with his usual tact, to interest the passions of the jury in favour of his client, if he cannot bias their judgments."

" The case," said the judge, calmly, " is certainly, after the prisoner has pleaded, before the court, and it is competent for the counsel on either side to make any application relevant to the subject in hand, or that may further the ends of justice in the opinion of the court."

The counsel for the prosecution sat down with a bounce, evidently very much put out, when he fully expected to be in the commencement of his speech against the unhappy Rowland.

" I have then to apply," said Rowland's counsel, " that two material witnesses for the prosecution, who, I am informed, will swear to similar facts, be separated."

" What witnesses ?" said the judge.

" Bernard Varley and Samuel Twitter, my lord."

" You wish these witnesses examined separately and out of hearing of each other ?"

" I do, my lord ; and, likewise, I wish that Samuel Twitter should leave the court, in order that he may not hear the details which my learned friend isi n- structed to make on behalf of the prosecution."

" I dare say," said the judge, " the witness mentioned can have no objection."

" He has—he has," cried Varley, who all along was much afraid that Twitter would bungle in the evidence he had to give.

" Silence—silence !" said the crier.

" Let Samuel Twitter withdraw," said the judge.

Varley bit his lips, and Twitter, pale as a ghost, and scarcely able to sup- port himself on his tottering limbs, rose from his seat, and moved towards the door.

When he was fairly gone, the counsel for the prosecution again rose and said,—

" Before I proceed to open the case, may I presume to ask my learned friend, through the court, if he contemplates any more of the little happy interruptions I presume he is instructed to make ?"

" None," said the other counsel.

" Then, my lord, if you please, I shall proceed."

CHAPTER XXXVIII.

THE PROGRESS OF THE TRIAL.—THE FIRST DAY.

THERE was a breathless silence for some moments in the crowded court, and then the counsel for the prosecution of the innocent Rowland commenced,—

" My lord and gentlemen of the jury,—The prisoner at the bar stands charged with one of the greatest, if not the worst crime which can appertain to humanity ; and if it should appear to you that the facts it will be my duty to lay before you are not sufficient to support that charge, no one in this court, whatever may be their affinity—whatever may be their feelings or their sympathies to the prisoner, will be more rejoiced than myself.

" The duty of a counsel for a prosecution is ever, my lord and gentlemen, a more painful duty than that of a counsel rising to defend his fellow-man from an as- persion upon his character, which, if found to be true, must hunt him as a pro- scribed being from the ranks of his fellow-men, or bring him to a shameful and gnominious end ; but which, if unsupported by the accuracy of evidence necessary to support a criminal charge, disappears like a noxious vapour before the pure light of his innocence, and leaves, or ought to leave, no stain behind.

" My lord and gentlemen,—It appears by my instructions, that about one year or more since, the families of Sir George Rankley, deceased, and whose death forms the substance of this judicial inquiry, and Mr. Percy became intimate. The estates of Sir George joined the apparently thriving leasehold lands of Mr. Percy, and a friendship sudden and great sprang up between the families.

"Sir George Rankley had an only daughter—Mr. Percy an only son. Under the circumstances of intimacy and daily communication in which these young persons were placed, it is not a matter of surprise that feelings of the tenderest nature should spring up between them, and that in a short period Mr. Rowland Percy, who now stands charged with the awful crime of murder at the bar of this court, became the avowed suitor of the heiress of the large estates of the Grange, which, doubtless, are familiar and well known to the jury.

"You will, then, hear in evidence that Sir George Rankley, believing in the apparent respectability and prosperity of his neighbour, Mr. Percy, did not interfere to place any check upon the affections of these young persons, and this intimacy continued for some time uninterruptedly, until the prisoner at the bar, as will appear, acquired one of those extraordinary controls over the imagination of the daughter of Sir George Rankley, which we can only wonder at, but not attempt to explain or define.

"While things were proceeding in this quiet strain, it became known to Sir George that his apparently prosperous neighbour was engaged in reckless speculations, which had, in their failure, brought down upon him utter ruin. Then as you will hear sworn to, by some of the witnesses in this prosecution, Sir George became exceedingly indignant that the shattered fortunes of the Percy family should be attempted to be patched by an union with his only child and heiress.

"An angry correspondence which ensued, will sufficiently prove that fact, and finally, the prisoner at the bar was formally forbidden to visit at the house of Sir George Rankley, and to all appearances the intimacy which would, had it resulted in a marriage, have proved probably so very advantageous to the Percy family, was at an end.

"The quarrel, however, between the parents continued, and resulted in a duel, with which we have nothing to do, except to prove, by medical evidence, that the injury received by Sir George Rankley there and then, was not the cause of his death. Had it been so, my lord and gentlemen of the jury, the elder Percy, and not the younger, would have this day stood at the bar of this court.

"A duel, however, was fought—of that there is most abundant proof, between Mr. Percy and Sir George Rankley, in which Sir George was wounded, but far from dangerously. A slight flesh wound, which, certainly, by inducing fever, might have proved fatal—but, my lord and gentlemen of the jury, it had not time to do so. Sir George Rankley was hurried to eternity by some other means, which it is our object to discover, and punish the perpetrator.

No. 18.

" For the purpose now of making more intelligible some portion of the evidence, which it will be my painful duty to lay before you, I must mention that among the servants residing at the Grange, there had existed for a long period of time antecedent to the purchase of the property by its late lamented proprietor, a superstition of a strange and remarkable character. Many years ago one of the game-keepers on the estate was found murdered on the lawn. By whose hand the deed was committed, no one knew, except the perpetrator himself, but since then a superstitious belief has existed that the disembodied spirit of that murdered man has haunted the Grange.

" My lord and gentlemen of the jury, I have no doubt you will find every servant examined here to-day impressed with a full belief in the reality of what they call, ' the spectre of the murdered keeper.'

" Having then premised thus much, I shall proceed to state as shortly as possible the facts as I am instructed to state them, which occurred on the eventful night immediatly succeding the duel between Sir George Rankley, and Mr. Percy.

" The wounded Sir, George my lord and gentlemen, was conducted to a chamber, opening from a long corridor, from whence many bed chambers were approached. The medical gentleman who attended him, remained until a late hour with his patient, but having satisfied himself that he was doing quite well, departed, leaving him in the care of an elderly female, whose evidence will be laid before the court.

" From that moment, my lord, a rapid succession of events took place, which terminated in the death of Sir George, and the apprehension of the prisoner at the bar, who it will be proved in evidence was a very long way from this country, until the actual day on which the duel was fought, when by design or accident, he unquestionably found his way to the scene of action, which was to him so very important—so very important indeed."

The counsel made a slight pause at this part of his speech, and it was evident to every one in court that he considered the arrival of Rowland at the Grange from a considerable distance off on that very day, as the first link in the chain of circumstantial evidence, which was to connect him with the fearful deed he stood charged with committing.

The attention of every one in the crowded court to what the counsel was saying, appeared intense, but was curious to note the effect which his narrative had upon those who were most interested in the result.

Rowland Percy listened with calm attention. His eyes were fixed upon the face of the counsel, to whom he seemed to be attending rather with curiosity, to know what could possibly be said against him, than the feverish excitement which might have been supposed to affect him.

The face of Bernard Varley presented a remarkable contrast to that of the prisoner. Any one might well have believed that life or death to him hung upon the result of the trial.

The counsel proceeded,—

" At the hour of midnight, my lord and gentlemen, Mr. Bernard Varley, an intimate and dear friend of the murdered baronet's, together with Samuel Twitter, the valet, purposd and arranged in their anxiety, that Sir George should be well attended to, and relieved the nurse for an hour or two, in order that she might take some repose previous to resuming her duties.

" You will hear detailed in evidence, gentlemen, that at that most solemn hour when men's imaginations are frequently more active than their reasoning powers, there appeared to Mr. Bernard Varley and Samuel Twitter on their route to the chamber of the wounded baronet, what at that moment they might be excused from really believing, was the much talked of spirit of the murdered keeper.

" A figure dressed in green darted past them, and they ascended to the chamber with a firm conviction that some being not of flesh and blood was in the house along with the living.

" They then took their station in the room, relieving the nurse according to arrangement. To this point, my lord and gentlemen, I have thought it necessary t go, in order that without waste of time what the various witnesses shall depose to should be clear and intelligible. What followed I shall now let you hear from the lips of those witnesses, and I can only say that it is my fervent hope that Heaven will enlighten us all sufficiently upon this painful inquiry to enable us to arrive at the truth."

The counsel for the prosecution now sat down, and a feeling of relief from intense excitement pervaded every breast; that mingled buzz of sounds arose which always follows any great effort of silence and attention on the part of the multitude, and by tacit consent every one seemed disposed to rest a few moments before proceeding with the investigation.

The first witness that was called was the medical man, who had attended Sir George immediately after his wound. He merely recapitulated the evidence he had given on the inquest, namely, that the death of Sir George Rankley certainly was not attributable to the wound he had received, but must have arisen from some other cause, being, in his opinion, from the appearance of the body suffocation.

"Was there any wound in addition to that inflicted by the pistol shot in the duel, perceptible on the deceased when you saw him after death?" asked the counsel.

"There was a scratch upon the face."

"You will swear the scratch was not there previous to your departure from the Grange, when you, as you believed, left your patient out of all danger?"

"I will swear it was not there."

The counsel for the prosecution sat down, and the able and intelligent lawyer, who had been retained by Mr. Anderson for the defence, immediately rose, and said,—

"Have you had any opportunities of judging of the feelings of Miranda Rankley towards her father?"

"I have. Her conduct has always been marked by the greatest affection. I never saw greater grief than she exhibited at her father's mischance in the duel."

"Did she make any remark concerning the supposed murder?"

"None further than declaring her belief in Mr. Rowland Percy's innocence."

"That will do, sir," said the counsel, sitting down at once.

The nurse was now called, and she merely deposed that Mr. Varley very kindly offered to sit up an hour or so with Sir George, in order that she might get a little rest, and that she had left the baronet asleep and moaning, as if in pain.

No questions whatever were asked of this witness by Rowland's counsel. There was a pause for a few moments now, and all eyes were bent upon the counsel for the prosecution, who, at length said,—

"Bernard Varley!"

"Bernard Varley!" echoed the crier of the court.

Varley rose as if under the influence of a shock of electricity, and in a deep hollow voice said,—

"I am here. Who calls on Bernard Varley?"

His ghastly pale face—his livid lips—the clammy perspiration that stood upon his brow, and the wild demoniac expression of his eyes, conspired to make him an object of fearful interest to every one in court. The judge took a long look at him, and then whispered something to the mayor, who replied, by a shrug of the shoulders, and many in the crowded court turned their eyes instinctively from Varley to Rowland; it seemed to them something strange and unnatural, that he, Varley, with his guilty looks and awful excitement, should be the accuser, and he, Rowland Percy, with his calm unmoved glance, and general appearance of dignified innocence and candour, should be the accused. The jury whispered together, and it was not until the counsel for the prosecution, who saw how the tide of feeling was going, said,—

"Mr. Varley, attend to me, if you please," that the eagerness to hear what Varley should say, overcame every other feeling in the breasts of the auditory.

While Varley was being sworn, he trembled so excessively, and looked so very ill, that the judge said to the counsel for the prosecution,—

"Cannot you take some other witness's evidence before Mr. Varley's? He seems very much indisposed."

"No—no!" cried Varley. "I am ready—I am quite ready and quite well, never was better."

"Proceed then," cried the judge.

Varley made great efforts by grasping the rail of the witness-box, to assume an air of composure. He forced himself to look round the court, and his effort to appear calm and at ease sat so uneasily upon him that it was evident to all it was an effort. As his eyes, however, wandered over the crowd of eager faces in the court, he carefully avoided meeting Rowland's eye. That he could not stand. Nor, at that moment of mental agony, would he have chosen to meet the gaze of Miranda, much as he would at any other time have given but to behold her face, and look into the depths of those beautiful eyes, which contained all of Heaven he had ever pictured to his mind.

CHAPTER XXXIX.

VARLEY'S EVIDENCE.—THE PROGRESS OF THE TRIAL.—THE CROSS EXAMINATION,

"State what you know of this transaction, which engages the attention of the court," said the counsel.

"I will," gasped Varley, "I will. When Sir George Rankley, who was my dearest and best friend, came home wounded from the unhappy duel between him and Mr. Percy, I naturally felt the extreme of anxiety concerning his welfare and recovery. I could not think of returning to rest on that night, and I accordingly sat up with Samuel Twitter, Sir George's valet. I had every reliance upon the nurse who was attending upon the wounded man, but I knew she was aged, and I believe it was I who proposed to Twitter that, as we were sitting up, at any rate, we might as well afford her an hour's rest, while we ourselves kept watch by the bedside of Sir George—the hour was twelve, and we had told the nurse that she would be relieved at that time. Therefore in accordance with our promise, when we heard the Grange clock strike the hour of midnight, we prepared to proceed to the chamber of Sir George. On our road thither, we were astonished by a figure gliding away from the neighbourhood of the chamber—we pursued it, and by the occasional glimpses we caught of it—we saw that the dress was green, and in all respects similar to what had been described to us as identifying the reputed apparition of the murdered keeper which was said to haunt the Grange.

"Fear took possession of our faculties for the moment. The hour, the exciting circumstances of the day, the danger, for aught we knew, which hovered over Sir George—all conspired to awaken in my mind those superstitious fears which all men feel more or less, and I am not ashamed to confess that I believed the appearance at the moment to be the supernatural being, which popular belief had pointed out, as gliding from chamber to chamber of the Grange.

As Bernard Varley spoke, he seemed to gather courage, and all the dark malignity of his nature revived—he glanced round him with something of his usual expression of ferocity—and began to dwell upon that portion of his evidence which he thought would tell against Rowland Percy, and to put in with emphasis various words which gave a marked signification to some of his statements.

He proceeded in his evidence with a fuller and more assured voice, as h said,—

"When we had overcome in some measure the shock our imagination had sustained by the supposed supernatural visitation we had been subjected to, we proceeded at once to our destination, and without saying anything to the nurse of what we have seen, for fear of alarming her, we allowed her to go to rest, determining to sit up with Sir George beyond the time we had promised, for the nurse looked wearied, and we had no desire for bed after what we had seen, or thought we had seen.

"In a few moments, then, the light which we had, began to show symptoms of expiring, and recollecting that there was a candle in the room below, which we had recently left, I asked Twitter to fetch it. It appeared, however, that he had been much affected by the supposed supernatural appearance, and he trembled so, being a nervous, timid man, when I asked him to go, that I went myself, leaving him in care of Sir George, who was asleep.

"I was away rather longer than I intended, for in endeavouring to find the candle I struck it off the table, and it took me some time to find it again; I could not, however, have been absent many minutes: when I returned, I was a little surprised to find the door of the chamber which I had left shut, wide open. With a presentiment that there was something wrong, I walked into the room—all was silent, and, to my surprise, I could not see Twitter anywhere.

"I lifted up my light as high as I could, and approached the bed; Sir George was as I thought, still asleep, but, upon a closer inspection, I found it was the sleep of death."

Varley now paused a moment, and not the smallest possible sound disturbed the solemn stillness of the court. The counsel for the prosecution made him a sign to go on, and he resumed,—

"I started back from the bed in horror, and then I saw Samuel Twitter lying in a state of insensibility on the floor. I tried to raise him, but in vain—he had fainted; and while I was so engaged, Miranda Rankley entered the room, inquiring with apparent interest and eagerness for her father. I tried to stop her, for I feared the shock she must receive upon finding her father was no more. She, however, persisted in coming in, until I should have to use actual force to prevent her. That I could not do; and accordingly allowing her to pass into the room, I rushed down stairs to give an alarm, when I again was crossed by the figure in the hunting dress; this time, however, I saw its face—I will swear it was the prisoner at the bar.

"The moment he saw that he was known, he made an attempt to murder me by striking me on the head, and so hard was the blow that I was rendered for a few moments quite insensible.

"I know not how long I was recovering, but when I did so, I went to the chamber of Sir George Rankley on the instant. As I entered it, I trod upon something, and upon picking it up—found it these tablets."

The set of ivory tablets was here produced, and the clerk of the court handed them to the judge, who at the request of the jury, read what was written on them, commencing by saying,—

"Here is the prisoner's name upon the first page, gentlemen, and a lengthened memorandum further on. I need not remark to you that there must, to connect this piece of evidence with the prisoner, be the fullest proof that not only the tablets were his, but the writing his also—as without throwing aspersions upon anybody, we cannot imagine anything easier than to write a few words of very serious consequence to the prisoner on an ivory tablet. The words are,—

"'An account of the Grange property, which would descend to M. R. in case of G. R's sudden death without a will. Five farms, two tenements in York, seven hundred acres of cultivated land, the Deer Forest, the Grange—estimated value twelve thousand per annum. Mem.—To be at Grange by seven o'clock, after duel, if that not fatal. A good exchange by wedding simple M. R. from difficulties to splendour.'

"That is the whole of the memorandum," said the judge, "and it is for the prosecution to prove that it has any connection whatever with the prisoner now at the bar."

"That of course," said the counsel for the prosecution, "it is for us to prove. Now, Mr. Varley, be so good as to answer my questions."

Varley bowed his head, and the first question was,—

"Do you know the causes which led to the duel between Sir George Rankley and Mr. Percy?"

"I can guess them, or rather the principal one," said Varley; "Sir George told me that he had good reason to believe a marriage between Rowland Percy and his daughter was sought eagerly by the Percys on account of their distressed circumstances."

"Did he repeat that circumstance more than once?"

"He did. Such were, in fact, very nearly his last words to me before he composed himself to sleep early on the evening after the duel."

Are you acquainted with the handwriting of the prisoner at the bar?"

"Only through casually seeing it."

"Could you swear that the memorandum on one of the ivory tablets is in his writing."

"I believe it, but should not like to swear it."

Varley thought this piece of affected candour would do more against Rowland than were he unhesitatingly to swear to anything and everything which could advance thei nterests of the prosecution.

"I have no more questions to ask," said the counsel. "Call Samuel Twitter."

"Let Samuel Twitter wait a little," said Rowland's counsel, calmly. "I want to have some conversation with Mr. Varley first."

Varley turned a trifle paler, as he said with affected ease and calmness—

"I am willing to answer any question to the best of my ability and belief."

"Then, Mr. Varley," said the counsel, raising his voice to a loud clear tone. "have you any objection to state to the jury what passed between you and a strange horseman in the bridle path between the Grange and York?"

A cry of terror burst from Varley's lips as the counsel spoke, and clutching with frantic violence the rail of the witness-box, he cried,—

"What—what—devil—prompted you to—to——"

"Answer me," cried the counsel, who saw in a moment what an effect the words had produced upon Bernard Varley's mind. "Answer me, I charge you."

"Water! water! water!" shrieked Varley, and he would have shrunk to the floor had he not been supported by those near him, for he thought that all was discovered, and he was a doomed man.

Judge, jury, and audience, all seemed alike astonished at the effect which the apparently simple and unconscious question of the counsel had had upon Bernard Varley; nor was Rowland Percy a whit less surprised than any one else, for he had not the remotest idea of the tendency of the question, or how it had so wonderful an effect upon the nerves of his great enemy.

"Several officers supported Varley in their arms, while others eagerly brought water from the table, at which sat the counsel, while the spectators seemed to forget entirely where they were; and in the excitement of the moment, they pressed roughly forward, surrounding Varley and the officers so closely that danger began to be apprehended of personal injury to the most forward.

Cries of all kinds arose on every side. Some females who had been driven into the court, amid the throng, which first made good their entrance, began to scream, imagining that something fearful must have occurred. There were loud cries of—

"Open the door, open the door—more air—air—down with Barnard Varley; he is a murderer. Mr. Percy is innocent. Down with Varley—he is a murderer!"

As this last expression caught the ears of Miranda, she rose from her seat, as if by an impulse she could not resist, and throwing back her veil, she cried in a voice which was heard above all the surrounding tumult, on account of its musical beauty, and the clearness of her enunciation,—

" Yes, Bernard Varley is a murderer—I am not mistaken. A voice as it were from Heaven tells me he is guilty ; look in his face. Can you doubt it ? See see—does he not in every feature look like the murderer of my father ?"

The judge having in vain several times tried to quell the tumult, now rose from his seat, and stretching out his hand, while he strove to raise his voice above the tumult in the court, he said,—

" I shall leave this court if my authority is to be held so lightly, that common decent behaviour cannot be obtained when the life of a fellow creature is at stake. Officers, take into custody all that you can depose to taking part in this outrage."

Several of the most foremost now were seized, and a universal panic for the consequences of their conduct began to spread among the people. A rush was made to the doors by those who knew themselves guilty ; and the judge observing that such was the case, prudently ordered the officers to let them go if they would, so that in a few minutes the court was half cleared of its motley contents, and the tumult was sensibly on the decrease.

" Keep the doors fast, now," said the judge ; " allow no one to enter the court. Where is the witness whose extraordinary agitation has caused all this indecorum ?"

" He is recovering," said the counsel for the prosecution, who was as much puzzled as anybody else, to account for Varley's extraordinary and sudden break down, when he was giving his evidence so triumphantly, and so clearly.

" Let the examination then proceed," said the judge.

The counsel stooped, and whispered to Varley in a tone of alarm,—

" For God's sake, Mr. Varley, what is the meaning of all this extraordinary scene ?"

" The—the meaning—" gasped Varley, looking wildly about him, " what has happened ?"

" Tell me who it was you met in the bridle path between the Grange and York ?"

" The—the enemy of mankind," whispered Varley.

" The what ?"

Varley shuddered.

" He's quite mad," thought the counsel, as with a vexed air he resumed his seat, and began chewing his pen, believing that the prosecution was knocked on the head, and that some strange disclosure was about to take place.

CHAPTER XL.

THE CROSS-EXAMINATION CONTINUED.—VARLEY'S CONFUSION.—THE EVIDENCE OF TWITTER.—MIRANDA'S FEARS.

WHAT would be the nature and issue of the cross-examination which in its commencement had produced so startling an effect no one could surmise ; and yet all were in the greatest state of excitement to know what would follow, for they could not but expect some tremendous revelation to succeed so startling a beginning.

Little did judge, jury, and opposing counsel imagine that the question which had been asked of Varley, would lead to nothing, but merely shattering his nervous system, and depriving him of that self confidence with which he had been giving his evidence.

But of all who were surprised at the effect of those few words upon Varley, and annoyed that they could lead to nothing, the counsel for Rowland was the most so. He was completely lost in conjecture as to the cause of the extraordinary emotion of the witness and he could not help surmising something of very great importance to the interest of his client, Rowland Percy, lay hidden in the breast of Varley.

In the course of five more minutes, Varley stood again in the witness-box, pale, trembling, and aghast awaiting with terror, what would next be said to him, and when the counsel again propounded the question,—

" What passed between you and the strange horseman on the bridle path between York and the Grange ?" he could only reply by a deep groan.

The counsel for the prosecution then rose and said,—

" I must submit to the court that my learned friend has no right to put to the witness so very rude a question. His duty is to examine the witnesses on all matters touching and concerning the murder of Sir George Rankley ; and who shall say that this question, which may relate to some of Mr. Varley's own private affairs, bears any relation to that calamitous and much regretted event ?"

" The question is regular enough," replied Rowland's counsel.

" If," said the judge, " you can say that it is essential to the ends of justice that the witness should answer the question, there can be no impropriety in it."

" I require an answer," said the counsel.

" I advise then," said the counsel for the prosecution, " that an answer be refused, provided the witness is in a position to declare on his oath that the matter concerns not this trial."

Here was a loop-hole for Varley to escape by—a faint gleam of hope came across his mind, that after all, the counsel might know nothing, but had only been put in possession of the bare fact of his encounter with the mysterious person of whom he, Varley, had such a dread, by some accidental spectator of the meeting.

" I do declare," he said, " that the affair has nothing to do with the trial."

" On your solemn oath ?" said Rowland's counsel.

" On my solemn oath," replied Varley.

" Then I admit," said the counsel, " that I am not in a condition to press the question."

These words gave Varley new life. The colour slowly revisited his cheeks—he breathed more freely, and altogether the remarkable change for the better that took place in his appearance, surprised every one, and made the curiosity to know what the question could possibly refer to, ten times more intense.

A short whispered consultation now took place between the counsel and Mr. Anderson, after which, the former turning to Varley said,—

" I shall still trouble you to answer some questions which I hope will be more readily done than the one I have already put to you."

Varley merely inclined his head, and by the curl of his lips, and the knitting of his brows, it was clear that he had recovered nearly all of his former confidence and tact.

" How long have you known the deceased, Sir George Rankley ?" was the first question.

" Nearly twenty years," said Varley.

" What were you then ?"

" I was clerk in the banking house in which he was a partner."

" What occupation have you followed since ?"

" None. When Sir George retired from business, he allowed me a sum per annum in consideration of my faithful services to him."

" Oh, indeed, and then you came to live at the Grange ?"

" On Sir George's pressing invitation I did do so."

" After which occurred all this quarrelling between Sir George Rankley and Mr. Percy?"

" Yes. Through some commercial friends, I ascertained the state of Mr. Percy's affairs, and I thought it my duty to communicate the same to him. Since then I am aware I have incurred the hatred of the Percy's, as well as the ill will of other parties."

" What other parties ?"

" Sir George's late solicitor, Mr. Anderson, and—and——"

"And who?'

"Miranda!" gasped Varley, glancing in the direction where she sat.

"On your oath have you, or have you not, made proposals of marriage to that young lady?"

Varley paused for a moment, and then said, faintly,—

"I have."

"Which were rejected with contempt?"

"Rejected!" said Varley.

"In favour of the prisoner at the bar," said the counsel, raising his voice, "that more fortunate suitor being now accused by you of murder."

"I—I don't accuse him," said Varley. "I only state that which I know."

"Now, sir, on your oath, have you not then offered to Miranda Rankley, to save Mr. Rowland Percy altogether from this prosecution, provided she would become your wife?"

This question produced a great sensation in the court, and the judge shook his head as he saw Varley move about uneasily, before he said—

" No."

" You swear that ?"

" I do."

" Has Sir George Rankley left a will ?"

" He has."

" Leaving all to you, Mr. Bernard Varley, I understand, and making his own child quite dependent upon your charity for common sustenance."

"He—he has left all to me."

" Did you not offer to destroy that will if Miranda Rankley would marry you? On your oath, sir, before Heaven, answer me."

" No," said Varley.

" Gentlemen of the jury," said the counsel, solemnly, " I shall be able to place a witness in this box, who upon oath will depose to these facts, and prove that this man would go through fire and water to obtain the hand of Miranda Rankley. Aye, gentlemen, that he would go from a faint lie to a charge of murder to accomplish his ends."

" 'Tis false," cried Varley.

" Silence, sir," said the counsel. " Answer my questions, and make no remarks. Did Sir George Rankley's usual solicitor draw up his will ?"

" No."

" Certainly not. He would have started at such a monstrous document—a document which, I hope will be successfully resisted by the deceased gentleman's daughter ; but admitting for one moment that such a will would stand the test of legal proceedings, on your oath tell the jury, sir, what provision, out of twelve thousand pounds per annum, which I understand you claim under that will, you have been pleased to make to Miranda Rankley ?"

" I have made her offers," said Varley.

" What offers ?"

" Large ones. Offers which I am always willing to renew. She may be mistress of the Grange if she likes."

" But uncoupled with the odious condition of wedding you, what offers have you made her ? What offers will you now, in presence of this court, make her ? On your oath, what income do you propose paying to her from her father's property ?"

Varley was sorely puzzled what to say to this ingenious mode of either committing him to make an allowance to Miranda, or to leave the impression on the minds of the jury that he was actuated by the worst feelings in retaining the property. His grand hope, however, was to reduce Miranda to great poverty, and he would not forego it. After a pause, he said,—

" I shall abide by the conditions of the will."

" And allow her nothing ?"

Varley was silent.

" You may go," said the counsel, "and enjoy as well as you can your position as the robber of the orphan Miranda Rankley and the prosecutor to death, if you can, of the only friend she has on God's earth. You may go, sir. You may go. I am sickened with this most hideous case."

A faint murmur of execration came from the people in the court as Varley stepped from the witness-box, and slunk among the crowd to endeavour to avoid the many eyes that were upon him. The effort of the counsel had been altogether directed to weaken the effect of his evidence by representing the motives which would induce him to give it, and he had thoroughly succeeded in loading him with infamy as well as in resting a strong suspicion even upon the distinct story he had told concerning the events immediately preceding and succeeding Sir George's death—a story which Varley had too well arranged to enable it to be attacked directly.

Twitter's evidence, however, as the counsel well knew, was of much more importance than Varley's, and unless he could throw so much discredit upon his estimony as well as upon Varley, as to almost prove a conspiracy between them, he in his heart despaired of the acquittal of Rowland Percy, although he himself had a strong belief in his innocence, and no slight opinion concerning the real facts of the case. The evidence, however, as far as it had gone, was but circumstantial, and upon that he had certainly succeeded in throwing as much suspicion as possible.

It was generally known that Twitter's evidence was very important, and when his name was loudly called at the doors of the court, every eye was eagerly bent upon catching the first glimpse of him as he entered the place.

He ascended the two steps leading to the witness box with more the aspect of a prisoner going to execution than a witness coming to tell what he knew on his oath before a court of justice. His mean, diminutive figure—his pale, unwholesome looking complexion, and his evident dreadful nervousness, caused a painful sensation in all who saw him. While the oath was being administered, his eyes wandered round the court in search of Varley, but in consequence of the position of the witness-box, he could not see him, so he was left to his own conjectures as to how the case had hitherto proceeded, and those were, to such a man as Twitter, of the most painful and tormenting nature.

At length the oath was taken, and the counsel for the prosecution rose and said,—

"Samuel Twitter, state what you know concerning the death of Sir George Rankley."

"I will," said Twitter; "I was Sir George's valet. I knew nothing of the duel I only saw my master brought home wounded, and was told by Mr. Varley that he had fought a duel with Mr. Percy, because——"

"We don't want to hear anything of the duel," said Rowland's counsel. "I submit that that is not before the court, and besides, what nonsense it is for a witness to come here and swear to the causes of events, which cause might be merely the sheer invention of some one who had his own bad ends only in view."

"Go on—go on," said the counsel for the prosecution.

"Mr. Varley," resumed Twitter, "spoke to me about the probability of the nurse falling asleep, if unrelieved all night in her attendance upon my master. He offered to sit up with me, and allow her to have an hour's rest, to which I of course assented. It was twelve o'clock when we thought of going. I carried the light, and as we were proceeding, I think it was I who first saw the figure we supposed to be the spectre of the murdered keeper. We attempted to follow it, but it eluded us, and we proceeded to the chamber of my master. He was sleeping, and when the nurse was gone, I sat down by the foot of the bed, as I felt very much overcome by the, as I then thought, supernatural appearance I had seen on my passage to the chamber. The candle we then had was nearly burnt to the socket, and Mr. Varley asked me to go down to his room, and get one which was there. Seeing, however, my agitation, for I am very nervous, he went himself, he—he went, I say, himself."

Here Twitter paused, and seemed unable to proceed for some moments, while he looked round in vain for an encouraging glance from Varley.

"Take your time," said the judge.

"He—he went himself," repeated Twitter, "leaving me alone with my master who was moaning as if in pain. But scarcely had he been gone a moment, when the same figure, dressed in green, which had so much alarmed me before, entered the room. I was paralysed with terror—I could not move nor speak. The fire light fell upon the face, and I at once recognised Mr. Rowland Percy. I was nearly hidden by the bed furniture, and I saw him glance round him a moment, as if to assure himself he was alone. Then he drew the pillow sharply from under Sir George's head, and laid it upon his face. I know no more—no more—no more."

CHAPTER XLI.

TWITTER repeated the words "no more" as if a tremendous weight had been suddenly taken off his breast. He breathed more freely, and seemed to anticipate that the worst he had to go through was now over.

The counsel for the prosecution, however, rose and said,—

"I have but a few questions to ask of you, Samuel Twitter, and the first is, how long have you been in Sir George Rankley's service?"

"Five years," said Twitter.

"He placed the greatest confidence in you?"

"He did."

"Are you left anything in the will?"

"Nothing beyond what every servant has, a twelvemonth's wages."

"You are quite sure that Sir George Rankley was alive when you sat down at the foot of the bed?"

"Quite sure. He was moaning and tossing his arms now and then about."

"And you have no doubt concerning the identity of the prisoner at the bar with the person you saw enter the chamber in a green dress?"

"None whatever."

"I have done."

The counsel sat down with quite a triumphant air, as much as to say,—

"You can make nothing out of this witness, but what is favourable, to the prosecution."

Rowland's counsel now rose and said abruptly,—

"How did you get a living before you entered Sir George Rankley's service?"

"Get—a—living!"

"Yes. What did you do?"

"I was assisted by my friends."

"What do you mean to do now?"

"I shall remain in the service of Mr. Varley, in the same capacity as that in which I served the late Sir George."

"What happened when you recovered from your swoon in the bed-room?"

"Miranda was there, and there was much confusion. I scarcely know what happened until I saw the prisoner in custody, and I felt much relieved in my mind when I found that he was the supposed ghost."

"Do you know a poor idiot, named Bold Hawk, or Mad Martin?"

"Yes."

"Does he not prophesy that Bernard Varley will be hanged at York?"

"He—he—does."

"I believe it, and so do you. Look at him, my lord and gentlemen of the jury—look at him."

The counsel pointed his finger at Twitter, who was seized with such a fit of trembling that he could scarcely stand.

"Gentlemen of the jury," continued the counsel, "the fear and agitation of these two witnesses for the prosecution, who play in each other's hands so, is certainly the most extraordinary thing of the kind I ever saw in my life. I have done with you, Samuel Twitter, and Heaven have mercy upon you, if you are a perjured man."

"Call George Hessel," said the prosecuting counsel.

This George Hessel was an old servant of Mr. Percy, and when he appeared and was sworn, the counsel said,—

" Do you know the handwriting of young Mr. Percy ?"

" I do," was the reply.

" Is that his writing ?"

The ivory tablets were handed to the witness, opened at the page where was the memorandum. The man paused some moments then he said—

" It is very like."

" You cannot swear it is not ?"

" No."

" But you cannot swear it is," said Rowland's counsel; " and now, George Hessel, do you think if you were going to commit a murder, you would made a memorandum of it on some tablet ?"

" No. Oh dear no !"

" Do you think you are wiser than young Mr. Percy ?"

" Oh dear no! I be but a poor man, and he has a mart o'larning."

" That will do. My lord these tablets are nonsense. If the prisoner were convicted on such evidence, I would move an arrest of judgment on account of lunacy. Who but a madman would have made such a memorandum ? It's a forgery."

Varley rose from a seat he had pushed himself into, and uttered an angry exclamation, but in an instant he seemed to be aware of the folly of what he was doing, and as rapidly sat down again, his sudden emotion being only perceptible by those immediately around him, and by Twitter.

Several witnesses were now examined to prove the chase for Rowland Percy through the house, and his ultimate capture in the identical green dress, concerning which so much has been said. Here closed the case for the prosecution, and it was evident to every lawyer present, that unless Twitter's evidence could be materially shaken, it must suffice to convict the prisoner.

The dim shadows of evening were now beginning to steal over the face of nature, and objects in the still crowded court became more and more faint, and confused ; judge, counsel, jury, witnesses, and spectators were alike exhausted, when, after a whispered word or two to the mayor, the judge said,—

" If the counsel on each side are agreeable, I will bind over the jury to appear to-morrow, and we will adjourn the case at this point before the defence is entered into."

" I have no objection, my lord," said Rowland's counsel, " myself and the prisoner's solicitor being allowed free access to him."

" That may be," said the judge, " but he must see no other visitors."

" I consent to the postponement," said the counsel for the prosecution ; " but the jury, I trust, will, by your lordship's direction, be prevented from holding communication with any one."

At this, one of the jurors rose and said,—

" Please you, my lord, I've got a wife."

" The court cannot help that, sir," said the judge, " however it may sympathise with you."

A smile passed among the counsel, and the discomforted juryman sat down.

" The jury," added the judge, " will be accommodated within the precincts of the court. I think it quite impossible that either they, myself, or the counsel engaged on this case, can do their duty efficiently for perhaps six or eight hours longer, after the fatigue of both mind and body we have already undergone. The court stands adjourned until ten o'clock to-morrow morning, when it is understood the defence is to be entered upon."

The adjournment was most welcome to every one, for, in truth, all were exhausted by so many hours' intense excitement. A rush was made to the door of the court, and Miranda, rising, cast her eyes towards the bar just as a turnkey laid his hand upon Rowland Percy's arm to remove him.

" Rowland !" she cried, and in a moment she was as near to him as she could get.

He stretched out both his hands, and could just take one of hers in his grasp.

"Hope, Rowland, hope !" she said.

" I will, Miranda," he replied—" my trust must be in Heaven—Oh, what things have we heard to day !"

"All false, Rowland, all false."

"You must come," said the turnkey.

"One moment only—be of good cheer, Miranda.   Tell my father not to despair."

"God bless you!" was all that Miranda had time to say, and then he was hurried from her sight ; for the officers feared censure for pausing even a moment in their duty under the eye of the judge.

Mr. Percy had not been able to reach the dock in time to speak to his son ; but now he took Miranda's arm in his, and said—

"Come, my child, come ; we will go home and pray for our innocent Rowland."

The throng made way for them as they left the court, and a more curious sight could scarcely be imagined than the daughter of the murdered man, whose death was the subject of inquiry, leaning upon the arm of the father of the accused, and in the minds of every one almost, after the conclusive evidence of Twitter, guilty Rowland Percy.

They were joined at the door by Mr. Anderson, who took Miranda's other arm in his, saying,—

"Come home with me, both of you, and we will talk over the strange events of the day.   Come, I can indeed take no denial."

Miranda would not pain the honest lawyer by refusing his proferred hospitality and accordingly she and Mr. Percy at once accompanied him home.   When they had arrived, Miranda could control no longer the question which was uppermost in her mind, but looking into Mr. Anderson's face, with an expression that showed the intense interest she took in the answer which might be returned to her, she said—

" Tell me now, my dear friend, and tell me candidly, for I can bear to hear the truth—what hope has Rowland of escape from the hands of his vile enemies ?"

"Miranda, I hope for the best," said Mr. Anderson.   " Your evidence, which will be called for to-morrow, I believe, the first thing, will be in direct contradiction to some of the sworn statements of Bernard Varley.   As far as I can judge of human nature, I should say the jury can have no sort of difficulty in deciding between you and the ruffian, who carries his character in every lineament of his face."

"Heaven grant the truth may prevail," said Miranda.   "Oh, what a web of falsehood have they woven round poor Rowland, and he is so entirely innocent—he is so kind, so noble—he who I have seen turn from his path to save the life of a fluttering insect—oh, it is so shocking—shocking to think of."

"Do not distress yourself, Miranda.   Reserve your strength for to-morrow.   It may be all required in the cross-examination you will be as a matter of course subjected to."

" I will be firm," said Miranda, " for Rowland's sake. He shall not fall if I can save him.   Time was when I should have shrunk in terror from the public exhibition of to-morrow, but now a far higher motive nerves me, and my trembling heart shall be as firm as adamant.   I would face a world in such a cause, for it is one of holy truth—of heavenly justice [warring] against vice and awful iniquity."

A servant now came into the room, and whispered something to Mr. Anderson, who, turning to Miranda, said,—

" The counsel who is for us has called."

"Oh, let me see him," cried Miranda.   "I must ask him, too, the same question, which you, with what I know you think a kind evasion, have not answered."

"Miranda, no human being can tell what may occur.   Let me entreat of you to be calm, and hope for the happiest result. Show Mr. —— in."

The counsel in a few moments entered the room. He was a humane man, as well as being a man of most acute mind, and great professional tact.

"I hope," he said, "I am not an intruder here, but I consider we have an advantage over the common enemy, by the adjournment of the trial, for, having heard the whole of his case, it gives us an opportunity of knowing better where to attack him."

Miranda walked up to the counsel, and while her clasped hands and excited countenance showed the state of her feelings, she said,—

"Sir—you—surely know. Will they condemn the innocent—will they condemn the innocent?"

"My good young lady," said the barrister, "I trust not—I believe that a more rare circumstance in English criminal proceeding than the innocent being condemned, cannot be imagined. The guilty have always a great chance of escaping, but the innocent have the smallest possible chance of being condemned, except where the grossest perjury is resorted to, to accomplish that end."

"But here we have that," said Miranda. "The principal part of the evidence to-day sworn to, I know to be false."

"I am a believer in the innocence of Mr. Percy," said the counsel, "although my acquaintance with him is very slight. I cannot say what the jury may do—but I would not believe either Varley or Twitter on their oaths."

"You give me new life," said Miranda, "by saying so. There is then hope for Rowland?"

"I think there is; but what I principally wished to see you for, was to tell you that the questions I shall ask you to-morrow will be for the purpose of weakening Bernard Varley's evidence, by casting discredit on it wherever we can. The circumstances sworn to by Twitter we cannot attack, but if we can gainsay some of Varley's statements, and then get any evidence calculated to prove an extraordinary degree of intimacy between him and Twitter, we may lead the jury to the point I wish them to arrive at, namely, that the whole affair is a conspiracy between Varley and Twitter, who are themselves the murderers, if Sir George was at all murdered."

"That is the truth," said Miranda.

"It may be, and I shall endeavour to elicit it, if possible. I am now going to Mr. Percy."

"To—Rowland?"

"Yes. I will willingly be the bearer of any message."

"Tell him," said Miranda, "you—you saw me smile, and left me full of hope. It will comfort him."

She sunk upon a chair as she spoke, and covered her face with her hands to hide the expression of despair which in spite of herself was depicted there.

CHAPTER XLII.

THE SECOND DAY OF THE TRIAL.—MIRANDA'S EVIDENCE.

THE intense excitement which the trial of Rowland Percy had excited, not only in York, but throughout the whole country, was by no means abated at the fact of the adjournment of the prisoner's defence until the following day—indeed, if possible, the fever of impatience which beset all classes of persons upon the subject, became much more intense, and nothing was talked of throughout York, but the probabilities or improbabilities of the verdict being favourable or unfavourable to the prisoner.

Never was there so much partisanship in favour of an accused person before, and at the very street corners, little knots of persons stood till a late hour on the evening of the first day of the trial, anxiously and vehemently commenting on the evidence.

Varley retired to his new lodging opposite to Miranda, in a perfect agony of suspense and terror—suspense as regarded the verdict, and terror lest from the question which Rowland's counsel had asked him, concerning the mysterious horseman on the bridle path, he had in reserve some information which he would produce at the last moment, to his, Varley's, absolute confusion and ruin.

So strangely did this idea take possession of his guilty mind, that he was more than once during the night tempted to fly, and escape the possibly impending storm of the morrow. He knew well, that he had communicated to no one the fact of his meeting with the stranger, and therefore it must be from that mysterious, and to Varley's heated imagination, terrible man himself, that the counsel for the defence had received his information; and so receiving it, what was to hinder a free communication of all, as well as of a part? Thus reasoned Bernard Varley, and as he did so, he passed such a night of horrors, that, had Rowland Percy seen him, he must have pitied him.

Retire to rest he could not, but he continued to pace to and fro in the room he had hired, to the great consternation and wonder of his landlady; only varying that most monotonous proceeding, by occasionally throwing himself into a seat, and fixing his eyes upon Miranda's window, while he muttered,—

"Miranda—Miranda. What do I not endure for you? You will not give me one kind word —one gentle look, to save me from despair. Oh, Miranda, Miranda —beautiful being! You might even now save Rowland Percy, for at a word from you, couched in the tone I fain would hear, I would take measures even yet to save him."

Then he would groan in a most awful manner, and a feeling of his own danger, as he considered it, on the morrow, would come over him, and he would slip down the staircase, and look anxiously up and down the street, to assure himself that no one was waiting to apprehend him.

Thus passed the wretched night of Bernard Varley, the much envied possessor of one of the finest estates in the country, and a man who, to all appearance, had reached the very summit of his ambition.

As the grey light of morning appeared, he sat down by the window, and stirred not, for he wished to see Miranda as she went forth—not knowing that she was at Mr. Anderson's.

Four o'clock pealed from the minster clock just as objects became visible. Then five, and he was still there, with his eyes fixed as those of a corpse upon the opposite window. Six o'clock still found him there, and then his wondering landlady knocked at his room door.

He started to his feet, and trembled in every limb, as he said in a voice of terror,—

"Who's there?"

"Please, sir, it's me," said the woman. "I thought you might want something, as you were up."

"Leave me," he cried. "Never think about my actions. I want nothing."

"Well, sir, I only thought——"

"Away! D——n, woman, am I to be pestered by you? Away, I say. Ha! who is that?"

A low single knock sounded on the street-door, and it could not have had more effect upon Varley's excited nerves, had it been the sudden report of a cannon close to his ears.

The woman bustled down the staircase to open the door, and Varley stood with his own room-door open in an attitude of listening, for, in his imagination, every alarm sounded like a summons to him to come and take Rowland Percy's place in the dock, and be accused of the murder of Sir George Rankley.

With a feeling of relief he heard the voice of Twitter inquiring for him, and in a few moments the valet came sneaking up the stairs, slowly and cautiously, as was his custom.

Varley threw himself into a seat with his back to the light, and when Twitter entered the room and closed the door, he said,—

"Well, well, Twitter—have you any news?"

"None," said Twitter, "but I thought I had better come and see you. The whole town seems to be in an uproar. Yesterday was nothing to it."

"Let the rabble shout," said Varley; "let them in their own minds condemn whom they please, sympathise with whom they please, I care not—I care not, Twitter."

"No—certainly not," said Twitter; "did I not," sinking his voice to a whisper, "did I not give my evidence well, eh?"

No. 20.

"You did—you did," said Varley. "What we two have sworn to should hang a better man than Rowland Percy."

"Yes—yes," said Twitter; "but I have come to you, Varley, to beg of you—to implore you to give up this insane love of Miranda. You must know how very hopeless such a passion must be."

"It may be hopeless," said Varley, bitterly, "but if she will not have my love, she shall have my revenge, Twitter—my deep and ample revenge."

Twitter groaned, as he said,—

"Varley, Varley, mark my words—upon that rock you will split. You will bring both me and yourself to ruin—to death."

"Peace, peace, ill-omened creature," cried Varley; "as soon might you move a mountain from its base, as move me from my purpose. I am a desperate man, and I will run my course."

"Varley, be advised."

"I will not. When you can move by your entreaties the stones that pave the streets of York, then expect to move me, but not before, Twitter—not before."

Twitter groaned, and turned to go, but Varley stepped up to him, and laying his hand on his arm, said in a nervous manner,—

"Twitter, you came along the streets—you heard men conversing. Are you sure we are not threatened with any danger?"

"Danger!" echoed Twitter.

"Yes—are you sure no being, perhaps of another world, has betrayed us to the —the counsel for the defence of Rowland Percy?"

"Oh! he is mad—he is mad!" exclaimed Twitter.

"Fool!" said Varley, "cease these exclamations, and answer me. Have you no hint of danger?"

"None—none," said the alarmed Twitter. "Good Heavens! what danger do you apprehend?"

"No matter—no matter—go now."

"I came for you because the difficulty of getting into the court is so great if we delay later."

"I shall wait here," said Varley, resuming his seat by the window, until she appears.

"Miranda has passed the night at Mr. Anderson's."

"Are you sure?"

"Quite sure."

"Then—then I will go with you, Twitter."

"Have you breakfasted?"

"No—no—but I cannot eat till all is over. On the road I will take some wine. Come—come."

Varley was now in quite as much haste to leave his new lodgings as Twitter could be, and the two false witnesses left the house together, each in his own way, full of all sorts of painful apprehensions, and as thoroughly wretched as any two human beings could possibly be.

As they neared the court, they found a throng of people rapidly bearing towards it, with the same intention as themselves, namely, to be there early enough to secure admission on the first rush which should take place when the door should be opened.

Varley felt very faint and exhausted from his long fasting, combined with the great anxiety of mind he had undergone; and observing a small public-house a few doors down a narrow street, he turned towards it, saying to Twitter, who walked by his side,—

"I will go in here and get some wine; eat I cannot, but I shall find a stimulant that may enable me perchance to go through the day."

It was a little old-fashioned house, and Varley was glad to find that he was not recognised by any one in it, although there were two persons in the bar, and a third talking to them.

"A pint of sherry," said Varley, trying to assume a tone of ease and confidence.

The wine was quickly placed before him, and as he drank, he was compelled to be a listener to some little conversation, no way flattering to himself.

"Yon see," said the man, who was talking to the two persons within the bar, "I can't stand a crowd, but my son went, and he came home quite in a taking, he did."

"Indeed—what for?" said the landlady of the house.

"Why, I'll tell you : 'Father,' said he, when he came in, 'there's an innocent man being tried to-day for his life !' that's what my son said. Then I said to him, 'Ned,' says I, 'what puts that in your head ?' 'I'm sure of it,' says he, 'and 'atween you and me, if Sir George Rankley has been murdered at all, some one else did it.' "

"Lor bless us, who ?" said the landlady.

"Hum—hum !"

"But you can tell me, sure, neighbour ?"

"Well I don't know; it aint safe to speak one's mind always."

"But among friends," interposed Varley, "you know sir, it is safe enough. Pray take a glass of wine, and let us know who your very clever son accuses of the murder ?"

"You are very good, sir," said the man, whose intellects were not sharp enough to detect the tone of irony in which Varley spoke.

Varley poured him a glass of wine, and the man as he raised it to his lips, said,—

"Well, as we is among friends, I don't mind telling you my Ned's opinion, and though I say it as shoulda't perhaps, Ned is no fool !"

"Children do not always take after their parents," said Varley, bitterly.

"That's true, sir," said the man, who took it as quite a compliment. "Well, then, my Ned thinks as Bernard Varley did it."

"The murder ! Lor bless us," ejaculated the landlady.

"Does he indeed ?"

"He does. I assure you that's my Ned's opinion, sir."

"Then you may tell your Ned that Mr. Varley will prosecute him for his opinion."

"What ?"

"Prosecute him."

"My Ned—eh? Mr. Varley prosecute my Ned ?"

"Yes, sir. My name is Bernard Varley."

So saying, Varley walked from the house, leaving every one who heard him perfectly aghast, and as terrified as if they had just been visited by some awful spectre.

"Curses on them," said Varley, when he was once more in the high street leading to the court, "what makes them suspect me ?"

"I don't know," said Twitter ; "I'm very full of apprehensions."

"Pshaw ! you always were ; but this is no place to converse in. Ah! who is that ?"

"It is old Mr. Percy."

At the same moment that Twitter pronounced his name, Rowland's father saw Varley, and immediately stepping up to him, he said,—

"Bernard Varley, you have borne false witness against my boy. May he be your accuser before that eternal Judge who cannot err !"

"Old man," said Varley, "your grey hairs protect you, or you should rue you insult to me."

"Did Sir George Rankley's grey hairs protect him from the hands of a murderer ?" cried Mr Percy.

"No, sir," replied Varley, "your son had not so much kind consideration it appears in his nature.

"Villain," said Mr. Percy, "you are now at large, and can brave this matter out; but the time will come when you, without that aid from Heaven which will surely be rendered to my innocent boy, will stand in the same position he is now in."

"Old man," said Varley as he passed on, for he saw that in a few moments they would be surrounded by a crowd, "your wits are wandering—you know not what you say."

"Vain subterfuge, Bernard Varley. Your own heart tells you what I mean better than I myself could explain. Oh, man, man! what a fearful account have you to settle when that you shall be called upon by an immortal Judge to answer."

Varley walked hastily onwards with a flushed brow, and curses at his heart.

CHAPTER XLIII.

THE CONTINUED TRIAL.—THE VERDICT.—A SCENE OF STRANGE EXCITEMENT.—
THE DENUNCIATION.—VARLEY'S TERROR.

WHEN Bernard Varley reached the entrance to the court, he found so dense a crowd there assembled, that it was next to impossible for him to make an entrance for some time. In vain he attempted to pass forward, and receiving little or no assistance from the cowardly and trembling Twitter, his progress was but very slow indeed.

Determined, however, to hear the progress of the trial, he still pressed onwards until he reached, after an hour's struggling, the door of the court.

There he was repulsed by some of the officials on duty, until he declared who he was, when he was admitted, together with Twitter, into the body of the court.

The doors as yet were not thrown open, and none had been allowed to enter but such as were in some manner connected with the future progress of the important trial which was about to be resumed.

Suddenly coming from the open daylight, it was some moments before Bernard Varley became acquainted with the presence of Miranda, who, with her extreme anxiety as regarded the fate of Rowland Percy, had even at an earlier hour than he, Varley, had thought proper, sought the scene of his acquittal or his condemnation.

When, however, his eyes fell upon the graceful form, to him more beautiful, if possible, in grief than it had been in joy, he grasped the arm of Twitter so tightly as to cause a slight exclamation of pain from the valet, and said,—

"She is here! She is here! The arbitress of my destiny—she is here, Twitter. Look upon her and bewitch your mind with her rare beauty. She is here, and yet, oh God, she will not smile upon me!"

"Hush! for Heaven's sake, hush!" said Twitter. "This wild emotion may yet be our ruin."

"I must speak to her," murmured Varley. "Even in the height of her scornful beauty, I must speak to her—see, her eyes are wet with tears. She weeps for him who shall die."

"Are you distracted," whispered Twitter, as he laid hold of Varley by the arm and held him back for a moment from advancing towards Miranda. "For your own sake, as well as for mine, forego the mad exhibition of any emotion now. There are a hundred eyes upon you?"

"Were an universe watching me," said Varley, "I must speak to her."

With these words he tore himself from the detaining grasp of Twitter, and with a slow, unsteady step he walked to where Miranda was sitting. She did not observe him, for her thoughts were with Rowland Percy in his lonely cel[1] and it was not until, with a frantic tone, he said,—

"Miranda!—Miranda!" that she became aware of his presence. Then turning she faced the man who had worked her so much woe, and with a tone of loathing horror, she cried—

"Away—away! Haunt me not, Barnard Varley—thou murderer of my father —false witness against the innocent—away—away."

"Hear me," said Varley, in a low tone of agony as he leant forward towards her. "Hear me, Miranda, even now I can save Rowland Percy."

Miranda rose on the instant, and cried,—

"Listen to the perjurer—listen all to him who has taken in vain the name of Heaven. The false witness even now condemns himself."

There was a rush of the few persons in the court towards Miranda, and Varley shrinking back, while a spasmodic change came over his face, cried,—

"'Tis false—'tis false. The girl is mad, because her lover is a murderer. The girl is mad."

"Mr. Bernard Varley," said Mr. Anderson, who at that moment entered the court, he having been home on some important business, after escorting Miranda to her seat; "I will not allow you to insult the lady by addressing her, for such she considers an insult."

"Indeed, sir," said Varley, all the devil in his nature showing itself in the diabolical expression of his face; "there may come a time when you—but no matter—no matter—I'm done now."

Smothering, then, as best he might the expression of the deep hatred that he felt towards Mr. Anderson, he slowly walked to the opposite side of the court, still followed by Twitter, who was in a state of the most pitiable agitation, for he feared each moment that Varley, in his wild passion for the beautiful Miranda, would say something that, while it committed himself, would likewise involve him, Twitter, in an inextricable dilemma.

The hour for resuming the business of the court was now rapidly approaching, but from the precautions which had been taken, in consequence of the proceedings of the day before, there was not a tithe of the confusion which then had reigned. The court instantly became densely crowded, but all was comparatively still, and when the judge, accompanied by the mayor of York, took his seat upon the bench, there was every appearance of the proceedings, deeply interesting as they were, proceeding tranquilly to a close.

Precisely at ten o'clock Rowland Percy was placed at the bar, and he appeared with the same unaltered mien as before, although Miranda, as she gazed at him, saw, or thought she saw, that he was much paler than before, and that the smile with which he recognised her presence was fainter than it had been.

There was no demonstration of feeling on the part of the crowded auditory when he appeared, and but for the low hum of voices which suddenly broke, and the low sententious "silence!" of the crier of the court, no one would have imagined that he whose life hung that day upon the opinion of twelve of his fellow men, had made his appearance.

The jury were sworn again, and as the bustle which was inevitably consequent upon this proceeding subsided, a look of care and gravity came over the features of Rowland's counsel, for it became his turn to address the court in favour of the prisoner, and to produce what witnesses he could in support of his innocence.

There was a perfect silence for some moments, and then he rose. He glanced at the prisoner, and then around the court before he spoke, and then, in a clear, manly voice, but slightly tinctured with an emotion which gave it truthfulness, he commenced,—

"My lord and gentlemen of the jury,—I appear before you in one of the most onerous positions in which one man can appear before his fellows, namely, to defend the fame and the life of a fellow creature, who, from my heart, I believe is innocent; and who, before Heaven, I here, to the best of my judgment, proclaim the victim of as awful a conspiracy as was ever concocted against a human being.

"Gentlemen, I am not here to make charges, but to rebut them ; but still, whatever the pains or the penalties of such a course of proceeding may be, I, as one man talking to my fellows, and with the ear of Heaven open to my words, declare my firm conviction that the principal witnesses for this prosecution are perjured men—aye, gentlemen of the jury, perjured men !"

There was a great sensation through the court at this bold declaration, and Varley was only prevented from some outburst of passion by the earnest and agonising whispered remonstrances of Twitter.

"Perjured men," repeated the counsel, in a still louder tone, "and, gentlemen of the jury, having in the face of this court made to you so solemn a declaration, I owe to them—I owe it to you, and lastly, I owe it to myself, to state to you the grounds upon which I found such a belief.

"My lord and gentlemen, I shall, in the first place, detail to you the simple facts of this case as I have had them from the lips of the parties who now most anxiously await the issue of this judicial investigation, and having stated these facts, I will proceed to bring before you what evidence I may in support of them.

"So far as my learned friend, who opened this case, went in his description of the contiguity of the estates of the Percy family and the Rankley family, as well as the reciprocal attachment which sprung up between the prisoner at the bar and Miranda, the only daughter of Sir George Rankley, I can agree with him ; but when he states that any scheme, plot, or contrivance, entered the brain of the Percys, for the purpose of amending their shattered fortunes by an union with the Rankley family, I am compelled by the exigencies of the present occasion, gentlemen, to contradict him in the most positive and unequivocal terms.   No such plan —no such plot—no such contrivance—was ever imagined, and in evidence I shall be able to prove to you that it was not many days before the duel took place, of which you have heard something, that Mr. Percy the elder was aware himself of the embarrassed state of his finances, and that Mr. Percy, the younger, the prisoner at the bar, was not at all aware of that fact until after the present charge had been made against him ; for he, when in custody, begged of his father to extend to Miranda Rankley, who has been robbed of her patrimony—robbed is my word, gentlemen—the fostering care of a parent from his ample resources, and the news that those resources were fled, fell like a thunderbolt upon the mind of my client, gentlemen.   So much for the gratuitous assumption that any one action, any one thought of my much injured and innocent client was engendered by a desire to rescue himself from embarrassment, and so much, gentlemen, for the principal, if not the only alleged motive, for the commission of the terrible crime with which he is charged.

"My lord and gentlemen of the jury, my learned friend on the other side elt himself in a difficulty to get up an imaginable motive for a young gentleman remarkable for humanity—remarkable for probity—remarkable for every manly virtue, committing so atrocious a crime as murder ; and he has stumbled over the supposition, that by killing the father and marrying the daughter, he should better his condition ; but, gentlemen, when I disprove the fact of his knowledge of any embarrassment, I humbly assume that the ingenious fabric my learned friend has based upon such a foundation must topple down likewise into the dust.

"That then, gentlemen, is the first point I shall seek by evidence to establish in favour of my client.

"And now, my lord and gentlemen of the jury, if taking up the admirable and ingenious line of argumentation of my learned friend, I admit with him that where we can produce a strong motive for crime there must be crime, and if I succeed in divesting my client of such strong motive, at the same time that I shift that great weight on to the shoulders of the prosecutor in this case, I apprehend it will wear a very different aspect—aye, the prosecutor, gentlemen.   Look at him."

Varley had risen to his feet in spite of Twitter's detaining grasp, and now the counsel for Rowland pointed full in his face, and kept repeating,—

"Look at him, gentlemen.   Look at him."

Varley tried to speak, but his words died away in his throat, and he could but gaze, like one fascinated, into the face of the counsel, who, in so searching a manner, was diving, as it were, into the secret of his inmost heart and turning against his breast the weapons he had used for the destruction of the innocen Rowland Percy.

"Silence!" cried the usher of the court.

"For God's sake sit down," said the counsel for the prosecution, addressing Varley.

"No, let him have his say," interposed Rowland's counsel. "People labouring under great agitation sometimes speak the truth, when in their cooler moments we cannot get it from them."

"We really cannot have these most irregular proceedings," said the judge. "If the witness, Bernard Varley, cannot maintain his equanimity, he must be removed from the court."

Varley sunk into his seat, and resting his head upon his hands, remained in that position during the continuance of the counsel's speech, which seemed to have lost none of its force or pungency by the interruption which had taken place.

CHAPTER XLIV.

THE SPEECH FOR THE DEFENCE.—THE EVIDENCE OF MR. PERCY.—THE WRITING ON THE TABLETS.

The counsel continued —

"My lords and gentlemen, notwithstanding the interruption which has taken place, and which might, or might not, have been intended to intimidate me, I shall proceed to show you that the prosecutor in this case, and not the prisoner at the bar, was the person deeply interested in the death of Sir George Rankley. It appears that the late Sir George was in possession of very large property, and although what I am going to say is known well to you all, it nevertheless is an astonishing circumstance taken in connection with this trial, that the whole of his property should be left in the hands of the prosecutor in this case; i n trust certainly, but on such revolting conditions could the daughter of Sir George only enjoy one penny of it, that the Grange and other property belonging to the late Sir George, has become, subject to any questions that may arise in a civil court concerning it, wholly and solely Mr. Bernard Varley's, the prosecutor in the case, gentlemen, one of the principal evidence against the prisoner, and a man who has, notwithstanding the circumstance, had the singular audacity to instruct counsel to talk of people benefiting by the death of Sir George Rankley as a suspicious circumstance against them.

"My lord and gentlemen, this is monstrous—my learned friend who addressed you for the prosecution, made a grand and particular point of this as a motive for a young gentlemen, notorious for his humanity, his rectitude of conduct, and his good feelings, committing a most heartless cold-blooded murder—and if such as proposition be correct, gentlemen—if we can stoop to the humiliation of believing such a libel upon human nature, what can my learned friend think of the prosecutor in this case, who has actually benefited so largely by the death of Sir George, and who, you have not heard, was ever notorious for humanity at all, and who, I here declare, to be a man destitute of the common feelings of human nature."

"I must really object to that," said the counsel for the prosecution.

"Then I must justify it—Benard Varley retains in his own hands the property, that of right belongs, or should belong, to Miranda Rankley, with the hope that by poverty's severe sufferings, he may induce her to submit to the loathsome alternative of becoming his wife, gentlemen of the jury. Whereever she goes, he follows her with his hideous addresses ; and you will recollect that the prisoner at the bar is the affianced husband of Miranda Rankley. So much for motives, gentlemen ; if the prisoner had a motive the size of a grain of sand, for murdering Sir George Rankley, the prosecutor himself seems to have possessed one as large as a mountain.

"Now it appears likewise that the prosecutor was the fortunate man to find those tablets upon which some stress had been laid by the prosecution. My lord and gentlemen, the prisoner at once owns the tablets as his, but he unhesitatingly calls Heaven to witness that beyond his name, when he purchased them, he never wrote one word in them.

"These words which have been read to you, gentlemen, from those tablets were never written by the prisoner. Let him who did write them beware of that awful day when an immortal Judge shall read his heart ! But, gentlemen, reasoning for one brief moment upon this question, how absurd is it,—how monstrously ridiculous that the man who could conceive an exceedingly artful murder—the man who had such a nice perception of the results of his crime, should at the very time when he was placing himself in great personal danger—when as yet he could but calculate upon success—not know it—that he, I say, should purchase some tablets, write in them words of such fearful import to himself, and then deliberately place them in his pocket, with a strong chance of losing them, on the spot, of all others, where if found, they would do him the most injury.

"Gentlemen, such a thing lies not within the compass of belief, and I repeat that if I thought the prisoner at the bar was a guilty man, and had written those words, I would apply for his acquittal on the ground of insanity.

"But, my lord, and gentlemen of the jury, he stands before you an innocent man, craving at your hands the verdict which shall restore him to that society of which he is so eminently—from his education, his talents, and his warm, good feelings—calculated to become an ornament. He has been, as yet, the victim of some conspiracy, artfully contrived and carried out with singular boldness and rare effrontery; but he is innocent, gentlemen. He is innocent, and in support of the allegations I have made, I shall now proceed to call before you some witnesses in every way worthy of the highest credit from this court."

The counsel sat down, and it was clear that his address had created a strong feeling in favour of Rowland. The jury whispered together, and cast some very suspicious glances at Bernard Varley and Twitter as they both sat looking ghastly with rage at the insinuations of the counsel, which to them were more desperately annoying because they were true.

After a slight pause, the first witness called was the elder Percy, and his appearance in the witness box to speak for his son, created a strong sensation in the court.

While he was being sworn, his eyes wandered to the face of Rowland who answered his anxious look by a smile ; but it was a sad smile, like a faint beam of sunlight illumining the heavens for a moment on a day of gloom.

His examination was then immediately commenced by the question—

"You were on intimate terms with the late Sir George Rankley?"

"I was."

"Are you aware of an attachment on the part of your son to Miranda Rankley?"

"Perfectly so. He loved her well—loves her still with all his heart."

"Was that attachment sanctioned by Sir George?"

"It was virtually, although we never but once had any conversation upon the subject, and that was scarcely in a serious strain, although amply sufficient to convince me that Sir George would place no impediment in the way of their union. He said he had the happiness of his dear child too much at heart to control her affections, so long as they were directed to a worthy object."

"You swear to these words distinctly, Mr. Percy?"

"I do."

"My lord and gentlemen of the jury, how does that tally with the will which Sir George Rankley is said to have made in favour of the prosecutor in this case?"

All saw the force of this observation, and the judge was observed to take a note of it.

"State what circumstances broke up this desirable state of things Mr. Percy."

"Since the residence o Bernard Varley with Sir George Rankley, there seemed a kind of waning of that hearty good feeling with which the deceased gentleman was in the habit of treating me and my son. Finally, I received a very insulting letter indeed, purporting to be from Sir George."

"How did it insult you?"

"The substance of it was, that I wished to repair my shattered fortunes by a union between my son and his daughter. I believe I wrote an angry reply."

"In what state, then, were your circumstances?"

"I thought myself for days and weeks after that letter a rich man; for I was not aware that an agent in London, in whom I had confided much, had absconded."

"But if Sir George wrote the letter you speak of, he must have been aware of it?"

"Certainly. I suspect strongly that he never wrote it, but that it was the production of some enemy of me and mine, who by some means had acquired the information earlier than I, and was desirous to use it in effecting a breach between Sir George and I."

"Proceed, sir."

"An angry correspondence ensued during which I sent my son a considerable distance from home; for I was so vexed at the insinuation contained in the first letter, that I would not allow him even to be on the spot. Sir George and I finally fought a duel, which was fomented and got up by Bernard Varley."

"Do you swear that solemnly?"

"I do. The quarrel would, in fact, have been made up, even on the ground but for him."

The counsel paused to allow these words to have their effect upon the minds of the jury before he said,—

"Now, Mr. Percy, on your oath, did or did not your son hear from you the state of your finances before the death of Sir George Rankley?"

"On my oath, he did not."

"Then he still thought you a rich man?"

"He did; and it was some days after the death of Sir George that he, hearing that Miranda was destitute, by the appropriation of all that should have been hers by Bernard Varley, implored me to take her to my heart, and treating her as a child of my own, not to let her know the want of those comforts and elegancies of life she had been accustomed to. Then—then——"

Here Mr. Percy became much affected, and the counsel said, kindly,—

"Take your time, sir; pray, take your time."

"Then I told my boy that I was as destitute as she was, but that I would beg for her from door to door, rather than she should ever want."

"Oh, my lord and gentlemen," said the counsel, elevating his hands, "what becomes now of the motives of this young man, to murder Sir George Rankley? What becomes of the pretended writing in the tablets now? I have nothing more to ask you, Mr. Percy, except if that is or is not your son's handwriting?"

The tablets were handed to Mr. Percy, open at the page containing the memorandum.

"It is a very good imitation," he said, "but I will swear these words were never written by my son."

"That will do, sir. You can go down."

CHAPTER XLV.

MIRANDA'S ELOQUENT APPEAL.—DOUBTS AND FEARS.—THE CAUSE OF THE TRIAL.

THE evidence of Mr. Percy had been so decidedly in favour of the prisoner, that Mr. Anderson whispered to Miranda,—

"Hope and expect the best, Miranda. Things could not be going on more satisfactorily than they are."

"Thank Heaven," said Miranda, in a low voice.

"Miranda Rankley," said the crier of the court, and Miranda started up exclaiming,—

"I am here."

"This way," said Mr. Anderson, as he handed her into the witness box. Every eye in the court was fixed upon her, and when she slowly removed her veil, and her lovely countenance could be seen, there was a murmur of astonishment at her rare beauty, brightened as it now was by a gentle flush of excitement.

She was sworn—and then there was a death-like silence for a moment or two before the counsel, in a kind considerate tone, said,—

"You are acquainted with the prisoner at the bar, Miss Rankley?"

Miranda turned her eyes upon Rowland, and in a voice which reached every heart she said—

"Rowland Percy is my affianced husband."

" You are aware of the crime of which he stands now charged. Pray relate to us what you know of the circumstaces connected with this inquiry."

" We were happy once," said Miranda in a low tone, of such exquisite pathos and feeling, that it brought tears into many eyes, "very—very happy—I was happy in my father's love, and in his approval of him I had chosen for my companion through life; but then Bernard Varley came, and all was changed. Soon—too soon I found that, from some most inexplicable cause my father could not resent even insults from that man. He obtruded upon me his hideous attentions, and when I complained, my father could do nothing. Then, for why I could not discover, Rowland was banished from the house, and there succeeded a period of uneasines and restless conjecture, which the few words only which my father ever said to me upon the subject did not alleviate.

" That was all before the duel, with the exception that once I was compelled to implore my father to send me somewhere from home, to escape the importunities of Bernard Varley, and then he wept and said he would do something soon to relieve me from him.

" Then, one morning, I was awakened by my maid, who, with cries and screams told me that Mr. Percy, and my father were fighting a duel. In a few minutes I rushed from the house, and found my father lying bleeding on the ground. My feelings I will not attempt to describe—that were impossible. The remainder seemed like a waking vision. I could not rest, and after taking leave of my father for the night, I sat for some hours in my own room deaf to all the solicitations of my maid to retire to rest. I heard the clock strike twelve and a desire came strongly across my mind to see my father again before I attempted to procure any repose.

" Believing no person but the nurse to be in his chamber, I crept from my own room, and crossing the corridor opened the door of my father's chamber, when to my surprise I saw there Bernard Varley, who made every effort to stop me from entering the room, but I persisted, and finally sat down by the bed-side of what I thought my seeping father."

Miranda paused —but she shed no tears,—and after a deep sigh continued :—

" That sleep was the sleep of death. My father was no more, and I was watching a lifeless form."

Miranda again paused and the counsel said,—

" Did you see any one in the room, or become conscious in any way of the presence of any one but yourself while you thus watched?"

" No no."

" What followed?"

" I can scarcely tell. My brain seemed on fire. I raised an instant alarm, and then I saw Rowland Percy surrounded by the servants."

" That is all you can tell the jury of the actual circumstances which occurred that night?"

" That is all."

" Have you since then had any conversation with the prosecutor in this case ?"

" Yes Bernard Varley has sought several interviews with me since that fearful night, and the purport of them all has been to promise Rowland Percy's acquittal if I would give him, Varley, my hand. But I knew that Rowland Percy would rather suffer death, although innocent, than purchase life on such terms."

" A thousand times rather—a thousand times," cried Rowland.

"I knew it said Miranda, "I knew it,'

" You will swear," said the counsel, "that he said he could procure the prisoner's acquittal ?"

" I will," replied Miranda. "He even tauntingly admitted his innocence to me saying at the same time, that I might state so much if I pleased, but no one would believe me."

" You have a full and entire c onfidence in the innocence of the prisoner ?

" As full and entire as I have in the villany of his accusers. Thinks any one here that I, loving my father with an affection that knew no bounds, could thus step between justice and his murderer? Rowland Percy is innocent. Let Heaven in its own good time discover the guilty."

"I have no more questions to ask," said the counsel; "perhaps you have?" turning to the counsel for the prosecution.

"No," he said, "I shall not interfere with the witnesses for the defence at all."

"Very well—then we need detain you no longer, Miss Rankley."

Miranda was very doubtful in her own heart that the ordeal was passed, for she had never imagined she could have gone through it as she had done, although she felt immeasurably dissatisfied with herself, and thought she might have said more yet for Rowland.

This feeling she communicated to Mr Anderson, who replied,—

"No—Miranda, you said quite enough. Any stronger or more energetic advocacy of him would have been injudicious. You must see that the whole question at issue turns upon the credibility or otherwise of the evidence of Twitter."

"Yes—yes." said Miranda. "Oh! how deeply, terribly perjured is that man."

Mr. Anderson was now called at his own request, for he wished to make one statement, which he did to the following effect.

"Ever since Sir George Rankley took possession of the Grange estates, I have been his legal adviser, and had the preparation of every legal document with the one exception of the monstrously unnatural will which is produced by Mr. Varley I have with me now the rough draft of a will which Sir George gave me more than a year ago wherein occurs this passage—

"'To my beloved child, Miranda Rankley, I give and bequeath the whole of my real estate, to have and to hold at her will and pleasure, and may Heaven send her h alth, happiness, and long life to enjoy it, with her father's blessing.'

"These I will swear were Sir George's own words, written after his dictation; and judge, therefore, of my surprise when another legal gentleman produces so very contrary a document."

"I have no question to ask you, Mr. Anderson," said the counsel.

"You are the solicitor for the defence," said the counsel for the prosecution.

"I am, sir," said Mr. Anderson, "and I trust in Heaven I may always be as now, on the side of innocence."

"I thought my learned friend," said Rowland's counsel sarcastically, "was not going to interfere in any way with the witnesses for the defence."

"Your learned friend," said the other, with some show of bitterness, "only thought it a little strange that the solicitor for the defence should be made a witness on the trial."

"We seek the truth," replied Rowland's counsel, "and come it from friend or foe, it is to us as welcome as the sunlight from heaven."

The next witness called was a man who answered to the name of Job Jackson, and who had all the appearance of a London ruffian, of the lowest grade, so much so indeed, that the counsell looked visibly chagrined at having him at all; but he soon became reconciled to Job's appearance, when he remarked the effect it had upon the nervous system of Twitter, who, at the mere announcement of the name, started up, and when he saw the witness enter the box, he showed such signs of trepidation, that all the connsel's fears about what Job Jackson should say, being believed by the jury, vanished before such confirmatory symptoms from Twitter himself.

"Now. Mr. Job Jackson," said the counsel, "do you know Samuel Twitter?"

"I should rather think I did," replied the witness.

"What do you know of him?"

"He and I were on the dodge in London some years ago."

"On the what?" said the judge.

"The dodge, my lord," said the counsel.

"But I want to know what that is?"

There was a suppressed laugh in the court, and Mr. Jackson cried,—

"Bless your innocence, old gentleman, being on the dodge means, a-going on he grand cadge."

"Well, I'm no wiser now," said the judge, "I don't understand the witness a bit."

"My lord," said the counsel, "I rather think he means that he and Samuel Twitter, the principal witness in this case, were in that condition in London, which induced them to seek the means of subsistence, without being particular as to the honesty of them."

"And that's being on the dodge, and the grand what, did he say?" remarked the judge, very carefully making a note of the same, to the great amusement of Job Jackson, who winked at the crowd, and in a variety of ways disturbed the gravity of almost every indifferent spectator of the trial.

"Now, Tell me," said the counsel to Mr. Jackson, "was this same Samuel Twitter ever suspected of a theft?"

"In conrse!"

"Can you see him in court?"

"I should think so—how do, Sammy—how do—ta! ta! How *air* you?"
Great laughter was excited at this, and Twitter, in a half frantic voice, said—

"I don't know you. Never saw you. I thought you were transported years ago."

"So I was, Sammy, but I comed back in consikence o' my uncommon genteel behaviour."

"Can you specify, Mr. Jackson, any special act of iniquity perpetrated by Samuel Twitter?"

"Can I speechify what?"

"I mean what did he do in the robbery line?"

"Oh, why, he was always a grabbing of what ever comed to hand, he was. He'd think no more o' boning your wig, or the old gentleman's specs up there, than I would—that is, I mean, than I'd think o' bringing 'em back agin."

"Then you imagine Mr. Twitter to be rather a bad character, Mr. Jackson?"

"Rather on the brink o' that ere. You doesn't look well, Sammy."

"Curses on you," muttered Twitter.

"You must tell us of some one particular thing that Samuel Twitter has done," said the counsel.

"Oh, why, he used get places in families, and lay his hands on all sorts o' things, and whenever there was a row, he used to put a spoon in one of the poor servant's boxes—he used."

"It's false— false," cried Twitter.

"Sammy—Sammy, take it easy," said Mr. Jackson.

CHAPTER XLVI.

A NEW WITNESS.—THE CROSS-EXAMINATION OF A GENTLEMAN AT LARGE.—
TWITTER'S OLD FRIEND.

Notwithstanding Mr. Jackson's recommendation to Twitter to "take it easy," he was so exasperated at the revelations his old companion in guilt was making, that had he possessed any means of inflicting a deadly injury upon him, he would have done so on the spot without scruple.

The counsel for Rowland was quite delighted with Twitter's rage, for it offered the very best confirmation of the truth of Mr. Job Jackson's statements that he could possibly wish for.

"Was he ever apprehended on any charge?"

"Yes—a dozen times. Sometimes he got off by crying and fainting away, and sometimes the beak wouldn't be gammoned no how, and guved him three blessed months of it."

" Was he ever committed for trial ?"

" Once—yes—but the old blokes as was on the grand jury did what they calls hignorein the bill.''

" You are quite sure of his identity ?"

" Don't I know Sammy's dentity ? I should think so," was Mr. Jackson's pithy reply.

" Really, my lord," said the counsel for the prosecution, " this witness, I beg to remark, is a most extraordinary one, and although I certainly did say that I would not interfere with the witnesses for the defence, yet the extraordinary course my learned friend has pursued in bringing forward this man, absolves me from such a promise, and I insist upon asking him a question or two."

" As you please," said Rowland's counsel.

The counsel for the prosecution then assumed a very severe aspect, and bending his brows upon Mr. Jackson, he said—

" Now, my fine fellow——"

" Thank you," said Job, promptly, " the same to you."

" Do not let us have any impertinence, sir," said the angry counsel, turning rather red, for he began to have a disagreeable suspicion that his cross-examination of Mr. Jackson might not result in anything very agreeable to himself.

" Very good," said Job Jackson, making a movement to leave the box.

" Stay where you are, sir," roared the counsel.

" Oh, I thought as you said as you'd done with your impudence," said Job.

This was almost too much for the gravity of the judge, and a slight smile forced itself into notice in spite of him.

" Who are you, Mr. Jackson ?" was the next question.

" Job Jackson," was the brief reply.

" But I mean what are you ?"

" I aint a lawyer—I tries to earn a honest penny, I does."

" Then how comes it you are so very intimate with Samuel Twitter, o whom you have given us so entertaining an account ?"

" Ah, that was long ago—I spoees as you've picked up with him since."

" Come, come, this won't do."

" I thought it wouldn't.   You're a out-and-out oracle, you are."

" On your oath, sir, now tell me—have you ever been apprehended for felony ?"

" Felony ?"

" Yes, sir.   Let us have no prevarication—felony, I mean, and felony I said."

" Why, you know wirtuous people is always a getting suspected."

" Answer me yes or no."

" Which would you like best ?   You look like a comfortable old pump, and I'll oblige you if I can."

" I appeal to the court," cried the counsel, " I really must appeal to the court."

" Do," said Job, " but don't over exert yourself.   You'll be ill arter this, I know."

" You must answer the questions put to you," said the judge. " We cannot have the time of the court wasted in this way."

" Now, sir, were you ever in custody on a charge of felony or not ?''

" Yes, I was.   Sammy, there, is such a artful card he'd bring a sucking dove into trouble.   He's been my ruin, he has.   O Sammy ! Sammy ! you *his* a wretch and no mistake !"

" I have done," said the counsel. " This witness has been brought from London, for no other purpose than to throw discredit upon the sworn testimo ny of Samuel Twitter, by stating that he has been accused of felony.   Now, my lord, and gentlemen of the jury, what face can my learned friend put on this matter when, from the mouth of his own witness I have proved a similar allegation as regards him. I submit that this man is quite unworthy of belief, and his evidence falls to the ground."

" Nay," said Rowland's counsel. " Two blacks don't make a white, and you may prove Mr. Jackson as bad as you like without cleansing Samuel Twitter from the spots on his character."

" I submit——"

" This is quite irregular," said the judge.

" Call Martha Monkton," said the counsel.

This was the nurse who had been with Sir George on the evening of the duel, and the first question put to her was,—

" Are you a nurse by profession ?"

" I am," was the answer.

" Are you accustomed to sitting up at nights with invalids ?"

" Of course."

" And you don't go to sleep, leaving your patients to take care of themselves ?"

" I go to sleep, sir! I should think I never did such a thing in all my life."

" You recollect nursing Sir George Rankley ?"

" Certainly, I do."

" Then you were not particularly anxious to be relieved from your duties by Mr. Varley and Mr. Twitter ?"

" No, I wasn't; but it was very kind."

" And very extraordinary ?"

" Yes."

" Call Mr. Querral. I have done with you, my good woman."

Querral, the attorney, entered the witness-box, with an air, as much as to say, you won't get anything to serve your turn out of me—oh, no.

Rowland's counsel, however, had been well instructed by Mr. Anderson, in the man he had to deal with, and, as he only wanted to elicit one fact from him, he determined so to nail him to that, that he should not have the smallest opportunity of escaping from answering it.

" Your name is Querral ?" he said.

" Yes."

" You are an attorney in this city ?"

" I am."

" You made a will for Sir George Rankley ?"

" I did."

" Who gave you the instructions ?"

" Who—gave—me—"

" Who gave you the instructions, sir ?" thundered the counsel. " Answer me at once, who gave you the instructions for the will ?"

" Mr. Varley."

Down sat the counsel, for he had got just the answer he wished, his object being to lead the minds of the jury to the supposition that Varley had all along had an eye to the property, and was a likely man to concoct plots and conspiracies to further his own ends.

" Is—is that all ?" said Mr. Querral, who had prepared himself for cross-examination, in which he intended to show how very clever he was at doubling, turning, shifting, and equivocating.

" That is all," said the counsel.

With a disappointed air Querral stepped from the witness-box.

Several influential gentlemen of the county were called, who, one and all, gave Rowland the very highest character for humanity, and the best feelings that could appertain to human nature.

Miranda felt her heart heave in her bosom as she heard the kindly sentiments which were uttered concerning Rowland, and clasping her hands, she silently breathed a prayer to Heaven to save the innocent.

There was a pause now of some minutes' duration, during the continuance of which the counsel for Rowland and Mr. Anderson earnestly consulted together.

The subject of this conference was the probability or non-probability of the mysterious man coming forward who had suggested the question which had had so great an effect on Bernard Varley, and effect which could not be carried out for want of further information.

" Shall we not attempt an appeal to him if he be in the court?' said the counsel.

" It can do no harm," said Mr. Anderson. " Sometimes, on the spur of a moment a man's good feelings may get the better even of all prudential motives, and he may come forward."

" As you say, it can do no harm. I will take upon myself to call him, and do you watch the effect it has upon Bernard Varley."

" I will."

The counsel then rose, and then, in a loud clear voice, which was distinctly heard by every one, and produced no little surprise, said,—

" I call solemnly and earnestly upon the man who met Varley on the bridle path between the city of York and the Grange, to come forward if he be here, and declare before God and man what he knows of this transaction."

Varley sprung to his feet, and his eyes looked like those of a maniac as he expected each moment to be blasted by a sight of the being who had taken such a strong hold of his imagination, and who, he verily believed, could reveal his most hidden actions.

There was a profound silence in the court, for all seemed to expect something strange as the result of the singular call made by the counsel on one he could not name.

Second after second passed slowly away, and there was no response to the call.

The counsel shook his head and sat down, while a look of disappointment came over the face of Mr. Anderson, who had entertained sanguine hopes that at the last moment the mysterious stranger might make his appearance.

Each moment that passed seemed to give Varley new life, and when he saw the counsel sit down, as if giving up all hope of the appearance of the witness, he, Varley, likewise sunk into his seat with a feeling of inexpressible relief.

Ned Witlet was in the court, but as we know, he knew nothing which could be at all beneficial to Rowland, of whose guilt or innocence he might, like others, entertain an opinion, but could have no positive knowledge. Accident alone had given him the power he held over the mind of Varley, and he felt that should he come forward at his own personal risk, and do all he could do, namely, blacken the character of Twitter, he should lose all the power which might eventually be exerted much to the benefit of Miranda, without materially advancing the interest of the prisoner.

Everybody now felt that the case was concluded for the defence, leaving the direct sworn evidence of Bernard Varley and Twitter untouched, except very remotely in the way of character.

The counsel for the prosecution had a right to reply if he chose to exercise it ; but he looked up to the judge, and shook his head, for he was, in his own mind, notwithstanding the numerous aggravations he had endured in the course of his cross-examination, quite satisfied that the case for the prosecution stood firm and unshaken, as not a tittle of the evidence had been shaken, except in the sworn opinion of Mr. Percy, that the words in the tablets were not in his son's handwriting ; and, after all, that was but a collateral piece of evidence, which might have been altogether given up by the prosecution without injuring the case in the least.

CHAPTER XLVII.

THE JUDGE'S SUMMING UP.—THE JURY AND THE VERDICT.

ALL eyes were now most anxiously turned towards the judge, whose duty it was to sum up the case and charge the jury. A profound stillness reigned in the court, for although the professional men present had no sort of difficulty in predicting to each other upon what points the judge must of necessity dwell, and what would be the verdict of the jury— but we will not anticipate.

The judge commenced his address in a calm, low, dispassionate tone of voice, now and then only referring to his notes, when he wished to quote particular words which had been used by any of the numerous witnesses who had been under examination.

"Gentlemen of the jury," he said, "this important case, you must perceive, entirely rests upon the degree of credit you feel disposed to give to the evidence of Mr. Bernard Varley and Samuel Twitter. I cannot myself see anything in the depositions of the other witnesses but what may be considered as decidedly in favour of the prisoner at the bar; but, gentlemen, in a court of justice we must not forget that the sworn statement of one

No. 22.

person, always provided that person be one worthy of belief, that he saw a crime committed, is of more importance than the statements of hundreds who may consider the commission of the crime by the man charged with it as improbable and contrary to the usual tenour of his habits.

"I am far, very far, from wishing to prejudice the prisoner at the bar, but we have frequent instances of such anomalies in human nature as persons upon whose integrity we would have staked our fortunes, committing thefts, and persons upon upon whose humanity we have the fullest reliance, becoming guilty of dreadful cruelties.

"In point of fact, gentlemen of the jury, the evidence for the prosecution in this case, I grieve to say, has gone to establish the fact that the prisoner committed a murder, and the evidence for the defence has only proved that to the best of everybody's knowledge, nobody thought he was the sort of person to do such a thing.

"You are all, gentlemen, residents in this city, and familiar with the parties concerned in this most singular case, but I pray you to dismiss from your minds utterly and entirely any previous feelings or affections which you may have in connexion with the individuals affected by this investigation.

"It appears by the evidence which has been produced, that an intimacy sprung up between the families of the Percys and the Rankleys, which promised to result in a marriage which would unite their interests very closely, but that some pecuniary difficulties which came upon Mr. Percy caused a cessation of that friendly intercourse. One mysterious circumstance connected with this part of the business is that, from the evidence, it would appear that this pecuniary difficulty was known to Sir George Rankley before it was known to him, whom it more nearly concerned, namely, Mr. Percy himself. How Sir George arrived at that knowledge, and through whom he obtained it, I cannot pretend to say; but at all events, the result seems to have been some very insulting insinuations with respect to the Percys' motives in wishing the marriage, which insulting insinuations terminated in a duel, from which Sir George Rankley received a wound, that we are assured upon respectable medical evidence could not have caused his demise, and hence we are compelled to look for other causes for that melancholy event.

"A series of circumstances now occurred on the evening of the same day, on which it appears this duel was fought, that terminate in one point—that point being the apprehension of the prisoner at the bar, on the charge of murdering Sir George Rankley.

"Now, gentlemen, that the prisoner was at the Grange, on the night in question —that he was there secretly and in disguise—is admitted, and I must say that even all that is quite compatible with innocence; for it does not follow that a man has committed a murder, because he is placed in circumstances so to do if he feels nclined.

"We have the evidence of the nurse, who states that Sir George Rankley was alive at twelve o'clock, and that she wanted no assistance whatever in watching his sick chamber; but that Mr. Varley had rendered such assistance, and thinking it very kind of him, she accepted it and left her charge. You see, gentlemen, that after that, the nurse has nothing to do with the affair, and the living Sir George Rankley is left in the hands of Bernard Varley and Samuel Twitter, they having to account for him, until he was found dead by his daughter Miranda some time afterwards.

"Now, gentlemen, you will see that the whole weight of this case rests upon the shoulders of these two men. They accepted the trust of tending a living man, and they are placed in a situation, consequently, which compels them to account for how he became a dead one!

"You will perceive, gentlemen, that the whole case narrows itself to this small compass, and comes to this, that either Bernard Varley and Samuel Twitter, or one of them, committed the murder, or they have accurately told you who really did so.

"These two witnesses with great exactness, and tallying well together, describe to us first the supposed mysterious appearance of the spectre on the staircase, which it is admitted on all hands was the prisoner at the bar—then the incident of the light nearly expiring, and Bernard Varley's absence from the room to procure a fresh one, thus leaving Samuel Twitter with the still living Sir George, and throwing upon him the onus of accounting for his death. This he does most frightfully—circumstantially; he describes the prisoner at the bar, to whom he distinctly swears, entering the room—glancing around him, as if to see that he was alone, and then with awful deliberation, smothering the unhappy Sir George Rankley with a pillow.

"Now, gentlemen, if we choose to receive this account as it is given us, it throws an everlasting slur upon this man, Samuel Twitter, whose cowardice must have been great indeed, to allow him to become a passive spectator of such a scene. Moreover, it is to be wondered at, that his fear did not induce a cry or a scream, which would have frightened the murderer from his purpose; but instead of that Samuel Twitter, being at first hidden in some strange manner, by the bed furniture, comfortably faints away, leaving his master, mind you, gentlemen, quite at the mercy of this strange appearance; which, however, he had previous to such fainting, ascertained not to be supernatural at all! But we, nevertheless, have this testimony upon oath, and it is for you to believe that witness or not, according to the best of your judgments. If you have any doubt with regard to any portion of his evidence, it is your duty to give the prisoner the full benefit of such doubt, and acquit him; but if you believe the witness Twitter, you can have no course open to you, but to bring in a verdict of guilty.

"I regretted that the counsel for the prosecution in this case thought it necessary to search for some motives for the prisoner's commission of the crime with which he stands charged, for, gentlemen, if all the counsel in the world were to prove to you that no imaginable motive could have acted upon his mind, and yet you believed the evidence of Samuel Twitter, you could not help convicting him.

"I may likewise add that his attribution of motives to the prisoner has signally failed, and recoiled on the prosecution, for the witness, Bernard Varley, seems the only man who has benefited by the decease of Sir George Rankley.

"With regard to the credibility of the evidence of Samuel Twitter, you must bear in mind, gentleman, that this could not be a concocted plan on the parts of Varley and Twitter to ruin the prisoner at the bar, for by the evidence on both sides, and by the instructions of the prisoner's counsel, his visit to the Grange is represented as a most secret one, he being thought to be a long way off from this part of the country.

"Evidence has been produced to show that Twitter was but an indifferent character, and if the allegations against him of the witness Job Jackson, who describes himself and Twitter as being upon some expedition, or under some circumstances called the 'dodge,' be true, they tend to prove Samuel Twitter as despicable a character as ever came into a court of justice; but, gentlemen, if Samuel Twitter's evidence were to be rejected because he has committed felonies and misdemeanours, the very evidence of Job Jackson accusing him of such lapses of morality, must fall to the ground from the same cause, leaving us without any allegation at all against Samuel Twitter. As thus, gentlemen:—If B is unworthy of belief because he has done something that A charges him with, A's charge is not to be believed against B, because he, A, admits himself to have done the same thing, and B's evidence upon a distinct matter stands untouched."

The jury looked very hard at each other as the judge put this case, and a doubtful mystified expression sat upon their faces, for A and B had quite bewildered them.

"I repeat, therefore, gentlemen," continued the judge, "that you must judge this case entirely upon the evidence of Samuel Twitter, who you must either disbelieve entirely, and acquit the prisoner, or believe wholly, and at once convict him.

"With respect to the tablets which have been produced in evidence, I do not lay much stress upon them. If indeed you can come to any conclusion that the words there set down, and which seem to hint at the murder, are in the han writing of the prisoner, it would be a circumstance tending to strengthen the credibility of Samuel Twitter's evidence; but on the contrary, if you think that those words were forged, in order to make another link in the chain of evidence against the prisoner, I should direct an acquittal, for such a circumstance would throw strong doubts upon the whole of the evidence for the prosecution, and induce a belief that Bernard Varley and Samuel Twitter were in a conspiracy together to destroy the prisoner at the bar.

"Some of the proceedings of the prisoner's counsel I must own myself completely at a loss to understand. I allude to the calling of a person with whose name even it appears the learned counsel was unacquainted, to depose to some facts with which he appears equally unacquainted. Some mystery seems to be lurking somewhere in this business, as was evident from the extraordinary agitation of the witness Varley, but what that mystery is, I cannot take upon myself to say, or even in the most distant manner conjecture.

"I pray, gentlemen of the jury, that Heaven may guide you in your deliberations, and that you may be enabled to come to a correct conclusion with regard to the credibility or non-credibility of the witness Samuel Twitter."

The judge ceased, and the jury sat for a few moments looking at each other in silence. The most intense excitement showed itself upon every countenance in the court.

"Would you like to retire, gentlemen?" said the judge.

The foreman whispered to his neighbour, and the whisper went round. That whisper was,—

"I think he's done. The idea of smothering a gentleman with his own pillow!"

"But what about that A and B," remarked one; "I don't quite understand that?"

"It means that if the prisoner didn't do the murder, who did?" said another.

"Oh!"

"Gentlemen of the jury, are you agreed?" said the clerk of the arraigns.

"Yes," said the foreman.

"Do you find the prisoner at the bar guilty or not guilty?"

"Guilty!"

CHAPTER XLVIII.

THE SENTENCE.—MIRANDA'S DECLARATION.—VARLEY'S DANGER FROM THE CROWD.—
THE RIOT.

FOR a few moments after the verdict was pronounced by the foreman of the jury, the dense crowd in the court looked in each other's faces, as if seeking for some confirmation of the dreadful verdict from each other. The awful word guilty, appeared, as it were, to hang in the very atmosphere of the place, exciting a stunning deadening influence upon the hearts of all who heard it.

The foreman of the jury still stood facing the clerk of the arraigns, and it appeared as if he too felt almost doubtful if he had been heard aright, for in a very low voice, but a very clear one, he again repeated the word—

"Guilty!"

The sound of his voice acted like the removal of a spell from the faculties of all present, and that confused murmur arose which is also produced from a multitude of persons, when they are released from any circumstances which have claimed their attention, and wrapped them in silence, either voluntary or compulsory for a time.

Several voices cried—"shame—shame—not guilty—not guilty!"

The officers looked confused, for those sounds arose from various parts of the court, and they knew not who to pounce upon for the breach of decorum.

Then suddenly, like a flash of light, uprose Miranda, and casting aside her veilt she lifted up her hands to Heaven, in such an attitude of solemn abjuration, that every sound was in a moment hushed, and all waited in breathless expectation for the words which were about to issue from her lips.

Twice the judge opened his mouth as if he would have stopped her, but as often, he produced no sound ; and finally, he sank back in his chair as though resolved to hear her.

"I appeal to Heaven," she said, "against human error, and human iniquity—to the spirit of him whose death is the subject of inquiry, I now appeal, and oh God, let it not be in vain—save the innocent—he is not guilty—he is not guilty—he is not guilty!"

These words were pronounced with so much earnest solemnity, and such a tono of soul-felt truth, that the feelling of the crowd, before excited in Rowland's favour, became doubly so, and had not the judge then risen on the moment, doubtless a great outcry would have followed Miranda's words.

"Officers," said the judge, in a voice that rung loud and clear through the court, "remove that lady."

"No, no," cried Rowland, "she will now be still. If I am really standing on the brink of eternity, for a crime of which I am innocent, do not deprive me of the sight of those whom I love, and may not long look upon."

"We cannot be interrupted," said the judge. "God knows I have no desire to oppress the last hours of the prisoner, but we must not forget that this is a court of justice."

The officers, who had made a move, towards Miranda, seemed now to take this as a permission for her to stay, and they fell back in their former position, leaving her unmolested.

"Prisoner at the bar," said the judge, in a voice that slightly trembled, "have you anything to say why I should not pronounce the sentence of death against you?"

All eyes were turned upon Rowland, who, drawing himself proudly up, while a slight flush of colour visited his check, and then as suddenly left it pale as before said, in a mild firm voice,—

"I have something to say, why I should not be unjustly condemned to death—it may be that the false witnesses against me will prevail—it may be that the most deep-laid awful plot that ever sprung up, like a rank weed in the brain of man, may fully succeed—for a time—for a time."

He cast his eyes upon Bernard Varley, as he said these words, and the villain shrunk back as if Rowland's gaze carried death with it.

"I say for a time," continued the unjustly condemned ; "for as sure as that to morrow's sun will light the world—as sure as that the bleak winds of winter will succeed the balmy gales of summer—as sure as there is a world beyond the grave, and a God in heaven, the blood of the murdered will rise up in judgment against the real murderer, and justice will be done. I shall be sleeping the long sleep of death. Those who love me will perchance have all gone to their last calm resting-place, where sorrow ceases, and the stilled heart knows no further anguish. Some there may be of those who hear the tale of my accusation and my death, who will live to see the issue of this dark mysterious story ; but be it early, or be it late, the day of retribution will come at last. And long, long perchance, before some human tribunal shall pronounce the doom of death upon the head of him who now hugs himself that an innocent man shall suffer for his crime, the torture—the exquisite agony—the hell of his own conscience shall begin, and as a double murderer shall he walk about, accursed ! accursed ! accursed !"

The blood retreated from the heart of Bernard Varley, and then flew back with a frightful gush, as Rowland's words came upon his ears, like the voice of judgment from Heaven.   He rose from his seat and staggered forward a pace or two.   Then as he found he could not get out of the court from the immense crowd which hemmed him in, he said,—

"Air, air!   Help—I suffocate—save me—air, air!"

The heat was, indeed, oppressive, and many voices joined in the same cry, but above them all rose the clear voice of Miranda, sweet as a silver bell, and making itself, in the excitement that gave it energy, heard to all above the din.

A judgment! a judgment!" she cried, "'Tis Bernard Varley who is my father's murderer!"

The crowd seemed to want but this as a watchword, and a hundred voices immediately shouted—

"Varley is the murderer!   Varley is the murderer!"

A rush was made to where he was standing, and but for the timely intervention of the officers, who threw themselves in a body between him and his assailants, he would, no doubt, in the excitement of the moment, have met with some serious injury.   As it was, he was saved, and the judge said—

"This is too much.   Officers, I must have the court cleared, and as many of the ringleaders in this tumult as you can secure, placed in confinement."

There was something this time in the tone and manner of the judge which convinced the crowd that he was serious, and almost as frightful a rush ensued to get out of the court as before had taken place to get into it.   In obedience to a signal from the judge, the officers did not impede any one in leaving, so that in few moments more than two-thirds of those who had made the place so uncomfortably full were outside.   The doors were then closed immediately, and comparative comfort and quiet reigned in the court.

The judge glanced at Rowland, as much as to say, have you finished? and the young man understanding so, said,—

"I have done.   I can but assert my innocence, call upon Heaven to witness it, and implore that in its mercy it may yet save me from an unjust death."

" It is my duty," said the judge, "to pass the sentence of the law upon you.'

He then sat down a moment, and there was an awful period of suspense, Miranda had buried her face in her hands, and appeared to be quite unnerved, while Mr. Percy looked at his son as well as he could though the blinding tears that rolled from his eyes, and which he was unable to control.

Bernard Varley had shrunk again back to his seat, and pale, ghastly, and trembling, was waiting the conclusion of the scene of woe and excitement.

There was a short whispered conference then between the judge and the mayer of York; after which the former placed something on his bench before him. It was the black cap!

Most reluctant did he appear to put it on, but at last, with a desperate determination, he placed it on his head. A shudder passed through every heart; and then in a voice of much emotion, the learned judge commenced,—

" Prisoner at the bar,—You have had a long and, I think   am justified in saying a most patient trial, and I do not see how, consistent with their oaths, the jury could return any other verdict than that they have returned.   Certain distinct facts have been distinctly sworn to, and either these witnesses are perjured, or you are, as you have been this day declared to be by the jury, a guilty man.

" My duty is now a simple, although, to me, a most grievous one. It is to pass upon you the last sentence of the law—it is my duty, and I must not shrink from it.

" There have certainly seemed, during the progress of this case, some extraordinary circumstances, and, upon the whole, I think I may call it one of the most singular cases that ever came under my notice. Nevertheless, I do not see how the evidence against you is to be got over, and we are bound to take facts instead of, and even in strong contradiction to all probabilities. I cannot help thus concurring in the verdict of the jury, and I grieve to say, that I dare not hold out to you the slightest hopes mercy on this side of the grave.

"The sentence of the court is, that you be taken now to the place from whenc you came, and that on Tuesday morning next you be removed to the place of common execution, and there hung by the neck until you be dead. May God have mercy upon your soul!"

The voice of the judge was scarcely audible as he pronounced the last few words, and when he had done, he sunk back in his chair evidently deeply affected.

Miranda could stand this scene no longer, but springing from where she was towards the dock, she stretched out her arms to her lover, crying,—

"Rowland—Rowland! They shall not—they cannot kill you. You are innocent!"

"Miranda!" was all he could say, and reaching as far from the dock as he could, he just succeeded in clasping her hands.

One of the turnkeys advanced officiously to pull Rowland back, but the judge said suddenly,—

"Officer, let the prisoner be. God help us all! we need not deprive him of one moment's joy."

"But he is innocent—he is innocent!" said Miranda. "He, Rowland Percy, murder my father? 'Tis too absurd—you cannot believe it!"

The judge rose, and with tears in his eyes, turned to leave the bench.

"Stay, oh, stay!" cried Miranda—"but a moment—another word and I am done. Let him live a month—a week—Oh, God! be merciful."

The judge shook his head, and with a heavy heart passed out of the court.

"Come," said one of the gaolers, "we can't wait here all night."

"Farewell, dear—dear Miranda!" said Rowland. "Hope still—hope still!"

"Hope, Rowland—oh, what hope have I yet to cling to?"

"Hush—hush! it may be, I shall yet escape a scaffold, Miranda."

"Escape."

"Hush, we shall meet again. 'Tis a privilege not denied to the condemned to see those they love, and towards whom their hearts yearn, ere this mortal life closes on them for ever. We shall meet again, dearest."

"I—I will be with you, Rowland. They shall not part us now. They shall kill me ere they part us, dear Rowland. I will cling to you, though the whole world should turn against you and call you guilty."

"I know you would, my Miranda—I know you would, and hence it is that death has no sting—the grave no victory. Farew llaew ier a brief space."

"I cannot—cannot leave you."

"But you must," said the gaoler, "this won't do. Come, young sir, we can't wait."

"One moment. Miranda, do not think too much of the mere passing pang that will take me somewhat earlier from a world that, after all, is but an abiding place for a brief season—we shall meet again, dearest, never—never to part."

"We shall, Rowland; but yet my heart is breaking!,"

"For—for my sake, Miranda, preserve more courage—I—I need support."

Miranda clung to him with a convulsive energy that he could not without actual violence free himself from, and with a deep sigh he turned to his weeping father, and said,—

"Father, take her—comfort her—love her, for your poor innocent Rowland's sake."

The gaoler pushed slightly against Rowland's arm, which nearly deprived Miranda of her hold of him, and she screamed loudly.

"Heaven help me!" cried Rowland; "I cannot bear this!" and disengaging himself from her frantic clutches, he added, "father! father! to you I consign my heart's best treasure! 'tis the only legacy your poor Rowland has to leave!" He resigned himself to the gaoler and officers, who quickly hurried him away.

CHAPTER XLIX.

MIRANDA'S APPEAL TO THE CROWD.—VARLEY'S DANGER.—THE RIOT.—THE PUR-
SUIT.—TWITTER'S AGONY AND ALARM.

THE mayor of York only was on the bench during the brief and impassioned
interview between Miranda and Rowland, and had lingered with evident curiosity
to watch the progress of the singular scene which was taking place—a scene singular
as well on account of the relative situations of the parties concerned in it as on
account of the circumstances under which it took place. There was the daughter
of the murdered man, whose death had been the subject of such solemn inquiry,
clinging with all the frantic agony of despairing affection to him who by the solemn
verdict of a jury had just been declared the murderer, and who was condemned to
suffer death for his supposed great crime.

Soon, however, the mayor was awakened from his contemplations by a still
greater source of inquietude, for when Miranda saw that Rowland was indeed taken
from her, instead of, as many a commoner mind would have done, sinking into an
agony of grief, a feeling of resentment rose up in her heart against him who had
been the author of so much misery—against Bernard Varley.

She glanced in the direction where she had last seen the villain standing pale
and haggard, watching the face of the judge as he pronounced the awful sentence
of death upon Rowland, but she saw him not. Then with an anxious eye she
looked round the court, and just caught a sight of his retreating figure, followed by
Twitter, as he was gliding towards the door. In a moment she raised her voice,
and pointing towards him and Twitter, she cried—

"See! see! there are the murderers! My father's blood cries for vengeance! I
denounce these men as my father's murderers!"

Twitter, with a cry of terror, tried to get past Varley, but all the devil in his
nature was aroused by the taunts of Miranda, coming so very near the truth, too,
as they did, and he turned upon her with a face in which every demoniac passion
was struggling for pre-eminence, crying—

"Miranda Rankley, you are mad? you make a bad cause worse by this affected
show of violence. Rather plead for mercy than defy and threaten."

"I do defy and threaten!" cried Miranda. "I defy villany, and threaten
guilt!"

"Indeed, I have heard that when a young maid falls so desperately in love as
Miranda Rankley has done, she forgets all things but the object of her fond idolatry,
clinging even to her father's murderer!"

"Do I cling to thee?" said Miranda, with startling earnestness, that made
Twitter push Varley on a pace or two, as he said,—

"Oh, for God's sake, come away, Varley? Do not, I pray you, stay to reason
with her! Come away—oh, come away!"

"She is beautiful," muttered Varley. "She is most rare and beautiful in her
passion and disdain."

"There again—there again," groaned Twitter. "He is beginning his madness!"

"Are you men?" said Miranda, turning to the throng of persons who were
pressing around her. "Are you fathers? Have you warm glowing hearts, in the
inmost shrines of which you cherish holy feelings? and will you see this monstrous
injustice done? Will you see the innocent condemned, while the forsworn, perjured villain walks to the home he has robbed from the destitute orphan, with a
smile, such as that—such as that?"

She pointed to the face of Bernard Varley, and then there was a cry from several
persons of,—

"Down with the villain! Down with Varley! The false witness and the murderer!"

"I tell you what it is, my good friends," said one man, "human nature is human nature, and I ask you if ever you in all your lives saw such a countenance as Bernard Varley's? Why, I wouldn't take his oath about the twisting the neck of a gosling."

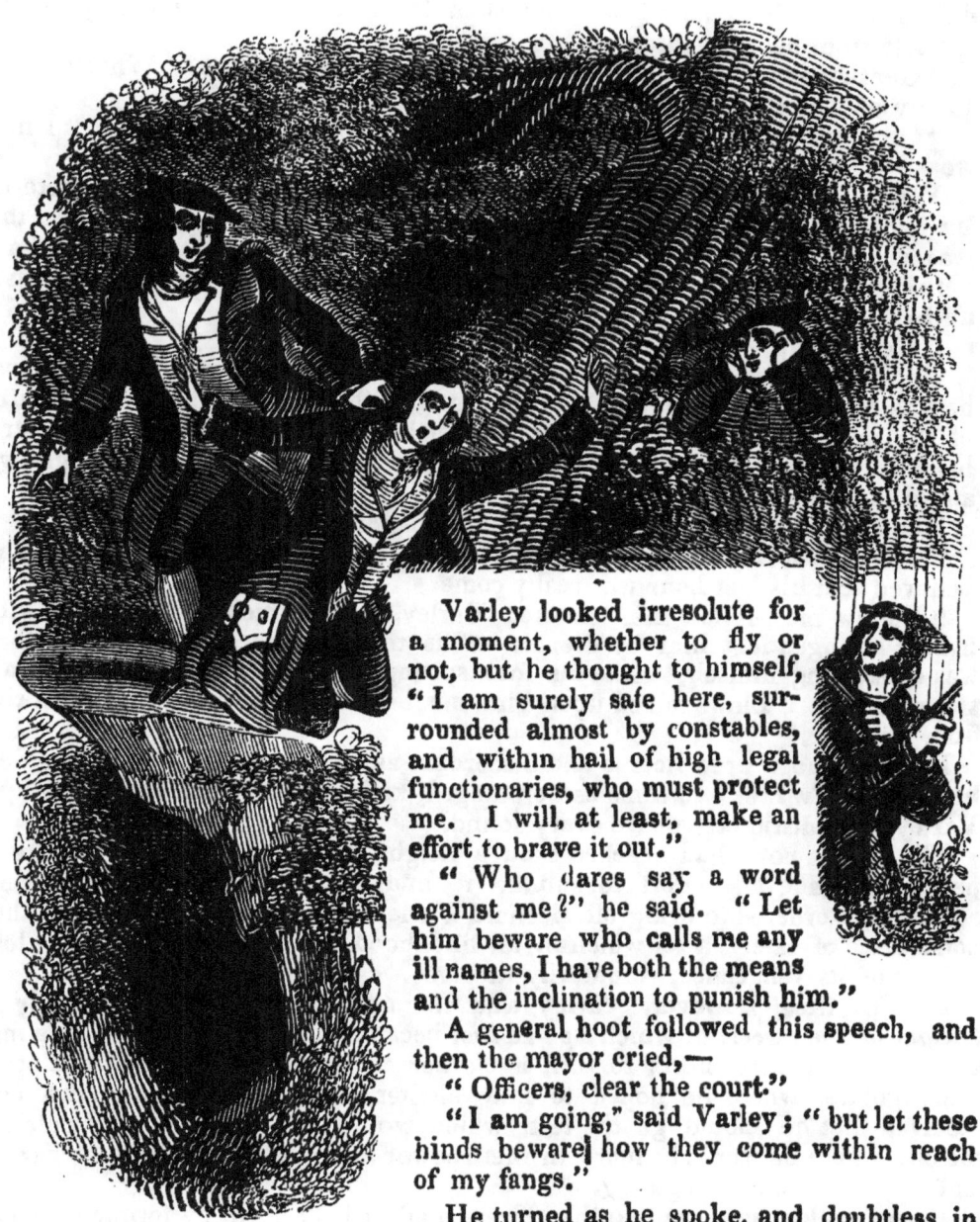

Varley looked irresolute for a moment, whether to fly or not, but he thought to himself, "I am surely safe here, surrounded almost by constables, and within hail of high legal functionaries, who must protect me. I will, at least, make an effort to brave it out."

"Who dares say a word against me?" he said. "Let him beware who calls me any ill names, I have both the means and the inclination to punish him."

A general hoot followed this speech, and then the mayor cried,—

"Officers, clear the court."

"I am going," said Varley; "but let these hinds beware how they come within reach of my fangs."

He turned as he spoke, and doubtless in the surprise of the moment, would have got clear off, had not one of the mob cried out,—

"Let's show him out at any rate, if it's only out of politeness," and coming forward, he was followed by a number of others, and Varley, as well as Twitter, although they were not struck, were projected into the open street, with much greater speed than they had anticipated performing that transit with.

There now occurred a circumstance which had not at all entered into the calculations of Varley, namely, the appearance outside of not only all those who had left the court, from the alarming words of the judge, but a dense throng of idlers

No. 23.

who, in the early part of the day had been occupied in various ways, but who now were free, and willing to take part in anything which promised diversion.

These received Varley and Twitter with open arms, and without inquiring what offence against the majesty of popular opinion they had committed, gave them so rough a reception, that Varley called loudly for help.

Help, however, was far more easily called for than procured; for the constables, either from indifference or inability, in consequence of the density of the crowd, did not reach him, and he was compelled to make a desperate attempt to release himself from his persecutors.

"Gentlemen—gentlemen," he cried, "what have I done? What have I said to any of you that you should push me about in this way?"

"Oh! what—what—what have we done?" returned Twitter, "I'm sure we ——"

What further Twitter was about to add, was lost to the crowd and posterity by his hat being suddenly struck down to the very extremity of his nose, so that he was completely in the dark as regarded future proceedings, although he had a vivid perception, that directly afterwards some gentleman behind tore his coat open right up to the very collar.

"Help—help—officers!" cried Varley.

He then made a desperate attempt to get back to the court, in which, however, he was completely foiled, and was at length, with a terror of death from the hands of the mob creeping over his heart, compelled to endeavour to fight and struggle his way towards the next street, which being full of shops, he thought would, afford him some sort of shelter.

The cries of the mob sounded terrible in his and Twitter's ears.

"Down with the murderers," was shouted by hundreds of them, and Twitter believed that his last hour was really come.

"Follow me—follow me," shouted Varley, as he struck right and left with the frantic strength lent him by despair. 'Tis true he overcame many, but then he was exhausting himself, while his foes sprung up each moment around him fresh and vigorous. Blows rained upon him on all sides. His coat was torn in ribbons from his back.

His voice now grew hoarse and discordant as he shrieked, rather than cried for help, while Twitter's screams as he plunged, kicked, and struggled to keep up with Varley, rose distinctly above every sound.

The tumult now had reached such a height, that the magistracy were compelled to make an effort to subdue it, and a strong body of constables were accordingly ordered to bring off Bernard Varley and Twitter, and lodge them in some place of safety, after which in all likelihood the crowd would, having lost the objects of its vengeance, voluntarily disperse.

By this time, however, Varley and the mob had, together, got nearly to the bottom of the street, in which he had first became surrounded, and he was making the most desperate efforts to turn a corner to his right which led to a principal thoroughfare, where he hoped to find shelter, while the crowd seemed equally resolved that he should go the left, which would conduct him to the outskirts of the city where he would be more in their power in consequence of the opener spaces and the more deficient lighting.

It was at this juncture that the officers made a bold push, by forming themselves into a strong, compact body, to rescue Varley and Twitter. The effort, however, was a vain one, for they only succeeded in getting firmly wedged among the crowd and were carried along with it, without being able to do more than lay violent hands, if they were so minded, upon those persons who happened to be immediately next to them.

Faint, weary, bleeding, and exhausted, Varley now still pushed on, and from the few dangerous blows he had received, it would seem as if the people were rather more intent upon punishing than taking his life, although it was rather rough work to be pushed about, hustled, struck, and half trampled upon by a hooting hissing crowd.

By a lucky chance for him he was swayed against some houses at the corner of the street, pertaining to which was a small shop with a glimmering light in the window of it. There Varley cast his eyes, and calling loudly to Twitter to follow, he tore down the few persons who were between him and the little haven of safety, and dashing open the door, entered the humble shop.

Twitter had followed him with a degree of desperation which had enabled him to keep close to him, and he now fell on to the floor of the shop directly Varley had crossed the threshold.

There was no one but a woman in the place, and strange to say, she did not seem in the least alarmed by the tumult, nor expressed any surprise till the entrance of Varley and Twitter caused her to utter a loud scream.

" Peace, woman—peace !" cried Varley, as he strove in vain to close the door against the mass of persons who were determined to push it open.

" Murder ! fire ! thieves !" cried the woman.

" Is there any back way from here?" said Twitter, in a low voice to her.

" Of course I bark away for fear," replied the woman, who was one of that numerous class of deaf persons who always make a guess at what you say.

" D———— !" said Varley as he was compelled to give way at the door, and had only time to throw down a chair, over which the foremost three or four of the mob fell, and gave him a moment's time.

There was a small door at the further end of the shop, to which he now rushed ; and opening it, he found that it led into a little back room, into which he dashed, still followed by Twitter, who, disfigured with blood and dust as he was, presented a most awful object.

The key of the door was in the inner side, and Varley's first act was to turn the lock.

" Help me, Twitter," he then cried, as he commenced throwing up against the door every article of furniture he could lay his hands on.

Twitter, with trembling hands applied himself to the task, and in a few moments there was a barricade erected, which, at all events, would give the scared fugitives a few moments in which to endeavour to conceal themselves from their pursuers.

CHAPTER L.

VARLEY'S ESCAPE.—THE EMPTY HOUSE.—THE SOLDIERS AND THE MAYOR.—THE SUPPRESSION OF THE RIOT.

A CRASH at the door, which had been barricadoed, announced that his enemies were aware of where he had taken refuge, and were determined to continue the chase. It would, however, necessarily take some time to enable them to surmount the difficulties he had placed in their way, and before that was done there was a hope of escape. Glancing eagerly around him in the small room, he observed another door, that opened apparently into a narrow, dark passage. All seemed quiet in that direction, and saying to Twitter, in a low voice.

" Follow ! follow !" he darted through this last doorway, and, taking the right hand direction, pushed open another door, which conducted them into a very small garden, at the futher end of which was a brick wall, the sides of the little slip of ground being only separated each way from those belonging to the neighbouring houses by slight, dilapidate palings, which were no obstacle whatever to any one who might desire to pass them.

" This way, this way," muttered Varley, as there came upon his ears the proof of the crowd, who were close upon his heels, had now suceeded in removing all obstacles to entering the little back room.

"Haste!" he added, as, seizing Twitter by the arm, he hurried him, half dead as he was with terror, towards the palings on one side of the garden.

"Oh, save me! save me!" said Twitter. "What a death will this be, to be torn limb from limb by an enraged multitude—to feel oneself dying in the frightful crush! Oh, save me, Varley, save me!"

Varley replied not, but, climbing over the palings into the next garden, he dragged Twitter after him, for he was most anxious to save his companion in guilt, who, he made sure, if taken in his present state of mind by the mob, would volunteer a full confession in an attempt to save his life.

By the very dim light that shone from the evening sky, the garden in which they now were appeared in a state of utter neglect and uncultivation. What plants had been placed in it were completely choked up by rank weeds, and it was evident that the little spot of ground had not, for a long period of time, been tended by man.

"We shall be more secure here," gasped Varley. "Let us listen—let us listen!"

He grasped the arm of Twitter convulsively as he spoke, and the sounds of pursuit and anger at losing their victims came from the mob in loud denunciations upon his head.

Hundreds by this time joined the throng who were not at all aware of the slender grounds upon which Varley had first been merely hustled by the crowd, and these latter accessions to the multitude it was who were most violent, and who, in all probability, would have taken his life, hearing as they did that he was denounced as a murderer, and not having time to inquire how it had come about that he was known as such.

"Hunt the murderer! Hunt him! hunt him!" was the cry; and, full of terrors that he might yet fall a victim to the fury of his assailants, Varley made the best of his way to the house in the garden of which he now was.

Not a light was visible in the whole of it. It looked black and gloomy, not exhibiting the least sign of human inhabitants. Varley tried the back door, and found it only on the latch. He then entered with a cautious step, and listened attentively; but no sound met his ears—all was still as the grave.

'Come, come," he said; "we will find refuge here."

Twitter with a groan followed him into the house, and Varley closed and bolted the door.

"It's—it's—very dark here," murmured Twitter.

"Darkness is better than danger," said Varley. "May my bitterest curse fall on all who have taken up the wild cry of Miranda, and followed me like bloodhounds seeking their prey!"

"We—we shall be murdered if we remain in York," said Twitter.

"Did you," asked Varley, "notice any of the faces of those who assailed us, so as to be able to swear to their identity, Twitter."

"No," groaned Twitter. "I noticed nothing—saw nothing—know nothing, but that I was upon the point of death."

"I will be revenged! I must be revenged!" growled Varley. "Am I to be hunted like a wild animal through York! By all the powers of hell I will be avenged!"

"Oh, Varley!" moaned Twitter, "be advised by me. For your own sake as well as for mine—for your life's sake, leave York, and take up your abode somewhere far away from where you are known."

"Miranda," was Varley's brief reply.

"Can it be possible," urged Twitter, "that you can think of her with any feelings but those of deadly hate. Can you cling to a desperate passion for one who would doom you to death if she had the power."

"I—I cannot help it," gasped Varley; "I love her—I love her still!"

"Oh, Varley, this is indeed infatuation!"

"It is—it is—I know it; but it is my fate, and I may not free myself from it. I love her still! I love her still!"

" But you surely must mark her deep loathing—her freely expressed horror of you—a hatred which, on her part, is to the full as violent as her love for him who soon will be no more."

"Name him not to me!" cried Varley with vehemence. "Tell me not that Miranda loves him, for, although that fact is written on my brain in letters of undying flame, I cannot bear it."

"You will leave your mad pursuit, Varley."

" With my life—with my life!"

Twitter groaned, and struck his own breast as he said—

" Then we are lost—lost!"

" Peace, evil croaker!" said Varley. "I love her; she is my very breath of life. Oh! surely, surely, some day, after, perhaps, years of duration, she may even smile at Bernard Varley."

" Never! never?" cried Twitter. "Varley, Varley, upon all other matters you are clear and acute, but upon this you reason like a child. The end of all this will be destruction to us both."

" Hark! hark!"

As Varley spoke the crowd had made their way into the garden of the next house, and their cries, shouts, and inprecations upon his head came to his ears with a painful distinctness. Then a broad gleam of light flashed through a window of the house the fugitives were in, for the mob had procured links to aid them in their pursuit.

"They come. They come," said Twitter. "What shall we do, Varley. What shall we do?"

" Hush! hush. They cannot know we are here. We are safe for the present. Be still."

Twitter sat down on the first of three steps which led to the front part of the house, rocking to and fro. In an agony of terror he gave himself up to the death which he believed was really awaiting him.

Varley still stood by the door, and listened attentively to all that was passing without, and if, by one word he could have taken the lives of every one of the throng that had pursued him, how gladly, and with what fiendish malice would he have spoken that word and gloated over their destruction.

"Twitter," he said, as he heard the low moaning of his guilty comrade, "we will disguise ourselves so that we shall not be known on Tuesday next."

" On Tuesday?"

" Aye, that will be a busy day in York,"

" I dread it," said Twitter. "Something seems to tell me, that despite of all, Rowland Percy will yet triumph over us, and be saved."

Varley laughed, a short unnatural forced laugh, as he said,

" Then, Samuel Twitter, if Rowland Percy be saved, you will be hung. Upon your evidence has he been committed, and nothing but your own confession that you have spoken falsely could save him now."

"You made me learn by heart the tale I was to tell," said Twitter, "I wonder I had strength to tell it."

"And so do I. But I give you great credit for your evidence, Twitter."

At this moment such a prolonged shout came from the mob, that it was evident something very particular had occurred, and such, indeed, was the fact, for the magistrates had become really alarmed at the numbers of the multitude, and the tumult that the whole city was in.

After a short consultation together, feeling the utter inefficiency of the constabulary force to subdue such a throng, the mayor sent a message to the nearest military station, and the shout from the crowd arose from the sudden arrival of several mounted magistrates, with a troop of dragoons behind them.

Many of the crowd scampered away now that real danger presented itself, for although they had no objection in life to hunting or persecuting anybody, they had the very strongest objection to encountering the soldiery.

The magistrates saw how quickly desertion was thinning the ranks of the mob, and purposely waited a few moments, until only the obstinate few were left to disperse, when more stringent measures would be required.

Then the mayor, with the riot act in his hand, cried in a loud voice,

" I call upon you all to disperse in the king's name."

" Down with Varley—down with Varley and Twitter, the murderers," cried many voices.

" Down with the mayor," roared a drunken cobbler, who, with his leathern apron and red nightcap, had joined the crowd. " Down with the king, and his name too. D—d—down with me. Down—down with everybody—down with everything, d—e !"

" Hurrah !" shouted the mob.

" Secure that fellow," said the mayor ; and several mounted police made a dash to get at the drunken cobbler, but they did not succeed, for the people near him hustled him out of the way, and finally pushed him through a parlour window, where he was perfectly safe, and accomplished one part of his wish, namely, that of being down himself.

" Once more I call upon you to disperse," said the mayor, " or, in pursuance of my duty I must read the riot act, and then take violent measures to put an end to this unlawful and tumultuous proceeding."

He then commenced reading the riot act, and as he did so the mob slowly dispersed, so that by the time he came to the end there were but some small lots of persons left who exhibited the most peaceable demeanour that could well be imagined.

The mayor laughed as he turned to the officer in command of the dragoons, and said,

" We shall not have to trouble you, but I never saw our city in such a state of excitement; we have had a criminal trial which has terminated contrary to the feelings and wishes of the populace. At the execution of the man who is convicted of murder, I fear we shall have some more rioting."

" You allude to the case of the murder of Sir George Rankley," said the officer.

" I do."

" It is a strange case, I am told."

" Very, but there was no getting over the evidence. It was quite clear."

Those of the rioters who had entered the house kept coming out now by twos and threes, and looking about them in very great surprise to find their companions, who in some instances, had literally pushed them in, all gone.

The mayor let some of them go, but he whispered to one of the police authorities to lay hold of some three or four, for the sake of example, in the morning, so that those who had emerged from the house into which they had pursued Varley and Twitter were taken into custody and marched off escorted by the police and dragoons.

Where Varley had taken refuge the magistrates did not trouble themselves to inquire, and as he did not make his appearance, they supposed he had got housed somewhere much earlier than he really had.

The streets so lately a scene of so much confusion were now, for the time of the evening, much quieter than usual, for the shopkeepers had hastily closed their shutters, and decent people, who dreaded a street riot, had betaken themselves to their homes, when first the tumult commenced and shewed signs of being a formidable one.

It was some time, however, before Varley thought proper to venture from his hiding-place, but when he did so he became perfectly sure that the mob had been dispersed, for a wrapped stillness reigned around, a stillness the more profound and remarkable, contrasting so immediately as it did with the so very recent scene of bustle and intense excitement.

"We are safe now, Twitter," he said. "We will now leave this friendly shelter."

"Are—are you sure?"

"Quite."

"But—but, Varley."

"Pshaw! mobs cannot be quiet if they would, and this was an affair in which no one or two individuals would act alone. All is still now, and we may proceed in safety."

"Come on—come on."

Twitter crept after Varley, who again crossed the palings into the garden of the inhabited house, and made his way to the parlour, against the door of which he had piled the woman's furniture.

The moment he made his appearance in the shop, the woman gave a loud scream, and it was in vain that Varley did all in his power to quiet her.

"Curse you," he cried, "do you want to bring a mob about your place again?"

"Murder," cried the woman, "murder."

Varley struck her a blow on the head, which half stunned her for the moment, and then rushed from the shop into the now quiet and deserted street.

"Meet me to-morrow," he said to Twitter.

"At what time?"

"At two. Come to me at my lodging, and now good night. Such a-day's work as this we shall never see again."

CHAPTER LI.

ROWLAND IN HIS CELL.—THE PRISON CHAPLAIN.—THE PROPHECY OF BOLD HAWK.

WHO can picture the feelings of poor Rowland Percy, who was removed from the court with sentence of death hanging over his innocent head. He began almost to think that the rapid events which had cast him down, as it were, from the "pleasant height of joy" could not be real, and that he surely must be suffering under some mental delusion which presented to him all the frightful images by which he had been and was surrounded.

He was placed in a cell of very small dimensions, and as it was not then the custom for any one to torture the last moments of a condemned criminal by sitting with him and watching his every look and gesture, Rowland had, at least, the comfort of being alone, if he could not have with him those he loved.

"God of Heaven," he cried, "when will all this be at an end? Is this frightful tragedy really to terminate on a scaffold? Am I, innocent even in thought of the crime laid to my charge, to suffer the most ignominious of deaths in a Christian country, where the meanest animal that crawls is affected to be protected from wanton cruelty, if he really be not so? Can it be possible that such a monstrous injustice can ensue? Surely, surely not; and yet I have heard and read of such things as the innocent suffering death, and then years afterwards when their remains have mouldered to corruption in the damp of the grave, their innocence has, by some strange accident, become apparent to the wonder of all men. Good Heaven, am I doomed to be one of these frightful examples of human fallibility? Oh, hard, cruel fate. Miranda—Miranda—! What will become of thee, unfriended, alone and deprived of that wealth which should have placed you at least above the fear of that most sad aggravation of all other ills, poverty—What? oh, what will become of thee, my own, my beautiful, my fond, trusting Miranda?"

These thoughts were sad and bitter ones for the prisoner in his lonely dungeon, and he sat himself down upon the solitary wooden seat, with which it was furnished, giving himself up for a time to grief, that was not for himself, but for her, the good and beautiful, he was denied by inexorable fate, the, to him, high and grateful privilege of guarding from the storms of fate, and protecting through the weary pilgrimage of life.

More than an hour passed thus, and then he was aroused by having the door his cell opened, and immediately closed again. He looked up and saw before him a mild, gentlemanly-enough-looking man, dressed in black, who, when he saw that he was regarded by Rowland, said, in a voice that had a slight twang of the conventicle in it,—

"My dear sir, I hope you will receive my visit with the same pure feelings and pious hopes that dictate it,"

"Who are you, sir?" said Rowland.

"I am the chaplain of this place."

"I can have no objection, sir, to a visit from any gentleman who comes to me in courtesy," said Rowland. "But before you say another word, I tell you plainly and distinctly, that I am an innocent man, and, therefore, require no further spiritual consolation or hope, than I have been accustomed to cherish in my heart as a consequence of my profound and deep appreciation of the goodness and justice of Heaven."

The clergyman shook his head, and with more of a whine than even he had used before, he said,—

"Oh, young man, repent—repent."

"I am innocent," said Rowland, "if you allude to the crime for which I am so unjustly condemned. If you allude to the necessity of repentance for many other errors, venial perhaps, but still errors in the pure sight of Heaven, I do repent me, and have ever acknowledged them to God."

"But, young man, I fear your heart still yearns towards the world and its vain creatures."

"It does yearn to the world, and to some of God's creatures, that inhabit it. Creatures of his, that he has made beautiful and good, that they might be loved with such love as I shall carry to my grave."

The chaplain gave a deep groan.

"Quite understand me, sir," added Rowland, "I will hold no sort of conversation or communication with any one who comes here presuming me guilty."

"Harden not your heart, young man."

"I don't understand you, sir."

"You will find that you will be welcomed to another world by ten thousand angels, to realms of bliss, if you will cast from you all earthly feelings, and live only for the life which is to come."

"Sir, sir," cried Rowland. "Here am I an innocent man—condemned to death for a crime I shudder at. Is it fair—is it just—is it religious that I am to be tormented in my last few hours by implied doubts of my solemn assertions of innocence, and inuendos of my guilt?"

The preacher looked rather confounded at this, and muttering to himself something about a hardened sinner, he left Rowland to his own meditations, with a resolution of attacking him again when his mind should be more enervated from his confiement.

And what were the sad thoughts of Miranda on the morning of that eventful and terrible day which had begun in doubt, mingled with hope, but had ended in despair. There was no comfort to offer her, for what could even the kind heart of Mr. Anderson invent, that could give her one solitary ray of hope? He felt that nothing short of some special interposition of Providence could save from his most undeserved fate the innocent Rowland, (for his, Mr. Anderson's, belief in his innocence was as firm as Miranda's.)

The words of the judge had held out no hope of mitigation of the sentence. Either some discovery of Twitter's and Varley's perjury must take place, or Rowland must fall a victim to the too successful conspiracy against his existence.

Mr. Anderson could only clasp the hand of Miranda, and beg of her again to come to his house, but she clung to old Mr. Percy, saying in a voice of deep dejection,—

" No, no, I will not bring sorrow into your dwelling, Mr. Anderson. Such deep grief as mine should court solitude, and not obtrude itself upon others. Heaven reward you for all you have done for the innocent."

Mr. Anderson was deeply affected by her tone and manner, so much so, indeed, that he could not command his voice sufficiently to speak, and the counsel for Rowland, who had been

No. 24.

unrobing, coming at the same moment, saw the agitated little group, which he immediately joined, saying,—

"Do not yet despair. I advise a memorial to be got up to the secretary of state, setting forth the strange conduct of Varley and Twitter at the trial; their previous bad character and motives for themselves committing the murder, and then accusing an innocent man."

"Oh, sir," cried Miranda, clinging to his arm, "is there still hope?"

"While there is life, certainly," replied the counsel, "I declare to you all, that I have a most perfect conviction of the innocence of Mr. Rowland Percy."

"Heaven bless you for those words," said Miranda. "He is innocent—indeed he is."

"I firmly believe it, and as there is guilt somewhere, between ourselves, I think all our suspicions point to the right quarter."

"I know it, I know it," added Miranda. "From the first it seemed to me as if a voice from Heaven cried to me, ' Behold in Bernard Varley the murderer of your father.'"

"Let me advise you now to go home," said the counsel. "Leave to me the preparation of the memorial, which I will undertake to have forwarded to London by an express within two hours, and should an answer not come by Tuesday morning, I have no doubt but the judge will grant, himself, a temporary respite till Wednesday."

Miranda looked in the face of the counsel as he spoke, and she saw a glistening tear in his eye, as he returned her gaze. A convulsive sob burst from her heart, and she said,—

"All can weep for my poor Rowland, but myself. Tears are denied to me, and yet, oh, Heaven, what sorrow sits brooding at my heart."

"Let your motto, be Hope, Miss Rankley. I will hasten to prepare the memorial."

He shook hands kindly with the heart-stricken girl, and then hurried away to perform his self-imposed task, while Miranda, with a feeling of hope newly awakened in her breast, accompanied old Mr. Percy to his humble home, while Mr. Anderson walked with them to the door.

As Miranda turned upon the threshold to bid him adieu, she saw standing close to her the poor idiot Bold Hawk, who had so strangely interested himself in the fate of the unfortunate Rowland.

He laid one finger lightly upon her arm, while he lifted his other hand above his head, and said,—

"He will be saved. He will be saved!"

Miranda was interested by the manner of the poor creature, and in her distress and despair, even words of hope from such as he, were sweet and welcome to her ears ; even as the fond parent or lover, when the object of boundless affection lies stricken by disease, and expiring, will listen with eager confidence to the wildest empiric, who will promise restoration.

"Who—who will be saved?" she said.

"Rowland Percy. He who has a hand open as the day, and a heart as kind as a summer's sunshine. He will be saved—he will be saved."

"All love him?" faltered Miranda. "Even this poor creature, whose immortal part seems wrapped in strange mists, even he is sensible of Rowland's innocence."

"I know it," resumed the idiot. "Some call me Martin, but my real name is Bold Hawk, because I can look at the sun and the twinkling stars without winking. You understand me? Sometimes at night when all the tiny lamps of Heaven are lighted in the deep blue sky, I go out into the pleasant fields, and I lie me down upon the dewy grass. Held up am I then by a world to look to the Heaven above it. Then—ha! ha! ha! then Bold Hawk asks questions of the stars and in their way they answer him."

There was a mild and beautiful romance in his language that interested Miranda, despite her better reason; but the heart is never so ready to bend to superstitious impressions, as when it is a prey to great grief, and is suffering much oppression.

"Go on," she said. "Tell me what they said of Rowland Percy?"

"Ah, they spoke of him. I'll tell you how. You have marked the broad starry belt that goes across the sky,—they call it the milky way, because such floods of pale star-light are over and about it, that it glows with a faint beauty, outshining all the firmament beside?"

"I have. I have."

"Of these small stars ask my questions, and when I do so, they dance before my eyes for awhile, like motes in the sunbeams, until they arrange themselves into some word, which gives me an answer."

"And thus you saw——"

"That he would be saved. I did—I did, and I saw that Bernard Varley would be hanged at York. Yes, hanged at York, surrounded by such a shouting, screaming crowd, as never yet awakened echoes in the ancient city."

"It may be in the mysterious ways of Providence," said Miranda, "that even such a one as this poor mindless man may be gifted with a prophetic knowledge of coming events. Heaven grant it may be so."

"Let there be peace here," said the idiot, indicating with his finger Miranda's breast. "Let there be peace here, for all shall be well. He shall be saved. The stars have said, and who shall gainsay them?"

"I thank you for your kind wishes," said Miranda.

"Speak again—speak again, lady. Your voice is music to Bold Hawk."

"Good night," said Miranda.

"You neither hoot at me, nor pelt at me with stones," he added. "You don't belong to this world. Ah, no, for real human creatures are cruel, revengeful, malicious, and always torment where they can. They say I am mad, and if it be so, 'tis a sore affliction from God. Then why should I be hooted at, and stoned? Heaven help me, and save me from human beings. The dogs are kind to me. A horse will not kick me more readily than any one else. No, no. 'Tis only human creatures made in the image of God, and endowed with heavenly intellect, that persecute poor Bold Hawk!"

CHAPTER LII.

MIRANDA AT HOME.—THE WEARY HOURS OF THE NIGHT.—THE RESOURCE
FOR THE MIND.

THE words of the poor idiot made a deep impression upon Miranda, and she pleased herself with thinking that Heaven in its mercy had really made use of Bold Hawk, as an insrument of hope and comfort to her heart.

As for poor Mr. Percy, he seemed thoroughly weighed down with grief. He looked years older than he had ever looked before the trial, and he could do nothing when he reached his home but sit down, and, leaning his head upon his hands, rock himself to and fro, murmuring,—

"My poor boy! my poor murdered Rowland."

The sight of his affliction was a great additional source of anguish to Miranda, although probably the effort she made to instil some hope and comfort into his mind, in some measure distracted her from too close a contemplation of her own sources of grief.

"I pray you, Mr. Percy, to be more calm," said Miranda. "Even I have some hope lingering around my heart. Why then should you despair?"

" Can nothing more be done for my poor boy ?" was the answer of the sorrow-ing man.

" Yes, something can and something will be done," said Miranda; " I am but a weak girl, but think you I will let him who has my heart's best love, perish without yet more struggles to save him ?"

" Miranda, what can you do ?"

" To-morrow early I will see the judge who presided at the trial. On my knees will pray for delay, if it be but for a week, and should he be moved by Heaven to grant my prayer, I will, during that time make some attempt to wring from Varley's guilty heart, an acknowledgment of Rowland's innocence."

" Pray Heaven you may be successful, my child," sobbed old Percy. " You are capable of more than I, for I feel as if I was already half claimed by death."

" Be of better cheer and retire now to rest," said Miranda, who was terrified at the unmoved paleness of his face, and the trembling of his hands.

" I cannot rest. There will be no rest for me again, Miranda. Thoughts of my poor boy in the gloom of his prison, crowd too thickly round my heart to let me attempt to sleep."

Miranda could have re-echoed this sentiment from the bottom of her heart, but she forbore to do so, and replied merely,—

" Then we will together sit up until the morning's dawn and talk of him we are both so deeply interested in, or shall I strive to withdraw for a brief space both your mind and my own from our sorrows by reading to you ?"

" I should not comprehend what you read, Miranda, but it may wile away a tedious hour."

" It will," said Miranda. " But first I must breathe a prayer to Heaven for poor Rowland."

She knelt and silently breathed a faint aspiration to the throne of justice in behalf of the persecuted, the good and the innocent. Tears coursed each other down the cheek of old Mr. Percy, as she remained in her mute posture of supplication, and when she rose, and, in a more softened and resigned voice, said,—

" May Heaven hear my prayer, but if it must be that this world is to be to me a vale of tears, oh, grant I may, without murmuring, be enabled to say, God's will be done."

" Amen !" sighed Mr. Percy. " Yet we are weak and cannot steel our hearts against sorrow."

Miranda went to another table, and with a heavy heart took from it a book which contained small fugitive pieces that had now and then, when sleep would not be wooed to her couch, wile away a few tedious hours of the night.

" 'Tis strange," she said, " that almost every episode in human life, to which is attached any interest, involves the persecution of some innocent and gifted person by a villain who knows no honour, no remorse."

" It is ever so, my dear Miranda. There is a constant contest between vice and virtue."

" Shall I read to you ?"

" Do—do; I can think of my boy the while."

Miranda opened the book at random, and read the first brief picture of life that presented itself, commencing thus :—

" Arthur Wollaston was the son of a country gentleman of considerable wealth and influence, and being an only son was humoured in every whim, which so influ-enced his self-love and turbulent passions, that his conduct and behaviour were quite intolerable to all who knew him.

" Strange, however, as it may seem, at the age of eighteen, he entered the univer-sity as a student for the church, and instead of practising self-denial so essential to fit him for his sacred calling, he was engaged in every species of riot and extra-vagance.

" At the expiration of his terms he took a low degree, left the tradesmen, who had supplied him, creditors to a large amount, whose claims his parent had to pay, and came forth to the world as a fit person by whom the souls of thousands were to be instructed in the lessons of holiness and brotherly love.

"For some time after leaving the university the better part of his time was spent in hunting the harmless animals on the paternal estate, and seducing the daughters of the tenants, till, at last, a curacy was appointed him, and he went to a distant part of the country to perform the duties of the holy office for which he was so badly qualified.

"Scarcely had he entered the reading desk of the parish church of A——, before his eyes roved over the forms and faces of his congregation, especially the female portion, and he was not long before he detected the soft and gentle mien of Eliza Melville, daughter of a surgeon in the hamlet.

"As she bent low before the throne of grace in pure devotion, her simple beauty fired the passionate admiration of the curate; (for even devils can admire the virtues of the saints, though at the same time they would despoil them of their glory by their innate malice and hatred of the virtues they cannot reach); he secretly determined she should be his, and whenever her eye was turned in direction of his desk, he practised his most eloquent delivery to captivate her ear, and assumed an air of the most exalted piety to captivate her eye, and by these means to allure her to his bosom.

"By these means he secretly resolved upon her ruin; he knew the heart of woman well, and Eliza Melville was still but woman, though in its fairest and purest form.

"The position which Wollaston held in society, gave him access to the homes of the best families in the town of A——, and amongst the rest he was invited to the family of Mr. Melville, where he had abundant opportunities of conversing with the charming Eliza, and pouring the poison of his insidious flattery into her ear. Disguised by the semblance of religion, which harmonised with her feelings and seemed to raise her own esteem, he thus appealed to her in her imagination until Eliza, unconscious of the power which directed her yielded her affections before she knew they had parted from her.

"This was the point to which Wollaston wished to lead her and when once secure of her esteem, determined to bend her to his wishes. although it should seem her actions were of her own free will.

"He had carried on this amour with Eliza for some time, but, in order to mature his plan of villany, so that he might not seem implicated in her ruin, he resolved to give up the curacy of A——, and for some time to return to the residence of his father.

"'Ah, my dear Eliza,' said he, one evening, as he met her in a meadow, near the parsonage, 'it wanted only your cheering presence to make this evening one of perfect bliss.'

"'You do me too much honour, Mr. Wollaston,' returned Eliza, 'but I am quite sure it is out of my power to enhance the beauty of nature.'

"'Perhaps I was wrong in using the word enhance,' said Wollaston; 'I should rather have said, when your loveliness is added to the splendour of this scene before us, it fills my soul with sublimest feelings.'

"To this Eliza could make no reply, but holding down her head she blushed with the mingled emotions of undeserved flattery and pride that a man of Wollaston's (as she imagined) exalted mind, should descend from his mental pedestal to seek her love.

"'Yes, Eliza,' continued he, 'I feel I can no longer live without you; but I have received intelligence of my father's illness, and must leave you for awhile.'

"'Leave us?' ejaculated Eliza.

"'Yes, my dear Eliza; the wishes of a dying parent are imperative.'

"'They are so,' sighed Eliza.

"'Ah, my dear girl, how gladly would I stay to bask in the sunshine of your love; but——'

"'You ought not to repine at the will of Heaven,' murmured Eliza,

"'I do not,' returned Wollaston, meekly; "but it is hard to be separated from those we love.'

"'Your father's death, no doubt, would be a great trial and affliction.'

"'It would, dear Eliza; but it was of your love I spoke."

"' Nay, think not of me—forget me in the more important claims of filial tenderness.'

"'Much as I admire the generosity of the sentiment, dear Eliza, be assured my soul is, and ever will be, present with you.'

"Eliza trembled from head to foot.

"'Yes, Eliza,' continued he, pressing her hand, 'your love is more precious to me than life itself; neither do I see why we should be separated.'

"'You speak in riddles,' said Eliza; 'what can you mean?'

"'That as our spirits are united, I do not see why our bodies should be separate.'

"' Have you asked my parents' consent to our union?' asked Eliza, as she fancied her lover's overtures were honourable.

"'No, I have not, my loved one; time and circumstance will not admit of it. But you love me, Eliza?'

"'I do.'

"' Then why not waive your parents' consent, and fly with me?'

"'Surely you, for the present, must forget the proposal you are making me,' said Eliza, as a flush of indignation fired her brow.

"'If you love me you would not long hesitate, Eliza. You do not doubt my honour?'

"'No—no; but——'

" Since you mistrust me, I must now say farewell; and the chaise in half an hour will bear me hence.'

"' So soon?' sighed Eliza.

" Yes; and since you will not be the partner of my journey, once more, adieu.'

"'Stay—oh stay!' cried Eliza: 'that coldness freezes me, Do not leave me thus.'

"' What wouldst thou?' said Wollaston, with the utmost *sang froid*,

" To tell thee—but 'tis—'tis nothing,' returned Eliza, with an emotion she could ill suppress.

"' Thou wouldst say, dear girl, that it is pain to part?' urged Wollaston.

" I would, dear Arthur; and since thou has penetrated the secret of my bosom, I confess thou art more dear to me than I imagined.'

"' Sweet angel,' sighed the libertine, 'would that we could never part.'

"' And must we?' urged Eliza.

"' It is absolutely necessary. Would to Heaven we had never met. Farewell!'

" As Wollaston gave his hand in token of adieu, he heaved a sigh, as if from the deepest recesses of his soul; while the nigh heart-broken Eliza sobbed audibly. Neither spoke for some minutes, and at length, as if with an impulse he could scarcely conquer, the seducer again sighed ' Farewell !' and hastily walked away.

" ' Oh, stay—stay! Do not leave me broken-hearted,' sobbed the agitated girl. ' One moment longer. Oh, stay !'

" This was the point Wollaston wanted to bring her to. He now felt thoroughly convinced of her affection, and, without looking to the right or left, lest his guilty soul should be tempted to sin, he walked steadily forward to the inn, where a chaise waited his attendance, and before many minutes he was lost in the distance.

" For some time Eliza stood as if rooted to the spot where the curate had left her She gazed upon him until her weeping eyes refused their office. and when out of sight, with an effort, as though her heart would break, she exclaimed,—

" ' Gone—gone for ever !'

" A choking sensation affected her throat. She placed her kerchief to her eyes, and it was with the greatest difficulty she prevented herself sinking to the earth.

" After some time she tranquillised her spirits, and having bathed her face and temples in an adjacent brook, whose cool and refreshing water greatly aided her recovery, she proceeded homeward.

" She had not proceeded many yards before she was overtaken by William Fitzhurst, the son of a neighbouring gentleman, and who long, but unsuccessfully had paid court to Eliza.

" ' Bless me, Miss Melville, how ill you look!' said he. ' Permit me to assist you home.'

" ' No, I thank you, sir,' sighed Eliza.

" ' You are really much excited,' continued William; ' and I should never forgive myself if I allowed you to go alone. I hope nothing serious has happened in the family ?'

" ' Nothing has happened, thank you ; they are all quite well,' stammered Eliza and at the same time she trembled so violently that she was compelled to support herself by leaning on his proffered arm.

" ' There, you will be better now,' said Fitzhurst, who evidently saw her excessive agitation, and to a certain extent, guessed the cause.

" ' Thank you,' replied Eliza. ' I am indeed a little indisposed ; but I will not trouble you to attend me further.

" ' The pleasure of being able to afford you assistance, Miss Melville, is indeed great, and if I could only prevail upon you to listen to my suit, it would——'

" ' I have already given you an answer, Mr. Fitzhurst,' faltered Eliza, ' and therefore beg you will not further importune me on that subject,"

" ' Excuse me if I ask you if your affections be really engaged ?'

" To this Eliza dared not reply in the affirmative, feeling assured her answer would be carried to her family, who knew not how deeply her heart was engaged, and that, too, clandestinely. She, therefore, held her peace.

" ' If another has claimed your heart,' continued William, ' I value your happiness too much to wish you to forego it ; but if not, I trust you will not refuse me what you would another, a fair and candid hearing.'

" ' At present your conversation troubles me,' replied {Eliza ; ' I am too unwell to bear it.'

" ' Dear lady, I would not cause you a moment's pain,' sighed Fitzhurst.

" ' Then leave me.'

" ' At your home I will, Eliza.'

" ' I feel better now ; you need not come so far, thank you.'

" ' Oh, Eliza,' continued Fitzhurst, ' if you knew but the ardour of the passion which consumes me, I am convinced you would be less cruel."."

" ' I cannot be answerable for your inclinations, sir,' replied Eliza, coolly.

" ' No, you cannot ; but I here declare, in the face of Heaven, never was maiden wooed with love more pure.'

" ' Cease this language, sir ; it distresses me.'

" ' I love you," continued William, heedless of the veto, ' more dearly than my own existence. In pity do not refuse to give me your society, and if I do not prove the truth of my declaration, treat me as you will.'

" ' I have already spoken my mind upon this subject, and will not retract it."

" ' Kindness, time, and assiduity may work wonders in my favour.' replied William.

" ' I am now at home, sir,' said Eliza, without further remark to what William had advanced, ' and beg to thank you for your attention. Good day.'

" Fitzhurst raised his hat gracefully, and returned her salute ; but it was with anxiety he saw the traces of deep tribulation on her features, and, as he walked away, he said, mentally,—

" ' There is some mystery here I will unravel. I have no doubt that parson is the cause, for I met him but a little before I saw Eliza. He, however, is about leaving the parish, and there will be little to fear from him.'

" No sooner had Eliza gained her home than she sought her chamber. She cast herself in despair upon her couch, and before long a burning fever raged within her, which, to keep it under, required all the skill her parent was possessed of.

" For some days she lingered in this condition, when she at length partially recovered ; but a pale and melancholy expression had settled upon her hitherto cheerful countenance. She avoided all society, and was more frequently to be found in the walks where she had listened to the seductive discourse of Wollaston.

" A month had nearly elapsed, when one evening, as she loitered in the meadow where she had last parted with her lover, he suddenly presented himself before her.

" ' Merciful Heaven !' cried Eliza, who at first deemed it to be an apparition.

" ' Nay, start not, dearest girl,' said Wollaston, in a calm, soft voice ; ' you see I cannot resist the temptation of haunting the spot that is hallowed by your presence.'

" ' You surely jest,' remarked Eliza.

" ' No, my beloved,' said Arthur, rapturously seizing her hand with an impassioned air. ' Since last I parted from you, my life has been but one continued dream of thee.'

" ' You wrote not to me.'

" ' No, angel of my soul. Day after day I resolved to visit you ; at length I could not delay any longer, and here I am, never, I trust, to part again.'

" ' Are you serious ?' asked Eliza.

" ' Yes, my beloved, here beneath the blue canopy of heaven, and in the face of my Maker, I vow never more to leave you.'

" ' You have a license, then ?' stammered Eliza.

" ' I have left it in town,' replied the artful man ; ' but I am sure that little circumstance will not matter much. You will go thither with me ?'

" ' No, Wollaston,' returned Eliza, calmly.

" ' And wherefore, love ?'

" ' Is it decorous ?' asked the trembling girl. ' My friends do not even know of your attentions.'

" ' Perhaps not.'

" ' Then, why wish me to leave without their consent ?'

" ' They will be sure to acquiesce after our marriage, at present they might object.'

" ' They would agree to anything that would enchance their daughter's happiness.'

" ' Possibly, Eliza ; but I trusted more to your love, and felt convinced I should not meet with a denial.'

" ' My love you have, Arthur.'

" ' And must put it to the test ; fly with me now, Eliza, or I must leave you for ever."

" Cruel man !' sighed Eliza, ' why thus do you tempt me ?'

" ' That you may be my bride before it is too late ; I have accepted a chapliancy on a foreign station ; to-morrow the vessel sails.'

" Eliza stood irresolute,

" ' Come, come, loved of my soul !' gently urged the libertine, ashe pulled her by the hand, " a chaise now waits in yonder lane.'

" ' I cannot ; I dare not.'

" ' Time presses, love—come.'

" ' Oh, my dear parents, what will you think of your ungrateful child ?' murmured Eliza.

" ' You blame yourself too severely,' said her admirer; ' the ceremony will be performed soon after you reach town,'

" ' On your sacred word ?' said the hesitating girl, as she regarded her seducer with a scrutinizing eye.

" ' On my salvation,' replied Wollaston, with the blandest and most earnest expression ; ' you then yet mistrust me ?'

" ' No, no, Arthur,' returned the yielding girl, ' as a proof that I trust you, I at once yield myself to your honour.'

" ' Sweet girl, ten thousand thanks for your condescension ; in a few hours we shall be united ; a clergyman, a friend of mine, will perform our marriage ceremony at the apartments I have engaged for you.'

" With a kiss upon her blushing cheeks and lips, Wollaston pressed her hastily forward, and seating himself beside her in the chaise, they were soon whirled along hastily towards London.

" As they thus journeyed rapidly onward, and were some miles from A——, a single horseman passed them on the road. Eliza shrunk back into the arms of Wollaston, for she had met the gaze of William Fitzhurst.

" A consciousness that something was wrong, filled the mind of William, and when he had progressed some little distance he turned his horse's head, and followed in the direction of the chaise, which stopped at a village about ten miles from town.

" Wollaston then alighted to bring refreshment to Eliza, and at the same instant Fitzhurst rode up and accosted him, with,—

" ' You must excuse me, sir, for questioning your conduct ; but when I see a lady (with whose family I am intimately acquainted) travelling alone in your company, and to whom I am well aware you are not married, I cannot help expressing my doubts as to its legality ?'

" ' Am I then compelled to satisfy the inquiries of every man who chooses to question me'

" ' No.'

" ' Then why do you inquire ?'

" ' I am personally interested in the lady's welfare,' plied William.

" ' Are you her father ?' demanded Wollaston, with a sneer.

" ' Not so ; but I feel equally bound to protect her.'

" ' She needs not your protection.'

" ' I do not know that.'

" ' Although I treat with contempt your impertinence,' said the irritated curate, ' yet I will allow you to satisfy your doubts—the lady is within 'the chaise and you can ask her if her actions be voluntary or not.'

" ' I will avail myself of the liberty,' said William, and stepping to the carriage door, he continued, ' Miss Melville, allow me to inquire if you are here of your free accord, and whether your parents are cognizant of your mode of travellin ?'

" ' Yes,' stammered Eliza, with confusion.

" ' They know you travel with Mr. Wollaston ?'

" ' My father is waiting to receive me in town where I am about to be united to Mr. Wollaston upon my arrival there.'

" There was a manner in Eliza as she uttered this falsity, that more than ever confirmed the suspicions of Fitzhurst, and he replied, with a sigh,—

" ' If such be the case I beg you will forgive my apparent rudeness, which nothing but an earnest wish for your welfare could have tempted me to.'

" ' Certainly ;' returned Eliza, with a confusion that he noted well, and immediately she crouched in the corner of the carriage.

" ' I hope your impertinence is now satisfied ?' cried Wollaston.

" ' Yes.'

" ' And had I time to waste upon you, it should not go unpunished ; but we shall meet again.'

" ' You then threaten me ?'

" ' I do.'

" ' Villain !' cried Fitzhurst, 'you shall not escape me.'

" He here made a dash at Wollaston and endeavoured to strike him with his riding whip, but the latter, without heeding this remark entered the chaise, and commanded the driver to go forward.

" The chaise immediately rattled off ; Fitzhurst pursued it for some yards, uttering impotent threats, and then returned to the inn from whence they had set out.

" Uncertain how to act, he here delayed some minutes ; he had had Eliza's word that her father waited her arrival in town—could he take it ? to return to A—— to make inquiries might seem officious ; and yet if aught was wrong, to allow them to proceed without a knowledge of their whereabouts might lead to the most fearful results. At last he decided and rang the bell.

" ' Waiter,' said he, ' have you a man you can trust with a message ?'

" ' Yes, sir.'

" ' Send him here immediately.'

" In a minute the ostler entered.

" ' Lend me your frock and hat and take this note to Surgeon Melville, of A——,' said William.

" The man scratched his head.

" ' Ride post haste, and here is a guinea for your trouble.'

" ' That's sum'ut like, zur,' replied the ostler, and immediately doffed his stable frock and hat ; the latter was somewhat greasy, and William declined it, prefering his own with only the band around it. He then put the following note into his hand with the injunction not to deliver it unless he saw Mr. Melville, or was assured he was in London.

" DEAR SIR.—I am following your daughter's movements with Mr. Wollaston ; proceed to the village of C—— till you hear from me.

" ' Yours in haste,   WM. FITZHURST.' "

" When the ostler had started, Fitzhurst disguised himself in the stable frock, mounted his horse, and at his utmost speed, pursued the fugitives, whom he overtook at a distance of two miles, and kept the chaise steadily in sight until they reached town, when they alighted at a house in one of the fashionable streets.

"No sooner had Fitzhurst noted the number of the house, and the name of the street, than he sought an hotel, and immediately posted a letter with the information to the inn at C——, where Mr. Melville received it as the former had expected, and without losing a moment, pursued his journey to London to join his friend.

* * * * *

"But to return to Eliza; upon alighting from the chaise, she was ushered into a suite of apartments, which on all sides bespoke ease and luxury.

"'These apartments, my love, I have chosen for you,' said Wollaston, 'do you like them?'

"'They are handsome,' replied Eliza, 'but your friend has not arrived.'

"'I thought he would have been here before this; he said he would be here.'

"'It is very negligent,' returned Eliza.

"'Very; but we will have supper, he will most probably arrive by the time we have finished.'

"With anxiety Eliza complied; and when the repast was ended her agitation became great.

"'You seem unwell, my love,' said Wollaston, 'let me fill you a glass of wine.'

"'Thank you.'

"'I assure you it is excellent, and will tend to raise your spirits.'

"Eliza put the glass to her lips, but something in the taste of the wine caused her to put it down again; she felt weary from the journey, and would fain have retired to rest; but the idea of being united to the man she loved, and imagining that the clergyman would each moment arrive, kept her in a constant tremor.

"Hour after hour thus passed away, and as the clock from a neighbouring spire tolled the hour of three, Eliza begged permission to retire.

"'Surely my love!' said Wollaston, 'you would not suffer me to seek a lodging at this hour?'

"'Really, Mr. Wollaston,' returned Eliza, 'you must have very little respect for me to remain, seeing that your friend has not arrived.'

"'The morning, love, no doubt, will see him here.'

"'But my reputation must suffer with the servants, sir.'

"'I have already informed them that we are wedded.'

"'Merciful Heaven!' cried Eliza, 'what will become of me!'

"'That you will become my bride,' returned the libertine, 'and surely a few hours can make no difference?'

"'What, sir?'"

"'My beloved Eliza!' returned Wollaston, 'since we are so soon to be united you cannot treat me thus cruelly.'

"'Was it for this, insolent man,' cried the indignant girl, 'that you brought me from my home?'

"'Calm yourself, my love!' cried Wollaston, 'I meant not to offend you.'

"'Then leave me.'

"'Never.'

"'Although my love for you were ten times more firm, I would now despise you.'

"'Consider, Eliza, you are now in my power, and if I wished—'

"'You could take advantage of the unsuspecting girl who had confided to your honour.'

"'You treat me cruelly—consider the ardour of my passion. You are at my mercy, Eliza.'

"'But I tremble not—I will cry for help!'

"'There are none here to aid you.'

"'Thou hast then betrayed me,' cried the fearful girl, 'and under the garb holiness I find a villian.'

"'You then insult me—come, my pretty fair, that tone must change'

" ' Unhand me,' cried Eliza, as Wollaston seized it, and attempted to kiss her cheek.

" ' No,' replied the libertine, ' when I catch a pretty bird, I do not let her fly so easily.'

" ' Merciful God ! assist me,' cried the fainting girl, as her unresisting form was borne in the arms of the remorseless man.

At this moment, a slight noise was heard outside the door, and in an instant after, Fitzhurst and Mr. Melville entered.

" ' Villain ! ' cried the former, as he levelled the libertine with a blow, ' now we meet again.'

" ' My poor child,' said Mr. Melville, raising the fainting girl.

" ' Dear father, I am innocent—mercy—mercy—oh ! spare me—spare me—I cannot brook thy anger,' cried Eliza, and again fainted on the couch.

" ' Speak ! speak ! ' cried the agonized father ; ' I forgive thee ! '

" ' Dear father, I am innocent ! '

" ' Monster of iniquity,' said Mr. Melville to Wollaston, ' if thou hast a spark of pity in thy wolfish nature, assure me that my child's honour is in her keeping still.'

" ' It is,' said the fallen man.

" ' Swear to me by the sacred calling thou hast disgraced ! ' said the father.

I swear it by the God that made me ! ' returned the libertine, ' her soul is too pure to be easily misled.'

" ' And dost thou love him, child ? '

" ' Once, dear father—I acknowledge it ; he has now broken his faith, and I now despise him.'

" ' Well said, my noble girl. Come let me press you to my heart.'

Eliza raised herself from the couch, and the old man straining her to his bosom shed tears of love upon her cheek.

" ' These apartments are mine ! ' said Wollaston rising. 'You have your daughter unharmed, therefore quit them ! '

" ' We go,' said Mr. Melville.

" ' And you, Mr. Go between,' continued the libertine, addressing Fitzhurst ; ' I would square accounts with you—here are the means. He pointed to a pair of pistols, which he drew from a drawer.

" ' The place is not fitting,' said William.

" ' It shall be,' cried the infuriated Wollaston, ' or meet your fate.'

" In self-defence Fitzhurst snatched up the remaining pistol, and standing at the length of the room, the pistols were fired with a loud report, and the curate was wounded in the right arm, while his own pistol missed fire.

" Eliza screamed, and was borne away from the scene by her father, while a crowd of servants and police entered the room. A coach was procured, and before many hours had elapsed Eliza was at her quiet home at A——

" Upon the arrival of Mr. Melville in town, he did not wait till the police courts were open for a warrant, but went direct to the residence of a magistrate, who, after hearing the nature of his business, readily granted a search warrant, and they thus obtained admission to the house.

" A case of abduction was instituted against Wollaston, who was mulcted in a heavy fine and lost his gown ; and soon after William Fitzhurst had the happiness to lead Eliza, who now saw her error, to the altar."

A faint streak of grey light was illumining the eastern sky as Miranda ceased reading, and she closed the page with a sigh that caused Mr. Percy to look in her face as he said,—

" By such a villain has my dear boy been betrayed, and such a villain would cast himself at your feet, Miranda."

CHAPTER LIII.

THE TEMPORARY RESPITE.—MIRANDA AND THE JUDGE.—THE PRISON ORDER.—
THE MEMORIAL.

THE counsel who had promised Miranda that he would prepare a memorial to the Secretary of State, praying for a postponement of Rowland's execution, was as good as his word. He lost no time in the preparation of the document. His object was to get to it, before sending it, the signatures of some of the leading members of the circuit who had been present at the trial, and whose joining in such a request might have considerable effect upon the mind of the Secretary of State.

Such signatures he readily obtained, for to say the least of it, almost every lawyer he spoke to considered the case a most serious one, and that there must surely be yet something behind hand which was highly for or against the prisoner.

Varley's own counsel, now that the case was over, and he had as he considered done his duty, did not refuse his name to the memorial, remarking that he should be as happy as any one at any new fact being elicited, which should save the unhappy young man from the ignominious death to which he seemed absolutely doomed.

Lastly then, the counsel repaired to the lodgings of the judge, who he made no scruple of awakening up, although the hour was most unseasonable. That he, the judge, was humane and considerate, the counsel well knew, and could he induce him to grant the delay prayed for, he felt how much anxiety would be spared to the prisoner and his friends ; but even should the judge feel that his duty would not allow him to grant the temporary respite, still there could be no doubt but upon such a representation from the most respectable of the bar, he would consent to such a postponement of the sentence as should enable the answer of the Secretary of State to arrive, which it could scarcely do by the time appointed for the execution—seeing that it was then Sunday morning.

The judge heard the counsel with patience, and read attentively the memorial. Then turning to his visitor, he said in a mild, compassionate voice,—

" Believe me, my dear sir, talking with you now in a friendly way, which, now that the trial is over, I can do, I give you the greatest credit for your humanity and kind consideration in this case ; but I am decidedly of opinion that you are awakening hopes in the mind of the prisoner and his friends, which cannot be realised."

" While there is life there is hope," said the counsel ; " and my opinion of his innocence is so strong, that I expect everything from delay. Some fortunate accident may save him."

The judge shook his head, as he said,—

" You speak more like a friend than a lawyer. You must know there is no getting over the evidence."

" If these men, Twitter and Varley, are perjured."

" If they are," responded the judge, " how are we to know ? Heaven only can see into men's hearts. The prisoner, you see, himself admits everything up to the very point where their evidence begins. They then circumstantially accuse him of a monstrous crime, and all he has to say is, ' I did not do it.' "

" The case is certainly strong, but I believe him to be the victim of as base conspiracy as can be imagined

" We cannot listen in courts of justice to anything but sworn evidence, and they weigh the same in our imaginations. I cannot consistently with my duty recommend the prisoner to mercy."

"I cannot—I cannot—I dare not."

"At least, then, my lord, let me hope that you will postpone the execution till Wednesday in order to allow time for the answer of the Secretary of State to come."

"Certainly I will do that, in deference to your own feelings, and those of the gentlemen who have signed this memorial. I will, notwithstanding the very few precedents we have for such a course, respite the prisoner until Thursday morning, which will give ample time."

"We are much beholden to you, my lord," said the counsel, "and I pray that Heaven, between this time and that, will in some manner interpose to save the innocent."

"If he be innocent, I echo your prayer, with all my heart and soul," said the judge; "and now, before we part, can you give me any information of who that mysterious person is, and what might be the nature of his connection with this case, the very mention of whom, without a name, caused such unwonted emotion in the heart of the prosecutor?"

"That," replied the counsel, "is a mystery I would fain solve, and a most earnest and anxious search shall be instituted for him immediately. If fonnd, he shall, by every means, be urged to come forward on oath with all he knows."

"Then your knowledge of him really extends no further than you were able to give at the trial?"

"No further, my lord. It appears this man, the very mention of whom excites such emotions of terror in the breast of Varley, accosted the attorney for the defence in the street, and desired that the question might be propounded as you heard me. Wherefore I know not. I asked the question with a hope that he who suggested it would come forward, if its effect answered his expectations."

"Well, there is a mystery somewhere; and that it may be unravelled favourably to the prisoner, is my earnest prayer. I need not say that, upon any affidavit, altering the complexion of the case, being sworn before me, I will immediately extend the respite, in order that a searching investigation of its truth may be made."

The counsel could not but be satisfied with the judge's conduct, and, thanking him warmly for his kindness, he bowed and left him, pleased that some time had been gained.

His next visit was to Mr. Anderson, who had arranged the mean of sending the memorial immediately to London.

The moment the counsel entered the room, Mr. Anderson, with a pleasurable exitement of manner he could not conceal, handed to him an open note. It was addressed to him, Mr. Anderson, and contained these words:—

"Meet the solitary horseman to-night, in the bridle path leading from York to the Grange."

"Thank Heaven," said the counsel, "the man will make himself visible at last. Meet him! I'd travel a thousand miles to meet him. He must know something important, or Varley would never have exhibited the terror he did at his mention."

"I hope he does," said Mr. Anderson. "He mentions no precise time in his note, so I suppose I must go about sunset, and wait his coming."

"I will accompany you," said the counsel.

"Do so. We mean him well, and in fact we could not take any advantage of his presence, if we would; for an unwilling witness would be of no use. But what about the memorial?"

The counsel then detailed his proceedings, terminating with his interview with the judge, when he concluded by saying,—

"It is important now that the prisoner and his friends should clearly understand the precise signification of this respite, and not be deluded into too much hope from it. I will myself proceed to the prison, if you will undertake to explain the matter fully to Mr. Percy and Miranda Rankley."

"That I will do," responded Mr. Anderson. "This note from the mysterious man has given me new hope; I will, however, say nothing of it to Miranda, as it would only cause her the most intense anxiety and surprise."

"Which, indeed, she may well be spared. I will trespass upon you, Mr. Anderson, for a breakfast, as I see the morning is close at hand."

* * * * * * *

The morning sun was shining in at the window of the room where sat Miranda, when Mr. Anderson was announced. She descended rapidly the staircase, and pausing for a moment ere she opened the door of the little parlour into which, by the courtesy of the people of the house, he had been shown, she then, with as much composure as she could assume, entered the room.

He took her extended hand silently, and then led her to a seat, when she looked up in his face with such a sweet beseeching glance, to read therein if any new hope for Rowland had arisen, that the kind-hearted man had much to do to command his voice to any degree of firmness, as he said, in a low tone,—

"The memorial is sent to London, Miranda."

"Yes—yes," said Miranda, in a half choked voice. "Surely it will save him."

"Hope without being too sanguine, Miranda. We must all bow to Heaven's decrees, and yet we should always hope."

"Always," gasped Miranda. "Always till death."

"The judge has kindly granted a delay."

A slight cry of joy escaped Miranda's lips, as she convulsively seized Mr. Anderson by the arm, saying,—

"The—the judge—delay. They will not then murder him—I thought they were human, and could not."

"Hush—hush, Miranda. For Heaven's sake do not misconstrue my words—I said delay—delay only."

"Yes—yes—I heard—delay is life. Dear precious life. What is a long existence, but a little delay ere the dawn of eternity bursts upon the soul. They will not murder him. Oh! Mr. Anderson, you are not feeding my heart with false hopes. You said delay—you did."

"I did, Miranda, but I pray you do not give the word a wider signification."

"No—no—I will be calm—quite calm. How—long?"

"Till Thursday."

"Thursday—Thursday?"

"Yes, so as to give full time for the answer of the Secretary of State to com which may grant yet further time."

"God help them all," said Miranda. "They are trifling with that gift of God's which when once thrown back to Him may never—never be reclaimed—life—life. The life of the innocent—the good—the gentle. 'Tis very gracious of them not yet to dip their hands in his blood. God forgive them—God forgive them."

"Indeed, Miranda," said Mr. Anderson, who was sorry to find her in such a frame of mind, "There is nothing but sympathy and good wishes to Rowland among high and low."

"Sympathy—sympathy, and yet they will murder him while Heaven looks down upon the deed."

"Miranda, Miranda!"

A shudder came across her frame.

"Forgive me—forgive me," she said, in a low plaintive tone. "I will bless them for letting my Rowland live even another day. But he is innocent, and sometimes my heart will swell till it is nigh bursting, and you see, Mr. Anderson, I have no tears—I cannot weep, so the vexed spirit shews itself in bitterness.— Thank God that he will live till Thursday. That is a boon—a great boon, for I shall be nearer death myself ere we part."

"Far be it from me, Miranda," said Mr. Anderson, with emotion, "to awaken too much hope in your breast, but still, dark and gloomy as the prospect around you seems, I would not have you despair."

Miranda gave him her hand, as she said,—

" I ought not indeed to despair while I have such hearts as yours to feel for my distress—I am very ungrateful, Mr. Anderson, but you will forgive me ?"

" It would be a poor heart, indeed Miranda, that paused for words and expressions of gratitude from a wounded spirit such as yours. What I do, I do from a deep and sincere sympathy for one, who from my heart I believe as innocent of the crime for which he now lies condemned as I am myself. Heaven help both him and you."

" In all affliction," said Miranda, " we may see the hand of Heaven in some ray of mercy—some gleam of light mingling with the otherwise universal desolation around us—a something which robs pain of its sting—a rest for the wounded heart. In my misery—in my heart's sadness and affliction you have been to me that one bright spot—which has saved me from utter annihilation and despair."

Mr. Anderson was very much affected, for Miranda pronounced these words with such exquisite pathos—such a majesty of feeling, and such a purity of candour, that it is impossible we can give any idea of her manner by description. He turned aside for a moment to hide one tear that would, despite his efforts to control, roll down his cheek, and then partially mastering his emotion, he said,—

" I will leave you to tell Mr. Percy of this trifling change in the immediate aspect of affairs, Miranda, and again I reiterate my offer of my home for yourself and poor Mr. Percy."

" You have my heart's best thanks," said Miranda, " but let us be here where we can cast no shadows upon the domestic joy of any house. Here we can talk to each other of Rowland, and when the old man weeps for his dear son, I can talk to him of hope and chase away the tears. Let us be where we are, Mr. Anderson. It is better—believe me it is—far better."

" At all events, Miranda, it is a point upon which I have no right to press you, and I can only say that my offer still remains open whenever you please to accept of it, and believe me it is made with all sincerity."

" I know it, I know it," said Miranda. " Now tell when—oh! when can I see Rowland ?"

" There will be no difficulty now, Miranda. There are stated hours of visiting prisoners, but in the case of you as well as in that of Mr. Percy, the judge will not scruple to give you an order to visit him when you please, within the hours that the prison is open for ingress or egress at all."

" The judge !—he who condemned my poor Rowland.—Yet he wept, and none save I saw him weep."

" A more compassionate man never lived. The duty is a most painful one to him. I will get an order from him for you to visit Rowland."

A faint hope came across Miranda's heart, that if she had an interview with the judge, she might possibly move him to look upon the case somewhat differently—she might suggest something he had not thought of; acting upon this impulse of the moment she said,—

" Would he see me ?"

" Doubtless he would," replied Mr. Anderson. " However he might wish to avoid what to him and yourself might be a painful interview, he would not refuse."

"Time was," said Miranda, while a faint flush of colour visited her cheeks, " when I would have shrunk from inflicting an interview upon any one in the least averse to it, but the most timid grow bold when those they love are in great peril, and it seems to me now as if the ordinary feelings which I possessed were all overcome by the one great object of my soul—the preservation of Rowland. I will see the judge, Mr. Anderson, even should he accord to me an unwilling interview—still will I see him."

" You will receive nothing but courtesy from him, at all events ; but if you do call upon him, let it be this evening when the court closes."

" Cannot I go now, for I would fain visit Rowland ere then ?"

" Yes, certainly ; any time within the next hour and a half he will see you, I dare say, and now I bethink me, perhaps he would rather in the morning than evening. If you say you will be ready in half an hour I will come again and take you to where he is staying."

Miranda rose with more animation than she had for some time exhibited, as she said,—

"Yes; let it be so. I will be ready."

Mr. Anderson, when he reached the street, felt rather pleased than otherwise, that she had determined herself to solicit the order of the judge, for the effort appeared to arouse her from the state of deep despondency into which, when inactive, she seemed, from the pressure of her sorrows, inclined to fall.

CHAPTER LIV.

THE YORK ARMS.—THE CONSULTATION.—
HONOUR AMONG THIEVES.—NED WITLET'S
PROPOSAL.

WHILE this conversation was proceeding between Miranda and Mr. Anderson, there was scarcely a small public-house in York that had not its little knot of eager talkers on the all-engrossing subject of popular interest—namely, the preceding day's trial. The great man of every parlour—and there is a great man to every parlour—became tremendously oracular. and many were the opinions hazarded pro and con upon the subject. With only one of these little throngs of persons however, have we anything to do, and that was assembled in a dim, back parlour of a public-house, known as the York Arms, and situated in an out-of-the-way, curious street, where it could not be supposed that any business would be done; and it was a wonder to every person how the York Arms continued to keep its doors open, and to wear a thriving, bustling look.

The fact was, that the house had its regular customers—customers of a peculiar class—who getting money lightly—somewhat in the style and after the fashion of our friend, Ned Witlet, spent it as lightly, to the great content of the landlady, who was one of those masculine females, who certainly do not depend upon the weakness of their sex for protection.

In this back parlour there was a collection of some twelve or fourteen persons, who, while they indulged themselves very freely with strong ale, argued and re-argued the trial and its result with noisy pertinacity.

"The jury be bothered!" said one. "He didn't do it. I'll lay my life on it he didn't do it."

"Oh! what a werry slippery sneak that 'ere Samivel Twitter is, to be sure—all on one end—kivey, kim up!" exclaimed the witness, who on the trial had deposed to several little disagreeable particulars with respect to Twitter's early life and pursuits, and had afterwards so effectually got the better of the counsel for the prosecution. What he meant by "kivey kim up!" nobody ever knew; and it was only supposed that he used these euphonious words as a kind of garnish to his discourse, instead of an oath.

"You may say that," remarked another gentleman in a white top coat, and an awful black eye:—"Look at my hi."

"How cumed you by that ere?"

"Guved it myself, out o' a mistake."

"Gentlemen," said Ned Witlet, advancing from a dark corner, and taking a seat near the fire, "we all seem in one mind about this affair. That young man never did the murder, and it will be a murder to hang him for it."

"So it will," said several.

"Howsomdever, swing will he, and no mistake," rejoined Jones; "kivey, kim up!"

"Unless ——"

Witlet paused, and a dead silence pervaded the room—for every one was anxious to hear what he had to say.

"Unless" he continued, "we get somebody to confess who really did it, comrades."

"We!" said several.

"Yes," resumed Witlet; "I said we when I ought perhaps not to have done so; but it does so happen that I have seen and heard perhaps, more of this affair than most men in York who really know so little of it. We well know what Twitter is. We all know what he would lend himself to. He didn't do the murder—he hasn't courage and nerve enough, but ——"

"But what, Neddy," said Jones; "yer goes on a speaking as if yer was a bolting hot peas, and some on 'em sticked in the vay."

"But I think he, Twitter, might be frightened into confessing the real truth."

"You may frighten Twitter into confessing a lie," remarked a man in a surly voice, who had not yet spoken—"that's the risk of meddling with such fellows."

"Granted," said Ned; "but such a man as Twitter——"

"A sneak yer means," interposed Jones.

"Well, well, such as he, if frightened into confessing a lie, if he thought it was what was wanted of him, would not have cunning enough in his fright to make it tally with circumstances already known past dispute, whereas, if he told a tale that really did come in well, there would be every probability of its truth, do you see?"

"My eye," exclaimed Jones; "Neddy, yer can come it above a bit. A lawyer with a hextra wig, is a fool to yer—Kivey, kim up."

"You see my position," said Witlet.

"And we feels it too," replied Jones, "for you're a kivering up all the fire."

"Jones," said Witlet, "none of your nonsense. You aint over particular in some matters as we all know, but I never yet knew you to do a downright smoking action. I am not joking, my friends. I wish you to agree with me, some of you to undertake this job of frightening Twitter. I can pounce upon him at any time."

"What's the good to us?" growled one.

"A thousand pounds divided among all who have any hand in the affair, provided it saves the life of Rowland Percy," said Ned Witlet in a clear voice.

There was a silence of some moments among the gentlemen, and then Jones gave a long whistle and exclaimed,—

"Say it again, Neddy."

"A thousand pounds to be divided among us," repeated Ned Witlet, emphatically.

"How many will it take to do the job?"

"Two or three might easily; but as we are all here, only let us act fairly towards each other, and divide it."

"Well said—well said," cried several.

"Stop a bit—stop a bit," said Jones. Kivey kim up! who's to pay the blunt?"

"I will undertake that it shall be paid. Listen to me, friends, what we say here among ourselves will go no further, I am quite confident; now I am convinced that the murder of Sir George Rankley has a good deal to do with the disposition of his large property, and that a discovery of who really did the deed will in all probability, in one way or another, alter the disposition of that property very considerably."

"Go on—go on," said Jones, "go on, my oracle. It's as good as a sermon, it is."

"Well, then," resumed Ned Witlet, "I am quite certain that the reward I have named will be forthcoming, and rather increased than diminished."

"Very good," said Jones. "Now, how's it to be done, Ned?"

"Leave that to me. Agree among yourselves that some four or five are to meet me for the purpose of undertaking the job, and I will manage everything else. I wish that number of you to come, because we ought to have ample evidence, by a number of witnesses, of anything that Twitter, in his fright, may reveal."

"Agreed, agreed!" cried several.

"Then," said Ned, as he rose to leave the room, "let it be this evening. You know the green lane that leads out by the new cottages on the south side of the city?"

"Yes, yes."

"Meet me there then, one hour after sunset this evening, and I will undertake to bring Twitter to you."

He then left the house, and although his scheme for attempting to discover the truth, as regarded the murder, was something of the wildest, yet it was the only one that occurred to him by which he could hope to carry any information worth the hearing or bearing to Mr. Anderson, should he keep the appointment made for that same evening in the bridal path leading to the Grange estates. Witlet had taken a great and absorbing interest in the fate of Miranda and her lover; for although his notions as to the rights of property were entirely of a very loose description, he was like many other persons in this world, who feel particularly shocked at any species of iniquity but the one which long usage has made them familiar with.

The offer of the thousand pounds was a step ventured upon by Ned Witlet from a conviction that should the result of the experiment be to implicate Varley in the murder, and the release of Rowland Percy, something would arise to restore to

Miranda the property which had been wrested from her; for at the worst, even if the will could not be attacked, even should there be no evidence to prove it a forgery, in the event of Varley's conviction for the murder, the property would revert from his hands to the crown, when, without the shadow of a doubt, Miranda would be permitted, as the real heiress, to take quiet possession, when her ability and inclination to pay the thousand pounds would be as equal as undoubted.

Net Witlet's object now was to make sure of the presence of Twitter at the appointed spot, and that he thought he should have no difficulty in doing, as he held in his possession funds belonging to the valet, which were the result of sales of plate &c., effected by him, Witlet, in London for Twitter.

The highwayman knew that avarice was the reigning passion of the guilty wretch, and he wrote him the following note, which he knew, if anything, would bring him to the place of appointment.

"Samuel Twitter,—You know who has money for you; if you will, meet him this evening an hour and a half after sunset, half way up the green lane, where he met you once before, on the south of the city. Be punctual."

This note he sealed, and sent to the lodgings which had been jointly occupied by Twitter and Varley, but which, owing to the wild maniacal manner in which Bernard Varley haunted Miranda's steps, had been now for some days in the sole possession of Twitter.

No invitation could be more welcome to him, Twitter, than one from which money was to result, for he had become so thoroughly and dreadfully alarmed at the infatuation of Bernard Varley, with regard to Miranda, that he had determined in his own mind, to gather together as quickly as possible, by every means in his power, as large a sum of money as he could, and leave England, to avoid the danger which, like the sword of Damocles, he believed to be hanging over his head from the indiscretion of his companion in guilt, whose very intellect seemed to suffer from the excess of his passion for her who was his victim.

CHAPTER LV.

MIRANDA'S INTERVIEW WITH THE JUDGE. —THE ORDER,—THE VISIT TO THE PRISON.

MR. ANDERSON returned to the humble abode of Miranda at the expiration of the appointed time, in order to conduct her to the judge's lodgings in compliance with her wish.

He found her ready for the street, and after a few moments' conversation with old Mr. Percy, during which he seemed to be so much depressed as scarcely to be conscious of what he was saying, the benevolent attorney and his beautiful client departed arm-in-arm, on the errand which Miranda had a vague hope might possibly result in something beneficial to Rowland, and which Mr. Anderson was sure could do no harm if it did no real good.

The distance was far from great, but there was one circumstance which made it wearisome and full of excitement of the most painful nature. That was the fact that she had not proceeded with Mr. Anderson a dozen paces from the door of the house in which she resided, ere Bernard Varley had left the window opposite, from which he had been watching her movements, and hurrying to the street, followed her at a distance only of ten or twelve paces.

Mr. Anderson first saw Varley, and it was the sudden start of surprise that he gave which made Miranda cast her eyes in the direction of her arch enemy.

She shuddered and clung closer to Mr. Anderson, as she whispered to him,—

"That dreadful man; my soul's enemy—my father's murderer—the prosecutor of my betrothed husband; he follows me like an evil genius. Oh, Mr. Anderson think you he is really human ?"

"I am sorry to say I do," replied Mr. Anderson; "but heed him not, Miranda. If I mistake not, that man with all his villany has not the power to inflict upon his greatest victim one tithe of the misery that rends his own heart, and makes him the miserable, despicable wretch his appearance at once indicates."

"Heaven save me from him ?" said Miranda.

"If ever," added Mr. Anderson, "a human being suffered in this world for his crimes, that man suffers; he carries the index of it in his face, he betrays it in every movement. I do verily believe that his wild attachment, if I may give it that name, to you is a retribution from Heaven against him, for it can bring him no feeling but despair."

"And yet, oh, yet," said Miranda, "I would it were not so; I fear him while I loathe him."

"Fear him not, Miranda; he dare not even annoy you; but there is one piece of advice which I would give you in the present juncture of affairs, which, however unpalatable it may be to you, and I confess disagreeable to me, I ought to give you, for the sake of him in whose fate we are all so deeply and so feelingly, but you most of all, Miranda, interested."

"You speak of Rowland ?"

"I do."

"What advice, Mr. Anderson, would you give me? Cóming from you, I am sure of its value and its sincerity."

"If my advice to you, Miranda, was as valuable as from my heart it is sincere, I should be rejoiced; but what I have to say concerns that man whose eyes are now glaring upon you, and whose whole guilty soul seems engrossed in watching your every movement."

"Concerns him ?"

"Yes, Miranda. He is evidently labouring under an infatuation which may for a time overcome his caution. Should he some of these times speak to you and make wild and strange proposals, I would advise, while you abate not one jot of your aversion—while you still show him by every word and every look what an abhorred thing he is to you—to listen to him."

"Listen to Bernard Varley ?"

"Yes, Miranda. Some chance word—some wild chance assertion or promise of his may give us a clue which, if properly followed up, might possibly change the present sad aspect of affairs, and open Rowland's prison gates. You understand me, Miranda ?"

"I do—I do. For Rowland's sake I will even listen to Bernard Varley. Your advice is kindly offered, Mr. Anderson. I will strive to act upon it."

"We should neglect no chance of righting the innocent, and the finger of Heaven may make itself visible in this transaction, by words, after all, out of his mouth, convicting him."

"It may—it may. I will not yet abandon hope."

They had now reached the judge's door, and Bernard Varley seemed in a moment to guess that Miranda's walk was ended there, for he crossed to the opposite side of the way, and stepping into a door way, he folded his hands upon his breast, and with eyes, from which shone wild and unholy lustre, watched the beautiful form of her he loved, and yet had worked so much woe to, till it disappeared within the house.

"She is more beautiful than daylight," he muttered. "The sun that shines upon her has its beams reflected back with tenfold loveliness. Her voice is like the gentlest music. Oh, how blessed must he be who hears it in accents of tenderness. Who can help loving her? The very air around her is glowing as if with a divine halo, created by her pure breath, made glorious and beautiful by her rare loveliness. Miranda—Miranda! if I could win you, I would renounce all else. The world contains no other charm to bind me to it. Thou, and thou only, art the one blessing that my heart covets. Can it be possible that such love as mine is in vain.

Miranda—Miranda! beautiful being—beautiful in thy pride—beautiful in thy scorn, but, most of all, beautiful in thy sorrow. I would for thy dear sake, consent to die, if that a smile from thy lips lit with beauty the last convulsive throb that parted me from life."

With clasped hands and upturned eyes he stood like one possessed, awaiting the appearance of her who was at once his only dream of joy, and his bitterest curse.

In the meanwhile Mr. Anderson had accompanied Miranda into a waiting room, from whence he sent up a card, on which he wrote Miranda's name, with a request for a brief interview.

An answer was speedily brought from the judge to the effect that he would see Miss Rankley in a few moments. Those few moments rapidly glided by, and then a servant came to conduct the beautiful girl to the presence of the man who, in pursuance of his sad duty, had been compelled to condemn her Rowland to a shameful and ignominious death.

Her heart palpitated painfully in her bosom as she entered the room, and every object for a moment seemed to swim before her eyes. Then a kind, soft, musical voice said to her,—

" Miss Rankley, pray be seated. I shall be most happy to comply with any request consistent with my duty which you may have come here to make to me."

She glanced at the face of the judge, and she saw that it was full of humanity and kindly feelings. Then making an effort to recover herself, she said, in those low, sweet accents that reach the heart,—

"Sir, my errand here is but to solicit your leave to visit him who now lies condemned——"

She paused, and the judge said, kindly,—

"You want an unconditional order to see Rowland Percy?"

" Yes," said Miranda, "and—and——"

" Pray take your time, and tell me, without reservation, what you wish."

" I wish," said Miranda, "now that I am here, to tell you how truly, how firmly I am convinced of the innocence of him who is condemned for my father's murder. Oh, sir, can you think for one moment that I who loved my father fondly, could think and speak as I do of his murderer? Nature would cry out against me—reason would shame me—imagination would terrify me. He is innocent—he is indeed innocent!"

The judge was silent for a moment, and then he said, in a tone of quiet consideration,—

" That you are sincere in what you say Heaven forbid that I should doubt. Human judgment is fallible, and God help us if we err in judging each other. By the light which Heaven vouchsafes us alone can we be guided."

" He is innocent—he is innocent!" repeated Miranda, in a tone of such exquisite anguish that the judge was much moved, and a tear trembled in his eye as he said,—

" Under any other circumstances than the extraordinary ones of this trial, which is now concluded, I should have felt myself justified in refusing to hold a conversation with any one concerning what came before me in my judicial capacity, and in which I have no sort of discretion. I sit but to administer the law. I am called a judge, and yet Heaven knows I judge not. He in whose fate you are so much interested has been pronounced guilty."

" And yet so innocent even in thought," said Miranda. " Oh, sir, think of the maddening regret—the frightful pang that must come across the hearts of all who have had to do with this great, this terrible error of judgment, when it shall come to pass in the fulness of time that his innocence shall be apparent to all men."

" If he be innocent," replied the judge, " I pray to Heaven as truly and as fervently as you can, that it may be manifest in time; but what more can I do?"

Miranda was not so absorbed in her grief even but what she felt how powerless the judge must be after the unqualified verdict which the jury had returned against Rowland, and she said,—

"Pardon me, sir, for my importunity. I know I cannot expect you to do more than you have—namely, to administer your office with the kind gentleness for which I feel so much your debtor; but I was anxious—very anxious to tell you personally that I, the daughter of the alleged murdered man, believe in the innocence of the accused Rowland Percy as I believe in Heaven."

"Your sincerity I cannot doubt," said the judge in an under tone. "Do you doubt the fact of your father having been murdered on that night?"

"No—no."

"Then who, think you, did the deed, if not he who now lies waiting the sentence of the law?"

"Bernard Varley."

"Well," said the judge, "I expected from you that answer, and having heard it, let me entreat you to be more discreet and guarded in what you say. That this Bernard Varley is a man of violent and bad passions it needs not much penetration to discover. I pray you, young lady, not to put it in his power to revenge himself for the words you may believe true, but which he would find no difficulty in getting a jury to declare libellous."

"I take your caution, sir, in good part," said Miranda; "but no power on earth shall prevent me denouncing to God and man Bernard Varley as my father's murderer!"

The judge shook his head as he wrote an order for Miranda to visit the prison at any hours between the time when the gates were opened in the morning to when they were closed for the night.

"Be prudent," he said, "and leave the issue of this matter in the hands of Heaven."

"I have to thank you, sir," said Miranda, "for as much kindness as it was possible for you to show to me and the innocent prisoner, under the melancholy circumstances in which we are placed."

The judge inclined his head, and Miranda, who was now anxious to visit the prison, took her leave, and in a few moments was in the street again with Mr. Anderson, who listened attentively to her account of what the judge had said to her, from which, as he expected, he derived not the least shadow of hope.

Varley, the moment he saw Miranda emerge from the door of the udge's house started from the listless attitude in which he had been standing, and pulling his hat down upon his brows, he followed her at about the same distance he had before pursued towards the place of Rowland's confinement.

"He follows me still," whispered Miranda to Mr. Anderson. "Am I ever to be haunted by this fearful man?"

"Endure it for a little time," said Mr. Andeason. "I will find means to free you from it eventually. Do you have interview with Rowland, and I will wait for you in the vestibule of the prison. Then I would advise you to go on alone, although I will keep you in sight, and be at your side any moment you wish. Let Bernard Varley speak to you if he will."

"For Rowland's sake," said Miranda, with a shudder. "I will even do that; but do not leave me quite."

"Be assured that I will not."

They had now reached the wicket-gate of the prison, and upon Miranda presenting her order, she was at once admitted within the vast gloomy building.

CHAPTER LVI.

THE PRISON.—THE APPEAL.—ROWLAND'S DESPAIR AND RENEWED HOPE.—THE UN-
EXPECTED MEETING.

ALTHOUGH Mr. Anderson, on account f being the solicitor of Rowland Percy would have been admitted with Miranda to his cell, he would not avail himself of that occasion of his privilege, but remained in the vestibule, leaving the lovers to talk over their hopes and their fears—alas how much the latter predominated over the former—by themselves.

The man who conducted Miranda through the gloomy passages to the still gloomier cell wherein was Rowland awaiting his doom, strode on with all the indifference of custom, which will so habituate one human being to the distresses of others as to make us look upon their tears as things of course—their sighs as nothing to awaken any sympathy in his obdurate bosom.

He even whistled a few bars of a lively air as he moved the dungeon door, and when he turned to Miranda he seemed surprised to see the look of suffering depicted on her face, and the death like paleness even of her very lips.

" Ain't you well, miss ?" he said.

" Yes—yes," replied Miranda ; " as well as, perhaps, I can ever hope to be."

" Oh," was the brief reply of the official, as he selected one from among a bunch of keys, which opened into a little octagonal room, on each of the sides of which was a door opening into a small cell.

" These here," remarked the man, " are the condemned cells, miss, and uncommon snug they is."

Miranda made him no answer, but she dropped the thick black veil she wore, over her face, and stood mutely waiting his pleasure to open Rowland"s cell.

Upon this, seeing that the visiter was not disposed to enter into conversation, he began whistling again, and having selected another key from his bundle, he approached one of the doors. The turnkey, with great deliberation, for he was in no hurry, not he, turned the lock, and then pushing the door open a little way, he put his head into the cell, and after completing the bar of the tune he was whistling, he said,

" A visiter, Percy."

" Rowland !" cried Miranda,

A cry of joy came from the lonely prisoner, and in the next moment she had rushed past the turnkey, and was hanging on her lover's arm.

" Miranda—Miranda—my own Miranda. So you have come to cheer me; to light with the glory of your presence this gloomy abode. Oh, how can I thank you, my own noble Miranda ?"

" I hopes as she ain't smuggled in no gin or 'baccy," was the remark of the turnkey to himself, as he locked the door upon the unhappy young persons, who, under brighter auspices, might have passed through life with scarce a shadow on the sunshine of their joy.

" Rowland, did you not expect me ?"

" I did, Miranda, with a fever of impatience that I could not moderate. I knew well, though deserted by all the world, you would still be true to me."

" If I deserted you now, Rowland, I should indeed be most unworthy of your love. You have heard that some time has been granted ?"

" Yes, dear Miranda, that news was communicated to me most quickly."

" Has—has it, Rowland, awakened hopes ?"

He turned aside his face for a moment, and then in a voice struggling with emotion, he said,

" It is indeed hard to be torn from love and from thee, Miranda ; and I am in the spring-tide of life—the season of existence, when hope, like the vine's tendrils, will cling around even a ruin."

Miranda silently pressed his hand, and for some moments their hearts were too full to speak. It was Rowland, who at length broke the silence by saying, in a more composed and cheerful tone of voice,

" Life is a strange dream, Miranda. Let us look upon it but as a fitful vision; the cares, the griefs, and anxieties of which are but like the phantasies of the imagination ;—here a moment, and then vanished in the dim records of the dreary past."

Miranda looked in his face, as she said,

"Rowland, your philosophy should have a higher, a nobler source—a source you overlook."

She pointed upwards as she spoke, and Rowland said in a low tone, as if doubtful of his own words,

"I—I trust to Heaven and my own conscience, but—— "

"Rowland, Rowland," cried Miranda; "this is the sharpest pang of all. There should be one thought—one hope which should support you, and that belongs to Heaven."

"'Tis hard for the moment, Miranda. And to suffer in such a manner. To be made the spectacle of a gaping crowd; to be brought out as if unfit to be trusted among my fellow men, with the faculties that God has given me; to be held up to execration; to be the object at which the finger of scorn will point; and then—then, innocent though I am, my Miranda, to be—be—strangled like a dog.—Oh, God! oh, God! If there be a Providence which will not let the fall of a sparrow pass unheeded, why——"

"Forbear—forbear," cried Miranda, as she clung convulsively to Rowland's arm. "Oh, how little did I expect to hear such words as these."

"They are forced from me."

"No—no—no, Rowland. Dear Rowland, for dear you are to me, and surely at such a time as this I may confess so much, let me beg, implore, on my knees beseech you to reconcile yourself to God, and doubt not His mercies. Oh, Rowland, Rowland! think again; your better judgment will surely step in, and I shall yet hear you say, "God's will be done?""

"Miranda, would you have me to submit?"

"To all! to all! and by so doing triumph over all."

"A poor triumph."

"No, Rowland, a glorious one. One that will reach the skies, and there be chronicled when mortal victories are forgotten in the dust of their heroes."

There was something that seemed almost inspired in the tone and manner of the beautiful girl as she thus nobly pleaded with her lover's heart, and combatted the gloomy philosophy with which he had in vain sought to cheat his situation of its terrors. He passed his hand across his face, and then in a humbled tone said,

"You—you would not surely, Miranda, wish me to undergo the fate I have pictured to you?"

"I would give my life for yours, Rowland."

"I want not that. I cannot—will not—make the show which shall bring about me the gaping crowd to gloat upon my dying agonies."

There was in his manner a hesitation, which, for some moments, Miranda could not comprehend; and then all at once there darted across her mind a dreadful supposition—a supposition which never for a moment previously had crossed her mind, but which now came with such an exquisite pang of anguish that made her brain reel, and seemed to threaten to overturn her reason.

Rowland saw the sudden change in her appearance. He saw the fixed look of terror with which she regarded him, and in a voice of alarm he cried,

"Miranda, Miranda! For the love of Heaven speak to me; for your looks terrify me. Miranda! speak—oh, speak?"

"For the love of Heaven," were Miranda's words, "can aught be done! For the love of Heaven? Rowland, you yourself have used these words. Search into your heart and ask yourself the cause of my emotion."

"My—own—heart!"

"Yes, Rowland. Is there not a frightful secret—a hideous spectre there which steps between you and your better self—casts a shadow between you and Heaven?"

Rowland trembled, as he replied,

"What—what—spectre?"

"Its name is temptation, and it whispers——"

"What—what?"

"Suicide!"

As Miranda spoke she sank to the floor of the cell, and covering her face with her hands, her bosom heaved with emotion, and a sharp cry of anguish escaped her lips.

"Miranda—Miranda!" said the agonised Rowland; "you have conquered."

She arose up, and flung her arms around him, as she said,

"Dear Rowland, you will not make me the widow of a self murderer. You will not take yourself that life which God has given you? and which, if it be His will to resume, you may be sure is for some holy and wise purpose, unscanned by mortal eyes, but visible in that bright world which is to come, and without the hope of which, dear—dear Rowland, what could have supported your Miranda amid her sea of troubles?"

Rowland's eyes were humid with tears, as pressing Miranda to his heart, he said,—

"You are my good angel, Miranda. You have saved me from myself. Bless you, Miranda. They may murder me, but they shall not call me the coward I thought of becoming."

Miranda laid her head upon his breast, and then looked up in his face as she said,—

"Heaven's will be done."

Rowland put his hand in his breast and took therefrom an exceedingly minute phial.

"Miranda," he said, "I wrote to one who I knew would comply with my wish and he sent me this."

"Poison!" shuddered Miranda.

"Yes, poison; one drop of this subtle essence would stretch out a corpse on the floor of my cell. I thought to have disappointed them when they came to fetch their victim; but you have conquered, Miranda. Take it; take it from me. I will submit."

Miranda eagerly took the bottle, and concealed it in her bosom.

"Rowland," she said, "this is, indeed, a triumph. Hope—hope, dear Rowland. It seems to me now as if a something whispered me that the worst was over. My heart is lighter than it has been for many a day."

"And mine; and now, Miranda—my father—is he well?"

"Not ill, Rowland, and yet much shattered."

The key turned in the lock of the door at this moment, and the turnkey, putting in his head, said,—

"Are you ready to go, mum?"

"To-morrow," whispered Miranda to Rowland, "to-morrow at this time I will be here."

"Heaven bless you, Miranda!"

There was a silent pressure of the hands, and Miranda turned from the cell.

CHAPTER LVII.

SAMUEL TWITTER AND THE GENTLEMEN OF THE ROAD.—THE MUTUAL SUSPICIONS OF VARLEY AND TWITTER.

NED WITLET, by writing to Samuel Twitter the note which we have presented to the reader, certainly took the most effectual method of inducing the avaricious and cowardly valet to meet him. As we have stated, Twitter had but one hope, and that was to escape from the great danger of an association with Varley by entirely leaving England; but then to do that he required, or fancied he required a much larger sum than he was already master of. His attempts to procure a, sufficient reward at once from Varley had, as we have seen, failed, and his only chance now of accomplishing his object was by degrees, and by such peculations as he could find an opportunity of committing upon Varley, with the assistance of Ned Witlet, who he still believed would be his ready agent in the disposal of whatever portable plunder he could lay his hands upon, either at the Grange or elsewhere.

Hence Twitter most readily determined to be punctual in meeting the highwayman at the place appointed, little suspecting the reception he was about to get from men unscrupulous by what means they fulfilled their purposes, and to whom the large reward mentioned by Witlet was indeed a most powerful incentive to action.

Varley had, during the day, insisted upon Twitter accompanying him to the proper authorities, in order to back him in a formal complaint of ill-usage he had received during the riot, notwithstanding Twitter would gladly have allowed the affair to pass over, for he dreaded nothing more than making himself well known by numerous appearances in public; but Varley was inexorable, and he was compelled to comply with his humour.

The magistrates, however, could only express their civil regret, and fine some of those who had been taken by the officers in various sums.

As the evening approached, Twitter became extremely anxious to know what Varley was going to do, or where he was going to remain. In fact, so extremely fidgetty was he, and so very inquisitive—for he was in a perfect fever when absent from his companion in guilt, lest he should seek an interview with Miranda, and, in the excess of his wild adoration of her, sacrifice both himself and him, Twitter, by some incautious admission—that to see him any one would have thought Bernard Varley was some dangerous lunatic, and that he, Samuel Twitter, was under heavy responsibilities as regarded his safety.

The suspicious, crafty temper of Varley never deserted him, except in his intercourse with Miranda; then, indeed, the now master spirit of his soul drowned in its flush of power every other feeling, and his passion for her eclipsed even his love for self. But widely different was he in his intercourse with others, and, most of all, with Twitter, who he was aware was smarting under the pang of disappointment at not reaping as suddenly as he expected—and, in fact, had been promised—a large pecuniary benefit from his share in the murder of Sir George Rankley.

This Varley would not permit him to do, for his knowledge of human nature had been derived from the very worst specimens, and he believed that he should not have a moment's safety if he permitted Twitter to be otherwise than entirely dependent upon him.

Hence he determined to keep him his slave, and to watch him with vigilance and activity. Moreover, Varley had another reason, if reason it could be called, in which there was so little judgment. He was not without a wild and clinging hope that at the last, when hope was dead, and despair ran riot in her heart, Miranda, to save Rowland Percy from a scaffold, would make some agreement with him, either to become his wife then, or at some distant period, provided he saved the innocent Rowland from the awful fate that seemed so inevitably waiting on him.

This Varley intended to do, if it were to be done at all, by a concocted tale, which should denounce Twitter and sacrifice him to the law; if he did not from the lack of evidence do that, at least Rowland Percy could not be executed in the face of recantation on the part of a principal witness of the principal evidence against him.

This recantation he would have transmitted to the authorities on the eve of his own departure to another country, to which he would have repaired under such circumstances, provided he could carry with him any promise from Miranda, which would in some measure give him hopes of one day calling her his own.

So wild—so extravagant—so improbable a fabric of the imagination could never have entered, or if it had, maintained a place for one moment in so politic a brain as Bernard Varley's, had his reason not been thoroughly besotted upon that one subject, and his love for Miranda not amounted to what it really was—a species of mania, that when once it began to act in his brain, disordered all reasoning, and presented him with the most absurd mental combinations.

Hence was it he looked upon Samuel Twitter as one to be sacrificed, and upon Miranda as the reward.

It was towards evening that Twitter, who felt his great danger until Rowland Percy should be no more—for, after that, what had Bernard Varley to offer Miranda —endeavoured in a cautious manner to elicit how he, Varley, was going to spend the next few hours.

The very fact of his making such cautious inquiries let Varley know at once that he, Twitter, expected to be engaged in some scheme which would prevent him from watching his movements, and it came into his mind immediately to execute the very project of which Twitter was so much afraid, namely of seeing Miranda if possible, and tempting her with her lover's life, to assume a smile towards him she abhorred, even as her pure spotless soul abhorred evil and crime.

"We shall feel easier and more comfortable," whispered Twitter, as he took a side glance at Varley's face, "when Thursday next is over."

"Thursday?" replied Varley, with a start.

"Yes, Thursday—to that day the execution is, as you know, put off, Varley."

"The execution—yes, the execution," in an abstracted tone. "Time is short —time is short."

"The better it should be," said Twitter. "When that is over we—we shall be much more safe."

"Are we not safe now," said Varley.

"Yes; but——"

"But what?"

"Nothing—nothing; only, you know, the excitement of the affair will altogether subside after he is dead, and then, Varley, we can begin to enjoy a little the fruits of that which, at least to me, has yielded nothing but bitterness and terror."

"What has it yielded to me?" said Varley, in a tone that seemed as if it came from the depths of the grave,

"There is one thing," said Twitter, not noticing Varley's remark, for he wished then no contention with him, "which I think would be very desirable, Varley."

"What is that?"

"That you should visit the Grange as early as possible, and see that all is safe there. The servants owe you no good will, you know—at least, the few of the old ones that remain—and, were to go, they would no doubt dispute my authority completely."

"Think you so?"

"Yes; I am sure of it. Now, if you were to ride over to-night, I would come after you, which would be better than my going with you, I think, as, just now, it may be desirable that we should not appear too much together. You understand, Varley?"

"I hear you," said Varley. "At what time would you meet me at the Grange?"

"It wants now but a short time of sunset. Suppose I was to come over in about two hours from now."

"Agreed—let it be so, and I will proceed thither at once."

"Very well; I shall merely stroll gently on the road, so as to get there about the time mentioned. You will probably overtake and pass me, for I shall walk."

"No doubt."

Twitter, after making a few more remarks about different matters which he suggested required seeing to at the Grange, even before it could be advertised to be let to any one, he then left the room, quite felicitating himself that he had succeeded in getting Varley from the immediate neighbourhood of Miranda, while he should be engaged so as not to be able to interrupt any interview that Varley might otherwise have sought with her.

"Every hour," muttered Twitter, when he was alone, "is an hour gained. Let Rowland Percy once be dead, and I shall be rid of my chief dread. Miranda, then will have nothing to hope. The very worst will have been realised, and Bernard Varley can have no possible motive to indiscretion, for, as it is, I verily believe he would place his neck, and mine too, in the halter, if that girl chose, by a little of woman's duplicity, to give him any hopes of becoming her husband."

"What can Twitter be aiming at this morning?" thought Varley. "He has some secret enterprise in hand. He wants to get me away from York to-night. Did he think, by shallow excuses and mock reasons, to persuade me to go alone to the Grange? No; I will this evening, unencumbered by him, endeavour to procure an interview with Miranda. And yet, am I in danger of Twitter? What means the mystery of his conduct? He is disappointed; and yet—yet surely he would not, could not be so mad as turn against me now, after swearing to so much. He did not do the deed. There he has an advantage over we—a door of escape would be opened to him were he to confess all, which mould for ever remain closed upon me as the actual perpetrator of the murder. His evidence would then destroy me—and yet who would believe the uncorroborated testimony of such as he? He could but swear to his new statement, and he has sworn to his old one. Yet I will endeavour to discover what he is doing this evening that makes him so anxious to get me out of the way. He will no doubt keep his word as to going to the Grange. I should overtake him on the road, he said. I will do so, and then after getting some distance, I can return on foot and keep an eye on him. After that I will visit thee, Miranda—beautiful being! Death even, at thy hands, were sweeter far than life without thee. If I could win but one smile—if I could be permitted to hold her hand in mine—if I could feel the soft, velvet pressure of her lips, I would sacrifice all—all!—yes all!"

The shadows of the evening were rapidly approaching, and Varley, after remaining for some moments silent, while his thoughts were with Miranda, suddenly rose, and, ordering his horse to be brought to the door with all convenient speed, he by many reasons, all of which were tinctured with the wildness of his mad passion, strove to convince himself that Miranda would some day be his.

It was strange that on that evening there should be so many persons interested directly or indirectly in the fate of Rowland Percy, bound to the outskirts of York—but so it was. There were Witlet, Twitter, Varley, Mr. Anderson, and the humane counsel, as well as the questionable companions of Ned Witlet, who hoped to reap so golden a harvest from the, to them, common-place job of frightening a timid man nearly out of his wits.

Twitter fully intended to go to the Grange, for he had about the premises several secret places, in which, from time to time, he had deposited the proceeds of his various robberies, until they amounted to sums which, through a London agent, he could place at interest in the public securities. These secret hoards he wished to visit, and empty of their treasures, since he resided no longer on the premises. For these purposes, as well as to keep faith with Varley, he intended to strike across the country to the Grange, after his meeting with the highwayman, which he judged would, as usual, be a very brief one.

While he was hurrying to the place mentioned by Witlet in his note, that personage had met six of his companions who were to form the expedition, and collecting them round him, he said to them,—

" Now, quite understand me in this matter. You must give it up on a signal from me, for I know how far to go with any chance of success. Twitter knows me, and were I to show myself in this business, it would spoil any future hope of thinking of another scheme the accomplish to object we have in view. So you six must waylay him, and do the job of frightening him without my assistance. I will blow my whistle when you are to leave him alone; but should he confess anything of importance, I will make my appearance directly.'"

" All right," said one.

" Remember the thousand pounds," said another.

"If we succeed, you will find it is not forgotten," replied Witlet.

The party now started by different routes to the scene of action, some of them happened to be upon such intimate terms with the police of York, that, had they all gone in a body, some troublesome member of that force might have been smitten with a notion of following them, which under the circumstances, would have been very awkward indeed.

Fortunately for the secresy of the enterprise, the night set in uncommonly dark for the season of the year, and a cold north-easterly wind was not likely to act as an inducement to any one to take a rural walk in the suburbs, except upon pressing business.

The lane which had been named by Twitter was a wild, secluded place. It was very seldom visited by any one except to admire the natural beauties by which it was surrounded, and which itself exhibited; and, as they could be only appreciated by daylight, it was, except when a full moon shone from a cloudless sky, rarely intruded upon after sunset. The fact was, that a discovery of extensive strata of gravel had been made years since about the spot, and hence the lane and its vicinity had been cut up into pits and small excavations, which, in time becoming covered with vegetation, gave the place a wild and very picturesque aspect, at the same time that it ill adapted it for a thoroughfare.

CHAPTER LVIII.

TWITTER IN AN AWKWARD POSITION.—ATTEMPT TO EXTORT A CONFESSION.—THE RESCUE.

WITLET and his companions were on the appointed spot some time before Twitter could fairly be expected, and the highwayman posted his force in an advantageous position at a narrow part of the lane, where it would be impossible for any human being to pass without being observed.

Close, likewise, to that was one of the deepest, if not the deepest of all pits or excavations which had been made for the purpose of procuring the gravel. The bottom of this pit—long since neglected and exhausted—had become a reservoir for all the rain water which had flowed from the higher ground, and even in the dryest weather there was commonly a black stagnant looking pool at the bottom of this pit, while at seasons when much rain had fallen, and there was a considerable humidity in the air, the pool increased to a miniature lake, in which stood up, like fairy islands, the tops of masses of rubbish and huge stones, which had fallen to the lowest depth of the excavation.

"Conceal yourselves here," said Witlet, "and I will go to the other side of the lane ; I know the man well and shall recognise him even in the dark. When you hear my whistle, one only of you step out and seize him. Then let the remainder of you appear when he is much frightened, and the sudden additional shock may alarm him into a confession."

"I say, Ned," remarked Jones, who formed one of the party, "I supposes as you haven't no sort o' objections to us all being lords o' this here blessed manor ? Kivey kim up. Eh, Ned ?"

" What do you mean ?"

" I mean this here. Yer knows as them ere lords o' manors has some on 'em, as we all knows uncommon well, no manners at all, lays their hands on what they calls waifs and strays."

" Well, what then ?"

" Why, 'sposing as some covey was to lose his way on this here dark night, and come down the lane, you know, Ned."

" Well, Jones, what have we to do with that ?"

" Wouldn't he be a waif and a blessed stray ? Business is business you knows, Neddy, and as we is here, why all's fish as comes to net."

" Nonsense, Jones," said Witlet. " You know as well as I how very dangerous it is to run after stray game when we are on any particular expedition, Let all pass free to-night but the man we seek."

" What, not go for to rob nobody ?"

" Certainly not. Besides the danger is excessive so near York. Leave all that alone to-night."

" Well," said Jones, with a disappointed tone, "we has 'pinted you governor for to-night, and I 'sposes as you must have your own way."

" Hush now," whispered Witlet, " I don't know a moment when our man may come, and the sound of voices would scare him off like a startled hare."

The Minster clock now sounded in the distance with gloomy grandeur, and Witlet counted eight.

" He will be here soon," he said. " Not another word."

The highwayman then stepped across the lane, and ensconced himself in a deep hollow on the other side, while his comrades kept a profound stillness and not a vestige of them could be seen amid the mass of dark vegetation that concealed them so effectually.

At the same time that Ned Witlet was listening to the Minster clock strike eight, Twitter had arrived at the entrance of the lane, and paused likewise to listen to the sonorous announcement as the wind bore it to his ears,—

"I'm just in nice time," he muttered. "Ned is sure to be here. He is a man of his word, but when I come to think of it, he can't have much money to give me—saving the proceeds of the ring, which I never yet had of him."

He looked up at the dark frowning sky a moment, and then he strove to pierce the imprenetrable gloom in which the lane was shrouded, and to enter which resembled plunging into some deep hollow that went far from the light of day into the very bowels of the earth.

"This," muttered Twitter, "would be a fearful place to be attacked in. I never saw it so dark as this. When I came here last a harvest moon was shining, and I could see my way as if it had been broad daylight."

A step into one of the hollows of about a foot in depth, now suddenly warned Twitter that he must be exceedingly cautious how he proceeded, and with a muttered execration he cautiously felt his way with his feet before he trusted all his weight upon them.

"I will get Witlet," he thought, "to go part of the way home with me. That is to say towards the Grange, for I might be robbed on my road of all that I have to receive from him. The lane gets surely darker and darker, I wish he would make his appearance."

Thus muttering to himself his fears, Twitter slowly proceeded up the lane, until he came to the narrow part, where those were posted who intended making so trying an experiment upon his nerves.

According to arrangement, Witlet blew his whistle, when he saw the dusky form of Twitter slowly approaching.

"Is that you Witlet?" said Twitter. "How dark this place is to-night,"

"Stand!" cried Jones, coming forward, and grasping the terrified Twitter by the collar.

"Murder!" gasped the assailed man. "Murder! murder!"

"Jist say that agin," cried Jones, "and if you'd as many lives as a cat I'd take 'em all, one after the other."

"Spare me—oh, spare me. Witlet—Witlet, save me."

Jones upon this gave Twitter so tremendous a shaking, that had he left go at its termination, he must have fallen to the ground, so confused and bewildered did he become.

"Take my money," he whined, "take it all—and—my watch, but spare my life. Oh, Witlet, Witlet, where are you?"

"I don't want your money," cried Jones, "nor your watch either. I wants a atomy."

"A—a what, sir?" said the trembling Twitter.

"A atomy, to be sure. Let's see."

Jones accompanied these latter words by divers pinches on Twitter's arms, who was perfectly in the dark as to what his assailant meant.

"For heaven's sake let me go," he said. "I will give you freely all the money I have with me. True, it is not much, but that I cannot help. You will let me go if I give you all?"

"You are more valuable nor money," said Jones, "and as you don't seem quite to understand what I means in conskense o' your ignorance, I'll expiflicate to you. By a atomy I means a stiff un. There's four doctors in York as have subscribed a handsome sum a piece, you see, for a atomy to divide among 'em. One on 'em wants a head—another on 'em wants two legs. You've got two, have you?"

This question was accompanied by several not very gentle kicks upon Twitter's shins, which made him jump again.

"Good God!" he said, "you don't mean to say that you will murder me?"

"Murder's an uncommon ugly word it is," said Jones. "We only means all for to make you sarviceable in a skientific way."

"You—you are surely only jesting with me?"

"It's no joke."

"It must be. You have chosen this dark lane in which to carry on a mere joke to frighten any one who migh come down it. I—I—could almost laugh myself. Tell me you are only jesting—I was frightened,—so you see you fully succeeded, and you will now let me go."

"Werry sorry," remarked Jones, " to find you is a labouring under sich a delusion."

"Nay, nay, you are carrying it rather too far now. Oh, Witlet, Witlet, where are you ?"

"Who do you mean ?"

"One who I was to meet here, but I will go back now to York. I—will not say anything about this little bit of amusement."

"I'm wery glad as you considers it so dreadful funny," said Jones, " and I hopes as you'll keep it up. Back to York you sartinly will go, but it will be in four different bags, and one of which belongs to each of the doctors, you see, so don't let's have any more gammon about it."

A cold perspiration broke out upon the brow of Twitter, for a though the story of the four doctors was too improbable, yet he began really to think that he should be murdered for some purpose, in that lonely place, where no aid was likely to reach him, and where it was far from likely that]even a chance passenger should come. His only hope was, that Witlet might arrive, and rescue him. Time, therefore, became to him the very breath of life, and he said in a voice of abject entreaty,—

"Set some fine upon my life, and you shall have it, I swear to you to-morrow, if you will meet me in York. If you are going to murder me for the dreadful purpose you speak of, you can but receive money. Whatever sum then has tempted you to the deed, I will double, if you spare me."

"All werry fine," said Jones, " but we arn't sich unprincipled fellows as you seems to think. We have been paid aforehand, and we is pinks o' honour, we is."

"But why murder for such a purpose? Surely some grave-yard would have supplied you, and saved you the great crime you contemplate."

"Ah!" said Jones, "there's the dodge. You don't understand these here matters. I'll exipflicate that ere, and then you'll be satisfied as all's right. I shouln't like you to think that everythink wasn't proper."

Twitter groaned at the idea of any explanation reconciling him to being knocked on the head or his throat cut for anatomical purposes.

"You must know," resumed Jones, "as these doctors wants a *corpus* as hasn't been ill ; that's the dodge."

"Have mercy upon me," cried Twitter..

"Holloa," cried Jones, "come on, pals ; bring them ere bags. The gemman is a getting impatient."

At this summons the five desperadoes, who were concealed, and who had half stifled themselves with laughter at the conversation that had taken place between Jones and Twitter, made their appearance, and at once destroyed the faintest hope that the valet might have had of the affair terminating otherwise than with [his destruction.

He dropped upon his knees, and in a shrieking tone said,—

"Oh, spare me, spare me. I will pay you well, on my sacred honour ; I will."

"But what are we to do for a body ?"

"Some one else," suggested Twitter, "may come down the lane and then yon will make double profit; for I swear to pay you handsomely if you let me go."

"That's uncommon considerate o'you," said Jones, "as regards some one else ; but we wait sometimes a week here and nobody comes."

"But, to-night," said Twitter, " I assure you some one will be here ; a better subject than I—a tall, fine man in robust health—he will be here. You can let me go and take him.?'

"Who's he ?"

"His name is Witlet. You will spare me."

"The infernal scoundrel," muttered Ned Witlet to himself, as he heard this kind suggestion of his friend Twitter.

"No," said Jones, in a tone of voice, as if he had been considering the matter. "No, we will have you, so there's an end of it."

"No no no. Help—murder—mercy, mercy !"

"Hold your noise, will you? I tell you what'll be the best way, pals, let's tie a rope round him, and let him down into the pool close by; when he's dead, then we can pull him up again and cut him up atween us without any bother."

"Aye, aye," said several, "that's the way."

Twitter now made a desperate effort to get away and run for his life; but he was foiled by Jones, who held him with the strength of a vce, while another of the party slipped a rope round h s neck, despite his struggles.

Shriek after shriek now came from the miserable wretch, as he was dragged to the very edge of the precipice below, which was the black pool into which he expected momentarily to he hurled.

Then when sensation had nearly deserted him and he was half-dead with terror, Jones said,

"Your name is Samuel Twitter, and on that account you have one chance for your life."

"A chance," he shrieked, "a chance! Oh, tell me what?"

"Disclose to us the real truth, as regards the murder of Sir George Rankley, and you shall live."

CHAPTER LIX.

THE RECSUE.—RECRIMINATION.—THE MEETING OF WITLET WITH MR. ANDERSON.—DISAPPOINTMENT

THE mental agony endured by Twitter, was beyond description. The pain of a hundred deaths could not, in reality have been equal to the awful sensations that beset his brain, as he believed himself within a few moments of eternity, while the crimes that lay heavy on his soul, rose up before his mental vision with awful distinctness.

"My life, my life!" he howled. "I know nothing—I can tell nothing. My life—spare me. Think of the horror you will one day feel, when my blood cries out for vengeance. I tell you, your feelings will be terrible—you will spare me. You will."

"Who murdered Sir George Rankley?" said Jones.

"The man who did the deed is condemned. The law has him in its clutches. You may see him hung at York on Thursday. Why do you ask me?"

"Because we have a fancy you know, but as you don't why such an ignorant indiwidual surely aint fit to live. Come on, boys."

They dragged him to the brink of the chasm. He gazed down with despairing eyes. The next moment he firmly believed would be his last. A thousand frightful images of horror gushed through him. A voice seemed to ring in his ear, saying,—

"Save yourself by denouncing Bernard Varley."

"Pitch him over when I say three," remarked Jones to his comrades.

"Shall I—shall I tell all," thought Twitter.

"One," said Jones.

The man tightened his grasp on him, and placed him so near the edge of the precipice, that a few loose stones crumbled down beneath his feet, and fell dashing from rock to rock, till they reached the still waters of the black pool, which they broke into a thousand eddies.

The sound was like a death knell to Twitter, and he groaned aloud, as Jones said in an assumed hollow voice,—

"Two."

"Now for it," said one of the men, "push him clean off, my pals."

"1—I will tell—I will tell," cried Twitter. "Save me—take me back to York —I will tell all."

The moment he uttered these words, a loud voice cried,—

" Hold !

It was the voice of Bernard Varley.

The men, with Jones at their head, shrunk back from the edge of the gloomy chasm, and glanced at each other irresolutely for a few moments. Then Varley's voice again cried,—

"Twitter, you are rescued. Officers, follow me."

" "Oh, d—n it," said Jones. "We——"

" "Silence !" cried Witlet, suddenly appearing among them. "Be off with you all. The game's up for this time. Off—off. Quick,"

Twitter was thrown down on his back where he lay insensible, partly through fear, and partly from the blow that Jones had given him, to put him there, so that he did not recognise Witlet, who after giving this advice to his wild lawless comrades, who availed themselves of it by disappearing very quickly, advanced in the direction of Bernard Varley's voice, and stood directly in his way.

Varley had, in pursuance of this intention, ridden on for the purpose of overtaking Twitter, and ascertaining that he was really going to the Grange. The road which he had taken, was some distance from the old gravel-pits, but in the stillness of the night, he had heard Twitter's first cry of alarm, and fastening his horse's bridle to a tree, he walked cautiously in the direction of the sound, when he saw quite enough to convince him that Twitter was in some danger. He listened to the conversation, that took place between him and his captors incredulously. The whole affair seemed too improbable, but when he heard the condition upon which his life was offered him, he understood it in a moment.

He only waited now to see how far Titter would go, before he proffered a confession. When he, Varley, heard him do so, he called out in the manner we have described, affecting to have officers with him, and succeeded, as we have seen, in the rescue.

Ae was always armed, and with a pistol in each hand, he now advanced in direction of the place where he had heard Twitter speaking, for by the sound of feet in different directions, he judged that his captors, whoever they were, had taken the alarm, and disappeared.

"Twitter—Twitter," he called, in a loud voice, "where are you now?"

"Stop, Bernard Varley," said Witlet, solemnly—"your evil genius is here."

A sharp cry of terror burst from Varley's lips as he heard the voice of him he so much dreaded, and who, in his own imagination, he had invested with a supernatural knowledge, and perchance power, he trembled to think of.

"Mysterious being," he said, "wherefore do you haunt me? What have I done to you that you should fill my soul with such terror?"

"You are alone?"

"I am."

"Humph !" thought Witlet; "we have been too precipitate after all." Then he said aloud,—

"Bernard Varley, beware! The blood of Sir George Rankley is on your hands, and you know it. Sooner or later the day of retribution will come. Beware—beware."

"In the name of Heaven," said Varley, trembling, "tell me who you are, that I may give a name to the object of my fears."

"It matters not who I am," said Witlet; "for a time you are safe, but the day is coming."

Varley could scarcely stand; a mist seemed to spread itself before his eyes, and when he recovered from his temporary stupor, his mysterious companion was gone.

"Speak again—speak—speak !" he gasped.

There was no reply. A solemn and unnatural kind of stillness reigned around him. Once more, then, in an agonised voice, he cried, "Appear to me, thou being not of this world, or else whence comes your knowledge? I would know all. If you can see the past, which was hidden, I know well, from all mortal eyes you can read, perchance, to me the future. I would know my destiny, and oh, most of all would I hear of Miranda!"

All was as still as the grave.

" He is gone," said Varley, with a shudder—" he is gone !"

Even as he spoke a faint gleam of light came from the moon, which had been struggling through a mass of clouds in the southern sky. It was not sufficient to make objects clearly visible, but it defined the grass from the bushes, the light gravelly soil from the luxuriant vegetation that grew around, and Varley did not feel quite so lonely as he had done in the intense darkness that had before prevailed.

Being convinced now that the much dreaded being who he firmly believed knew all concerning the murder, was gone, his next effort was to find Twitter, who, he thought would surely not leave the spot after hearing his voice.

He called him loudly by name, but received no answer ; and then he cautiously walked forward in the direction whence the sound of his voice first proceeded. A few moments brought him nearly to the verge of the chasm, when he saw Twitter lying, to all appearance dead, within a few paces of the extreme edge.

With a feeling something between hope and fear—hope that he was dead, and fear to touch the ghastly remains of his companion in guilt, if such should be his fate—he stooped and lifted one of his hands.

Twitter uttered a hollow groan.

" He lives," muttered Varley ; " but what is to hinder me from completing the work they have begun, and ridding myself of this trembling coward ?"

A sudden thought then came across his mind that the mysterious man he had just parted with had his eye upon him from some secret nook around, and the notion was one which gave Varley such a sudden fright, that he sprung to his feet, and looked around him with an expression of tremor truly pitiable.

" I dare not—I dare not," he murmured. " He is watching me. I feel, as it were, his eyes upon me. No—I dare not kill Twitter."

He then stooped again over the prostrate man, and, shaking him roughly, he cried,—

" Twitter, Twitter—arouse yourself."

" Spare me, and I will tell all," murmured Twitter.

" Curses !"

" It was Bernard Varley did the deed. I—I will tell you all, but spare my life."

Varley gave him a savage kick, that made him give a shriek of pain, and open his eyes, when he saw leaning over him, with a deep scowl upon his face, the very man whom he was damning.

" Varley !" he said.

" Aye, Varley. Rise—rise, I say, and follow me. Samuel Twitter, we must have some conversation together of importance. Come on, or by the fiends, I will blow your brains out, and throw your corpse down yon chasm."

He presented a pistol at Twitter's head as he spoke, and the trembling valet could only gasp out,—

" Varley—Bernard Varley—I have said nothing—on my soul I have said nothing. All is safe—quite safe."

" Did I not hear you proffer to tell all ?"

" Yes, but I would not have done so. With some coined tale, that should have fixed guilt still more strongly upon Rowland Percy, I would have amused those who sought my life, but I would not have committed you, Varley."

" Indeed !"

" You may believe me. What hope have I but in you ? Am I not quite dependent upon you even for subsistence ? Think you, then, that I would betray you ? Oh, no ; you may trust to me Varley, as you would trust to yourself, indeed you may."

" You protest strongly," said Varley ; " but how came you here ? 'Tis out of your route to the Grange."

"Ha!—how came I here? Why, I was dragged hither by those men; how could I resist so many?"

"Samuel Twitter," said Varley, peering into his companion's face, and speaking with intense bitterness through his clenched teeth, "you have been this evening engaged in some piece of treachery and villany, which in some strange manner recoiled on your own head. I do believe from my heart that you would have denounced me; and if I were sure that, apart from the mortal peril you were in, you had harboured a moment's intention against me, this instant should be your last."

"You much wrong me, Varley, by your suspicions," said Twitter, "indeed you do. I harbour any bad intention towards you! Impossible!"

"Recollect that this night I have saved your life," said Varley.

"You have—you have, and I am grateful."

"Be so, and beware of tampering with me. I am one standing on a precipice, down which I would rather hurl any one who was too dangerously close to me— you understand—than risk a fall myself."

"I comprehend you."

"'Tis well. Go then on to the Grange. I have my horse close by here, and will follow you."

Twitter walked on, while Varley, slinking across a meadow, made towards the spot where he had left his horse.

It would have been difficult to have decided on that eventful evening which of the accomplices in crime was in the greatest state of terror; for circumstances had happened to awaken the most lively fears of them both.

CHAPTER LX.

MEETING OF WITLET AND MR. ANDERSON.—DISAPPOINTMENT. VARLEY AND MIRANDA.

WITH a feeling of disappointment, that was very vexing to him, Ned Witlet hurried from the gravel-pits to keep his appointment with Mr. Anderson.

"A dead failure," he muttered, "and all through the very scoundrel who would perhaps have been brought to the gallows, if the affair had succeeded properly. Twitter's forced confession would not have been worth much, for he would have disputed it afterwards; nevertheless, if we could have got him to give a detailed account of the real particulars concerning Sir George Rankley's murder, it would have surely contained some circumstances that would have placed the case in a very different light, and saved Mr. Percy. However, that chance is over. Well, well, if the young man must die for what I am sure he is innocent of, I can't help him; and if poor Miranda breaks her heart, which she will surely, and dies too, I can't help that."

With these melancholy reflections, Ned Witlet walked rapidly on till he came to the appointed place of meeting; he then lingered about for a few seconds till he saw advancing towards him two persons.

One of them he thought was Mr. Anderson, but the other was a stranger to him. The moon had now acquired greater brilliancy, from the dispersion of the vapours, which at an earlier hour of the evening had dimmed some of its lustre.

"It is Mr. Anderson," said Witlet, "but who on earth can he have brought with him—an officer! No, no; I will trust him."

Witlet then advanced slowly to meet the two persons; and, when Mr. Anderson was sufficiently near, he called to him, saying—

"Do you come to meet the solitary horseman, sir?"

"I have."

"But alone?"

"This gentleman is the counsel who defended Mr. Percy at his trial, and who is as convinced of his innocence as I am. I have brought him with me, and I know you may rely upon his honour, and he is likely to be a better judge of the importance of what you have to tell than myself,

"Gentlemen," said Witlet, "you are both welcome; but it is with deep regret I inform you I have nothing to tell you."

"Nothing!" exclaimed Mr. Anderson.

"Nothing whatever; but do not believe that I brought you here upon so foolish an errand. I had a great and well-founded hope that I should by this time be able to communicate something to you that would have saved Mr. Rowland Percy. My scheme, however, has failed, and I know no more than yourselves."

Mr. Anderson and the counsel looked at each other for a moment in doubt and surprise; then the latter said—

"Whoever you are, rest assured that in any communication you may make us you shall be personally protected, and if you wish it, most liberally paid."

"I understand you, sir," said Witlet, with a mortified air. "You think I am trying to have a high price put upon my services, but I declare to you, before Heaven, that were you to offer me the wealth of this kingdom, I could tell you nothing which would be of any legal use, as regards the condemned Mr. Percy."

"We cannot but believe so solemn an asseveration," said Mr. Anderson; "but if such is the case, explain to us how it is that you have acquired so great a power over Bernard Varley. At a very hint of your existence, he is quite unmanned and terrified beyond expression. Surely that must arise from his conviction of your power to harm him, from your knowledge of some very grave and criminal transaction."

"Aye," said the counsel, "that's the point. Pray, as we have come so far to see you, explain that to us?"

"I will, gentlemen, as well as I can. Strange as it may appear, although I believe I have such a power as you mention, and can terrify Bernard Varley, I know nothing to criminate him. I met him accidentally one night, and having my mind full of suspicions, both of him and Twitter, I dropped some hints, which I presume came so near the truth that he imagined I knew all. His mind was evidently in a state of great excitement, and I firmly believe that he looked upon me as a something scarcely human. He trembles when we meet; he believes I know all, when I really know nothing, although I suspect just what you do yourselves, namely, that he had far more to do with the death of Sir George Rankley than any other living soul."

"This is very strange," said the counsel.

"And yet I believe it," added Mr. Anderson. "There is an air of sincerity about the tale, which convinces me of its truth."

"I see no reason to doubt it."

"It is true, so help me Heaven," said Witlet, "and I have only to regret bringing you here for no good purpose."

"Never mind that," said Mr. Anderson, "we believe you intended to give us information of importance, and we have still to thank you for the intention, although some accident may have interfered with its completion."

"You do me but justice, gentlemen, when you call it an accident. If it should happen that I can yet accomplish anything for Rowland Percy, it shall be done."

"Will you tell us who and what you are?" said the counsel, as Ned Witlet turned away.

"Let me remain as I am, unknown, but in person," said the highwayman. Then, as a faint smile crossed his countenance, he added, "We may some day be professionally acquainted."

He then walked rapidly away, and was soon lost to sight in the gloom of the deep shadows of the ancient trees.

"Well," said Mr. Anderson, "so this last hope seems to have crumbled away."
"It has," replied the counsel. "I have now scarcely a hope."

Discoursing thus, in a melancholy mood, they walked to the city, with a painful conviction on their minds that after all poor Rowland would suffer an ignominious death for a crime of which he was as innocent as the babe unborn.

Bernard Varley, when he left Witlet, mounted his horse with all possible expedition and galloped to York, for his mind was full of his project of seeing Miranda, and succeeding in making some sort of compromise with her for Rowland Percy's safety.

The exciting scene he had been a listener to, and a spectator of, at the old gravel pits, had by no means tended to lessen the fever of his brain or enable him to judge more calmly and dispassionately of his hopes, in any interview he might be enabled to procure with the beautiful girl, who owed so much misery to him, and whose evil spirit he had certainly been.

All he kept muttering to himself, was, "that for Rowland Percy's sake, she would surely sacrifice even herself."

But he knew not—he could not imagine the high and noble sentiments of the heart he projected attacking ; he was not capable of comprehending that loving Rowland Percy as she did, believing his innocence as she believed in Heaven, still Miranda could bear to see him sacrificed, with a conviction that they should meet again where there would be no sorrow, rather than secure a few fleeting years of existence in this perishable world at the sacrifice of her integrity of heart.

Nor did Bernard Varley properly estimate the character of Rowland Percy, or he would never have reasoned regarding him as if his mere love of life was the ruling principle of his conduct.

But so it is, men reason upon all men from their experience of their own passions. Clever men fail in their plans and projects because they present motives of action to men of lower mental power to themselves. Villains destitute of all the nobler feelings of humanity, reason upon human nature from their own despicable hearts, and they fail by encountering purer, abler natures than their own.

The difficulty of procuring his much desired interview with Miranda, was ever staring Bernard Varley in the face, ever intruding itself upon his thoughts; but still he rode on, and would not suffer it to interrupt his hasty progress to the city.

It was one of those difficulties which are of such great magnitude that they will not bear reflection, and he speeded towards Miranda's temporary home without any fixed resolve, or arranged mode of action to be put in practice when he should reach it.

He trusted, as hundreds and thousands of men do, to accident befriending him at the moment. That he could receive no very serious interruption he was very well aware, for the weak, enfeebled Mr. Percy was far from in a condition to offer any ; and he alone who would have been dreaded and shrunk from, was occupying the condemned cell of a felon.

The night was considerably advanced, when, with a recklessness that only the state of mental excitement Varley was in could ever have lent to him, he reached the door of Miranda and Mr. Percy's humble abode, and knocked as if he thought himself a welcome visitor.

He had previously given his horse into the care of a boy ; and, when the door was opened by the woman of the house, she started at the pale face and strange tone of the visitor, who asked for Miranda Rankley.

"Shall I take your name to her, sir ?" she said.

"No, no," said Varley; "show me into some room, and then go and tell her that a person wishes to speak to her concerning Rowland Percy."

The woman hesitated some moments, for she really thought her extraordinary visitor was mad; but Varley himself finished her irresolution by stepping to an open door which led into a neat little parlour, into which he walked, and sat down, saying,—

"Take my message—I will wait here."

The woman had now no other resource but to go to Miranda, to whom she communicated the strange message.

"A man?" asked Miranda.

"Yes, miss; and not the handsomest in the world, nor the best behaved," was the reply.

"You don't know him?"

"No, miss."

"Is—is he tall—dark?"

"Yes, he is; and has peculiar, deepset eyes, that look one through and through in such a way that it's quite disagreeable."

"I will go to him directly."

The woman left the room, and then Miranda clasped her hands, as she said—

"'Tis he, Bernard Varley, the murderer of my father—the false witness against Rowland—the despoiler of my patrimony—'tis he, 'tis he! Oh, Heaven!

grant me strength to go through this interview for Rowland's sake—for the sake of the innocent, grant me patience to suppress for a time my deep, unutterable loathing of this bad man."

She then slowly, and with trembling steps, descended the stairs, and stood a moment by the parlour door before she could gather strength to open it. When she did so, she saw Varley standing but a few paces from the entrance. At her appearance he shook fearfully, and, clasping his hands, cried—

"Miranda, Miranda! Do not fly from me—do not curse me! By your hopes of Heaven!—by your dearest affection, I conjure you to hear me!"

Miranda held the back of a chair for a moment as she said, in low, agitated accents—

No. 29.

"Bernard Varley, what brings you here?"

The advice of Mr. Anderson was present to her mind, or with what scorn she would have repulsed the villain who dared to pollute with his presence the home he had driven her to seek.

"Hear me—hear me!" he said. "Miranda, beautiful being, hear me."

"I hear," she said, in a low, choking tone.

"I never knelt to Heaven; but I now kneel to thee, for thou art my heaven—my hope—my trust. Oh, Miranda! when first my eyes beheld thee, I felt a new existence dashing wildly through my veins, and I told myself that with thee I would not envy the seraphim that crowd around the throne of God—without thee hell had no torment that could equal my despair. Miranda, you were young then —a pure, beautiful spirit, at that sweet spring-time of existence when the world is all new, and life, like a budding rose, is but just expanding to the glory that surrounds it. Then I loved you—then I adored you—then I worshipped you; but another stepped between me and the choice of my idolatry. Rowland Percy came. Can you wonder that I hated him? Miranda, can you wonder that he became the shadow on my soul that dimmed the sunshine that the love of you had cast upon it? Love and hate! Love and hate! The two master passions of humanity were struggling in my heart:—love for you, hatred to him. Oh, Miranda, Miranda! turn not from me; kill me, but smile upon the ruin you have made ere you consign it to the tomb!"

He covered his face with his hands, and hot scalding tears flowed between his fingers as he there knelt, such a picture of moral debasement as human nature seldom exhibits.

Miranda was terrified. She fain would have called for help, or rushed from the room as from the cell of some maniac, but the image of Rowland in his cell came across her mind, and she paused for his sake.

"In this man's wild passion," she thought, "in his extasy of despair, he may confess something that may save the innocent. I will hear him—I will hear him."

"You do not speak to me," continued Varley. "You do not look upon me. Oh! let me hear your voice, even if it breathe curses on my head. Let the light of your eye fall upon me though it sear me like the forked lightning. Miranda, where will you find such love as mine? Where such wild, fervent devotion?"

"Rowland Percy," said Miranda.

"He cannot love like I. His blood flows temperately through his veins. Ah! no. He cannot love as I love."

"You are his murderer!"

"But I can save him. Miranda, Miranda. I can save even Rowland Percy, were the fatal noose round his neck even now I could save him—I and no one else. Think of that Miranda. I have come to tell you I could save him yet!"

"He is innocent."

"Hush—hush—Miranda. Come nearer to me. I may not speak aloud. Come nearer, beautiful Miranda, the air is more serene and balmy near you. I do not think you quite mortal. You should live among cloisters. Nearer yet, Miranda, nearer."

"Rowland is innocent," said Miranda, as by a violent effort she forced herself to stoop towards Varley, who replied in a hissing whisper—

"He is!—he is!"

CHAPTER LXI.

THE ANSWER FROM LONDON.—THE SECOND VISIT OF MIRANDA TO THE CON-
DEMNED CELL.—THE BALLAD SINGER.—RENEWED HOPE.—THE MYSTERIOUS
EPISTLE.

PERHAPS of all the severe trials which Miranda had endured, this one was that
in which she had most need of self-control, and most difficulty in exercising it.
Loathing Bernard Varley as she did—a stranger to guile and dissimulation as she
was—how very difficult a task it was for her to listen with common patience to
his words, loaded as they were with the fulsome adulations which, from any one,
would have been distasteful to Miranda.

She absolutely shuddered as she looked upon Varley kneeling at her feet ith
uplifted hands, and a countenance of such imploring agony, that any one would
have supposed him some object wretch, pleading to an offended Deity for that
mercy he could scarcely expect.

In low, moaning accents, he spoke again—

"Oh, bethink you, Miranda, how much hangs upon your answer to me this night.
The life of him who who would fain rescue from the death to which the law has
doomed him. The mortal agony of your own mind—an agony which, in its climax,
will almost tempt you to doubt Heaven's mercy—my destruction for ever and ever ;
for I vow, that if you reject me, I will do some deed to shut out all hope of mercy
hereafter. My soul's perdition shall be heavy on you, and in the agony of countless
ages my writhing spirit shall shriek your name as the cause of its destruction.
Think what an awful thing is death, and such a death as that which awaits
Rowland Percy; think of that, Miranda, and in blessing me spare him."

With great reluctance Miranda answered him.

"Spare Rowland Percy," she said. "What power can you, Bernard Varley, have
to snatch him from death ?"

"I have—I have power, Miranda. Believe me, improbable as it may appear, I
have such power."

"You then admit that he is innocent ?"

"I can save him," was Varley's reply.

"And, for your reward, you ask me to sacrifice myself, and all the hopes of
happiness this world can afford me."

"I ask you to be mine, Miranda. What greater happiness can you look for
than in being the bright particular star of the heart's worship of such as I. My
love is not the old common feeling which profanes the same name. Oh, no,
Miranda, it is as a mountain torrent, wild, free, and irresistible, compared to
placid lake, whose stagnant waters show no signs of vitality. Say you will live
the object of my idolatry, and Rowland Percy shall be saved."

"Tell me how he is to be saved," said Miranda.

Varley was silent for a moment, and then said—

"Upon that may I build a hope ?"

Miranda could not for worlds have said yes. She turned away with a loathing
shudder ; and when she could command her voice, she said—

"Bernard Varley, if you yet can and will save him, who you know to be
innocent, from an ignominious death, I can offer you but one reward."

"Name it—name it," he said.

"Forgiveness," said Miranda ; "forgiveness for the past, and my prayers to
Heaven to have mercy upon you."

"Is—that—all ?" gasped Varley.

"Surely," added Miranda, "it is much from me to you. Could you have
ever hoped for so much from me, upon whose head you have brought so much
misery ? Oh, Bernard, if there still lingers in your heart one germ of human

feeling—one lingering hope of a hereafter, save him who, upon your false testimony has deen condemned to death, and at least release your soul from the conseqeences of another murder."

"Another mnrder ?"

" Yes, another—for as Heaven is my judge, I do believe you the contriver, if not the executor of my father's death."

" This—is—your—fixed purpose, Miranda ?   You will make no other terms with me "

" No other."

" Then all is over.   He—he shall die—die the death of a felon ; and I shall exult in his agonies, while you, Miranda, tell yourself you might by a word have saved him."

He stood by the door and looked wildly at Miranda.   He seemed to meditate some further appeal to her, but the words stuck in his throat, and he could not do other than heave, from the bottom of his heart, deep and heavy groans.

Miranda would fain have left the room, but he stood in her way, and she was afraid to pass him.   Each moment seemed an hour of suspense, and then the door was opened from without, and Mr. Anderson showed himself.

Miranda sprung forward, as she cried—

" Save me from the presence of this man."

Varley waited not to say another word to Miranda, but muttering some unintelligible words between his teeth, he strode past Mr. Anderson, and left the house.

" Has the villt'n confessed anything?" asked the attorney.

" No, no ; 'tis all in vain," was Miranda's reply.   " Rowland ! Rowland ! each moment seems to decrease even the fragile hope to which I would fain cling."

Mr. Anderson was silent for some minutes ; and, when he did speak, it was with a painful effort that he said—

" Miranda, you ought to know all.   It is not right that anything should be kept from you."

" Heaven help me !" said Miranda ; what new calamity can reach my heart ?"

" Nothing new, but the confirmation of present fears.   The answer of the secretary of state has arrived.'

" And—and————"

" It is unfavourable !"

Miranda shook like an aspen leaf, as she resesumed—

"And this is Tuesday night!   God of Heaven ! must I count the existence of him who is so dear to me by hours !"

" If," said Mr. Anderson, with much emotion, " any new hope should arise, you may depend upon it being eagerly seized upon by myself and the counsel."

" I—know it," said Miranda, " we have much to thank you for ; God knows we have, Mr. Anderson.   And—and—this is Tuesday night.   Oh, Rowand ! Rowland !"

" Nay, do not give way thus to despair ; put your trust even yet in Heaven."

" We never know," said Miranda, " how heavily we have lent upon some fragile hope, until it is suddenly drawn from us.   Despair is thickening around me.   I think my reason will fail, and perhaps I shvll then be happier.'

" Miranda, Miranda," urged Mr. Anderson, " consider you have still a high and holy office to perform.   If it be the will of Providence that Rowland Percy shall be sacrificed, do you be the ministering angel which shall light his path to the tomb, and rob death of its sting."

" You are right, you are right," said Miranda, clasping her hands.   " Rowland, you shall not be forsaken because I despair.   I will cheer him in his dungeon, I will bless him with kind words softly spoken, and I will promise him, which Heaven knows I may, that I will meet him soon in that world where there are no false accusers, no weak, fallible judges, no sorrow, no tears.   My heart will break, and then I shall die, and join him and my murdered father.'

" Will you," said Mr. Anderson, " undertake the task of communicating to old Mr. Percy the result of the application to the secretary of state ?"

" Yes—yes. That shall be my duty. I will do so."

Mr. Anderson still lingered, although the hour was getting late. He would fain have found some words of consolation for Miranda, but what could he say ? What new hope could he awaken ? How even could he preach patience to that wounded heart ? After remaining silent for some minutes, he silently pressed Miranda's hand in his, and then walked to the door. He turned, however, upon the threshold, and a faint " God bless you !" came from his lips.

In another moment Miranda was alone with her griefs and her despair.

Mr. Percy she knew was sleeping, and she would not have him awakened to listen to the extinction of a hope which he had clung to much more strenuously than she, Miranda, had.

" The morning—the morning will be time enough," she murmured, " to communicate such tidings."

She then sought her own chamber, but not to sleep ; for the whole night she lay in a kind of stupor of despair, while her fancy over and over again depicted to her the fearful scene of an execution, in which Rowland Percy was the victim.

That Wednesday morning dawned gloomily upon the ancient city of York, and with what different sensations was it received by many who watched its faint increasing light. How many welcomed it with joy, and converted its gloom into beauty by the sunshine of their own hearts ! How many saw its first streak of grey light in the eastern sky with shudders and aching hearts, that would have cast a shadow over the most glorious sunshine ?

Some there were who had lingered long upon a death-bed, to whom that day was the least sad one of this mortal career. Some there were in the pure spring tide of existence, who on that day were to make some move in life which was to tincture the future with its colours, be they bright or gloomy. But of all the varied hopes, the fears, and agonies that were the adjuncts of that Wednesday, there could be none equal to those which in different manners affected the DRAMATIS PERSONÆ of our veritable narrative.

What awful images chased each other through the mind of Bernard Varley, peopling vacancy with terrors, and wringing the very soul with anguish—what sufferings Twitter, in his frightful state of mental anxiety and dread, endured, we will not pause to attempt to pourtray. Let those evil-minded men writhe under the stings of conscience which will make itself heard in the most seeming callous breast, while we follow Miranda once again to the lonely prisoner, awaiting his dreadful doom.

Mr. Percy had not made his appearance when Miranda was ready to visit the prison, and still without having told the heart stricken old man of the answer that had been received from the secretary of state, she with hasty steps walked to the prison,

Her order from the judge gained her instant admission, and with a trembling heart she entered Rowland's cell, which was another only nearer to the outer walls of the prison, than that which she had before visited him in.

Miranda was dreadfully shocked at the change in his appearance, which one night had produced, and the faint smile with which he strove to welcome her, was far more harrowing to her feelings than would have been the greatest extasy of grief. For some moments they held each other's hands without speaking, and then Miranda said, faintly—

" Rowland, you know all ?"

" Yes—they removed me here last night, immeidately upon the unfavourable answer of the secretary of state being known. My only other remove will be to my grave."

His lips quivered as he spoke, and his whole appearance betrayed that death, and such a death, was a subject of frightful contemplation to him, and from which he found it impossible to turn.

" Rowland—my Rowland," said Miranda, " I cannot yet believe it. They will, not murder you."

" What hope is there now, Miranda ?"

She covered her face with her hands, and shook palpably, as something seemed lmost to whisper in her ear,—

"Be Bernard Varley's wife, and save him."

" Oh, God ! no, no, no," she said.

" What, Miranda ?" said Rowland, alarmed at her extreme agitation.

" Rowland, hear me. I have had a visit from Bernard Varley."

A flush of colour crossed the pale cheeks of Rowland Percy, as lifting his hand, he cried—

" May heaven punish ——"

" Hush—hush. Curse no one," interrupted Miranda. The vengeance of Heaven will reach the gnilty, without being evoked by a human voice. Hear what I was about to say to you, Rowland. Bernard Varley came to tell me that he could save you, even now."

" Yes, Miranda, he could; but such men as Bernard Varley do not sacrifice themselves so easily."

" But he named a condition."

" What condition, Miranda ?"

" One that, if you will consent to, Rowland, I will accede to, but if you don't, I fear——"

" Tell me, Miranda, what condition this is you almost dread to tell me ?"

" It is, that I consent to become the wife of Bernard Varley."

" The villain ! dared he—oh, Miranda, you know well my answer. Were death ten times over to be my fate, unless averted by such means, I would smile upon the torments that awaited me, and defy the villain, who to save a life, would break a heart."

" But, Rowland, bethink you."

No, no, Miranda. I will not deny that life is dear to me. I will not deny that death is terrible, but you have now shown me that there is something yet more hideous."

Miranda looked in his pale face, and again she thought.

" I should soon die were I to consent to what Varley requires—but Rowland would be saved. I should die before probably my promise to become his could be ratified. I feel that my heart is breaking. Shall I not save him ?

" Miranda, you look strangely and fixedly upon me, as if some fearful thoughts were passing in your brain you would not trust me with."

" No, no, Rowland. No—do not despair, I will come to you again soon—very —very soon. This is Wednesday—Wednesday."

" And to-morrow——"

" Hush, Rowland, hush. Speak not of to-morrow. You may perchance see m any suns rise and set yet, and even should I not be among the living, you will always think of your poor Miranda, and spare a sigh for her love, a tear for her memory."

" For Heaven's sake, explain yourself, Miranda," he cried.

" Yes, yes—I will be back soon," she answered, "very soon. Farewell for a brief space."

She drew closely around her the cloke she wore, and hurried from the prison.

CHAPTER XLII.

THE WRECK OF A MIND.—MIRANDA'S NEW GRIEF.—THE FATHER AND SON.

THE new idea which sprung so rapidly in Miranda's mind, was a self-sacrificing one, and in consonance with her nature. It was to save Rowland at the price of her own life, for she felt that if she gave a consent to become the wife of Bern . Varley, she must die, as the only source of relief she could find.

"Perhaps," she thought, " I can induce him to wait for a time the fulfilment of my promise, and then I shall be wedded to the tomb long before he can claim me as his bride. That will be the only way of saving Rowland. He is young, and life is all before him. It may be that time will enable him to forget me, and be happy with some other, who may not love him as I do, but still may create for him a home of contentment."

With these, self-denying thoughts crowding through her brain, the noble-hearted girl walked swiftly towards her own home, for she had not made up her mind quite, how and in what manner she should signify to Bernard Varley, that she was at length prepared to listen to his offers.

Sudenly she felt some one touch her arm, and on turning she saw a tall man, with his face muffled up, who said, in coarse, but not uncourteous tones,—

"Is it you, Miss Rankley?—kim up!'

"What?" said Miranda, who was far from knowing anything of Mr. Jones, or his peculiarities, for it was no other person than that gentleman himself.

"I axes yer pardon, miss," he said, " I mean, is you Miss Rankley, without the kim up? That's only a way as I've got, and don't mean no harm no how."

" My name is Rankley."

" Then jist read that ere kivey."

He placed in Miranda's hand a small piece of paper as he spoke, and then made off, as fast as he could.

Miranda opened the paper, which was folded, but not sealed, and on it she read the follwing words,—

" A friend to Rowland Percy will suggest something to Miranda Rankley, that may be serviceable, if she will receive him this day at twelve o'clock, at her own home."

Miranda read the little epistle twice before she could believe that she had read it right, and then crumpling it up in her hand, she said —

" Oh, is it possible, that without the dreadful sacrifice I contemplated, there is still a hope? Has Heaven not quite deserted us? I will see this mysterious stranger, be he who he may. At twelve. Yes, even then there will be time."

An itinerant ballad-singer at this moment commenced singing a strain, the words of which rooted Miranda to the spot—

HOPE! HOPE TO THE LAST.

"When the heart full of anguish
    Knows nought of despair,
And cast is its shadow
    O'er all that is fair ;
When bright hope has vanished,
    And pale is the cheek ;
When so lost are the sad ones,
    No mercy they seek.
Even, then, straight from Heaven
    A ray will be cast
On the dull blighted heart,
    And 'twill hope to the last !
'Hope! hope to the last!"
    Some angel's voice whispers—
'Hope! hope to the last!"'

'When guilt seems to triumph
    O'er all that is good,
And virtue is cast from
    The rock where it stood ;
When the innocent suffer
    And might governs right,
When the heart's wild despair
    Is darkling as night—

> Even then, straight from Heaven
>   A ray will be cast
> On the dull blighted heart,
>   And 'twill hope to the last.
> 'Hope! hope to the last!'
>   Some angel's voice whispers—
> 'Hope! hope to the last.'

"I thank thee, Heaven," said Miranda. "I will hope to the last. There is boundless mercy yet."

Nervously then clutching the little epistle in her hand, she hurried with re-freshened feelings to her home.

She found old Mr. Percy in anxious expectations of her return, and the moment he saw her, he, with trembling eagerness, said—.

"You have seen my boy—he will be saved—he will be saved, Miranda!"

"Saved!" echoed Miranda.

"Yes—yes. I have slept long, and had happy visions. My poor boy Rowland will yet be saved. The answer from the secretary of state must and will be a favourable one—all will be well, and we shall be so happy."

There was a strange earnestness about the old man's manner, and an alteration in his voice, that much alarmed Miranda. Moreover, she saw, or fancied she saw, in his eyes a wild and unnatural lustre, which they had never worn before to her observation.

"Mr. Percy," she said, imploringly, "there is, I trust, still hope, but the answer of the secretary of state is——"

'Well, well,—Miranda—speak——"

"Against us."

Mr Percy sunk into a chair with a deep groan, and his face became deathly pale. He opened and shut his hands convulsively for some moments, then he heaved a deep sigh, and almost immediately he placed one hand upon his head, as if some sudden pain had come across him; a look of anguish came over his face, and then calmly died away. It was succeeded by a smile—a smile of insanity—then a loud frightful laugh followed; and in a screaming voice he said—

"Saved—saved—saved! My boy is saved at last, and we are rich again. Ha! ha! ha! Let the bells take up the joyous sound!—Saved—saved—saved—and my boy too!"

Miranda clasped her hands in despair. There could be no mistaking that laugh; reason was overturned, and the unhappy father was a harmless lunatic.

"Mr. Percy," cried Miranda, clinging to his arm, "speak to me—Mr. Percy."

"God bless you!" he said; "for my poor boy's sake, God bless you! We will have a merry wedding—a very merry wedding. Rowland loves you, and I will love you, Miranda Rankley. Have you told your father yet?"

"My father?"

"Yes. He should know. We must not settle all without him. And do you hear, Miranda, you need not repeat my words, but from my inmost heart I con-sider Bernard Varley to be a villain."

"Alas! alas!" cried Miranda, "What shall I do? How shall I encounter this new horror? Mr. Percy, think again; my father is no more."

"Ah! so they said," replied he, "but I know better. Where is my boy?'

Miranda was too overcome by her feelings to answer him; but answer he required not, for he went on talking with strange garrulity, mingling together the living and the dead, but showing no symptoms of anything like violence.

At the request of Miranda, the people of the house, who were as compassionate as they could be, procured the attendance of a medical man, who gave it as his opinion, that the aberration of intellect under which Mr. Percy was labouring would subside in time, and even while it continued, would be quite a harmless fatuity.

"You need be under no apprehension, young lady," he said to Miranda; "he will in all probability be perfectly docile."

"For so much comfort I thank you," said Miranda. "I believe he has no one but myself in this world to look to for a kind word."

"Pardon my curiosity," said the medical man; "but may I ask if this gentleman is in any way connected with the unhappy young man now lying under sentence of death?"

"His father, sir."

"Oh, indeed."

"And I am Miranda Rankley."

The surgeon bowed, as he said,—

"I have heard your story from many mouths, and if it be any satisfaction to you to hear such an individual opinion, I beg to say that I have a strong conviction of Mr. Percy's innocence."

"I thank you, sir," said Miranda, with much emotion. "He is innocent Heaven knows that he is innocent, and I even yet hope for some interposition in his favour.

No, 30,

"I fervently wish that such a hope may be realised," said the surgeon, as he took his leave.

"How strange is it," sighed Miranda, "that nearly all but those whose opinions would have saved poor Rowland, believe in his innocence."

The hour of twelve at this instant sounded from the minster clock, and Miranda listened with breathless eagerness to the sounds. She looked again at the little note which had been handed to her in the street, to assure herself she had made no mistake, and that twelve was indeed the hour named. While she was doing so one heavy knock at the street door aroused her to a hope that it might be her mysterious visiter.

She stepped to the room door, and heard a voice say—

"Is Miss Rankly within?"

"Yes," she herself cried, as she opened the door; "I am here—I am here."

In a moment she recognised in the visitor Ned Witlet, for she had never forgotten him since he had given her her father's ring.

"You know me?" he said.

"I do, and trust you," responded Miranda. "If you can tell me aught that will give me any hope for Rowland Percy, I will bless you."

Witlet spoke very seriously and diffidently, as he said,—

"Miss Miranda, I have something to suggest; but it is a wild scheme, and will require upon your part, perhaps, more nerve than you, under your present circumstances, can be mistress of."

"Never!" said Miranda. "Shew me, tell me how I can rescue Rowland, and you shall see that I can do anything."

Miranda then conducted him into the room which, by courtesy of the people of the house, she was permitted to use in case of any one calling.

"I almost regret," said Witlet, "that I have ventured to suggest to you a hope which may never be realised; but under desperate circumstances, Miss Rankley, desperate measures are required, and this is a most desperate one."

"Name it, and let it involve what risk it may, it shall be done. I will thank you, from the bottom of my heart, for the least shadow of a hope."

"We must be very cautious, then," said Witlet, lowering his voice, "for there is danger even in the supposition of the course I am about to recommend."

CHAPTER LXIII.

THE PLAN OF ESCAPE.—MIRANDA'S GRATITUDE. — THE FIRMNESS OF A LOVING HEART.—HOPE LIVES STILL

The manner of Witlet was such as to raise in her heart the most conflicting and contrary emotions. There was something of hope, something of fear—a glimpse of sunshine amid the gloom which surrounded her, and yet so small, so very indistinct a glance of that celestial light, that she could scarce separate it from the darkness around. That Witlet had some proposition, which he, extensive as his knowledge of human nature was, deemed possible, although perchance beset with danger, was evident, and slender as that foothold for hope was to Miranda, she clung to it with an eagerness that afflicted Witlet for he judged how great would be her disappointment in the failure of what he had to propose, and that failure was far more probable than success, he could not conceal from himself for one moment.

"Miranda," he added, in a voice which sounded rather mournful than hopeful, "hope little but try all. Had I a better suggestion to offer to you, I would bring it, but circumstances grow desperate as time rolls on, and then desperate, strange, and unlikely remedies suggest themselves to the mind."

" Speak—speak," said Miranda. "That you are a friend to him who is innocent] yet condemned, my heart assures me. Oh, if you can suggest a means of saving him—if you can suggest a means from which I can extract the faintest hope, I implore you to tell it to me, and bless my ears with happier sounds than have greeted them for now many a weary day."

" From my soul," said Witlet, " I sympathise with you, and I believe Mr. Rowland Percy to be innocent."

" He is—he is!"

" It is—it has ever been my most firm conviction. But what can we do now to impress our belief upod these who alone have power to snatch him from death?"

" You surely know enough, nay, you have shown that you do," said Miranda, " of the strange tangled web of circumstances connected with my poor father's death, to assist you with some power to stay, what in this case is the hand of revenge, not justice?"

" I would I did—I would I did."

" Does not Varley tremble at a mere hint concerning you ?"

" He does."

" Then——"

" Nay, hear me, Miranda. It is Bernard Varley's own guilty fears that make him tremble, not my knowledge. As there are many timid depredaters who fancy that they see in each bush an officer, so Bernard Varley has, upon most slight grounds, invested me, to his imagination, with a power that makes him suffer much mortal agony, but is productive of no other result."

" Then," said Miranda, faintly, " you cannot save Rowland?'

" Not from my knowledge. I am in the same situation as yourself. I suspect much, know nothing."

" Alas—alas !"

" Nay, Miranda Rankley, do not quite despair until the period for action has passed away ; I have not come merely to tell you how powerless I am, but to suggest a plan which, if successful, will restore Rowland Percy to liberty, and which, even should it fail——"

" Heed not the consequences of failure, if I alone am to be the sufferer," said Miranda.

" You alone would be."

" Thank Heaven."

" Have you, do you think, courage, personally to aid in a most perilous and uncertain attempt to rescue Rowland from his prison?"

" Rescue Rowland ? Have I courage ? Tell me what to do; point out to me some path existing with danger ; shew me some daring act which men might well start appalled from perpetrating, and you shall see that a weak girl's fond trusting heart will nerve her to the task."

" I cannot, will not, doubt you, Miranda. Listen, then, to my plan for Rowland's escape."

" Escape!"

" Hush! —we must be cautious, beyond the ordinary bounds of caution. Even walls have ears."

" Yes, yes," said Miranda, in a low tone, " I will speak with bated breath—I will be very cautious. Oh ! speak again—say on—say on. Speak again of Rowland's rescue."

" I will, but calm your agitation, I pray you. What you will have to do will require nerves as still as iron—a cool collected brain—a firm step."

" When the time shall come," said Miranda, " that all these qualities are essential for Rowland's safety, you shall find I will not shrink. Oh ! tell me how—when—where I am to call to my aid all the firmness of nature in the cause of him, the innocent, the young, and the gifted."

" You are," said Witlet, with unfeigned admiration, " the noblest specimen of gentle, loving woman, that ever I beheld. Heaven help you, and him who has won so great a treasure as your pure heart. The plan I have to propose is this :"

Miranda came close to Witlet, and the expression of deep and earnest attention and anxiety that beamed from her face, was almost painful to look upon. Her very breathing seemed nearly suspended, and it was evident that each word which fell from Witlet's lips, went direct to her very heart.

It was in a tone of some emotion that the man of many vices, but whose heart was still susceptible of some of the best and noblest sentiments of human nature, continued—

"My plan for the escape of Mr. Rowland Percy from prison is based upon two circumstances. The one is your possession of a written order from the judge to visit the prisoner when you please; the other, my acquaintance with one of the officials of the prison, who will do what he can to aid me in any enterprise so near my heart as this is, for I have set my mind upon rescuing Rowland Percy, if such a thing be possible, at any risk."

"How can I thank you?" murmured Miranda.

"If I succeed, one smile of joy, Miss Miranda, upon your sweet face will amply repay me."

"And—and your plan?"

"Pardon me, lady, I will tell you briefly. My plan is that to-morrow evening —that is, the evening before the——"

"Execution," said Miranda, with a shudder.

"I would have spared you the word, lady, but it was what I meant. To-morrow evening, then, I would have you go to the prison in the same large cloak and long habit you have hitherto worn on your gloomy visits."

"Yes—yes."

"Persuade Rowland Percy to disguise himself in that cloak and habit. Then he who I know being at the gate——"

"I see it all—I see it all!" cried Miranda, clasping her hands. "There is hope —there is hope!"

"A slender one."

"But still a hope."

"Truly. He, then, with whom I am acquainted being on duty, as he will be, I have ascertained, at the gate, will, unquestioned and unscrutinised, permit Rowland to pass out."

"Yes—yes! good friend! Oh, yes!"

"Should all this succeed, I will be there to receive him, and with my own life I will answer for his safety, if once he be clear of the prison walls."

"You are our deliverer!" cried Miranda, with animation.

"But remember," added Witlet, "you cannot escape yourself. You will be left in the gloomy cell now occupied by Rowland."

"Gloomy cell! It will be to me a palace of light, radiant and beautiful. Gloomy! —ah, no! The sunshine of my own joy will irradiate it, and make it glow with sunny lustre."

"By Heaven!" cried Witlet, "if ever human heart deserved the greatest happiness, it is yours."

"And Rowland will be free," said Miranda, evidently not hearing, or if she did, not comprehending Witlet's words. Once more he will breathe the pure air of Heaven—once more I shall see him smile as he has smiled of yore, before the blight of affliction fell upon us all."

"From my soul I hope that such will be the case," said Witlet. "We can but try the enterprise; and would that its practical execution lay with myself; but the circumstances are such that none but you can afford the least glimpse of hope to the prisoner."

"That do I rejoice at," said Miranda; "for who but I feels for him in his helplessness and persecution sufficiently to dare all for his preservation? I feel even now a conviction at my heart that Heaven is working with us—that the full tide of our misfortunes has reached its flood. The future contains hope—a hope that will be realized in joy. Rowland shall be saved!"

" You are enthusiastic, and sanguine of the success of the scheme," said Witlet, " and you have by your confidence made me think better of it than before. I would advise you to go at once to the prison and prepare Mr. Percy for the effort that will be made to save him, and in that going be sure you wear as much over your face as may be the cloak that he is to conceal himself in. Indeed, as you come out of the prison, affect so much concealment of your face as to excite surprise, if not suspicion,"

" I understand."

" Should you be stopped even, it will be a step gained towards the success of our plan."

" It would—it would."

" I would not desire a more favourable circumstance than that you should be stopped by some meddling officer, who should insist upon seeing your face. Affect then indignation at such want of courtesy, and threaten an appeal to the judge who gave you the writen order of admission. Rowland, then, will be more likely when so muffled up, to pass free."

" Thanks, thanks," said Miranda. " I will treasure up in my memory every word you say. I will forget nothing—all shall be as you direct."

" All that I can tell you, then, is, that he upon whose friendly silence I can depend will be on duty at the outer door of the prison at nine o'clock this evening."

" That is the hour the gates are closed against all visitors," said Miranda.

" It is, and here some management and caution will be necessary. You must affect the change in Rowland's dress as speedily as possible after your arrival, and take care to keep the door of the cell fast until you hear nine strike. Then he must not wait for the turnkey to come and warn you to begone, but he must step out of the cell, closing the door behind him."

" Yes, yes—it shall be so done."

" When you are yourself left in the cell, place yourself at the table with your back towards the door, and appear to be leaning your head upon your hands, in deep affliction. You must have Rowland Percy's coat on, and conceal your hair as much as possible."

" Fear not," said Miranda, " all shall be well arranged."

" I have no doubt. Exactly as nine strikes my friend will be at the outer gate. He will let Rowland Percy out as quick as possible, and it may be hours before the affair is discovered."

" Perhaps till morning. "

" No ; the cell will be visited every two hours during the night, but at the first visit you may not be discovered, if you affect to be sleeping."

" And in the meantime you will provide for Rowland's safety ?"

" I will. At the second visit to the cell, which will be at one o'clock in the morning, I would advise you to declare yonrself. They dare not then keep you in the cell, for that is only destined for condemned prisoners, and although you will be detained, it will not be in a place so replete with unpleasant associations."

" But there would then be pursuit."

Witlet smiled as he replied—

" There might, but I would consent to forfeit my head if it were successful. I have means of concealment which may defy all the police of York. When you hear one o'clock strike, you may tell yourself that Rowland Percy is quite safe."

" Oh happy thought."

" Farewell, now, lady," said Witlet, " Heaven help you. If our enterprise should be successful, I will take care to find means by which Mr. Percy can communicate with you in writing."

" Before we part," said Miranda, earnestly, " tell me who, and what you are." Witlet shook his head.

" The knowledge would avail nothing. I am one who, too early thrown upon a bad world, took up bad weapons in self-defence."

" But your name ?"

" Pardon me. There are reasons why you had better remain is ignorance of who

I am. Pray take the good which I can offer you alone. My life has been a chequered one. I have done much wrong, and am in some things a proscribed man, but all natural feeling is not quenched within my breast."

" Let the world say of you, think of you, what it may," said Miranda, " my fervent gratitude is yours, and while I have a voice, it shall ever be raised in defence of you, my friend, and the friend of the innocent."

" God bless you, lady," said Witlet, with emotion, " when we meet again may it be under far happier circumstances, till then, farewell."

CHAPTER LXIV.

THE PRISON.—THE FATHER AND SON.—MIRANDA'S PROPOSAL.—ROWLAND'S SUPPLICCA-TION.—THE ARRANGED PLAN OF ESCAPE.

IN the meantime, little aware that such generous and self-sacrificing exertions were being made for his release, Rowland Percy was a prey to all the alternations of hope and despair. As the time crept on, he began to think that his fate was indeed inevitable, and that he was doomed to form a cruel illustration in after years, of the fallibility of human judgment.

One thing which particulary annoyed him, was the manner in which the chaplain of the prison took his guilt for granted, and paid no more attention to his assertions of innocence, than as if he had raved a few delirious sentences.

Still he urged him to repent and confess, treated him in all respects with such hildish folly, that Rowland at length would not permit his visits at all, and requested Mr. Anderson, by note, to send him some books to read in lieu of the mass of evangelical tracts with which the limited intellect of the chaplain had provided him.

This request Mr. Anderson lost no time in complying with, and to the great horror of the chaplain, Rowland persisted in endeavouring to assuage the gloom of his most unjust confinement, by persuing works of fiction, with the hope of with-drawing his mind from too painful a contemplation of the real, by pleasing the imagination with the ideal.

This was horrifying to the evangelical chaplain, who wished to see him groan-ing and sighing, and in a state of religious delirium rather than in any manner reconciled to his melancholy state, by the exercise of those gifts of mind which God has given his creatures.

To avoid the importunities of the chaplain, Rowland opened a book of tales, and when he announced his intention of reading one, the bigotted man left the cell, in a state of horror.

The tale was one which interested Rowland much, and weaned him more from his sorrows than any other had done. It was this :—

" During the civil war that raged with such fury in La Vendee, many curious incidents occurred that rendered some individuals more famous or infamous, as the case might be, and gave the same notoriety for the time. Many acts of bar-barous ferocity were performed, as were also some of heroism and generosity, that would not have disgraced the most exalted.

" In the neighbourhood of the camp formed by the troops, and which was a kind of magazine, was a little cabaret, kept by a widow woman and her daughter. They were civil and obliging, and obtained the good will of both sides, when they visited honest Marie and her daughter Antoinette. They were so poor and so help-less that it was deemed an extreme barbarity to place any burden upon them, and thus they escaped much that their neighbours suffered.

" Before the breaking out of the Vendean war, Antoinette was courted by a youth of the name of Paul Desslines. He was the son of the proprietor of a very pretty estate, or farm. He cultivated much of it himself, and employed his leisure hours with his fowling-piece, of which he was passionately fond ; and in his excursions he chanced to be near the bower of the widow Marie's dwelling, and entered it for the purpose of refreshing himself after his fatigue.

" Antoinette served the stranger. Her modesty and beauty attracted his attention. He gazed upon her with interest, and saw that she was extremely beautiful and that, too, without its prudery.

" He came often to the same place, and would spend an hour in pleasant chat with Antoinette, as well as in the contemplation of her charms. They were, indeed, of no common order, and they were not marred, as the beauty of Frenchwomen were then ; her dress was simple, decent, and national, while her hair was bound up tastily, and her complexion was her own.

" Antoinette's poverty was a heavy drawback to her other good qualities; for the young fowler looked upon her and loved her, but yet he knew not how to declare his passion.

" ' How could I'' he would say,'' take to my parents the daughter of a widowed proprietor of an obscure cabaret? It is not to be expected. They would refuse to receive her ; I would be degraded and thrown upon my own resources, which would be my own labour, and beggary would be our lot. No—it will never do.'

" He often reasoned thus in his walks to the cabaret ; but the modest simplicity, and the bright, clear blue eye of Antoinette, always dispelled these gloomy fancies and brought pleasanter reflections.

" I could live in poverty, and be happy, too, with such a wife; but it would never come to that; my freinds would surely assist me, and I could do much of myself.

" Thus he would reason pro and con, as the absence from Antoinette was greater or less, with the inevitable effect of all such reasoning, that it for a long time ended in nothing; but Paul continued his visits as before, becoming daily more enamoured of the charming rustic than ever.

" Antoinette, notwithstanding all her simplicity and modesty, was a woman, and had her perceptions. She at least saw that Paul admired her, if he did not feel a stronger sentiment for her, and that there was a struggle in his own breast which made him silent, and prevented him from declaring his passion to her.

" Being convinced of this, she exerted a little coquetry, and attended to the conversation of the other swains who frequented the house. This was more than Paul could bear, and before he had considered what was best to be done, he found Antoinette on a seat in the little harbour attached to their garden. Entering it, he seated himself by her side, and thus began—

" ' Well, Antoinette, how is it you are alone to day ?

" ' Alone ?' she exclaimed, in surprise, ' there can be nothing unusual in that.'

" ' Why, I thought you must have had some swain or other uttering praises to your beauty and good sense.'

" ' And if I had, it does not follow that I must believe all that is told me. They mean it in kindness, no doubt.'

" ' I dare say they do, but women often prefer a score of lovers to one.'

" ' How do you know that ?'

" ' I have heard it said so, and I am inclined to think, not always without truth, for some women do love the flattery of many, to the real affection of one.'

" ' It is possible they may,' rejoined Antoinette, ' but they are not women of sense ; but I suppose, by the way you make the remark, I am one of the many.'

" ' No, I meant not that ; I did not think you would think so. But if I were to say I loved you, nay, I did more, would you be able seriously to say, that you could love me in return ?'

" ' It is a serious question to put thus, but I think much of the nature of my answer would depend upon circumstances.'

" ' Then, dear Antoinette,' said Paul, taking one hand in his, and putting his own round her waist, ' tell me truly, and put aside all banter, for I really and truly love you, can you think favourably of me ?'

" ' I do think favourably of you,' she replied in an under tone.

" ' Ay, but can you love me—can you reward affection with affection ?'

" ' It must be won first, and I will not say but you have partially done so, but sincerely is the best.'

" ' And my affection is sincere ; I have loved you since I saw you, and I have daily increased in affection, until I could no longer live without seeking your heart in return.'

" ' You know that I am poor, Paul,' she said, looking on her own humble attire.

" ' Yes, I do ; I have thought of all that,' was Paul's reply.

" ' And that I will never desert my mother while she lives. She has been a good mother to me, for if I were to leave her here, she would be ruined.'

" ' I beleive you, Antoinette ; you are, indeed, her sole support, and I would not wish you to turn your back upon her ; but, you must know that I have friends whom I must consult ; I wish to put this off as long as I can, to give me time to render myself as independant as possible.'

" ' I understand you, and can assure you that I am in no haste about such a matter ; there is time for us both."

" ' Then it is a bargain,' said Paul, pressing her lips to his own.

" Antoinette did not reply, but the colour rose to her cheeks, and she escaped from him, but with a half formed smile upon her lips as she entered the house.

" Paul was a constant visitor to the cabaret, where he was always treated with respect, yet he was received within the little room, which was entirely occupied by themselves. Many whisperings took place, as to the impropriety of admitting a wealthy lover to such intimacy, for few could beleive that Paul would take Antoinette for his bride.

" Things were in this state when rumours of various kinds reached La Vendee. Tumults took place—the population became discontented, and the La Vendeeans considered that they were not bound to acquiesce in all that other parts of the kingdom had borne, and they determined to resist. The country being extremely irregular and broken in its surface, had many woods and bogs, and above all, the unanimity of its population caused a general outbreak ; and at first, several attacks of the troops had been unsuccesful. Tired by success, she arose *en masse*, and attempted to repel the invasion of the regular troops.

" Many desperate conflicts ensued, in which both parties suffered dreadfully. Paul Desslines took an active part against the troops, and became well known, and was also proscribed, and, taken where he might be, would be shot as a malignant rebel. The feelings of Antoinette might be better imagined than described, when the first saw the troops quartered in the neighbourhood.

" But their simplicity soon secured them from all molestation, and that morn many of the officers and men visited her cabaret, much to their benefit. Notwithstanding the vicinity of the troops, Paul would often visit his mistress in the dead of the night. The ground was so well known to him, that he could elude all their sentinels without any danger.

" It was at these meetings that he learned much of the situation and number of men composing the posts, and various other particulars, that enabled him, with a small band of followers, to defeat the troops in detail, and which surprised them much. Whatever Antoinette heard in the day, she would relate at night to her lover.

" This had been carried on for some time, when it became dangerous for Paul to traverse, and his visits were fewer, and at greater intervals. There was quartered at Marie's cabaret, or rather he had taken up his quarters there, a young officer of Grenadiers. He was a handsome man naturally, but, with the addition of his uniform, which sat gracefully upon him, he appeared perfectly irresistible among woman. He was well educated and possessed a considerable ease and fluency in his speech.

"Alexander De Bois, his name, was scarce two-and-twenty, and yet he commanded a company with great credit, and had deserved approbation from his superior officer on more than one occasion. At the widow's, however, he was constantly in the presence of Antoinette, and as constantly did he pay homage to her singular beauty, which the young captain could not fail to observe.

"At first this was excessively annoying to Antoinette, but she became familiarised to it, and it excited no emotion. The officer was far from disagreeable either in person or manners, and she began to consider that he was really a gay, pleasing, handsome man, and she felt pleasure in his company. But, since he had been in the house, she had not been able to see her lover often.

"This was at first an irksome affair, and De Bois perceived there was something on her mind, and knowing the connection the peasantry had naturally with such places

as these, he resolved to worm out what appeared to him a secret of impor
tance. Could it be possible that she held any secret communications with the in
surgents? She might have lovers or relatives among them, for aught he knew,
and yet her youth, beauty, and simplicity were, he thought, evidence against such
a supposition. He could not look upon her, and believe that she was a traitress.

"But what would not woman do for a lover? He knew that in all ages the
most gentle and beautiful creatures of the mind had become very heroines, and
braved death and danger to serve those they were bound to by the ties of love. 'It
must be so,' he thought; then how was he to proceed? That was a difficult inquiry, and not very readily pointed out. To question her at once would be to
put her upon her guard, and defeat his objects at once.

"He thought that he could do nothing better than to win her confidence, and
esteem—nay, her love. That would be, perhaps, the surest way. He had some
compunctious visitings of conscience about the course he was about to pursue; but
he thought his duty enjoined him to prosecute the solution of the mystery, and
added to which there was much to tempt him.

"In prosecution of this purpose, he became attentive to Antoinette, and conversed much with her in such a strain as to leave an impression on her mind that
he was struggling with his own feelings, which were strongly excited in her favour.
Indeed she became convinced that he was in love with her, but that various circumstances compelled him to remain silent, when he would gladly have acknowledged
his passion for her.

"Under this impression, the thought often crossed her imagination how she
could have given her promise to Paul, who was now, with his whole family, insurgents and beggars. De Bois was so much superior to Paul in every respect, mentally, personally, and in respect to rank and station.

"These thoughts were continually passing and repassing before her mind, and
this, together with the constant presence of the young officer, gave very soon the
ascendancy to the latter. De Bois was not slow to perceive this, and resolved to
break the ice, which he did in a very masterly manner, by declaring his love for her
to be pure and honourable, but that he was prevented from marrying at that moment from pecuniary embarrassments, but that the first favourable occurrence, such
as the capture of any insurgent leaders, he should mend his fortune, and be pro-
moted, at which time he would offer his hand and heart to her if she would take
them.

"Numerous blandishments he used, and his constant presence gave him a complete control over her actions. He protected her and her mother, promising to
make her happy for life. These and other things of a similar nature completely
effaced all impression from the mind of Antoinette that Paul had formerly caused,
and she confessed that she loved De Bois tenderly.

"To do her justice, he really loved her, and the thought frequently passed across
his mind that it was possible to make her his wife, and if he should be enabled to
capture any of the insurgent leaders through her means, it would be a merit that
might balance her want of birth or education; but then she had waited on his brother
officers in the menial capacity, and even his subordinates had been served by her
hands; this thought would always efface the better feelings of his heart, and he
would again devote his energies to the completion of his plan as he originally
designed.

"He inquired one day if Antoinette could not assist him in procuring promotion
and fortune, thus securing both their happiness and a speedy union.

"'I would do so,' replied Antoinette, 'but I have no influence with those who
can direct these things.'

"'Would you if I could show you how you could?'

"'Yes, I would.'

"'Then, tell me where to find any of the insurgents, or one of their leaders,
and this will do all I desire.'

"But Antoinette was unwilling to betray her old lover, and evaded his direct
question. He pressed her to his bosom, and declared his love and swore that he

only desired the means of their speedy union. This conversation lasted near two hours, at the end of which time De Bois had triumphed over the honour and virtue of Antoinette. He had also secured enough information to enable him to make a capture of importance. Paul Desslines, with several others of more consequence, were taken prisoners and strongly guarded, and next day sent to the commander of the division, who ordered them to be shot.

" On being marched to the spot, Paul requested to be allowed to speak with Antoinette, who knew nothing of what had happened. The meeting was an affecting one. She saw what she had done, and madly accused herself of being the sole cause of his death. Paul, who had heard something of this before, but would not believe it, now became convinced of her crime, and in the height of his indignation, said,

" Thou wilt find my blood lie heavy at thy door, and a bitter reward shalt thou receive, traitress, for thy treachery."

" He then passed on to the place of his execution. A roll of musquetry soon announced that he had fallen, and Antoinette was carried away insensible, and placed in bed in that state,

" De Bois obtained his promotion, and was ordered to another spot, at his own request, where the scene which he had witnessed, and in which he had been an actor, might soon become effaced from his mind; but the other unfortunate actress became daily more melancholy from the inward sense of her own unworthiness and criminality. Her mother soon died, leaving her to support herself by what means she could. After a few years spent in vice and crime, she ended a life of misery, by poison,"

" Poison! Poison!" repeated Rowland Percy. " That was to have been my resource, had it not been that my guardian angel, in the form of Miranda, stepped between me and the dreadful unhallowed purpose of my soul.

A deep sigh then escaped him, and for many minutes he remained in bitter contemplation.

" To die thus," he then muttered, " even in the morning of life. To linger for a few moments on the verge of existence, and that for an imputed crime, of which Heaven knows my innocence—to be held up to execration as a monster and spiller of human blood—one destitute of that great principle in the social code which forbids man to shed man's blood. Oh! 'tis a sad—a fear ul fate. And what is death? What sights and sounds are to greet us when once we have passed the dreadful portal which separates the 'mortal from the immortal part of God's creation?"

He paced his narrow cell with unequal steps, and strove, with what human judgment Heaven had endowed him, to plunge among the mysteries of the world that was to come. How soon was he then in

" Wandering mazes lost."

How inadequate did he feel his mortal powers to grapple with the great questions of immortality and eternity. Witht a shudder he sat down again, and muttered,

" No—no. There human wisdom and human research availeth nothing. We shrink before the rush of images that crowd upon the brain. We are lost—in an unfathomable depth of thought."

He started suddenly, his prison door opened, and the turnkey made the usual abrupt exclamation when announcing any one, of—

" Visitor!"

" To me ?" exclaimed Rowland ; " is it—is it——"

" Miranda," said she herself, as she entered the cell, and took both the hands of Rowland in hers. " It is Miranda, dear, dear Rowland."

The turnkey gave a grunt, as he left the door of the cell.

" Once again—once again," said Rowland, as he gazed fondly on the face of Miranda, " once again you have, like a blessed messenger of holy peace and love from heaven, sought the dreary dungeon of the solitary prisoner. My own Miranda, my beautiful and good. My latest breath shall be a blessing upon thee."

" Rowland," said Miranda, as she clutched his hands with convulsive earnestness, " Rowland, there is no one who can overhear what we say ?"

" Certainly not, Miranda. We are, I believe, as much alone here as if we were
in the wilderness of nature. But wherefore do you ask ?"

" Because, Rowland, I wish to ask if you really love your Miranda ?"

" Love you—love you! Is this a time to doubt ?"

" No, Rowland, not to doubt, but to prove the dear love I do believe glows
brightly in your heart."

" How prove it ?"

Miránda looked beseechingly in his face, as she said—

" Hear me say all that now gushes from my heart to my tongue, Rowland.
The time is now come when I have that to ask you which will try your feelings—
cause much false sense of honour—cause you to start and possibly oppose yourself to your own and my happiness in this world while either of us are doomed
to be sojourners in it. But you must promise me, Rowland. You must say you
will consent. You must not doom me to the unspeakable misery of thinking I
might have saved and——"

" Miranda, Miranda," said Rowland, despairingly, " oh, urge no more that
theme. You do indeed wring my heart. To see you another's—to purchase life
—a life of wretchedness and remorse—by the sacrifice of you to such a monster."

" You mistake me, Rowland," interrupted Miranda, " I came not to urge
again that dreadful suggestion. No—no—God be thanked, no. That has passed
away."

" What hope would your words and glances instil into my heart, Miranda ?
You do look hopeful. You have something yet to tell me which—which—Miranda
—keep me not in suspense, my Miranda. If I am saved——"

His colour went and came like the flashing sunlight of an April morn, and he
trembled more from the excitement of revived hope, than ever he had done from
the abandonment of despair. The idea had got possession of him that some
favourable turn must have taken place in his affairs, and that Miranda was fearful
of communicating it to him, lest sudden joy should do him more harm than all his
misery had accomplished.

Miranda saw in a moment that such was the idea of Rowland, and she hastened
to undeceive him by saying—

" Rowland, there is no secret—I know nothing—have no news. On my word,
Rowland, I am keeping no intelligence from you."

He became very pale as he said—

" Then tell me, dear Miranda, what has given new colour to your cheek, and
fresher brilliancy to your eye ?"

" Hope—hope !"

" For me?"

" Yes, Rowland, for you—a hope founded on an act of energy, of enterprise and
danger—that is, the danger of failure, for we have all to gain—fortune can place
us no lower on her wheel."

" True. An ignominious death ——"

" Hush, hush. I came, not unadvisedly, to breathe to you a hope of—of—escape."

"Escape from here ?" Alas, Miranda, you know not what you say—it is impossible."

" By force truly impossible, but stratagem may succeed where force were vain.
I think I must make you promise me you will consent. For my sake you will ;
you cannot say me nay, Rowland—I know you will not. They cannot harm
me. You will consent to escape—to allow yourself this night to be enveloped in
my cloak—to attempt a passage from the prison. All this you will do for my sake
—for your poor suffering father's sake—you will, Rowland—oh, tell me you will !"

These words were uttered with a pathos that went to the very soul of Percy,
for Miranda well knew that he would shrink long from exposing her to the

consequences of aiding in his attempt to escape ; and so strong did the feeling that he would not consent become in her mind, that it assumed to her imagination the shape of the greatest difficulty connected with the project.

Miranda was right, for if, indeed, there was any plan likely to aid him from which he would shrink more than from another, it would be such a one as Witlet had proposed, and Miranda in her despair, adopted.

Rowland turned away his face for a moment to hide the sudden gush of feeling that came over his heart, and exhibited in his countenance, at this instance of pure, disinterested, and self-sacrificing affection on the part of Miranda.

" Oh, is there such another heart like this ?" he asked himself. " Shall I— dare I accept so great a sacrifice ?"

Miranda knew not for a moment, when he turned from her, how to construe the action ; but when, in the next instant, he again looked in her face, and said, in tones of deep emotion—tones that gushed fresh and feelingly from the heart,

" Dearest—best ——," she uttered a cry of joy, and throwing herself upon his breast, said,

" You consent, Rowland—you consent; my Rowland, you will save yourself."

" Miranda," he said, " I were, indeed, the veriest wretch that ever crawled beneath the canopy of Heaven, if I felt not deeply, appreciated not fully, the generous, noble sacrifice you would make for me. It is indeed, in misfortune and bitterness of heart that the purest, holiest feelings of human nature are sum- moned from the dreamy rest, which might for ever have hung upon them had the spangled veil of prosperity still hidden their proper sphere of action. My Miranda— my own beautiful Miranda, you would expose yourself to evils you dream not of by an attempt to take my place in this dreary abode. Think of my agony, even were this plan successful, to escape myself, the dread of to-morrow, by entailing upon you a portion of the miseries I have undergone. Could I see you arraigned ——"

" Rowland—Rowland—think of my greater agony."

" But, Miranda ——"

" Nay, hear me. You 'yourself have called my love self-sacrificing; do you imitate it, and let yours likewise be self-sacrificing."

" My life, Miranda, were it freely mine, instead of holding it now, as I do, upon so frail a tenure, should be at a moment cast away to save you a passing pang."

" And so inflict a never-ceasing agony. Rowland, your argument is false. Feelings blind your judgment ; you would die to save me for a few days, perchance, the tiresome *ennui* of a prison, and by so dying, Rowland, you would break the fond heart that clings to you—you see, Rowland, you are wrong. Upon my own account I came to you on this mission. Surely you will, of two evils, strive to ward the greater from your own Miranda. You see I am selfish, Rowland, and you will consent."

Rowland Percy was silent for a moment. His judgment could not but acquiesce Miranda's reasoning, but his feeling revolted from purchasing liberty at the price of her freedom.

" Miranda," he said, " this plan might fail."

" It might—all human plans might fail. It is for Heaven above to say, let this be, and command the results of human action ; but should it fail, I then shall know of the failure—were it untried, I should ever predict its success, and it would be a new source of woe and anguish. You see, Rowland, it must be done. To-night I will be here. Oh ! I am full of hope. Heaven help us, Rowland."

" My —my noble Miranda."

A tear glistened in Percy's eye as he looked upon her beaming face, eloquent with the best feelings of humanity. Oh ! what would the apparently triumphant Bernard Varley have not given to feel for one fleeting instant the pure sunshine of the heart that irradiated the breasts of those two innocent beings, as in silence—a silence more eloquent than words, they thus for some minutes gaze upon each other, making a very palace of that dungeon, by the light of love and truth that beamed upon its frigid walls.

Miranda first spoke as she clung closer to her lover's heart. In soft whispered accents, she murmured—

"You consent, Rowland—you consent?"

"Yes—Yes!"

"Joy—joy and hope," said Miranda, "Till this evening, Rowland, farewell. I am happier now than I have been since last I saw my poor father in life. Heaven has not forgotten us, Rowland. Farewell—till night."

He clasped her to his heart. He could not speak, but he imprinted one kiss upon the marble brow, took one look at the beaming face, and then threw himself into the chair.

Miranda gathered her cloak about her and stepped lightly from the cell.

"Now to awaken suspicion," she said. "Let me be questioned now that Rowland may pass unquestioned to-night."

CHAPTER LXV.

MIRANDA AND THE TURNKEYS.—INTERVIEW BETWEEN TWITTER AND VARLEY.—VARLEY'S NEW HOPES.

MIRANDA, when she left the cell, proceded for some distance through the tortuous passages conducting to the outer gate of the prison, before she was met by any one, and then she heard footsteps approaching her which she guessed to be those of a turnkey, who had his post in a little nook in the passage, some short distance from where she was.

Pausing immediately, Miranda, in pursuance of the advice given her by Witlet, muffled up her face as much as possible with the ample cloak she wore, and purposely affected a wish to pass the officer without showing her face.

The man's suspicions were awakened in a moment, and giving what he considered an amazingly knowing wink, he followed Miranda until she arrived at the vestibule of the prison, when he suddenly stepped forward, saying—

"Perhaps, before you go, miss, you will have the kindness just to let us see as it is you?"

"Sir?" said Miranda, in an assumed tone.

"We just want one look at your face."

"Why this insult?"

"Just for the sake of satisfaction. It rather strikes me, too, that you've got a cold, for you don't speak just as I have heard you, miss—ahem!"

Miranda withdrew the cloak from her face as she said in a mournful tone—

"'Tis very hard that grief should not be permitted even to hide its face from rude curiosity. The thoughts of to-morrow may well weigh heavily upon my heart, and even impart to my voice an unnatural tone. You see my face and even have the poor satisfaction of having added an additional pang to sorrow already too—too—but I will not, for the few hours that I shall have cause to visit this place, be treated thus. I will see the governor, and surely he will give permission that I may keep my tears sacred from the observation of his menials."

The officer who had thought himself so very cunning, and who really had suspected his prisoner was attempting an escape, looked confounded when he saw Miranda's pale face, and heard her talk of an appeal to the governor, for he knew perfectly well he should be just as much abused for his mistaken zeal, as he would have been praised for his cleverness, had his suspicions turned out well founded.

"I—I," he stammered, "I beg pardon, but you see, miss, I—I—really——"

"Enough, enough," said Miranda, "I ought not to complain. The wretched should suffer perhaps such things as this in silence. 'Tis time to appeal to a higher authority should the insult be repeated."

So saying she passed out at the gate which the man who was on duty there was holding open for her. When she was gone, he turned to the discomfited officer, and said,

"Well, Sammy, you've put your foot in it, I think."

"Well, I never," said Sammy. "Here is a kick up. Why did she look so blessed 'spicious !"

"Feelings, Sammy, feelings."

"Feelins be bothered; I never had none, and I don't see the use of em—not I."

"I can't say as I sees the use on 'em, Sammy, but you know people as comes to see other people as is a going to be hung, always comes it strong in that ere line."

"They does—they does."

"Well, you ought to make 'lowances, Sammy."

"So I does. When Dick Lee, the cracksman was hung, and his wife comed with a bottle of gin the night afore, didn't I make 'lowances ?"

"Yes, you did, for you lowanced it out atween you and her, curse you, and never said to me so much as, Bill, will you take a drain ?"

"Feelins purwented me."

"You be bothered, and I tells you what, if that there young ooman complains to the guvner, I wouldn't give twopenee for your place, Sammy."

"Thank you for nothing," said Sammy, as he walked away, and then muttered to himself. "Blessed if she may n't come out and in, in a bag tied up tight at the top, afore I'll have anything more to say to her. How do I hate feelins to be sure. I ne'er had none—ain't got none, and don't want none. Feelins be blowed !"

Having thus vented his indignation, Sammy sat down, with a conviction that he was a very greatly injured man.

In the meantime, strange as it may appear, Bernard Varley was in a more hopeful state than he had been since the trial. In the first place, he thought he saw symptoms of wavering resolution in Miranda's manner, and he nourished an expectation that perhaps at the last moment she might save her lover at the sacrifice of herself, and giving him a solemn promise, which he could rely upon, enable him to take the necessary steps for saving Rowland Percy.

He arranged then what he meant to do with singular clearness and perspicuity. The only one point upon which his mind was evidently unable to think rationally, concerned Miranda. His hopes of ever winning her to become his, were based upon the most extraordinary improbabilities, and yet he clung to them with dogged perseverance, while his judgment would have at once detected their fallaciousness, had they presented themselves in any other shape.

After his interview with Miranda, he hurried homewards, not to his lodging opposite, but to where he expected ro find Twitter, with whom he wished to have some more conversation concerning the adventure by the gravel-pits.

Neither of them had visited the Grange, and Varley found Twitter at home, seriously ill from the fright he had sustained, and in a state of mental and physical prostration, which was of the most alarming nature.

He was, however, Varley thought, more likely to return truthful answers to what he should ask of him than if he were in his usual state. The great fact which he wished to ascertain was, if Twitter had seen the mysterious man from whose supposed knowledge he, Bernard Varley, shrunk aghast, in any way interfering with the course of examination that he, Twitter, had undergone by the brink of the chasm, down which he had been threatened to be hurled.

That the mysterious horseman had a part in that transaction, appeared to Varley more than probable, and what he wished to please his mind with as a consequence was, that the knowledge of the mysterious horseman concerning the murder of Sir George Rankley must be limited, or, perhaps, only conjecture ; for if it were otherwise—if he really possessed ample information, why should he seek by threats to wring from Twitter a confession of that by which, if known to him already, he could insure the destruction of them both ?

Hence it was that Varley, most anxious to rescue his imagination from the bugbear that was ever present to it, in the shape of the solitary horseman, would gladly have associated him with the attempt upon Twitter, which, if he could thoroughly succeed in doing, would calm his mind upon the subject.

These, then, were the two sources of Varley's consolation and easier state of mind.   Hopes of Miranda at the last hour relenting, and becoming his, to save Rowland, as well as a rescue from his dread of the unknown horseman.

His question to Twitter was—

" Were you aware of the presence of a tall man, wearing a short riding-cloak, when you were assaulted by the ruffians, and threatened with death ?"

" No, no," said Twitter, " I saw no one distinctly but him who held me and catechised me.   You know, Varley, that I was staunch and faithful—telling nothing that could injure you—breathing no sort of suspicion upon your name."

" Peace—peace !" said Varley.   " I know better than perhaps you are aware of, what you said, and well can I guess what you would have said, had I not interfered to save you from what, after all, I believe firmly was but an empty threat, that never would have been carried into execution."

" You think they would not have killed me ?"

" I am sure they would not.   The thing was a mere trick of Percy's friends to wring a confession from you, for well can I perceive they suspect the truth."

" Then we are in great danger."

" Wherefore ?   Let the whole world suspect what it may, provided nothing can be proved, and Rowland Percy in the meantime will be hanged, unless——"

Varley paused, and Twitter said anxiously—

" What can save him now ?"

" Nothing, nothing, Twitter, but what would destroy us.   The next hanging in York will be Rowland Percy's, or——"

" Oh, cease, cease," cried Twitter.   " Can you command voice and nerve to indulge in such dreadful speculations?"

" Yes when the result is certain.   Now, Twitter, I have but one piece of advice to give you, and be it upon your own head if you neglect it."

" Advice, Varley ; what is it ?"

" This—until Rowland Percy is hanged, you must not stir from this house. Who knows what other plan would be adopted to scare you into a confession that would be our destruction?"

" I will not stir," said Twitter.   " Believe me, Varley, I will not cross the threshold of this house until he is dead.   I would not encounter such another attack for worlds."

" You are prudent—very prudent, Twitter."

" And you too, Varley—you will be cautious.   Oh, be warned and abandon your mad chase after Miranda.   It can end in nothing but ruin.   Varley—Varley, hear me.   Be warned in time.   If there be any one circumstance fraught with danger to us both, it is that—it is that."

With a smile of contempt upon his lips, Varley left the room.

" He is gone—he is gone," muttered Twitter.   " Shall I know more peace when Rowland Percy has met his doom?   Will the horrible images that now persecute me through the long hours of the night then leave me ?   Surely yes. They will—they will, and I shall be more calm—more composed—my blood will not then boil through my veins one moment, as if it would burst its bounds, and then suddenly pause, and seem to curdle round my heart, as if it never meant to flow again.   Yes—yes, I shall feel a greater relief when Rowland Percy is dead."

He lay then for some minutes silent, but his restlessness would not be appeased, and he spoke again.

" I must force myself from Varley," he muttered.   " By robbery, and by what I can wring from him, I must get enough for comfort, and then leave him.   If my

—my nerves and strength would let me, I would some day take his life. I would—I would. Oh, how I hate him. Curses!—curses!"

He lifted up his hands, and his countenance assumed an awful expression as he showered bitter maledictions on the head of the man who had tempted him to such iniquity, and then deceived him as to the promised wages of his crime.

Exhausted then by his own wild emotion, he remained passive for hours, only occasionally dropping off into an uneasy slumber, which was visited by crowds of frightful images, which gibed and mocked him, until with cries of terror he would awaken, and start half from his couch, gaze into vacancy, with eyes glazed with terror.

Varley, when he reached his room, opposite to where Miranda resided, sat down, thoroughly to arrange his diabolical schemes.

The unprincipled attorney, who had assisted him so far as Sir George Rankley's will was concerned, had made him an offer for the Grange estates, far below their estimated value, and Varley's scheme was this :—

Should Miranda consent at the last moment to become his, in order to save Rowland, he would at once proceed to the attorney and accept his offer, with a deduction of a large per centage, provided there and then he gave him the cash, which he knew he could do of his own, or some one elses.   Then having extracted so solemn a promise from Miranda to be his, that she could not retract it, he would write to the judges, denying all his evidence upon the trial, and flatly accusing Samuel Twitter of the murder.   At the same time, then, that he forwarded his letter, he himself would start for the Continent, in some obscure part of which he would wait the result of the affair.

———

CHAPTER LXVI.

THE NIGHT BEFORE THE EXECUTION.—MIRANDA'S COURAGE.—THE CELL.—THE DISGUISE.—WITLET'S ANXIETY.

WHEN Miranda reached her home after the agitating interview she had had with Rowland Percy, her first inquiry was for the afflicted father, who had shown such fearful evidence of what a wreck sorrow could make of the strongest minds. Had her mind not been engrossed as it was even to overflowing with the condition of her lover, and the million of hopes, fears, and anxieties that waited on the enterprise of the coming evening, she might have felt more keenly and more deeply the state of Mr. Percy ; but as it was, she felt how true it is that great griefs in their wild intensity and overwhelming power, swallow up all lesser ones, making the human mind look with comparative calmness upon events, which, had they come alone, would have filled the heart with terror and the imagination with dismay.

Insanity in any shape or form, is always terrible, and to a mind constituted as Miranda's was, it presented ever the most lamentable aspect, for the greater the degree of mental power, excellence, and beauty there may be in one mind, the more keenly and bitterly will such an intellect commisserate with those who, from temporary or permanent causes, have lost the god-like power which lifts humanity so near the pure throne of Heaven.

To her relief, she was told that he slept.   After talking much of his Rowland, and indulging in many visions of the happiness he should himself have, by witnessing the joy of Miranda and his son, who he supposed were about to be married with the consent of Sir George Rankley, whose death he would not believe, he had quietly laid down and dropped into a peaceful slumber, from which the medical man anticipated the most beneficial results.

" If this sleep," he said, " should continue calm and unshaken for some hours, it may carry off his mental hallucination ; but should he, during it, be tormented with dreams, the mind will scarcely be able to recover its equilibrium, and the temporary insanity may continue for some time longer.   There is every appearance at present of the happiest results."

Such was the state of affairs when Miranda reached her home, where she resolved to wait and see no one till the time should arrive for her to start upon her heroic expedition of love and devotion.

She sat down in silence by the bedside of Mr. Percy, and her thoughts wandered back again to Rowland's gloomy cell.   A bright smile played like sunshine upon her face, as she thought what a glorious habitation it would seem to her for the few hours succeeding the successful escape of Rowland, should Heaven in its mercy, will that that escape should succeed, and save the innocent even in the hour of greatest peril.

Thus she pictured to herself what the future might still be, should Rowland escape destruction. Surely, she thought, some day will come when his innocence will be apparent, and he will be able to walk abroad among his fellow-men with an unclouded brow, an unshrinking heart—now all men's hands are raised against him, and he stands alone, with nothing but his consciousness of right to guide him through the tangled paths of mental disquietude, and save him from despair, or the worse fate which has befallen his poor suffering father.

Miranda was silent now for a time, but her thoughts were very busy. They carried her far back, even to her happy childhood, when all around her was sunshine and joy. Not the dimmest shadow of the cloud which since had burst with such awful vehemence over her, and all she loved then, showed itself in the sunny heaven of her heart.

"We were so happy," she murmured, "so very happy, so full of life, of joy and love. Oh, who would have believed that of four human beings, upon whom the sun of prosperity was so brightly shining, there should be one yet so far unscathed as to have even the liberty of action. My father murdered—Rowland condemned for a crime he never for one instant contemplated, and which the tenor of his life and constitution of his mind should at once give a contradiction to—his father, the wreck of what he was, a maniac—and I—I, a poor, helpless girl, striving against such an accumulation of miseries, as formerly to read of would have tortured my brain and given me hours of disquietude."

She clasped her hands upon her head, and leaning down upon the bed, she strove to weep, for she felt as if tears would be a world of relief to her.

A voice seemed then to whisper to her, "Not yet, Miranda—not yet—no tears yet."

"I cannot weep," she said. "'Tis very strange. Time was when the death of a bird, the untimely fading of a flower, would have wrung my heart, and each fond pet had its tributary tear; but now, feelings that lie deeper than the source of tears are awakened, and I cannot weep."

She sunk then upon her knees by the bedside, and offered up an artless, eloquent prayer to the Author of all good, to aid her in her enterprise to save the innocent. She asked not that the guilty should be punished, but with gentle, holy supplication, she wished the innocent to be saved, and virtue to be rescued from distress.

When does prayer ever fail to relieve the oppressed heart? Miranda, when she rose again, felt a holy calm stealing over her, her brain had ceased to throb, and her heart beat in more regular cadences. Who will doubt that the supplications of that young, pure being had reached the throne of mercy, and been accepted by Him who has said, "Come to me in your sorrow, and you shall be comforted."

Scarcely had she risen from her posture of prayer when she heard a slight tap at the chamber-door; upon opening it she saw the woman of the house, who said:—

"Mr. Anderson is below; he wishes to speak to you, and to know how Mr. Percy is now."

"Mr. Percy sleeps," said Miranda. "Tell him I ——"

She paused, for she shrunk from refusing to see the faithful friend, who throughout all her dire adversity had clung to her with so much disinterested devotion, and yet she felt the necessity of not seeing him, for she would not for worlds have him a party to the scheme for the liberation of Rowland, so far as to commit him professionally in the matter, for, should the scheme fail, what an additional source of anguish would it be to her to reflect that in its trial she had inflicted injury upon others as well as herself.

These thoughts flashed through Miranda's mind with great rapidity, as she said:—

"Give my best regards to Mr. Anderson, and tell him to see me in the morning. Just now I am not equal to the task of seeing even my best and dearest friends."

This message was communicated to Mr. Anderson, who of course instantly departed, grieving sadly over the melancholy and despair which he felt sure were gnawing at the heart of the beautiful girl who must look forward to the morrow with such exquisite anguish.

"Yes, to-morrow," said Miranda; "to-morrow—Heaven send he may find me in Rowland's cell. Oh, with what joy he will see me looking upon those dingy walls. Methinks I could for ever take up my abode within them, were Rowland free."

An uneasy movement on the part of Mr. Percy now arrested her attention, and she looked earnestly in his face. He slowly opened his eyes; one glance of those orbs was enough for Miranda. They spoke not of mind—the wild restless glare of insanity still shone from them. The sleep had not done its gentle office well, and the mind was still a chaos of disjointed images.

He knew Miranda, for, as a smile played upon his lips, he said—

"You are my dear son Rowland's beautiful bride. God bless you, Miranda. How happy we shall be for many, many years. Bless you and my boy—where is he? Surely he is not still tossing on those restless white-crested waves I saw him on?"

Miranda sighed deeply.

"Hush, hush," said the old man. "Do not sigh—I think that was a dream—have I slept?"

"You have."

He laughed a strange, wild laugh, as he added—

"I thought so—I thought so. Yet it was so very, very like reality, I will tell you. My boy Rowland, who lies so near my heart, I thought I saw him in a stormy ocean. Oh! how the wild winds howled, and how fearfully the waves dashed hither and thither the tiny bark which, like a shell, danced over the curling foam. My boy held bravely on—his eye flinched not—he looked like a spirit of the waters watching them in their wild, boisterous play. Oh! it was beautiful to see how the one small boat, fashioned by the hands of man, thus sported with the wildest element of nature, and defied its utmost wrath."

Mr. Percy spoke in a tone of strange, wild enthusiasm, and Miranda was greatly interested by the romance of his singular dream.

"What more?" she said. "What more?"

"I will tell you. I watched the little shell-like bark, with its living freight, till my eyes ached again. It was my Rowland who was in it, and his face was very pale. He seemed wound up to some great pitch of mental endurance. I never saw him look so pale—except once—except once."

"When was that?"

"Hush—don't speak of it. But it was once when I thought they accused him of murder."

Miranda shuddered, and cried—

"Alas! alas! how strangely reality mingles with fiction. How the fevered imagination trenches on the memory, making strange havoc and confusion in the brain."

"That was a worse dream than this," continued Mr. Percy, "and it very nearly drove me mad—mad—mad. They accused him of murder, Miranda. My son, my own gentle, brave, tender, gallant Rowland."

"But—but the dream," said Miranda. "I pray you go on with the dream. What happened to the small boat in which Rowland was? Tell me all."

"I will—I will. The fierce wind from the south came rushing on like a wild creature shrieking for prey. It curled round the misty waves, mingling them together in a wild confusion, till the sea looked like a seething cauldron stirred by millions of evil spirits, and all for the destruction of that small shell-like boat and its pale human occupant."

"And what did he?"

"Sometimes I saw him not. Sometimes on the topmast pinnacle of a surging wave I saw it balanced for a moment as if in mid air. Then down—down it flew, like a guilty thing, into the deep abyss below."

" But there was a Heaven above," said Miranda. " There was an eye which never sleeps gazing down upon that boat and the soul that was cradled by that wild waste of waters."

" Yes, yes—and then I lost it for a time, and a loud voice screamed in my ears one word which seared my heart.

" What word was that ?"

" Guilty ! guilty !"

" The trial again," murmured Miranda, " that ever mixes its dread realities up with his wildest ravings. I pray you say on, Mr. Percy. Was the boat then lost, or did it reach its wished-for haven ?"

" When next I saw it, it had raised a snow white sail, no thicker than a gossamer. I scarce could see it, save when it stood against the black waters that like a wall, nearly submerged it in their rage. It was so very frail—of such light texture, that I trembled for it—but it was of such a pearl-like whiteness that it looked most beautiful, and as the mild reflection of its colour fell upon the face of him who was in that boat, it seemed to shed a halo of light upon it, and to bring that blest composure to his heart which innocence should impart."

" And the result ?" said Miranda. " Oh ! tell me, did the boat come safe to land ?"

" Hush—hush ! As the thin white sail fluttered in the blast, and rose and fell with the tiny boat upon the world of waters, I saw the one word 'innocence' upon it, and in another instant it was rent to atoms by the howling wind."

" Lost—lost !" said Miranda. " Innocence would not suffice to save him."

" Tossed at the mercy of the lashing sea—now down as if seeking the depth of some hidden cavern of the earth, and then up, as if summoned by Heaven itself to mount to its radiant gates—I saw that boat. In the foremost part there sat a female form."

" A female form ?"

" Yes. How very strange was the vision of my slumbers. That form resembled you, Miranda. You were pale too—pale as my boy, Rowland ; but I saw you take the tiller of the frail vessel and point to the shore. I saw you smile, and my heart became glad, for there was hope, I felt, for my Rowland."

" Was he saved ?"

" He was—he was ! Saved—saved !"

" Heaven, I thank thee !" said Miranda. " Let me accept this vision as thy voice, telling me that he I would succour shall be free. Innocence has not saved him, but shall. So says the dream. I will let it nerve me, even at the risk of superstition."

Eight o'clock sounded from a time-piece on the staircase, and Miranda sprung to her feet.

" Time—time !" she cried.

" Time for what ? Where is Rowland ?" said Mr. Percy. " I want to speak to your father, Miranda. I did not like to tell you before ; but do you know I have not been successful lately in what I fear your father will call rash speculations. I would fain speak with him."

Miranda could scarcely speak from the excitement of her feelings at this allusion to one who was in the cold grave, and alike indifferent to the world and all its concerns ; but she managed with difficulty to say—

" Remain here till I return, Mr. Percy. Let me beg of you to try and sleep now."

" Where go you, Miranda ? Send my son to me."

" You shall see him soon. Be patient till I return."

" I will try to sleep. I would fain have more dreams. They look so like the truth—only some are dreadful. Some one accused my son of a murder, and that was the most absurd of all. Good night—good night. Blessings on you, Miranda. Rowland is very happy."

" Good night," said Miranda, in choking accents. " Good night !"

With a quick step she left the room and hastened down the staircase. She then called to the woman of the house, and when she came to her, said—

"Should I not return by to-morrow morning early, or by to-night even, please to send for Mr. Anderson. He will arrange all that should be done in my temporary absence."

"Yes, miss," said the woman. "I hope you will keep your heart up. We never know what good may come even when we least expect it. My husband says as he is quite sure Mr. Rowland Percy didn't do the murder.

"Thank you—thank you!" said Miranda. "I am much beholden to your kind opinion. Thank you. Good evening."

"Good evening, miss."

In another moment Miranda was at the door. A gush of cool fresh air from the open street was welcome to her fevered brow, and she drew her cloak more closely around her, as she hurried on in the direction of the prison.

A cold wind swept through the streets, but Miranda heeded it not. Her heart was glowing with hope.

"He will be saved—he will be saved," she said, "and I shall know the exquisite joy of being the means of rescuing him. Oh, what an anxious time will be the next two hours! All seems now to me like a dream. Can the pages of fiction, adorned as they may be by the most brilliant imaginings, excel the romance of such truth as this? Oh, Rowland, Rowland! if you should be saved, I shall ever look upon you as some gift from Heaven—as one snatched by the hand of God himself from destruction."

"Miranda!" said a voice close to her ear.

She started, and turning hastily, saw Witlet gazing anxiously upon her animated face.

CHAPTER LXVII.

NINE O'CLOCK.—THE DISGUISE.—THE BAFFLED OFFICIAL.—MOMENTS OF SUSPENCE.
LIBERTY.

"My friend," said Miranda.

"Thank you for calling me such," said Witlet. "I will not detain you a moment My only object was to assure you I was here, and ready to do what in me lay, to further the noble object in view."

"I thank you from my heart."

"The moment," added Witlet, "that Mr. Percy leaves the prison-gate, I will meet him, and in another quarter of an hour he shall be on his route to London, where, I have bethought me I have much more ample and available means of concealing him than I have here, although I have friends in York who would do their best for him."

"To you we owe everything," said Miranda. "Your advice I have already followed with success, and the probabilities are all in favour of Rowland's escape."

"Tell him to stoop as he comes out, and impress upon him the necessity of walking slow. Should there even be a moment's hesitation at the gate I will have him out, for I will not be alone here. Not a chance shall be thrown away."

Miranda held out her hand, which Witlet took respectfully in his, and she said—

"Come what may, happen what may, you will ever hold a warm place in my heart. Do not needlessly run yourself into any danger. Farewell, until we meet again; and whether in joy or in sorrow, you will ever find a warm welcome and a grateful heart from Miranda Rankley."

"God bless you, and success attend you," said Witlet, in a tone of emotion, as he wrung her hand, and then turned away.

Miranda once more adjusted her cloak, and hastened towards the prison.

It was strange, as Miranda neared the spot where she was to undergo so severe trial of nerves, that she should become more and more calm—but such was the case. Her's was one of these dispositions which suffer much during the idleness of expectation, and which become bold and firm, when the period for action arrives.

As she neared the gloomy mansion in which so many unhappy persons were sighing for the pure and beautiful light of Heaven, and the free air, which would invigorate their wasted energies, she felt a renewed hope, and a boldness which her heart had some hours before been a stranger to.

She repeated to herself a sentiment she had heard once attributed to Napoleon by an occasional guest at her father's hospitable table. It was this—

"The great element of success in all enterprises is to determine upon it—to believe we have the power, and confidently to anticipate the favourable result."

This she repeated to herself over and over again, until she gave herself a confidence which much emboldened her to proceed, and use every means for making success a certainty instead of a theoretical event.

She rung the bell at the wicket gate of the prison without a tremor, and the moment she had done so, she gathered her cloak over the lower part of her face, and waited impatiently the appearance of the turnkey.

In about a minute a small grating was opened, and a harsh inquiry of "Whose there?" saluted her.

"Miranda Rankley," she replied, "I come to visit Mr. Percy."

"Humph!" growled the man; "you know, miss, we close to all visitors at nine o'clock. Its over five-and-twenty minutes past eight now."

"I have an order," said Miranda, "as you well know, from the judge, to admit me at all hours, when the prison is considered open at all to strangers. Refuse me admittance, and I go directly to the judge's chambers."

"Oh! there's no occasion for that," said the man, opening the wicket in some alarm. "You can come in, of course; I only meant to tell you what a short time you would have to remain."

"I know it," said Miranda, and then added to herself, "Heaven send I may remain here till to-morrow's dawn, so that Rowland be safe away."

A passing tremor came across her as she heard the wicket-gate closed behind her. In another moment she was calm again, and all was as before. Her cloak she kept closely round her chin and, as she waited to be conducted to the cell, she said in a voice she purposely made rough and strange—

"Has Mr. Percy had any visitors since last I was here?"

"Eh!" said the turnkey, looking at her.

"Has Mr Percy had any visitors?"

As she the second time pronounced her question, she purposely allowed the cloak to drop from her face, so that there could be no difficulty in seeing who she was.

"No, mum," said the turnkey, as he looked in her beautiful countenance with some surprise. "There ain't been nobody here. Hem," he added to himself, "what an out of the way cold she has got, to be sure. I never heard her speak so afore."

Miranda followed him in silence, still keeping the cloak nearly entirely over her face, until they reached the cell of Rowland, when the man knocked. As he did so, he unlocked the door, and made the usual brief announcement of—

"A visitor."

"Thank you," said Miranda, and she passed into the cell.

The turnkey stood a moment on the outside, and then with what he considered an extraordinary clever shake of the head, he said in an under tone—

"Well d—n me, for a nice looking and pretty girl too, she has the most out and out extraordinary manners that ever I comed near. Hiding of her face, and then growling out thank you like a young bear. Well, she's a rum un; there aint much feeling there, I should say. She's like our sammy, se ain't got no feerrlng at all, nor don't want none.'

With these remarks, the man went to the vestibule, and did what Miranda wou:d have rejoiced to hear him do, namely, told all the officials, who were there assembled for a gossip, what an extraordinary masculine, odd, gruff sort of young woman she, Miranda, was. Then Sammy, whom Miranda had threatened to report to the governor, told circumstantially, how he had very nearly got into a scrape, all through suspecting her, and terminated by saying—

"I won't have nothing more to do with her or say to her, not I, I can tell |you. She'll go and make a complaint to the guvnor, and get a fellow guved the sack to in half a minute. If she was to come in in a blessed hogshead, and only speak through the bung-hole, I'd just roll her out and in, and I'm blessed if I'd say a word to her no how. She's an out and out rum un, she is, and it's my belief and *verdit* as she wants to get us into some scrape cos we keeps her sweetheart, as is to be scragged to-morrow, too safe in quod."

"Werry right, werry right," cried another. "Sammy, you have hit the correct nail on the head this time, any how, my boy.

"I believe yer," said Sammy, "Look at me—do I look a ass?"

"Rather," said another; "only you hasn't so long ears as common. Howsomever, I recommends when this here young ooman comes out as we gets the better on her by paying no sort o' attention to what she says or what she does ay.

"That's the thing," said several. "We'll get the better on her, any w   We wasn't born yesterday."

How happy would this conversation have made Miranda; but still without a knowledge of it she was full of hope, and the moment she stepped into Rowland's cell, she cast the cloak from her, and holding out both her hands, she said, in a voice full of joy—

"Dear Rowland, you will yet be saved."

"My Miranda," he cried, as he clasped her to his heart, "do you still intend to sacrifice yourself for me?"

"Sacrifice, Rowland! No; by saving you, I intend to save myself; you will escape, and I shall be happy. All has succedeed to the utmost of my wishes. There is no one circumstance which has gone awry. Rowland, dear, dear Rowland, you have, I believe, but to walk out of your prison, and you will be free. Trust implicitly a tall man who will speak to you outside; he is your friend, and has arranged everything to facilitate your escape and permanent concealment."

"But you, you, Miranda. Oh, what pangs should I not suffer with the thought that you were exposed to the insolence of the officials of this place, and——"

"Hush! hush, Rowland!" interrupted Miranda, "there are pangs of different degrees; what frightful misery would be mine if I were to leave you here to perish, and know that to-morrow morning would find you a corpse!"

Rowland perceptibly shuddered.

"I have your promise," continued Miranda; "time presses. Envelope yourself in this cloak, and be firm, bold, and resolute. Stoop as you leave the prison; hide your f:ce; heed not what you hear, but walk slowly—mind, slowly, Rowland—to the outer gate."

The prison-clock at this instant struck the three quarters to nine, and Miranda took the cloak from the ground, saying—

"Quick, Rowland, quick, they will soon be here to warn you to go, and this will be your only chance."

Even as she spoke, and while she held her cloak in her hand towards Rowland, the door of the cell was opened, and to Miranda's as well as the prisoner's deep vexation, the chaplain stood in the entrance.

He looked as grave and solemn as he could, making a very slight bow to Miranda as he entered the cell, and then, before either of them could speak, he said—

"I have come once more in your presence, young woman—I beg your pardon, lady—to exhort this unhappy young man, who is so near to eternity, to repentance and to a confession of his many sins and deep transgressions, in order, as I once before remarked to him, that he may be welcomed to another and a better world by ten thousand angels, who will sing requiems of joy over the brand which has been snatched by me, an unworthy labourer in the vineyard of the Lord, from the burning; and in order that grace everlasting, and——"

"Peace, sir," cried Rowland; "if I am even now hanging upon the brink of eternity, at least I should be allowed the consolation of taking leave in peace of those who are dearest to my heart, and for whom I would fain linger yet awhile in life."

"Ah," said the chaplain, casting up his eyes, "that is all vanity and vexation of spirit. Young lady, you should reason with this sinful man, and not uphold him in his obstinacy, which induces him to reject the means of everlasting grace, where ten thousand augels——"

"Cease, sir," said Miranda; "I have as pure, and I hope, purer notions of Heaven and its great Master, than you have. Rowland Percy is my affianced husband. I know his pure and spotless heart well. He is not sinful. Begone, sir ; your avocation is thrown away here. He is innocent, and even yet I do not believe Heaven will permit him to die the death of a felon. Leave this cell and make not the possibly last moments of an innocent man more bitter by your unwelcome presence."

"Do you, then, lost beings that you are, both utterly reject my ministry ?"

"We decline your services," said Rowland, "and request you will leave this place."

"Hell flames will be your portion," said the pious (?) man; "and there will be gnashing of teeth and deep despair, and all sorts of wailing, and the wicked shall know no rest, for that they repent not."

"Begone, profane man! Doubter of Heaven's mercy, begone!" said Rowland.

He advanced a step as he spoke, and the alarmed chaplain thought it prudent to make a hasty retreat. Nine boomed forth by the Minster clock the moment his back was turned.

"The cloak, Rowland ! the cloak !" cried Miranda. "Quick, quick, or we are loss !'

CHAPTER LXVIII.

FROM NINE TILL A QUARTER PAST.—THE SCUFFLE.—ROWLAND'S DANGER.— WITLET'S PROMPTITUDE AND COURAGE.—THE ESCAPE COMPLETED.

CONCIOUS that there was really not a moment now to loose, if he intended at all to avail himself of Miranda's generous self-sacrifice in his favour, Rowland accepted the proffered cloak, in which he hastily enveloped himself.

His next step was rapidly to roll up the legs of his trowsers, and then Miranda completed his disguise by placing her bonnet upon his head, and tying it securely under his chin.

"Wrap the cloak closely round you, Rowland," she said, in hurried accents, "and you will be safe. Speak not to any one. Do not hurry through the passages. Rowland, Heaven aid and prosper you."

"My Miranda," was all he could say. For one fleeting moment then, he clasped her to his heart, and they heard the sound of a footstep leisurely approaching the cell. It was the turnkey. Rowland knew well that step—among the few incidents that relieve the tediousness of a prison life, the peculiarity even of the gaoler's tread becomes a subject of contemplation.

"We must part now, Miranda," he said. "I hear the turnkey even now coming."

"Hold the door a moment," said Miranda.

Rowland placed his back against it, while Miranda hurriedly put on his coat and hat. She then seated herself at the table in such a way that her head and shoulders only were in the light.

Scarcely had she completed her change of costume ere a knock came on the door of the cell, and the voice of the turnkey in no very gentle accents, said—

"Hilloa ! we don't allow doors fastened on the inside here."

"Are you ready ?" wispered Rowland.

"Quite, quite, farewell—Heaven help you."

"God bless you, my Miranda. It will be a happy day when we meet again."

"Hush ! hush ! let him in—hush !"

Rowland moved away from the door, and stooping so as to decrease his height as much as possible, he stood some few paces from it, in the direction where Miranda was sitting.

In a moment she dropped her head upon the table, as if too much affected to speak, and the truth was that she could not at that moment have said anything for the world, for her anxiety almost prevented her breathing.

The turnkey stood on the threshold for a moment in surprise at the silence and singular relative position of the parties. Then he said—

" Oh, there's been some feelings at work has there ; wel , there's a end of every thing, and if you please, mum, we is going to put the kiver on the jug, and in case you shouldn't understand what that ere means, wh y I explains it to be shut-ing up the prison."

The man's tone and manner at once proclaimed him to be in the first stage of intoxication, and Miranda trembled for what might ensue during Rowland's passage from the cell to the outer gate.

All the light the turnkey had with him was a lantern, which he held swingingly in one hand in such a manner as rather to confuse his vision than to afford it any essential asistance, and now he stood a little way outside the door, saying—

" Come o n, we can't wait all night, if you please, mum. Don't be going and saying I wasn't civil, cos I am, but we can't wait for you."

Without a word, Rowland passed from the cell to the great suprise of the turn-key, who cast a glance at what he supposed to be his prisoner, and then mut-tered—

" Oh, I suppose as the feelings business has all been settled afore I comed. Well, it don't matter to me, but I did expect the usual skrimmage of crying and pocket handkerchers to-night, always, considering as to-morrow morning there's to be the scragging."

It was not in human nature not to feel some terrors, situated as Rowland Percy was with his life hanging as it were upon a thread. He did tremble, but he took care it should not be perceptible as he walked after the turnkey, who now and then looked behind him to make some remark, savouring more of insolence than courtesy ; for now that he was in a state of partial intoxieation, his mistake in insisting upon seeing Miranda's face, and her threat of appealing to the governor came fully across his mind, and made him think himself a very injured individual.

He accordingly made what he considered some of the most cutting remarks to Rowland, every now and then, such as—

" Perhaps you'd like to complain to the governor to night about something— cos if you does, I'll ring his blessed bell for you, mum ?"

Of course, Rowland said nothing to this, which was ten times more aggravating to the turnkey than a regular wrangle would have been, and he got in such a rage at last, as he came near the vestibule, that he banged the lantern about to its imminent danger ; and when he fairly arrived there, he set it down with a bang and a curse that quite astonished the gate-keeper.

Here was the trying moment for Rowland. Immediately above the wicket-gate was a lamp, within which there was a strong reflector, that cast a broad glare of light down the vestibule.

Had there been no person there but the friendly turnkey, who was, what he technically termed, on the lock that night, all would have been well ; but there was also in the vestibule a keen, sharp eyed under-turnkey, who, while Row-land waited the brief moment that was necessary to have the gate opend for him, eyed him with the closest scrutiny.

Now, had this gentleman not been so amazingly cunning and artful, as he believed himself to be, Rowland Percy would have been discovered, and conducted back to his cell, from whence he would not again have departed, but to the place of execution on the morrow.

Such, however, did not occur, for although the under-turnkey did suspect some-thing amiss, he though how very clever it would be for him to follow the supposed young lady in the cloak, and if she should prove to be the prisoner escapei n in disguise, how amazingly to his credit and advantage it would be to bring him back himself, after he had passed out unsuspected by the other officials.

"I'm not quite sure," he thought to himself, "but I'm nearly sure that that's a man. If I was to say anything about it just now, I should have Sammy and all the fellows in the place swearing they knew it, and only were waiting to see how far he'd go. I know a trick worth two of that. If they let him go without following him, why they can't say as they had ever any suspicion. Very good. I will follow, and if I'm wrong, why, they can't laugh at me, for they won't know it, and if I'm right, I shall come in for all the credit."

This reasoning looked so amazingly plausible in the eyes of the turnkey, that he adopted at once a course of action resulting from it.

No sooner had Rowland, with a thrill of delight such as in his whole life he had never before experienced, passed across the threshold of the prison, than the clever under turnkey said to the man on the lock.

"Let him out—I sha'nt be long."

With a misgiving of the truth in his own mind, the friendly turnkey let him out and saw him dart down the steps, and walk off in the direction Rowland had taken.

"Ha!" he said, "it's all up now. The d—d prying fellow has his suspicions, I know. Well, I can do nothing. I promised Ned I would do my best, and I have."

He then threw himself into his chair, and calmly waited the result, which he expected would be the return of the prisoner in about a quarter of an hour.

The quarter of an hour, however, passed away, and another quarter at the back of it, without any such result ensuing, and suprise began to take the place of any other feeling in his mind.

How is it that the clever under-turnkey has failed in his cleverness? we shall see.

The moment Rowland Percy gained the street, Ned Witlet, who was watching the prison door with the most intense eagerness, walked across the road, and going up to him, whispered,

"Mr. Percy!"

Rowland started, and his first impression was that it was an enemy who spoke.

"Who are you?" he said, at the same time that he prepared himself to dash the interrogator to the ground, if the answer should not be satisfactory.

"A friend," was Witlet's reply. My name is Witlet; I am your friend and hers, who is now there."

He pointed to the prison as he spoke.

"Enough, I will trust you freely," said Rowland; "but moments are now precious."

"I know it. Take my arm and walk slowly till we turn the next coner.

Rowland did so, and still muffling himself closely in the cloak, he walked at a very deliberate pace with the highwayman, although his own impulse would have been to oustrip the wind in flight, if possible. That walk from the prison-gate to the corner indicated by Witlet was one of the greatest agony to Rowland, for now that there appeared every chance of escape, the love of life came more strongly across him than ever it had done in his cell, and he would have died upon the spot rather than again have visited, as a prisoner, the interor of the gloomy dwelling he had just left.

It took scarcely two minutes to reach the corner, but those two minutes were decidedly the most wretched Rowland Percy had ever passed during his existence. To him they were lengthened into two hours, and when he reached the corner, the perspiration of intense excitement was pouring from his brow.

Now—now," he whispered, "are we safe?"

"For Heaven's sake," replied Witlet, "be not yet precipitate. A false step even now might ruin all."

"How—how?"

" Hush, Mr. Percy, hush ?"

Witlet, without turning completely round, contrived to take a good look behind him. A slight exclamation escaped him, for he knew well by sight the man who was dogging their footsteps.

" What's amiss ?" said Rowland, anxiously; " you spoke."

" Hush—hush ! walk slower."

" Yes ; but——"

" But what ?—speak."

" We are followed."

A gush of agony came from Rowland's heart, and he pressed his hands to his breast as he uttered a deep groan.

" Do not despair," whispered Witlet; " there is still a chance. Walk slower still, and trust all to me.

" Oh, what chance can there be ?"

" Hush—hush ?"

" They shall not take me alive. If you are indeed my friend, I pray you, I implore you, for the love of Heaven to give me some weapon with which I may defend my life.

" Hush—hush."

" I will die fighting," continued Rowland. " I will not be dragged back to yon dungeon. Lead me past some spot where they sell arms, if you have none about you, and I will rush in and help myself."

" Mr. Percy, this is madness," whispered Witlet. " Leave all to m, I pray you. By any violence you sacrifice yourself and jeopadise my safety seriously."

Rowland said no more, but it was agony to him when Witlet said—

" Walk slower, still. Slower—slower ; it is our only chance now, Mr. Percy."

A thought came across him, that after all, this man, in whom Miranda had put so much trust, was the dupe of a plot which was to show off the efficiency of the officials of a prison, and sacrifice her liberty in an abortive attempt to succour him."

Such a thought as this was terrible, and he said to Witlet in a choking voice.

' Whoever you are, may the bitter curse of two broken hearts cling to you till your dying day, and follow you to another world, if you are betraying me and the pure innocent heart of her who told me to trust you.'

" Mr. Rowland Percy," said Witlet, " I forgive you, for you are not master of yourself, and know not what you say."

" If I do an injustice, it will be, for me to implore your forgiveness."

" Hush—hush ; no more of that at present. Slower—slower, still. All may yet be well.

The suspicions of the under turnkey were each moment growing stronger. There were numerous starts and infeminine movements about Rowland's arms and head, that confirmed him in the supposition that it was indeed his prisoner attempting an escape.

Oh, how he congratulated him, then, upon his own self deep and amazing cunning that had kept it all to himself. His object now was to take both Rowland and his companion, and that he would either do in some populous street, or he would see them fairly housed and then procure immediate assistance for their capture.

By chance Rowland and Witlet had to cross a drain, along which an ample stream of water was flowing, and on the opposite side of which several paving stones had been taken up for the the purpose of repairs ; the manner in which Rowland Percy, at one bound, cleared the obstruction, at once settled the matter in the turnkey's mind. He had no more doubt now about the identity of the presumed young lady, and he almost chuckled aloud in the excessive self-congratulation, and the thought of the reward which would be his.

" Let me see," he muttered ; " I shall be put in some snug situation safe, and in course the visiting magistrates will order me a reward, I shouldn't wonder, if I netted a matter of fifty pounds by this job. Besides the crow I shall have over Sammy and Joe, and old Grisket, who think themselves so uncommonly clever, all of them. Ha, ha, ha! He, he, he, I rather think I have taken the shine out of them all jist a bit—only a few. Ho! ho! ho!"

Thus chuckling to himself, and ever and anon rubbing his hands together like a fly who has just been gorging himself with treacle, did the under-turnkey closely follow in the footsteps of Rowland Percy and Ned Witlet.

Ned had now turned down a narrow street which was but very dimly lighted, and was promptly followed by the spy.

"Walk quicker now," he whispered to Roland, who could see nothing for the sides of his bonnet.

"Shall we escape, think you, by speed?"

"No—no; we should have a hue and cry after us in a moment were we to attempt it. Follow my instructions as if you were a machine."

"I will."

"Walk fast then."

They quickened their speed suddenly, and that at once put the clever turnkey upon his mettle.

"Ha!" he said, "they think they are all right now, and are putting on the steam a little. Cut away. That's your sort. I can come out a little in that way myself."

So saying, he hastened on rather faster than Rowland and Witlet, which had the effect of decreasing the distance between them considerably, and when after proceeding thus for some time, Witlet suddenly turned a corner, leading into a very dull out-of-the-way street, where there were but two dim oil lamps, and not a single prssenger, the turnkey made a run to get up to the corner, for fear they should pass into some house and elude him.

"Stop," said Witlet, the moment they had turned the corner, and he disengaged his arm from Rowland.

In the next moment the turnkey arrived quite breathless, when instantly on his turning the corner he was met by Witlet, who being a powerful man and a practical boxer, gave him one blow between the eyes which sent him down to the ground as if he had been struck by a cannon-shot.

"There," said Witlet, "our enemy is innoxious now."

"Was it he who was dogging us?" said Rowland.

"Yes, and my object was to lead him on till I could rid ourselves of him as I have. If I mistake not he will not recover that blow in time to do us much harm, for we shall be on the road to London now within ten minutes."

"How much I have wronged you by my unworthy suspicions of your good faith," said Rowland, as he held out his hand. "Will you forgive me?"

"Freely," said Ned, as he took the proffered hand, "and all I can say is I dare say I should have been more suspicious than you were, for my acquaintance with human nature has been greater, and it don't improve on intimacy."

He then laid hold of the perfectly insensible turnkey, and laid him on the step of a door, after which, turning to Rowland, he said—

"Now sir, make what speed you like, and follow me."

CHAPTER LXIX.

VARLEY'S VISIT TO MIRANDA'S LODGINGS.—HIS INTERVIEW WITH OLD PERCY.—
THREE O'CLOCK IN THE MORNING.—HIS DESPAIR AND AGONY.

IF the hours as they slowly winged their leaden flight on that most eventful evening were to Miranda and Rowland Percy fraught with deep anxieties, how much more were they full of ghastly images of despair to the guilty soul of Bernard Varley, who as each one passed away found his hopes diminishing—his fears growing to a monstrous size.

Each moment his expectations of hearing from Miranda decreased, until he came to the desiring conclusion that with all her love for Rowland Percy; she would suffer judicial murder of the morrow to proceed rather than suffer him to call it.

By a strange perversion of intellect, then Varley got angry with her, and he of all people in the world—he, a murderer and a false witness, began to accuse her of hard-heartedness, not towards himself, but towards Rowland.

"So," he muttered, "this is her boasted love for the innocent Rowland Percy. She might save him, and she will not, because her silly, girlish fancies stand in the way—and so much for the arts of women. My curse light on her head. May she some day experience the pangs I feel, and she will—she will—and surely to-morrow's work will wring her proud heart, and cause it to weep tears of blood. He shall die! he shall die! and she shall have the bitter, sorrowful feeling of knowing she might have saved him, but would not—ay, would not, forsooth."

Till he commenced this tirade against Miranda he had been sitting by his window in gloomy meditation and in darkness, for he would have no light, lest he should be seen from the opposite house, or from the street, in which case he might have been foiled in his wish to see Miranda as often as possible.

When, however, this burst of hatred and rage overcame him for a moment, he rose from the sofa he had wheeled over to the window, and paced the room to and fro with hasty and perturbed strides.

Surely Heaven was working for Miranda and her innocent lover, for it was precisely at that moment of Varley's absence from the window at which he had kept watch so long, that Miranda, enveloped in her cloak, walked from her humble house towards the prison.

When he returned again to resume his watch, it was without the least thought that she was gone; and while Miranda was conversing with Witlet, and afterwards in the cell with Rowland, Varley was watching the house to which it was improbable she should ever now return.

Ah, how little did the villain Varley—the author of so much misery, imagine as he heard the Minster clock strike nine, with what different feelings it was listened to by Miranda and Rowland Percy, and what dear hopes to them hung upon the next ten minutes.

Could he have seen into that narrow cell, and watched his victim escape him, what torments would have been his—what agonies of baffled rage would have filled his bursting heart.

Still, and with the exterior appearance of calmness, he sat with his eyes rivetted upon the house, but no Miranda came forth to bless his eyes for one fleeting moment, and give him new hope.

The quarter past nine sounded from the various clocks, and then the half hour and all remained silent and still as before. Then Varley's impatience rose again to a wild burst of excitement—the air of the room felt to him close and pestiferous —hot flames seemed to be scorching his heart and brain—he could no longer remain in that room, and seizing his hat, he rushed down the staircase, and made his way to the cool, open air, which he let for some minutes play unrestrainedly upon his fevered brow.

"What shall I do—what shall I do?" he asked himself, as he uneasily paced to and fro in front of the house in which he believed Miranda to be waiting, with a heavy heart, the tragedy of the morrow.

A thousand wild plans and conjectures rushed through his brain, but he could fix none sufficiently long to give them the consistency of shape and outline. They were all vague, wild imaginings, dealing but little in the probable, and shadowing forth with just a faint hue of possibility, the wishes and aspirations of his guilty heart.

"She comes not forth," he muttered. "Why keeps she in on such a night as this? Surely she has not removed from here? No, no—I have watched too well for that. Perhaps a little more urging—a little more painting of the horrors of the execution, which will make a holiday show for the idle rabble to-morrow might move her; but come what may, I can no longer endure this suspense;—would soon drive me mad. I will call upon her again—at least I may see her although she taunt me with bitter reproaches—and to see her, is as if a d—d soul was allowed in its despair one radiant glimpse of heaven in all its beauty."

This resolve gave him some calmness and relief, for it was a something to do, saving his mind from preying so hopelessly upon itself.

He approached the door, and knocked cautiously, for he was afraid that if Miranda suspected who it was demanding admission, she might order herself to be denied to him.

The door was opened by one of the children belonging to the woman of the house, who knew not whether Miranda was at home or not.

" That will do," said Varley, as he slipped a piece of silver into the child's hand. " I am a friend, and will go to her if you will tell me which room she occupies."

The child directed him to Miranda's apartment, and before the woman herself, who heard some conversation going on in the passage, without knowing its purport could get up stairs, ascended to the room indicated to him.

With a firm expectation of seeing Miranda, he knocked gently at the door, but receiving no answer he turned the lock and passed into the room. It was empty; the mouldering remains of a fire were crackling and expiring in the grate, and the room presented every appearance of recent occupation, but she alone, whom he sought, was not there. With a pang of disappointment he glanced around him, and then he saw the door which led into Mr. Percy's chamber. A hope sprung up in his mind that Miranda might be in that inner room.

He approached it, and listened for some few moments, but all was as still as the grave. Then just as he was on the point of opening that door the woman of the house made her appearance in the front room.

" What may you please to want, sir ?" she said.

" Is Miss Rankley at home ?" he said, endeavouring to speak as calmly as he could, and hiding his face as much as possible from the light which the woman carried.

" No, sir, she has been out nearly an hour. Are you a doctor, sir—come to see the old gentleman ? He ain't much better, I'm very sorry to say."

" Out one hour !—an hour, and I—I not know it. Curses—"

These words were ground through Varley's teeth in a manner which prevented the exact signification of them from reaching the ears of the woman, and she again put her question of—

" Are you a doctor, sir, come to see Mr. Percy ?"

The thought struck Varley that he might for some time, perhaps, even till Miranda should return, take advantage of such a character and wait; so he said—

" Yes, I am. Is he no better ?"

" No, sir. He keeps on dozing; and when he wakes he don't seem to know anybody."

" Indeed !"

" Yes, sir. Ah! poor man, he won't be long for this world, I'm sure. It's all grief about his son, who you know, sir, is to be hanged to-morrow morning for the murder of Sir George Rankley."

" Yes—yes," said Varley. " I know all that; and—and, Miranda, how is she ?"

" Ah! poor thing, she is an angel if ever there was one; but she gets thinner and thinner every day, and paler, except to-night, and then she did look beautiful.

" To-night !"

" Yes, sir ; when she went out she seemed to me as if something had quite set her up again, though she did not tell me what it was. Perhaps, after all, sir, they mig't hang the young man,"

"Never doubt it," said Varley, with a bitter smile. "I will trouble you no further, madam. Is there a light in the next chamber? for I will remain here a short time."

"There is, sir; and should you want anything, just please to touch the bell and I will come."

"Yes—yes—thank you—thank you."

Varley then opened the door, and in a moment stood by the bed-side of the father whose mind had fallen beneath the pressure of woe he, Varley, had placed

upon it. Mr. Percy was in an uneasy slumber, and moaning occasionally, as if he were disturbed by frightful images. Now and then, too, he would speak, and it was ever on the one subject—that of his boy Rowland.

"No—no," he muttered; "not guilty—not guilty. He is innocent. Heaven have mercy!"

"He raves," said Varley. "Can I act upon his disordered brain sufficiently to discover whither Miranda has gone? I will awaken him and try."

No. 34,

He laid his hand upon Mr. Percy's shoulder, saying—

"Awake—awake—Mr. Percy, awake."

The sick man opened his eyes and said, in a low voice—

" Who calls on me ? Was that from the grave, or was it you, my dear boy—my Rowland ? Yet no, it was not your voice, it is softer, sweeter far, and comes like music to your father's heart. Bless you, Rowland—bless you. You have made a worthy choice, for Miranda is beautiful and good."

" His brain is quite unsettled," said Varley. " I shall find but little to rely on in his conversation. Mr. Percy, do you know who I am ?"

Mr. Percy started at the voice of Varley, and raising himself partially in the bed, he gazed in his face long and earnestly ere he said—

" I did know you well—I do know you well; but latterly have thought you a fiend, which, having performed its hellish mission of destruction and despair among several hearts, had descended again to its hated home. Man or devil, what want you now with me ?"

" Can you name me ?"

" I can ; but it shall not pass my lips."

" Hear me, Mr. Percy; and if you have any love for your son, any pity for yourself, ponder upon my words. I can even now save Rowland. It is in my power, and mine only, to snatch him from death and restore him to your arms, provided you can induce Miranda to consent to my terms—those terms she knows ; and her refusal makes her the virtual murderer of your son."

" How came you to know my dreams ?" said Mr. Percy. " What have you to do with my Rowland ?"

" Mad—mad," said Varley, with a bitter execration. " Where is Miranda ?"

" Perhaps on a visit to some kindred soul in heaven, where you may never, never be."

" Pshaw! answer me at once, old man. She has left the house. Where has she gone ? When will she return ? Answer me at once, I say."

" How long shall the fiend be allowed to mock me? Oh, save me from him, Heaven ! Rowland, where are you now ? They told me the shot was not fatal ; then how could he kill Sir George Rankley ? Another hand did that deed, and thrice have I dreamt that Bernard Varley was the man."

Varley rose and stood for a moment with his hands clenched, and a feeling at his heart that he would like to quench for ever the wild yet truthful ravings of the broken hearted father. His fears of the consequences in a house full of people restrained him, and, with a malediction too awful to record, he walked from the room, determining rather to wait in his own room opposite and watch for the return of Miranda than remain to have his conscience goaded by the remarks that fell from the lips of Mr. Percy.

He took his station once again at the window, and without a light, with nothing to commune with but his own dark and unholy thoughts, where he remained until the Minster clock struck three.

CHAPTER LXX.

MIRANDA IN THE CONDEMNED CELL.—THE CHAPLAIN'S VISIT.—THE EXHORTATION.—MIRANDA'S JOY AND EXULTATION. — THREE O'CLOCK. — THE TURNKEY'S THREAT.

WHEN Miranda found herself alone in the condemned cell, she for some minutes could not have removed from the position she had assumed at the table, even if the whole success of the plan for Rowland's liberation had depended upon her so doing. Her feelings for the succeeding ten minutes were of the most powerful and agonizing description, A hundred times she asked herself,—

"Is he clear of the prison? Has he passed the gate?"

The slightest sound that met her ears from any part of the building, filled her with the most lively alarm; and when she did rise from her seat she stood in the centre of the floor so pale, so wan, and so tremblingly alive to the least alarm, that any one who could, Asmodeus-like, have glanced into that gloomy cell, would indeed have thought her the criminal awaiting the coming day to be dragged to the place of execution.

But Miranda's thoughts never for an instant wandered to herself. It was of Rowland—of him upon whom her heart's best, holiest love was fixed, that she reflected with a painful intensity that made thought an actual agony.

"Has he passed the gate?—has he passed the gate?" she repeated in a whisper, that made the question still more terrible to her imagination. Then she strove to consider how many steps it would take to convey him from the door of the condemned cell to the open street. She could not tell, but she thought that by then he surely must be free.

"Yes—yes, he is saved—he is saved," she cried. "By this time I should have heard some indication of his apprehension; they would have dragged him back here. Some noise would have reached my ears; he would not have yielded perchance, without a struggle; and all is still. He is saved—he must be saved. I will believe it now, Why does my heart beat thus tumultuously? Why do I tremble? Can there be a doubt now? No—no. There has been ample time, I think—I am sure now that he is safe. Rowland, Rowland, if I could see you now at liberty, I should be happy."

She clasped her hands, and the colour which had retreated from her very lips during the awful period of doubt, which, although short as to actual duration of time, had concentrated such an age of anxiety within its brief space, slowly returned. Her heart ceased to palpitate with such fearful vehemence, and she no longer drew her breath with short, quick respirations. She turned her beautiful beaming eyes upwards as she said,—

"The innocent are not deserted by Heaven! My Rowland saved! He must be safe now. Thank Heaven, thank heaven!"

"With a deep sigh, which had in it much relief, for it appeared to carry with it a world of anxiety from her heart, she sat down again by the table. Then a holy and beautiful calm spread itself over her spirit, and a smile, such as she had not worn for many a weary day, broke like sunlight over her face. She repeated the same words that she had used before; but with how very different a tone did she now tell herself,—

"He is saved!—he is saved!"

There was an awful doubt still lingering at the bottom of her heart when first she strove to convince herself that he had effected his escape, but now she was sure. There had been ample time to traverse the distance from the cell to the outer gate of the prison three times over. He must, therefore, be free.

By the light of the lamp which was in the cell, Miranda now glanced round her and oh, how different appeared the aspect of it as she now viewed it with feelings of hope and joy, to when it had presented to her nothing but the dreary vestibule, as it were, in which her lover tarried ere he was ushered to the tomb.

It would have puzzled many a philosopher and deep speculator upon human nature to have accounted for the look of happiness that lit up the countenance of that beautiful girl in such a place. What a delicious contrast did her feelings then present to what they had been at that same hour the preceeding evening, when all was despair—when there appeared not one ray of hope to illumine the universal gloom in which her fortune and her lover's were shrouded.

Once free of the prison, she believed that Rowland would be safe; for her faith in Witlet was great, and she was now only anxious to give the fugitive as much time as possible before a discovery should take place, and pursuit be commenced.

She paced the cell with firm steps—she could have sung for very gladness. It was more than as if she herself had been rescued from death; it was more than as if a pardon had reached the prison, and rescued from the scaffold him who she loved ; for a more fond, unselfish being than Miranda could not exist, and she felt much more acutely the sufferings of those to whom she was attached, than she would any amount of misery touching herself personally. Moreover, how delightful a thought it was to her to feel that she had been the direct cause of rescuing Rowland from the fate that else had surely been his !

How exquisite was the gush of pleasurable thought with which she pronounced the words—

" I have saved him !"

Could Rowland Percy then have seen his Miranda in the prison to which he had so lately bidden adieu, he would have dismissed from his mind much of the anxious, painful thought that beset it while he was rapidly accompanying Willet from York.

The time which had for the few minutes after Rowland's departure from the cell lagged so fearfully, now flew on more swift and joyous wings. Ten o'clock struck by the Minster timepiece, and no one had disturbed Miranda in the cell. The sound, however, recalled her to a consciousness of the necessity, or at all events of the desireableness of getting over the next periodical visit of the turnkey without a discovery taking place.

Again she arranged her long silken hair so that it would show as little as possible, and placed Rowland's hat on her head. She then listened attentively at the door of the cell, but there was no sound of any one approaching, and she sat down by the table, permitted her thoughts to wander sweetly to the time when she should again meet Rowland, and they should be able to talk over the events of that anxious, yet joyful night.

What was to be her own fate, and what consequences were to arise from the position in which she had placed herself never for a moment crossed her mind. She had succeded where success was life—where failure would have been death and despair. What then cared she for the result—how immeasurably short of the evil she had avoided must they be. What a solemn farce would appear to her the legal consequences of her act. How she could smile upon the detail of what would be called her crime, and with what joy, what exultation she could say—

" I am satisfied. He is saved—he is saved."

Then they would meet, she and Rowland, in some other land, and calmly await the course of events which, from her inmost heart, she believed would some day proclaim his innocence, and welcome him back to his native land in contentment and honour. Then how gladly she would thank all those who had lent a willing ear to her assertions of his innocence, while those who had declared him guilty would shrink in terror from the judicial murder they had been near committing, and pause ere they again adventured to take the life they never could restore, and usurping God's high and holy prerogative.

These thoughts and hundreds such like filled the lonely cell, with crowds of speaking, moving images. No longer was Miranda alone, for fancy peopled vacancy, and in her mind's eye she sketched a future full of light, of joy, and love.

The sudden turning of the key in the lock of the door roused Miranda with a shock from her reverie, and she instantly moved the lamp, so as to cast herself very much into the shade. and waited anxiously for the result of the visit of, as she supposed, the turnkey.

She heard the door open, and there was a silence of a few moments. as if some one was contemplating her from the threshold. That silence, she thought, was ominous of detection, but she assured herself that Rowland had already had time enough, although she would gladly have given him more. Her fears, however, were vain, for in a moment more she heard the voice of the chaplain.

" Young man, young man—are you so sinfully attached to the vain world that you have not spirits sufficient on this eve of your departure from it to look round even to see who enters your cell ?"

Miranda made no answer, and he continued, after a pause—

"Sinner, sinner! repent ye. Time is but short—repent and confess."

Miranda made a gesture of impatience, and with a deep groan the evangelical man added—

"Satan is in your heart, and I believe that you think more of the sinful young woman, who is evidently a vessel of wrath and not one of the godly, than you do of your future state. Cast from you the evil spirit, and walk in the paths of righteousness; which, albeit they be not so flowery and pleasant to the eye at the commencement, yet do they abound with saving grace."

Here he paused again, and blew his nose with a true conventual blast, but as Miranda said nothing, the holy man waxed just a little wrath, and added,—

"Young man, young man, I would fain snatch you as a brand from the burning, but I fear the old man is strong within you, and that you are one of those who, rejecting the word of life, will descend to everlasting flame and torrents of burning brimstone, where you will wallow in liquid fire, and your soul, for ages to come, by the mercy of Providence, be tortured alway.—Amen!"

Miranda was so provoked at this atrocious speech, that she had an answer on the tip of her tongue which would have been couched in the form of advice to the chaplain, to study and comprehend the pure and holy precepts of christianity, ere he again adventured to use the name of Heaven as a sanction for his exhortation; but she controlled the impulse, for she considered even five minutes more time given to Rowland Percy as of infinitely more importance than a wrangle with a bigot.

"You will not speak?" continued the chaplain.

Miranda made a gesture indicative of her determination to remain silent.

The chaplain then got up a series of extemporaneous groans, after which he commenced a prayer for the conversion, as he called it, of Rowland Percy, all which Miranda listened to with more patience than could be expected, or than she could have commanded under any other circumstances—but she was giving Rowland time.

Not for long, however, could she felicitate herself upon preserving her incognito for when the prayer was over, and no effect ensued therefrom, the chaplain got still more impatient, and said in a tone of rather worldly asperity—

"Young man, I never had such a hardened sinner and obdurate rascal as you in this gaol before. Eh? oh! you won't speak—very well—it's dreadful. Come come, young man, repent and confess."

As he spoke, he laid his hand upon Miranda's arm, and she, feeling that concealment for another moment would be impossible, calmly rose, and taking off the hat, allowed her long hair to fall in dancing ringlets on her neck and bosom, as she said—

"Thank Heaven—that Heaven of love and mercy, the name of which you use profanely—Rowland Percy is not here—he is innocent, therefore he has nothing confess. His and my reliance upon the goodness and mercy of God to his weak erring creatures is unbounded, therefore we have no fear."

The chaplain actually staggered back, till he could get no further than the wall, his amazement, and his little sleepy eyes opened to their utmost width, while dropped on the floor of the cell a bundle of tracts which he had brought with the first of which was entitled, "The Fast Coach to Hell, or Sinners put Drag," and gasped several times before he could say—

"Who—are—you?"

"Miranda Rankley," was the reply.

"Where—where—where is the murderer?"

"What murderer?"

"Young woman—young woman—I—I—where is Rowland Percy?"

"Escaped!" said Miranda, in a voice that made the pious man give a jump that brought him at once to the door of the cell.

"Escaped?"

"Yes, and free as the air of Heaven. Make what alarm you like—use you utmost exertions. He is, I believe, under the protection of that power which sees all hearts, and, in its own good time, saves the innocent."

"Help—help—murder—Jones—Jenkins. Fire—murder. He has escaped!"

Shouting these words of alarm, the chaplain rushed from the cell, and, with his gown streaming behind him, sped along the passages towards the outer gate.

The word fire was the one which happened most of all to catch the ears of the turnkeys, and, catching up a pail of water, he ran with it in the direction of the cry, shouting—

"Where?—Where?—Where?" till he met the parson, when they ran against each other with a violence that brought them both rolling to the floor deluged with the water.

"Curse you," said the turnkey. "Who are you?"

"Murder," shrieked the chaplain.

A mob of officials now, with lights, approached the prostrate pair, and the turnkey, when he saw who his opponent was, became very contrite indeed, but was cut short by the parson saying, in an angry tone—

"I'll have you discharged to-morrow, my man; but first of all, the murderer, Percy, has escaped."

"Escaped?" echoed every one.

"Gone—gone—and left another vessel of wrath behind him."

"Gone off in a *wessel*?" said Sammy. "Oh, my eye and Elizabeth Martin!"

"Call the governor," said another. "Call the governor."

"What's the matter now?" said the governor himself, who had been alarmed by the tumult, suddenly making his appearance in his dressing gown.

"Oh, Captain Price," said the chaplain! "Percy has escaped."

A flush of surprise crossed the governor's face, and he said in a tone of great annoyance,—

"Pho—pho—it can't be. How could he—from the condemned cell? Impossible."

As he said so, however, he strode down the passages towards the cell with a very uncomfortable feeling that if it were true there would be something in the shape of a tremendous row made about his ears.

CHAPTER LXXI.

ROWLAND AND HIS FRIEND WITLET.—THE OLD NAG'S HEAD AT YORK.—THE SECRET CHAMBER.

NED WITLET and Rowland Percy proceeded at a very rapid pace through a great many streets, after the quietus had been so nuceremoniously given to the cunning turnkey, who, with all his cleverness, and all his bruises, lay doubled up in the doorway, as innoxious as any very clever under-turnkey could possibly be.

"You have freed me from this danger," said Rowland, "most admirably. To your skill and courage I owe my life, and it shall go hard with me indeed if I find not some means of showing you that you have not thrown away your services upon an ungrateful heart."

"I am quite satisfied, Mr. Percy," said Witlet, "that you are an innocent man; that is enough for me, if I did not believe Miss Rankley to be, as I sincerely do, as brave and noble-hearted a girl as ever stepped."

"You do her no more than justice," said Rowland, with animation; "she is —but how can I find language adequate to a description of Miranda?"

"No how," said Witlet, "so don't try it. We are very near our first place destination now. Yonder dim light, which is just on the out-skirts of the town, is at an old public-house, called th Nag's Head. You will find there a friendly shelter for an hour, within which time I will return to you with means for your conveyance to London, where I will accompany you."

" I place myself solely under your guidance," said Rowland.

" Do so, and all will be well. Now, come on. Here we are at the door. Say nothing, but sit down among the company I shall introduce you to."

" Without any hesitation Rowland entered the public-house, from which rose the sounds of jovial merriment, and rather boisterous enjoyment.

The few words of " A friend of mine, who don't want to be inquisitive himself, nor to be bothered," from the Witlet to the landlord, seemed a sufficient introduction, for he nodded, and said—

" All's right—we have none here but good hands. Will the gentleman walk into the snuggery?"

" Yes," said Witlet ; " come on."

Followed then by Rowland, he led the way through very intricate winding passages, until he came to a door covered with green baize, which he opened. Another door of the same outward material then appeared, at which he knocked. It was on the instant opened by a brawny fellow, who seemed fully capable of maintaining it against any one. The moment he saw Witlet his eyes danced with glee, and his mouth widened to a grin of pleasure.

"Come to stay, of course," he said.

"No. I have important business, but here is a friend of mine who will remain half an hour. He don't wont to see any one, mind."

" All right."

" Remain here till I come," whispered Witlet. " I had hoped to have had a conveyance ready for you at once, but have been disappointed. You will be quite safe here, for even should any officer come here in pursuit of you, the people here will hide you."

" I trust you and them implicitly," said Rowland, "and I'm sure I need not say come back to me as soon as you can."

" You need not indeed ; expect me within the hour."

Rowland passed on, and in a moment found himself in a room filled with men, who were all conversing in loud tones at the moment. Before, however, Rowland could seat himself, one cried loudly—

" Order—order. Hear the poor devil—hear what he has to say."

" Gentlemen," said a meagre specimen of humanity. " I am a poor devil for I am an author. I wish for your opinion upon my last little production. Here it is, gentlemen—founded on facts.

" It was one bright December morning, when Harry Moreton, a hard-working country labourer, took down an old fowling-piece from above his mantel-shelf, and began to examine the lock, which he pulled several times, emitting sparks as the flint touched the steel of the pan, much to the amusement of the little ones."

" ' Now, Harry," said their mother, who at that moment entered, ' what are you going to do with that horrid gun ? I hate the sight of it ; let me beg of you to put it up again.'

" ' Not I.' returned Harry Morton.

" 'Surely you are not going to use it ?' exclaimed his wife.

" ' Indeed I am,' was the reply; ' we have not a bit of food within the house, and it is now three weeks since I have been employed.'

" ' You surely are not going to poach ?'

" ' Certainly not ; but there are many small birds that will make a meal.'

" ' And if a hare or a partridge should cross your path, you would be tempted to fire at it, and what should we do then ?'

" ' No, no ; trust me,' continued her husband. ' I am not going to run myself into danger for the sake of a hare or pheasant ?'

" ' You know, Harry, you are very easily led astray : do not run yourself into danger.'

" 'Pshaw! can't a man take care of himself, think you?'

" 'Not always.'

" 'The women are always preaching,' said Morton, again furbishing the barrel of the gun.'

" 'Then put up that gun, or it will bring you into trouble.'

" 'And even if I were to shoot a hare or a pheasant, I do not see the harm of it; and I know those who would be very glad to eat them if I should shoot them.'

" 'We can all eat when we get it, Hal; but not by breaking the law.'

" 'I'll tell you, woman, I'm not going to do any such thing.'

" 'Well, well, you were always an obstinate man, Hal.'

" 'And mean to continue so?'

" 'No doubt of it; but if ye had ta'en my advice, ye'd had plenty of work.'

" 'Nonsense, nonsense!'

" 'And I also had an unlucky dream, Hal,' continued the wife, 'so don't go out with that gun to-day.'

" 'Fiddlesticks!' said Harry; 'where's my powder-horn and shot!'

" 'Nay, then, Morton, and I'll not tell ye, for it will only bring you into trouble.'

" 'Then I will find them myself.'"

" So saying, Harry Morton rummaged an old drawer, and found the articles he desired. He then, with a careless air, shouldered his gun, and whistling an air, left the cottage.

" After walking through many fields, without killing a single bird, he began to tire, and sat down upon a gate to ponder whether he should return and give up his intention, when the idea struck him there was no better fare at home than abroad; he therefore resolved to reload his gun, and try his luck once more.

" Scarcely had he done so, when, looking up, he perceived what he considered to be a hare.

" 'There's a chance,' said he, 'if I dare but fire. No, no, it will not do;' and, to avoid being tempted, Morton turned his head in another direction.

" When he imagined the hare had left the spot behind the hedge, he turned to look, but to his surprise saw it there still, and seemingly very busy, the back being alone visible.

" 'The devil take the thing,' said he; 'one would imagine it stopped there on purpose for me to hit her; 'pon my soul, it is a pity to let her escape, and the youngsters a-crying for food. Let me see, there's no one coming; I don't see why I should not pop her off.'

" For some time Morton stood irresolute; at last he levelled the gun, and fired the fatal shot.

" 'Dead as a door-nail.' said he, running to the spot, eager to secrete what would have transported him had it been discovered; but, to his horror, instead of a hare he found he had mortally wounded a man, and what he had mistaken for a hare was nothing more than his seal-skin cap, which was seen by Morton above the level of the trench in which the farmer was digging.

" For a moment Morton was completely bewildered, but on raising the body his agony was intense, for he discovered it to be his aged father who had become his victim.

" 'Father! father!' he cried, in wildest accents, 'forgive me—forgive your son?'

" A deep groan was the only answer.

" 'Merciful God!' ejaculated Morton, 'thou knowest it was not wilful.'

" 'No, no! my boy!' uttered the aged man, in a low, guttural tone, 'I feel conscious you are innocent.'

" 'I am, dear father.'

" 'I forgive thee, I forgive thee,' said the aged man; 'my hour must soon have come, and it might be as well now as any other time.'

" 'But by any other means than the hand of thy son.'

"'Fly! fly! my boy, ere it is too late and punishment await thee; I may not live to vindicate you.'

"Without loss of time, Morton conveyed his dying parent to his lonely cottage, and having despatched his wife for medical assistance, fled he knew not whither— in the interim old Morton had died.

     *   *   *   *   *

"Harry Morton travelled all night without molestation, and by the light   f

morning arrived at a distant town where he heard the fife and drum of a recruiting party; distressed and without a home, he enlisted in an assumed name; and the same day he was sent to London, and on the following set sail in a transport to join the army in a foreign land.

     *   *   *   *   *

"Many years now rolled away, when an aged soldier, supported on a wooden leg, stopped to rest beneath one of the alcoves of Westminster Bridge, where also sat a middle-aged female, apparently much careworn.

No. 35.

"For some minutes they engaged in conversation, but neither seemed interested in the topic.   At length they raised their heads to regard each other, when a certain expression of feature on the instant revealed to them that they were man and wife—the next they were locked in each other's arms—it was Harry Morton and his wife.

"As they walked from the spot, the former said, 'Would to heaven, Mary, I had never touched that gun.'"

"Now gentlemen, what do you think of that ?'"

A general laugh was the reply, and one shouted—

"I say, hav'n't you got never something about a fogle-hunting, fly-faking, spice-toby, out-and-out family cove ?"

The poor poet shook his head and crept into a corner.

"They are rough fellows here," whispered an intelligent-looking man to Rowand, "but they are not unkind in their way, for they keep that poor devil from starving."

CHAPTER LXXII.

MIRANDA AND THE GOVERNOR.—A TROUBLESOME AFFAIR.—THE PURSUIT.—
UNWILLING PRAISE.—THE REMOVAL.

WHEN the governor reached the cell, Miranda was awaiting his appearance with anxiety, certainly, but still with feelings of such an exultant nature, that they triumphed over any shade of disagreeable anticipation as regarded herself, and her own fate.

The object she proposed to herself now, was to put off to the last moment anything in the shape of an active pursuit of Rowland, not that she doubted his safety, but she would, if she could, have made assurance doubly sure, and could she gain for him another five minutes by parleying with the governor, she would.

The moment that official personage entered the cell, he saw that it was no false alarm that had been raised by the chaplain, and that in lieu of the person who the following dawn would have been led to an ignominious death, he had in his custody a beautiful and heroic girl, whom he found it even difficult to speak harshly to.

The governor had been on officer in the army, and all his preconceived habits and notions tended to make him in his own heart admire what Miranda had done, notwithstanding the disagreeable train of circumstances which was likely to ensue, and the trouble and annoyance, not to say censure, he would in all likelihood receive from the enraged authorities.

"Young lady," he said, "for Heaven's sake tell me where the prisoner is. How in the name of all that's dam——I beg your pardon—wonderful !—came you to project this scheme ?"

"He has escaped !" said Miranda with fervour.   "He is safe—the innocent Rowland Percy is now far beyond the reach of his enemies.   Sir, your appearance speaks you a gentleman.   I know what I have done is a crime, but I glory in it, and all I have to ask of you is to let the consequences of my act fall upon myself alone, for I assure you old Mr. Percy, the father of the injured Rowland, knows nothing of my proceedings. '

"But do you mean to say that you have had the—audacity—I mean the courage—no, the criminality——"

"Sir—sir," said Miranda, "your heart is struggling against what you consider your duty.   I do grieve that in rescuing one more dear to me than life itself from death, I have drawn you probably into some trouble.   Accept my regrets—more I cannot say. I am, I presume, your prisoner, and thus I throw myself upon your humanity.'

The govenor looked up at the ceiling, and stroked his chin, and coughed several times—in fact, he had never felt himself so thoroughly puzzled before. What on earth to do, or what to say, he knew not.

Miranda seeing the state of doubt and hesitation he was in, said,—

"Sir—heed me not—but do your duty. God forbid that I should be a source of greater anxiety to you than necessary. You never injured my, Rowland. He came here, and was detained by you in the due process of your duty—without then, any hesitation, I beg of you to continue the exercise of that duty. I will not blame you, sir."

"For God's sake, young lady," said the governor, "save yourself, and let the law take its course."

"What!—surrender him again? Never. No, sir, sooner should the scaffold, which is now preparing in expectation of him who by the mercy of Heaven is far away, receive me as its victim, than I would breathe one word to place upon Rowland Percy's track the blood-hounds that would hunt him to death."

"I have already ordered a pursuit."

"'Twill be a vain one. Hear me, sir, I have set myself a task in this world, which, with Heaven's assistance, I will perform. When the awful word 'Guilty' fell upon my heart in the Court of Justice, from the misguided lips of him who uttered it, I told myself that from that moment it should be the aim of my future life to blot it from the minds of men, and substitute for it the more glorious word 'Innocent.' Sir, I loved my father—a mother's tenderness I never knew. The concentrated affection of my young heart was all given to him. He was murdered! Think you I mourned not for him? Think you, because you see no tears now that my heart feels no pang at that sad bereavement? Then Rowland Percy was accused, and I knew him to be innocent. For him I have placed myself a prisoner here—yet, sir, I loved my father. Can human nature in its sanity become the slave of such contradictions, that the fond doting heart of a bereaved child could risk all—dare all in behalf of its father's murderer? No—no. He is innocent —he is innocent. If Rowland Percy be guilty, then he and I must both be mad."

The govenor listened to her with rapt attention, and then he said—

"Lady, I cannot blame you—your noble faith in him—your—hang it, I dare not, Miranda Rankley, say what I think, but from my soul I admire——"

"Where's the hardened sinner?" said the chaplain, appearing at the door of the cell. "Oh! young woman—young woman."

"Sir—you are the governor of this place," said Miranda, appealing to him I request you to protect me from this man's impertinence—as you are a gentleman I claim your protection."

"Impertinence!" cried the chaplain.

"Come, come, Mr. Salver," said the governor, "I don't see that either you or I have any right to annoy this lady. She has certainly made herself amenable to the law, but we cannot call her morally guilty in any way."

"Not guilty! Is she not one of those vessels of wrath which look fair to the eye in order to lead men from the proper path into the way of ungodliness?

"Just as you please," said the governor; "but she is not even my prisoner at present."

"What! not a prisoner?"

"Charity, charity, sir."

"Oh, the time will come, when there will be howling and gnashing of teeth; when the everlasting flames——"

"I tell you what, Mr. Salver," said the governor, "I think you and I will quarrel some of these days. My dear girl, don't mind what he says."

"I do not, I do not," said Miranda.

"I shall make a point," said the chaplain, with bitterness, "of representing your conduct to the magistracy."

"I hope you will; and very glad am I that you and I have at last come to a fair understanding. What is wanted in a person as a chaplain is a man of education, talent, and liberality. One who knows human nature, and can make allowances for its weakness and great temptations. One who will kindly lead the unhappy person with whom he may come in contact to a better and happier mode of thinking. Such a one, I am sorry to say, sir, you are not ; and I am resolved that either I will no longer be governor here, or you shall no longer be chaplain, for I intend to explain what I mean and what I complain of to the magistracy."

The chaplain looked perfectly thunderstruck at this calm and reasonable speech; he stared at the governor with his fish-like eyes wide open, and could not say a word. To Miranda, the temperate rebuke of the governor gave the greatest pleasure, and to find herself in the hands of one of such proper feelings and kindred sentiments to her own, joined to the conviction that Rowland was saved, gave her so much joy, that could she have commanded tears, she would have bid them flow to relieve her throbbing heart.

The governor then said to Miranda, in a kind tone, "You shall not be long confined here, I will return soon."

"I shall not be lonely," said Miranda; "this once gloomy cell will be to me a palace full of rare thoughts. My now free and unfettered fancy will people it with pleasant sights. I have not been so happy since I last saw my poor father in life."

The governor stood by the door of the cell, and waited for the chaplain to come out; but the latter, with an assurance that was quite inexcusable, said, with a conventicle snuffle,

"I shall remain here. My heavenly duties place me far above any human denunciations."

"Remain here ?"

"Yes, I shall reason with this sinful young woman."

"Indeed," said the governor, "you shall do no such thing. If you are still chaplain here I will let you know that I am still governor, and if you don't come out of this cell directly by fair means you shall by foul."

"If you dare to assault me, I will get you removed from your situation for a surety."

"I believe you wish me to assault you," said the governor, "and under the circumstances I shall gratify you. Are you coming ?"

"No, I am not."

"Then you shall."

So saying, the governor took him by the collar, and handed him out in a moment.

Miranda then heard the cell door locked, and for a time all was silent around her.

The governor said no more to the chaplain, but leaving him just outside the cell door, he walked to the lobby, and directed several of the officers connected with the prison to disperse themselves about the city in search of the escaped prisoner, while he himself repaired to the nearest magistrate, to know what was to be done with Miranda.

Without any clue to direct them where to look, the search of the officers for Rowland was not likely to be successful, and they could do nothing but wander up and down the city, visiting such houses as they thought by possibility he might be concealed in ; among which, to the great surprise of Miranda's landlady, they searched her house, although they would not say what was their reason for so doing.

While this languid pursuit of Rowland was going on, the governor had attired himself for the streets, and started for the nearest magistrate, whom he knocked up and insisted upon seeing on very urgent business.

When he explained the circumstances, the magistrate looked astonished and remarked—

"Something must be done directly. I will go with you to another magistrate and we two can take some step in the business, which is a very awkward one to act alone in. You have, I presume, taken all the steps in your power to recover the prisoner ?"

" I have."

" Then, then—really I don't know what can be done."

" No," said the governor, with a smile. " But what am I to do with the young lady who has played us this trick ?"

" Why, to tell the truth, you have no right to lock her up, and she might bring an action against you for false imprisonment, as you have no warrant for her, detention."

" I don't think she will," said the governor; " but what do you advise me to do?"

" Why, you bring her before me and Mr. Angerstein, my brother magistrate, the first thing in the morning. We must commit her for the misdemeaour of aiding comforting, and abetting a felon, you see."

" Very well; and in the meantime I must, of course, keep her in custody ?"

" I suppose so. Dear me, it's an awkward affair altogether. Your turnkeys must certainly lose their situations."

" Why, one would think," said the governor, as he rose to go, " that the most ordinary circumspection would have prevented such a thing from occurring."

" She must have accomplices."

" So I think; but you will as easily make the sun shine at midnight, I am sure, as get her to name them."

" Indeed ?"

" Yes. A more resolute, determined spirit, I never encountered in all my life."

" Well, well, we must make the best of the affair. Good night, sir, rather, good morning. We shall see you, I suppose, with your prisoner in the morning."

" Certainly."

With this the governor went back to the prison again, feeling more entertainment and pleasant excitement from the whole affair than annoyance.

When he reached the gloomy abode of crime and sorrow, he went at once to the cell in which Miranda was confined, and, unlocking the door, he entered its narrow precincts.

" Miss Rankley," he said, " I am far from disposed to be unfriendly towards you, and now that we are alone, permit me to compromise myself so far as to say that while in my official capacity I am compelled to blame, and should certainly had I any suspicion of the trick, have thwarted your proceedings, yet I cannot as a man, blame you. On the contrary, your courage and perseverance in the case of one you believe to be innocent, (for who can doubt you?) does you infinite credit."

" I thank you from my heart, sir," said Miranda, " I have much to be thankful for to many kind friends since my career of unhappiness commenced with the death of my father; but, least of all did I expect to find within those walls the kind sympathy you have shown to me. Once more sir, I thank you."

" You half convince me of Rowland Percy's innocence," added the governor, " and if such be really the case, and yourself be not deceived, I rejoice that I was not in the way to mar this night's work."

" Thank Heaven !" said Miranda.

" I have come now to tell you that it will be my duty to take you in the morning before the magistrates, when they will deal with you as the law directs."

" I shall not shrink from the consequences of my act," said Miranda, " I will not say that I reflected upon the consequences, and so prepared myself to meet them, for such was not the fact. I thought of nothing but the preservation of Rowland Percy, and that accomplished, I knew would bring me strength to bear all else. I can remain here well till morning."

" Nay," said the governor, " I have no authority to keep you here in a condemned cell. In the building you must remain ; but I must confine you in a much more gloomy and dreadful place than this. Are you willing ?"

"I will follow you wherever it is your duty to take me," said Miranda.

"Come then we must proceed at once."

Miranda followed the governor through many devious turnings and long gloomy passages, where in nooks sat here and there a guard, who touched his hat to the governor as he passed, and much wondered who it was that was with him. Then he led the way up a long flight of stairs, and, taking a key from his pocket, unlocked a very massive iron door, which revolved on its enormous hinges slowly and with difficulty, immediately on the other side of this door was another, covered with green baize, and yielding to the slightest touch. Miranda felt the soft tread of carpetting beneath her feet, and the governor turning to her, and raising the lamp he held in his hand, said,—

"We are near our destination, Miranda Rankley. I wish you to make yourse f as happy as you can while you are my prisoner, and if you bring an action against me for false imprisonment, do not say I aggravated its terrors."

He walked across the small room into which the door, covered with green baze led, and opening another, discovered a large, handsome well-lighted apartment, in which were a lady and a young child of about five years of age. The lady and child had evidently both newly arisen from bed and merely thrown on some loose covering.

"My dear," said the governor, "this is the heroic Miranda Rankley. Treat her kindly. Miranda, my wife and child."

CHAPTER LXXIII.

THE MORNING OF THE INTENDED EXECUTION.—THE SCAFFOLD.—THE EXPECTANT
CROWD.—THE STRANGE MESSAGE.—THE PLACARD.

By six o'clock on that eventful morning, many hundreds of persons were up and stirring, who ordinarily never thought of showing themselves from their bedrooms for full two hours after that period. The excitement and interest the approaching execution had created among all classes was unprecedented. By the hour we have named a dense crowd had assembled at the place of execution, and each moment increased the pressure of the throng. House-top, far and near, so that they commanded any view at all of the scaffold, were rapidly becoming covered with anxious spectators, and from the neighbouring counties many persons had come on horseback, having ridden for hours in order to be present at a scene which, from the peculiar condition in life of the parties concerned, and the singular train of evidence which had conspired to fix the guilt upon him who was to suffer death, had not its parallel in the history of the county of York.

So dense became the throng towards seven o'clock, that the workmen who were erecting the scaffold were compelled to desist from their labour, until some constables could be brought to take the pressure of the throng off them.

By that hour, however, there was not an official person in the city who had not been made aware of the escape of the prisoner, but no orders were given to suspend the arrangements for the execution, as no one individual seemed inclined to act by himself in the matter.

A meeting of the magistracy and civic authorities was hastily called, and the judge, who was still remaining in the city, was pressed to attend, which, however, he would not, saying that he had nothing to do with the failure of the executive portion of the authorities in carrying the law into effect.

By a quarter past seven every magistrate who could be found, was with his colleagues in solemn conclave, considering what was to be done under the unexpected circumstances.

Where they sat they could hear the clank of the hammers used by the workmen in putting up the now useless scaffold, and it was not until one rose and said—" Gentlemen, as yet we know nothing but that we have no prisoner to execute," that they roused themselves to send for the governor and Miranda.

The noise of the putting up of the scaffold still continued, as if in very mockery of the attempted jurisdiction of those assembled: men, who, in their short-sighted human wisdom, would have solemnly put to death an innocent fellow-creature.

The chairman of the bench then proposed that, in order to disperse the mob, a placard should be placed upon the prison gate, offering a reward of a hundred pounds, to be paid by the county, to any one who would apprehend or give such information as should lead to the apprehension of Rowland Percy, the convicted murderer.

This resolution was carried just as the Minster clock was sounding the half hour past seven, and it was immediately written out, until some could be printed for general use, in a large bold hand by the clerk.

Even while the document was being signed by some of the magistrates, the confused hum of the dense multitude assembled to witness the execution came upon their ears like the sullen roaring of the sea upon a rocky beach.

A strong body of police was despatched with orders to bid the workmen to take down the scaffold, while they were to post the placard, and then endeavour to induce the multitude to disperse, and quietly seek their homes.

A magistrate on horseback preceded the officers; and tremendous was the difficulty they had in forcing a passage through the dense throng of persons that were in their way.

Within about a hundred paces of the prison gates they were completely hemmed in; and the magistrate, waving his hand, said—

" Disperse—disperse! There will be no execution."

His words were only heard by those immediately about him, but they took up the cry, and a thousand shouted—

" No execution! no execution!"

Then one man, who had clambered up a lamp-post about the middle of the crowd, and who had resisted, by heavy kicks, the many attempts that had been made to pull him down, drew a night-cap of red cotton from his head, and said—

" Guv him a cheer, my covies! They daren't hang him. My name's Jones. Hip—hip—hip—Hurrah!"

The mob, more from diversion than any real sympathy with Rowland Percy, joined in the lusty cheer; and such a shout as was raised had not been heard in the ancient city of York for many a day.

The magistrate then called, in a loud voice, to the men who were at the scaffold—

" Remove it—remove it!"

" Lit's help 'em, said Jones. " It will make beautiful fire-wood, and boil half the tea-kettles in York to day."

A suggestion of a mischievous character thrown out to a mob, is like a lighted match in a powder magazine. The scaffold in five minutes was taken piece-meal, in spite of the efforts of the astonished workmen, who stood gazing on the scene of demolition with silent wonder.

' Run back to the magistrates," whispered he who was mounted, to the constable nearest him. " Tell them we shall have a riot for a certainty unless they send more force."

The officer went on his errand as quickly as he could; and then the magistrate made a foolish attempt to take Jones prisoner, who, being the popular idol of the moment, was quite in a condition to defy him; and accordingly, when the magistrate pointed to him and said,—

" Seize that man."

Jones pointed back again to him, crying, in a loud rough voice—

" Seize him !   seize him !—a handful of mouldy coppers reward.   Seize him !
He's a-getting wild—he is."

A roar of laughter followed this speech ; and the magistrate was fain to content
himself with a good look at Mr. Jones, in order that, on any future occasion, he
might be able to swear to him as the cause of the riot ; for had he not spoken, the
mob would in all likelihood have gone quietly away from the spot.

"Put up the placard," said the magistrate then, as he passed forward to the
prison-gate, in which direction, as he was away from Jones, he was now allowed a
tolerably easy passage.   In a few moments the placard was fixed, and the last tack
that held it to the gate was struck in at the moment the Minster clock struck eight,
and when, but for the heroism of Miranda, Rowland Perey would have been
judicially murdered before the eyes of assembled thousands.

The foremost of the mob read the placard, and turning to those behind, they
shouted—

" He has escaped !—he has escaped !"

The impression had been, that Rowland Percy was reprieved, and the news that
he had escaped, came with all the freshness of a first announcement to the ears of
the multitude.

" Well done he," said Jones.   " Another cheer !"

Another shout then rose, which might have been heard for miles around.

At this moment the gate of the prison opened, and at the top of the steps, which
were sufficiently high to be seen by every person that assembled, stood the compassionate governor and Miranda Rankley.

Her face was beaming with pleasure ; and she stood for some moments looking
upon the vast throng before her, contrasting her present feelings at eight o'clock
then, with what they might have been had she been unsuccesful in her attempt
to liberate Rowland,

CHAPTER LXXIV.

THE LONELY WATCH OF BERNARD VARLEY.—THE FRENZIED CRY AND INSENSI-
BILITY.—THE CROWD AND THE MAGISTRACY.

IT must have been the rare, exquisite beauty of Miranda, as she stood in that
commanding situation, accompanied by the governor of the prison, that at once
attracted all eyes and all hearts towards her. Some there were who certainly knew
her by sight, but the majority of the immense throng of human beings that assembled had not the slightest conception of whom she was beyond the fact that a more
truly beautiful girl had never blessed their eyes.

There must be surely something in the old philosophy that beauty of mind is of
necessity associated with exquisitely enchanting forms ; at least, let our reason do
for us what it will, let our modern systems of philosophy rise up in battle array
as they may against the beautiful theory, still in all hearts will be found a place for
it, and there never was yet a human cause pleaded by a human advocate that did
not acquire one half of its complexion from the peculiar physical appearance of the
accused.

A more striking exemplification of our remark could not have been found than
in the universal cheer from thousands of hearts which immediately greeted the
beautiful and heroic Miranda.

Her beauty they allk new, and there was not a soul among them that did no
feel its magic power, but, her heroism none knew but he who stood by her side,
and who felt full as proud of his lovely companion as if the circumstances which

called forth such feelings in his heart had not been, as they were, inimical to himself and greatly derogatory to his efficiency as a public officer.

Miranda clasped her hands, and with a look of appealing emotion she turned to the governor, saying.—

"You see, sir, Heaven is showing the innocence of Rowland to all men. Every heart here present appears to sympathise with him, and those who are come to see his execution are clamourous that he is saved."

The governor shook his head as he replied,—

"My dear Miss Rankley, you don't know mobs so well as I do. I could give you a different interpretation of the clamorous shouts of this vast assemblage."

"A different interpretation?" echoed Miranda.

"Yes, Miranda, a far different one. There is one feeling common to humanity, and that is the admiration of such rare and unequalled beauty as yours."

No. 36.

"Nay, sir," said Miranda, "I would much prefer my own interpretation of those who thus cheer at the sight of me, or it may be that you are the special favourite, and I am assuming a character that I am not entitled to."

The governer smiled, as he said, in a deprecating tone,—

"No, Miranda, no. The choice of right belongs to you. The public officers seldom come in for any great share of popular favour or applause."

"But surely such as you," said Miranda, "must have won even the hearts of the most obdurate beings who have been confined within these walls. I migh have smiled at every aggravation of the miseries of my situation, and laid to my heart, as an antidote to all other evils, the delightful recollection that I had saved the innocent Rowland Percy from an ignominious death; but still it would have been no small aggravation of the anxieties of the situation into which I had plunged myself, if I had met with harshness, instead of the kindest sympathy I have experienced at your hands."

"I am more than repaid," said the governor, "by hearing you say so much. Heaven prosper you, Miranda Rankley, and my fervent wish is, that the noble confidence you have shown in him to whom you have plighted your faith, may be verified by the course of events."

"At least," said Miranda, smiling, "let me cherish the thought that I have made one convert. Tell me that you believe him innocent."

"Miranda, before I saw you," replied the governor, "I had no opinion upon the subject, but received Rowland Percy as my prisoner in the ordinary course of my duty. It seems to me now, however, as if Heaven spoke from your mouth —from my soul I believe him innocent."

"Thank Heaven !" cried Miranda, "I am fulfilling my mission, and that is to proclaim to all men, heedless of censure or reproach, the innocence of Rowland Percy."

"You'll have many converts," said the governor.

The mounted magistrate, who was in the midst of the throng, now made various signs to the governor to follow him with his fair prisoner, at the same time that he sent forward as many of the officers as he could spare from about his own person, to serve as an escort for them from the prison to the place where the magistrates were holding their extraordinary sitting.

Before, however, the governor could descend the steps in obedience to the summons, an extraordinary commotion in the outskirts of the mob attracted universal attention.

"Hold," said the governor, "we may as well remain on the advantage ground until we can ascertain the cause of this tumult, for mobs are by no means particular whether friend or foe comes in for a share of their violence."

Miranda, as we have said, was considerably elevated above the level on which stood the enormous throng of persons, so that she could see the cause of this tumult more clearly than those who were mingled with it. The mob was swaying to and fro like the vexed waves of the ocean, when many miles of water move with a restless impulse in enormous masses, sad precursors of a coming hurricane. Shouts, cries, and curses filled the air, and, at one particular spot, she could see as if the black, moving mass was being mowed down as by the irresistable hand of death. Then, as she removed her sphere of vision to the particular spot from whence diverged so much tumult and confusion, she perceived one tall, gaunt figure from whom she found it impossible to withdraw her gaze.

Sweeping forward like something endowed with more than mortal strength, came that one frightful, palid human form. Bold and stout men shrunk from before him. The crowd he tore down as with a giant's grasp; the strongest he dashed aside as if they had been weeds upon his path.

But one word came from his lips as he thus proceeded through that dense crowd of human beings, and that was shrieked forth in a voice which betrayed such a tone and an air of abandonment and despair, that had he striven not otherwise to force a passage through that living throng, one would have been accorded to him through pure horror of the preternatural tone in which he so spoke,

"Escaped—escaped—escaped!" was the one word which, as often as he could gather breath to scream, he shrieked out with a bewildered wildness of intonation.

Well might Miranda cling convulsively to the arm of the governor. Well might her cheek grow pale and her limbs tremble, as she gazed upon that frantic form, rapidly approaching the prison gate. Too vividly upon her memory were those features stamped. Too often with shrinking horror had she gazed upon that countenance, to be doubtful of its identity, although distorted as it was now with demoniac passions. She might well have been excused for her want of knowledge even of him, who she believed had wrought her so much woe—her cruel enemy, Bernard Varley.

Yes, it was indeed he, who with such wild demoniacal gestures—such an agony of heart, that it was nigh bursting in his bosom—was now rushing through that throng of persons intent upon but one thought, one object, namely, to satisfy himself that the, to him, dreadful report were true, that his victim—he, whom he thought was so securely entangled in the toils, that no chance or accident of human fortune, could protract his existence to another sunrise—had escaped.

In his lonely room, opposite to the lodging of Miranda, he had waited the livelong night, with the expectation of seeing the gentle girl, in whose bosom he had planted such bitter thorns, emerge, with tottering steps, at early dawn, to take a last long farewell of him who was to be snatched from her encircling arms to the cold embrace of death.

As we are aware, he was grievously disappointed in his expectations; and oh! what a night of horrors was that to Bernard Varley—what thronging phantom forms in the still watches of that night appeared to people the silent vacancy around him. The sinful thoughts, the wild aspirations, and the deep crimes of other years rose up from memory's depths, and mingled strongly with the more stupendous circumstances in which he was now placed.

His former impulses had been those of avarice, or ambition, mingled with revenge against those who crossed his path in those unholy pursuits, and so might he have floated easily onwards in the present case with scarce a pang, had it not been that with wild vehemence, that master passion of the human soul, the wild and ungovernable love of woman, engulphed in its whirling vortex all of her thoughts.

The midnight hour tolled solemnly from the Minster bell, and by the dim flickering oil lamp that burned in the street, he kept his painfully strained eyes fixed upon the door of Miranda's temporary home. Slowly the small hours of the coming morn waned, but she whose sight to him was light and life itself came not—he saw the first faint streaks of the approaching day struggling with the artificial lights still gleaming in the streets of the ancient city—but still she came not.

One by one the bright stars retired in the blue vault of Heaven—warmer and warmer grew the first grey tints of the coming dawn—he heard the hum of life slowly arising from the myriads of waking beings around him, and still she came not.

Despair seized upon his heart, the very silence around him became pregnant, to his imagination, with frightful sounds. He leaned from the window, and scarcely knowing what he did, or what might be the consequence of his mad display of passion, he cried—

"Miranda, Miranda—come forth, scornful but beautiful—bless my eyes again—although you blast my ears with words of hatred and detestation. Miranda—Miranda—time is flying—think, oh! think what a morn is this—come forth, and by one word light up a heaven of joy in my heart, and save yourself from everlasting regret, Miranda—Miranda—awake—awake—God of Heaven, she hears not—she must be dead—dead—dead!"

With one gasping sob he reeled across the floor, and just as the first faint gleam of sunlight fell upon the topmost windows of the house, he pped insensible in the lonely apartment, which had witnessed his melancholy ils.

The people in the house, who in the early part of the evening had been alarmed at his ghastly countenance, and the singular expression of his eyes, were disturbed by the frantic manner in which he spoke, and they stood shuddering upon the staircase, afraid to venture into the room, where they might encounter one bereft of sense.

Nearly an hour thus passed away, and Bernard Varley remained insensible to the despair, which, had he been in active existence, might, indeed, have driven him to destruction.

Then hearing that all was still, the master and mistress of the house gathered courage slowly to ascend to his door, which after listening at it for a long time, they proposed to themselves cautiously to open, sufficiently wide only to reconnoitre their strange, and as they began to think, mad lodger.

The man himself was armed with an immense kitchen poker, which he protruded into the room some distance before himself, in order that Bernard Varley might be held *in terrorem*, and made cognisant of what desperate courage actuated the breast of his landlord.

At the suggestion of the good woman of the house, the poker was shaken menacingly for several moments before she would allow her worser half, as she most certainly considered him, to venture his life by entering the apartment. For as she acutely reasoned, a very indifferent husband was better than none, and in, consequence of a court mourning, all the paraphernalia of outward grief was exceedingly dear in York at that moment.

Like most people's the man's courage was greatly increased as there became apparently less and less occasion for it, and he felt very much like the soldier who ran hard for five miles, till he placed a battery between him and the foe, and then cried,

"By God! if they caught me, what a drubbing they would have had."

"Speak to him, John' said the woman, " then he says any thing we can rush down stairs like a flash of lightning."

John then suggested, in a low tone, " What would be the use of speaking to him he said nothing in reply?"

Upon which John was declared an idiot and a curse to any woman ; being finally told that he was no man, or he would have before that cried, " Hilloa Mr. Varley !"

Thus urged, the no-man did cry " Hilloa, Mr. Varley !" and receiving no answer, he ventured to open the door a little wider, when he discovered his strange and troublesome lodger lying insensible in the middle of the floor.

CHAPTER LXXV.

THE AWFUL COMMUNCIATION.—THE WILD FEELINGS OF VARLEY.—THE STRANGE INTERVIEW AT THE PRISON GATE.

THERE could not be much danger for a man in such a situation, " unless, indeed," as John's wife suggested, " that it might be only his artfulness, and he might spring up the moment he thought any one was sufficiently near him to murder ;" but John was liberal in his estimate of human nature, and thought otherwise, so he entered the room on the instant, and approached the postrate form of Bernard Varley, who it would have been a mercy to leave in the state of forgetfulness he was then in.

" He has fainted, wife," cried the ma ; " run for water. Perhaps he may be dead, and if so——"

" We would never let our lodgings again," cried his wife, filling up the sentence, as she hurried down stairs for some water.

By dint of various remedies Bernard Varley was restored to a state of conscious-ness, and then looking wildly around him, he said in a deep sepulchral voice,

"Where am I?—where am I? Is this a place for damned spirits? and have I indeed passed through the portals of the tomb?"

"No, sir, if you please," said the woman, "you are in our first-floor front, and your week's up to-morrow. We'll let you go without any notice whatsomdever, if so be as you'll go at once."

"Hush, wife!—hush!" said the man. "He is not in a condition now to talk of such matters. We ought, I think, to send for a doctor."

During this brief conversation between the landlord and landlady, Varley's memory was recovering from its state of stupor, and he was beginning to compre-hend the situation in which he was placed.

"Tell me," he said, faintly, "what has happened. I now see where I am, but what has happened to me I know not."

"You must have fainted, sir," said the man.

Varley placed his hand over his eyes for a moment, as if by shutting out the external world he was endeavouring to call to mind the circumstances which had preceded his temporary oblivion from the many cares and deep anxieties which be-set him.

"We heard you, sir," said the woman, "calling to somebody from the window, and then, as they wouldn't come, you were pleased to faint away with a great dab."

"Calling from the window?"

"Yes, you called Miss Miranda, sir, who you know is——"

"Yes—yes," cried Varley, suddenly springing to his feet from the arm-chair in which the couple had placed him. "Miranda! Miranda! Has she not yet come forth? Watch for her. Let me see her, if but for a moment, as she takes her melancholy way to the execution—ay, the execution."

"He's thinking of the hanging that's going to be, John," said the woman. "Poor man, he's quite a wandering, he is."

"The time—the time!" cried Varley—"what is the time?"

He dragged his watch from his pocket with vehemence; and when he saw it wanted but a short time to the fatal hour of eight, he dropped the watch upon the floor, and clasping his hands, he cried,—

"Time—time—time is flying. All will soon be over, and another spirit will be kneeling at the throne of Heaven, to prefer its plaint against me. Where is she? Miranda—Miranda, can you see him die? God of Heaven! can there be such constancy in woman?"

At this moment a loud monotonous voice from the streets immediately below the window, was heard, shouting with painful reiteration and distinctness, what had been prepared the day before by a speculative printer, in the full expectation that Rowland Percy, must be hanged. He had certainly suggested to the hawkers of the document the propriety of waiting till the Minster clock struck eight ere they commenced their avocation; but this one, ever with a laudable desire to be first in the field, began before that hour.

"Here you have," he cried "the last dying speech *and* the confession *of* Rowland Percy, who *was* executed *for* the murder—the most, atrocious and sanguine-*hairy* murder of Sir George Rankley! Here you have it—here you have it, for the small charge of one halfpenny—the dying speech and the con-fession, in which he says—here you have it for one halfpenny—with many curious and interesting and odd particulars never before heard of and never to be heard of again—here, for the small charge of one halfpenny, the very last dying speech and confession of Rowland Percy, who was hanged this morning, with a copy of verses, and all for the small charge of one halfpenny—here you have it—here you have it—sold again and pocketted the browns. Now, young woman, for the small charge of a halfpenny!"

Bernard Varley listened to the singular harangue as if his very soul's salvation depended upon the hearing every word of it.

"'Tis done—'tis done!" he gasped, "and she came not—she came not!" I—I thought that even at the last she would have saved him ; but—but she came not—the tragedy is over—over, and what am I now—who am I now ?"

"He forgets *hisself*," remarked the woman. "Please sir, you are our lodger, you know, sir."

He sank back in the chair, and covering his face with his hands, cried aloud,—

"Horror—horror—why do I live ? Death—death wrap me in the elysium of forgetfulness !"

Then in strange discord to his feelings, rose the voice of the man in the street, as he commenced with a sentorian voice repeating the copy of verses which had been composed for the occasion, commencing with—and we presume the commencement will be quite enough for the reader,—

> "Attend to me, ye mothers dear,
> Wot hugs a precious bady,
> And while your blood turns curds and whey,
> Let all your flesh feel flabby ;
> By heaping of bad com—pa—ny,
> And fostering of his malice,
>   An *unfort'nate* young man you see
> Has comed unto the gallows ?"

"Lost—lost—lost !" groaned Varley, as he rocked himself to and fro in the chair in which he sat.

"John," said the woman, "just run down and buy one of them papers ; I never heard anything so affecting in all my life."

On the instant then, and before John could execute his mission, another voice rose with stentorian power in the street, and but that the gentleman who owned it had a bad cold, it might have been clear and dulcet.

"Here you have," he cried, the full and interesting particulars of the most wonderful and extra—ordinary and unkimmon escape of Rowland Percy, who was to be hanged but wasn't—here you have it, just printed and published."

"Hilloa, spoony," cried he who was thus abruptly stopped in his recitation of the affecting copy of verses—" what do you mean by that ?"

"What I says, my *werdant*," said the new comer. "Here you have it—here you have it. Don't attend to the humbug *oppersite*. Here, for the small charge of one halfpenny, you have the full particulars of the most wonderful, the most extra-ordinary escape of Rowland Percy, from the condemned cell, last night—just printed—leaving his sweetheart behind him—for a halfpenny."

The man with the last dying speech and confession, cast his eyes around him in despair.

"Here's a blessed do," he gasped. "I feels briled brown. You out and out wagabond, will you be off ?"

"The miraculous escape, for a halfpenny," shouted the other.

"The last dying speech and confession," bawled the first comer.

"Be off with you, will you ?"

"No, I shan't—for one halfpenny and a copy of verses."

"The extra-ordinary escape, with the full and interesting particulars—and what he said, and what his sweetheart said—and what the neither of 'em said. I'll just walk into you if you don't cut."

"He was hung !" shouted the man with the dying speech.

"He wasn't," said the other.

"Then it's a shame of him not to be. That's the way people takes the bread out o' others' mouths. I'd a been hung twice, afore I'd a been so desperate shabby—for the small charge of one halfpenny."

"Take that," said he, who cried the escape, the particulars of which he had received from an acquaintance who was an under turnkey, and giving his opponent what, in vulgar parlance, is called a bonneter, he effectually put a stop to his literary pursuits for some minutes.

Varley had listened to the words of the new comer with an interest that was fearfully manifest in his countenance.

"Escaped—escaped," he cried. "No no—that cannot be. I never dreamt of such a thing as that. 'Tis false—false. He is dead—dead."

"Please, sir, if you mean the murderer who is going to be hanged," said the woman, "it ain't struck eight yet."

"Hark," cried Varley.

Solemnly and slowly the Minster clock went through the chimes, indicative of the lapse of four quarters of an hour, and then struck eight.

Varley counted the sounds with painful exactness, and when the air had ceased to reverberate to the last tone, he said,—

"Now—now 'tis over—over. He is struggling—I think I see him writhing in his death agony. I see the contortions of the body, and fancy shows me, beneath that covering which hides them from all else, the frightful convulsions of the face. He—he is now dying—dying—oh, horror! horror!"

"John," said the woman, "I am quite scared, and feel *sterical*."

"Don't be a fool," said John.

The man who cried the account of the escape of Rowland, having by this time overcome his antagonist, had all the field to himself, so that Bernard Varley heard him again proclaim the fact, which, while it would, if true, unburden his heart of one great weight, would load it with a thousand anxieties instead.

With a sudden impulse he rose from the chair, and darting past the astonished couple, he rushed down the staircase, and out into the street with the speed of a maniac.

"Here, here," he cried, to the man. "I—I want to know the truth. Tell me, on your soul, tell me if you speak the truth, and you shall have gold."

"He has escaped, sir," said the man, gazing at Bernard Varley's wild looking face with wonder and astonishment.

"You are sure?"

"Quite, sir."

"How—how. Tell me how?"

"Why, sir, his sweetheart went to the prison last night all for to see him, and they changed clothes you see, and she stayed in the condemned cell, while he walked out."

"She—she—Miranda. Mean you her?"

"That's the cretur, sir."

Varley threw the man a piece of gold, which he immediately pocketed, and then ran from the street, muttering—

"That ere mad gentleman's keeper will be coming out, and wanting this here *suverin* back again if I ain't off quick."

Varley stood a moment irresolute, with his hands clasped, and his whole countenance distorted by a contrariety of emotions. Then he said in choking accents—

"I must know the truth. I must know the truth. To the scaffold—to the scaffold."

Darting off then in the direction of the place of execution, he reached the outskirts of the immense mob which had assembled, to witness the sickening sight of a fellow creature deprived of life.

Then in the frantic manner we have recorded, he battled his way through the throng of persons, keeping his eyes fixed upon the one face which he saw by the prison gate—that was Miranda's, and by an impulse he could not control, and sought not to question, he felt that he must ask her if the truth had been spoken by the man in the street, for from no other lips could he assure himself of the fact,

Nor was Miranda's gaze less fixed upon Bernard Varley's face, with scarce the power to withdraw it, than his upon her's, for she was full of dread that he might be rushing to her with some news of evil import,

CHAPTER LXXVI.

THE CONFIRMATION OF VARLEY'S FEARS.—THE AWAKENED SUSPICION.—NEW
DANGER FROM THE MOB.

PARTLY from fear of his wild vehemence, and partly from curiosity to know where he was making such desperate efforts to get to, the mob made way for Bernard Varley, as, with his glaring eyes fixed upon Miranda, he strove to reach the steps on which she stood.

"Who is that," said the governor, "who fixes his eyes upon you, and you alone in so strange and terrible a manner?"

"'Tis Bernard Varley," said Miranda. "'Tis he, who, as I shall have to answer it before Heaven, I fully believe to be the author of all the misfortunes which have broken in upon my otherwise happy life; and although I cannot give a definite shape to my accusations, my heart tells me that in Bernard Varley I see my father's murderer, and the false perjured witness who would have sacrificed Rowland Percy to his wild passions."

"His countenance is far from prepossessing," said the governor. "I have heard much of the man, and was anxious to see him. My duties have prevented me from attending the trial. With what a frantic perseverance he strives to reach this spot."

The magistrate now called with a loud voice—

"Bring your prisoner, sir, if you please. Hilloa there, constables, clear the way. Keep off the mob."

"Now, constables, do you hear his *washup?*" cried Jones, from his elevated position, in a tone which was one of such capital mockery, the roar of laughter arose from the multitude.

"Some other time, my man," said the magistrate, "when I am not so occupied as I am now, I shall have the pleasure of making your acquaintance."

"Oh, don't trouble yourself," said Jones. "My *wisiting* list's uncommon full, and I don't much like you."

"Scoundrel," muttered the magistrate. "If it would not, as I see too well it would, create a general riot, I would take him at all risks."

"Stay yet a moment," said Miranda, to the governor; "I would fain hear what that ill-omened man has to say to me."

Varley by this time had arrived within about a dozen paces of the prison steps, and then with another desperate effort, he dashed those aside who were between him and Miranda, and stood at the foot of the small stone flight, unable to speak and scarcely able to stand, from the violent exertion he had gone through to reach so far.

His apparel was torn, and his hands and face were disfigured by blood. He reeled from side to side like a drunken man, and when he in some measure found breath sufficient to utter an articulate sound, all he could say, was—

"Miranda—Miranda—Miranda."

"Bernard Varley, what have you to say to me?" cried Miranda, with a loathing of the man she addressed. "Monster! perjured villain, what have you to say to me?"

"Is—is—it true?" grasped Varley.

"What true?" cried the governor. "Say what you wish at once, for we must be going."

"Tell me—tell me," almost shrieked Varley, "has he escaped—has he, the doomed one, escaped?"

"He has," said Miranda. "To your confusion—to your dismay, Rowland Percy is free; and hear me now, Bernard Varley, while I speak to you in the voice of prophecy, which for its own wise purposes is sometimes lent by Heaven to its weakest creatures. The escape of Rowland Percy, who you know to be innocent, is, and shall be the first in a chain of events strikingly in contrast to those which have preceded it.

"What—what mean you?" said Varley,

"This," cntinu ed Miranda, "that, whereas every accident, every combination of events had conspired to fix guilt on the innocent Rowland Percy, and to make you fancy that Heaven was so unmindful of its creatures, as to abandon them to the mercy of such as thou, this escape shall be the first in a new train of events, each one of which shall do something for the innocence of Rowland, and the condemnation of the real murderer of my father."

"No—no—no," gasped Varley,

"Hear me, and tremble," added Miranda. "My words have sunk into your heart, and there shall they remain a never-ceasing torment."

The effect of Miranda's words upon the guilty conscience of that miserable man, was full as great as she could have anticipated. He drew his breath short and thickly, a clammy moisture came upon his brow, and although he would fain have spoken he could not, for his tongue seemed glued to the roof of his mouth, and his parched lips could not shape themselves to a human sound.

"I am ready, I am ready," said Miranda, to the governor. "Take me now where you will, I am ready. Let me not look longer on that hated and fearful man."

"Clear the way," cried the governor, to some officers who were at hand, and he commenced descending the steps, leading Miranda by the hand.

At this appearance of Miranda going, all Varley's fears seemed to unite to drive him to distraction. He recovered his power of speech, and, spreading out his arms, as if to detain her, he cried,—

"Miranda—Miranda—form of more than earthly beauty—can you doom me to despair? Me, your worshipper—your adorer? Miranda—Miranda—I will be your slave! Trample on me; but, oh! do not, in my deep debasement, look such killing scorn upon me. Mercy—mercy—as you are beautiful have mercy!"

He clung to her dress, and, shrinking back, as from the touch of some loathsome thing, Miranda cried,—

"Unhand me—unhand me, monster!—unhand me!"

"Take your hands from this lady's dress," cried the governor, "or you shall repent your temerity. Away, sir, away."

But for the words of the governor Bernard Varley would have disregarded the thousands of eyes that were gazing upon him, and further debased himself, in the vain hope of wringing from Miranda's pity or disgust that which she could not accord him from opinion,—namely, a smile.

At the sound, however, of the governor's voice, he turned his eyes from the face of Miranda, and then, like one who succeeded in wresting his gaze from some fascinating object, which held in control all his faculties, he seemed to become at once conscious of the situation in which he was placed, and the fearful risk he was running of committing himself past recovery by incautious expressions, which might be wrung from him in the extremity of his despair and anguish.

He drew himself up to his full gaunt height, and in a deep, gutteral voice, he said,—

"Pass on—pass on, Miranda; you are the sun of my destiny, the star of my divinity; but the time may come, proud and scornful beauty, when you may yet feel the power of Bernard Varley, and tremble again at his testimony."

"Away! away with you," said the governor, "you are a madman; I would not take your testimony against the life of a dog."

A flushing accession of colour came across the pale and ghastly countenance of Varley, and his eyes seemed to kindle with fire as he turned them upon the governor's face.

"Fool," he said; "do you set so little value on your life that you taunt a man as desperate as I?"

"It matters but little to me," said the governor, "whether you be desperate or calm; but if you prove any further annoyance, I shall give you into immediate custody."

For a moment, then, Bernard Varley seemed to measure with his eyes the athletic proportions of the governor; and, half maddened as he was, a something seemed to whisper to him that he would stand but a poor chance in a personal encounter with the calm, determined-looking man before him. He therefore contented himself with muttering through his clenched teeth,—

"There may come a time even for you—I never forget."

"Let us proceed, let us proceed," cried Miranda; "the very air is oppressive while this man breathes it."

The governor again placed her arm in his, which he had momentarily let go during his brief colloquy with Bernard Varley, and motioning to the officers to clear the way, he and Miranda proceeded rapidly from the prison-gates.

As if then actuated by the infernal spirit of a fiend, Bernard Varley sprung up the steps which had been so lately occupied by the governor and Miranda; and turning his face to the astonished crowd, he with the most frantic and violent gesticulations, cried,—

" A thousand pounds for the apprehension of Rowland Percy. A thousand for the murderer, dead or alive—dead or alive. A thousand pounds to him who will show me his face."

The persons composing the immense assemblage one and all stood aghast and terrified at the wild tone and manner of him who offered so large a reward individually for the apprehension of him who was an escaped criminal. Varley, when he had done speaking, maintained the remarkable and striking attitude which he had assumed while uttering the words that had produced so great a sensation, and for the space of more than a minute, so intent was every mortal soul there present in gazing at him, and listening if he should speak again, that not a sound came from among them, and they might aptly have been likened to a forest which had grown up in some wilderness of nature, and was there reposing in the unwonted placidity of an elemental calm.

Mr. Jones, however, who was not at all of a romantic turn, and who saw nothing in the whole proceeding but that Bernard Varley was in a great rage, and that he, Mr. Jones, would be happy to put him in a still greater, suddenly cried—

" Will you give it us now, old Wire-wove, or let us wait till we get it ?"

A straw will turn the tide of popular feeling, and Mr. Jones's remark seemed to unburthen every one's breast ; not only was every heart which had been filled with astonishment, and not a few with avaricious longings at the largeness of the offer, at once convinced of its unsound nature, but a feeling of indignation began to pervade them that they had been tampered with for a moment by such a golden dream.

Shouts of derision arose from many, loud laughter from others, and not a few who raised loud hoots and groans at the man who so far overshot his mark in the reward he had offered.

Varley darted a glance of intense bitterness towards the lamp-post on which Mr. Jones held his enviable station, and in a voice nearly inarticulate with rage he cried—

" Down with that man—down with him—throw him into the next horse-pond, and come to me for your reward."

Uncommonly obliged to you," cried Mr. Jones, " but I come of a modest family, and I don't like to give trouble ; perhaps you will come and do it yourself ? Try if you can't borrow a stick long enough, you sack of bad-looking bones."

Bernard Varley's tall, gaunt, misshapen form made Mr. Jone's simile far from inappropriate, and it tickled the mob so amazingly, that had Varley then possessed sufficient discretion to retire, he might have accomplished an escape before the loud roar had subsided. But such was not the case ; it is an old saying and a true one, that the last drop of water overruns the cup, and so it was with Bernard Varley ; he had stood up against a world of disappointments, and battled with deep cares and anxieties, the effort to subdue which had driven him nearly distracted, but now he forgot all self-command, and rushed wildly into a throng of at least six thousand persons to punish one who had added the last drop to his already full cup of wrath by a jeering remark.

The mob, as might be expected, was in a complete ectasy when it saw that Bernard Varley was fairly intent upon placing himself in collision with its mighty power.

Shouts, oaths, groans, hisses, and every discordant noise the human voice was capable of, resounded on every side. Above all which arose the ironical voice of Mr. Jones, offering a thousand pounds down on the nail, and no gammon, to any one who would catch him, Bernard Varley, and bring him to him.

Varley did succeed in getting about a dozen paces from the prison-door, and then the numerous bonneters, and the awful hustling he received, although no one struck him, so completely bewildered his faculties that he knew not in which direction he was striving to proceed.

It was well for him that at that moment there arrived a strong body of police headed by two mounted magistrates who had been delegated by their body so specially assembled to attempt the dispersion of the crowd and read the riot act if necessary.

At the same time, from a neighbouring barracks, a troop of horse was in readiness in case the civil authorities should not be sufficient to allay the tumult.

The magistrates and police had for one of their objects the apprehension of Mr. Jones, who had been such a source of deep aggravation to their brother officials, and who had made himself so obnoxious to the law by being the suggestor of the destruction of the scaffold and appropriation of its fragments.

Who the man was that seemed to be tossed to and fro by the mob like a frail weed in a boiling torrent, they had no means of knowing, for, although the governor and Miranda had arrived at the police-office, they had made no mention of Bernard Varley, nor were they indeed at all aware of his danger.

The last Miranda had heard of him, and that when she had gone some distance from the prison, was his wild offer of a thousand pounds for the ap rehension of Rowland Percy.

His words fell upon her heart with a shudder which was, however, changed in a moment to a feeling of hopefulness that the innocent Rowland was surely by that time far beyond the reach of his utmost malice.

" Who is that ?" remarked one of the magistrates to the other, pointing to the struggling Varley

" I really don't know," said the other raising himself in his stirrups ; " but something strikes me very forcibly that it must be— and yet I can't say for certain."

" Who—who ?" said the other.

" Ned Wilks, the hangman."

" Bless me ?" said the first speaker, with great indifference ; " it is extremely likely. A mob may, very probably, fall on the hangman after tearing the gallows to pieces. How very imprudent of him to come out."

" I suppose we must bring him off, eh ?" said the other.

" Well, I suppose so. Do you see to him, while I endeavour to take possession of yon knave on the lamp-post."

Union in the case of the magistrates and the police might have been strength ; but they did not, when separated, possess much of that desirable quality, for the more they diverged from each other, the more they began to discover how extremely innoxious they were to the mob, and that the extent of their possessions consisted of the small piece of ground on which they stood.

Mr. Jones waved his hand in an encouraging manner to the magistrate, who was endeavouring to approach him, crying—

" Come on—come on. It's all right—fair play, and no favour."

By a desperate effort the magistrate succeeded in getting within almost arm's length of Mr. Jones ; but further he could not get, and as each of the officers happened to be shut up in a sort of living sentry box, composed of four men, the whole of the party became as harmless and inoffensive as any one could desire.

" Disperse—disperse," cried the magistrate, waving his arm authoritatively. " This assemblage is unlawful ; disperse in the king's name."

" Don't you hear his worship ?" said Jones. " You'll put him in a passion now if you don't go. Why don't ye disperse, ye *warmint* ?"

The magistrate shook his clenched hand menacingly at Mr. Jones, and said—

" Never mind—never mind, my fine fellow, I'll have you yet."

" Oh, thank you," said Jones, " I don't mind a bit. I am sorry I can't return that ere compliment, and as for having me, I wouldn't give you that trouble on no account.

" You scoundrel !"

" Listen to his worship—listen to his worship : where's your manners ?" cried Jones.

The mob were delighted beyond anything, but when the magistrate nearly wrenching the skirt off his coat, got out the riot act, and waving it in the air, brought it so near Mr. Jones, that the latter was enabled to lay hold of it, and by one jerk possessed himself of that mysterious document, the crowd could, as of one accord, have fallen flat down and roared with laughter.

Before, then, the magistrate could speak, Jones cried, as he affected to read the riot act.

"Oh yes—oh yes—oh yes—here you have it. God save the king and hang the crier, his head in the ditch, and his feet in the fire. Missle—cut—notch your poles."

Mr. Jones had got thus far when the red coats and burnished helmets of a party of dragoons appeared flashing in the morning sun at the further end of the street.

"Game's up," cried Jones; "drop the blessed curtain."

Then placing his fingers in his mouth, he produced a whistle of such astounding shrillness, that the unlucky magistrate involuntarily put his hands to his ears, and before he removed them again, Mr. Jones had slid from the post, and disappeared among the now rapidly dispersing crowd.

A more popular man than Mr. Jones did not that night exist in York.

CHAPTER LXXVII.

ROWLAND PERCY'S JOURNEY TO LONDON WITH NED WITLET.

In order that our readers may keep pace with the circumstances of our varied and veritable narrative, we must leave for a brief space the beautiful and gifted Miranda, in order to return to the fortunes of her innocent and persecuted lover, Rowland Percy.

The hour during which Ned Witlet had promised to return passed away; to Rowland Percy, amid the strange motley group among which he was thrown, slowly and uneasily. His tastes were far from sympathetic with the rude and boisterous throng around him, and but that he felt conscious that Ned Witlet had good reasons for placing him in such a situation, and that no doubt that his safety was best assured by so doing, he could almost have blamed his generous friend for exposing him to the rough contact of such uncongenial spirits.

At length when the hour had elapsed, with the addition of some ten minutes or a quarter added to it, the landlord of the house entered the room, and walking up to Rowland Percy, he whispered in his ear—

"Follow me."

Rowland said immediately—

"Has my friend come?"

"No," said the landlord, "but your enemies have. Hush, not a word; follow me, and you shall be placed in perfect safety."

Ned Witlet had told Rowland to trust this man implicitly, and without another word, or the least hesitation in his manner, he arose and followed him out of the room. The landlord took a course directly opposite to that which led into the open street, and threading his way noiselessly and cautiously along a narrow passage which seemed to Rowland to be interminable, he suddenly opened a door, when a gust of fresh air fell welcomely upon the young man's face.

"Come," said the landlord, and in a moment they stood in the open air, in what appeared to be a garden of considerable extent.

The clouds which had hung heavily in the air during the early part of the evening were rapidly retreating before a brisk breeze from the north west, and the moon's rays were alternately hidden by the black masses, and then partially illuminating the spot where they stood, but for such short periods that it scarcely sufficed to enable Rowland Percy to distinguish very minutely the subjects around him.

" Are we safe in speaking now?" whispered Rowland.

" Quite," replied the landlord; " but we may as well keep it to ourselves as much as possible. There are three or four officers below who described you to a tittle. Now, baring that you are a friend of Ned Witlet's, you may be the man in the moon for aught I know, for I be hanged if ever I clapped my eyes on you before."

" My name is Rowland Percy."

" What! the fellow who was to be hung in the morning?"

" The same," said Rowland Percy; " but I solemnly assure you, on my soul's hope of salvation, that in aiding me you aid an innocent man."

" I believe you," said the landlord, " or else Ned Witlet had not been the man to take you by the hand. Now come on, we have about as pretty a hiding place about these premises as any one would wish to see."

Rowland followed the dusky form of the landlord for some minutes, and then the former, suddenly stopping, took from his pocket a very small dark lantern, the magnifier of which he turned upon a water-butt of most extraordinary dimensions. It stood upon some brickwork about four feet from the ground, and from that elevation it rose at least twelve feet higher, seeming to be the depository of rain water from a multitude of pipes and spouts that came from all parts of the house.

" What do you think of that?" said the landlord, " there's a hiding place for you."

" You may be a very clever fellow," said Rowland, in a tone of disappointment; " but I should consider it the height of folly to get into an empty water-butt, with the view of hiding myself. Why the merest child could ascend these steps which are so handy, and at one peep discover me."

" Clever, uncommon clever," said the landlord, and then he laughed as if he enjoyed some joke exceedingly, after which he added—

" You make a little mistake—just a slight mistake; it ain't an empty water-butt."

" Why you don't expect me to get into a full one?" said Rowland, with a slight degree of impatience.

" Clever again, clever again," said the landlord tapping his nose mysteriously with the edge of the lantern; " that's just what I do expect, the very thing, the out and outer, the caper, the ticket."

Rowland knew not whether to be amused or angry, and suspecting that there possibly might be some trick in the matter, he quickly ascended some steps that were placed against the wall very conveniently. He brought his head to a level with the top of the water-butt, when he saw at once that it was nearly running over.

" It is full," he said. " You are jesting with me, or betraying me. Moments may be precious to me now. I will seek my own safety in flight. Attempt to stop me at your peril."

" Not so clever," said the landlord. " No hurry,—no, I ain't—no, you won't."

" What in the name of Heaven do you mean?" said Rowland.

" Why, in the first place, there's lots of time, for the fellows are taking it easy in searching the front of the house, while there's a couple of them marching up and down just on the other side of that brick wall, so that they know quite well tha you can't get out at the back. All's right, you see."

" Right! said Rowland. " Upon my word, you have a strange notion of right and wrong; and is my only resource to drown myself in a water-butt?"

" That's it," said the landlord; " there never was such cleverness. Just take the lantern—fix your eyes on the top of that tree, and don't say anything till I call out " oh!"

"The man must be mad," thought Rowland, but he took the lantern mechanically, and looked up in the tree indicated, and for which purpose he had to turn his back upon the burly landlord.

Scarcely had he remained in that position half a minute when he heard a strange chuckling noise behind him, which sounded more like a cock attempting to crow with his head in a beer-pot, which was followed by a singularly smothered "Oh," in the voice of the landlord.

Rowland turned instantly, but no landlord was to be seen; all was still as the grave, and he looked around him for some moments in mute astonishment. Then a curious sound came apparently from the inside of the water-butt, and Rowland said, in a low voice—

"Where are you?"

"In the blessed butt," was the answer; but the voice sounded so strange and unearthly, that Rowland involuntarily shrunk back a pace or two.

"Cock-a-doodle-do," added the landlord. "Cockoroo—cockoroo—cockoroo— cockoroo!"

"Oh," thought Rowland, "he has got some means of letting the water off," and ascending the steps, he again looked into the water-butt, which, to his surprise, was as full as ever, and not a bit ruffled. He put his arm in up to the elbow to convince himself that it was water.

"Cock-a-doodle-do—time's up," said the landlord, and before Rowland could descend from the steps, he saw by the light of the moon the two gaitered legs of his landlord projecting from under the brickwork, from whence the body of that important individual emerged.

"Been in the water-butt," he said; "but we don't get in at the top; there's a false bottom, three foot from the brim, and there's some comfortable sticks laid across lower down, for a fellow to sit on. Just pop your head under, and you'll be able to draw yourself up in a moment.

Rowland took the lantern, and peeping under, he saw there was space sufficient, actually, within the butt to hold three or four moderately sized persons.

"That's ingenious," he said.

"Clever," said the landlord. "In with you, quick, don't move or speak, and you have a thousand chances to one of safety."

Rowland's slim figure accommodated itself in the water-butt in a moment, and scarcely had he done so, when he heard the back door of the house open, and the trampling of several feet on the walks of the garden.

"Halloa," said a voice; "so you are here, landlord, are you? That don't look altogether the thing."

"No, it don't," said the landlord; "but I was afraid you'd have asked me to trust you half a pint of something, and I am so tender-hearted I should have done it. So I came out here to get a pail of water."

"Ah, we know you of old," said one of the officers. "You'll get into a mess some of these days, and if the fellow we seek is upon your premises, you won't come off so easy."

"Oh, what a way I'm in," said the landlord, affecting to tremble, so that he shook the pail in a most ludicrous manner.

"Keep an eye on the door," said one of the officers to another. "I'll soon ferret my gentleman out, if he is here."

While the landlord ascended the steps, and dipped for his pail of water, thus giving a convincing proof of what the butt contained, the officer stooped down and cast a full glare of the bull's-eye of his lantern between the two pieces of brick on which the butt stood.

"Found him, my grand inquisitor?" said the landlord.

"No, euss you," said the officer to the landlord; "if he ain't under the butt he may be in it."

"There's cleverness," said the landlord; "how uncommonly true. You'll be found a corpse some morning, smothered in your own wit."

The officer muttered an oath, as he ascended the steps, adding,

"I did pull a fellow out of a water-butt once, who was up to his chin."

A glance, however, sufficed to let him see that such was not the case in this instance.

In another minute Rowland Percy was safe, and the search, although it continued actively in the neighbourhood of the immense water-butt, never again approached it.

Various and numerous were the jeers with which the landlord of the inn saluted the officers, who he knew would make so unsuccessful a search for Rowland Percy.

The low, common wit with which he assailed them was fully understandable by them, and had all its due weight and effect upon men who entered upon their professional pursuits with a kind of partisanship in the capture of criminals, which made the pursuit more of a personal than a professional nature.

They, however, very soon satisfied themselves that a further search was quite useless, and one of them, turning to the landlord said—

"Well, old Paunch, laugh away, it's your turn now, but ours may come; our man aint here, that's clear, and all I have to say is, that it is well for you he is not, for had he been, the magistrates were determined to put down your house once and for ever."

"How uncommonly kind," said the landlord; "I wouldn't give the magistrates so much trouble on any account whatever. Give my compliments to them, and tell 'em to take things easy, for if they put themselves out of the way so much they are safe to be ill."

So saying, Boniface escorted the officers from the garden, but it was far from his policy to allow them to leave the house in anything like an evil spirit towards him, so when they reached the bar he said, in a friendly tone—

"Now, my lads, a joke's a joke, and I know you can give and take one as well as myself. It's dry work looking for something one can't find, so let's have a glass round for old acquaintance sake."

This was a proposition which no mortal constable could refuse, and accordingly declaring their entire concurrence in what he said, and their unanimous conviction that a joke was a joke, and that they always knew he was a good fellow, they fully acquiesced in the proposition of the glass by adding to their remarks, that in their opinion no liquor was like brandy, and that they, the magistrates, would put their foot in it rather, if they attempted to interfere with his licence.

"I believe you, my rummy pals," said the landlord, "you know very well I never harbours a sneak. Don't I give him up to you if one of 'em comes into my place? and as for murder, oh, what an out an' out odd idea to suppose as I'd harbour one in such a house as this; no, I scorns it. Here's better luck to you next time—a highwayman is a gentleman, and an out an' out good cracksman mind you, isn't small beer; but a sneak's a sneak, and a murderer is like touching a shovel full of hot ha'pence."

"That's true enough," said the officers, as they finished their glasses. "Good night to you, and good luck to you—you know we never trouble you except when we can't help it."

After all this politeness the officers departed from the house, leaving the landlord with a broad grin upon his ruby countenance.

"There's fools!" he said; "well, if ever I come near such a set of ninnies as officers is.'

He then at once proceeded to the long room, where for a brief space, Rowland Percy had found refuge, although among so strange and motley a group.

A glance from the landlord within the door brought Ned Witlet, who had arrived during the search, from the room.

"They're off," said the landlord—"all safe."

"Are you sure?" said Witlet.

"Quite," was the reply.

"Thank Heaven!" said Witlet, "I would not have had him taken for the best thousand pounds that ever mortal man set eyes on. I believe him innocent, as I believe I am in existence."

"So do I, Ned," replied the landlord; "I have seen a pretty goodish many chaps in my time who have done one thing or another, and I pretty well know by this time by the cut of a fellow's face, what he is capable of, and what he isn't. Why, that young chap couldn't commit a murder if he wished it, and he wouldn't wish it if he could. I can see what he is—he's one of your out an' out humanity

coves, and whosoever says he murdered Sir George Rankley has got the wrong sow by the ear."

"You are right," said Witlet; "he is as innocent as you or I."

"And we is more like suckling doves than nothink else."

"Pooh—pooh!" said Witlet, "I mean only with regard to the murder we were talking of—but where did you conceal him?"

"Oh, in the old place—in the old place."

"The water-butt?"

"Yes, to be sure; they looked into it and underneath it, but, unless he had hung

No. 38.

out his foot and said, "here I am my kiddies," it wasn't very likely they should see him."

"It is a good hiding-place," said Witlet.

"I believe yer," said the landlord, "I should never be the man again as I am if that ere water-butt consarn was found out. I calls it the triumph of modern ingenuity, I does ; and if I don't drown the fellow on the top of it as finds out the place at the bottom, if so be as ever that ere conwulsion of nature ensues, I ain't me, that's all."

"But do you think," said Witlet, "the environs of the house are perfectly safe ?"

"Think the what ?" said the landlord.

"I mean—do you think the door is not watched ?"

"Look at me," said the landlord, and after a desperate struggle, which he was forced to assist with a stamp of the foot, he succeeded in winking with one eye.

"Well, I see you," said Ned.

"Did you ever catch a pig with a greased tail ?" said the landlord. "Did you think, now, Neddy, I was such a fool as to walk this ere young chap out of the door as if he was a wisitor come for a kivarton, or a blow out of heavy ?"

"No," said Ned, "I scarcely supposed so much."

"Just come up them ere stairs, will yer, and I'll soon bring your man to yer. We've got two doors to this here house, one of 'em opens to the street, and 't's easy watching that ere—but the tother is rather in the attic-ceiling, and it ain't so easy by no means to watch that ere."

"I should think not," said Witlet ; "but do you mean him to escape by that means ?"

"Yes—to be sure. There's an empty house five doors off ; as it wasn't incommoding anybody, I just walked along the parapet, and took possession. You and your man can do the same, with the advantage of letting yourselves out three doors round the corner."

"That will be admirable," said Witlet. "I am most deeply indebted to you, Joe."

"Stew your gammon," said Joe. "I suppose you wants to pick my pocket now, and I never was wery much complimented but once, and then I'm blowed if the fellow didn't steal my watch. I was *green* afore that, and it did me *brown*, and I haven't been half so easy took in since."

With this practical remark, the landlord departed to release Rowland Percy from his somewhat disagreeable position.

In a very few moments he brought him into the house, saying as they entered—

"All's safe. Your friend, Ned Witlet, is here, but if it hadn't been for my water-butt, you'd have been in the condemned cell again before now, and as it isn't many hours to eight o'clock, that wouldn't have been so pleasant—follow me, and don't say a word."

Rowland Percy obeyed him in silence, although he was about to utter some expressions of gratitude for the really kindly protection that had been extended towards him.

The landlord led him up the various staircases, until they reached the topmost story of the house, where Ned Witlet was already awaiting their coming.

It was a small attic, with a slanting roof, to which the landlord introduced the fugitives, and setting the candle upon the table, he pointed to a trap-door in the roof, which was secured by several massive bolts.

"There," he said, "is a great deal better door than the front one. You'll find the steps in that corner, Ned, and I'll show you the way to the empty house, for it isn't quite safe to be crawling along the roofs of houses, you know, at such a time of night as this."

The steps were placed, and the trap-door was speedily removed, leaving an orifice that was only just sufficiently large to allow the bulky landlord to pass through, which, however, he accomplished with greater ease and dexterity than could have been supposed, from his appearance.

Rowland Percy followed, and Ned Witlet ascended last of all, saying—

"You keep close to the landlord's track, Mr. Percy, and I will come after you, for, I dare say, you are not so much used to these kind of adventures as either of us."

"I am greatly beholden to you both," said Rowland, "and I do hope and trust, that the day will come when I can more adequately thank you than at present is in my power."

"There, there," said the landlord, "that'll do; lean towards the house as you creep after me, and if you do make a slip it can only be into the gutter."

It was somewhat a perilous journey, amid the darkness and obscurity of the night, to perambulate the housetops, secured only against falling into the deep abyss below by a narrow coping stone, which, the houses being very old, was, in many cases, in a state of great decay, and in some wholly gone.

Their progress was slow and tedious, and to get across the roofs of the five houses consumed much time, for the landlord was himself extremely cautious, and crept along in a crouching posture, with his body much inclined towards the slanting roof.

After a time, then, he paused, and in a low voice, said—

"Hist—hist, pull up here, all's right."

"Have we arrived?" said Rowland.

"Yes; here's the empty house. D——n, what's that?"

One of the crazy coping stones had given way beneath a slight pressure from the foot of Ned Witlet, and it fell with a tremendous crash into the area of the next house to the empty one.

"Below there!" said the landlord, peering into the depth of darkness below.

In a moment a window was heard to open, and a female voice cried,—

"Gracious! what's that?"

"Nothing, mum," said the landlord, in a deep mysterious voice. "You had, better pull in your head, for there's another coming."

"Gracious!" cried the woman again, and the window was immediately closed with a bang, sufficient to break every pane of glass in it.

"All's right," said the landlord, "just creep up this sloping roof after me, and we can drop through the trap-door of the empty house as pleasantly as possible."

To Rowland it was a matter of great difficulty to ascend the roof, for the tiles, overlapping each other as they did, presented no sort of foothold, while the slope being considerable, he fancied that every moment he must inevitably roll back again into the gutter.

Such, however, was not the case, and at last he succeeded in getting a firm hold of the edge of the orifice which had been produced by the displacement of the trap-door.

"I have took the door," said the landlord, "to my place, and a fine rousing kitchen fire it made. I thought if anybody ever happened to see me on the roofs, and got crawling about out of curiosity to find out where I was going, they might just as well drop into a hole as not; howsomever, this is the way to do it."

Letting himself down carefully by his hands, he disappeared through the trap-door.

There is always something fearful in darkness and undefined heights; to Rowland Percy it seemed like dropping down a well, to let go his hold of the edge of that narrow opening, and trust himself to the intense darkness below it. It requires all his reason at the moment to induce him to do so, and when, at the solicitation of the landlord, he did leave go, he received a greater shock than if he had fallen from a great distance, by finding that he had not been six inches from the floor.

Witlet immediately followed, and the landlord then said,—
" Lay hold of me, and I'll guide you down stairs safely. I daren't have a light here, because its known as an empty house, and the neighbours opposite would of course take notice of it."

Rowland held by the dress of the landlord, and the party proceeded noise-lessly and carefully down the attic staircase. Just, however, as they ar-rived at the first landing, the loud sound of a watchman's rattle struck upon their ears.

" Who the devil's that ?" said Witlet.

" I'll lay any wager," said the landlord, " it's the woman who expected the other coping stone on her head. If there's an old maid in the street, she's sure to keep a rattle."

A voice now sounded clear and loud, crying,—

" Watch ! watch ! thieves—thieves—murder—murder !"

" There," said the landlord, " that's the woman's voice. I knew it. Come, as quick as you can—we shall be out of the house before she can get anybody to her assistance."

The whole three rushed down stairs with great precipitancy, the landlord opened the door, and they were in the street in a moment.

CHAPTER LXXVIII.

THE CHARGE AGAINST MIRANDA.—THE INDECISION OF THE MAGISTRATE.—THE PLEA OF GUILTY.

Escorted by more than one half of the persons who had formed the outskirts of the mob, and who, as they had taken no part in the disturbances that had ensued, the police and magistrates did not interfere with, Maranda and the governor proceeded to the meeting of the justices.

The proceedings of the authorities were upon this occasion, as is too frequently the case, when anything like extraordinary energy and decision is required, cha-racterised by a flurry and anxiety, and a want of fixedness of purpose that gave those persons against whom they fain would have acted, an ample opportunity of making the most of the lapse of time, between the necessity for prompt measures and their actually being resorted to.

Thus the small party, which, by the command of one member of the magis-terial body, was sent through York, in pursuit of the prisoner, comprised the only active step taken on the emergency, and even while Miranda was proceeding in the custody of the governor, a violent altercation was taking place in the council chamber, as to whose fault it was that the prisoner had escaped.

Miranda had not proceeded half her distance, when with a face beaming with satis-faction, and an excitement of manner that showed the exhilirating feelings that were at his heart, Mr. Anderson made his way towards her. The voice of popular report had informed him of what was taking place, and from the deep melancholy h ewas experiencing at his own home, he at once started into life's energy and activity, upon hearing that the prisoner had escaped, and that York and its autho-rities were spared the future reproach which would thereby have been theirs, had the judicial murder, which was contemplated, been really consummated.

He seized Miranda's hand, and while his voice was almost inarticulate from emotion, he cried,—

" Miranda, Miranda, you have saved him. You have saved him, Heaven bless you, Miranda, for a heroine as you are."

" He is saved," said Miranda, returning the smile of Mr. Anderson. " Heaven would not allow the innocent to perish, and has made me the humble instrument in the work of his preservation."

"I am sorry, sir," said the governor, "that we cannot now delay a moment. You can follow me and this lady if you please, to the magistrates."

"I am her professional adviser, sir," said Mr. Anderson, "and never did I in my life undertake a cause with the intense gratification I shall her's to-day."

"Very well, sir," said the governor, with a smile. "I have my duty to perform, from which I cannot shrink, but believe me it is with no regret that I see this young lady so well surrounded by friends and able defenders."

"From my heart I thank you, sir," said Mr. Anderson, "and with pleasure I perceive that the heroic Miranda Rankley has found a friend in you."

"I have indeed," said Miranda, "and what might have been a night accompanied by some painful circumstances, has been stripped of everything of a disagreable nature, and made replete with kindly sympathies. But I want no defence, Mr. Anderson ; believe me I am prouder of what they call my guilt, than any one circumstance in my mortal career."

"I believe it," said Mr. Anderson, "yet it shall be my duty to watch over your safety."

They had been walking on rapidly during this brief dialogue, and now reached the hall in which the magistrates were assembled, discoursing together in eager knots of two or three, concerning the unprecedented event which had called them together, and over and over again talking upon the peculiar line of evidence upon which Rowland Percy had been convicted, for his escape from the dreadful fate which had awaited him, seemed in every mind to have opened the whole case anew, and with many to have suggested grave doubts with regard to the nature of the evidence.

The assizes being not yet over, the court was densely crowded by barristers and attorneys, of all grades and degrees, and had Miranda required fifty defenders, she could instantly have procured them, so anxious was every professional man present to have something to do with the most extraordinary case they had met with on any of their circuits.

He who had been Rowland's counsel on the occasion of his trial, was surrounded by some eight or ten of his brethren, to whom, with a flushed countenance and an eager voice, he was again running over all the principal points of defence, ever and anon earnestly declaring his conviction of Rowland's innocence, and that the day would come when some circumstances would arise to make it apparent, until when he said, he hoped that Heaven would interpose between the persecuted young man and his enemies.

There was an earnestness' of manner, and a devotion to the cause which he espoused, about the general tone and bearing of the young barrister, that were almost sufficient to bring conviction to every heart that the cause he espoused was one of truth, [and [that the group around him was nearly presenting the singular anomaly of eight or ten lawyers being led away by feeling.

In a few moments then the attention of all was arrested by the senior member of the magistracy taking his seat.

Then immediately followed the loud, "Hush, hush !" of the crier, and in a few moments every discordant sound was subdued to silence.

The chairman of the magistrates then rose, saying :—

"Gentleman, I understand that the sheriff has a communication of some importance to make to us, concerning the non-execution of a criminal, who was to have suffered, this morning, the last penalty of the law."

Immediately upon the magistrate taking his seat, the sheriff rose and said—

"Having received due warrant for the execution of Rowland Percy, convicted at this present assizes of the capital felony of murder, he was by me, and under virtue of my warrant, confined in the gaol which is usually allotted to criminals.

"My duty, this morning, was to see that the sentence of the law was duly carried into effect, and all I can further state is, that upon arriving at the gaol, I was told that the criminal had escaped. However, in what manner you will hear from those who held him in actual custody; for myself, gentleman, I can only deeply regret that the majesty of the law has not been fully vindicated as yet by the execution of this criminal."

A flash of indignation came from the eyes of Miranda as the sheriff thus spoke, but Mr. Anderson, who guessed her feelings, whispered to her—

"Pooh, pooh, Miranda, heed not what he says; those are mere words of course, which he is forced to use in the discharge of his official duties; he is as kind-hearted and humane a man as ever lived, and I am quite sure would last night have given a hundred pounds out of his own pocket to have ensured the escape of Rowland Percy, in order that he himself might be spared the pain of presiding at his execution."

"I am foolish," said Miranda, "to heed what any one says. Rowland Percy is free, and I am satisfied."

The record of Rowland's conviction for murder was then put in and read by the clerk of the court. After which the sheriff produced the warrant for his execution, and the receipt he had received in the due form of official business from the governor of the gaol upon the occasion of Rowland being delivered into his custody.

This ended the preliminary proceedings, and it remained but for the governor to explain his non-production of the prisoner upon the formal requisition which had been made at seven o'clock that morning.

Miranda saw with some pain the shade of anxiety that crossed the face of the governor as he rose to speak, and if a feeling of uneasiness crossed her mind at all at the moment, it was that one, whom she had so much reason to esteem, should be placed in so embarrassing a situation.

"I am aware, gentlemen," said the governor, "that although the sheriff is presumed at law to be answerable for the safe custody of the prisoner who was committed to my charge, yet that I, and I alone, am virtually so answerable."

"Hear, hear," said the sheriff.

"Keep order, Mr. Crier," said the magistrate, who was in the chair, and the "Hush, hush," of the crier resounded through the court.

The governor continued—

"All I can take upon myself, gentlemen, distinctly to state is, that as the various apartments of the gaol were constructed for different purposes, which were pointed out to me upon my assumption to office, so I used them.

"Rowland Percy, as cast for death this morning, was placed in the cell appropriated to condemned criminals, and I rather think that if any blame is ultimately to rest upon any one in particular, it would be found to belong to the learned, upright, and humane judge who presided at the recent trial, and who gave an unlimited order for the admission at all times to the gaol and the cell of the prisoner, of one who, in her deep conviction of his innocence, would dare all for his liberation."

The magistrates looked at each other with some little degree of amazement, as the governor thus adroitly shifted the principal blame of the transaction, for which he was called upon to account, to the shoulders of so much higher a personage than himself.

"Gentlemen," he continued, "you will readily perceive the peculiar position in which I am placed by this transaction. True it is that I hold prisoners in my custody, but I am as one in whose custody might be placed a chest of plate, while some other person had the liberty of lending the key to whomsoever he chose. Thus, gentlemen, I humbly conceive it will be seen, that if the worthy and enlightended judge had not given the unlimited order, to visit my prison, to the person who aided the escape of Mr. Rowland Percy, such escape would not have taken place, and, therefore, I humbly throw myself upon the consideration and able advocacy of that learned personage to drag me out of the mire, into which, with the best and purest motives, he has unwittingly plunged me."

Some of the magistrates looked very grave at this, others laughed, and many looked extremly puzzled, as not knowing what to make of it.

The presiding magistrate then said,

"Perhaps, Mr. Governor, we are, or at all events as are presumed to be, very much in the dark with regard to the particulars of this transaction, you will have no objection to detail to us how it was that you came to permit your prisoner to escape?"

"I assure your worship and this honourable assembly," said the governor, drily, "that such a circumstance was completely without my permission, and that no man, nt even Mr. Sheriff, could feel more shocked than I do at the untoward occurrence."

The govenor's looks betokened anything but a man whose mind was very much shocked, and was so strikingly at variance with his words that a very irreverent laugh burst from some of the spectators.

"Keep order in the court," said the presiding magistrate; "have the kindness to proceed, Mr. Governor, with your statement ?"

"Will you allow me to ask, Mr. Chairman," said a little fat local magistrate, who had come to York in order to be present at the assizes, "if we are in order in conducting the business of this court in so desultory a manner?"

Then, before the chairman could reply, the under-sheriff, who prided himself much upon his facetiousness, said,

"After the grossly disorderly act which has been committed by Rowland Percy, in not being quietly hung according to law, it is not to be wondered at that the proceedings of this court, for a short time, should not be of so regular a character as might be wished; but, if he would have the kindness to surrender now, and undergo the sentence of the law, there could be no doubt but that the court would suffer a relapse into its usual state of regularity."

"I beg your pardon, sir," said Rowland's counsel, in a loud, clear voice, that was heard by every one in court. "The warrant for my client's execution appoints the morning of this day, at eight o'clock, naming both the month and the year. Now, gentlemen, if my client were brought in this moment a prisoner, I defy you to hang him, for you have no authority so to do. What at eight o'clock this morning would have been an extremely legal act, cannot be perpetrated at a quarter past ten. Gentlemen, I humbly presume we cannot be too particular in cases of this nature."

"We should certainly hang your client," said the under-sheriff, "and leave him to bring his action."

A general laugh succeeded this sally, and it was with some difficulty that the president of the court made himself heard, and then he said.

"I shall certainly commit any person who interrupts the proceedings of the court, and I must, at the same time, express my great surprise that my brother magistrates and the legal gentlemen connected with the circuit, now present, should treat this affair as the capital joke they seem to consider it."

"Really—really," said the mayor, rising, "I—I don't see the joke; it don't appear to me to be funny at all. Upon my life, I don't see any joke."

The mayor looked so uncommonly stolid, as he uttered these words, and presented to the assembly a face about as full of intellectual fire as might be supposed to reside in a large turnip, that it upset the gravity of those who had suppressed their mirth, and a roar of laughter, which alike defied the crier and chairman, succeeded.

"This is frightfully irregular," said the presiding magistrate; "if such scenes as these are allowed to proceed, there will be an end of all order, law, and justice."

"Only think of that, my covies," said the voice of Jones from the throng. "Penny polonies would riz, and you wouldn't get a ha'penny faggot for tuppence."

"Seize that man—seize that man!" cried the magistrate, from whom Jones had abstracted the riot act; "officers, seize him—hold him fast—handcuff him—bring him before the bench! Whatever you do, secure that scoundrel.'

The officers made a great bustle in the direction that Mr. Jones's voice proceeded, when the crowd pushed into their arms a mild, inoffensive man, who seemed struck dumb by the horror of his situation, and allowed himself to be conducted before the bench.

"That's not him!" cried the indignant magistrate.

"I humbly thank your worship," said the man, trembling in every limb. "I know it isn't me; I assure your worship, upon my honour—my wife's here—and she ——"

"Go along about your business," said the magistrate. "Gentlemen—gentlemen!" he continued, "I shall leave this seat unless you assist me in the preservation of order. I wish Mr. Governor to proceed with his explanation, upon which we may found some substantial act that will restore us to regularity."

Comparative silence then being obtained, the governor continued.

"From my own knowledge, I can avouch that up to half-past eight yesterday evening the prisoner was in safe custody; about that period, however, as I have since ascertained from the officials under me, the prisoner was visited by Miss Miranda Rankley, the young lady who had procured from the learned judge so comprehensive an order, to enable her so to do.

"Of that visit, so long as it terminated, which to all appearance it did, at nine o'clock, the hour at which the prison is cleared of all strangers, I could know nothing. The first alarm that I received was a hasty message, in the dead of the night, to the effect that the prisoner had escaped; such escape, it appears, having been discovered by the chaplain, concerning whom, at a fitting time and place, I have a presentment to make to the visiting justices.

"Upon then proceeding to the cell of the prisoner, gentlemen, I found, instead of the young man, Rowland Percy, who had been committed to my charge, this young lady, Miranda Rankley, who, at my own risk, I detained, although I had no means of charging her with anything beyond a trespass, and who, for all I know, may bring her action against me for such detention."

"Ridiculous!" cried the chairman.

"I humbly thank you, sir," said the governor, "for your legal opinion, so luminously expressed."

The chairman looked very red, and the juniors among the barristers tittered amazingly.

"That is all you have to say then, sir?" said the magistrate.

"All," replied the governor. "Here is the lady, she can now answer for herself if any charge is brought against her."

"She must be considered in custody, and Mr. Sheriff must prosecute," said the magistrate,

"I suppose I must," said the sheriff.

Miranda rose on the instant, and in a calm, clear voice, that sounded sweet as the tinkle of a silver bell, she said.

"I need trouble no one. I am guilty, but in that guilt is my triumph and fulfilment of my earnest prayers to Heaven."

CHAPTER LXXIX.

THE LEGAL PROCEEDINGS AGAINST MIRANDA.—A STRANGE SCENE AND A STRANGE
WITNESS.

IN an instant, as if by magic, every angry and every mirthful feeling in that assemblage seemed hushed, and they bent all their energies with one accord to admire the surpassing beauty, and listen to the lute like sweetness of the voice of Miranda Rankley.

"Miranda," said Mr. Anderson, hastily, "you are not yet charged with any crime, and I can hardly suppose the magistrates are serious in intending to charge you with any."

"I certainly must disagree with you," said the presiding magistrate. "I consider Miranda Rankley as actually in custody, and brought before me as charged with aiding and abetting in the escape of a person convicted of a capital offence, and Mr. Sheriff as I understand, will support that charge."

"Certainly," said the sheriff, "with whatever evidence I may. The act of Miranda Rankley is a misdemeanor of the highest class."

"Then so charged she comes before me; and now, gentlemen, we are I believe, strictly regular. We can take whatever evidence may now offer in its due course."

"I will spare all this," added Miranda, "by pleading guilty to the charge."

"I think," said the magistrate, "that the ends of public justice would best be answered by allowing the inquiry to proceed. Mr. Sheriff, call your witness to prove how the prisoner escaped from your custody."

The sheriff held a brief consultation with one of the barristers present, who then rose and said,—

"I appear on behalf of the prosecution, and have to request that the governor of the prison may again relate his statement of facts upon oath; leaving out the extremely irrelevant matter with which he has thought fit to garnish his tale."

The counsel true to the cause in which he had embarked, made this first hit at the governor, because he plainly saw his animus in favour of the prisoner.

The statement was calmly and dispassionately made by the governor, and when he had

finished the counsel said,—

"Now, Mr. Governor, how often do you visit your prisoners?"

"Whenever I think proper," said the governor.

"Were you a thief-taker before you were thief-keeper, Mr. Governor?"

"No," said the governor, "nor was I a hired thief-defender. I was in his majesty's service; and the last puppy I kicked was asking impertinent questions."

The governor looked very hard at the barrister as he spoke, and the barrister

No. 39.

looked very hard at the governor. Then the counsel gave his wig a pull that brought it very near the bridge of his nose, and shook his head, as much as to say,—

"This won't do at all—I must try another tack."

"Now, Mr. Governor, who was keeping watch at the outer door last evening?"

"Samuel Twigg," said the governor.

"Any relation of yours, Mr. Governor?"

"No," said the governor; "but he is an impudent dog, and I believe has a connection that goes the York circuit."

"Oh!" said the counsel, with a jerk of his head.

"Exactly so," said the governor, with a nod."

A titter ran through the court, and a cold prespiration broke out on the brow of the counsel, for he found himself in that most disagreeable of all predicaments, of a man who has been attemping to shine amazingly, and finds that his light is quietly put under a bushel by the sun of some one else's superior intellect.

He looked despairingly around the court; a broad grin sat upon the face of every professional man present; there was no sympathy to be found anywhere and it was something in the shivering manner of a man who had been trying to show off in skates to a party of ladies, and found himself, in the course of a few minutes indebted to the Humane Society, and dragged out of the water like a half-drowned rat, that he said—

"Mr. Governor, this—this—affair may cost you your place, Mr. Governor. Do you hear that, Mr. Governor?"

"He ain't deaf, Mr. Minikin," said Jones, from an obscure corner of the court.

The discomfitted counsel sat down, while that disagreeable titter, which is really so frightful to the feelings of a nervous man, ran through the court. The sheriff, however, came to his side, and it is to be presumed, whispered some words of consolation in his ear, for in a few moments he rose and said—

"Call Samuel Twigg."

"Samuel Twigg!" said the crier of the court, in a loud sonorous voice, and the man who had really known Percy in his disguise, but connived at his escape, came forward.

"You kept the key of the outer gate of the prison," said the counsel, "on the occasion of this escape?"

"I did," was the reply.

"Who passed on that evening?"

"Miss Miranda Rankley, as I believe."

"Then, my man, you are unfit for your situation. You may go down."

"I wishes to be examined," said a voice, and there came through the throng an individual, the examination of whom, if conducted personally, would have taken up no inconsiderable time of the court.

In the first place, there was an amazing quantity of straps of sticking plaster placed across his nose in every possible direction, until his face looked as if it were meant to represent the sun in some astronomical diagram. Across one eye was tied a bandage, and the other was ornamented with a green shade; his head was completely shaved, and sundry pieces of adhesive plaster on sundry parts of it, betokened that some one must have been, with malice aforethought punching the same.

This singular apparition had not before attracted any particular attention, for he had kept a large hat very much slouched down over his face; but now, when in a singular voice, the peculiarities of which arose from the recent violent extraction of his front teeth, he said—

"I wishes to be examined—I wishes to be examined," and at the same time took off his hat; the people shrank from him right and left, and permitted him easily to approach the table.

"Who are you?" said the counsel for the prosecution, looking rather alarmed, and beginning to wish his job at the very devil.

"They calls me Tommy Goggles, but my real name 's Tommy Green. Ain't I a apparition?"

"Why—why—I must say, you—you rather are ; and now, Mr. Tommy Green—alias Goggles—what have you to say with regard to this business?"

"Why, I've been rather in the thick of it," said Mr. Goggles. "I wants wengence, and I'll have it, or my name isn't Green—I mean Goggles."

"Well, Mr. Green Goggles," said the counsel, delighted at his own wit, "this I must say, is the very place to come for *wengence.*"

"So I thought," said Mr. Goggles. "I am rather like you, old chap, in one particular."

"In what particular do you mean Mr. Goggles?" said the counsel, with a laugh —"pray don't be shy."

"Why, I means I was trying to be remarkable clever, and put my foot in it."

"Come, come, sir," said the counsel, "let's us have none of your low insolence here : remember you are on your oath."

"Oh, I knows it," said Goggles. "I ain't going to inwent nothink. The blessed truth's a stinger. I am under-turnkey at the prison, and as I was standing in the sanguinary westibule, I seed the chap as was to be hanged come out with my own eyes, all for to make his escape in female toggery. Then I thinks to myself as I'd come it uncommon clever, so I doesn't so much as wink at nobody, but walks out arter him—oh, dear, worse luck! "I follers him down the street, and then another cove jines him ; but I didn't think nothink of that, but went a follering on ; then, arter awhile, they takes to running like mad, then I runs arter them like a streak of lightning : when all on a sudden they pulls up in an uncommon deserted street like a clap of thunder and afore I could stop myself, or say so much as Jack, not to think of Robinson, one on 'em hits me this here blow, which cumflummoxed my nose, sent three or four of my ivories into my stomach, doused my ogles, and did me up in a small heap—that's what's made me such a apparition as I is."

The roar of laughter that followed this speech transcends all description ; nobody tried to stop it, for nobody could help joining in it, although the counsel for the prosecution nearly bit his lips through in the attempt.

Mr. Goggles alone, who dare not laugh, had he even felt so inclined, for fear of disarranging the adhesive plaster by which his face was covered, looked solemn and serious, and added largely to the shrieks of merriment, by the rage he seemed to be getting in.

In vain he tried to make himself heard, the only words that were audible, being the occasional remonstrance of—

"It's all very fine, but——"

When, however, at length from sheer exhaustion the laughter subsided, the counsel for the prosecution merely said,—"That is my case—that is my case!" and sat down quite in a huff.

Then up rose the barrister who had defended Percy on his trial, and in a tone of voice which at once changed the feelings of his audience from the ridiculous to the decorously attentive, he said,—

"Gentlemen, my client, Miss Miranda Rankley, pleads freely and unhesitatingly guilty to the charge which is brought against her of aiding and abetting in the escape of Rowland Percy, the alleged murderer of her father, from prison, and from an ignominious death. I mention the fact, gentlemen, of his being the alleged murderer of her father, to prove how deep, how sincere, how heart-felt, must be her conviction of his spotless innocence.

"This young lady, then, possessed, as she truly is, of the higher and nobler feelings of human nature, while she still proposes to herself the task of crying aloud to Heaven for justice upon her father's murderer, through the agency of human tribunals, felt, when this innocent man was accused of the foul deed, that a purer, a higher, a fair holier duty called upon her to rescue him from that terrible imputation.

"Oh, gentlemen, if it be consistent with human nature—if it be praise worthy

—if it be great—to seek for the vengeance of the law against an evil doer—and to cry aloud in the emphatic words of scripture—' he who sheddeth man's blood by man also shall his blood be shed'—how much more praise worthy—how much more just—how much greater—how much nobler—how much holier—in the sight of the great God that sees us all, must be that effort, which, heedless of all human consequences, has urged this young and shrinking girl to rescue an innocent man, and step between the erring ministers of the law and the perpetration of a judicial murder, for which, in after years, when grey-headed old men and trembling on the graves' brink, they will be shrunk from with horror.

"Yes, gentlemen, guilty is the plea—but glorious, great, noble, and God-like, is the guilt!"

    *   *   *   *   *

So wrapt was the stillness of the throng in that densely-crowded court, during the delivery of these fervent and eloquent words, that the very echo of them seemed to remain for some moments in every heart, preserving the stillness of deep attention, even after the young and enthusiastic counsel had ceased to speak.

Then ensued that buzzing noise, which is heard in every assembly, when the minds of all are suddenly released from something which has encharmed every sense—there was a loud and very general clapping of hands, and a most striking illustration of the power which one human mind may acquire over a multitude, by the utterance of sentiments at once recognised as just, in appropriate and graceful language.

The under-sheriff leaned over to the counsel for the prosecution, and said,—

"What do you think of that?—and what do you think a jury would say to it?"

There will be only one chance,' whispered the counsel for the prosecution; "but that would be a good one."

"Indeed!"

"It's rather too good, and I don't think they quite understand it."

"I presume, then," said the presiding magistrate, "that the affair is now fairly in our own hands. The case is quite an unprecedented one, and I am of opinion it can be dealt with both by fine and imprisonment."

"I beg to suggest," said an elderly magistrate, rising, "that the prisoner be called upon to enter into her own recognizances, to the amount of five hundred pounds, and produce two sureties of two hundred and fifty pounds each, to appear and receive judgment when called upon."

A majority of the magistrates immediately cried, "Hear—hear!"

Mr. Anderson and the counsel for the defence at once proposed themselves as the required sureties, and in five minutes more Miranda was at liberty.

CHAPTER LXXX.

THE ROUTE TO LONDON.—NED WITLET'S NOTIONS OF PUBLIC AND PRIVATE MO-
RALITY.—THE ALARM AT THE ROAD-SIDE INN.

FOR a moment or two Rowland Percy and his two friends stood on the door-steps of the empty house, while the rattle continued springing violently from the neighbouring habitation.

"We shall have a glorious row in a few moments," said the landlord, "I dare say that old lady thought the coping-stone that fell with such a bang was some out-and-out cracksman who had dropped from the parapet, with an idea of getting in at the window as he came down."

'She is making noise enough," said Ned Witlet.

"Ah, curse her for an old cat!" continued the landlord : "the worst of women is, they never know when to leave off anything—but here you have the watchman."

"Had we better not leave this place?" said Rowland.

"Not at all," said the landlord, "there's nothing to fear." Then stopping the first watchman who made his appearance, he said,—

"It's a chimney on fire, and an old gal in hysterics—there, don't you see her up at the window? You hold on by the street-door, while somebody else runs for an engine."

While the watchman was stupidly staring up at the window, Rowland and his friends walked gently away, the landlord quietly remarking,—

"If there had been any time now for a bit of fun, I'd have had it with that old cat; I'd have called out fire till an engine came, and wouldn't I have drenched her then a little; but, however, there's a time for all things, and she and I are too near neighbours not to provoke each other a little occasionally."

"You had better leave us now," said Ned Witlet; "I believe that the worst danger is over, and that my young friend here has nothing more to fear. I have a chaise-cart waiting out in the London road with a good horse that will go fifty miles in little better than six hours; we shall be in London in all probability much earlier than any one would follow us, even were the route we have taken suspected."

"Good night, then," said the landlord, "and good luck attend you.'

"Stay yet a moment," said Rowland Percy; "how am I, proceeding to so great a distance, to obtain information concerning the fate of her who has so nobly saved me from destruction?"

"Fear not," said Witlet, "I have arranged all that. We shall receive full intelligence of everything that occurs to her from a friend of mine, who will find out everything, and write to me daily, and whose letters I will communicate to you."

"I am much—very much beholden to you," said Rowland; "I never was a disbeliever in the existence of warm hearts and generous dispositions, but I certainly never expected to meet with the disinterested friendship you have shewn me."

"I hope," said Witlet, "all may turn out fortunately as it has begun. In London you will, without doubt, be safe enough, for there is no hiding-place equal to it, and you must just wait with what patience you may for better news."

The deep solemn tones of the Minster bell struck at the moment upon Roland's ears.

"It may be the last time," he thought, "that I shall hear those sounds. It seems like parting from a dear friend to leave this ancient city, in which so many of my happiest hours were passed. Ah! what a world of unhappiness and deep anxieties have been crowded into the last few months of my existence. Already do I seem aged, if I count my years by the multitude of the events that have oppressed my life. Farewell, Miranda, for a brief space only, I hope, farewell. Thou best, noblest, dearest one—farewell."

A deep sigh arose from his heart, and Ned Witlet said in a kindly tone,—

"Come, come, Mr. Percy, cheer up; sorrow is the worst enemy to succumb to, for when you own yourself beaten, it gives you no quarter."

"You are right—you are right," said Rowland, "viewing my situation now, comparatively to what it was, it is, indeed, a blessed one, and I of all men should not repine."

"Besides," said Witlet, "there are happier days in store, and a merry peal from the old Minster bells may some day welcome you in triumph back to York."

"True—true—I will not despair."

"Besides," added Witlet, "you have a treasure which an emperor on his throne might envy."

"I know it—I know it," cried Rowland; "you mean the love of Miranda Rankley."

'I do," said Witlet.

"Oh! that is indeed a treasure," said Rowland; "could I for one moment forget that no human malice, or human weakness, could rob me of that Divine possession. My good friend, you have properly corrected me; I ought, indeed, to find ample materials in my own mind for joyful felicitation."

"Here we are," said Witlet, as suddenly turning a corner, he pointed to a chaise-cart a few paces down the street.

"We must make ourselves as comfortable in this conveyance as we can," said Witlet, "although it will be rather a cold one, and some of the road between here and London not so pleasant as might be."

"I ought to be, and am thankful for any conveyance that will assist me in leaving York," remarked Rowland.

In a few moments they were seated in the chaise-cart, which had been in charge of a boy, to whom Witlet spoke some words in an under tone, among which Rowland thought he heard the name of Miranda.

"Did you not mention her name?" said Rowland.

"I did," replied Witlet. "It was to tell the boy by no means to forget his father's promise to write to me concerning her every day."

"Who is his father?" said Rowland.

"The man named Jones, who gave evidence against Samuel Twitter at your trial."

"He is a strange, rough man, but seems an honest one," said Rowland.

"Why, as for his honesty," said Witlet, "that's neither here nor there—he has his little peculiar notions upon that subject, as well as the rest of us—but he is a good fellow in the main, and I believe never did a deliberately sneaking action in his life. You must understand, Mr. Percy, that there are grades even in what is called dishonesty."

"So I believe," said Rowland, "although dishonesty is so positive a thing as to be governed by one great principle."

"Ay, that may be very true," said Witlet, as he spoke cheeringly to the horse; "I have had so many ups and downs in my life, that I scarcely know what is honesty and what isn't."

"Now that we are doomed to so long a journey together," said Rowland, "will you not confide in me, by telling me really who and what you are?

"Oh, certainly—cetainly. My name is Ned Witlet, although they call me in the profession the 'Slashing 'Squire,' and sometimes other names."

"But that profession?" said Rowland.

"I am a highwayman,?' said Ned, as coolly as possible. "Kim up, so you'll shy at the first mile post out of York, will you?"

"A highwayman!" repeated Rowland Percy in some surprise.

"Yes," replied Ned; "there must be people of all professions in the world, and what would become of the lawyers and judges if there were no gentlemen of my way of thinking?"

"I ought, certainly," said Rowland, "to be the very last person who could think about being captious about who or what you were; the great assistance you have rendered me, demands the warmest sentiments of gratitude that one man can feel towards another. I regret that I asked you the question of what you were, for there could be no occasion for my doing so."

"I am glad you've asked if," said Ned Witlet; "and, if you had not, I should have taken the first opportunity of telling you, for I thought it would be no bad thing to convince such as you, that a man who sets at defiance one of the great principles of what is called social life, might not necessarily be a great scoundrel. I have a peculiar way of thinking with regard to my professional pursuits. In early life I commenced in what they called the honest line. I went into business; but I failed signally, because I was not rogue enough. I found out then, by degrees, in my intercourse with society, that the breaches of good order, morality, and honour, were those which the law took no cognisance of. It is only the great staiiring crimes about which there can be no mistake, that society seems inclined to arm itself against."

"There is some truth in that," said Rowland Percy.

"I know there is," resumed Ned; "I think a great deal of truth in it. The deep inducement of vices, that are the most pernicious of all, and strike at t.he very foundation of happiness and all sorts of contentment, remain untouched, because it is quite impossible to define them. So you see, I found myself a touch too honest for society at large; and, as I was not an independent gentleman, I was compelled, in order to earn my living with as little self-reproach as possible, to turn a high-wayman."

"I certainly," said Rowland, "never heard such an excuse before for what is commonly considered a very criminal line of conduct; at the same time, however, my reason cannot but at once admit that a highwayman may be an angel of light in comparison to many a man who might sit as one of his judges."

"That's the thing," said Ned Witlet; I think we now understand each other, Mr. Percy. I am very far from defending myself from the charge of taking other people's goods and money; but what I do mean to assert is, that when I say I am a highwayman, I do not necessarily imply a greater degree of criminality than as if I had said I am a lawyer, or a doctor, or a parson, or any other gentlemanly pursuit, which, without its little species of rascality, would never succeed."

Rowland laughed as he said—

"You certainly are a philosopher on a grand scale. But when do you think we shall reach London?"

"If our nag holds out well to its work, and meets with no particular accident on the way, I think we may venture to say that we shall hear the next midnight chimes at St. Paul's."

"Thank Heaven!" said Rowland, "that I shall at least be removed so far from the scene of the greatest dangers that in all likelihood I shall ever endure."

The road they were now on was a hard and level one, and they proceeded at a capital pace for a number of miles, when the country became more hilly; and, in a hollow, after passing the first eminence, Ned Witlet drew up at the door of a small roadside public-house, from one window of which proceeded a long stream of light, indicating that at least some one was up in the establishment to receive any chance guest that might arrive.

"We shall bait here for a short time," said Witlet; "you must be in need of some refreshment; and as for myself, such has been my hurry and anxiety for the last four-and-twenty hours, that I have scarcely tasted food."

"How far are we from York?" said Rowland, as he got out of the chaise-cart.

"A trifle over thirty miles," was Ned's reply; "and if your enemies were only to start after you now, we have as fair a chance of beating them as we could desire."

"I do not see," said Rowland, "how they are to guess at our progress in this direction."

"Leave them alone for that," said Witlet; "let us rather hope to baffle them than that they will not attempt to find you. Come into the house, for it appears to me that we shall have rain to-night, and that shortly too."

Rowland, on hearing this, looked up towards the sky, and could see the clouds were chasing each other across the moon's disc, and ever and anon throwing the earth in deep shade, while a dampness pervaded the air, that rendered him chilly. The wind, too, came moaning across the country, and whistled past the gable ends of the solitary house, but would, having spent its force, again sink into a sullen silence.

But though the gusts were short, yet they rose and fell, and, as they did so gained gradually, though slowly, in strength and duration, while the clouds came heavier, and a freshness pervaded the air, that surely indicated the coming storm so soon as the wind should entirely lull.

"We shall have a stormy night," said Rowland Percy.

"That I am sure of," said Ned Witlet, "for there is every indication of it."

Even as he spoke, the sound of horses feet came plainly upon their ears.

CHAPTER LXXXI.

MIRANDA AT FREEDOM.—THE REITERATED PROPOSAL OF MR. ANDERSON.—MIRANDA'S NOBLE SENSE OF HER DUTIES.—THE MAGISTRATE'S PLAN FOR ROWLAND'S CAPTURE.

THE news that the high spirited Miranda Rankley had escaped so easily from the consequences of her devoted act in favour of her lover, spread like wildfire throughout the city. It was carried from mouth to mouth that the magistrates dared not harm her; and Mr. Jones remarked to a number of his popular admirers, that he thought he had rather scared them, and "they'd be afeard to do nothing. 'Sides," he added, "I have boned the blessed riot-act, and you may kick up the jolliest rows you like in York afore I'll read it."

This reasoning did remarkably well, both for Mr. Jones and his admirers, for they seemed to fancy the riot-act was a something which, when once they had got possession of it, fully exonerated them from pain and penalties of future disturbances.

As for Miranda, her feelings were certainly joyful and enviable. True it was that Rowland Percy was a fugitive, but the mere fact that he was so, implied his rescue from a fate that she shuddered to reflect upon. True that she herself was in a state of comparative destitution: that in the course, perhaps, of a few short weeks she might not know where to turn for sustenance; but then, was not Rowland free, and, as a consequence, was there not hope—dear hope, which, had he fallen a victim to his enemies, must have been extinguished for ever; for could all the lament—could all the sympathy of a nation, or a world, restore to her arms he who, but for her own intrepidity and exalted courage, would ere then have been a murdered man?

Oh, how sweetly delightful to her seemed the sunny sky that smiled upon that ancient city as she once more emerged into its crowded streets, free to go whither she listed—free to search for him whose danger had caused her such exquisite pangs—whose safety such exquisite delight.

She was immediately recognised by the crowd which had waited outside the court during the legal proceedings against her; but now that all excitement was over—now that she had achieved everything—now that that night, which had been so full of deep anxieties had passed away, and she told herself she had little to fear, while what she had to hope—namely, the complete establishment of Rowland's innocence to all men, might be very far distant, although she looked upon it as a circumstance which in Heaven's own time must happen—she shrunk from the popularity with which the events of the last eight-and-forty hours had invested her.

Besides, she could not but recollect that the very mob whose cheerings and vociferations now sounded in her ears was the same mob that had assembled to gloat on the dying agonies of Rowland Percy, and find an hour's amusement from his execution.

With these feelings, was it to be wondered at that she shrunk from the shouts of those persons who, with the same cries, would not have hesitated to herald into eternity him who was her heart's best, fondest treasure.

Turning to Mr. Anderson, she said,—

"How shall I escape these people? My self-imposed duty now calls me to visit the unhappy father of Rowland Percy : before his present mental blight had fallen upon him, he declared that my fortunes should be his, and that he would cling to me, protecting and comforting me while he should live, through that stormy season of my life that had begun with such accumulated horrors : but now that his mind has become a wreck, and he is the shadow of his former self, it is my duty to cling to him, which I will do as well for Rowland's sake as for his own."

"You are right, Miranda," said Mr. Anderson, "as you always are when real feeling has to be consulted."

"And, moreover," said the barrister who had conducted her defence, "Miss Rankley is quite right in the estimate she sets upon popular applause."

"Where can I go," said Miranda, "for a brief space, to free myself from what amounts to a persecution from these people? I am fearful they should follow me to my home, and there commit some indiscretion that might much aggravate Mr. Percy's malady."

No. 40.

"You shall come to my house, Miranda," said Mr. Anderson; "and although they may certainly follow you there, they will soon be tired of looking at my uninteresting street-door."

"I don't know that," said the governor with a laugh, "since the fork which was the companion to the knife with which Margaret Nicholson tried to stab the king, became a popular exhibition, and attracted a crowd of people, I can believe anything of popular credulity; however, Mr. Anderson's plan may answer for an hour or two, if he adds to it a little cold water from one of the windows, and the intimation that he is a lawyer."

Miranda turned to the governor as he spoke and with a grateful expression of countenance and tone, she said—

"I have much kindness and courtesy to thank you for, sir, and I have only sincerely to hope that your advocacy of the cause of the unfortunate Miranda Rankley may not expose you to any evil consequences from those who are really, and those who are compelled to become her enemies."

"Far from it," said the governor; "I am quite sure from another reason, that I should not have held my situation long."

"And what reason may that be?" said Mr. Anderson.

"Why, I have quarrelled with the evangelical chaplain, and as the mass of mankind are fools, not even excepting visiting justices, he is sure to get the better of me, for, of course, they would rather offend me than one who seems on such intimate terms with the infernal regions, that he can send anybody there at pleasure: so, Miranda, I beg you will have no uneasiness on my account, for I have no doubt, for the reason I have mentioned to you, I shall lose the situation I never was particularly well calculated for. Farewell, and may health and happiness attend you, and believe it would give me as sincere pleasure as ever I have experienced in my life to hear some happy day that you have succeeded in clearing your lover's character, when after which I wish you all the happiness as a wife, to which I am sure you are so eminently entitled."

With a graceful bow the governor then walked away, before Miranda could reply to him.

"That man," said Mr. Anderson, "is a gentleman in the truest acceptation of the term; he is no more fit for the governor of a prison than for the situation of a slave-driver, or the overseer of a factory. But here we are at my door, come in, Miranda Rankley, and I can truly say that a more honoured or truly welcome guest never crossed my threshold."

When Miranda had entered the house, Mr. Anderson turned to the throng that had followed her to his door, and said,—

"Now, my good people, you won't see any more of her. She is going to stay here for a month, and never stir out of doors; besides, I won't have a crowd round my door, and when I say I won't, I won't. So you had better walk away, all of you, recollecting that I am a lawyer, and can get consequently more law and justice for a penny than you can get for a shilling."

"Well," said Mr. Jones, "I never did hear a more sensible speech than that ere in all my life, it beats nothing into unkimmon small bits. One cheer and let's mizzle. Hurray—hip, hip, hip, hurrah."

The mob seconded the cheer with right good-will, as all mobs are always willing to do upon any and every occasion or excuse. Then Mr. Jones, who guessed that Miranda was anxious to be clear of the assemblage, and be left free to act as her feelings might dictate, drew off the throng more quickly and easily than such a feat could have been accomplished by threats or remonstrances.

When Miranda and her friends had left the court, the chairman of the bench, after a short consultation with some of his colleagues, ordered the court to be cleared of all persons but themselves, and the parties holding official situations connected with the administration of the law.

When this was accomplished, he arose and said,—

"Gentlemen, in consenting to the easy and somewhat triumphant manner in which the prisoner, Miranda Rankley, has left this court, I dare say we each had the same natural motive.

" If any one circumstance more than another was likely to lead to the reapture of Rowland Percy, that circumstance is the leaving Miranda Rankley apparently at perfect liberty, but at the same time keeping upon all her movements and her correspondence, such a watchful eye as may speedily lead to a discovery of the hiding-place of the prisoner.''

" Hear! hear!" cried several of the magistrates.

" Gentlemen," continued the presiding magistrate, " there has not been a capital conviction in York for some years, and let it not gain currency that when we are so unhappy as to have among us a notorious criminal, we cannot execute the sentence of the law upon him.''

" Hear! hear!" was the response again to this remark, and one of the magistrates rising, said,—

" I would propose then, in accordance with the very accurate view taken of this subject by our chairman, that two of our most active and intelligent officers be specially appointed to watch Miranda Rankley, and follow her from house to house, wherever she may go."

This resolution was agreed to, and after informing his brother magistrates that he, the chairman, had already taken care Miranda's immediate steps should be made known to him, two officers with full instructions and a *carte blanche* as to expense were deputed as spies upon the movements of Miranda.

That the magistracy of York, considering their peculiar position, were sufficiently justified in taking this course, we are not prepared flatly to deny, for although we and our readers are aware of the innocence of Rowland Percy, and the vile machinations by which his name had been blackened, and he had been made to appear the ruthless murderer that many believed him, they were not; and as administrators of the law, they were compelled to take every legitimate means of again securing the escaped criminal.

Leaving then the magistracy to adopt what measures they might think proper, in pursuance of their duty, we shall again follow the fortunes of the heroic girl, who, we hope, has placed herself so near the affections of our readers.

When Mr. Anderson saw that the mob was fairly away from his door by the interposition of Mr. Jones, he insisted that Miranda should partake of some refreshment, before he would speak to her concerning her ulterior views or future objects. This, at his earnest solicitation, she was compelled to do, and then with great earnestness of manner he said to her,—

" Now, Miranda, you must be extremely cautious in your future acts, for although, as circumstances are at present, you will never be called upon to answer the charge laid against you, yet were it to be discovered, as no doubt it will be attentively watched for, that you hold any communication with Rowland Percy, it may lead not only to his recapture, but your own lengthened imprisonment.''

" I will be cautious,'' said Miranda, " both for his sake and for the sake of those dear friends who have so kindly assisted me in this exigency. I must strive, Mr. Anderson, to meet him. I must strive again to look into his face with calmer feelings than those which necessarily agitated us when last we parted. It may be wrong, and I may be foolish, but I do wish again to see him smile, and hear him tell me that I have saved him.''

" You run the greatest risk, Miranda," said Mr. Anderson; " besides how can you tell the direction in which Mr. Percy has proceeded?''

" He will go to London," said Miranda, " of that I am aware, and thither must I go to follow him. Believe me, Mr. Anderson, I will be most cautious, and doubly so, when I consider that indiscretion upon my part may commit, in some manner, you, and the kind friend who, with you, has become a surety for me.''

" Nay," said Mr. Anderson, " understand that, clearly, Miranda. All that we are committed to, is, upon pain of forfeiting a certain sum of money to produce you, should you be called upon, so that we are safe enough. Your commission of any new act obnoxious to the law, cannot affect us, so long as you surrender yourself to its consequences ; but it is for your own sake, Miranda, that I implore you to be careful, as well as for the sake of Rowland."

" I will, I will," said Miranda.

" Do not, oh do not," continued Mr. Anderson, "be lulled into any fancied security ; do not imagine that you will be unwatched, or yonr minutest actions unnoticed. Our greatest, deaiest hope must still be rather in circumstances arising to clear Mr. Percy of his alleged guilt, than from a continued success in secreting him from the ministers of the law."

" You are right, you are right," said Miranda, " it is indeed on the establishment of his innocence that I build my dearest, my fondest hopes."

" Do so ever," rejoined Mr. Anderson ; " and now, Miranda, I am sorry to say, that the expectation I once entertained of rescuing from the general wreck some private portion of old Mr. Percy's property, has proved fallacious—he is utterly and totally destitute."

" And so am I, and so am I," sighed Miranda. " Our trust must be in Heaven, for it alone can step between us and the miseries of want."

Mr. Anderson, for some moments looked as if a little confused, and then he said in a low tone,—

" Miranda, you will, I am sure, pardon me for repeating to you the offer I have before made you, that is, that you shall honour my humble abode by becoming its permanent guest. You can remain with me in peace and tranquility, awaiting calmly that happy time which I hope will soon dawn upon your fortunes."

" I cannot, I cannot," sighed Miranda.

" Nay, think again, think again, Miranda," urged Mr. Anderson.

" I have thought," she said, mournfully, " thought deeply of this, the kindest offer I shall ever meet with ; but I have duties, Mr. Anderson, which prevent my accepting it. You wish me to sit down here in peace, waiting with serenity for a happier day. Think you I could know peace or serenity, while my mind was tortured with uncertainty concerning the fate of those with whom, now that my own parents are in the cold grave, I must henceforward remain ? We may suffer greatly, but we must suffer together."

" I am answered, Miranda," said Mr. Anderson, " but it is with grief that I say so. At least, let me have the consolation of knowing beforehand, of any step you may take for the furtherance of those views so near and dear to your heart."

" You shall know," said Miranda, " and, let my fate be what it may, there is no name that will mingle itself more purely with my better and happpier feelings than yours."

Miranda then rose to depart, and Mr. Anderson strove to conceal his emotion by affecting to search for his hat, in order to escort her to her lodgings.

CHAPTER LXXXII.

THE CONVERSATION BETWEEN VARLEY AND TWITTER.—THE DISCOMFORTED VIL-LAINS.—THE CRAFTINESS OF VARLEY, AND THE DEFEAT OF THE AVARICE OF TWITTER.

It was some time after Miranda's liberation upon bail, that in the lodging first occupied by Bernard Varley, sat Samuel Twittei, confionted by the dark instigator of his more recent crimes, and trembling in every limb as he listened to Varley's account of the escape of Rowland Percy from prison, and the manner in which Miranda Rankley had succeeded, after all, in foiling their villanous schemes.

Bleeding and disfigured as he was from the violence of the crowd, and his clothing rent in mary places, Bernard Varley's exciting narrative carried with it to the shrinking soul of Twitter, a terrible truthfulness, and filled him with an alarm that seemed almost sufficient to stop the even current of his existence.

He rung his hands despairingly as Varley concluded his narrative.

"What is to be done?—what is to be done?" he cried. "We are lost—we are lost. All will be discovered. I think I see the scaffold even now being prepared for us—I see the fatal noose—I hear the infuriated populace. Oh! Bernard Varley—Bernard Varley—what a pit of horrors have you brought me into, and how can I escape?"

Varley looked upon Twitter for some minutes in silence; but during those moments, such an expression of ferocity crossed his countenance, that Twitter shrunk as far from him as possible, as if anticipating some sudden act of violence from his hands.

Nor were his fears diminished, when Varley took from his pocket a large knife, which he deliberataly opened, the blade of which was secured by a spring, so that the weapon became as formidable a dagger, as could be constructed.

"No—no—no!" cried Twitter. "Have mercy, Bernard Varley! Do not murder me. I cannot—dare not die; and, at least not from your hands should the blow come.'"

"Listen to me," said Varley, in a tone of such concentrated rage, that it sounded more like the voice of a wild beast than the voice of a human being. "Listen to me, Samuel Twitter. If you favour me with any more of your reproaches, about what you say I have led you into, I will cut your throat, and so be rid at once of the dastardly coward who shrunk not from the wages of murder, but avoided in abject fear, the deed itself."

"Mercy—mercy!" said Twitter. "I did not mean, Varley, to accuse you. You have been a great friend—an excellent friend to me; but I was so sadly grieved at the escape of Rowland Percy, that you may believe me, I know not what I said."

"Beware, for the future," said Varley; "upon any, even the slightest motion of treachery from you—or, if you dare to goad me with reproaches, you shall die."

"You—you—do not suspect me?" said Twitter.

"Of what?" said Varley.

"Treachery."

"I shall, if you protest too much; and if my supicions be once aroused, I will, wash away the uncomfortable thought in your blood. Now, beware of what you say or do."

"Yes, I will," said Twitter. "You may depend upon me, Varley; but you know, I have not your bold, daring spirit; and, after all—I—I— but no matter—excuse me?"

"Speak," cried Varley. "Whatwere you about to say?"

"Oh, it was nothing—I'd rather not say it.—You would be angry—and—beside —I forget it, Varley."

"This moment let me hear it," said Varley, "or——"

He opened the knife again, and pointed it significantly at Twitter's throat, who, under such compulsion, really said what he had so prudently stopped himself in, for he was in too great a state of mental perturbation to invent anything less true and less offensive.

"It—it—was merely a casual remark, Bernard Varley," he stammered, "and what it meant, was not that I am in any hurry, oh, far from it; but as yet I had not pocketed any of the profits of the murder, although you know I have had several ot the disagreeables; that was all, Bernard Varley, don't be offended, it doesn't mean anything—a mere passing remark, that's all."

"Indeed," said Varley, "I shall give you some of what you call the profits when I please, aad not before; in the meantime I permit you to exist, for which you ought to be sufficiently thankful."

"But you know," gasped Twitter, "I was to have had six hundred-a-year, Varley."

"And shall have, unless I cut your throat before the first twelve-month comes round. You did not expect it in advance, did you?"

" No, no, no, not exactly, but it would have been a little pleasanter."

" Once for all, Samuel Twitter," said Varley, " understand your position. When all these affairs in which I have so great an interest, and which run so cross as if hell itsel had stepped in to cross me, are satisfactorily concluded, I will reward you handsomely ; but till then, Samuel Twitter, I tell you candidly, I will not trust you ; eat what you like—drink what you like—and sleep where you like, at my cost, and then, if you provoke me not in the interim to cut your throat, or blow out your brains, the time may come, when I shall place money in your hands, and such a sum too, as shall gratify your avarice, at the same time I shall bid you adieu for ever!"

" Oh! thank you, thank you," said Twitter ; " it's a very pleasant arrangement, but I have scarcely eaten anything for two days, my appetite ain't near so good as it was, and as for drinking, I am positively afraid to begin upon it."

" In those matters you may please yourself," said Varley ; " you see I have been quite confidential, and told you of my plans and intentions."

" I can't sleep either," whined Twitter ; " could you be so good as to name when you think you can quite conveniently give me some money, provided the little contingencies you mentioned do not occur in the meantime ; I should rather like to know, too, how much you intend to make it ?"

" These are considerations which will keep," said Bernard Varley ; " for the present, one sole consideration must be, in what manner, so as to present us with the greatest chance of success, we can commence an attentive search for Rowland Percy, for until he is surrendered to the law and executed, we shall be kept in continual apprehension on the score of the murder, all questions concerning which will be set at rest by his execution."

" Yes, yes," said Twitter, abstractedly, " who would have thought of him getting away ?"

" Besides," added Varley, as much to himself as to Twitter, " his death would have at once crushed all Miranda Rankley's energies, for she is not one who would fight up, against great sadness, for the mere ultimate prospect of revenge."

" Certainly," groaned Twitter, " if he had but been hanged it would have been much more agreeable ; but what is to be done, Bernard Varley ? What is to be done?"

" The proper authorities." said Varley, " will of course, as bound to do, use their best endeavours for the prisoner's recapture ; but as we are much more largely interested than they, so will our exertions be more earnest, and more likely to be effectual ;—we must ourselves seek him, and if possible deliver him again to the hands of justice."

Although Miranda spoke trustingly of her hopes of the future to Mr. Anderson, each moment, as her mind became more and more relieved from immediate anxiety concerning Rowland, the melancholy destitution of both his and her own situation would obtrude itself upon her mind, filling her with uneasy thoughts, and suggesting much prospective misery.

There was likewise one circumstance which rendered both her and Rowland's situation considerably worse than what it might have been under circumstances of ordinary poverty ; that circumstance was, that Rowland Percy, from the peculiarity of his position, could not have the free use and action of those powers with which Heaven had gifted him ; nor could she, from the necessity for extreme caution in all her movements, as associated with him, he said to be quite free to turn those accomplishments to account, upon which she shuddered to think she must rely as a provision for the future.

These were thoughts which she would not communicate to Mr. Anderson, because she feared that his generous spirit would outrun his means in some attempt to better the condition of those for whom he felt such true sympathy.

As for inhabiting the house on the footing of a guest, whose period of stay should be unlimited, and entering into, or attempting to enjoy, a life of comparative luxury, while Rowland Percy might be wanting the common necessaries of existence, it was a thing she could not think of—dream of for a moment, without such an exquisite pang of agony, that she at once discarded the thought from her bosom.

Nor could she make up her mind to tell Mr. Anderson of her immediate intention of following Rowland to London, which, from her previous communication with Ned Witlet, she was aware would be his place of destination.

It will look, she thought, so like begging of him the means wherewith to acomplish the journey, and that she so much shrunk from that she could not bring her lips to utter the words,

"I am going to travel nearly penniless from York to London, having, too, in my care one whom the heavy hand of misfortune has made prematurely old, and shattered the god-like power of reason to its base."

"And yet—and yet," she asked herself, "how are we to travel the many weary miles between here and London, upon a sum something less than twenty shillings, which I have in my possession ?"

This was a question she could not answer, but the painful thoughts it gave rise to brought her to the street in which she lived, when, taking a kind leave of Mr, Anderson—a farewell which he thought temporary, but which lasted for a long weary time, she approached the step of her own door.

Before, however, she could make any application for admission, a singular-looking creature stepped up to her—it appeared to be a woman by the apparel—although the size of the lady was prodigious, and Miranda was not a little surprised to hear the voice of Mr. Jones say.

"Don't be arter being skeared, mum—miss, I means—the people takes me for a female in an interesting 'sit——on, I means an interesting female—excuse me mum—miss, I does'nt know what I was going to say."

CHAPTER LXXXIII.

MR. JONES'S SYMPATHY.—THE LETTER TO ROWLAND PERCY.—THE FIVE-POUND NOTE.

MIRANDA looked with the most intense astonishment at Mr. Jones in his singular disguise, the purport and object of which she could not for a moment imagine.

"I do not know you," she said, " but I recognise your voice as one which has uttered friendly sentiments to me and mine."

"That ere is the blessed ticket, mum," said Mr. Jones, " though more politerer than I could have said it, notwithstanding, mum, my edication ; the slashing 'squire, that is to say, mum, Neddy the Night Owl, and we is elderly pals, we know what's o'clock, mum—and we's up to a whole blessed jar of snuff, and ever such a pile of pinches above it. I thinks it's right and proper to be explanatory, mum, as you mightn't know what a slashing toby was, and not belonging to the family, mightn't understand crummy pattern."

Miranda looked, as well she might, rather amazed at this explanatory speech, and a slight suspicion crossed her mind that Mr. Jones must have been sacrificing largely to the rosy god.

"I dare say," she said, "either to congratulate me upon my success, or sympathise with me for my sorows ; in 'either case I thank you, and as I am now at my own home, I will bid you farewell."

"Niver so fast—niver so fast," said Mr. Jones ; "is that ere the way you treats a lady, mum? I tells you what it is, it won't be safe for you to be a writing walentines and love letters to youug Mr. Percy. Neddy and I knows that—so I am to be what he calls the blessed medium of correspondence. You are to tell me as you isn't particular down on your luck, and I'm to write to Neddy, when, you see, he'll shew your sweetheart the hepistles."

Miranda now began to have a glimmering of what Mr. Jones meant, and she said—

"By Neddy you mean he who so kindly assisted me in effecting the escape of Mr. Percy?"

"Right, again," said Mr. Jones. "I am going to send off my blessed letter to-day, and I only wants to know what I shall say in the tender line on your account."

"Say that I am well, very well," said Miranda; "say that I have met with kindness, sympathy, and protection ; and say that I am happy in the hope of soon meeting him who is dearer to me in his misfortunes than he ever was in his prosperity."

Mr. Jones listened to this speech with the most ludicrous air of attention, which shewed that he was indeed making a violent mental effort to understand it.

"I'll try and say it, mum," he remarked, when Miranda had done speaking? "but I'd ha' preferred it being in English, mum, as I ain't larned in furrin languages."

"What I have said, I have endeavoured to say simply," said Miranda; "but shall I write it ?"

"No, mum, that wouldn't answer," said Jones ; "Neddy and I has a perticlar way of speaking about people, that you'd be never so long in larning, so that if our letters should come across the hands of the beaks, they wouldn't know what to make on 'em."

"But why are you in this singular disguise ?" said Miranda.

"'Cos of the blessed riot act," said Jones ; "they is making wiolent exertinos to nab me on account of that ere, so I thought I'd come it in the delicate young female line ; I'm rather afeared of the fellows, to be sure, but only let one on 'em follow me too close, and if I don't fetch him a rum 'un on the right ogle, my name isn't Jones ; and now, mum, just look down the street at them ere two gentlemen as is pretending to converse about nothing."

"There are certainly two persons conversing," said Miranda.

"It's gammon—it's gammon, mum," said Jones." You've been to a theatre, I suppose ?"

"Yes," said Miranda, "I certainly have."

"Then you've seen fellers purtend to drink goblets of rosy ; but that's gammon—broad-wheeled gammon—they don't drink nothing. So it is with these ere fellows, they ain't a-talking nothing, but they've got such an eye on you as never was."

"An eye on me !" said Miranda.

"Yes, mum. Them's officers : they're 'pinted to watch you, and you'll see if they doesn't ; so just put the kibosh ou them. if you please, mum."

Miranda quite despaired of asking Mr. Jones what the kibosh was, so she merely said,—

"I thank you for your caution and doubtly thank you for the kind feeling you have manifested towards me and mine."

Miranda then knocked at the door of her humble dwelling : while Mr. Jones proceeded down the street, with the most ridiculous affectation of a female walk and manner that can be imagined.

He was quite right when he pointed out the two individuals, apparently conversing, at the corner of the street, as officers, for they were those who had been deputed by the magistracy to watch Miranda's minutest proceedings, and immediately that they saw her fairly within the house, they walked up to the door. One then said to the other,—

"We must take this job, now, by turns. You stay here, and if she should come out again, you must follow her closely, and see where she goes, and in the course of two or three hours, if you fairly get her housed anywhere, you can get some boy to come to me at my house, and I will relieve your watch."

"That will do," said the other. "There's no occasion for two of us at once;

but my own opinion is, that we may watch her about York to no purpose, for Percy is off long before this, and a great fool he is if he don't get out of the country."

"Do you really think he did the murder!" said the other.

"What's that to us?" was the reply. "We're officers, and it's our duty to get him hanged if we can, while, certainly, he's a great flat if he lets us."

The one officer was then left as a sentinel at Miranda's door; a proceeding, however, which, now that she had been warned both by Mr. Anderson and Jones that she was watched, was not likely to be half so effective as it otherwise might have been.

Her first inquiry of the people of the house was concerning Mr. Percy, and she was told that he had slept nearly the whole of the time she had been absent, only waking now and then at long intervals, to utter some incoherent words respecting her and his son, and then again to relapse into a deep and quiet slumber.

With many thanks to the people of the house for their attention to him during her absence, she repaired to her own room, on the table of which was a letter, with the simple address of—

"Miss Miranda Rankley."

Miranda timidly opened it, in some suspicion as to whom it could come from. The inside was a complete blank, but from the enclosure fell a Bank of England note for five pounds.

Small as this sum was, it was indeed a treasure to Miranda Rankley, for the harassing, and, to her, dreadful thought, had arisen, that her small amount of cash could not possibly suffice, even to discharge the rent due at the temporary lodging,

No. 41.

a matter which, in the hurry and excitement of the last deeply anxious week, she had not thought of previously.

"From whom," she said, "can this kindly donation come? From Mr. Anderson, doubtless, or from Rowland's counsel. Either of them are capable of this generous and delicate act. Heaven reward and bless them both, for their kindness to me in my deep affliction, and the best present thanks I can give them, is without scruple to make use of their kind bounty."

Miranda was wrong, for the five pounds had come from Ned Witlet, whose resources, being rather of a variable nature, would not at that present moment permit him to bestow more upon Miranda, or he would have lacked the means of reaching London with Rowland Percy.

The letter had been left there by Mr. Jones, who had received a strict injunction from Ned Witlet not to mention it to Miranda.

As Mr. Percy still slept, Miranda sat down in the silence of her own little chamber, fully and carefully to consider what should be her next step. Her thoughts all tended towards London, where alone there could be a hope of meeting with Rowland, and the more she considered her situation in York, and the many disagreeables it would give rise to, the more did her plan present itself to her in attractive colours.

Besides, the idea of being under police surveillance at York, was to her painful and harassing. Such, she thought, would not be the case in London, so very far as it was from the scene of the events which had placed her in so remarkable a position.

While she was immersed in these reflections, all of which were tending towards her resolution to leave York as speedily as possible, a circumstance occurred which materially strengthened her resolution, that was, the entrance into the room of the woman of the house, who, with a hesitation of manner that showed she rather shrunk from her task, said.—

"If you please, Miss Rankley, I am very sorry, but my husband thinks we shall want the apartments. There's been so much noise and disturbance in York about you, you know, miss, that my husband thinks, you see——"

"Enough—enough," said Miranda; "I quite understand—I will leave you to-morrow."

"Thank you, miss," said the woman. "There's no particular hurry; but my husband's such a quiet man, that he can't bear notorious characters."

"I will go to-morrow evening," said Miranda.

There was nothing in Miranda's tone to encourage further conversation, so the woman left the room without another word.

"Now I am decided," said Miranda; "I am become a proscribed being in York—a person to be shunned, and shut out from the ordinary feelings of humanity, because I have been so unhappy as to have my father murdered, and my betrothed husband wrongfully accused of the same. Well—well, be it so, I am decided—I am decided. To-morrow night I will leave York. Far from here, I shall, at least, have the satisfaction of sinking into obscurity, and avoiding that terrible notoriety which I percieve, in York, would become so harassing and full of evils. To-morrow night—to-morrow night. Shall I, or shall I not, comunicate my intention to Mr Anderson? What would be his course of conduct? He will try to combat my intention by every means; he will try to dissuade me from this step, and I should then have the pain of acting in contradiction to the urgent remonstrance of my best friend. Then, when he found me obstinately fixed upon my purpose, he would think himself called upon to make some effort to assist me, that might prejudice himself and family. I will tell no one—I will tell no one, trusting only in that Providence which has already saved Rowland Percy from the death which seemed inevitable. I will, with no other company than the melancholy one of his afflicted father, proceed to London."

Miranda had been so brought up as the child of luxury, with not a wish ungratified, and so little care, knowledge, or concern about money, or its value, that when she had formed this resolution, she had not the slightest idea of how far her limited pecuniary resources would second her inclination.

Nay, how far she should be safe in making inquiries on that subject she knew not. That there were frequent conveyances from York to London she was well aware; but what a frightful risk of detection in her flight, and of being followed should she run, by proceeding in a public conveyance.

From these considerations Miranda certainly correctly enough concluded that her best and safest plan would be to proceed on foot on her journey however long and toilsome it might become.

By such a course of proceeding, too, there would be the greatest possible facility in discovering if she were really followed. While among the passengers in a stage coach how could she pick out any one in particular on whom to fix the suspicion of following her to the metropolis.

The constant recurrence, however, of the same face halting where she should halt, and keeping pace with her and old Mr. Percy to London, would be conclusive evidence that a spy was watching her movements, and she could accordingly make what deviations in her direct route such a circumstance might render politic.

Now she wished repeatedly that she had asked of Jones during her recent interview with him, some direct clue by which she could find Witlet and Rowland Percy in London: for she had heard sufficient talk of that vast metropolis to be aware of the extreme difficulty of finding any stranger within its populous precincts, particularly when that stranger was using his utmost endeavours to render his name and abode a secret.

But where was she to seek Jones, in order to procure this information? This was a question which Miranda could not answer, and after much more anxious and painful reflection, she felt herself compelled to trust to chance, and what good fortune might occur to her in the prosecution of her arduous undertaking; but having once made that resolution, she swerved not from it, and looked upon her approaching journey to London as a thing determined upon, and not to be set aside.

She then rose, and gently approached the bedside of the slumbering Mr. Percy.

He opened his eyes at the moment, and fixed them upon her's with a mournful expression, as he said—

"Is it indeed you, Miranda Rankley, or some pure spirit that is borrowing new grace and beauty by assuming your face and form?"

"It is I—it is I," said Miranda.

CHAPTER LXXXIV.

THE PURSUIT FROM YORK.—JOE AND HIS TURNIPS.—A TOO ACTIVE OFFICER.—NED WITLET'S SCHEME OF ESCAPE.

WE left Rowland Percy and his friend, Ned Witlet, at the road-side inn precisely as the sound of horses' feet proceeding from York caused a pang of alarm to pervade Rowland's bosom, and to proclaim to Witlet the necessity of extreme caution and circumspection in their proceedings.

"Hush—hush!" he said; "do not betray the slightest flurry or alarm. If those who are approaching be enemies, you may depend they will at least receive no assistance from the people who keep this house. Get into the cart again, and trust to me."

Rowland did as he was desired, and sprung with celerity into the chaise-cart, while Witlet was busy opening a gate by the side of the house, which led to some stabling and a wilderness of a garden at the back of the premises.

Meantime the clattering sound of the hoofs of the approaching horses came more and more distinctly to their ears, now and then intermingled with the sound of voices, as if those approaching were conversing in loud and eager tones.

Ned Witlet, without another word, took the head of the horse, and leading him through the gate, then closed it, saying, in a low tone to Percy—

"We must give them the double if possible—always provided they are our pursuers, which we shall have but little difficulty in discovering."

At this moment a side-door of the house opened, and a man appeared with a lantern in his hand.

"Hilloa!" he cried; "make yourself at home, do, whoever you are, there's nothing like it. Open people's gates at any hour of the night, and tramp in. Curse you, who are you?"

"Find out," said Ned.

The man laughed as he immediately added—

"I suppose I'm getting a fool in my old age, for I ought to have known, too, that nobody but you would have had such infernal impudence. Well, well, 'squire, the road from London to York, I believe, is all your own, and is likely to remain so for many a year to come."

"Silence," cried Witlet. "You hear the sounds of those horses' feet?"

"Rather," said the man. "They seem in a hurry, but they have got the hill to come up, and won't be here for five minutes yet, though you'd fancy by the sound of their hoofs that they were almost at our door.

"When they do came up," said Ned, "mind there's nobody here; and I'll trouble you to ask them what they want, and repeat their answer in as loud a voice as you like, and leave me then to take care of myself."

The man seemed to think this was very funny, for he chuckled enormously under his breath, and then said—

"Leave you to take care of yourself;—I rather think I may. Going to London, eh?"

"Yes," said Ned,

"Ah, well," added the man, "you must have begun business soon out of York, if so be as these horsemen are after you."

"You're right," said Ned. "Good night to you."

He then led the horse in the dark for some four or five hundred yards over an uneven piece of waste ground at the back of the house, when he took down another gate, whispering to Rowland :—

"If these are our pursuers, and I must say it looks a little like it, they had better be before us than behind us, for we don't want to catch them, and they do us."

"But think you they will go on," said Rowland, "without the news that we are before them?"

"Yes," replied Witlet, "no doubt they will. At least, for some considerable distance. My principal object, however, is to find if we are pursued so closely or not. If this should turn out to be a false alarm, we have amply sufficient start of them to pursue our journey without further trouble; but if the officers are really upon our heels, why, we must even make the best of it, and outwit them if we can't outrun them."

By this time the horsemen had reached the door of the little old-fashioned inn, but not a light was visible, and the man who kept it was too determined to seem profoundly asleep to pay the slightest attention to the bawling and shouting of the four well mounted and well armed men, for there was that number, who drew up at his door.

"Hilloa! hilloa!" cried the foremost. "D—n him, he sleeps too sound for it to be real."

He flung himself off his horse and applied the butt-end of his whip with violence against the door of the house; scarcely, however, had he done so, when with a loud oath he rushed into the road again, for from one of the upper windows the landlord had precipitated some fluid of a very questionable character upon his head, at the same time that he cried out :—

" So, I've nabbed you at last, have I? You won't try that again, any how."

" Why, what do you mean, you fool?" said the horseman.

" Why, this is the third night you've been hamering at my door," said the landlord ; "but I'm even with you at last."

" Come, come," cried one of the horsemen, " none of that. My name is Viggers, I dare say you've heard it before."

" Oh, dear yes," said the landlord ; "how's Mrs. Viggers and the little Viggerses? Are you any relation to Viggers the officer ?"

" You know well I am Viggers the officer," was the reply.

" Oh !" said the landlord ; raising his voice to a stentorian pitch, " you are Viggers the officer from York, are you ?"

" What the deuce makes you hollah that way ?" said the officer.

" Because I've got a stiff neck," was the reply.

" D—n you and your neck too," muttered the officer to himself, and then in a loud tone, he cried—

" Has there been a chaise-cart past with two men in it ?"

" Yes," said the landlord.

" Ay, indeed !" said Viggers the officer. " When ?"

" Why, let me see," said the landlord in a deliberative tone of voice.

" Tell me the exact time, and here's a guinea for you," cried Viggers.

" Throw up the guinea and I'll tell you, honour bright."

" Thank you for nothing," cried the officer ; " you shall have the guinea when I come back. I've got a stiff neck too."

" Oh, indeed," said the landlord, " you'll never get rid of that till a good strong rope is put round it, I'm thinking."

" Come, come, nonsense—earn your guinea, Joe. When did the chaise cart come past ?"

" Last Monday was a week, my fancy maggot," said Joe, as he shut the window with a bang.

The officer stood for a moment uttering some diabolical curses, for he was sadly provoked at being outwitted in the little dialogue, before his three companions. He then said—

" Here, Ned Wilkins, dismount and come with me, we shall soon find if any chaise-cart is on old Joe's premises. You, Evans and Smith, keep a good eye on the road."

The voice of the landlord had been quite sufficiently high to reach the ears of Witlet and Rowland Percy, so that they became well possessed of the danger which awaited them.

" It is as I suspected," said Witlet, " we have been seen by some one, and are now pursued hotly from York, but it will go hard with us but we will get the better of them. It is a great object to know where the foe is situated, and those fellows will now go galloping a considerable distance on the road with the notion of overtaking us at last, little suspecting that we are behind them."

" But still we must meet them," said Percy, " for as they precede us the whole of the way, I do not see how we are to prevent ourselves encountering them on their return."

" We shall certainly encounter them," said Witlet, "unless by some rare piece of good fortune we are housed somewhere and pass by them on their return ; but our object, now that we know our danger, must be to render a meeting with them as harmless as possible, which, if you will leave it to me, I think I can accomplish."

" I am but too thankful," said Rowland, " to be in such good hands."

While this conversation was proceeding in a low and cautious voice, Witlet had led the horse through the second gate he had opened, which brought them into a meadow, over the long grass of which the wheels rolled noiselessly, and which seemed of immense length.

" This meadow," said Witlet, " is nearly seven acres in length, and takes us a considerable distance parallel to the road back again to York ; from another gate, at its extremity, we can emerge into the high road, allowing our pursuers to proceed at as hard a pace as they please a-head of us."

" We are succeeding in avoiding them," said Percy, " and one great uneasiness off our minds consists in what I think we may fairly presume to be a fact, namely that we shall have no other pursuers from York."

" True," said Witlet ; " and in consequence we need not be listening with apprehension to the sound of every horse's foot behind us. Hark, now—our pursuers are off again."

As he spoke the whole party of officers were heard leaving the door of the public-house at a hard trot, in the direction of London, fully beleiving that those they sought must be still in advance of them, and that they must speedily overtake one horse encumbered with a chaise-cart, and the weight of two men.

Ned Witlet then took down the gate which terminated the long meadow, on the other side of which was the road, and then got into the cart, saying—

" Now, Mr. Percy, I have better hopes of your escape than ever I had. This man Viggers is an active and daring officer, and it is something to know what he is about, and that he is not behind us."

" Who could have given notice," said Percy, " of the direction of our flight ?"

" Oh," said Witlet, " that may have been quite accidental. Very diligent inquiry would be almost certain to obtain a description of every kind of vehicle that passed from York on the London road, combined, too, most probably with some sort of notion of the persons within it. But here we are again at Joe's door."

The landlord seemed to be well aware that Ned Witlet would make his appearance, and was waiting for him at his door-porch, accompanied by the lantern, with which he had not condescended to lighten the darkness of Mr. Viggers and his companions.

At Witlet's suggestion Rowland alighted from the chaise-cart, and they entered the doorway of the ancient road-side inn.

" Come in—come in," cried the landlord, as he held the lantern up in Witlet's face. " I thought you would come back, and it does my heart good to see you." Then, as his eyes suddenly fell upon the pale pensive face of Rowland Percy, he cried, " Hilloa, Ned ! who the devil's that ? I have heard you say you would never have a pal in your line of business."

" Nor is this gentleman one," said Witlet. " He is merely a friend of mine, in a little difficulty."

" Then it was arter him that Muster Viggers come ?"

" It was ; but when I tell you that he is a friend of mine, that is sufficient for you, Joe."

" In course—in course," said Joe. " Walk in sir. Perhaps you ain't aware that Dick Turpin stopped here on his famous ride from London to York, to give his horse a mouthful of wet hay. I remember him as if it was yesterday, although I was but a youngster then, for it's a matter of five-and-forty years ago. " Joe, my lad," said he, " and he throw'd me a guinea, that hit me a rap edgeways on the poll that made me grin again—" Joe," said he, " there's some gentlemen coming up, and they are rather warm ; tell 'em some cold brandy and water is the best thing they can take, and that Dick Turpin will pay for it." Then off he cantered like a hemperor. Oh them was times—them was times !"

" There now," said Ned Witlet, " when you begin about Dick Turpin there's no knowing when it'll end ; so shut up your domino slap at once, Joe."

" But it's enough to make a fellow punch his own head," added Joe, " to think of the times as is gone. I could kick myself, I could with vexation."

" You could trouble a friend on these occasions," said Ned, as he nearly disturbed the equilibrium of Joe, by something between a projection forward with his oot and a kick. " But, hark ye, Joe, you must pull up a lot of turnips, for I mean to take them to London with me."

" Do yer ?" said Joe. " That's a rum start, anyhow."

"I want a smock-frock, too," said Witlet, "and a carter's hat; so bustle, Joe, bustle."

"How many do you want?" said Joe.

"Enough to fill the chaise-cart," was the reply.

"Then it will take me and Bob a full hour to dig 'em, purwided we works ike niggars."

So saying, the landlord departed to do Witlet's bidding, singing as he went the one song which delighted his fancy above all others, and which ran thus :—

> "The good old times we ne'er shall see,
>   The times beloved by all ;
> When highwaymen were on the road,
>   And stopped both great and small.
>
> When not a lord in all the land,
>   Though he were young or old,
> Could say he travelled scathless for
>   Dick Turpin stout and bold.
>
> The moon was high on Bagshot heath,
>   A bishop sleek was driving,
> Quoth Turpin, bold, I love the church,
>   For it is always thriving.
>
> But as my tithes I cannot count,
>   As I am but a dunce,
> Your watches, rings, and purse, hand out,
>   I'll take them all at once."

The landlord was better than his word, for in less than an hour the chaise cart was tolerably filled with good bunches of turnips, and the necessary materials of dress for changing Witlet's appearance were procured.

"Now, Mr. Percy," he said "we can get on a little. I think I shall make a cavity down among these turnips, upon which I will spread my cloak, where you may lie comfortably, and should it become necessary, you must not mind me covering you up face and all, with some of the bunches. You will find plenty of cavities through which to breath, and every petty village and farmer"s name between York and London is so well known to me, that you may trust to me for making a good story should we be questioned. Moreover, you must hide yourself as we go through every turnpike, so that there shall be no report current of a chaise-cart, with two men in it, being upon the road. Good night Joe."

"Good night," said Joe. "Lord love you, you put me more in mind of Dick Turpin than anybody else I ever seed, only you are a trifle taller. Ah, well, the times as is gone won't come back again."

With this sage remark, Joe closed his door, just as the sound of Witlet's chaise cart was dying away in the distance.

CHAPTER LXXXV.

TWITTER AT HOME.—THE LETTER TO VARLEY.—THE SCHEME OF SAFETY.—THE
SILVER SPOON AND A LITTLE MISUNDERSTANDING.

If to Miranda the city of York had become a peculiarly uncomfortable place to abide in, in consequence of the notoriety which had attended the spirited action she had committed, how much more disagreeable was Varley's position on the theatre of action in which he had been so singularly worsted.

He was certainly in full and undisturbed possession of the Grange estates, the ample revenue of which had touched his cupidity before his wild adoration of Miranda had grown to its maddening height, but so replete was the superb mansion, in which the death of Sir George Rankley had taken place, with the most frightful reminiscences, that he, Varley, shrunk from even a visit to the spot, and had been even for some days past possessed with a notion of getting rid of it for a large sum in cash, and never again blasting his eyes with the sight of it.

The sudden and unexpected escape of Rowland Percy had sadly deranged all his thoughts and plans, and confounding that chaos of conflicting thoughts and feelings, some portion of which might have been allayed by the death of the innocent Rowland, he felt towards that unhappy victim of his malice and his hatred all the revengeful feelings which actuate such minds towards those whom they have deeply injured.

Nothing but Rowland Percy's death could possibly satisfy him that he had nothing to fear from the fearful retribution which he felt that Rowland Percy had a right to exact from him.

Then his passion for Miranda was far, very far from being weakened by the crowd of insurmountable obstacles that seemed to surround it. It seemed to gather strength and fresh fire, as he lost hope, and when he spoke of following Rowland Percy to the metropolis, he had full conviction that he should be likewise following Miranda, for he felt that with her spirited determination and devotion she would not be long absent from the side of him, for whom she had already sacrificed so much.

His fears of Twitter were decidedly on the increase, for he saw that the valet deeply regretted his involvement in the whole transaction, which had called upon him for so much personal exertion and deeper anxiety than he had ever calculated upon. To regret his connection with him, Varley, must surely be but the precursor to the adoption of some means of severing it, and Varley was resolved to keep him destitute of finances, in the manner he had openly avowed, for the purpose of having a hold upon him from hour to hour, which he could not otherwise obtain.

The proposed journey to London, in search of Rowland Percy and Miranda, provided it were to be found that she had left York, presented itself to Samuel Twitter in far from alluring colours, and yet what could he do?

"I might turn king's evidence," he groaned, "and Bernard Varley would be hanged, which certainly would be a great satisfaction to me, and exceedingly pleasant to my feelings; but what should I get by it? Nothing—just nothing: I could expect nothing from Miranda, for she would hardly reward me for telling the truth, because I was disappointed of being paid for keeping it a secret. I dare say they would'nt hang me—that is, I don't think they could: but they would be sure to put me in prison for a good while, or transport me, and what is called in all the newspapers, the learned and humane judge, would tell me to think myself well off that a merciful view was taken of my case by his majesty's advisers, and that I was not to be hanged upon my own confession, but transported beyond the seas for my natural life, or put in prison for a long while to hard labour."

Twitter uttered a deep groan as he summed up these reflections, by saying, "I should like very much to turn king's evidence, but I dare not. Fool that I have been, I was a great deal better off before this transaction than I am now, for then I had my salary as valet to Sir George, and besides, he was very unsuspicious and I kept on robbing the house wholesale. Now what a wretch I am; I've no salary from anybody, and since I have been in this house I have only got possession of one silver tablespoon, and that I'm afraid to sell, although I have got out the man's initials, by working it to and fro on the window-sill."

Tremblingly alive likewise, as he was, to the perils of his situation, or to what he supposed the perils of it, from the violence of the York mob, he feared to venture into the streets, although Varley's prohibition extended not after the morning appointed for Rowland's execution, and perhaps, had he been not so tortured and afflicted by Varley's want of faith with him, and the manner in which he found himself so completely in that villain's power, he might have looked upon his journey to London with no very disagreeable sensations, but as it was, he shrank from it, as entailing upon him additional trouble and inconvenience, literally for nothing.

He was thus reflecting, and in this most unenviable state of mind, when a letter was brought into the room, addressed to Bernard Varley.

Twitter, upon an examination of the post-mark, found that the letter came from

Liverpool, and concerned as he was with Bernard Varley, he became seized with an earnest curiosity to know what it could contain, since, during the whole period of Varley's residence at the Grange, not one communication had arrived for him.

"Varley has but recently left me," he said. "He cannot know of this letter coming; if I could but obtain a glimpse of its contents, it might possibly give some hint as to my future action, that would force him to draw his purse-strings in my favour. If I could possibly convict him of any other transaction, which

No. 42.

would make him amenable to the laws, than this one in which I myself am so deeply involved, it would give me more hold upon him; if I dared now open this letter, my wish might be gratified, and yet I tremble—I tremble—lest he should discover it."

As he spoke, Twitter turned the letter over and over, and carefully examined the large black seal with which it was fastened.

"I will try—I will try,'" he muttered. "I have before opened letters, and re-sealed them without detection, and why should I not this one? I will try—yes—I will try."

He then rung for a light, and when one was brought to him, he heated the blade of his penknife, which he carefully slipped under the waxen seal, so as to release it whole, and unblemished, from its hold.

There was scarcely a mean act of this description which Samuel Twitter had not at one time or other during his life practised; he, therefore, got through the present manœuvre with tolerable cleverness, and there lay Bernard Varley's letter open before him.

It was short, and to the following effect:—

"SIR,—Agreeably to your written instructions, I have purchased for you a small yacht, which, with her complement] of five" men, will cruise off the mouth of the Mersey, awaiting your good pleasure to come on board of her, for the trip you mention to the Mediterranean, but which I would not advise you to under take at this season of the year as you will scarcely derive that pleasure from it you anticipate.

"The name of the yacht is the Argus, and I have given full instructions to the intelligent men on board to attend particularly to your signal words of—'New Owner B. D.,' which you say you will use should you feel inclined to board her in an open boat.

"The price of the vessel, with her stores and fittings for three months, has rather exceeded sixteen hundred pounds, so that I have placed to your account the fifteen hundred pounds, transmitted to me, per cheque upon the Liverpool bankers, and shall feel happy to attend to your further commands.

"I am, sir, your very obedient and most humble servant,

"THOMAS SINGLETON, Shipping Agent."

Twitter read this epistle thrice over, before he uttered a word concerning its contents; then he drew a long breath, as he said,—

"So Bernard Varley contemplates escaping. I see it all—I see it all. He will convert, some day, all his ill-gotten property into money, and leave me to destitution and despair; that is his plan—that is his plan, or why should he keep me in this state of abject dependance upon him. I am lost—lost—lost! what will become of me? what will become of me? This letter is conclusive; it is as clear as the sun at noonday. Why should he buy a yacht at such a large expense but for such a purpose? What shall I—what can I—do to thwart him? I must adopt some instant action, and——"

A loud knock at the street door at this moment made Twitter's heart, to use common, but expressive words, leap into his mouth; for the dreadful supposition came across him, that it might be Varley, and what time had he to reseal the letter with that nicety and exactness which should defy the scrutinizing eyes of his companion in guilt.

To attempt it were madness, and in his agony of apprehension he blew out the candle, thrusting it, candlestick and all, into his pocket, together with the letter and his open penknife, after which he stood in the middle of the floor in such an agony of apprehension that no one could have avoided suspecting he had been guilty of something which he was frightfully anxious to conceal.

In another moment the door opened, and Bernard Varley entered the room. The first glance he bent upon Twitter, showed him that something extraordinary must have occurred, and, in a voice hovering between alarm and anger, he said,—

"How now, Twitter? your countenance betrays that you have some unusual ause of uneasiness, or——"

"Or what?" gasped Twitter.

"Or of concocting some villany against me," said Varley.

"No, no," said Twitter, whose lips were perfectly livid with fear, "indeed you are mistaken;" then he added, quite unconsciously adopting the concluding words of the letter, "I am, sir, your very obedient humble servant. I am, sir, upon my soul—I am, Bernard Varley. Don't look at me so; I—I—don't feel certainly very well just at this moment. It's a kind of dizziness, God bless me— and I can only just at this moment repeat that—sir, I am your very obedient and most humble servant."

So saying, Twitter sank into a chair with a deep groan, for he had a glimmering perception that he was saying a little more than he ought, and the more he kicked and floundered the more he should get into the mire.

Bernard Varley bent a keen, scrutinizing glance into his face, as he muttered between his clenched teeth,—

"Cowardly scoundrel, what have you been about? Your looks betray you; with all the will to become a villain, you lack the nerve, Samuel Twitter, to carry you through any one act; speak, or this moment shall be your last."

"Your most humble servant," groaned Twitter, in a perfect agony of fright, "I did'nt do it—I'd scorn the action,"

"What action!" said Varley, seizing him by the throat.

"N—n—n—nothing; I'm like a babe unborn, and, sir, your very obedient servant."

"Are you mad?" said Varley, "or has temporary fear of my discovery of something you have done deprived you of your reason for a time? Tell me all, this moment, or, by the infernal powers, I'll stop your breath—"

"Have mercy upon me," said Twitter, "give us our daily bread, as we forgive them that trespass against us!"

Varley shook him to and fro so violently that the candlestick in his pocket swung about, and rattled against his knife with an ominous sound.

"What have you in your pocket?" he cried,—"what have you in your pocket?"

"Nothing," said Twitter, gasping for breath, "I never had anything in my pocket in all my life—it's all a joke—amen! Don't you see me smile?—what will you take to drink?—I am, sir, your obedient and very humble servant."

Bernard Varley remained for some moments silent, for he really knew not what to say next, nor could he imagine what on earth could occasion Twitter's extreme emotion. Then suddenly a thought came across Twitter's mind that was as welcome as a ray of light from Heaven to some benighted wretch sinking from fatigue and hunger; as welcome as the word forgiveness to a shrieking soul which feels itself condemned by Heaven. He really laughed, and his face changed from a ghastly hue to its usual tallowy, but not so horrible a complexion. He plunged his hand into his pocket, and, in a tone between a scream and a laugh he cried,—

"Bernard Varley, I have stolen a silver spoon, and I had been afraid they had found it out. Don't be angry; there was W. M. B. on the handle, but I've nearly scrubbed it out. Here's the spoon, and I am, sir, your very obedient servant."

"D—n you for a fool, as you are," said Varley, as, snatching the spoon from Twitter's hand, he threw it in his face, and then in great anger left the apartment.

CHAPTER LXXXVI.

THE WANDERINGS OF A BLIGHTED BRAIN.—MR. JONES'S SECOND VISIT, AND IMITA-
TION OF A DELICATE YOUNG LADY.

MR. ANDERSON, although far from being a rich man, still felt that he could do
something for Miranda, even out of his limited resources, and with him to feel such
a conviction was to act upon it immediately, to its utmost extent.

After Miranda had left him, he proceeded immediately to the young barrister
who had taken so warm an interest in her cause, and with him held a consultation
as to what could be done for Miranda's permanent benefit.

It was then arranged and fully agreed upon between them that, without saying
anything to her upon the subject, they should go among the friends of the late Sir
George Rankley, and those influential and wealthy persons in and about York,
who might be induced to believe in Rowland Percy's innocence, and admire the
heroism of Miranda, in order to raise quietly, and without any public *eclat*, a
subscription which should enable her to turn the abilities and acomplishments she
possessed to some permament advantage.

The delicacy which Mr. Anderson felt of communicating any such proceeding
to Miranda prevented him from visiting her that day, and thus it was that a want
of free and unreserved confidence arose between Miranda and the kind-hearted
attorney, from the highest and purest motives in both cases.

Had Miranda communicated to him her intention of leaving York, he would
have prayed her to delay until what he was about had been accomplished, and
she would have been spared much misery and many fearful scenes through which
she had to pass.

But such was not to be; and these two persons, with the best feelings, were
acting at cross purposes, for while Mr. Anderson was pleasing himself with the
idea that he was doing all that mortal man could do for Miranda, she was, with a
sad and lonely heart, making her quiet preparations for her departure to London.

Mr. Percy, at whose bedside we left her, seemed refreshed by the sleep he had
obtained; but too soon did the saddened Miranda find that his mind was still
lost, for his words presented nothing but a mass of chaotic images, without form
or speculation.

"You're better, Mr. Percy," she said, as she bent over him.

"Much better—much better," he said; "but it is strange we should change
our nature in sleep, and fancy such horrors—such frightful horrors, that it requires,
dear Miranda, many moments of waking reality ere the soul can shake itself free
from the mysticism of dreams. Who would suppose I was a king?"

Miranda heaved a deep sigh as she said,—

"Mr. Percy—Mr. Percy, think again—think of your son Rowland, and by
reflecting upon him, you will know yourself."

"Ay that was a dream again," he said, "I thought, Miranda, that I saw
your father; he was in his shroud, and dabbled in his heart's best blood."

Miranda shuddered, and he added instantly,—

"You weep, Miranda—weep at a dream."

"No," she said, "I do not weep—'tis strange and unnatural; but from the first
moment that I heard the frightful word accusing Rowland Percy of murder, my
feelings seemed to rise above tears, and although there have been many times
when they would have been merciful relief to my overcharged heart, I could not
command them. I know not when I shall weep again, for common sorrows
cannot touch me, and those I have lie too deep for ordinary expression."

"Ay, 'tis well," said the old man. "There should be no tears from such eyes;
I have heard my Rowland talk of their brightness until I have thought the boy distracted, but you shall be a princess yet, Miranda; nay, your beauty shall make you

one of nature's queens, and who shall dare dispute your sovereignty? But for my dream—my dream—I have not told you all."

"Hear me first," said Miranda imploringly. "Hear me first. Do you think Mr. Percy, that with me you could undertake a journey?"

"A journey?" he muttered.

"Yes," said Miranda, in a low tone, for she was fearful that any one might be within hearing, and arrive at a knowledge of her intention of seeking Rowland in his place of concealment. "I wish you to proceed with me to London to see your son, Mr. Percy—your son, who is so dear to both of us."

"Ay, but my dream," said the old man, abstractedly.

"I must hear it," thought Miranda, "however much it may harrow my feelings. And yet, what does it matter. He cannot tell me aught of what I know already, and no words from any one can plant more vividly in my mind the circumstances of distress and terror I never can forget,"

"Yes, I knew it was your father," continued Mr. Percy, "for there was on his finger a bright diamond he so much loved to wear."

These words, for the first time since her father's ring had been given to her by Ned Witlet, brought the circumstance to Miranda's mind, and it was with mixed feelings of pain and pleasure, that she thought, after all, should she be driven to great extremity, the ring would present a valuable resource, although to part with it, as the last sad memento of her father, would inflict upon her the greatest misery.

"You remember the ring, Miranda?" said Mr. Percy.

"I do," said Miranda, sadly.

"Then by that I knew him. The bright gem shot forth its long rays of sunny light, as if in mockery of the cold hand it adorned; then, as dreams will strangely shift from place to place, I thought you and I sat in a crowded court—there was the sound of many voices, but among them all, I heard my Rowland's, declaring he was innocent, but ere I could ask of what he was accused, the dreadful words 'murder,' and 'guilty,' rung in my ears. Miranda, how could my boy Rowland be guilty? how could he have done murder? what could they mean by accusing him?"

"Do you not know," said Miranda, "that the dream is true, and but the echo of events which had preceded it? He was accused of murder—they did call him guilty, but how wrongfully, Heaven knows; he is innocent, and the day will come when his innocence will be apparent as the light of heaven. Till then, however, there must be gloom and darkness over us all, and we must endure with what patience we may, the afflictions with which a gracious and benign Providence chooses in its great mercy and great love for its creatures to visit us."

"No, it was a dream," said the old man.

"I would it were—I would it were," sighed Miranda; "but answer me, Mr. Percy, are you willing to acompany me to London?"

A sudden change seemed to come over his feelings, and from the composed and rather exalted tone in which he had been speaking, he turned to one of deep grief and despondency, saying,—

"Miranda, Miranda, where is my boy Rowland? where is he? what have they done with him? oh, can it be true, Miranda, that they have taken his life?"

"No," said Miranda, in a tone of grief. "It is not, but they would have done so, Mr. Percy; they fain would have done so—he is saved, and it is to seek him in his place of concealment from his enemies, that I wish you to come with me."

"Yes, yes, I will come, Miranda," he said, "to the world's end I will come, in search of my poor boy, Rowland. So they would have taken his life, but Heaven would not let them, and he is saved. He is saved. Let us go at once. Are we not now in York, Miranda?"

"We are, we are," she said, eagerly, for her heart hailed the question as some proof of returning reason. "Do you not remember, Mr. Percy, misfortune has come upon us both, but it is not so bad as it might have been, since Rowland still lives. Oh, try to think."

He passed his hand across his brow, as if making a mental effort at clear reflection, and then he said, sadly,—

"There have been so many events, Miranda, that I know not which preceded which. You must tell me all as we go to meet Rowland. Let the carriage be ordered, and we'll proceed at once."

"Alas! alas!" thought Miranda, "my hope is a vain one. His reason is completely shattered. Time alone may ameliorate his sad condition, and to that must I trust."

At this moment a low knock at the chamber door attracted Miranda's attention, and upon gliding to it to ascertain who demanded admission, she found her landlady there, who said,—

"If you please, miss, there's a most singular female, of the name of Mrs. Jones, who wants to see you."

Miranda in a moment surmised who the Mrs. Jones was, and as she was in reality most anxious to see Jones before her departure, she said,—

"Will you oblige me by allowing me to see her in your parlour below?"

"Oh, yes, miss, certainly," said the woman, "and if you please, as I was coming up at any rate, I have just brought my little bill."

"Very well," said Miranda, "it shall be discharged after I have seen this person."

Upon this assurance the woman's respect seemed greatly to increase towards Miranda, for she had had her own suspicions, which, when duly given utterance to, were of course greatly increased at a tea-drinking with some five of her neighbours given on the preceding evening, that the little bill would have been found a little inconvenience when presented, and just possibly a very great one.

She was, therefore, agreeably surprised upon finding that such was not the case, and that it was to be settled so promptly and, easily.

She preceded Miranda to the passage in which stood Mr. Jones, who in his female garments nearly filled it up, and who was standing most unfemininely with his arms akimbo, whistling with great power one of the popular tunes of the day. When he saw Miranda, accompanied by the woman of the house, he thought it neccessary to keep up his female character, and he accordingly executed a curtsey from which he recovered with such a sudden jerk upwards, that he brought his head in violent contact with something hanging in the passage, bearing a remote resemblance to a lamp, and which as nobody was insane enough to attempt to light it answered its purpose—we beg pardon, a hall-lamp—at number seven.

Upon this untoward circumstance occurring, Mr. Jones rather for the moment forgetting the delicacy of his assumed character, exclaimed,—

"D—n it, what's this? Is a delicate female's knowledge-box to be pummelled in this sanguinary way, mum?"

"Gracious! you've broken the hall-lamp," said the landlady.

"Have I," said Mr. Jones;" then I advise you to save the pieces." I was never so insulted in all my life. A female, a female, I hope mum, and delicate, quite natural. Oh! my blessed narves, I'm a good mind to faint, and if I does, I shall come down with a whop that would break the passage in. Beware of love, mum, hip, hip, hip, hurrah—beware of love!"

The landlady looked perfectly aghast at the specimen of female delicacy before her, and it was with difficulty that she stammered out,—

"Will you walk into the parlour?"

"Suttenly, mum," said Mr. Jones, as with one kick he sent a chair that was in the way quite down the kitchen staircase, where its sudden arrival set the maid of all-work screaming. "It's all the same to me, mum, whether I goes into the parlour or the tap-room—I means the drawing-room, mum, excuse my wulgarity. I was brought up in a band-box, and fed upon carroway-seeds, but some how or other I have fallen into the company of rum ones, and evil associations, mum, corrupts good manners, so I ain't so delicate as I once was. Here's a d—d lock and be cursed to it."

This latter exclamation arose from a little difficulty in opening the parlour-door, which Mr. Jones solved by the immediate production of a skeleton key, with which he opened it, and then walking into the room, he sat down upon the flimsy sofa with a crash that made it groan again.

"Well, miss, I must say," remarked the landlady " that of all the extraordinary females that ever I came near, this one beats them."

"In course," shouted Mr. Jones from the parlour, "my father was a whopper, and my mother a stunner—and as I was the only young lady as they produced, I takes arter them, in course. I should like to see the blessed female as I can't beat."

Miranda knew not what to say, but she thought her best plan would be to proceed at once to the parlour and get Mr. Jones out of the house as speedily as possible.

She accordingly, without making any remark to the woman concerning the peculiarities of the supposed female, walked into the parlour, and closing the door she said,—

"For Heaven's sake, Mr. Jones, be more careful and circumspect; you will bring down, both upon me and yourself, the greatest suspicion and danger, if you proceed as you have done. What on earth can induce you to think that violence and disorder would enable you to pass for the character you assume?"

"I begs yer pardon, miss," said Jones, "but I really thought I was coming it rather; people shouldn't hang things in the passages to nob other people's heads. I'm sure, miss, you'd a swom like one o'clock if you had had such a cracker."

The parlour-door was at this moment opened again, and the landlady made her appearance with the exclamation of—

"Four and sixpence! four and sixpence! as I'm a sinner."

"Guv us hold of it," cried Jones. " 'Never despise trifles,' says the blessed proverb."

"I mean you are to pay it, you wretch," said the landlady. "A likely thing indeed that I am to have my hall-lamp broken by such as you. It will take four and sixpence at the very least to repair it, and that I'll have or I'll know the reason why."

"Don't make a noise and disgrace your sex, mum," said Jones. "Can't you take pattern by me and behave with delicate propriety? I'm always ready to faint away at the least provocation, and I'd go into histrikes at a minute's notice for nothing. There's breeding for you."

"The wretch," said the landlady, turning her nose up.

"There's the money," said Jones, throwing down two half crowns, "and there's sixpence change you know, mum."

The landlady, who had evidently expected a row, took up the two half-crowns with rather a quiet look of astonishment, and after a moment's hesitation, during which she regretted she had not asked more for the lamp, she said,—

"I will send up the sixpence."

"The change yer means," said Mr. Jones.

"Yes, four and sixpence is considerably under the walley of the lamp, but I consents to take it."

"You'r werry good," said Mr. Jones, "and as for the change——"

"Yes," said the landlady, eagerly expecting to be told she might retain it.

"Why," said Mr. Jones, "you may send it up in gin."

CHAPTER LXXXVII.

MR. JONES'S PROPOSAL.—A NEW PHILOSOPHY.—THE PROMISE OF ASSISTANCE.

WHEN the indignant landlady had retired, Mr. Jones carefully closed the door, and then turning to Miranda, he said,—

"If you please mum—miss, I have made so bold as to kim and pay you this here visit, with the werry best of motives, as the prig said when he picked the gentleman's pocket in the fair. It ain't for me, oh no, kim up, for to pretend as my manners is so genteel as they might be. The blessed school as I was brought up in, mum, didn't teach them ere, leastways they were something extra, and the man as wholloped me by wirtue of being my paternal relative, wouldn't pay it, so you see the other man as wholloped me by wirtue of being my schoolmaster, wouldn't teach 'em, that ere then's the consequence, Miss Miranda, why all my perliteness is nateral talent."

"Let sympathy and kindness be clothed in what rough guise it may, it is ever welcome."

"Wery good," said Mr. Jones, "what I comes all for to say to-day is, that we have put up a crack, and you shall have your share of the swag."

"You've what?" said Miranda.

"Ignorant people as ain't wersed in the dead languages," said Mr. Jones, "calls a crack a robbery, and the swag what we gets by it."

"Good Heavens!" said Miranda, "you can never mean to proffer me a share in the proceeds of a dishonourable action?"

"Bravo—kim up," said Mr. Jones, "me and some friends of mine goes on the good old plan of keep who may—catch who can—it saves a world o' trouble, and makes people blessed sharp. All I means then to say is, that as the people have sarved you as they sarved me, why we must lay hold of the same plan to save ourselves from being drowned."

"I really cannot comprehend your meaning,'" said Miranda, "further than I am sure you mean to do me a kindness."

"Why you see there was a blessed conspiracy against me, and the folks wouldn't let me be honest, though I tried hard and fast. 'No,' says society, 'you sha'n't be honest, Jones, for if so be as you tries it, it sha'n't be a go, we'll starve you out, prigs is wanted, and you shall be one.' So then I says to society, 'Blow yer,' says I, 'if so be as that's the caper, why there's no perwenting it, so I suppose I must do it,' Now that ere reminds me unkimmon of you; if people would let you have your own, you'd have been as right as nothink, but they would'nt, and what is you to do but sarve 'em out the best way you can. We are going to go down upon somebody as I needn't mention, who can spare a few silver spoons, and you shall have your share, never fear."

Miranda was fairly puzzled with Mr. Jones's notions of morality, and what answer to make him which should convince him of his very erroneous logic she knew not: moreover she felt his proposal not as a deliberate attempt to draw her into guilt. She was certain such was not the motive, and she, therefore, hesitated to speak to him with that harshness she would have used if resisting a similar proposal from any one else. After a few minutes thought, she said—

"Mr. Jones, you and I differ most materially upon the subject of which you are speaking, and I doubt if ever we should understand each other concerning it. You see no crime in retaliating upon society for the difficulties it has imposed upon you. To me your proposition carries with it a feeling of absolute terror, and I beg you will not mention it again, and I am sure you will not when I tell you that to my mind, absolute starvation would not be worse than the frighful resource you have pointed out."

"That beats me hollow," said Mr. Jones; "I can't come over that at all, Miss Miranda; howsomdever, you may be right, and I wrong, I don't deny that ere. You is a creatur with a hedication, I isn't—whether it's betterer or worserer to be able to read writing, and think upon, and like a printed book, I leaves to wiser heads nor mine, but what I wants to know is where's the prog to come from? and what are you to do when yer feels yer inside tantalised for want of grub? Where's wirtue then, miss—mum, I mean—and what's to become of that ere rum dodger as people calls morality. When I'm all of a heap, Miss Miranda, and some people in just such a fix would take to crying, and some to religion, I takes to gin—that's what I calls philosophy—a *kivorten* and three outs I calls a home argayment, and it beats the other things all to fits. I repeats my humble *kivestion,* as the parson says to the sinners, 'What is yer going to do, my werdant tulip?'"

"I can comprehend what you mean," said Miranda rising, "although not all the words in which you express it; and in unhesitatingly rejecting your offer, and repudiating the false reasoning by which you endeavour to support it, let me assure you that it detracts in no way from my grateful feeling towards you for what you have done for me."

Mr. Jones likewise rose, as he said—

"Werry well, mum, I hope there ain't no offence; what I said wasn't intended to give none. Is there anybody in York as you'd like me to give a blessed nob or two?—'Cos if there is, only say the word, and I'll do it."

"No," said Miranda; "I have no enmities. All I wish is, that you would give me a piece of information that may be of the greatest service to me."

"In course, mum. What is it?"

"Tell me where, in case I should go to London, I should find your friend Witlet?"

" What Neddy?" said Jones.

" Yes," said Miranda.

" If I tells yer, will yer tell me one thing ? and that is, do yer mean to go ?"

" I scarcely need keep such a secret from you," said Miranda. " I therefore say unhesitatingly, I do mean to go."

" When ?" said Jones.

" This very night, if possible."

" You've made up your mind, and no flinching ?"

" I am thoroughly resolved."

" Then I'll tell yer. You must go to the Star and Tinder-box, in Steeple-court, Drury-lane, and ask for the Slashing Squire. Then the landlord will say to yer—' What's the dodge!' and you shall say—' The old caper,' when he'll tell yer where Neddy is to be found."

" I thank you," said Miranda. " It would, indeed, be a great object with me, when I reach London, if I should be so fortunate as to be able at once to find your friend Witlet and Rowland Percy."

" They are together no doubt," said Jones, " and you need never fear for Mr. Percy's safety, as long as he's with Neddy."

" I thank you for the assurance," said Miranda, " and that is all I require of your kind services."

" Then I'll go mum. But, first of all, tell me when you means to go ?"

" At midnight," said Miranda.

" Precisely ?" inquired Mr. Jones.

" That I can scarcely say," replied Miranda, " as I must be much guided by circumstances. My greatest uneasiness now arises from the fact, which you have informed me of, namely, that my proceedings are watched by the police."

" Don't be troubled about that, Miss Miranda," said Jones. " I'll make that all right, you may depend."

" If you could do that," said Miranda, " you will be conferring a great benefit upon me, and I shall be much your debtor."

" All's right," said Mr. Jones. " You will see me to-night."

So saying, he left the parlour ; but when he reached the passage, he walked to the head of the kitchen stairs, and called out loudly,—

" I say, mother thingammy, where's that ere gin as was to come out of my change ? Don't make a bilk of it, old lady."

" You horrid wretch," said the landlady, as she flung some halfpence up the staircase ; " there's your beastly change, you low feller, for a feller you are, I know, though you pretend to be a delicate female. Oh, you Grogan !"

It may be presumed that the landlady meant Gorgon ; but Mr. Jones hearing the word grog, cried,—

" Well, make it grog, if you like, old'un." Then making a noise with his feet, as if he were about running down the kitchen stairs, to the great alarm of the landlady, who began screaming, he walked out of the house.

Then the landlady, after deep consideration, had what she thought the greatest revenge that was in her power, that was to proceed at once up stairs with her bill.

Miranda had ascended to her apartment, but the vindictive landlady followed her, and in a voice trembling between passion and anger, she said,—

" Now, miss, that your highly respectable visitor is gone, perhaps you will look at my little account."

" I will pay it," said Miranda. " What is its amount ?"

" Four pound seven," said the landlady, as she placed the uninviting document in her lodger's hands.

" So much," said Miranda.

" Oh, dispute it—do, by all means," said the landlady, in a sarcastic tone. " Certainly dispute it."

" I have no intention to dispute it," said Miranda, sadly, " I was only for the moment surprised at its amount. Take it from that, and give me the change. I shall leave your house to-night."

As she spoke, she handed to the landlady the five pound note which had been anonymously sent to her, and it is doubtful whether that lady was not more indignant at being paid so promptly, than as if she had been refused, for she flounced out of the room as if some deep insult had been put upon her, and then returned in a few minutes with the thirteen shillings change, and receipt, both of which she banged on the table, as if Miranda was far from being entitled to them.

To this gratuitous insolence the persecuted girl made no reply, but was glad when once more left alone to her thoughts.

She gazed upon the small sum which made up all her possession, and with a shudder, she asked herself,—

"How far would this carry me on my long and weary journey to London? What would become of me when this small fund is exhausted? Shall I, indeed, so early have to rely upon the proceeds of my father's ring, which I would fain reserve for the wants of Rowland, when I shall meet him in that great metropolis, of which I have heard so much, and where he must have but a fugitive and uncertain existence, an existence which would be ever trammelled with alarm, until it shall please Heaven to make manifest his innocence. Alas, if direful circumstances should indeed compel me to make use of that resource, it must go. Heaven help me, Heaven help me. Ah, that we, Rowland and myself, whose fortunes are so strangely mingled, were together. It seems to me as if misfortune was never so bitter, misery never so acute, when endured in the sweet companionship of those whose dear sympathy robs distress of half its wretchedness."

CHAPTER LXXXVIII.

TWITTER'S PECUNIARY DESTITUTION.—THE APPEAL TO VARLEY.—THE PLAN
OF ESCAPE.

WHEN Bernard Varley came to consider alone the interview he recently had with Twitter, he found more and more reason to feel suspicious of the conduct of that individual, and as is ever the case with such persons ; he extracted the greatest food for alarm from the most trivial circumstances. The confusion, so unnecessary to him, of Samuel Twitter, had in it a something fearfully mysterious, and to account for it merely as Twitter himself had accounted for it, by his possession of the silver spoon, was far from sufficient to satisfy the suspicious mind of Bernard Varley.

"What can he mean?" he thought; "he must be plotting something, he must be contriving something against my peace, or he would never have shown so much confusion and wretchedness while in my presence; and yet, what has he power to do? destitute of pecuniary resources as he is, I am surely safe from the utmost reach of his malevolence. What could he do to me that would not fall doubly upon himself? and yet, although my reason tells me I need not fear him, my imagination tinctures every word he has said with suspicion, and I am full of dread when I reflect upon his slightest actions."

Varley had taken up his apartments at an hotel, in a magnificent room of which he now was, and by the splendours that were around him, he had hoped in some measure to mitigate those pangs of conscience from which he was never free.

He had deputed, since the escape of Rowland Percy, a person to watch the lodging of Miranda, and give him notice of wheresoever she should go, for he thought himself safe now in adopting such a course, inasmuch as he could lay it to his anxiety that the ends of justice should not be frustrated ; and as the magistrates had taken up the notion, that by watching Miranda there would be a chance of discovering the retreat of Rowland Percy, he felt himself at liberty to think the same, and to act accordingly.

'Twas some hours after Miranda's interview with Mr. Jones that Varley again sought an interview with Twitter; but this time the valet was not in such an abject state of fright as he had been upon a former occasion, for during Varley's absence he had contrived to place the letter in its original, or nearly original state, and it was lying on the table, as if but newly arrived, and waiting but the coming of him alone who had a right to it.

Varley purposely entered the room abruptly, and fixing his keen scrutinizing eyes upon the trembling Twitter, he saw at a glance that he was far from being in the agitated state he had exhibited so short a time before.

Twitter certainly did start at the sudden appearance of his fell tempter—the man who had urged him to deeds from the commission of which his own poor spirit would have shrunk in dismay, although he wanted not, at the bottom of his soul, the inclination to be as desperate and blood-thirsty a villain as ever trod the earth, or libelled humanity.

"So, Twitter," said Varley, "you have recovered from your extreme fright at the commission of a petty larceny, which one would have thought so incidental to your existence as scarcely to have disturbed your equanimity."

"Yes, Varley—certainly Varley," said Twitter, "I was alarmed, and surely there are circumstances enough in our present situation to make us both nervous."

"Yes," said Varley; "but not so suddenly and strangely nervous as you were even now; besides, Twitter, why are you better? Circumstances still remain the same, and while time is so young, Twitter, each moment is rather against than for us. It seems to me, from my knowledge of human nature, and particularly of your nature, Twitter, that something unusual has occurred to disturb you, which now no longer exists. Learn this, Samuel Twitter, that your slightest secret movement, inimical to me or my interests, or my wishes, shall be your death. You had better be confidential, Samuel Twitter."

"I—I am very confidential," said Twitter, "upon my life I am. Indeed you mistrust me without reason, Bernard Varley, you know I would do anything in the world for you—anything. I will risk my life for you, for what hope have I in this world but in you."

Varley laughed bitterly as he said,—

"Protest not to me, Samuel Twitter; such words to my mind go for nothing, and you may spare your breath. I doubt you, and let that doubt be ripened into certainty, and I will kill you. My words are plain, and I would have you reflect upon them deeply."

"There is a letter for you," said Twitter, who was most anxious to change the conversation.

Varley immediately took it from the table, and, to Twitter's great relief, opened it so hastily, that had it been resealed again much more clumsily than it was, the cheat would not have been discovered.

"'Tis well," he muttered, as he read the epistle; "'tis well. Money indeed, does wonders. My orders have been promptly enough obeyed. I shall remember; yes, I shall remember."

"So shall I," thought Twitter; "and, perhaps, my memory may be effective earlier than yours, master Varley. I have but two hopes in this world, the one is to make money, and the other to see you hanged."

"Safer, much safer," continued Varley to himself; "by post-horses, the journey could be performed quickly—very quickly—and then away."

"What did you say?" remarked Twitter.

"What matters it to you what I say?" exclaimed Varley. "Nevertheless, I will tell you, for I know your suspicious character. I was remarking that, with the aid of post-horses, to employ which some one must have supplied him with means, Roland Percy could have escaped with great speed from York, and been away before the officers of justice were thoroughly alive to the fact of his escape. Are you satisfied now, Samuel Twitter?"

"Oh, quite," said Twitter, "I was before. As you say, post-horses will carry people away quick that have got the money; that are not like me, so dreadfully poor."

Here Twitter gave a deep groan, as the consciousness that he had no money came disagreeably across him.

"I have none—I have none," he muttered.

"Nor want any, most admirable Twitter; you are like a king or queen, whose wants are so abundantly supplied that it is of no consequence if you never see a coin."

"But I should like to see a few," groaned Twitter.

"Oh! I understand," continued Varley, in the same bantering tone, "from motives of curiosity, you would like occasionally to see a few; you shall be gratified now and then, Twitter, when I have a leisure hour; but in the meantime my post-horses will suffice to carry you to London, saving you a world of trouble. You see how mindful I am of your happiness, Twitter, and likewise to shew that I am not unheedful of what is of vast importance to us both, look at that bill."

As he spoke he took from his pocket a printed handbill, and laid it before the eyes of Twitter. Its head line contained the words, " One thousand pounds reward," and it went on to state that, "Charles Rowland Percy, condemned to death for wilful murder, at the York Assizes, had broken prison and escaped.' Then followed a description of his person, and the whole concluded by stating tha one thousand pounds reward would be paid one hour after his, the said Rowland Percy's execution, to any person who would be directly instrumental in apprehending him, and safely lodging him in any jail.

"What think you of that?" said Varley; "will it re-produce the prisoner, destitute of means as he must be, and surrounded by those to whom such a sum would appear an exhaustless treasure?"

"It may," said Twitter. "It may, Bernard Varley. I should like to earn it myself, for as you are perfectly well aware I have no money, and it's of no use stealing silver spoons here, for I've nowhere to sell them. I took another to-day, and I have got it in my coat-pocket; but it is only an aggravation."

"Ever—ever harping about money," said Varley; "once for all, Samuel Twitter, I tell you you shall have none until the circumstances by which we are surrounded have assumed a pleasanter complexion."

"Do you think they can ever be very pleasant?" suggested Twitter.

"Peace," cried Varley, "I will hear no more of this. It seems to be now well ascertained by the authorities at York that Rowland Percy has proceeded to London, for they have sent officers in pursuit of him. I should follow to-night ay, this very hour, were it not that the air of York is hallowed to me while breathed by Miranda Rankley; when she leaves, I leave, but not before."

"Varley—Varley," said Twitter, "let me once more, if it be for the last time, warn you against the terrible insanity that has come over you as regards Miranda. This infatuation of yours concerning her is the only one thing I dread as likely to produce our ruin. Oh, be warned! be warned, Bernard Varley, be warned, of that fatal passion which has sprung up so strongly in your soul, and which seems to deprive you at times of your reason. I implore you, not for my sake, but for your own, to relinquish the mad pursuit of one who evidently looks upon you with terror and hate."

"Speak to me no more on that head," said Bernard Varley, " if I am mad in my exceeding love for Miranda Rankley, mad I shall remain until my dying hour. It is in vain you argue with me, Twitter, my adoration of the angelic beauty of Miranda will overcome all your reasonings; say no more—say no more, it's in vain."

Samuel Twitter groaned aloud as he thought to himself, " It s indeed in vain."

Varley then left the room, and the trembling Twitter was again alone.

"What will become of me? What will become of me?" he said, "how shall I carry into effect my intentions? Escape I must from the meshes around me. To tarry were certain destruction, for Bernard Varley will be warned by no one, and soon, too soon, will he commit himself in some manner which will bring destruction to us both. It may be then, at the last moment, he will begin to see his own danger, and adopt those means of escape which his wily nature has pointed out to him; leaving me to perish as the victim at once of his indiscretion, and his crimes. There is no other resource, I must rob him, and that quickly too— to as great an extent as possible, and then make my escape with the proceeds. Yes that yatch at Liverpool shall serve my turn instead of his. That were a deep trick to serve Bernard Varley, and it shall be played."

CHAPTER LXXXIX.

THE PREPARATION FOR DEPARTURE.—THE MANIAC.—AN UNEXPECTED INTERRUPTION.

As the midnight hour drew near, Miranda made her few brief and hasty preparations for leaving York. The few articles of apparel she had to take with her were easily confined within the compass of a small bundle; and before the hour of eleven had struck, she had completed everything for her hasty journey.

Of the road to London she knew nothing—all her information extended merely to which direction out of York she intended to go, and now her greatest anxiety arose—namely, to get Mr. Percy, in his present state of mind, to comprehend the object of her journey, and to set about it cheerfully.

An hour or so before she had persuaded him to rise, and he had been seated some time in the front room, gazing with a meaningless eye upon the preparations she was making.

Then the Minster clock chimed the quarter past eleven, and a solemn stillness seemed to reign about the ancient city.

From eleven to nearly twelve, in all large cities, is generally a quiet period, for many persons then are at home for the night, while those who are accustomed to later hours, are either making merry at the houses of their friends, or shut up in the various places of public amusement, which, not until a much later hour, would disgorge their multitudes.

But occasionally a footfall sounded down the narrow street in which Miranda resided; but there were persons in that street, whose attention was wholly and solely fixed upon the one house then inhabited by that persecuted and noble-hearted girl, but which she was so soon to leave, in all probability for ever.

Of them we shall speak anon; but let us, for the present, listen to the gentle stirring Miranda, as with quiet earnestness she urged Mr. Percy to be up and

Approaching him, clasping her hand affectionately upon his arm, she said, in a low, soft voice—

"Shall we seek Rowland? Shall we seek Rowland? He is sighing for us, and shall we not seek him?"

"You were speaking of my dear boy," said the bereaved father, with a fain smile. "Say on, my darling Miranda—what of him?—what of him?"

"I said that we should go to seek him," said Miranda; "he is far, very far from us, and shall we not go to him? He is very lonely without us, and who else can love him as we love him?—who anticipate his slightest wishes as we shall?—who watch over him as we should watch? Let us go to him, Mr. Percy—let us go to seek Rowland."

"Yes, yes," replied Mr. Percy, "you say well, Miranda, you say well. We will seek him. Come, let us hasten—let us hasten. It seems long since I have seen him."

"It is long," said Miranda. "Time counted by sighs is ever long."

"And then, besides," said Mr. Percy, "I have had such dreams of him as have vexed me sorely. I thought they wished to hang my boy; and, although I know they have not, for you have told me so much, I would fain see him—very fain see him with my own eyes, and assure myself that he is well."

"Hark!" said Miranda, "do you know that sound?"

"It is the Minster bell," said the old man; "I have heard it often. What is the hour, Miranda?"

"It is half an hour to midnight," she said; "see here, Mr. Percy, is your hat and cloak. Will you come with me?"

"To the world's end," said the prematurely aged man, as he rose from his seat. "To the world's end, beautiful Miranda, I will come with thee."

With an anxious eye Miranda watched his step as he crossed the room. It was infirm and faltering, and she asked herself, with a deep sigh, "can he bear the fatigue of the journey I contemplate? Can he in his debilitated state ever reach London? Alas!—alas!—Heaven must speedily assist us, or we perish!"

"Come, Miranda," he said. "Come, are we not going to my boy, Rowland? Is it very far?"

"It is," said Miranda; "but we have time, and can take the journey at our leisure."

"Why not order the carriage?" said the old man. "Where are my servants? the idle knaves fatten on one's bounty, and then refuse their service when most needed. Where are they now? Call them, Miranda, call them! My voice is perhaps too weak and old."

Miranda uttered a deep sigh ere she replied, and then she said,—

"Oh, bethink you, Mr. Percy, there has been a sad reverse of fortune. Do you not recollect, we are not as we were? Our hopes are blighted, our fortune is not merely decayed, but gone. What is to become of us Heaven only knows, but we are fighting against great and deep calamities."

"Calamities, calamities," he said.

"Yes," added Miranda, "you will surely recollect."

"Dreams, dreams," said the old man. "Why will you let dreams disturb you? Banish these idle fancies, Miranda, and order the carriage."

Miranda felt for a few moments utterly hopeless, for if such feelings were to continue in the breast of Mr. Percy, how was she to hope that he would calmly accompany her the long and weary distance from York to London. Then a thought struck her, that perhaps by gently humouring his malady, she might succeed better than by attempting to awaken memory, or reasoning with the shattered intellect, that seemed by Heaven to be confided to her care.

"Listen to me, Mr. Percy," she said, "Rowland is in very great danger."

"Danger!" echoed Mr. Percy, "my son in great danger?"

"Yes, he has many and bitter enemies."

"Gracious Heaven!" said the old man.

"But be not too much afflicted," hastily added Miranda, "he has already gained one great victory over them, and by caution, he may escape their machinations altogether."

"Ay, caution," said the old man, while his face assumed that peculiar maniacal expression so often met with among the insane, when they think themselves peculiarly cunning "Caution is the word—we must be very cautious. We must use much art, and as you say, with art and caution, he may be saved."

"For that object," said Miranda, "we will dispense with the carriage."

"Of course, of course," said Mr. Percy, "they would laugh at us for being foolish were we to take it. We will send it another way, Miranda, and they will follow it. So shall we save Rowland. They will know the grey horses in a moment. Yes, we will be very cautious—we will save him—we will save him."

"Come then," said Miranda, as she assisted the old man on with an ample cloak which he had often worn in happier days. "Come come."

"I will follow you. I will follow you," he said. "You are my guardian angel, for you will save Rowland, and in so doing, you will save me ; but Miranda, yet a moment tarry."

"What would you say ?" said Miranda.

"Will not your father miss you?" said the old man : "he is apt to be hasty of temper, and of late I do not think we have been such good friends. Tell me, Miranda, think you he will not miss you ?"

"I am sure he will not," said Miranda. "Come, Mr. Percy, come."

"That is well," he muttered, as he followed her down the staircase.

There was no obstruction to their passing to the street door, but when that was opened, Miranda saw by the dim light of a neighbouring lamp, that some one was sitting upon the steps.

She instinctively shrunk back, saying to Mr. Percy,—

"Hush, not a word. Wait here a moment."

"Is that an enemy of Rowland's ?" whispered Mr. Percy.

"I know not," said Miranda, "but will quickly ascertain. For Heaven's sake be still."

These few words passed in much less time than it has taken to record them, and while they were being spoken, the person who was seated on the step appeared to be be aware, from the sudden opening of the door, of the necessity of rising.

In another moment the huge form of Jones in his female apparel, presented itself to the eyes of Miranda, and she instantly pronounced his name.

"Yes, mum," said Jones, "its me. Is you serious?"

"What mean you ?"

"I means, does yer really mean to notch yer blessed mahogany, and mizzel from York ?"

"I am even now about to start on my weary journey," said Miranda.

"Then just wait till I comes to yer again, or else you'll be watched like one o'clock, and never lost sight of by those who wouldn't do you a good turn on any account."

"Do the officers then keep so watchful an eye on my movements ?" said Miranda.

"Rayther," said Mr. Jones. "Mums's the word, and keep the door shut."

"I will wait," said Miranda; "but think you it will be long ?"

"Ten minutes ought to settle the hash," said Mr. Jones ; "but I thinks as it'll be out an' out cooked before that 'ere time. Shut the door, and if anybody comes give 'em an ewasive answer."

"An evasive answer ?" said Miranda.

"Yes; tell 'em you wasn't born yesterday, and to take it out o' nothink."

Mr. Jones then walked away from the door, and as Miranda could not see what was passing outside, we will, with the privilege accorded to faithful historians, place before the readers what there occurred.

As we are well aware that Miranda had not stirred from home the whole of the day, consequently the active watch of the two constables, set on by the magistracy had been signally unproductive of any result. They had continued to relieve each other at stated intervals, and those intervals happened to be at the even hours; that is to say, there was a change of guard at ten o'clock, and there would be another at twelve, so that while Miranda was making short preparations for her departure from York, one of the constables was pacing to and fro in the street, now and then dodging round the corner, and taking sly looks to see if he was observed; then getting up into a doorway for a time, and occasionally skulking behind a pump that was in the street, all of which proceedings, it so happened, excited a great deal of anxiety and suspicion in the minds of every person but those most intimately connected with his proceedings ; for although Miranda never saw the active officer dodging and fretting about the street, there were other of its inhabitants who did.

Many, and alarming, then, were the speculations which the phenomenon gave rise to, and on that eventful evening many shutters were fastened that were never fastened before, and divers intricate and ingenious fastenings were resorted to for dilapidated doors.

The bottom bolts of street doors were shot with suspicious energy, though usually

left undone, because people do so hate stooping, and the bottom bolt, moreover, always screams for want of use, and awakens the children.

It seemed as if society in that street was seized with a mania of apprehension as regarded that solitary man, and were determined to lock him out, and bar him out, and bolt him out in every possible way.

In the meanwhile the officer fumed and fretted exceedingly, for it is very provoking to be extremely cunning, and careful, and watchful, and nothing come of it.

No. 44.

So much aggravated, indeed, was he at the apparent calmness of Miranda, and the absolute no notice she took of him, that at a quarter past eleven o'clock he came up to the door and gave utterance to a great volley of oaths, which see med to have a sedative effect upon his system, for he sat down on the nex t step, and only came out with a hearty curse occasionally.

Now it happened, that, as he there sat, he saw a man with very suspicious movements, creep down the street, and when he came near the pump before mentioned, make a great rush and dodge behind it, as if he had suddenly achieved something very wonderful, and executed some feat of exceeding cleverness.

" What's the meaning of that, I wonder ?" muttered the officer. " There's something going on now, I'll be bound. If this infernally provoking Miss What's-her-name won't come out, I may fin d out something else quite as well worth looking after."

He saw the man behind the pump slowly and carefully peep out several times in the direction of the door of Miranda's house, and then suddenly draw back his head again, as if he expected a knock upon it from some invisible agency, if he kept it too long in that extremely artful position.

" I'll know what he's bobbing about there for," said the officer ; " or else I'll know the reason why."

Advancing, then, carefully under cover of the pump itself, until he stood close to it, he waited till the head should again peer forth, and the moment it did, he gave it a little rap with the stick he held in his hand, which so alarmed the owner that, with a cry of murder, he fell in a very complicated manner into the sink, producing a great rattling with the chain and the ladle, which, having been put up the week before, had not yet been stolen for old iron, as is the general fate of such public conveniences.

Immediately upon this successful achievement, the officer rushed round the pump and seized the mysterious man, crying,—

" Hilloa ! hilloa ! my man, what do you do here Come, let me see your face ; perhaps I may know you. I suppose there's some robbery put up to night ?"

" Bless my heart and soul, is that you, Green ?" said the man.

" Yes, I am Green," said the officer ; " and who the devil are you ?"

" Kiggs—Kiggs—don't you know me ? I'm Kiggs."

" D—n it," said the officer, " I know you now ; but what are you skulking about here for ? making yourself ridiculous by playing at bo-peep with the pump. Kiggs, Kiggs, I'm afraid you're arter no good."

" No good, ain't I ?" said Kiggs. " Half-a-guinea a day, and skulk as much as you like."

" Why, what do you mean ?"

" Just this," replied Kiggs, confidentially. " I heard that Mr. Varley wanted some one to keep an eye on the young woman as lives here. She who got the chap who was a-going to be hanged out of the condemned cell. So I called upon him, and told him I had been occasional messenger about the courts for some time, and was up to a thing or two ; and he gave me the situation."

" Indeed !"

" And it's not so bad, neither ; is it ?"

" I wish mine was half so good ; and here have I been watching all day long almost, and it only comes into regular duty."

" More flat you," said Kiggs. " I took my situation this morning ; and when I did, Mr. Varley he says to me,—" I will come between eleven and twelve myself and relieve your watch, while you go home and take a few hours' repose." So you see, I've jest come to meet him, and I haven't been here afore. Let him watch himself. Let him look after the young woman himself—let him——."

" But you forget the half guinea a day, Kiggs," said the officer.

" Do I ?" said Kiggs. " Catch me forgetting it, that's all. Hilloa !—hilloa ! —hi—hi—look—look——"

"What's the matter?" said the officer, turning round twice or thrice, like a man about to play at blind man's buff.

"On the steps," said Kiggs.

"The devil!" said the officer.

"Much the same—a woman," said Kiggs. "A fine woman, I should say. D—n if she didn't shake the area rails when she sat down."

"The devil she did!" said the officer.

"Mr. Kiggs and Mr. Green then both hid themselves behind the pump, and peeping one from each side of it, kept up a steady stare at Mr. Jones, who sat with great composure on Miranda's door step.

CHAPTER LC.

MR JONES AND THE OFFICERS.—A DELICATE FEMALE.—THE ATTACK AND THE ESCAPE.

"Who is it?" said Kiggs, in a mysterious manner.

"Don't know," replied Green. "Hark, she's a-singing."

To relieve the tedium of his waiting for Miranda, Mr. Jones hummed an air.

"Is it the young lady?" said Kiggs.

"Don't be a fool," said Green. "That female horse marine could put Miss Miranda Rankley in her pocket."

"Hark!" said Kiggs. "She's a-singing again."

> "Slash his whining, tap his nob;
> Grab his ticker, it's in his fob.
> Fal de ral, te tidy, tidy, tidy,
> Kim up, fol de ridy."

said Jones.

"What an extraordinary song for a female," said Kiggs.

"Rather," said Green; "but what a voice, too."

"I say," said Kiggs, "let's get over to the other side of the way, under kiver of the pump, and then cross over the end of the street, and walk past her as if we were thinking of nothing, and have a look at her."

Mr. Green thought this a good and reasonable proposal, so he accordingly adopted it, and he and Mr. Kiggs crossed over the road, as had been suggested by the latter gentleman.

Some good fortune did appear to be wanting on Miranda's flight, for it was just then she opened the door, and held the short conversation with Mr. Jones which we have recorded in the preceding chapter.

By the time Kiggs and Green arrived at the door, Mr. Jones was again seated upon the step, but this time he had drawn a black veil partially over his face, and exactly as they passed, he made a singular sound with his mouth, which sounded more like "Kick," than anything else, and added, whilst he saluted Mr. Green across the ancles with a stick—

"My dear, are you good natured?"

"Curse you," said Green, rubbing his shins, "what do you mean by that? I'll have you taken up."

"Oh, don't, oh, don't!" said Mr. Jones, in a tone of affected dismay. "I'am an unfortunate female, oh, don't. If I has strayed away from the paths of blessed wirtue, and made a beast of myself, what's that to you, cuss you!"

"What an extraordinary female," said Kiggs; "come, get up you—you can't sit there."

"Oh, you little sneaking, snivelling, never-grow-fat-must-be-hung-parish-brought-up-wretch. Is that the way you speak to the fair sex? It shows your broughtings up, you d—d humbug."

"Why, who the devil are you?" said Green.

"Larn politeness, and ax my elbow," said Jones.

"I'll be hanged," said Kiggs, "if I don't think it's a man."

"Oh, oh, oh!" said Jones, with great affected horror, "to compare me with a male cretur, and make me out an ante-female production. You murdering wretch, I'll be down upon you in a minute, kivey, kim up."

So saying, Mr. Jones rose and presented to Kiggs such Amazonian proportions, that he fairly ran away, leaving Mr. Green to stand the brunt of the contest as best he might.

Even he retreated two or three doors off, and had a passing thought that he had better leave the unfortunate female alone; but before he could settle his reflections into any form of action, Mr. Jones made a rush at him, at the same time that the officer was fairly bewildered, and knew not how, or when it occurred, but he found himself suddenly seized up by the arms and legs, and carried with great rapidity down the sreet by two men, who had started from Heaven knows where.

"Ri fol-de-di-di-dol-di-di," said Mr. Jones, "their geese is cooked."

"Thieves, thieves."

"What's the matter?" said a voice from a window.

"Nothing," said Jones, as he threw a handful of mud in the speaker's face; "it's rather a dirty night only, that's all."

The head withdrew with a faint scream, and down went the window.

"Curiosity," soliquised Mr. Jones, "is a very great failing—people often brings themselves to the dirt by that ere, and if they dosen't, why it's wery proper that the dirt should be brought to them. All's right now, and Miss Miranda may now be off without nobody seeing of her. I didn't think I could have come it half so well. One-eyed Bill said as how I wasn't delicate enough for a female, and what's the consekins, I have done it quite astonishing, and there's flukey Joe, and the badger will carry that unfortunate officer to the blessed sewer as is under repair; it's not above five feet six deep, and I think he is about five feet eight, so he cannot come to much harm—a miss is as good as a mile I have heard say, and two inches is a pretty good miss."

Thus speaking, Mr. Jones reached Miranda's door, at which he tapped carefully with his knuckles.

Miranda heard him, and immediately answered the summons.

"All's right," said Jones. "Come out now and take the direct road to London. You won't be quite deserted, for a friend of mine will keep on your track, just to give any one a nobber who may make themselves disagreeable the first mile or two."

"I am much beholden to you," said Miranda, "and shall never forget the service you've rendered me."

"Bother that," said Jones; "good-night, and good luck to you."

Miranda turned to Mr. Percy, and taking him by the arm, said—

"Come, Mr. Percy, come. We will now go and seek for Rowland. Quick, quick, let us go."

"Yes, yes," muttered the old man, "we will seek Rowland—my boy Rowland —we will seek him and save him from his enemies."

Mr. Jones darted away, and in another moment Miranda and her helpless companion stood houseless wanderers beneath the canopy of heaven.

CHAPTER XCI.

THE SLUMBERING CITY.—THE WANDERERS.—THE WALK FROM YORK.—THE
ALARM.

THE street was very dull and quiet, scarcely a breath of air was stirring, and
Miranda assured herself, by one glance, that she and her aged companion were
the only living beings within sight. She placed her arm within that of Mr. Percy,
and gently led him down the street, now and then as she went, talking to him of
Rowland, in order to keep him still assured of the object of the journey.

"You know where to find him, Miranda?" he said. "You are quite sure, you
know where to find Rowland?"

"I am," was her reply. "It will take us time, Mr. Percy; but that matters
little, we have ample time before us."

"Yes, we have," he said. "Yow are right, Miranda, you are right; we have
ample time. Wherefore should we not? Who should control our actions?"

"No one," said Miranda. "See, Mr. Percy, the night is brightening, and we
shall have plesant weather for our journey."

"But, Miranda," said Mr. Percy, "I must still think of your father. You know
he is scornful and proud of heart. Will not his anger be great to find that you
have gone without his knowledge?"

It was great grief to Miranda, to hear this constant allusion to her father, whose
unhappy fate she would fain have forgotten; but she controlled all expression of
her own feelings, merely saying.

"No, Mr. Percy, there will be no anger from him; think no more of him;
let all your attention be directed to Rowland. There will be no anger from my
father."

"That is a great assurance," said Mr. Percy, "for he is apt to be choleric, and
was ever proud of heart, so as to obscure at times some of his better qualities; but
which of us is perfect; which of us is perfect, Miranda?"

"Which, indeed," she said mournfully; "but, thank Heaven, we are unpursued,
and the night is brightened; come, Mr. Percy, can you hasten for a short space
that we may get free of the suburbs of this great city, and wander onward more
freely, among the works of God, leaving those of men far behind us."

The clouds which had obscured the early evening, now suddenly scattered before
a gentle breeze.

The moon rose in silvery radiance over the benighted city. But a very
different scene is it to that of a moonlight night in the country, where one can
wander beneath the shade of some spreading oak and watch the fleecy clouds as
they pass her pale face, or gaze upon the whitened walls of the mansion of the
gentry, which dot the country over in nearly all parts, or upon the rippling stream,
chastly illumined by her cold rays.

But though there be nothing of this kind, yet there is more of beauty,
more to contemplate, wonder at, and admire, than unthinking souls would at first
believe.

In the main streets, where there is a glare of gas, both from lamps and shop
fronts, the two lights are in conflict, by which they both suffer, and the passengers
look up at the moon, inwardly thinking it is a fine night, and no further notes the
matter, but passes on full of busy thoughts of the past day's labour, or reflections
on what the morrow may bring forth. In the quieter portions of the town, in the
squares, as they are called, the moon's beams throw broad shadows, which strongly
contrast with the white light in other spots, putting to shame the lamps which
flare on their respective ports; but even this is not the best spot to contemplate
moonlight in a city.

He who can clamber to the roof of some old tenement in a crowded spot, and quietly look round him and contemplate what he sees, will find much to occupy his attention.

Immediately in his vicinity he will trace the line of streets until lost by a mass of buildings, whose chimneys and variously formed roofs group themselves into odd shapes and masses, and then a church spire will strike his view, and near its lofty head, far above the neighbouring habitations, as if in scorn of their lowliness and comparative insignificance.

Then cast your eye over the broad expanse of house-tops,—ay, for miles, and then shall the senses be wrapped in wonder, as the sight becomes sensible of the ocean of roofs, windows, chimneys, and all kinds of projections, while the spires and steeples of the churches stand up in bold relief in the sky; some whitened by the moonlight, others standing in the shade, like a darkened pyramid, its vane, perhaps, reflecting back the soft light.

Such a scene as this has a sedative effect upon the mind, and only those who have contemplated such a scene in a quiet hour, can believe the charms it possesses. The moon's beams here and there illuminating many spots, while as many more are thrown into deep shade, causing a contrast so long and so distinct that the observer pauses and wonders he has never noted the scene before.

The whole town might not inaptly be compared to a river in which lay numerous vessels of all sizes and kinds; the tall tapering spires look like the masts of vessels lying at anchor, or at the wharfing, while the undulating and various formed house-tops might be readily imagined to be the hulls of the vessels lying idle.

Nearly filled as her heart was with the sad thoughts engered by her own hapless condition, Miranda yet could feel and appreciate the beauties by which she was surrounded.

It is said, and well said too, that God made the country and that man made the town; but still, much as man unavoidably does from the necessity, or apparent necessity, there is for congregating together in large masses, so destroying the beautiful charms in scenery which otherwise would surround him, the beauties of nature will still creep with a quiet gentleness into the most crowded thoroughfares, and sunlight and moonlight will make beautiful the darkest spots, and penetrate into the deepest recesses of cities.

The blight that was upon the mind of Mr. Percy, was, however, amply sufficient to deaden his feelings, despite the mild beauty by which he was surrounded. He walked quietly and sadly by the side of Miranda, now and then murmuring something about his Rowland, which required no reply, although the saddened girl as often made some gentle answer, calculated to soothe his perturbed feelings, and cheer him on his road with new hopes—hopes which she scarcely felt herself, but which certainly grew more full of reality as she uttered them to him.

There was evidently no pursuit; for as the singularly-assorted pair passed from street to street in the outskirts of the city, Miranda often looked back, and as often felt assured that they were unobserved.

It was a weary time before the houses diminished in their quantity, and becoming interspersed here and there with garden walls, and patches of sweet green verdure announced that the city was being left far behind, and the open country was near at hand.

Miranda felt her spirits grow lighter the further she proceeded from York, for what had that ancient city presented to her lately but scenes of unhappiness and terror? Soon, too soon, however, the saddest reflections began to cross her mind concerning the depressed state of her fortunes, and as she felt in the breast of her clothing to assure herself of the safety of the little purse,—a gift from Rowland Percy in happier days—in which she had placed the thirteen shillings, which comprised now all her worldly wealth, except a few halfpence, for some petty exigencies during the day had swallowed up the small sum she had calculated upon over the five pound note, she asked herself the often repeated question of—

"How shall we travel nearly two hundred miles upon this small sum?" and with an additional pang to her already burthened heart, she told herself that it must surely happen that her father's ring must be parted with to provide the exigencies of the journey.

When they reached the first mile-stone out of York, the morning was beginning slowly to break, and a dim streak of grey light could be observed low down on the eastern horizon.

Mr. Percy gazed long and earnestly at this first dim imitation of the coming day, and then in the same saddened, quiet tone in which he usually addressed Miranda, he said—

"Have we far to go, Miranda, to seek my boy? I am weary, I pray you let me rest awhile—the pleasant and beautiful day is coming : let us watch it, Miranda; as it gleams up from the lighting east, it will well repay the trouble."

"Nay, you forget," said Miranda, "we have far to go—very far to go. Scarcely two of the many weary miles we must traverse, ere we reach Rowland, are already passed. Oh, bethink you, Mr. Percy, how far we have to go, and let us walk on, however gently."

"Hark, hark," said Mr. Percy, whose external senses, like those of many persons in his unhappy state of mind, seemed preternaturally acute—"hark, I hear the sound of horses' feet ; the trot is a sharp one, just such a goaded trot as when the rider is in haste, or angry."

" I hear nothing," said Miranda. "Where comes the sound ? "

" There," said Mr. Percy, as he pointed up the road, in the direction of London; " it comes from there."

" Thank Heaven," said Miranda, " if there really be horsemen approaching ; so that they do not come from York, I have no apprehensions.

"But hark ! " again said the old man; "there come sounds from York."

Almost at the same moment Miranda heard the sound of wheels from the neighbourhood of the city, and the heavy beat of the horses' feet, which Mr. Percy's acuter perceptions enabled him to hear before her, rapidly approaching in the opposite direction,

"Let us draw aside," she said. "It is unlikely that these persons are either friends or foes to us ; they will pass us as mere wayfarers on the road, heeding not whence we come or whither we are going."

The sky was just sufficiently light to enable Miranda, as she looked in the direction of York, to be aware that some vehicle was approaching, but what it was she could not ascertain, although from the dreadful rattle it kept up, and the occasional screaming of the wheels, and a perpetual jolt, jolt, jolt, at each trot of the horse, she guessed that it was of a very common description, and most probably belonged to some of the market people, going from York to the large orchards in the vicinity,

The sound of the horses' feet became suddenly much more subdued, for the mounted party were ascending an eminence at a walk, which enabled the small dilapidated cart, for such it was that was coming from York, to reach Miranda and Mr. Percy some few minutes before the horsemen who were approaching from the opposite direction.

Whoever was driving the miserable horse, that with a convulsive sort of trot, as if kept in a perpetual state of galvanism, was approaching, seemed extremely jolly over it, for he was bellowing forth, with great strength of lungs, a popular ballad.

There was something about the tones of the voice which Miranda thought she knew, and as the vehicle came still nearer, she became convinced that it could be no other than Mr. Jones himself, who was proceeding with such glee. Rough and uncouth as he was, a sense of pleasure came over Miranda's mind as she heard him approaching, for she felt sure then that there was one friendly heart at hand, although what was his errand out of York she knew not, but that it in some manner concerned her and her fortunes, she at once supposed.

"There is, at all events, one friendly person approaching," she said to Mr. Percy ; "one from whom we shall receive as much active sympathy and good will as it may be in his power to render us."

Mr. Jones, for it was indeed he, appeared to have seen Miranda and Mr. Percy, and he made an attempt to bring his sorry steed up to the spot where they stood with some degree of eclat, and rather sharply; but the horse had not understood anything of that kind for many years, and resisted with all his might and main, sometimes backing a little towards York, then dodging from one side of the road to the other, and altogether exhibiting, in the most determined manner his indisposition to proceed otherwise than by the spasmodic looking jerks, which he no doubt considered a famous trot, and one fully entitling him to great admiration, and a handful of beans.

"Cus you," said Mr. Jones, "do you think I stole yer? infernal wretch! I only borrow'd yer a mile or two—you've had it all your own way, and be hanged to yer, and made my wery inside sore with that ere patent trot of yourn. What a d——d inwention that |is—you shouldn't be so ingenious, cus yer, take that and be d——d to yer. Oh! you wretch, I suppose your over forty, if yer a bit."

Whether it was Mr. Jones's verbal remonstrances, or the application of a stick which had the effect, we cannot say, but certain it was, that suddenly the horse made a great dart forwards, and so unexpected was that dart to Mr. Jones, that sitting as he had been, upon a little piece of board suspended by two straps, he in the most conclusively scientific manner as regarded the actions of momentum and inertia, lifted up his feet in front, as if he was doing it on purpose, and fell on the flat of his back in the cart.

The horse incontestibly would have had it all his own way now, had he chosen to indulge in any vagaries; but as the height of his ambition was to strike work whenever he could, he stopped exactly by the mile-stone, which, by the drooping of his head, and the watery twinkle of his one eye, he appeared to be reading attentively.

"Well, I'm d——d," said Mr. Jones, struggling to his feet, and rubbing the back of his head, "there's blood for yer. I suppose, old cock, as you used up the last drop of that ere sanguinary fluid in executing this ere manœuvre. Oh! cus yer, another time, just cut up that ere bolt into small bits, and make a trot of it. Miss Miranda, mum! I thought I'd catch yer; I've been taking off my female toggery, and I'se no longer the delicate cretur I was. 'I am rough and ready,' as the file remarked to the old nail. This ere's my carriage; leastways, it is mine, only the owner keeps me out of it, and is vexations enough to carry his own greens and taters in it, just as if there was no such indiwidual as me breathing. I thought you and the old gentleman would like a lift just as far as this ere rum combination of an old doormat, and a bundle of sticks, they call a hoss, is capable of taking yer. Hillo, what's that——"

The horsemen who were approaching from the direction of London, had now ascended the brow of the hill, and suddenly increasing their speed, were now coming at a rapid pace in the direction where Miranda and Mr. Percy were standing.

"Somebody's coming in a hurry," added Mr. Jones. "Woa, Buonaparte, don't you be arter being too fiery. I call him Buonaparte, mum, because it strikes me he's used up his inside, mum."

"If," said Miranda, "you can expedite us even a mile upon our journey, we shall be grateful, more especially so near York as we still are."

"I dosen't make the smallest doubt, mum, that Buonaparte will manage a mile if he's well whalloped, and we must manage to do that 'ere among us. Just get in, mum."

"Let those horsemen," said Miranda, "pass us first. I do not know that it is so, but something seems to whisper to me that there is danger from them."

"Danger," said Mr. Jones, "they're not coming the right road for that, Miss Miranda."

"I do not know," said Miranda; "but I have a presentiment of evil from their approach."

"They're in a passion, howsomedever," said Mr. Jones. "Hark how they are cussing."

CHAPTER XCII.

THE RETURN OF THE OFFICERS.—ROWLAND IN SAFETY.—MR. JONES AND BUONA-
PARTE.—A BIT OF BLOOD.

THE horsemen were, in a few moments, close to Mr. Jones and his cart, when, drawing up, the formost of them cried in a loud voice :—

"Hilloa—do you come from York ?"

"Yes spooney," said Jones, "I do; where do you come from ?"

"Come come," said the man, "no insolence nor nonsense. What's the news?"

"'Taters riz," said Jones, "and greens is fell."

"Damn your impertinence," said the horseman, "I want to know if anything has been heard of Rowland Percy, the murderer?"

"I believe yer," said Jones, "ever such a lot."

"Indeed!" said the horseman; "d—n it, and here have we been on a fool's errand half way to London."

No. 45.

"Well, if I didn't think as much," said Jones. "I judges people werry much by their looks, and I should say that's just the way you does your messages, old feller."

"Come, come, my man," said the officer, "you may earn a crown, and perhaps more, by being civil. What is known as regards Rowland Percy at York?"

"You want to know what's know'd?" said Jones.

"Of course I do," said the officer.

"Ah, then, there you have me," said Jones. "You asked me what has been heard? there has lots o' things been heard, and nothing knowed."

"You're an impertinent fellow," said the officer.

"Yes," said Jones, drily, "I comes from York. You're a clever, bustling sort of fellow in your way, but your ears are so precious long, and when yer brays into the bargain, people thinks as yer a hass—that's yer way—the first public-house as yer comes to is the Cat's Inside and a Drumstick—get yourself a pint, and tell 'em score it up to nobody. Who did you steal that ere hoss from? is yer mother out of gaol yet? what did yer get for that ere copper? did they bone yer father's toggery when he was hung? How about them silver candlesticks?"

The officer could make no head against this, what Mr. Jones denominated chaff, but shouting "Come on!" to his companions, he merely added, in a threatening tone to Jones,—

"If I were not better engaged, my man, I'd take you up."

To this Mr. Jones's only reply was an imitation of the braying of a donkey, which awakened echo far and wide, and so alarmed the old horse in the cart, that he suddenly woke up and nearly shook his head.

"Now, Miss Miranda," said Jones, "I'm glad I was with yer when we met those chaps, or perhaps you wouldn't have found out that they had been to London, or nearly as far, after Rowland Percy."

"Indeed!" said Miranda "then, of course, they have missed him. How could that be? for doubtless they have ridden harder than he could hope to travel."

Ned Witlet must have managed that, somehow," said Jones; "leave him alone for a bit of cleverness of that kind; there ain't much danger now, for this chap that spoke to me, though he asked such green questions, is about as good an officer as they have in York."

"Then you think he will escape?" said Miranda.

"He has a better chance than ever; the chase to London is given up, that's quite clear, and they'll be hunting in every hole and corner in York, while he's as safe as can be."

"Is it of my son Rowland you speak?" said Mr. Percy.

"Yes, old gentleman," said Jones.

"Go to my house, then, and tell them to give you of the best—tell them to stint nothing in your entertainment. I'm going now to find my son Rowland, of whom who have now spoken? when I return you shall be amply rewarded. You have an honest countenance."

"You mustn't take folks by their looks," replied Jones. "It's true I isn't a lawyer, or a parson, or any of them ere perlite perfessions, but I don't pertend to be more honester than my neighbours; but just please to get into this ere cart, and arter that I'll give you a leg up, Miss Miranda, and we may, by dint of uncommon persuasion, get Buonaparte to toddle."

With the assistance of Mr. Jones, Miranda and old Mr. Percy were seated in the frail vehicle, and Buonaparte, after some active persuasion, was induced to start at the extraordinary rate of three miles and half an hour.

Miranda felt the cold morning air acutely in that vehicle—the child of luxury as she had been so long, and accustomed to have every, and the slightest wish gratified. Even at the slow rate they were then travelling, she felt the air blow keenly and sharply round her, and shuddered several times. Poor old Mr. Percy, although his mind was so dreadfully shattered by the misfortunes he had gone through, and the ruin which had fallen upon him and his, was still alive to anything that affected Miranda, and taking off his cloak, he insisted upon wrapping it around her, which she reluctantly permitted him to do, for he was otherwise but lightly clad.

"Here's a potato sack," said Jones, raking about the bottom of the cart till he found one ; "put that on, old gentleman, I'm blessed if you won't look like an ancient Roman."

"I will," said Mr. Percy, "I will. It will be a disguise too, against my enemies. Yon horsemen were seeking our lives, Miranda, and how thankful should we be that they succeeded not in finding Rowland."

"Now, Miss Miranda," said Jones, in a low voice, so that Mr. Percy should not hear,—"now that Buonaparte is taking it easy up this ere hill, tell me how are you off for the mopuses?"

"The what?" said Miranda.

"The tin—the dust—the coal—the pony, I mean."

"Do you mean money ?" inquired Miranda, having an indistinct recollection of hearing it called tin once before.

"Yes, I does."

"Then I have very little indeed, and must husband well my small resources."

"Have you got enough to get to London with?"

"Far from it, without parting with a ring of my father's, which—which I would fain keep, at least until some very great exigency indeed."

"Oh, bother selling the ring," said Mr. Jones.

"But what else am I to do? "

"Werry good, we'll take a thought of that ere. Kim up, Buonaparte. Oh, you wretch, don't be purtending as you haven't got on the level. Now what do yer see down that 'ere blessed drain? nothing, I'll be bound—it's only one of your wicious excuses."

Buonaparte seemed to have acquired a kind of dread of Jones, and upon the urgent remonstrances used to him boldly stepped out six paces.

"This here wehicle," said Mr. Jones to Miranda, with the most unconcerned air imaginable, "and the singular cretur as walks afore it, was a standing at the corner of a street, so I guve the boy as was a minding on him a penny, and a bonneter, along with a solemn promise of tuppence, if he ever seed me agin—that ere being involved in great doubt; but I didn't diskiver as Buonaparte was such a rum'un to go, till I got into the wehicle, and begun to whollop him."

"Good heavens, Mr. Jones," said Miranda, "you don't mean to say that you stole this horse and cart ? "

"Stole it, mum?" cried Jones. "I steal a consarn like this ere? I'd be ashamed to do it."

"But, Mr. Jones, youv'e confessed taking it from its owner."

"Wery good," said Jones. "I have sartainly took a loan of Buonaparte, and the bundle of old sticks as is miraculously holding together arter his tail, but as to stealing on 'em, oh dear no. If I stealed a horse and cart, I'd take care as they was genuine, and not a blessed one like this ere."

"But what will the owner do?" said Miranda.

"That's a curious speculation," said Mr. Jones. "I rather think he ought to be grateful, but I rayther think he'll run about like mad till Buonaparte comes back."

"Do you know who he is ? " said Miranda.

"No, I don't, but according to law the name ought to be on the cart: but if it isn't, I'll lay an information against the beast, and we'll divide the penalty. Now, Buonaparte, what's the row? I'm blessed if he ain't getting aggrawated, and throwing his shoes away; there's one of 'em gone into that ere field just now."

The extreme coolness with which Mr. Jones took the capital felony he had committed, by the abstraction of Buonaparte and the vehicle, did not at all tend to assuage the alarm of Miranda, when she found that such was really the case, and to Mr. Jones's surprise, who thought her extremely fastidious, she expressed an earnest wish to quit the conveyance which had been so singularly obtained.

"Lor' bless you," said Mr. Jones, "these ere things happen every day. only wishes I had come across something worth borrowing, instead of this ere wretch. I had popped yer twenty or thirty miles on yer road in a twinkling —there goes another shoe! Cus yer, you tried to throw that at my head, I know."

"I implore you to let us alight from this vehicle," said Miranda. "My terror of pursuit is doubly increased by being here, and I do believe that the danger is far greater."

"Well, if so be you think so," said Jones, "you can get out. Let me see, we've been an 'our and three quarters coming a matter of four mile. Well done, Buonaparte, if you don't die arter that ere unnatural exertion, you are an astonishing cretur."

Jones then assisted Miranda to alight, and when she and Mr. Percy were again on the road-side, he turned Buonaparte's head towards York, saying—

"Now, my high-mettled racer, you had better pick up yer shoes as yer go home, or you'll be accused of disposing of 'em in wice—you will—there, now cut."

Buonaparte seemed to understand this speech tolerably well, and with the same deliberate pace which there was no getting him out of, he went leisurely back to York.

"There's a village," said Jones, "a couple of miles further ahead. You had better rest there, and take some breakfast, then walk on. Depend upon seeing me again before night."

So saying, Mr. Jones pushed through a hedge, and walked off at a brisk pace across the fields to the right of the road.

CHAPTER XCIII.

THE BREAKFAST AT THE VILLAGE INN.—TOBIAS POPPLETON, ESQ., AND THE RIGHT OF PATHWAY.—MIRANDA'S PROGRESS.

It was with a feeling of desolation that Miranda found herself again dependent upon her own resources, and her own courage, with that aged and mind-stricken man. She determined, however, to follow the advice of Jones, and seek the village he mentioned.

On the whole, however, she found Mr. Percy bear up much better than she expected, under the fatigues of the journey. His debility began to leave him, and by exercise his physical powers seemed in a great measure to improve instead of lessen. He still, however, talked very incoherently, and in a low tone, as if communing with himself rather than asking a question of Miranda, he would often say—

"Where is my boy, Rowland? I wonder if we have far to go? It seems a weary way—a weary way."

Then Miranda would strive to cheer him, by directing his mind to other objects —although it is, indeed, a sad and heavy task for those who are careworn and full of anxiety themselves, to minister comfort and consolation to others. It is only such noble natures as Miranda Rankley's that are equal to the task.

"Mr. Percy," she said, "you have been in London?"

"In London?—yes," he replied; "but that is very far from York."

"It is," she said. "Yet there must we go to meet Rowland. His enemies have forced him so far."

"To London—to London," muttered the old man—"a weary distance, indeed. Ah, Miranda, let us send for him. Nay, I will speak to your father. I will tell him to subdue the pride which has separated neighbours and friends. Yes, I will speak to him.'

"Alas!" said Miranda, "let me tell you, Mr. Percy—once again, let me tell you—my poor father is not of this world."

"Sir George dead—Sir George dead!' said Mr. Percy—" impossible! But if so grievous a thing has happened, Miranda, you shall live with us, and we will make up to you in love for all the tenderness you have lost. But see, some one is approaching. What manner of man is that?"

A singular-looking being was coming down in the opposite direction from Miranda and Percy. His attire was of that order which proclaims in every article the most elaborate and costly self-denial. His collarless coat proclaimed him a quaker, and his demure aspect, of course, showed how far above the vanities of the world he was. Although it is possible that any one inclined to be censorious might have detected in the general appointments of the man, and in his round, bluff face, abundant evidence that he had not wholly neglected the creature comforts, and had he (the censorious person) been quite wickedly inclined, he might have even gone so far as to intimate a suspicion which, of course, must be wrong, as quite opposed to the generally-received opinion, that the aforesaid quaker, like many of his brethren, was a painstaking humbug, making a trade of his piety and collarless coat, and succeeding wonderfully in taking in huge numbers of the population on the strength of a broad-brimmed hat.

In fact, we once head a wicked and malevolent person say that quakers had so high a character for honest and upright dealing, that they could afford to be rogues for the next half century, without being found out, except it was by troublesome and fidgetty persons, who were always finding out everything, seeing farther into a mill-stone than their neighbours—persons wearing a kind of moral spectacles, that enables them quite to overlook a collarless coat and a broad-brimmed hat—persons who, with a species of mental gimlet, bore deep holes beneath the surface of society, and peeping therein, make sad discoveries with regard to what things really are in point of distinction to what they seen.

These persons are apt, now and then, to proclaim that piety, whether real, or assumed, covereth a multitude of sins—that there lurks many times under a white neckcloth, tied in the most evangelical manner, the most deadly hypocrisy; and that it is just possible a man who would not wear a collar to his coat on any account, nor have his garments of other colours than sober brown or black, may be a thundering rogue.

But these kinds of people are very properly scouted by society at large, and considered very troublesome and disagreeable members thereof; so that their opinions are of no importance at all, and a quaker is a quaker after all, and an evangelical parson is a great creature.

But to return from this digression; the sombre-looking personage approached Miranda, and Mr. Percy, saying to the latter,—

"Friend, when thou gettest a little further on thou wilt see a small gate, which leadeth across a dry path, and as it is in thy way, friend, thee may take that path unadvisedly, seeing that the road is uncommonly muddy and dirty. Now, friend, that path leadeth by a circumbendibus to my house, although it hath a branch which leadeth to the high-road again. Now, I desire that thee and the young maiden will walk into the road, instead of using that path; for, truly, I wish to keep it clean for my own feet, for, verily, as thee are already muddy, thee might as well go into the road."

"Can you be so selfish," said Miranda, " wearing the garb you do, and professing such great charity, as to wish to turn us from a few hundred yards of pleasant walking?"

"Oh," said the quaker, turning up his eyes in great horror, " I perceive, maiden, that thee art one of the scoffers and the mockers, although my worldly eyes do tell me thee art beautiful, and thee mayest walk with me up the path, while the old sinner who is with thee may walk in the road."

"Who are you, man," said Mr. Percy, " that you dare speak thus to one who although she considers not that piety and the love of Heaven may be expressed by the colour and cut of the apparel, is as far above you as are the heavens above the earth. You are one of my boy Rowland's enemies, or you would not talk in such a guise."

"Come, come," said Miranda, "Come, Mr. Percy, do not speak to him."

"Tarry a moment," said Mr. Percy, as if in deep thought. "The world is taught many things by examples; and now I will make an example of this man, to teach them to despise mock piety."

"Murder—help—police—the devil!" said the quaker, as Mr. Percy advanced a step towards him; and then turning round, he set off at a most unquakerly speed —for they never drive anything hard but a horse or a bargain—towards his own house.

"How dare that man," said Mr. Percy, with great vehemence, "insult us thus! How dare he address us as he has done! He has gone to injure Rowland, and I must after him, and slay him—death—death——"

Miranda was much alarmed at the excited manner of Mr. Percy, and it took her much pains to sooth and subdue the irritation which had been produced in his mind by the man of peace, who, with such rare philanthrophy, wished to turn them into the road from the pleasant path.

The distance to the village mentioned by Mr. Jones was now not great, and it was with a thankful heart that Miranda saw the little cluster of houses peeping among the trees, and showing their white fronts, and old gable ends.

"We shall rest here," she said. "We shall rest in yon village, Mr. Percy; for there the only friend upon whom we can rely has promised to meet us."

The village was soon gained, and the wayfarers sat down in the neatly-sanded parlour in the one ale-house, to partake of the morning meal, which, after the, to them, long walk, they were much in need of.

The exercise seemed materially to have benefitted Mr. Percy's health; and Miranda thought, with deep thankfulness to Heaven, that she detected less incoherence in his manner than while he was in York.

She was most anxious for the arrival of Jones, as expedition upon their journey was to her a matter of vast importance. And not long had she to await for him; for within half an hour after their own arrival in the village, he walked into the parlour. There was an air of disappointment about Mr. Jones, which was fully observable to Miranda, and to her it was a great relief that she found it proceeded from only an inability on his part to supply them with money, for Miranda had been fearful that something had arisen in York to increase the peril of Rowland Percy, or render her own going more hazardous.

"I did hope mum," said Jones, "to have downed with some dust when I seed you, but half-a-bull is the outside as I have got, and that wont go very far. Howsomdever it'll cut up into two or three chops, and make an out and out breakfast and lunch. There's a waggon coming by here in about an hour; he's not much of a spirit the feller as drives it, and he'd guv yer a lift if you was to frighten him in to it; but perhaps you objects to wiolence?"

"I certainly do," said Miranda; and at the same time I must say, that I scarcely understand what you have been speaking about."

"Oh, I forget," said Mr. Jones. "There's the cuss of not recollecting nothink. What I means is, I have only got half-a-crown, but if you waits here for an hour or two, I shouldn't wonder but somebody will come along the road 'as'll lend me a trifle, leastways you had better wait for the waggoner, and see if he'll give you a lift."

"We will wait for you," said Miranda; "we have too few friends not to heed the advice of those who still cling to us."

"How did you get this far?" said Mr. Jones, "for you have come a mile or two since I left you."

"We met with but one interruption," said Miranda, "and that was from a quaker."

"A quaker!" cried Jones.

"Yes, he stopped us to prevent us taking a dry path, instead of the road which was heavy and dirty."

"Confound his cat's meat," said Jones, "I know him, then; it's Tobias Poppleton; he's got an estate here by, and makes a deuced good thing of being sleeping partner in half-a-dozen gin shops in London."

"Indeed," said Miranda; "it is strange, indeed, that there should be such a difference between what people profess to do, and what people really do."

"Is it," said Jones. "It strikes me it would be rayther unkimmon the other way; "but, howsomedever, that quaker's guved me an idea, and not a bad one neither. You wait here, Miss Miranda, until I come to you. I sha'nt be very long. How do yet get on, old gentleman?" to Mr. Percy. "Do you find yourself any better?"

"You are a rough, hardy fellow," said Mr. Percy. "I will give you a situation on my estate, for I think you mean well by Miranda; would you like to be a gamekeeper?"

"Yes, I should," said Jones; "but I am afeard I should keep it all, so I begs to decline the situation at the present time, and thank you all the same, old commodore;" then turning to Miranda, in a low tone, he added,—"There's nothing like humouring on him. I goes on the soothing system."

After that he hastily left the little ale-house, and proceeded rapidly on the road to York again. Mr. Jones was scarcely absent above an hour; but as, during that hour, his proceedings were more active and more amusing than Miranda's at the little ale-house, we will jog on pleasantly with him, with the view of discovering what was the idea which the mention of Mr. Tobias Poppleton had given rise to.

"The idea," he muttered, "of them ere quakers being such out-an'-out humbugs, it's enough to make a fellow savage, it is. I am bad enough, I dare say; but I ain't a quaker at all events. I ain't come to that yet. There's a difference atween borrowing a trifle of people whether they like it or not, and being an out-an'-out humbug, like Tobias Poppleton."

Mr. Jones then, as he neared the quaker's estate, saw no less a person than Tobias himself sauntering up and down, acting as his own scarecrow in keeping people off the path, which was quite a public one, and no more for his private use than the king's highway.

"Oh, there he is," said Jones, "and a precious pump he looks too. I think if I ever gets put to the bar of the Bailey, I'll buy an out-an'-out quaker's toggery, and then I shall be sure to be acquitted. "When they axes me what I have got to say, I shall just cry out,—

"'Please you, my blessed lord and gentlemen of the jury, I am an out-an'-out conwart, and sees the error of my ways. I guved all the family coves the bag, and turned a quaker, and blow me if I prigs nothing else except in such a genteel pious sort of way as 'll make me quite a 'spectable member of society.' Then I'll tip 'em a stave as I have made myself to convince 'em as honesty is the very best policy. I've called it, 'What's the use of grieving, when the world all lives by thieving.'

"'The little babby, when its born,
Will grab all it can catch at;
And so the boy as goes to school
Another's cake will snatch at.
The schoolmaster robs right and left,
The parents rob to pay him,
Sure how to prig is what he'll teach,
And don't the lads obey him.
Then what's the use, oh, what's the use—
Oh, what's the use of grieving,
As all the world—as all the world
Can't live except by thieving.

The doctors thieve of those who choose
   To take a nasty potion ;
And parsons are but thieves in black,
   A very common notion.
The lawyers rob you right and left,
   They are thieves sure by profession,
And every one you meet around
   Will rob you in succession.
      Then what's the use, oh, what's the use—
        Then what's the use of grieving,
      As all the world—as all the world
        Must do a little thieving.

King Solomon was very wise,
   But rather fond of stealing,
And surely 'gainst so down a prig
   There wasn't no appealing.
Young Mercury Jove's thunder stole,
   A wise example setting,
And mortals ever since that time
   The swag are always netting.
      Then what's the use, oh, what's the use—
        Then what's the use of grieving—
      As all the world—as all the world
        Must do a little thieving.

The learned judge upon the bench,
   With all his artful rigs,
Would little need his gown and wig.
   If it wasn't for the prigs.
Such facts as these are past a doubt,
   And seeing is believing ;
From kings to beggars, all the world
   Is getting grub by thieving.
      Then what's the use, then what's the use—
        Then what's the use of grieving,
      As all the world, yes all the world
        Must do a little thievin

I thinks as that'll rather astonish them," said Mr. Jones ; " there'll be werdict fo
the prisoner ; and the learned judge 'll say,—' Young man, take warning, an
don't let me see you here again ; and when you prigs, do it more genteeler, an
according to law ; mind what I say, and go away, you've had a narrow escape
young man, don't be a fool."

———

CHAPTER XCIV.

THE GIGANTIC WOMAN.—THE HIGHWAY ROBBERY.—THE SEASONABLE RELIEF.—
THE LIFT IN THE WAGGON.

   As Mr. Jones uttered these words, he made his way through a gap in a hedge,
and being tolerably well screened from observation on the other side, he undid a
bundle which he had been carrying on a stick across his shoulder, and took out
of it the female apparel in which he had figured so conspicuously in York.   There
was the bonnet too, but wrapt up to a perfectly flat shape, so that its appearance
was by no means improved, and it had a very singular look indeed, when Mr. Jones
bent about some of the wires with which it was provided, to make it what he
called remarkably nobby.

The gown was easily slipped on, only for the sake of convenience it was hin part before, as Mr. Jones was not provided with a lady's maid to do the hook and eyes ; by the assistance then of a variety of handkerchiefs, which by some means Mr. Jones had become possessed of at the smallest possible expence, he contrived to hide his face, and to tie on his bonnet. ｜　　　　　　　d

"I wonder," he muttered, "if that ere Tobias Poppleton would mind lending a trifle to a distressed female, I don't see why I shouldn't try it on—s here goes."

Mr. Jones then recrossed the hedge and appeared on the road-way as a gigantic female, a supplementary skirt of a different colour having been sown on the dress to make it long enough for him ; he then made directly up to Tobias Poppleton, who, being deeply engaged with his own thoughts, did not for some minutes perceive the singular apparition that was approaching him. When, however, Tobias Poppleton did see him, he gave a great start, saying,—

"Verily, in all my experience, I never saw such a woman; truly she is nigh unto six feet high, and will make hideous marks upon the new path."

No. 46.

"How is you this blessed morning, sir?" said Mr. Jones. "Is this ere a civilized country? and do you think of letting a female like me pass you without so much as saying, 'Oh, lady fair, where is you going?'"

"Begone, woman, begone," said Tobias, holding out his hands in horror.

"What, don't you know me!" said Jones. "Oh, you deceiver, I shall cry myself into fits; you are enough to make a bull kick his mother, you is. Don't you recollect Susanna? how can you be such a brute; lend me a guinea."

"Verily, I know thee not," said the alarmed quaker, "go thy ways."

"You needn't look about you, Tobias," said Mr. Jones, "there's nobody near; and if you attempts to set up a shout, I shall put your head in chancery in a minute. Just sit down, and let's talk it over."

Here Mr. Jones introduced his stick so rapidly between Tobias's ankles, that that pious individual forwith sat down with a great plump in some moist clay, while he looked at Mr. Jones with a rueful face, and muttered,—

"Dreadful female, art thee going to murder me?"

"No, I arn't," said Jones; "but I want to borrow a trifle, it's towards having the road scraped, so that the pathway up to your house may not be trod upon; people must pay for their luxuries. Give us a guinea, and get up and be kicked."

"Yea, it striketh me," said Tobias, "that thee art on the high road to the gallows."

"Never you mind about that ere," said Jones; "there's a good many little cross footpaths as goes to that same spot; but here's somebody coming. Now I tells you what, Mr Tobias, if so be as you opens your mouth by way of saying anything but just what I tells you, there won't be so many quakers by one in this ere world. You understands me?"

To make his meaning more clear, Mr. Jones took from his pocket a clasp knife, which he opened with his teeth, and drew suddenly across the neckcloth of Mr. Tobias Poppleton with a threatening gesture.

"Mur—murder! Oh, spare my life," said Mr. Tobias Poppleton.

"Very good," said Jones, "there's a fellow coming up on horseback, and if you don't say arter me, just what I says, I'll cut your throat first, and manage him arterwards."

"I will—verily I will," said Mr. Tobias Poppleton, with a groan; "for preservation of my life, friend, I will even say after thee whatever profane thing, curse thee, thee may put into my mouth."

The horseman who was coming up happened to know Tobias very well by sight and asked,—

"How do you do, Mr. Poppleton?"

"Speak arter me," growled Jones, "or I'll cut your head off. Tell him to axe your elbow."

"Thee mays't axe my elbow, friend," said Tobias Poppleton, to the intense surprise of the horseman, and he said "Sir?" with an enquiring tone, for he could scarcely believe his own ears.

"Has your mother sold her mangle?" whispered Jones.

"Hast thee mother parted with her mangle, friend?" said Tobias, in a groaning voice that betrayed great agony of mind.

"Bless my heart and soul, he must have taken a drop too much," said the horseman; "I never heard such a thing, or perhaps he's ill. How long has he been in this way, mum?" addressing Jones.

"As long as my arm, spooney," said Jones. "Where did you steal that ere hoss?"

"As long as my arm, friend," said Tobias, who thought himself bound to repeat what Jones said, on pain of having his throat cut. "Where did thee purloin that animal?"

"Ah, they are both mad," said the man on horseback. "Mr. Tobias Poppleton, I couldn't have believed it of you, and nobody 'll believe it when I tell them."

"Mizzle, you humbug. There you go with your eye out," said Jones.

"Thee must mizzle," said Tobias, " and proceed with thee eye out."

    " Oh, what's the use of grieving,
      Since all the world, since all the world
    Must surely live by thieving.
          To la looral, to la looral."

"Friend," said Tobias, with a groan.
    " What is the utility of grieving,
      Since all the world, friend,
    Have to la looral, friend, taken to thieving?"

"Now get up and dance," said Jones.

"Verily, I cannot," said Tobias, "for I have stuck deep in the clay."

"Gracious!" cried the man, " who would have believed it—Mr. Tobias Poppleton drunk?"

"Oh, he's all right," said Jones; " I am his new housekeeper, and we hob and nob a little now and then. Its right as a trivet, ain't it, Toby."

"Ay, truly," said Tobias, " as correct as a trivet."

"Well," said the horseman, " it's no business of mine. Good morning."

"Call him back," said Jones.

"Friend—friend," cried Tobias, "wilt thee come back?"

"Well, what is it?" said the man.

" Are you sure you shut the door?" said Jones.

" Confound you both," said the man as he stopped, and putting spurs to his horse, galloped away.

"Now, Mr. Tobias Poppleton," said Jones, " I advise you to make the best of this here business by just handing out to me what tinklers you have about you, and saying nothing to nobody."

" Friend I know not thy meaning," said Tobias.

"Money," said Jones; " and, mark me, if you say anything about it, or kick up any disturbance, don't show your sanctified mug on this road again; for so sure as you do, I'll be down upon you and you'll find me a dangerous female."

With a deep groan Mr. Poppleton produced his purse, and gave it to Jones, saying,

" Friend, I would gladly have given thee ten times as much if thee had not made me say, 'ax my elbow,' and other profane words ; but it will become known now that I did say so, and truly my brethren will cast me out, for verily they have no mercy upon those who cannot keep their frailties from public observation; ' if thee have a rent in thy garment,' they will say to me, 'under the sleeve of thy coat, keep thy arm down, and we will say nothing to thee about it, but if thee lettest it be seen, we will spew thee out.'

" Twelve pounds," muttered Jones, as he counted over the quaker's money ; " you may take your purse back again, old stick in the mud, and remember mum's the word."

" Verily, mum, I shall remember thee as long as I live," said the quaker.

Mr. Jones then left Tobias Poppleton seated among the clay, and hurrying forward till he came to a turn in the road, he took off his female habiliments, and tying them up again in the same bundle as before, he walked on at a rapid pace to the village.

"Miss Miranda," he said, " here's luck in a bag, and take it out as you want it." At the same time he handed Miranda a small leathern bag, in which he had placed the greater portion of Tobias Poppleton's twelve pounds.

A slight flush came across Miranda's face as she said, timidly.

" May I hope, Mr. Jones, without offending you, that this money was come by honestly?"

" Honestly, Miss Miranda," said Jones; "in course. I never did anything so outrageously honest in all my life. It's quite a hact of piety."

" I will take your word," said Miranda, " and thank you for this most seasonable relief. I have still hopes—very great hopes—that the day may come when I shall be able to repay all those who have so generously assisted me in my distress; but till then I must remain your most grateful debtor."

"Never mind that," said Jones, "here comes the waggon, don't you hear the horses' bells? It's not going to London, but it's going on forty miles of the road, and that's a good long lift. Offer the man a shilling piece and he won't refuse it."

"And shall I not see you again?" asked Miranda.

"You may or may not, as the case may turn out; but I intend to take easy stages to London, and borrow a little money as I go on. I rather think, though, that you will see me often enough, and if you do not, go right on without me. Be sure you never make any inquiries after me, and remember that ere address as I guved you where to find Neddy Witlet."

"I will remember," said Miranda, "with many, many thanks to you for all you have done for us."

The tinkle of the bells which adorned the heads of the waggon-horses, and which were placed there for the purpose of keeping them awake, but notwithstanding which the whole train was in a state of somnambulism by the time they reached the village, was now plainly heard, and Miranda, turning to Mr. Percy, said,

"Let us come now; forty miles will indeed be a long lift on our weary ourney."

He followed her to the door, and then the waggon was slowly dragging its length along through the one street of the village. The waggoner seemed as fast asleep as his horses, for he was going along with a monotonous trudge, neither looking to the right nor the left, nor upwards nor straightforwards, but intently on the ground, as if on his last journey he had lost some small coin, and he was in hopes of picking it up on this.

Mr. Jones went up to the leading horse, and taking hold of it by the ear, bellowed into it "whoa," upon which the leading horse shook his head, and came to a stand still, whilst the others bumping up against him, took that as a hint to stop also. so that at length, after much creaking, and wheezing, and groaning, the waggon came to a stand; while the waggoner, who was totally oblivious of the whole circumstance, walked on as if nothing was the matter; and it was not until Mr. Jones commenced pelting him with stones—at which exercise he seemed quite an adept, for he hit the waggoner almost every time—that the latter, after saying "woa" several times, stopped, and became aware that he had shot a-head of the amazing bits of blood that were dragging his team.

He then walked back and looked wildly about him for a few seconds, after which he said, fancying he was at a turnpike—

"Number thirty-seven."

"Two passengers," cried Jones; "an old gentleman and a young lady—four quarts of threepenny a-piece."

"Ah, ah, ah!" said the waggoner.

"That'll do?" roared Jones.

"Ah," said the waggoner.

"Get in," said Jones to Miranda. "You and the old gentleman will find yourselves comfortable enough, although it is tedious travelling."

Mr. Jones went again to the leading horse, and laying hold of his ear as he did before, he screamed in it, "gee-up;" and in about a minute the horse took it into consideration, and began walking on, the others all being roused by the process, and stepping out at the amazing pace of two miles and three-quarters an hour, while the bells kept up their monotonous tinkle, tinkle, and the waggoner resumed his dreamy career.

CHAPTER XCV.

VARLEY AND HIS SPY.—THE WATCH-HOUSE AT YORK.—MARTIN THE IDIOT AND
THE PISTOL SHOT.

MIRANDA was gone, and the tumult and excitement which had reigned in the little street where she had resided in York was over before, like an apparition of evil, Bernard Varley arrived at the spot, and as he gazed around him he muttered indistinct imprecations upon the head of his spy.

"Where can the hound be—where can the hound be?" he said. "D——n! he's off his guard. How dare he leave without my express permission? Who knows what might happen even in a temporary absence? I'll brain him if he has let her escape—I'll brain him. He's not here—'tis certain he is not here."

By this time he had arrived opposite the house in which Miranda had occupied apartments, and for awhile his attention was taken from the consideration of the delinquency of his spy in gazing with a wild rush of mingled feelings upon that house, which he believed contained the being who had cast a spell of fascination around him, and who by a strong contradiction of feeling he loved so intensely and had injured so deeply.

"There is a light at the window," he muttered, "and I see a shadow flit across the casement; it must be her's. Miranda, Miranda! even yet, methinks, you could save my soul from the deep perdition that awaits it; in your hands I could be a slave,—a willing slave; and I think even, terrible as death is to me, even in thought, I could consent to die soon, provided in the interim you would be mine, and light up my soul with some of these sunny smiles thou art so lavish of to others, but never—never allowed to beam on me. Oh, Miranda, Miranda! even now look down with pity upon the wretch you have made."

How common it is for such men as Bernard Varley, after a career of crime and villany, to attempt to shift the onus of their guilt upon the shoulders of some innocent person, who could have nothing whatever to do directly with their iniquities. Thus the thief, when sentenced to a trifling punishment for his first offence, would say, that if the judge, who in his impartial administration of the law, was compelled to sentence him, had spared him, he might have become a useful member of society, instead of persevering in a course of crime. The housebreaker, who when meeting with resistance, murders the person whom he came but to rob, might as well attempt to shift the onus of the crime upon that person's head, and say that he himself brought on his death.

It was quite as absurd for Bernard Varley to accuse Miranda of being indirectly the cause of his iniquity, because she could not love him; but the overburthened conscience will catch at straws to float itself upon the sea of hope, and strong minded as Bernard Varley was, he would fain have cheated himself into the idea that he was not quite personally answerable for his own iniquities.

For a considerable time he remained, musing and gazing up at the window of the room which he still supposed Miranda inhabited. At last one o'clock sounded from the various steeples of the metropolitan city. He then started from his dreamy posture, and in an angry tone he said—

"So, I have paid well for being duped; the rascal whom I set here to watch, has utterly and wholly neglected his duty. It will yet be some hours before the city is alive again, and during that time, what better occupation can I have than in watching yon window, within which is all I ever loved on earth."

As he spoke, he became conscious of some one slinking down the street on the other side of the way, and ever suspicious as he was, that where there was secresy and caution there must be danger to him, he stepped beneath a door-way, and stood in the deep shadow, watching the actions of the person approaching.

That person was Kiggs, who, having run home to Mrs. Kiggs, and informed her of the singular circumstances, by which his watch had been disturbed, was duly advised by that careful and exemplary woman to return to the scene of action, and earn his money, a piece of advice that was rendered wonderfully practicable by a blow with the fire-tongs, so that Kiggs, who had began somewhat to recover from his fright abroad, thought it best to flee from the wrath to come at home, and he accordingly hastened back to the street, to see what was then going on.

Now Mr. Kiggs was a politic man in his way, and he thought that if Mr. Varley should have been there, and duly missed him, that he, Kiggs, might still have a chance of saving himself from reproach by slipping behind the pump, and suddenly appearing with a " Lord bless me, sir, is it you ! why, I have been watching yer ever so long, and I didn't know you !"

It was in pursuance of this clever scheme, that [Mr. Kiggs slinked down the street in the manner we have described, and then screened himself behind the pump, all of which Bernard Varley saw clearly, looking as he was from darkness to comparative light.

" What is the meaning of this ?" he said ; " the manner and general bearing of that man leads me to think it is he that I employed to keep strict watch upon this house, and the scoundrel has deceived me, and thinks now to make some lying boast of his acuteness."

Varley then advanced to the pump with slow and cautious steps, and when he was sufficiently near, he bolted round it, and seizing Kiggs by the collar, he said—

" Scoundrel—you have deceived me."

" Lor, sir, is it you ?" said Kiggs, who could think of nothing but the speech he had determined to make ; " well, I never, I've been watching you ever so long. There hasn't a mouse been moving, sir, at the young lady's house—to be sure, I've had some of my clothes torn off my back by a mad woman, but your worship will no doubt make them good. Says I to myself, says I, Mr. Varley's a gentleman, and he'll make everything square. Oh ! murder—murder !"

These exclamations arose from Varley kicking Mr. Kiggs down the street, who was thus doomed on that eventual night to receive another practical opinion as regarded his attainments.

As fortune then would have it, Mr. Green, who by this time had been rescued from the tavern, arrived, nearly red hot with fury, accompanied by half-a-dozen other constables in the street, resolved to find the gigantic female if possible, or, at all events, wreak his vengeance upon somebody.

The first sight that met his anger flashing eyes was Kiggs, being kicked ferociously down the street by a tall figure.

" Seize him—seize him," he cried, and Bernard Varley was in a moment in the hands of the officers, and in another the whole party was rolling in the street, for Bernard Varley was not the kind of man to be taken quietly, nor was he just then in the sort of humour to be interfered with at all.

Nevertheless, no effectual resistance could be made against so many, and the consequence was, that Varley, in defiance of all explanation, was dragged off with scarcely a whole rag on his back, to the nearest watch-house. There, however, a general explanation ensued, and Mr. Kiggs, after some hard pressing, confessed his delinquency, while Green loudly explained how he had been maltreated by some fiend in petticoats, who had a dozen devils to do what she thought fit.

From all this Bernard Varley gathered abundant food for suspicion that something was going on as regarded Miranda, which he should miss the knowledge of, and with frenzied gestures he hastened back to the street in which she had resided.

It was a little before three o'clock, but without reflecting a moment about the unseasonableness of the hour, he knocked loudly at the door, nor ceased, notwithstanding he alarmed the whole street, until the woman of the house opened the window with a candle in one hand, and a watchman's rattle in the other.

" Woman !" shrieked Varley, " tell me this instant, is Miranda Rankley here or not ?"

"Gracious Powers!" cried the woman, trying to spring the candle instead of the rattle; "who are you?"

"Answer my question," shouted Bernard Varley, "or I'll not leave a whole pane of glass in your house."

"She is gone," cried the woman, "and I am very glad of it; and if you don't go too, I'll give you to the watch."

"Gone—gone!" said Varley, as he staggered across the street with clasped hands, not hearing or heeding the loud springing of the rattle which the woman then really commenced. "Gone—gone! she is gone, and I have missed her. Oh, fool, fool, to lose sight for one brief moment of her—to delegate a watch to others which only I myself could keep with fitting diligence. Whither has she gone?—whither has she gone? Her progress must be slow, for it is cramped by want of means, and the company of the elder Percy, whom I am certain she would not forsake. London—that must be her destination, and where she is there will be Rowland Percy. Where would he be likely to seek for refuge but in that great city—that grave of individuality, where one man may live entombed among the living, hidden amidst moving masses, so that it would be impossible for the most practised seeker to lay hands upon him, and point out his whereabouts— where would I go but to London, if I wished to hide from the consequences of some great crime?—if—if those consequences were pursuing me, as, of course they never will—they never can; for I have fenced myself too well round with precautions —my guilt is known but to one, and he dare not reveal it; blood is upon my hands, but they will look pure in the eyes of men; for who but Samuel Twitter could point out the ensanguined stains, and he dare not—he dare not. It would be to sign his own death-warrant."

He stood at the corner of the street, and breathed laboriously for several seconds. When he again spoke, it was in a lower tone, and his steps became more languid, for Bernard Varley's health was sadly failing him, and he was only powerful and violent by fits and starts, like the gusty wind, which one moment would rush on its career with headlong violence and fury, and the next subside into placidity and calm repose.

"To London—to London," he muttered. "To London at once. I may over-take them on the road—I shall overtake them on the road, and never again will I lose the track of Miranda Rankley. The Grange shall be sold. It is mine, indisputably mine. My title to it is as good as Sir George Rankley's, for no one doubts the authenticity of the will by which he bequeathed it to me. It shall be sold by auction, and I will never again while I live blast my eyes with the sight of it or York."

"Never again—never again?" shrieked a voice in Varley's ear. "Ah! ah! a wild, stray thought. Bernard Varley will be hanged at York—hanged in the presence of thousands—hanged at York—hanged at York. They call me an idiot, but that is the prophecy. You sped the bullet well at me, Bernard Varley, but it would not do its work, for you are to be hanged at York, and I am to see it."

"Devil!" cried Varley, as he aimed a blow at the retreating figure of poor Martin the maniac. "Am I in my bitterest moments to be tormented by such as thou art? 'Tis a fair chance, and I will now rid myself of at least one of the curses of my existence."

He drew a brace of pistols from his pocket, and pursued the figure of the flying idiot.

Rage lent to Bernard Varley the fleetness which he was far from ordinarily possessing, and he rapidly gained upon poor Martin, although the latter was no despicable runner. Varley, however, had not patience to wait until he was close to his victim, but levelling one of his pistols, he fired at the retreating form, which fell with a loud cry to the pavement.

"Tis done," muttered Bernard Varley, between his teeth, as he placed the other weapon in his pocket, "'tis done. Who dare cross my path, idiot or sane man, he shall perish."

A loud clapping of hands attracted his attention, and looking hastily in the direction from whence the sounds proceeded, he saw to his surprise the idiot boy standing at the entrance of a narrow court, and when he saw that Bernard Varley's eyes were fixed upon him, he shrieked in wild accents that rung far and wide,—

"Hanged at York—hanged at York—with a crowd to see it. Ah! ah! ah! Bernard Varley will be hanged at York!"

Upon the moment, then, he disappeared with extreme rapidity down the dark passage, and Bernard Varley felt that in the intricacies of the market-place to which it led, pursuit would be fruitless.

With deep execrations, then, he wrapped his cloak hurriedly around him, and hearing many windows open, and that a general alarm was created in the street by the firing of the shot, he hurried with great speed, and in a nearly frantic state of mind, towards the hotel which at he had temporarily taken up his abode.

CHAPTER XCVI.

ROWLAND'S JOURNEY.—THE TURNIPS.—THE TURNPIKE GATE.—THE ORDEAL PASSED.
—AND THE CHASE.

WE left Rowland Percy in far from a very enviable position as regarded his mode of transit to London, although it had the great charm of being a tolerably safe one.

His acquaintanceship with turnips in the chaise-cart was by far too intimate to promote warmth or comfort, and as those vegetable productions had been, at the requisition of Witlet, newly pulled from the parent soil by the landlord of the road-side inn, they brought with them various accompaniments of lumps of mould, &c., which by no means tended to make them agreeable travelling companions.

Still, while there was no danger there would be no necessity for Rowland's being entirely covered up with cold vegetable matter, and they jogged on for some time without anything arising to provoke such a measure.

"As I said," remarked Witlet, "the officers are sure to proceed a good way a-head until they are quite certain that you are not before them, for they will inquire diligently what travellers have passed through every turnpike."

"And then, I presume, they will return?" said Rowland.

"They will, and carefully, too, stopping every vehicle they meet on the road from York; if we escape them, then we shall be safe enough, for each moment will be increasing our distance from them."

"It may be premature," said Rowland, in a saddened voice, "for of course I am yet far from safe, but the thought will obtrude itself upon me, of what on earth am I to do when I get to London.—All the frightful misfortunes, under certainly, the severest of which I was near sinking, have come together upon my own family and upon Sir George Rankley's. My own father became destitute at the same time by a singular caprice of Sir George Rankley's, or by some deep-laid villany, yet to be discovered; Bernard Varley, my bitterest enemy, claimed everything which should have been Miranda's."

"Your position in London is certainly bad," said Witlet, "because by the peculiarity of your situation you are deprived of your proper chances; but you, Mr. Percy, who have been brought up luxuriously, never knowing what want was, and I dare say scarcely the cost of any one article of your daily consumption, can scarcely have a notion of how small a sum will supply a person's mere physical wants in London."

"Indeed!" said Percy.

"Yes; your peculiar situation, until your innocence is established, if it ever should be so, would prevent you from spending much money, unless you sat down and got drunk every day, or sent yourself into an apoplexy. I will undertake to get you boarded and lodged safely in London for a sum that will be to me very trifling indeed, until some change for the better takes place in your fortunes."

"My generous friend," said Rowland, "am I not only to owe you my life and

my rescue from a death which I will own now was most frightful to my imagination, but am I to make myself a perpetual burthen to you?"

"Oh, nonsense about perpetual burden," said Witlet; "lightly come, you know, Mr. Percy, lightly go. You know my profession; we have ups and downs, as there are in all trades. Sometimes we are overflowing with wealth; at another, we are poor, miserable devils, with scarcely a farthing to help ourselves; but where I mean to place you, they know me, and will have confidence for a few weeks at any time. So cheer up, for it seems to me you have got out of the fire pretty well."

No. 47.

"Thanks to you, indeed," said Percy, "I have—but what—oh, what is to become of Miranda?"

"Be under no anxiety on that score," said Witlet. "I saw enough to convince me before I left York that Miranda was surrounded by good and warm-hearted friends, and friends, too, capable of helping her. She will want for nothing this world can afford, you may depend."

"I thank Heaven it is so," said Percy. "But hark! do I not hear horses' feet?"

Ned Witlet pulled up instantly, and they both listened with the greatest attention; from afar off on the road they were taking, came the unmistakable sound of horses' feet at an easy trot.

"It may be them," said Witlet.

"The officers?"

"Yes, they'll be sure to return this way, and we had better provide against all chances. You must go down among the turnips, and we must see what a little bamboozling will do."

While Percy held the reins, Ned Witlet busied himself in making a hollow place among the turnips, where Rowland could lie down in a crouched-up position, and be easily and completely covered up by them.

"You'll have lots of room to breathe," said Witlet; "but hear what you will as to any proposition for searching the cart, or taking us back to York, do not be alarmed, but remain perfectly quiet."

"I will," said Rowland; "although, believe me, rather than again fall into the hands of my enemies, I would die resisting them."

"If the worst comes to the worst," said Witlet, "I won't tamely give you up. You are an innocent man, and you have a right to defend your life. Place these pistols in your breast, but do not use them except in great extremity. If they should insist upon moving the turnips, we'll give them a chase for it to the darkest part of the road we can find, and then trust to our luck; but we had better talk no more, lest our voices should be carried on the air, and they'll never believe I ha e been holding a conversation with the horse."

"I think that will do," said Rowland, as Witlet placed an amazing bunch of turnips on his face; "it's wretchedly cold, and something like being buried alive, I think."

"Hush—hush!" said Witlet—"not another word."

Ned then allowed the horse to go forward at an easy trot, while he hummed a provincial air, and occasionally smacked his whip as the burden of the tune.

There was a toll-bar about a quarter of a mile a-head, and from this there came a sound of voices, proceeding, as Witlet rightly enough guessed, from the returning officers, who were stopping to have a parley with the gate-keeper. Witlet would rather not have passed through the ordeal which he felt was at hand under the glare of light from the toll-house; but the sound of the wheels of his cart must have reached the ears of the officers, and to stop then would be to bespeak the very suspicion he wished so particularly to avoid.

Less then five minutes more driving brought them to the toll-bar; around the door of the little tenement connected therewith were several horsemen, one of whom had dismounted, and was doing something to his saddle girths.

"Now, stupid," said the toll-man to Witlet, who was jogging through without taking any notice.

"What's the row," said Witlet; "don't the Thorn-end ticket clear this ere end gate?"

"No, it don't, and you know that well enough, I'll be bound. Thruppence, stupid, perhaps you think it's hard."

"Yeas," said Witlet; "do yow?" At the same time he gave the man a hard nob on the head with three penny pieces, that made him jump back and rub the afflicted part with great fervour.

"Confound you," said the man, " what did you do that for? You're an idiot, I suppose?"

"Eh! eh! I coomes from Yark."

"The devil doubt you," said the toll-man.

"So, friend, you come fron York," said one of the mounted officers; " have you heard of Rowland Percy?"

"Chap as hoong?" said Witlet.

" No, the chap as was to be hung, but who contrived to get away."

"Eh! eh!" said Witlet; " where did he coome froom?"

"The fellow's an ass," said the officer, " Where are you going to?"

" Next fear with these ere nips."

The officer rode to the side of the cart and looked somewhat curiously into it, as he said,—

" Why, you have not brought them all the way from York?"

" Yeas, I have, though," said Witlet. " They're fine 'uns, ain't they?"

" They seem of the right sort. Are you sure you saw no suspicious characters on the road?"

" Noa," said Witlet, " not till I zeed some chaps round a pike, as seemed arter no good."

"Oh, the fellow's a fool," said the officer turning away.

"Thank ye," said Witlet; " we are all fools as coome from Yark."

With that he spoke to the horse, and jogged on at a very slow pace, while Rowland Percy blessed his stars that the investigation was over.

"Did you see the horse that fellow had?" said the dismounted officer to him who had ridden up to the side of the cart.

"No," was the reply, " I didn't notice it."

"On my soul!" said the other, " it was as fine a creature as ever stepped, and never cost less than a hundred guineas."

" You don't say so; that don't look a likely thing for a turnip cart."

"D—n him!" said another, " look how he's stepping out now."

This was a fact, for Ned Witlet really believed then that they had not the remotest suspicion, and when he got about a quarter of a mile off, he just put the horse to a canter, and away they went at a good eleven miles an hour.

This was certainly injudicious of Witlet; but the idea of his pace making any difference to the officers never occurred to him, nor would it have occurred to them, had not the question been raised about the value of his horse.

There was a moment or two's hesitation among the officers, and several of them spoke together, saying,—

" Is it worth while to go after him?" Then by one accord, they said " Yes;" and turning their horses' heads towards London, they were soon in full gallop after Ned Witlet.

It was some minutes after Ned Witlet had increased his speed in the manner we have related, before he thought it prudent to speak to Rowland Percy, and then he leaned down and said,—

" I think all's safe, but I'll keep on at this pace for a few miles; until we have put those between us and the toll-bar we may as well speak low."

" I thihk you managed it amazingly well, Witlet," said Percy. " The few moments we remained in suspense were far from pleasant ones."

" We are safer now than ever we were," said Witlet; " and if the magistrates should take it into their heads to send a party again up the road, we shall have got a good start, and—what's that—what's that?"

" What?" said Percy, as Witlet drew up abruptly.

"Pursued, by Heavens!" said Witlet—"at a slashing pace, too."

CHAPTER XCVII.

THE CHASE CONTINUED.—THE PARTING.—AN HOUR OF DESPAIR.—THE VILLAGE
BELLS.—A BETTER RESOLUTION.

As Ned Witlet spoke, he gave the horse the rein, and the animal immediately broke into a prodigious gallop, the turnips flying about in all directions.

For some moments Percy said nothing, for the speed at which they went was so great, that it was as much as he could do to keep his place in the cart. At length he said,—

"Surely Witlet, mounted men must overtake us. I will sell my life as dearly as possible, for, by the Heaven above me, I will not be taken back to that cell from which I have so lately emerged."

"Make yourself comfortable," said Witlet, through his set teeth, as he held the reins slackly with both hands, "The road's like a bowling-green for the next dozen miles, and a stern chase is a long chase. I know that we are beating them now, although we sha'nt be able to keep it up."

"And then what is to become of me?" said Rowland.

"Why," said Witlet, "I have an opinion that you won't get to London so quick as I thought. I tell you what you must do; there's a place some miles a-head called Wickford Hollow; it lies low, and is as dark a bit of the road as we could wish. As, I say, we are beating them now, and by the time we arrive there we shall have about five minutes to spare, your only chance then will be to get out and hide yourself on the roadside, while I gallop on. They are safe to pass you then, and your plan will be to walk on leisurely; you will then come to a roadside public-house, called the Old Moon, where you can wait till you see or hear of me. Tell them you are a friend of mine, and all will be right."

It may be supposed this speech of Witlet's was spoken under considerable disadvantages, and came jolting out of his mouth as the horse galloped in rather an unconnected manner; nevertheless, it was sufficiently explicit for Rowland Percy fully to understand it, and his immediate reply was,—

"But, my good friend, do you not expose yourself to considerable evil and suspicion from such a course; for when they overtake you, may they not arrest you on suspicion of aiding me in my escape?"

"I think not," said Witlet. "I shall go at my own pace, and they can't quarrel with me for galloping on the road from York to London, since they are doing the same themselves, and I rather think it will be a long job to catch me, and when they do, what can they find but a chaise-cart with a few turnips at the bottom, which they may take into custody if they like, and much good may they do them.

"Certainly," said Percy, "that presents a feasible aspect of escape; but in good or evil fortune, whether we overtake each other or not, I shall never forget how much I owe to you."

"Never mind that," said Ned Witlet. "The man who would not assist such a noble-hearted creature as Miranda Rankley must be a brute indeed, and I know by assisting you I am assisting her, not to mention my dislike and unwillingness to see an innocent man sacrificed to such an infernal scoundrel as Bernard Varley."

"I am deeply indebted to you."

"And then, again," continued Witlet, "we gentlemen of the road are the natural enemies of the law and all its paraphernalia of judges and officers. But hark! by Heaven they are coming at a slashing pace. They've good cattle, but it strikes me that, lumbered as our horse is with two persons and a cart, he's beating them. His reach in a gallop is tremendous. I'd draw up in a moment if I thought they were gaining six inches in a mile upon us."

Percy could plainly now hear the loud and regular beat of the horses' hoofs, which were in such hot pursuit of him, and as occasionally the road wound about in different directions, those sounds would appear to be nearer or further off as the vibrations of the air came directly to their ears, or were interrupted by intervening obstacles. Their own steed shewed not the slightest distress, but seemed rather to improve upon his speed than otherwise, galloping on at a rate which soon left nothing but the under stratum of turnips, and perfectly astounded the drivers of the few stray vehicles they passed.

There was something pleasurable in the excitement of that wild chase, notwithstanding its result was of such fearful import to Rowland Percy; and the cool air of the early morning, as it blew freshly in Rowland's face, for the speed they were going at created a tremendous artificial current, felt invigorating and delightful. On, on they sped, passed meadows, villas, cottages, and through long avenues of trees at undiminished speed, until at a considerable distance a-head, Rowland Percy could perceive what appeared to him so far off a perfect wood, to which they were dashing with such tremendous speed.

"There," said Witlet," "there, right ahead, you will see Wickford Hollow. There we will draw up for one moment to permit you to alight."

"It seems quite an impervious wood," said Rowland.

"Yes, but there is not a bad road going through it, although, except in the very height of summer, a damp one. Remember the Moon. Say you are to meet me there, and do not think of moving until I come to you, except something very urgent should arise, and then do not let me pass you as you proceed towards London, for I suppose you will hardly turn your face to York."

"Hardly, indeed," said Rowland. "What an extremely dark place this is."

They had now plunged into the part of the road where Witlet intended to draw up, and he began gently to moderate the speed of the horse, saying—

"Creep out at the back, Mr. Percy, and then hide yourself among the brushwood —less than five minutes will bring them here."

Percy did as he was desired, and clambering over the back of the cart, he hung for a moment to it, until Witlet very nearly stopped the horse.

"All's right," he said, as he dropped into the road.

"Good luck to you," cried Witlet, and giving a cheering whistle to the horse, he again started off at the same tremendous gallop that for the last half hour had carried them over so many miles of country.

The sudden transition from the rapid motion of the cart to perfect quiet and inaction, felt very strange for a moment or two to Percy, and he stood for a few moments, as if half bewildered, in the road, and incapable of action; then came upon his ears the fearful and tremendous beat of the horses' hoofs, that were pursuing him for his destruction. Death and disgrace came in the sound; and, excited as his imagination was, it was with a cry of terror that he rushed to the side of the road, and cowered down among the tall brushwood that grew there in such wild luxuriance.

Nearer and nearer came his pursuers, making the earth echo again with the loud tramp of their horses' feet; then, upon the dense morning air, he could hear their voices as they encouraged each other to the pursuit, some minutes before the purport of their words could reach his ears. It was, however, with great gratification that he noticed the gradual decrease in the sound of Witlet's horse's feet, and felt that that faithful friend was, in all probability, still gaining ground upon the half-maddened officers, who did not entertain the shadow of a doubt but that their victim was really before them.

There was but little time, however, for reflection, before the officers came on with the speed almost equal to that of the fabled wild huntsmen of the German forests.

He heard the voice of the foremost of them saying to his comrades—

"On—on—on! Never mind horse-flesh. We'll have him yet—we'll have him yet—they can't keep it up. On—on—on!"

Then there was one rush, as if a hurricane was sweeping through some trees. The pursuers were passing him, and for the moment Rowland Percy was safe.

With a bewildered feeling he half walked, half staggered into the road, and strove to pierce with his eyes the deep obscurity of the shaded hollow through which the horsemen had disappeared. Fainter and fainter came the heavy beat of the horses' hoofs upon his ear, and then, like a glimmering light which, after it has been extinguished, leaves its faint spectrum upon the eye, cheating the imagination into a belief of its continued existence, Rowland Percy thought he still heard, from afar off, the monotonous beat of those horses' hoofs, when they were too far off for the faintest sounds to reach his ears.

A few moments more, and even that delusion vanished. He felt h'mself utterly alone—a wanderer on the earth's surface—friendless, or, at all events, those who would have befriended him were helpless—houseless, proscribed, and a price upon his head.

A deep sigh burst from his labouring heart, and lifting his arms to Heaven, he said—

"When, oh when, am I to know again that dear heart's security that was mine in times gone by ?—When can I again take my place among my fellow-men, as free as they, and as little obnoxious to death and ignominy as the best and bravest, with all the feeling to make one, and that not the least kindly one, of the family of man? Why, oh, why am I picked out by cruel fortune for such a fate as that which I have narrowly escaped, and cast off from that society which I have never injured, for an alleged crime, at which my nature shudders, and which the world's wealth, and the world's power, would not have tempted me to commit? Miranda, too—Miranda, the pure and the beautiful—the sinless, innocent being, in whose composition the diviner elements of nature seemed to have entered—what a fate has been her's ! God of Heaven! is it possible that one bad man is endowed with a fiend-like power of crushing so many trusting, loving hearts? What will become of me—what will become of me ? "

As he spoke he crossed his arms upon his breast, by which action he felt the pistols which Witlet had given to him, and forgot to ask back.

" Ha !" he cried, " these are friends, indeed. While I have these I need not fear the felon's cell ; for I can tempt those who would take me to destroy me ; and, oh ! what would death be in comparison with again encountering the gloom of that prison-house, with the consciousness that but a few short hours were between me and death upon the scaffold."

The wind swept past him with a howling and melancholy sound, and the darkness of that nearly impervious shadow in which he was, seemed momentarily to deepen around him. A cold and shuddering feeling came across his heart, and it seemed to him as if nature was assuming around him a more stern and forbidding aspect—as if the natural elements of creation, as well as his fellow creatures, were arraying themselves against him.

" Am I repudiated—am I repudiated," he cried, " by all ? Am I to be alike cast off by Heaven and earth ; what deep sin have I unknowingly committed that I should be made the wretch I am, shrinking at ever y footstep, and trembling at the sound of the human voice ?"

The dark feelings then that a time had swept across his soul when in the condemned cell, found a place again in his heart, and the one frightful word suicide rose to his lips.

He plunged among the brushwood again, and sat himself down against the trunk of an aged tree ; he tried to extract hope from his position, but the feeling was dead within him ; he tried to tell himself that all was not lost ; but the reply he gave his own heart was, " all—all."

" If ever," he said, in a low, shrinking voice, " a mortal soul might be excused in unbidden standing before its Creator, it would be one placed in such circumstances as mine—persecuted without crime ; hunted without cause ; condemned, though innocent."

The wrapt stillness that reigned around, the entire absence of any sounds that would bring his thoughts back to earth and earthly feelings, {much assisted in nourishing the feelings which at that dread moment found a place in Rowland

Percy's heart; everything was forgotten but his own hopelessness—his own fearfully critical situation, and his despair.

For a time he covered his face with his hands; a convulsive sob shook his frame, then he gazed wildly about him for a moment, and cried in a loud voice,— " Farewell !"

It was his adieu to earth ;—in another moment the deadly weapon of destruction was in his hand—it was levelled at his head ;—but ere he could complete his fatal purpose amid the deep stillness of nature some sounds fell upon his ear, which he felt as if compelled to listen to, and which seemed one by one to be drawing him back with a gentle and sweet compulsion to earth—to hope—and to happiness.

The sounds were those of the bells of some distant church, which, mellowed by distance, came with a silvery and softened tone to his ears. It was but a rude attempt on the part of the ringers of these bells to perpetuate a simple melody; but it was a melody which Rowland Percy had heard and loved in his childhood, when all was bright and beautiful around him, when the summer sun shone for him with a more than heavenly lustre, and when the sunshine of the heart and the jocund merriment of a happy home carried him fleetly through the winter, making it but the shadow to the otherwise too bright and lustrous picture of his happiness.

Now each note of that simple melody fell like the voice of a friend long lost upon his heart, the dear companions of his early days seemed rising in thronging groups from the dim and fading past; all the bright, all the beautiful associations of his existence crowded about his heart, and then, with a gasping sob and a gush of tears, he cried—

" Miranda ! Miranda! I am saved again, I am saved again !"

More sweetly and with an evener cadence came the witching of that sound across his soul. It seemed to fill the air with a chaste and holy influence. The mists of despair cleared from the brain of Rowland Percy, and he arose from the foot of that aged tree with deep thankfulness to Heaven that had saved him from himself, and made him a wiser and a better man.

" Hope—radiant and beautiful hope," he said, " I will not peep too curiously into thy airy structure, thou shalt be to my cheering fancy as beautiful as rainbow tints, but not so fleeting;—I will cling to thee, and in whatever depth of misery the malignant fates may place me, I will not only be hopeful of emerging from it, but I will imagine a still lower depth, and raising my voice to Heaven, I will thank its mercy for that it has saved me from, and not question the wisdom in which it is inflicted. For thee, Miranda, for thee, I will live !—ah, how could I call myself lonely and desolate, when such a heart as yours was mine—when I had such a pure spirit to cling to me in the dark hour of my fate. Miranda, Miranda! my beautiful, my best !—a gift of God, which should fill my heart with thankfulness instead of murmuring."

CHAPTER XCVIII.

THE JADED STEEDS.—THE OFFICER'S MISHAP.—THE STAGE COACH, AND THE MEETING.

NED WITLET smiled to himself when he heard the horsemen in full pursuit of him, and the few turnips that still remained in the chaise-cart, with a malicious satisfaction he determined upon leading them a long, and useless chase.

" I will not distress my horse," he said, " for that I wouldn't do, for the lot of them ; but I can lead them a tolerable distance on the London road without doing so—as for poor Percy, he's safe for the present ; they'll be ready to gnaw their own heads off when they catch me, just to find they have been scouring somewhere between thirty or forty miles across the country after a man in a cart, whom they are not to interfere with when they catch him, and abut a dozen bunches of turnips."

At the end of Wickford Hollow there was a turnpike, but Ned Witlet's pursuers were not sufficiently near to him to give any alarm to the 'pikeman to shut the gate, so that shouting out the number enabled him to pass, and he dashed through it without abating a jot of his speed. The turnips made a terrible riot at the bottom of the cart, keeping up a constant dance, as if they had been instinct with life; but Ned Witlet would not waste time by stopping to throw them out, and the road being now more level and a great deal harder, he got on for five miles with amazing quickness.

Meanwhile, the horses of his pursuers became frightfully jaded, for although good cattle, they by no means started fresh to their work, having had a good share of hard riding before the chase commenced; the consequence of this was, that getting up the rise on the opposite side of the hollow nearly foundered them together, so that while Witlet was dashing on at a considerably increased pace, the only hope of his pursuers was to reach the next town, and there get fresh horses, for, with the tired animals they rode, the pursuit was becoming a most hopeless affair, and one which, without fresh steeds, would be much better given up, for while Witlet went two miles, they scarcely got a mile and a half, so that they were lagging fearfully behind.

"This won't do," cried the senior officer; "I have no doubt on earth that our man is before us; we shall be able to get fresh horses in another six miles, and that six miles we must push on by some means or another."

"I doubt," said one, "if it be possible—whip and spur will never get my horse half the distance."

"Try it," cried the senior officer, "and don't spare him. I warrant you I'll get my brute on—I never saw the horse yet that I couldn't make go till he dropped."

The horse seemed upon this to conclude it would be better to do so at once, so he picked out the next little hole he came to to stumble over, and away went the officer over his head into the hedge at the roadside, performing in his progress, many very curious gymnastic feats, and then embedding himself head foremost, like a congreve rocket, into the most vindictive quick set-hedge that ever was planted, for all the prickles by general consent seemed to assail the luckless officer at once.

"Murder—murder!" he cried, "help! d——n it, where am I going to? Pull me out—was there ever such a beast?"

It took the united exertions of the whole party to drag their leader from the hedge, and the process of so doing was torture of an infinitely worse character than getting into it, for the one was long and protracted, while the other had been so sudden an operation, that he was wounded fearfully before he scarcely knew it, or could think what was happening to him.

When rescued, he looked in the most pitiable plight, his face and hands streaming with blood, and his clothes torn in many places. His first fury seemed to be directed against the horse, and with the exclamation of—"Where's that infernal beast?" he rushed towards the animal, who, however, was not to be so easily caught, for, after tantalizing his late rider by dancing round him twice, he set off at a tolerable smart trot towards York.

"Catch him—catch him!" said the officer; "d——n it, what am I to do?" But at the moment the other horsemen set their steeds in action, the animal, who found himself unencumbered by a rider, increased his trot to a canter, and then the canter to a gallop, so that there was a fair chance, had they chosen to embrace it, of a gallop back again to York after the runaway steed.

This, however, they gave up as hopeless, and the officer who had been so anxious to push on, found himself most uncomfortably situated on foot and the six miles lying before him far from agreeable.

Fortune, however for once befriended him, for scarcely had he rubbed his face down with his handkerchief, and propounded the question of "what's to be done now?" than the sound of a horn announced the approach of a coach.

"All's right—all's right!" he cried; "I'll get on the coach and stop at the next town, where if you have not arrived, I'll order the horses in readiness, and we shall catch our man for certain, for the pace he was going at can't last many hours."

The coach soon reached the spot, and being hailed by the officers, it drew up, while their unlucky principal mounted on its roof, smarting most woefully from the scratches he had received, and feeling a great degree of personal indignation at Rowland Percy, whom he heartily cursed as the author of all his misfortunes.

The other officers followed the coach in a straggling and disorderly manner, the whole party reaching the market town, six miles off, at somewhere about the same period of time, although the horses were ready to drop from fatigue, and the riders themselves were more fit for bed than continued exertion.

Nevertheless, there was one circumstance which spurred them on, and that was, that at least, a dozen persons certified to the fact, that a man in a chaise-cart, with some turnips, had gallopped through the town, at head-long speed, to the imminent risk of several pigs, and numerous families of chickens.

"He must be ahead of us," cried the officer, "don't let us relax—remember the reward, besides the honour of the thing. The York police will be laughed at for ever, if we don't catch him."

No. 48.

Fresh horses, and tolerably good roadsters, were easily procured, and within ten minutes of their arrival, the whole party were again in the saddle, intent upon reaching the next turnpike, where another inquiry would be made to satisfy them, if he, who they were pursuing, were still upon the high road or not.

The answer convinced them that they were all right, for the turnpike man said,—

"That nearly an hour before such a vehicle had passed the gate."

"Was there one man or two?" was the question.

"One man and some turnips," replied the turnpike keeper; "and as nice a horse as ever I seed. I asked him how far he had come, but the chap only laughed in my face, and said, 'as there was some people coming behind him as would be able to tell me,' and, I suppose you are them?"

"Come on," cried the officer, and without another word he gallopped forward.

Now, Ned Witlet, for the last hour, began seriously to think that the chase was abandoned, although he was by no means unmindful of the fact that the officers might have stopped to change horses, relying upon the extra speed they would afterwards attain to, to make up for the trifling delay.

"But, then, after all," he said to himself, "it was only a suspicion they had of me, and, it is possible enough, they may have abandoned it. I'll lead them another dozen miles, and then trot gently back, when, if they are coming after me, we shall soon meet. I must not forget Rowland Percy, and the precarious situation in which he is placed."

It was in consequence of thus reasoning, that Ned Witlet slackened his speed considerably, and even waited some time at a little road-side inn, to refresh both himself and his steed; then he gave away the remainder of the turnips.

"Why, friend," said the landlord, "these are prime ones, and, if you have been to market, I wonder that they were left."

"I was going to market," said Witlet, "and had a cart full, but my horse took fright, owing to having something ugly behind him—and most of the turnips were left on the road side for the Lord of the Manor, so you are welcome to the remainder if you like."

"Very good," said the landlord. "I'll swap a jug of my old October for them."

The old October was duly discussed, and the horse being refreshed considerably by his temporary halt, and the attention which Witlet paid to his wants, they started on the road back to York at a comfortable and easy pace, which, the burden behind him being considerably lightened, was no hardship, and, perhaps, better than sending him at once to a stable.

The great speed which the officers were now making, was to be added to the pace at which Witlet was travelling, and the two combined, presented a very early prospect of the parties meeting; in fact, half an hour had scarcely elapsed, when Witlet saw his pursuers attain the brow of the hill and come sweeping down the declivity at a great rate.

"Now for it," said Witlet. "I shall see what sort of a humour they are in—if they ride terribly rusty, and think of taking me, I'll try to get a little start of them, and give them another gallop on their road home; but in case they shouldn't recognise me now, I just give them a taste of the quality of my horse, for I wouldn't miss the fun on any account."

Witlet then spoke to the horse, which immediately commenced stepping, but in that tremendous trot of which some horses are capable.

"Halt!" cried the senior officer; "halt—that's our man for a hundred pounds!"

"That's the horse—that's the horse!" cried another, "I should know him again among a thousand."

The horsemen immediately drew themselves up across the road, and Ned Witlet drawing his horse to a walk, said,—

"Gentlemen, I presume you are highwaymen; but it isn't of no use in stopping me, for I have not five shillings about me."

"Come, come," said the senior officer, gallopping up to the side of the chaise-cart, "where's all your turnips?"

"Why, the chap as I'm taking home this cart for," said Witlet, "tells me the horse took fright, after shying at some ill-looking rascals that he saw near a turnpike-gate."

The officer bit his lip as he saw the empty cart, and felt quite satisfied that Ned Witlet was not the man he sought.

"Done again by G—!" he muttered to himself, then, in a loud voice he said,—

"Hark you, my friend, I don't know who you are, but I very much suspect you had somebody with you when you passed this way before."

"Ay," said Witlet, calmly; "you look a suspicious chap."

"What have you done with the turnips?"

"Partly giv 'em away, and partly swapped 'em. How come you and the cat to fall out—have you seen your face lately.

"We will take this fellow," said the officer, "into custody, at all events."

"May I humbly ask," said Ned Witlet, "what for?"

"Suspicious circumstances," said the officer. "You have a suspicious look, my friend."

"Lord bless you," said Witlet, "it would never do to take up people for that."

"And why not," said the officer; "you seem a remarkably clever fellow in your way."

"Because you'd never be out of gaol," said Witlet.

The officers who were not engaged in the controversy, seemed to feel the joke of this retort of Witlet's fully, although he against whom it was directed did not, but reddening with anger, he turned to his companions, saying,—

"Ho! men, help me to lay hold of this vagabond, he's after no good, I'll warrant; and by laying hold of him, we sha'nt, at all events, return to York empty handed."

At the same moment that he spoke, he made an attempt to lay hold of the horse's rein, but Witlet, by a sudden movement, eluded him, and then, before the other officers could have moved towards him, he said,—

"Harkye, my friends—a joke's a joke, and I know what you can do and what you can't as well as yourselves. You have no charge against me, not the shadow of one. You can't take me either of you unless I choose to let you; but I don't see why I should put myself out of the way upon the subject; so, now I tell you candidly, that I have both means and inclination to trounce you soundly, if you attempt to lay hands upon me."

The officers drew back, leaving their principal to contest the matter alone; one of them remarking to the other,—

"It's no joke taking up a man for nothing. Bill White was let in for a hundred pounds damages on such a score."

"And who may you be?" cried the senior officer. "You talk big enough."

"I am not bound to tell you on the king's highway," said Witlet, "who, or what I am. Go to school again, stupid, and persuade your mother to give an extra twopence to teach you manners."

The officer ground his teeth with rage, and shaking his riding whip he said,—

"You are on the high road back to York now, my man, and so are we. If there be law to prevent my taking you into custody, which I am not quite sure of, only I wouldn't give a fellow like you an advantage, there's none to prevent me from keeping an eye on you."

"Oh! nothing in the least," said Witlet. "Would you like to go behind or before, a change would be desirable, as you are all on one side now?"

Witlet, then, at a sharp trot, proceeded on his road, followed by the officers, who kept within a dozen yards of the back of the chaise cart, their principal being determined to see him into York, and ascertain really who and what he was.

It was not part, however, of Ned Witlet's intention that such should be the case, and although he could, probably, have easily avoided the pursuit by turning his horse's head and going in the opposite direction, whither the officers, after their long ride, would have no disposition to follow him, the spirit of fun took possession of him, and forgetting for a brief space Rowland Percy and his perils, he annoyed the officers beyond description by his singular mode of travelling.

For a few moments he would start off at a gallop, when they would all clap spurs to their steeds to keep up with him; but when he found they had fairly got into the pace, he would draw the horse into a walk, or perhaps, stop altogether, and whistle a tune throughout, with a great many variations, while the officers were fain to wait, cursing and swearing the whole time, until, to them, the anything but melody was finished.

This kind of thing lasted for about half an-hour, and then Ned Witlet suddenly drew up, and clapping his hand over his mouth, said—

"Bless my soul, I have dropped one of my eye-teeth, and have got to go all the way back again."

Upon the word he wheeled the horse round, and giving it a long whistle, he started off again at a smart trot, leaving the officers looking at each other bewildered in the middle of the road.

"After him—after him," cried the senior officer. "D—n him, I'll take him handcuffed to York, if it cost me a hundred pouuds."

The others, however, hung back, and one of them said, shaking his head gravely—

It's better to leave him alone, sir, he's only poking his fun at us. If it should turn out to be some sporting gentleman after all, which, when you come to look at his nag, isn't at all unlikely, we shall get into a pretty mess."

"Mess, be hanged," cried the angry officer, "Follow—I say follow; d—n the fellow, he'll be out of sight in five minutes."

He seemed to make no doubt, then, but his companions must of necessity follow him; but such a supposition was an error in judgment, for, although he started after Witlet at a good round pace, they made uo movement to follow him, but continued in the middle of the road gazing after him, as if they were quite unconcerned spectators.

"I say," said one to another, "what shall we do uow?"

"Oh," was the reply, "I don't see that we are called upon to gallop on every fool's errand. Here has been something like a chaffing match, and he who has had the worst of it would get us all into a pretty scrape, because he happens to be in a passion. I vote for a quiet canter back to York.

This suggestion met with general approval, and rather to the consternation of the senior officer, far from being backed up by his companions, he found his distance increasing from them in a duplicate ratio.

Had he consulted, then, his own inclinations, he would most certainly have turned his horse's head to York; but his pride and anger got the better of prudence; he dreaded the laugh which would follow his return, and a laugh which, although from prudential motives it might be hidden from him, would be none the less indulged in; and with a bitter curse against him who had been the cause of his getting into so disagreeable a predicament, he determined to follow up the chase at all risks.

"It is but man to man," he muttered, "and I am armed. He would never be fool enough to resist me."

CHAPTER XCIX.

ROWLAND'S PROGRESS.—AN ANCIENT ENGLISH INN— THE LEGACY.

ROWLAND PERCY had perhaps never felt in so calm and clear a state of mind since he was first falsely accused of the dreadful crime of murder as he did when his better reason had triumphed over the frightful suggestion to commit suicide, and he emerged from the copse into the high road.

It seemed as if some accumulating mental vapour had been suddenly dispersed from before his soul, and he could see his situation more clearly in all its various bearings than he had been able to do before.

" I have numerous chances," he thought, " of yet emerging from the painful circumstances that surround me, and as yet what have I suffered to poor Miranda, who has supported herself amidst it all with an heroic resolution, which should have been a pattern to me, and enabled me to bear with my lighter ills most patiently.

" Has she not lost a father—a father she loved with an intensity of affection, that for so many years had no other object on which to expend its sweet impulses—lost him too in a manner calculated to rend her very heart-strings, and plunge her into the profoundest melancholy; yet for my sake, my sake alone, she fought up against all the accumulated evils that would have crushed a weaker spirit, and discarding her own miseries, risked all, dared all, to save me from the unjust death that threatened me.

" True, the hand of man is raised against me, and I am a hunted, proscribed being; but if I have lost one world have I not gained another in the dear love of Miranda Rankley, and have I not escaped a death which the most sanguine heart that ever beat would have pronounced inevitable ?

" Great God, let me be thankful for what I have, and the dear gifts that Providence has bestowed upon me, murmuring not that affliction has visited me, but seeking with a philosophy which shall surely be sublime to extract good from everything."

'Twas in a frame of mind such as this, and with a comparatively light and buoyant heart, that Rowland Percy walked rapidly forward in the direction where Witlet had told him he would find the road-side public-house, the landlord of which, for his, Witlet's sake, would afford him food and shelter until he should arrive.

The clear and beautiful morning air imparted a strength to his frame and tension to his muscles, such as he had not experienced since his weary imprisonment, and the pace at which he walked was an extremely rapid one, so much so that he soon arrived in front of the low, long looking, straggling house, the swinging sign of which proclaimed it the " Moon."

It was a very pattern of an old English road-side public-house, containing such a singular collection of architectural orders as would look absurd in a modern residence, but tinctured with age and with the green crust of antiquity about it, it afforded a pleasing variety to the eye at that ancient hotel.

There was no end of gable ends, and such multitudes of little windows that peeped here and there from out of the sly corners and old places, sometimes struggling to shew themselves amid an overgrowth of ivy, and at another, appearing as if jutting out from the house in order to find an additional support among the boughs of some ancient tree.

Each succeeding generation seemed to have added something in its own peculiar taste and style to that ancient and most interesting structure, and Nature, ever bountiful, had aided largely by its multitude of creeping plants in connecting the whole together, so as to make the structure as pretty and romantic a piece of habitable confusion as the most ardent lover of the picturesque could wish to see.

Then there was the rare old porch, still beautiful and sturdy in its old age, still admired for its blackened and ancient carvings that had resisted successfully the encroaching hand of time, and the clasp knives of the topers, who, for nearly three hundred years had quaffed from rare old flagons rich creamy ale beneath its tempting shadow.

Oh, how many a portly man of iron frame, and such sinewy strength that it would seem as if he could laugh at time and all its doings, has sat beneath that ancient porch, making the welkin ring with his loud and hearty merriment, but over whom now waves the long rank grass of the silent church-yard.

But then, as the stout forest leaves falling before autumnal blasts, are succeeded again by the pure freshness of the spring-tide vegetation, which, in their turn, become the glory and beauty of the forests; so as each three-quarters of a century rolled over the head of this ancient house, the song and the jest would still be heard beneath the ancient porch, although from new voices, and the sparkling ale would mantle in other cheeks than those to which it lent its gladdening influence some fifty years ago.

Rowland Percy could not but pause to admire the fine old structure ere he entered its portal. It was a pleasant and cheering thing to his heart, dear lover of the picturesque and the beautiful as he was, to find that his temporary sojourn was to be in a house the very exterior of which afforded him such ample food for pleasurable reflection.

"Ay," he cried, " I think I could be happy here, if free from the storm of fate and with my own beautiful Miranda by my side ; I think I could be happy here— the world forgetting, by the world forgot."

It was rather *mal apropos*, though Percy was pleased to hear it, but at that instant such a peal of jovial laughter came from the ancient porch, that it was evident some joke of a most titillating character had b een perpetrated, for a big stout man had rushed out into the road, with a face of about the colour and size of the largest and brightest conceivable warming-pan, and danced again in the very ecstacy of his mirth.

Rowland was forced to smile in spite of himself, and, as he walked up to the porch of the " Old Moon," he said—

" A pleasant morning, friends, it does one good to see you so merry."

" Merry," cried the man with the warming-pan face, who, having recovered a little from his convulsive mirth, had followed Rowland within the porch, " merry, dom'd if we ain't!   My ould aunt, poor creatur, worse luck, she's dead, and left me three hundred and twenty-seven quarts—dom'd if we haven't begun to drink 'em."

" Perhaps, sir," said a thin, lanky-loooking man, who held a fast clutch of one of the quarts, " you will allow me to attempt an exemplification, as Lindley Murray says.   I am the schoolmaster of the village nigh away here."

" Ay, ay," roared the fortunate legatee, " exploficate, will ye," at the same time that he dealt the schoolmaster such a blow between the shoulders, by way of encouragement, that he could scarcely draw his breath for three minutes.

" His aunt," continued the schoolmaster, " left him some chairs and tables, and what they come to just produce, according to an arithmetical sum I have made on the occasion, the number of quarts he mentions, which quarts are a-going.— My service to you, sir."

The schoolmaster, upon this, made a great vacuum in one of the quarts, and the man with the warming pan face shouted—

" Dom'd if that schoolmaster ain't a clever fellow.   Take a quart, my lad," to Rowland, " and we'll drink good luck to old Tabby Bullmuggin, my aunt, and the 'Old Moon,' too, bless it,"

Rowland did not refuse the draught, for, in truth, he was thirsty after his walk, and when he removed the tankard from his lips, he said,—

" I wish to see the landlord if he's anywhere here about."

"Oh—ay," cried the legatee, "he's asleep in some corner, I'll be bound. Hedges! Hedges! Hedges! here be some one wanting thee."

Upon this an indistinct rumbling sound came from the passage, and, in a moment an enormously tall man got through the door with a side wrench, which he could only have accomplished by long practice, but in the accomplishment of which he was fain to screw up his features into an agonised expressio, which shewed that it was an effort of no ordinary character.

"What's the row?" said Hedges.

"Are you the landlord?" said Rowland.

"Yees."

"Then I wish to speak to you a moment in private."

"It be no use," said Hedges, "t'other 'sizeman called last week, Stump."

"You mistake me," said Rowland Percy; and, coming as close to the landlord as his rotundity would permit him, he whispered,—

"Ned Witlet, known sometimes as the Slashing Squire, told me I might wait at the 'Old Moon,' and meet with a kind reception, till he came."

The landlord took a strong steady stare in Rowland's face, and then he looked right down him, beginning at the top of his head, and finishing at his boots; after which he gradually brought his eyes up again, when he began to make such extraordinary faces that Rowland became alarmed, and thought he was choking; but before he could interfere, the landlord seemed to recover, and, shaking his head, said—

"No go, no go, haven't succeeded in getting up a regular wink for a matter of thirty years; howsomdever, they say a nod's as good as a wink, and that's un-kimmon easy. All's right—no gab or guffery here; stay as long as you like, young 'un, and you'll see as much rollicking, roaring, tearing, at the 'Old Moon,' as will do your heart good. All's right—curse this door, it gets narrower every day."

The fat landlord, with a dreadful effort, during which he stamped frightfully upon the oaken flooring, to the immeasurable amusement of the topers in the porch—succeeded in forcing his way into the porch again, whither Rowland followed him, as he was anxious to tell him more at leisure how much his circumstances required secrecy and caution.

Having thus seen the persecuted Percy safely housed beneath the hospitable roof of the 'Old Moon,' we will return to Ned Witlet, who very soon became aware of the fact that he was followed by the officer, and he guessed, likewise, pretty correctly, that it was more from anger and spite than from reflection that such was the case; for first of all, there could be no charge against him; and secondly, it is very seldom that the police authorities place themselves merely upon equal terms in point of strength with those they wish to apprehend.

It was rather with vexation than any alarm that Ned Witlet became aware of the fact that he was still pursued, and he said to himself—

"What on earth can the fool mean by coming after me alone; he must be mad to think I'd let him interfere with me, when it is but man to man. His anger must have got the better of his judgment; but still he may prove a serious incon-venience to me, if he chooses to keep following me wherever I go; Rowland Percy is still but in a very precarious situation, and his escape, after all, depends upon a series of lucky accidents, which may or may not occur. Curse the fellow, he's getting his horse warm to the work, and making more speed."

Ned Witlet set himself seriously to consider how he could ged rid of the officer, and at last he came to an extremely natural conclusion for a man like him, and that was, to accomplish by violence what might be a very slow process by any other means.

"If he will come," said Witlet, "he must stand the consequences, for 1 cannot be pestered with him any longer. He seems determined on an encounter, and he shall have it—the sooner the better."

When Witlet had once made this determination he lost no time in putting it into execution, and turning round his horse's head again towards York, he advanced rapidly to meet his pursuer.

"Curse him, I have turned him at all events," muttered the officer, as he saw this manœuvre. "He knows I must have had him the next place he passed through, and he seems willing to spare himself the trouble. It will be a feather in my cap to capture the blade, come of it what may, and I'll trust to my own luck and reputation to set things right with the magistrates, even if it is a mistake."

The officer then planted his horse exactly in the middle of the road and drawing a holster pistol from the pocket of his over-coat, he presented it at Witlet, saying, as he approached sufficiently near to hear him,—

"Hark ye, my man; I intend making you my prisoner by foul means or fair, so you had better take it quietly, and give in at once. If you are an innocent man there is no harm done, and you know your remedy; but if a rogue, as I suspect you are, it is my duty to make you prisoner."

Witlet made no answer whatever, but came slashing on in the cart, directly in the middle of the road, as if the officer was not there at all, so that the latter was compelled, for his own safety's sake, to get out of the way of the wheel, which otherwise would have inflicted upon him some serious injury.

This contemptuous conduct on the part of Witlet increased his anger wonderfully, and he cried in a voice, hoarse with rage,—

"Surrender—confound you, surrender! Curse you, if you hesitate another moment, I will fire!"

"Fire away," said Witlet.

Even as he spoke bang went the pistol of the officer, but it was very unlikely he should hit so shifting a mark as was Ned Witlet, who had not failed to see the pistol, and whose great object was to get it discharged.

The moment he heard the report he wheeled round his horse, and was in a few moments by the side of the officer, to whom he dealt so heavy a blow on the head with the crab-stick he had, that it nearly knocked him from his horse, and taking immediate advantage of his temporary confusion, Ned Witlet sprung from the cart, and dragged his opponent to the ground.

The officer, however, was not so far stunned as to be incapable of resistance, and being far from a weak man, a tremendous struggle ensued between the two.

It was soon, however, perceived that he was no match for the sturdy highwayman, who, although not so muscular as the officer, was taller, and much the more powerful man. The consequence of this was, that in a few minutes, Ned Witlet was uppermost, and had his antagonist fast by the throat, and within a hair's breadth of choking.

"Mur—mur—murder!" gasped the officer.

"You are a very troublesome, meddling fellow," said Witlet. "What the devil possessed you to put your neck in this noose?"

"Help—help! D—d—n it, I am choking."

"Choke and be d—d," said Witlet. "You tried to take my life, and if I was as passionate a fool as you, I should just knock your brains out. Come, answer me, and if you don't it will be the worse for you. Have you any information respecting Rowland Percy?"

"None—none," gasped the officer. "I—I can't speak—you are choking me."

"Have you got any handcuffs about?"

"Coat pocket," gasped the officer.

Ned Witlet, holding him by the throat with one hand, plunged the other into his coat pocket, and there sure enough he found a pair of very well made, new looking handcuffs, which shut by a spring as comfortably as possible.

The officer made a desperate attempt to rise, when he found that it was Witlet's intention to place the handcuffs upon him, but the latter was determined to secure his enemy for some time at least, and as he continued his resistance, kicking and plunging in all directions, Witlet laid down the handcuffs for a moment, and dealt him two such tremendous open-handed whacks on each side of the head, that his face tingled again, and the tears started in his eyes in spite of himself.

After this the officer's spirit seemed completely subdued, and he allowed Witlet to put on the handcuffs without the least attempt to hinder him.

Ned Witlet's next movement was to take from him a pocket-book and a purse, both containing a good round sum; after which, with a hearty kick, he said,

"Now, get up, I'll trouble you to get on the other side of the hedge."

The officer could not have got up himself; but Ned Witlet lent him assistance by a tremendous pull of the collar, and when he was on his feet he pointed to a gap in the hedge at some distance off, saying,

"You'll just be pleased to walk through there, and as I am in a hurry, pray be quick.'

Witlet walked behind the officer, lending him each moment an accelerating kick, so that they were both of them in a meadow, adjoining the road, in a few minutes; but Ned Witlet made him cross that and enter the field beyond, after which he took a handkerchief and tied his elbows together at his back, which, combined with the handcuffs in front, as totally deprived him of all use of his hands and arms, as if he had not possessed those members.

No. 49.

A second handkerchief he then tied tightly round his eyes, after which, giving him another kick to bespeak attention, he said,

"Perhaps you'd like to know who I am now, after all this?"

A groan was the officer's only answer.

"Well," continued Witlet, "whether you do or not, I'll tell you: did you ever hear of the Slashing Squire?"

"The highwayman!" cried the officer; "the highwayman that the rector of Elwinkle offered two hundred pounds reward for, because he robbed him one evening when he was trotting home from a charity sermon?"

"Yes," said Ned; "I'm the man."

"Oh, what an ass I have been."

"There you are right, and it strikes me, that for a little while an ass you will remain."

So saying, Ned tripped up the officer's heels, bringing him down on his back with such a thump on the soft meadow, that he made quite an indentation, and there he lay as helpless as could possibly be, for not being a tumbler, and the grass very slippery, his efforts to get up without the assistance of his hands were for a long while perfectly useless.

When Ned reached the road he found that the officer's horse had trotted quietly off somewhere, while his own was nibbling the scant herbage that grew by the hedge side.

"Now for the 'Old Moon,' and Rowland Percy," said he, as he jumped into the cart and galloped away.

CHAPTER C.

VARLEY'S MEDITATION.—WILD LOVE.—THE SALE OF THE GRANGE.

It was on the morning of the third day after the departure of Miranda from York, on her long and perilous journey to London, to meet with Rowland Percy, that Varley rose from a sleepless couch and proceeded long before daylight to the Grange estate.

He thought the cool air of the morning would refresh his wearied body and heated blood, perhaps calm the harassing agitation of his spirits also.

No one was on foot, and he proceeded unmolested towards the spot he sought. He wished to behold it once more, ere he parted with that which had caused him to dye his hands in blood to acquire, and which he now sought to rid himself of. He was soon out of York, and in the green lanes which led towards the Grange; he, however, avoided the mansion, and sought a gentle eminence covered with verdure, from which he could see to a great distance; but it was as yet dark, but by the time he arrived the grey tints of the morning peeped up from the east and proclaimed the earliest dawn—the chilliness and gloom of night would soon give place to the light of glorious day, and all creatures would rejoice in the warmth of the sun's beams. The cawing of the rooks, in the distant rookery heralded the approach of morn.

All else as yet was still and quiet—nature reposed—but ere long the teeming earth would be filled with life and motion, and every living creature would be endued with cheerfulness and gladness.

The feathered tribe began to twitter in the hedge-rows and on the trees as the light became stronger, and before his beams had well illumined the hemisphere, the lark had risen to its giddy height, and then hailed the sunny morn.

The dark clouds of night slowly retired before the day, and ere they were fled they had felt the warm rays and glowing tints of the sun, rendering the heavens glorious as they departed, and adding a beauty to the scene they no longer became a part of.

Hill and dale, meadow and woodland, now became distinctly visible, and afforded a grateful picture to the eye. The dark masses of wood in the distance relieved the eye when wearied by gazing upon the sloping meadows or the sunny sky, and they in their turn served to enliven the scenery. Many were the delightful spots where the eye would rest for a moment to contemplate its beauties, as if it desired to wander no further in search of novelty, or seek another spot in which to calmly live and enjoy a pastoral life.

Soon the face of nature is changed, and what but a few short hours since was silence—a scene of still life—was now quickened into an active, busy scene; myriads of living creatures, peopling earth, air, and water, darted into life; the timid hare is seen to cross the grassy knoll, and the rabbit to dart in its wayward path through furze and brake; the feathered inhabitants of the air, filling it with pleasant sounds, flitted to and fro with joyous carol, while the many coloured tribes that have been loosened by the farmer and peasant from the roost, enliven the scenery by their presence, and loudly proclaim the day begun.

Such a sight as this casts over the most gloomy mind a sense of pleasure— earth and air contribute to fill him with emotions to which he may have been a stranger, and help him to feel, that praise is due to nature's God for so ordering such a succession of pleasant images.

But the heart of him who now gazed upon that still and beautiful morning was but little adapted to appreciate its varied beauties and the claims it would have presented to the admiration of a better nature.

We will not libel common sense, even to pay a compliment to human nature, by saying, that no one could be found less calculated than Bernard Varley to admire, and look with a kindly eye upon the glories of inanimate existence. There are many such, although we rejoice to say few in comparison with the mass of mankind.

Situated as he was, he could take in at a glance the whole of those broad lands and that splended mansion, for the acquisition of which he had risked his very soul's salvation, and now that he had gained all, the glory of possession had departed; and he would have trembled and been possessed with a thousand terrors in walking over that estate and entering the apartments of that splendid house, which he had coveted so fearfully as to dip his hands in human blood to obtain.

; For some time he remained silent with his arms folded across his breast, then deep sighs burst from his labouring heart, and he cried in a despairing voice,

"I might have known—I might have known, experience should have taught me, that it is not possession, but successful pursuit which brings contentment. Am I the happier that all this is mine own?"

As he spoke, he stretched his arm across the varied landscape, and then allowed it to fall to his side with a deep groan, as he added,

"No—no; did I say happier? Can I ever know even a negative state of repose? will there ever occur a moment, during which I shall not be haunted by the frightful images that now assail my soul? Will it ever be that I can lay my hand upon my heart, saying, ' Here is peace?' Oh, how have I lingered upon that estate, prying into every corner, counting its very trees, admiring its beauties, giving myself up to dreaming contemplation of its soft shadows, and basking in the mid-day sun, that shone upon its fruitful fields, until the wish that it should all be mine, grew into a raging fever. It took possession of my heart and soul; withering all reflection, shutting out all feeling, and making itself the sole object of my thoughts by day and my dreams by night.

"Then came the murder—the successful murder, the one deed of blood that gave me all I coveted ; and no sooner was all mine—no sooner could I smile at the storms of fate, and tell myself that I was far above every ordinary contingency of existence, than a new passion, strange, wild, and wonderful, arose within my soul, and I would have given all again for one smile from her who is and ever will be the load-star of my existence—Miranda Rankley—Miranda Rankley! Oh, God oh, God! was ever beauty like her's? Was ever adoration like mine?"

It was a moment of wild and ungovernable passion with Varley, with the consciousness that he was alone, and no human eye was a witness to his emotion. He felt no restraint in giving utterance to the terrible feelings that possessed him; deep sobs burst from his labouring breast; he struck his forehead frantically with his clenched hands, and shouted the name of Miranda till far and near the fields and trees re-echoed the sound. Any one who heard him would have considered him a maniac in one of the most dangerous paroxysms, for he addressed wild and strange arguments and appeals to Miranda, as if she had actually been there to listen to him.

"Where, oh where, can you find a love like mine? Where, oh where, could you find a heart, that for the privilege of being beloved by you for one short week, would consent to be torn from its home, and consigned to everlasting perdition? Will the puny passion of Rowland Percy bear comparison with such idoliatry? Miranda, Miranda, are you mad, that you reject a love like mine for the cold feeling which by the mass of mankind goes by such a name?

"Love, what do they know of the glorious impulse? What do they know of the god-like feeling, which has its true manifestations in such self-sacrifices as they would shrink from aghast? They call a preference for one being above another love, and their feelings glide on in peaceable, and quiet obscurity, like an over-charged puddle by a quickset hedge.

"But my love is like a torrent, foaming and whirling on its course, leaping from crag to rock, in the wild delirium of its progress, and dashing itself madly into millions of bright scintilla, rather than not reach the object of its destination; or it is like the seething lava from a burning mountain, scorching in its progress, and redolent of fiercest fires. Oh, Miranda—Miranda, would I could repay scorn with scorn—hate with hate! But no, I must love you, adore you, when you trample upon my very heartstrings!"

A solemn sound came across the waste of nature to his ears, it was the minster clock; eight pealed forth, and Varley cast his eyes hurriedly over the Grange estate, muttering to himself,—

"Time warns me—time warns me. I came not to rave, and hold communion with my convulsed heart, but to take a long and last farewell glance of this spot, which I feel assured I shall never—never see again. 'Tis fair and beautiful, if it were not full of such reminiscences as would soon drive my soul to madness.

"Besides, I have now a pursuit—the one only pursuit of my future life. I must find Miranda. I must see Miranda. I must see her—I must see her, though she load me execrations—though she revile me in the bitterest language that the human mind can conceive, that the human tongue can utter. Still I must be near her, for it is something to be near heaven's gate."

He was silent then for some time, after which he said, evidently pursuing a new train of thought that had arisen in his mind.

"The Grange estates should fetch a goodly sum; that sum I will securely invest, but not in English funds, for something that I now little expect may possibly arise at some future day to make it advisable for me to avail myself of the yacht I have purchased, in making my escape. My money shall be in the Dutch funds; in my yacht, then, I can go to Rotterdam, make my own financial arrangements, and provide for my personal safety as circumstances may prompt me. As for Samuel Twitter, my only encumbrance, now, if it should happen that I have to fly the country, why, of course, I would leave him to his fate; let them hang him or do what they will with him, it matters not to me.

"In the event, however, of no danger occurring, he may follow me as my valet, and most abject slave, and the first suspicion I have of any scheme on his part contrary to my interests, he shall die—he shall die! It would become a measure of self-defence, and I shall not scruple to put it into execution. The Grange shall be sold to-morrow, agreeably to my instructions, sold without reservation to the highest bidder, be he who he may, and then my life is devoted to a pursuit of Miranda.'

CHAPTER CI.

THE AUCTION.—THE INTERRUPTED SALE.—VARLEY'S RAGE.—THE AUCTIONEER.

BERNARD VARLEY had pursued his original intention of applying to the attorney who had assisted him in some of his machinations, to give a price for the Grange estates ; but that wily practitioner, who, in his own mind never entertained the shadow of a doubt of Varley's guilt as regarded the murder of Sir George Rankley, shook his head at the proposition, saying,—

"Why, you see, Mr. Varley, if young Rowland Percy had stayed in prison and been hanged comfortably as he ought to have been, I should have had no objection, for although I have not enough money of my own to buy the Grange estates, even at a bargain, but I could have procured you the means, and paid cash down ; but now the case is widely different, and by the escape of young Mr. Percy, the subject is not allowed to sleep in the public mind, and really there . is no knowing who may be hanged eventually for the murder, or what disputation there might be years hence respecting your title to the estates."

"Dare you insinuate ?" cried Bernard Varley.

"Oh, dear no, sir, I insinuate nothing—very far from it—there is a law of libel, and I know it—it is voluminous and comprehensive. I would not insinuate, or say anything for all the world, and being unusually busy, I must really wish you a very good morning."

The fact is that Twitter had paid the attorney a visit, and from what he had related to him concerning Varley's mad pursuit of Miranda, the professional gentleman, instead of thinking Varley the clever scoundrel he once believed him, began to think with Twitter, that his wits were a little deranged, and that he would be anything but a desireable acquisition.

Thus was Varley foiled in his original attempt to dispose of the Grange, and cursing the attorney in his heart, he proceeded to an auctioneer who was in a large way in the city, and requested him to undertake the disposal of the Grange estates for whatever they would fetch, in the then state of the market.

As a matter of business the job was readily accepted, and for some days past the provincial and London papers had teemed with attractive descriptions in the most vivid colours] of what the Grange was, and in a great number of instances what it was not, but at all events there were certain to be some good bidders for so importantly situated a property, although certainly many capitalists were deterred from attempting the purchase as a speculation, in consequence of the notoriety of the circumstances attending the death of its late occupier.

The ample revenue of the Grange estates, however, and its noble mansion, were not likely to go a begging, because one of its owners had been murdered, so that by twelve o'clock, the hour appointed for the sale, there was a crowded room, full of persons, ready, some to witness the proceedings merely out of curiosity, and others ready to bid for the important property.

By far the greater number, however, were strangers, come there for mere amusement, and the murder of Sir George Rankley, together with the criminal proceedings consequent thereon, had not a little added to that curiosity.

There is ever a morbid desire on the part of the public to be present at, and take great interest in, any proceedings which have grown out of others presenting features of peculiar atrocity. Thus there is no doubt if the furniture if the Grange had been sold by auction it would have fetched enormous prices, and most probably the bed on which Sir George Rankley was murdered would have sold for ten times its value.

The price, however, which the Grange estates must inevitably go at precluded the possibility of an exercise of this absurd feeling, which, to use a popular phrase of the day, might be called morbidity for the million. So those who attended could only take an interest in preserving one of the catalogues, glaring at the auctioneer, and taking an intense interest in the faces of those who bid for the property, as if by so doing they became in a remote degree connected with the murder—an object of popular interest themselves.

Half-past twelve o'clock came, and the auctioneer mounted the rostrum—all was breathless attention, and a shade of care seemed to pass over the rubicund countenance of the knight of the hammer—his very red whiskers seemed to quiver with anxiety, and as it was observed that he turned his little grey eyes in a very singular manner to all parts of the room before he ventured to speak, then a cadaverous expression crossed his face, and pointing with his ivory hammer tremblingly, to a corner of the room, he said,—

"You don't mean it; you don't mean it?"

"I do mean it," cried Mr. Anderson, stepping forward, and standing upon a chair, so that he could command a view of, and likewise be seen by, the whole apartment. "I do mean it. Ladies and gentlemen, I have something very important to say before this sale is allowed to be proceeded with."

"Oh! pho, pho—pish—pshaw," said the auctioneer.

"Ladies and gentlemen," continued Mr. Anderson, "many of you in this room know me; my name is Anderson, and I am sure I need not ask twice for a patient hearing while I make a few remarks of the first importance to those who may be interested in the disposal of the property now about to be put up for auction."

"Oh, rubbish—stuff—pho, pho," cried the auctioneer; "he's been to me last night, and I know all about it—pho, pho."

"Hear him—hear him," cried several voices.

"No, no," cried others; "let the sale proceed."

"Anderson, Anderson—hear Anderson," was loudly cried; "down with him—hear him—the sale—police—shame—knock him down—turn him out."

The auctioneer flourished his hammer, and turned redder in the face, until he looked like a new copper cauldron, while Mr. Anderson made calm but repeated efforts to be heard in the midst of the confusion which was each moment increasing.

Then when the riot was at its height, Bernard Varley suddenly stepped forward, and exerting his voice to the utmost, he cried "Silence," in so tremendous a tone, that the chaos of sound was stilled, as if by the voice of some enchanter; each one pausing, involuntarily, in the noise he was making, to look upon the pale face, distorted with passion, of the man who had so lately, in York, gained so unenviable a notoriety.

"I am glad you are here, Mr. Varley," said Mr. Anderson, "as you will now hear truly what I say, without being possessed of any garbled statements upon the subject."

"How dare you," cried Varley, in a tremendous tone, "interrupt these proceedings? Five pounds to the man who will bring me a police officer to turn this scoundrel out of the room."

"Hard words break no bones, Bernard Varley," cried Mr. Anderson, "and I would rather he abused wrongfully than deserve it and escape."

"Proceed with the sale," cried Varley to the auctioner; "time is a little too valuable to have it wasted in listening to this mad attorney, and his musty proverbs."

"True," said Mr. Anderson, "and that puts me in mind that I came here decidedly to stop this sale."

"Stop the sale," cried the auctioneer, "oh, pho, pho—rubbish."

"Don't be a fool, copper nose," cried somebody from the lower end of the room, and a roar of laughter at the auctioneer's expense succeeded.

"Stop the sale!" shrieked Bernard Varley. "How dare you attempt to stop the sale of property? police—police."

"Mad or sane, Bernard Varley," continued Mr. Anderson. "I mean to attempt it, and with every hope too of success. At all events, it will not be the threats of such a man as Bernard Varley that will deter me. I stand here as the champion, although, perhaps an inefficient one, of the innocent and oppressed, but I hope that God will give me strength to support my cause."

Loud cries of,—" Bravo Anderson ! bravo Anderson !" resounded through the room ; " hear him—hear him—let him speak !"

Mr. Anderson had fairly got the ear of the multitude, but Varley made another desperate attempt to stop him by saying,—

"This man is my enemy ; it is well known he is my enemy, my avowed enemy, and now he wants to prevent my selling the estate which was bequeathed to me by my friend, and which my feelings will not permit me, myself to inhabit."

" As God is my judge," cried Mr. Anderson, " I have but one object, and that is to save, if possible, some gentleman here present, from incurring heavy losses by purchasing an estate, the title of which may be disputed."

"Disputed !" cried Varley.

" Aye, disputed," cried Mr. Anderson, " I dispute it, and I advise all [here present to abstain from bidding for an estate which has been acquired at the expense of the destitute, the innocent, and the orphan, Miranda Rankley."

A loud burst of applause followed from those who merely came as lookers on, and even those who came to buy looked doubtful and dispirited.

" Ladies and gentlemen," continued Mr. Anderson, for he saw he had got the ear of the meeting, " I would fain have spared you all the trouble of coming here this day, and I called upon the auctioneer last night to tell him that I was determined to make this attempt to stop the proceedings of the day. The circumstances under which these estates have passed to this man, Bernard Varley, are full of suspicion, and I warn anyone against taking the estate off his hands, even at the lowest and most nominal price. Let him hold possession, ladies and gentleman, while he can, but do not let him, after reducing to destitution the gentlest and noblest creature God ever created——"

Here was a loud burst of applause, and when it subsided, Mr. Anderson continued,—

" Do not, I say, let him walk off in truimph after converting that estate into money. No, ladies and gentlemen, let it be a clog to his foot, a galling collar round his neck, a torment to him by day and by night, so long as he keeps it from that innocent, and heroic girl, who has shown an example of courage and heroism that would for ages to come be talked of, as along with her beauty, (as one of the characteristics of the ladies of York)——"

This was a most politic sentence of Mr. Anderson's, for it at once enlisted in his cause every female in the room, and several meek looking men, who rather hung back till now, were pushed headlong into the fray by their wives and daughters, and made to shout, " Hurrah ! bravo ! and go it !" till they almost terrified themselves.

In vain did Bernard Varley try to make himself heard. He grew hoarse with passion, and almost foamed at the mouth with his impotent rage. He sprung upon a chair in order to raise himself above the multitude, but it was kicked from under him in an instant, and he found that if there was the slightest chance of his being allowed to remain in the room, it was only on his good behaviour.

As for the auctioneer, he kept up a continual knocking with his hammer, and looked quite bewildered, until somebody threw somebody else's hat at him, and then he disappeared altogether, sinking down in the bottom of the pulpit, fully convinced that the end of the world was very near at hand.

As the hat went down with him in a very singular manner, the occurrence produced a perfect shriek of laughter, and a variety of brass articles which lay at hand, were pitched into the rostrum, producing almost a state of delirium in the auctioneer, who could not conceive what was taking place ; and when at last somebody shut up the writing-desk which was before the clerk, and taking it from him by force of arms, dropped that in, there was such a shout as transcends all description.

"I think the sale's over," whispered Mr. Anderson to the two or three friends by whom he was surrounded, and who had occompained him to the auction for fear of any personal collision with Varley.

"Quite—quite," said the young barrister, who was one of the party. "You need say no more. Our friend the auctioneer must fancy there is an earthquake, and he is buried alive among miscellaneous property."

"I think so too," said Anderson, as he alighted from the chair on which he stood.

"On my word," said the governor of the prison, who made one of the party, and was wiping his eyes, "I never was so amused in all my life. That auctioneer is a perfect treasure for a joke. Who could have supposed he would have gone in again so curiously; but you come away, Mr. Anderson; the sooner now we leave this place the better."

By this time Bernard Varley had recovered from the shock he had sustained in being decanted from the chair suddenly, and he roared out,—

"Auctioneer, do your duty. I will not have this sale stopped. The Grange estates are at auction. Do your duty, sir. As for you," turning to Mr. Anderson, "I will prosecute you for your interference, in the proper quarter."

"And I defend him," cried the young barrister; "and my first endeavours shall be to discover if the plantiff comes into court with clean hands."

"I understand you all," said Varley; "this is a conspiracy against me. Was there ever yet a man prosperous by his own industry, or the kindness of another, who did not make a host of enemies? But I will indict you all for a conspiracy, and this day's work shall be the worst you ever did in your lives."

"I should be glad, indeed," said Mr. Anderson, "to get you into court; you would cut no very enviable figure at the assizes, and I don't think, for my own part that you will relish another cross-examination."

"I despise you," cried Varley, "and your insane remarks.—Auctioneer, do your duty!"

The auctioneer, however, was quite deaf to the repeated calls which Varley made upon him; and as the room was getting rapidly clear of persons, for the crowd followed Mr. Anderson and his party into the street, cheering him as they went; and even Varley began to see that there would, indeed, be no auction that day.

Then he took it into his head that, if the auctioneer had acted with firmness, the sale might have proceeded; and, impressed with that conviction, he strode towards the rostrum, he mounted the steps leading to it, and looking in, shouted to the auctioneer,—

"Idiot! I shall make you answerable, by bringing an action against you for this day's disappointment."

"The Lord have mercy upon me!" said the auctioneer; "where am I?"

"Curse you!" cried Varley, making a blow with the heavy riding-whip, he carried, on the top of the miscellaneous property, which hitting the writing-desk, brought it in more violent contact with the auctioneer's head, making him believe he was in the other world, and the sport of malignant demons.

"Stay, stay," cried Varley, to the retreating throng of persons, "why are you going?"

"Ah! I hear him," said the auctioneer; "he says, going; the devil's knocking down human souls, and I am gone."

The crowd of persons would not be stayed, for they saw no further amusement, or profit, by remaining in the auction-room, so that, in a few moments more, there was none left but the half dead auctioneer, his clerk, and Bernard Varley.

"Now," said Mr. Anderson, when he gained the street, "come to my house, gentlemen, and let us think of some means of finding out where Miranda Rankley has gone."

"Ah!" said the young barrister, "I can well guess her feelings; she has that true nobility of soul that shrinks from being a burden upon any one; I declare to you, gentlemen, that if her heart were free at this moment, I should glory in making that girl my wife."

"A better," said Mr. Anderson, "could never be found to make a happy home and I long to see the day, should it ever come, when she and her first and only love,

Rowland Percy, for whom she has suffered so much, and done so much, may meet, never to part again."

"Amen." said the governor; "I never met or heard of her equal; the praises of her courage and heroism are upon every unprejudiced tongue in York. She deserves the happiest of fates; and it cuts me to the soul to think that she may be, even now, suffering great poverty, if not absolute want."

No. 50.

CHAPTER CII.

MIRANDA IN THE WAGGON.—THE JEW PEDLAR.—THE ROBBERY AND THE DIAMOND
RING.

IT was a slow and dreary mode of conveyance, that by the waggon, which
Miranda, for the want of a better, had been forced to avail herself of; but still it
was better, far better, than being exposed to wind and weather, and the chance
accidents of the road. If her progress was slow, it was certain; and, while old
Mr. Percy fell into a dreamy and disturbed sleep, she pleased herself with the idea
that she was each moment approaching nearer and nearer to Rowland Percy.

And, ho, how delightful would be their first interview, after so long a time, for
long, indeed, did it appear to Miranda, although it had been short in reality. The
multitude of events which had been crowded into it, would have sufficed for the
incidents of half a century; and it seemed to her, since that night in the condemned
cell, when her heart was fluttering between hope and fear, a long and weary time
must have elapsed.

She knew not how far she had travelled in the waggon, but her chequered
imaginations were suddenly put an end to by the stoppage of the vehicle; some
conversation then took place outside, and in another few moments a man scrambled
into the interior.

His aspect was far from pleasing—he had that indescibable low look which
belongs to a Jewish countenance of the worst order; and a small brass bound box
he had with him, not much larger then a writing-desk, would at once have
proclaimed to any more practised eye then Miranda's, that he was one of those
itinerant hawkers of mock jewellery, who makes the exhibition of their wares an
excuse in many cases, for committing petty larcenies, and in many others, for
obtaining information which leads to more serious robberies.

Miranda shrunk as far as possible away from the man, for his looks were
repulsive in the extreme, and she was not a little annoyed by feeling confident, for
the next half hour, he never took his eyes off her.

At length he spoke, and it was in a tone of insolent inquiry that he said,—

" Going far, miss—eh?"

" I do not wish to awaken my companion," replied Miranda, pointing to the
sleeping Mr. Percy, " and therefore decline conversation."

" Oh, you decline, do you?" said the man; " that's civil, anyhow. I didn't
mean any offence, miss—a handsome ring, by G—d."

As he spoke, he advanced so suddenly to Miranda, to look at the ring which she
wore on her finger, as the safest place to keep that last memento of her father, that
he was close to her side for a moment, but only for a moment, for she shrunk back
crying,—

" Help, Mr. Percy, help."

The cry acted like magic upon the slumbering senses of Mr. Percy, all the
maniac in his disposition seemed aroused, and springing to his feet, he seized the
man by the throat with a grip of iron, and flung him on his back in an instant,
shouting,—

" Fiend! fiend! monster, have I caught you? So you would comdemn my
innocent boy Rowland to death—you would see him writhing on the scaffold, and
exult in his pangs? Devil, devil, I will try if I cannot kill you."

He then bumped the man's head with such frightful violence and rapidity
against the bottom of the waggon, that it sounded as if some one was performing a
succession of double knocks at a street-door.

" Murder! murder!" cried the man; but the waggoner was fast asleep, and so
were all the horses, so that no attention was paid to the outcries of the pedlar, and
he would in all probability have paid with his life for his unwarrantable insolence,
had not Miranda sprung forward, and clinging to the arm of Mr. Percy, cried,—

"Spare him, spare him—it is enough, spare him, Mr. Percy—spare him—I implore you to spare him."

Her voice acted like a charm upon the troubled spirit which had been aroused to such an ungovernable pitch of fury, and with a smile he let go his hold of the terrified man, saying,—

"Ay, Miranda—ay, Miranda, at your bidding. Yes, my beautiful child, at your bidding. Yes, he shall live—the wretch shall live. God bless you, Miranda, is he not one of my Rowland's enemies?"

"No, no! let him be now," cried Miranda, "let him be, now, Mr. Percy; he is not—do not heed him—he is not."

Miranda clung to Mr. Percy's arm, and was quite as much terrified at the scene which ensued, as was the Jew pedlar, who slowly rose to his feet, as pale as a corpse, rubbing his head with great vehemence,

"You see," said Miranda, turning to him, "what your own folly brought upon your head."

"Upon my head!" muttered the man; "d—n, he's nearly knocked it off, Is he a madman?"

"Hush—yes," whispered Miranda.

"The devil!" cried the pedlar, as he sprung to the tail of the waggon.

"Again, again," cried Mr. Percy, in a loud voice.

"No, no," cried the pedlar; "for God's sake—it all right I didn't mean anything—how do you do, old gentleman? I hope you'ill be better soon. D—n my rags, I never had such a bump in my life. When one gets into a waggon, one don't expect to get into a wild beast show."

"Is he an enemy now!" said Mr. Percy, turning to Miranda.

"No, no," cried the pedlar; "for God's sake tell him no, young woman. It's all right, old cock—I tell you it's all right."

"Peace," cried Miranda, taking Mr. Percy by the hand; "there is no danger; will you sleep again?"

"Yes, sleep," he muttered. "I was dreaming of my boy. Wake me, Miranda, if the enemy should come. I will tear them limb from limb, and tread down the pulsation of their hears twith my heel."

"Good gracious!" said the pedlar, suddenly dropping his brass-bound box, and then, fearful that the noise would arouse Mr. Percy's fury, he said, in a whining tone,—"The Lord Almighty bless you, sir, and all your family. It's a fine day sir, I hope you're well, sir."

"We will let him," said Mr. Percy to Miranda,—"we will let him live for a little while. Now, I will go to sleep awhile, and dream of my boy, Rowland, and of you, my beautiful Miranda; Heaven have mercy on those who look awry on you, for I will have none."

"What a sanguinary old thief," muttered the pedlar; "but if I don't have that ring, my name is not Ikey Samuels."

The journey now proceeded some miles without interruption, no sound disturbing the stillness around, but the monotonous tinkle, tinkle, of the horses' bells, which they were so accustomed to, that the sound rather acted as a gentle lullaby than otherwise, and it is probable that if the bells had suddenly been taken away, they would have all started wide awake in wonder and astonishment to know what had happened.

The Jew, however, was too good a judge of the value of Miranda's ring, and of too avaricious and dishonest a disposition to allow even his dread of the violence of Mr. Percy to stand in his way of an attempt to possess himself of it.

"Miss," he said, in a low cringing tone, "I've got a pair of earings as is the very pattern and model of that ring you have on your finger."

"I do not wear such ornaments," said Miranda, shortly.

"But," added the Jew, "as it would match my ear-rings, I could perhaps sell the lot together, and as well to make up the little offence I made you, my dear, as for that reason, I will give you a more valuable ring in exchange for years.

"I want no exchanges," said Miranda; "there is no ring to me so valuable as this, and nothing short of absolute necessity to provide for the wants of my aged companion and myself shall ever induce me to part with it."

"But ——"

"Nay—nay," said Miranda, "I wish for no offers, and no conversation concerning it."

"I humbly beg your pardon," said the Jew, "and am glad you are so well provided for the journey you are going on."

Miranda felt instinctively for her purse, and she felt in her pocket, for, unlike some young ladies, she wore that useful appendage, and did not stuff everything down the bosom of her dress.

With a pang of alarm she assured herself that the purse was gone, and as the expression of her features could not be mistaken for a moment, the Jew said in a low tone—

"Have you lost anything, miss?"

"My purse—my purse," said Miranda, clasping her hands, "we are destitute now."

"Nay—nay," said the Jew, with repressed eagerness, "you—you have the ring, my dear, which, although of small value, will still, if given an honest and conscientious price for, carry you far on your journey."

"Small value," said Miranda, "I know well it is of large value."

"Indeed!" said the Jew. "Let me look again. Ah! you are right, it is worth a hundred pounds, and if you do ever part with it for less, he who purchases it of you will be taking an undue advantage of you."

"I have heard that sum named as its value," sighed Miranda; "but it—it—is almost like parting with my dear father again, to part with this——"

"But, my dear," said the Jew, "you are destitute, friendless; that is to say, you have no rich friends, and poor ones are not worth having at all; besides, I dare say the violent old gentleman is quite depending upon you, my dear."

"He is—he is," sighed Miranda. "Oh, heaven! what will become of us now?"

"Why—why," said the Jew, speaking eagerly, and creeping nearer to her at each word,—"you can sell the ring to me."

"To you?"

"Yes, my dear, rather than you shall fall into dishonest hands, I will give you the full value for it—the hundred pounds, as I am a sinner."

"My father's ring—my dear father's ring—my dear father's ring," cried Miranda, as she pressed it to her lips.

"Ah!" said the Jew, "I have a soft heart. Don't look at me, I am crying, my dear."

"If—if," said Miranda, in low, trembling accents, "if I sell it to you, will you tell me where I can find you, and promise me, in the name of Heaven, that you will keep it at least one year, in case I should be able to reclaim it of you."

"Oh, certainly—certainly, my dear," said the Jew, "as many years as you like. Do you think I have no feeling?" I had a father myself; he was hanged—no, I mean, he was drowned. You shall have it of me whenever you please, and without a farthing of interest too."

"That," said Miranda, mournfully, "would be a great consideration; I could part with it with less regret, if I thought that when fortune smiled upon me again, should such ever be the case, I could reclaim it."

"Reclaim it?—of course, my dear. Do you think I would keep your ring from you?—your father's ring, too!"

"But how should I find you," said Miranda, "if I were to part with it to you?"

"Have you ever been in London?" said the Jew.

"Never," replied Miranda.

"Oh, then," said the Jew, "my dear, I live in London, and you have nothing to do at any time but to ask the first person you meet for Ikey Samuels, and they will direct you to me."

'May I depend upon you?" said Miranda.

'On my word," said the Jew; "and you may well believe me, when I offer you the full value for your ring—the full value, my dear, that you have heard set upon it. Abraham forbid, my dear, that I should make a profit of you in your distress."

Miranda as silent for some moments, and it was evident that during that brief space of time her feelings were of the most painful nature; but then, when she thought of the heavy charge she had in Mr. Percy, who seemed committed solely to her care by Providence, and likewise how probable it was that when she reached poor Rowland, his circumstances would be far from flourishing, she chid herself for hesitating, and being sentimental about a ring, when so many more important feelings and interests were at stake.

"I will let it go," she thought. "A hundred pounds is a large sum and it will be a cheering think in the great city to which I am making my way, to have such a sum to present to Rowland Percy. Moreover, it will enable me to pay the man, Jones, who has so kindly assisted me with money. Yes; I will let it go—I will let it go. How could I hesitate when such considerations are at stake?"

Then turning to the Jew, she said,—

"On your solemn promise to restore me the ring again, if it should be in my power to make you ample restitution for so doing, I will sell it."

"I swear—I swear," cried the Jew, with eagerness; "I swear to restore it to you; my name is Ikey Samuels, and I would not break my oath for a thousand pounds, though if you knew me, you would take my word just as easily. My word, my bond, and my oath, are all alike. Did you ever know, miss, a Jew that was dishonest?"

"I know nothing upon the subject," said Miranda; "but with pain, I do consent to part with my ring, for what I have heard is its value, namely one hundred pounds."

"And you shall have it—and you shall have it, miss. A bank of England note for the amount you shall have; and here it is—how fortunate I have one about me."

As he spoke, he produced an ancient-looking pocket-book; and, after a great deal of fumbling about its contents, he produced a hundred pound note, which he handed to Miranda.

"Can you not give me gold?" said Miranda, "for I want money for current expences, and not in this condensed form."

"My dear," said the Jew, "you'll get change at the first turnpike you come to; they always keep a few hundreds in gold and silver, to give change to chance travellers."

Miranda hesitated still for a moment, and then she blamed herself for her suspicions: with a deep sigh she took the ring from her finger, and, handing it to the Jew, said,—

"Take it, and pray preserve it—you do not, cannot know how dear it is to me."

"I will preserve it with my life," said the Jew. "You have made a good bargain, miss, on my word, a good bargain."

He placed the ring, after carefully wrapping it in a piece of paper, deep in his pocket, and then he could ill suppress the chuckle of conscious knavery, that would make itself heard in spite of him.

Miranda placed the note in her pocket, and then, forgetting the very existence of the Jew, she fell into a deep reverie, in which painful reminiscences of the past, and hopes and fears of the future, mingled together in her mind

She was aroused from this by hearing the voice of the Jew calling loudly to the waggoner to stop, and glancing towards him, she saw that he was getting out at the back of the waggon.

When he saw her eyes fixed upon him, he said,—

"Good day, my dear—good day. Be assured I will save the ring. It is safer, a great deal safer then if you had it yourself, for you might meet, you know, my dear, with some rogue on the road that might deprive you of it. He! he! he! Good day, my dear—good day. Take care of the old gentleman—bless his heart."

"Good day," said Miranda, and, with another disagreeable chuckle, the Jew left the waggon.

CHAPTER CIII.

THE ATTEMPT TO CHANGE THE NOTE.—MR. JONES'S ARRIVAL.—THE DISTRESSING DISCOVERY.—MIRANDA'S SACRIFICE IN VAIN.

MIRANDA was extremely anxious to get change of the hundred pound note, for she had not, besides, a sixpence in the world; and it showed a very limited knowledge of society and its usages, to suppose for a moment that she could get change for it at a turnpike-gate.

An opportunity occurred of testing the accuracy of the Jew's information during the next hour, when the leading horse, after running his head against the gate, and producing an extra peal of all his little bells, came to a stand-still, and succeeded, as before, in stopping the whole team.

The waggoner then opened his eyes, and, after rubbing them for three minutes, said,—

"Thirty-six."

"All right," cried the toll-man.

"Stop a moment," cried Miranda—"stop."

"Woa!" said waggoner, and the old leading horse, who had slowly lifted up one leg, put it down again.

"What's the row?" said the turnpike-keeper.

"I wish to ask a favour of you," said Miranda.

"Sartenly, miss. What is it?"

"Can you give me change for an hundred pound note?"

"There's a d—n sell," said the turnpike-keeper, as he rushed into his little house.

"What does he mean?" said Miranda to the waggoner.

The waggoner shook his head, and then giving a crack with his whip, he said,—

"Kim up—gee."

A rattling of chains ensued, and a tinkling of bells, and the whole team was in motion; and, as Miranda looked from the back of the waggon, she saw the turnpike-man shaking his fist, and looking as angry as if somebody had just jumped on his corns.

Poor Miranda was quite at a loss to understand the meaning of all this, and she asked herself over and over again how she could possibly get change now for the hundred pound note; for, after the extraordinary conduct of the turnpike-man, unless it could be accounted for by insanity, engendered by the loneliness of his situation, she dreaded to ask another of the same class for the accommodation.

An hour and more passed away in uneasy thoughts, when a loud shout at some distance on the road attracted her attention, roused up Mr. Percy, and very nearly awakened the shaft horse.

"Hilloa! hilloa!" cried the voice. "Woa, there—woa. Stop the hunt. Good gracious! what a state you must all be in. You'll break all your blessed vinds at that speed. I never seed such coursing in all my life—neck or nothing—fifteen miles an hour—walk two on 'em, and dream the rest."

"That is Jones's voice," said Miranda. He will assist me in my dilemma."

In another moment Jones appeared at the tail of the waggon, into which he scrambled, and was out of sight before the waggoner had become thoroughly aware that there was a voice somewhere. When he did, however, his impression was that somebody had been run over, and he stopped the whole team, by spreading out his arms, and catching the leading horse round the neck.

Then he looked for five minutes under the waggon, by the end of which time he became satisfied that there was nothing to be seen but the wheels, the dirty road, the drag chain, and some turnip tops.

"Kim up—gee," he said, and again the cumbrous affair crawled on in total unconsciousness of the addition of Mr. Jones to the party.

"Well, mum," said Jones, "how is you and the old gentleman? I hopes as you is tolderido."

"We are very well, Mr. Jones," said Miranda.

"Nothing happened, I persume,"

"I have been very careless,'" said Miranda, "for the money with which you so kindly supplied me, I by some accident lost."

Mr. Jones gave a long whistle, and then added,

"Ah, well, it wasn't altogether unpleasantly, earned. I have got a few more of them same little tinkling goldfinches; some wagabone, I suppose, seeing as you was werdant, boned the mopusses."

"I think less of the loss," said Miranda, who had got into the habit of guessing at Mr. Jones's meaning, rather then trouble him to explain each word he uttered; "I think the less of it, because, by a sacrifice, which I ought not perhaps to have hesitated about before, I am enabled to provide amply for my present exigencies, as well as repay you the sums you have so kindly lent me."

"The deuce!" said Mr. Jones; "what's up now?"

"I have sold my father's ring?

"Sold it! my eye, who to?"

"A Mr. Ikey Samuels,"

Jones gave a comic sort of shriek, and then exclaimed,

"What a captivating name—done brown—done brown! tell us the peticulars; oh, crikey, here's a go."

"He came like myself," said Miranda, "to have a lift in the waggon."

"'Twas arter that," interrupted Mr. Jones, "you found as your tin had lewanted." ·

"Found what?" said Miranda.

"As the poney cut his stick—mopusses mizzled—the goldfinches emigrated.'

"Oh," said Miranda, "you mean the money; yes, it was after that I missed my money,"

"Oh, in course," said Jones, screwing up a terrible face. "Resoom—resoom."

"When I made known my loss," continued Miranda, "he offered to buy my ring; but I was very cautious, as you had warned me there were dishonest persons about."

Mr. Jones give a singular sort of howl, kicked the straw at the bottom of the waggon desperately, after which he cried,

"Resoom—resoom."

"I could not go wrong," said Miranda, "because I had often heard that a hundred pounds was the extreme value of the ring, and I resolved that I would not take a less sum than one which could come near that amount, and when he offered that sum in full, and at the same time promised to keep the ring for me in case I should be able to redeem it, I could no longer doubt the sincerity of his intentions."

"Fake away," said Mr. Jones, placing the tip of his thumb on the extreme point of his nose, and agitating his fingers in a mysterious manner.

"So," continued Miranda, "I let him have the ring on those conditions."

"Where's the tippery?" said Jones.

"He paid me with his hundred pounds note."

"That's the doge," said Jones.

"I have been trying to get it changed, but the turnpike man refused the trifling accommodation ; behaving very insolent, likewise, upon the occasion."

"What a ass he must have been," said Jones, unfolding the note and putting it carefully on his knees. "Here's a sanguinary do : 'Bank of Noland, I promise to humbug whoseever's green as grass, and doesn't know B from from a bull's foot.'"

"B what ?" said Miranda.

"What, didn't you read it ?"

"No ; I did not."

"My eye, what a extent of werdant vegetation you must carry about along with you—why, it's an out-an-out do : he's not only boned them ere mopusses as I guved yer, but this here note's just the walley of any other little bit of crumpled paper. It's a outrageous do."

"Gracious powers !" cried Miranda, " am I deceived ?"

"Gracious powers, you are regularly done brown," said Jones. "I never know'd such a splendiferous flabbergastation sort of do in all my life. Was he a feller with a little mahogany box, with brass edges ?"

"Yes,"said Miranda ; "he said his name was Ikey Samuels. Oh, how could I be so heedless as to lose my poor father's ring in such a manner ?"

"It's never no use of taking on," said Jones. "I meant to have gone the remainder of this here way with yer, but it's no go now. Howsomedever, I'll try to overtake yer yet ; but if I don't, stick to the vaggon till it's loaded, and come back with it—when I shall be sure to meet you. Here's something as'll do till I sees you again ; and, goodness gracious, Miss Miranda, whatever you does, don't be so outrageous green—it's puffictly putrifying."

"Where are you going, now ?" said Miranda.

"To ax for change for the flimsey," said Jones. "Ikey and me must settle this ere affair some how or other."

So saying, Jones, after thrusting the note into his breeches pocket, jumped from the waggon, and hastened off at a sharp walk in the opposite direction.

Poor Miranda felt this misfortune connected with the ring most acutely. She had only parted with it at the greatest possible sacrifice to her own feelings, with the higher and nobler object of providing first of all for the wants of h m who had been so strangely thrown upon her hands for support, and the pleasur eit would be to her to place in the hands of Rowland Percy a sum, at all events, that would rescue him for a time from poverty and its serious attendant evils.

But now to feel that she had made all that sacrifice in vain—to feel that she had lost that last and only memento of her father, and that her mind had nothing to fall back upon and console her for the deprivation, was grievous and heart-sickening in the extreme.

The only thing that supported her was, that Jones might be able to discover him who had so deceived her, and, before he could have disposed of the ring in any way, procure it for her, and once more give her the pleasure of having it in her possesion.

The supposition that the note was not a genuine one had never for an instant occurred to her mind ; but now that she felt its full force, she trembled at the danger she had unwittingly run into in attempting to change it.

"I ought to be thankful," she thought, "that I have escaped from this circumstance even as I have ; for what horrors might have been in store for me had I been arrested on what surely would have been the criminal charge of attempting to pass a false note ; what great delays my release might have been subjected to, while the safety of Rowland would have been greatly endangered by the steps I should have been forced to take in order to free myself from the frightful suspicion which would otherwise have attached to me. Ought I not indeed to be thankful—most thankful ?"

These were, however, but poor and sad reflections for Miranda as she proceeded on her weary and toilsome journey, yet they were the only ones with which her imagination furnished her.

The day was cold, but still fair, and occasionally bright, although any one not particularly weather-wise would have prognosticated change towards sunset. It was a relief to Miranda's feelings that old Mr. Percy slept so much as he did, for she was hardly in spirits to have talked to him, the anxiety she felt concerning her ring, added to her other sources of discomfort, completely distressing her mind.

The horses that drew the waggon seemed to be well accustomed to the road, and to be perfectly well acquainted with the different road-side public-houses at

which it was usual to stop for refreshment, for they drew up as leisurely as possible whenever they came to one, and the waggoner, when he got himself thoroughly awake, would come now and then to the tail of the waggon, and ask if Miranda and Mr. Percy wanted anything.

But slight refreshments, however, sufficed for those care-worn travellers, and they did not take during the whole day what was scarcely sufficient to suffice the waggoner himself at one of his numerous little halts.

As hour after hour passed away, Miranda became more and more anxious for

No. 51.

the reappearance of Jones ; but he came not, and a deeper feeling of melancholy than had oppressed her for some time, crept across her heart.

Towards evening the wind which had blown freshly and in sudden squalls fell, the whole atmosphere became charged with moisture, which spread its leaden-colour vapour over the country, and began to descend in the form of a heavy mist, which towards night turned to a heavy rain.

Nature wore her sombrest hues, and assumed her most melancholy garb, and as the light of day departed, darkness shrouded the earth.

The rain continued to fall, while neither the light of the moon nor the stars shed a solitary gleam of light to cheer the road of the weary, or give him hopes of an amendment in the weather. True it was that it was not so utterly dark that no object could be seen ; but for the intervention of the clouds there would have been moonlight—as it was, sufficient reached the way to enable any one who might be abroad to distinguish objects, though but dimly, and thus enable the peasant to plod over common and through field to his lonely home.

Rain may be necessary to vegetable life, and water we know is to animal life, but in the form of rain there is nothing so disagreeable and inconvenient to the human animal, and few things are there that it will not sooner encounter rather than suffer its influence longer than necessity alone compels it.

The earth is surcharged with moisture, which oozes out at every step, while in all the little hollows the water collects, and forms pools, while the ditches and drains gradually become filled, and help to swell the brook, which rushes onward with mimic force and impetuosity until it has discharged its discoloured burthen into the nearest river, until the last overflows its banks and inundates the surrounding country.

Thus one mischief produces many ; but this was not the case on the present occasion ; true it was the little brook rushed onward with fury, dashing its foam over any obstruction that lay in its way, but always overcoming it, and finding its way onward. The earth was damp—the air was damp—and the rain fell fast—the very hedgerows and trees were dripping, and when any suddden gust of wind came moaning over the country, the tall trees shook their branches, and discharged heavy showers of collected rain upon the earth beneath.

Gloomy and desolate was all around—no cheering sight or sound struck upon the senses—the dull hoarse howling of the wind which came up in gusts, sweeping the falling rain in showers in one direction, then suddenly ceasing, nought was heard but the sullen pattering of the rain which fell in big drops, and fast. Such a night would chill the heart of the boldest and stoutest, and gladly would they select the first shelter that afforded them warmth and the presence of their fellow creatures, for all else was lonely—so dreary—and exquisitely uncomfortable.

The road was now beginning to assume a more lively character, and Miranda on creeping to the front of the waggon, and looking out, saw some half a mile or more ahead the numerous lights of what appeared to be a large town.

" I shall soon have," she thought, " to leave this friendly shelter for awhile. Oh, that he would come ! oh, that he would come !"

CHAPTER CIV.

JONES AND THE JEW.—THE RESTORATION OF THE RING.—IKEY SAMUELS' DESPAIR. —COGENT REASONING.

" WHAT an aggrawation this is, to be sure," was Mr. Jones's soliloquy, after he had parted from Miranda. " The idea of that infernal Ikey Samuels a boning that ere ring—what wice there is in the world—there is people as thinks nothing of dishonesty, and as no more notion of what belongs to 'em, and what dosen't, then a pig in a turnip field."

Having thus declared to himself his opinion of Mr. Ikey Samuels' rascality, Jones proceeded at a very rapid pace in a contrary direction from that in which the waggon was proceeding, for he had no doubt the Jew would choose to make as great a distance between himself and her whom he thought he had so thoroughly victimised as possible.

It did not take very long for Mr. Jones to reach the turnpike, and when he did, he entered the small dwelling without any ceremony.

" Hilloa, friend," he said to the turnpike man, " who's been through here lately —a fellow with a brass-bound box ?"

" No," said the pikeman, " there's been nobody of the kind ; mine's a dog sleep ; I always looks on foot pasengers with one eye, and anything on four legs or wheels with two."

" Thank yer," said Jones, " thank yer."

He then walked on, saying to himself,—

" I'm after him, for a certainty ; it was just possible he might have doubled on his track after going some distance this way to let the waggon get ahead of him, and I am quite sure and certain that, if that had been the manœuvre, he would have gone just as far as that public house, and no farther."

Now the Jew pedlar congratulated himself extremely upon his meeting with Miranda, and the ease with which he had played upon her so heartless a trick. Danger he never dreamt of for a moment, for two beings moret horoughly isolated from society or friends than were that beautiful girl and her aged companion he thought he had scarcely ever met ; and certainly without a knowledge of the very peculiar circumstances which had brought Miranda in her present situation, it would, indeed, seem as if she were utterly friendless, and, with that old man, thrown completely destitute upon the world.

He laughed repeatedly to himself at what he considered his own cleverness in the execution of the trick.

" Not a bad day's work," he cried ; " ah, ah, far from a bad day's work ; how she came by the ring it matters net to me. I have it now, and that is amply sufficient and satisfactory. It will be hard, indeed, if I can't make fifty or sixty pounds of it. Thanks to my apprenticeship to the old lapidary of Hamburg, I know a real diamond at a glance, and this is one of the first water—a fine day's work, a brave day's work, ah, and a safe day's work, for I'd swear she came honestly by the ring, or she would never have parted with it so foolishly. Well, Ikey Samuels, you are a clever boy, a very clever boy ; what would Solomans, in Duke's-place, say to this ?—I shall be made an elder of the synagogue."

Here Mr. Ikey Samuels rapped his brass-bound box with his knuckles and laughed again in the most exulting manner as he said,—

" I have it, I have it safe—safe and firm, and the devil himself shan't get it away from me."

" How do you do, Ikey ?" said a voice behind him.

" So help me, Abraham ! who's that ?" cried Ikey, giving a sudden jump forward, and turning round, he saw the athletic form of Mr. Jones within a few paces of him.

" I don't know you," said Ikey Samuels, " so help my honesty, I don't know you,"

" Not know me," said Jones ; " lor', well, I thought everybody know'd me, and if you doesn't, you are the only one as is in such a state of werdant ignorance, and we must alter that ere afore we parts.—How is business, Ikey ?"

" It's no business of yours," said Ikey Samuels, walking on doggedly, with a determination to get rid as soon as possible of the chance acquaintance,

" No, but it's a pleasure," said Jones, " you can't think how far I have come on purpose to see you."

" What do you want with me?" said the Jew, hurriedly, and looking round him in some dismay, as he recognised he was on a part of the road, three miles from a public-house, and six from a private one.

" Why to tell you the truth," said Jones, " I am distressed for change."

"Change! what do you mean?" cried the Jew, as he plunged his hand into his pocket, and brought it out again with a clasp knife, the blade of which sprung up upon touching a spring, making it, indeed, a most deadly weapon in a close encounter.

"Ah," said Jones; "that's it, is it?" and he made a dart at the Jew so suddenly, that he succeeded in laying hold of his wrist with one hand, and his collar with the other.

"Murder!" cried the Jew.

"No," said Jones, "it's only a swindle; I doesn't accuse you of murder yet, whatever you might ha' done with that clasp knife if you had been able.—Now, drop it, will you."

The Jew aimed a savage kick at Jones, which, however, the latter adroitly avoided, and returned with such interest that Ikey Samuels set up a yell of despair, and danced again in agony.

"Drop it!" cried Jones, "drop it, I say."

The knife fell at his feet, and the Jew sinking on his knees, cried,—

"Mercy—mercy—spare my life! I suppose you are a highwayman?"

"If I am," said Jones, "I am not a sneak—do you know this?"

As he spoke, he unfolded the note within an inch of the Jew's nose.

Ikey Samuels replied in the negative, with a deep groan.

"Not know it!" cried Jones; "how can you say so to my face?—Come, I'll let you off easy; bolt the note whole, and give up the ring and purse, and then you may go."

"On my conscience," said the Jew, "I do not understand you. I am an innocent man; a poor hawker of Brummagem jewellery, and havent five shillings in the world."

"What a shocking thing a bad memory is," said Jones. "Just sit down, will you?"

The Jew obeyed, and with a face of absolute despair, sat down by the road-side, devoutly wishing that some one would come past to relieve him from his distressing situation.

"Now, you scoundrel," said Jones, "what I have to say to you is just this. You have a choice, either quietly to give up a ring which you got from a young lady in a waggon, who is a friend of mine, or to make a trouble of the matter, and place me under what people calls the pressure o' circumstances, which means as I shall have to break your neck."

The Jew wrung his hands, as he thought,—"There goes the result of all my cleverness in a moment." Then, however, a sudden thought, which conveyed a very faint hope, struck him, and he said,—

"I have not the ring here. I have sold it. On my conscience, I have, and know not where it is."

"Oh, indeed!"

"Yes—yes—as I am an honest man, I have parted with it to a man who has gone on to London, and all I can offer you, as I'm a sinner, is the amount he gave me for it."

"How much is that?"

"Twenty pounds."

"Why, you just now swore as you wasn't worth five shillings in the blessed world. I'm afeard, Ikey Samuels, as you sometimes gives yer mind to saying what isn't exactly the blessed and out-and-out truth."

"But I was confused, and knew not what I said. You will take the twenty pounds, and let me go?"

"Why, I will take the twenty pounds," said Jones.

The Jew's face brightened up in a moment, and he said,—

"You shall have the money. I'm very sorry the young lady was a friend of yours. You see I make nothing by the whole transaction."

"Absolutely nothink," said Jones. I made up my mind as you shouldn't when first I heard of it, and so as to make quite sure o' such a state o' things, I sha take the liberty o' overhauling that nice looking box of yours."

"No—no—murder," cried the Jew. "You don't know how dreadfully perish able the articles I have there are. The open air hurts them very much."

"I should say it would make some on 'em wanish quite outright," said Jones as he seized the box despite the frantic struggles of Ikey Samuels, who felt tha: his defeat was now quite certain, and that, in addition to losing the produce of hi; robbery, he should himself be a considerable sufferer.

"In the name of Abraham," he groaned " who are you?"

"A cracksman," was the brief response.

"Then—then," said the Jew, "you ought to have some feeling for me, as we are both of a trade."

"What do you mean, you humbug?"

"I never did an honest action in my life—I assure you—I'm a terrible thief, and surely we oughtn't to make war upon each other? You will spare me?"

"It's one o' my opinions." said Jones, "as all the world is thieves, but there's a precious difference as to how they does the prigging. Some is sneaks, and some is slashers, and if you takes upon yourself all for to try to make out as I'm as bad as you, I'll just break this box over your head, instead of over that ere mile-stone."

"Break my box!" shrieked the Jew. "Oh! for mercy's sake, don't. Heres the key."

"Bother the key," said Jones, and proceeding to the mile stone, he dealt the Jew's box such a whack against it that it fell into pieces, scattering the "Brumma-gem Jewellery" in all directions. It did not take Jones many minutes to find among the mock gems the real diamond ring of Miranda, and placing it upon his little finger, he said,—

"All's right, Ikey. Your friend as guv'd you the twenty pound for this here, must have been an uncommonly careless fellow, for he's left it behind him. Now I tell you what I'll do. I'll take both the twenty pounds and the ring, so when I meet him, you know, I can give him back his blunt in a honest way."

Foiled in all his tricks, and rendered nearly desperate, by seeing his stock in trade scattered upon the public road, Ikey Samuels actually yelled with rage, and would have rushed away in hopes of procuring assistance, had it not been that he could not possibly tear himself away from his beloved box, in a secret drawer of which was some momey, which he yet hoped would escape Mr. Jones's scrutiny. In this expectation, however, he hugely miscalculated, for Jones was too practised a hand in that profession of which he was certainly not the worst member—for there are degrees even in crime—to allow any part of his box to remain un-searched.

With a cry of despair the Jew saw his secret hoard discovered, and transported to Mr. Jones's pockets.

"I'm a ruined man," cried Ikey Samuels. "What will become of me now? I shall be cast off by my people, and come again to selling black-lead pencils with-out lead in them. Oh, dear, oh, dear."

"Hold yer noise, and listen to me," said Jones. "This here affair is all in the way of business. It's diamond cut diamond, you know, for me to get the better of you, and now let me give you a warnin', Ikey Samuels. You may make a hue and cry after me for robbing you, but so sure as you do, you won't catch me; and if I hear that you so much as grumbles in your sleep about the matter, that young lady as you robbed shall prosecute you, and a defence which only says as you was robbed of your swag arter you had boned it, you'll find is somewhere about pleading guilty. So, you see, Ikey, in this blessed business, the least as is said is the soonest mended."

To say that the Jew did not feel the full force of this course of argument, would be to libel the cunning of his whole tribe. He saw his position just as Jones painted it, and with a deep groan he replied —

"You are right enough, but do give me something to save me from starvation.

"Lying again," cried Jones; "why you've got the purse now that you stole. Come, fork, fork."

Ikey Samuels showed so much reluctance to comply with the demand to "fork," that Jones took up the knife and commenced whetting it upon his boot.

"What are you doing that for?" inquired the Jew.

"To cut your throat," was the reply. "I see I shall have to do it, and I may as well do it clean and nice as not."

"There's the purse; and now you leave me quite a ruined man."

"Very good," said Jones, as he colly walked away, without bestowing another word or look upon the half-distracted Ikey Samuels.

CHAPTER CV.

THE QUARREL BETWEEN VARLEY AND TWITTER.—THE COMPROMISE.—THE
JOURNEY TO LONDON.

STUNG nearly to madness with the agony of his feelings, and the successful opposition he had met with in the prosecution of his plans, Bernard Varley repaired from the auction room to the hotel, where for some time he had taken up his abode. Truly did he now begin to feel that the possession of the Grange estates was not equivalent to a power of doing what he pleased with the property, and the more he thought over the circumstances of the last few days, the greater grew his rage at everybody and at everything.

He felt that if the whole human race had but one head, he would glory in striking it off. He raved at Providence—at what he called fate and destiny, continuing for some hours in an irrational state of mind, which knew but one strong feeling, and that was an intense desire to inflict upon some one, he scarcely cared who, exquisite suffering.

His oaths and imprecations were terrible, and it was not until they could hear, by the comparative silence, that the wild storm of passion was abating, that any of the establishment would venture into the room, although he had repeatedly rung the bell for wine.

In this state of mind was he when Samuel Twitter was announced to him, and, with a shout of satisfaction that he should now have one upon whom he could vent the utmost bitterness of his spirit, Varley at once ordered him to be shown into the room.

Twitter started when he saw the maniac-looking countenance of Varley, and for the moment he thought the catastrophe which he had prognosticated had actually occurred, namely, that Varley, by excessive brooding over his passion for Miranda, and his utter hopelessness, had gone mad.

With a pang of alarm, he said,—

"Good heavens! what has occurred?"

"Occurred!" cried Varley, glaring at him like a wild animal preparing for a deadly spring, "Sneaking hound—can you—dare you—ask?"

"I—I—really don't know," said Twitter, keeping as near the door as possible. "I hope nothing particular has gone wrong?"

"How could things go right," cried Varley, "when I yoked myself to a man like you, with all the villany to ——"

"Hush—hush—for God's sake, hush," interrupted Twitter. "We may be overheard. Oh, Varley—Varley—think of the great danger you run by these bursts of passion. If indulged in at all, they should be far from sight or sound of human beings."

" Yes—yes," said Varley, " you are cautious—very cautious, Samuel Twitter. You excel in fear—that is your master passion—at least, with avarice. The one tempts you to crime—the other, to tremble at its commission."

" If," said Twitter, in a low tone, and turning supernaturally pale as he spoke, " if avarice tempted me to crime—what tempted you? Surely that feeling to a still greater excess, Bernard Varley, for, were I you, and you me, I should not refuse you your share in the profits of a deed which, although it might have been done single-handed, could not have been so done safely."

This was, perhaps, the boldest speech that Twitter had ever made to Bernard Varley, and for a moment the latter was quite silent from intense surprise. Then rage became doubly increased, and he seized Twitter by the collar before he could get out of his way, saying, through his clenched teeth, for Twitter's caution respecting loud speaking had not been totally ineffective,—

" Wretch, dare you presume to address me? At last, I will satisfy one item of vengeance, by taking your worthless life."

" Help!—help!—murder!" cried Twitter, as loudly as he could.

In a few moments the room was half full of people, and the alarmed Twitter was torn from the grasp of Bernard Varley, who began to feel terrified himself at the length he had allowed his passions, in this wild excitement, to carry him."

" What's the matter?" cried the landlord of the house, " What's the matter?"

" Ask him," said Twitter, pointing to Varley; " ask him."

" 'Tis past," said Varley. " This is my apartment. How dare any one enter it without my permission?"

" They were summoned by my cries of murder," said Twitter, who for once in his life, found a little courage.

" Fool, fool," said Varley; " what's your worthless life to me?"

" I call upon all here present to witness," said Twitter, " that I have been compelled to summon assistance against the violence of Mr. Varley. If anything should happen to me, remember, it will be his doing."

" Are you mad?" cried Varley.

" No," added Twitter, who was never in such a state of excitement in his life before. " No,—but I am determined to protect myself. This is no ordinary quarrel, and I will not for the future endure threats against my life."

" This—this is a matter between me and my servant," said Varley, rising from the sofa, on which he had sunk after his sudden burst of passion. " I had cause, ample cause for anger against him, and he knows it; but as for any serious intention of doing any harm, he is perfectly aware I should never intertain it."

" It's all very well, sir," said the the landlord, " and you and your friends or servants may settle your own quarrels as you please, but all I've got to say in the matter is, that the sooner you leave my house the better I and all my other guests will be pleased."

The landlord did not wait for a reply to this speech, but walked out of the room immediately, in a great fluster, for he was really enraged greatly at this disturbance, which was by no means calculated to do his establishment any good.

It was Twitter who first broke the silence which ensued for a few moments after he and Varley were alone.

" Mr. Varley," he said, " if you are not mad yourself, you will drive me so, if you go on as you are doing. Surely, I am much ill-used by you in not having faith kept with me as regards what I was to have for assisting you, and when you add to that violence and threats, you may drive me to some course which will eventually distroy us both."

Twitter then sat down, and trembled like an aspen leaf, while a dread of what Bernard Varley might do or say lay heavy at his heart.

Varley's thoughts were by no means idle for some minutes; and, as the paroxysm of his rage rapidly subsided, he began to think that it would be absolutely necessary to adopt another course of conduct towards Twitter, or to take his life a the first convenient opportunity. The latter mental proposition, however, was

he for far more mature thought; but the former required instant decision, and
Varley said, in a temporising tone, which Twitter was delighted to hear,—

"Twitter, are you a man who can make no allowances for a distracted temper?
You must feel assured that I should, for my own sake, be the very last person
eally to harbour against you any ill design."

"Bernard Varley," said Twitter, "I only know that you have made my life a
ositive burthen to me. I only know that I am poor and wretched."

"There is a hundred pound note for you," said Varley, as he took one from what
ppeared to Twitter's gloating eyes a well-filled pocket-book. "Let what has
assed be forgotten. The impolicy of our quarrelling needs no sort of argument."

"Now Varley," said Twitter, "you are more yourself; but tell me what had
.ccurred to give you so much uneasiness."

"Simply this," said Varley, "that I thought the Grange estates were freely
nine, and now I find it is not so."

"Not your's!"

"No I made an attempt to-day to sell them, which attempt was most audaciously
esisted."

"Think nothing," replied Twitter, "about the hindrance of the sale. In
London there are people who will buy anything, provided they get it a bargain,
and they don't care if the very devil himself were the vendor of the article."

"Ay," said Varley, "London is the place. This day, Twitter, we will post to
he metropolis, for I feel convinced that thither Miranda must have flown,
notwithstanding the absence of any positive proof upon the subject."

"Shall I make the necessary arrangements?"

"Yes, assuredly; and remember, Twitter, we understand each other better than
we did."

"Much better—much better," replied Twitter; "and I sincerely hope the good
understanding will never be broken in upon."

*   *   *   *   *

"I will kill him," muttered Varley, when he was alone; "I will kill him on the
very first opportunity. He shall feel what it is to have braved me. By Heaven
and hell, he shall surely die! It is but another murder—only another. Let his
blood mingle with that which already stains my soul. I will sell the Grange
estates in London. Oh, how I detest their very name; and never again will
I blast my eyes by a sight of that house, which once I so much coveted to
call my own. I have now but one hope—one pursuit in life, and that is thee,
Miranda, thee."

"Well done—well done," said Samuel Twitter, when he reached the street;
"Bernard is to be braved after all, if one can but muster up the resolution to
do it. Oh, what a fool I have been! Henceforward I will threaten, and talk
big to him. He evidently fears me. A hundred pounds to lul! the remembrance
of the little fracas. I am rejoiced that I treated him as I did! 'Tis well—'tis
vastly well—ag lorious beginning. Now, Bernard Varley, I will stay by you while
you have a guinea left."

CHAPTER CVI.

THE MEETING AT THE INN.—WITLET'S ADVICE.—THE JOVIAL COMPANY AT THE
OLD MOON.

JONES had been for a longer period of time away from Miranda than he had
calculated upon, for Ikey Samuels had made good speed on his way back to York,
and the little agreeable interview which Mr. Jones had had with him, had helped
to prolong the time.

Nevertheless his success in getting back the ring was sufficiently gratifying to
Jones to induce him to overlook other and more minor considerations; he would

gladly have taken some conveyance could such have been procured, in order to follow Miranda with greater expedition, for he was vexed at the idea that she should be left in the streets of the next market town, with her aged companion, and destitute nearly of means.

There was, however, no resource left him but to push on as quickly as he could, and this he did, not without a hope that some passing vehicle would give him a lift on his journey.

Slow as had been the progress of the waggon, when added to the distance that Jones had gone in the opposite dirrection, a good five or six miles were placed between him and the objects of his care. It was hard work to walk this in the hour, but being unobstructed on the even country road, Jones did come in sight of the town which had attracted Miranda's attention within that period of time.

That town he knew was the destination of the waggon, and he now quickened his pace, with the expectation of speedily coming up with that heroic girl, who

No. 52.

for truth and justice had suffered so much, at the same time that she had achieved so much.

Mr. Jones's encounter with the Jew, added to his long walk, produced a sensation of thirst, and an ardent desire to imbibe something a little stronger than the purest element of nature.

"Well, she won't have to wait for me long," soliloquized Jones; "I am as dry as a methody parson, and I don't see no reason why I shouldn't break bulk of that ere blessed twenty pounds as Ikey Samuels was so particular about; what an agreeable sight a swinging sign is, to be sure, when one's blessed clay is nearly cracking, like a common in July for want of a moistening. There it is, a creacking now and then, as much as to say, walk in ladies and gentlemen, and taste of the wonders of nature in the way of gin and other things. What would this ere world be if it wasn't for public-houses—an out-an'-out bit of the infernal."

With those sentiments Mr. Jones arrived beneath the swinging sign of the public-house, which was the first tenement in the town, the lights from which Miranda had seen in the waggon.

Before, however, he could enter, the door of a stable which was adjoining opened, and a boy, with a head of hair that resembled greatly some superfluous piece of an old flock bed, led forth a horse, crying, alternately, "woa," and "cum up," with a view, it is to be supposed, of keeping the animal quiet and in one spot, by involving his mind in great doubt whether he was to "woa" or "cum up."

"Well my kidney-bean," said Jones, "what's the sign of this ere house, for I can't make it out no how?"

"It's the Shovel and Shoe-brush," said the boy, "and I ain't the kidney-bean.—Woa, will yer; cum up—gee up—woa, woa,—gee up."

Mr. Jones walked to the front of the horse, and looking him intently in the face, he raised a kind of congratulatory shout that so alarmed the boy with the flock head, that he ran into the stable forthwith, and bolted the door.

"Why, how is you, yer love," said Jones, embracing the horse with great cordiality; "bless yer, you warigated tulip, the sight on yer is quite a treat—hurray, here's a meeting."

In his exultation, then, Mr. Jones laughed so uproariously that several people sallied out of the public-house, with a conviction that some admirable joke must be taking place.

"Hurrah, for the squire!" said Jones: "here's the horse, and where's his master?"

"Jones," cried Witlet, rushing forward, "how came you here?"

"Dreadfully dry," said Jones; "perfectly gasping."

Witlet took him by the arm, and led him into the public-house, saying in a whisper as he went,—

"Tell me of Miranda, Jones; where have you left Miranda?"

"Dry as dust," said Jones.

"And old Mr. Percy. Are they still at York, or where? tell me at once?"

"Baked as a pipkin," said Jones; "have'n't had nothing to drink for so long that I have quite lost the blessed calculation."

"How can you be such a sot, Jones, as to think of nothing but drinking—order what you like at once, and answer me the questions I put to you."

"There's gratitude!" said Jones. "A pot of ale. Where's Percy? I thought you and him had been in London long ago. Here's a unexpected meeting, as the fox said when he crept into the dog-kennel. Miss Miranda ain't far off, and I dare say is quite alive and kicking—you see, she wouldn't stay in York no how, and we've been on the road now some time. We've had a few little ups and downs; but taking it altogether, we've rather done the knowing ones."

"Do you mean to say that Miranda is on her road to London?"

"That's the werdict. She's had a lift in a waggon, and has been a coming it at the astonishing rate of a mile and a half a hour. I ha'n't been able to keep by her, you see, all the while, cos you see, some on us must 'arn a living as we go on;

and, I believe, I have only now got to prig something of the very devil himself, when I should have got over three of the most downy characters as is."

"What do you mean ?"

"Why, we've been a receiving woluntary contributions from a quaker and a Jew—they is rúm uns, as you well know, to get the better on."

"I trust," said Witlet, "you have not committed Miranda in any of your heedless robberies ?"

"I never commits nobody," said Jones. "Some of these ere days when I retires from business, and becomes a country justice, I shall go on committing all sorts of people, and myself to, as well as the best of them; but is Mr Percy here ?"

"No," said Witlet; "he is is at the Old Moon, some miles on ; but you give me great uneasiness, Jones, when you talk of having committed robberies, while having escorted Miranda. You know not the frightful mischief you might do to her, by implicating her in such transactions. You must be awar, that she regards with a very different eye to what we do, the rights of property and the usage of society."

"Oh indeed !" said Jones. "Where did you pick up that fine sentiment ? I tell you what it is, Neddy Witlet—there was a boy as was at the door with your hoss, and he was reading a astonishing moral lesson—he was—a lesson as just put me in mind of us, and society, as you speaks on."

"Indeed !" said Witlet ; "how do you make that out ?"

"This ere way, quite easy, unkimmon. That ere boy reminded me of society and us—one minute it says woa, and another minute it says kim up. Woa—says society when we prigs something, and then if we was to woa—society leaves us to starve, and human nature says kim up. What is then we to do? Of course we kims up, and cracks a crib or stops some confiding individual on the highway."

"There is certainly, some philosophy in what you say," said Witlet, "and I confess to taking a similar view of our position. I regret much that Miranda did not see the policy of remaining at York, where she was surrounded by so many attached friends, instead of throwing herself upon the world, and, I must say, adding greatly to Rowland Percy's danger."

"I have hinted all that ere to her," said Jones, "and it wasn't no use. I just adwises you to say nothing to her about, it—woman is woman, and the best on em is as obstinate as blazes."

"I shall certainly not endeavour to make her unhappy," said Witlet, "for no object ; imprudent as I consider the course she has adopted, she is made up of high and noble sentiments, and I can well understand, though I deeply regret, the feeling that has induced her to fly from those in York, who would gladly have given her a home."

"Werry good," said Jones. "She came here in a waggon along with the old gentleman, and, as I told her to stick by it till she seed me, there ain't never a doubt but we shall easily find her."

Witlet looked embarrassed for some moments, and a shade of great care and anxiety hung upon his brow.

"It's an unfortunate circumstance," he said, "and certainly increases the risks Rowland Percy is compelled to run most fearfully. It is quite impossible that we should all proceed to London in a body; such a step would be to ensure detection. You must continue your guardianship of Miranda, Jones, while I proceed by a different route with Percy."

"I sees all that ere," said Jones; "but it's difficult reasoning with her ; just you come along with me, and tell her in your own way what you thinks of the proceeding. She doesn't always seem to understand me when I speaks to her, in consekens, I suppose, of learning too many 'complishments, instead of being teached some of the beauties of the language."

By this time Mr. Jones had finished his pot of ale, and feeling wonderfully refreshed, he was thereby willing to proceed at once after Miranda, and in a few moments Witlet was mounted, and, with Jones at his side, proceeded at an easy pace through the high street of the town.

In the meantime Miranda's anxiety had considerably increased, as minute after minute passed without the return of Jones, and she began to think how difficult it would be to follow his advice, and keep by the waggon, should it be put up for the night in an inn-yard, into which she had no pretext for demanding access.

This turned out to be very much the case, for the horses of their own accord turned under a narrow roofed way which led into a large, badly paved yard, littered with all kinds of lumber and merchandise, and then they all stopped, some of them shaking their heads and producing an extra tinkling of the bells, as if in congratulation that their journey was over.

When the waggoner came to the back of the vehicle and looked at Miranda, it was with as great a stare of astonishment as if he had never seen her before; in fact, he had slept and awoke so many times since she first got into the vehicle, that had he been on his oath he could not have told upon which of his journeys it was that he had taken up a young female and an old man as passengers.

"Do you go no further than here?" said Miranda.

"No," was the reply; "here we be's."

"Then I presume I must alight. Come, Mr. Percy, we must now leave this friendly shelter."

"Yes," said the old man, "yes—but where is Rowland?"

"We are yet far from him, and we must wait here a short time, if we are permitted, for the friend who has already done us so much good service."

The inn-yard was an old and picturesque place, oddly built, but commodious. It ran some distance up the entrance ere you reached the yard, which opened into a wide space, around three sides of which ran the rambling old inn itself, and a large shed on the other.

Under this shed were stowed several waggons, for the most part laden with goods, others in the process of lading with bales of merchandise, crates of goods, and sacks without end or number; from under this shed appeared every here and there doors, from which, when opened, an odour escaped, which at once told you it was the stables,

From out of these doors would peep some curious faces, as if in anxious inquiry who it was that had now entered the yard, and whose services would be required next to take charge of the freshly arrived cattle.

On the other sides—formed by the inn itself—ran an old-fashioned gallery, along what is called the first floor, and which was accessible from the yard by means of a wide flight of steps, and from the house by various little doors from the several sides; besides this, it was conveniently protected from the weather by means of a covering, which was supported by little wooden pillars that took their rise from the old oaken balustrades that surrounded the gallery.

On this gallery were, as is invariably the case, several articles, such as clothes and linen, a collection of boots and shoes; and of course several female heads peering over, watching what was going on most attentively.

It was in the midst of this comfortless confusion that Miranda stood looking anxiously around her, and counting sadly each weary minute as it passed, that brought not to her the only friend she could calculate upon, who would really do his utmost to expedite her on her journey.

CHAPTER CVII.

THE TRANSACTIONS ON THE ROAD.—ROWLAND'S DANGER THICKENS.—A LITTLE MORALITY.

THE impatience of Mr. Percy was each moment growing greater, and it required, an exercise of all the gentle influence which Miranda had over him, to induce him to wait at all in the inn-yard.

She feared to go into the house, in case by so doing, she should miss Jones ; moreover, she dreaded the eccentricities of poor Mr. Percy becoming a subject of remark, as they undoubtedly would, if she entered with him into any of the public rooms in the tavern, and the state of her finances, dependent, too, as she was for them, upon the kindness of others, prevented her from dreaming for a moment of incurring much expense in the inn by calling for a private room.

How slowly and deliberately do the minutes pass to those who are in anxious expectation ; these same minutes, if of a pleasurable character, would be more swiftly fleeting than the most evanescent vapour of creation, lingering apparently not half their allowed space, lest too much pleasure should live too long in the imagination.

Poor Miranda had waited nearly half-an-hour, and she began to think that perforce she should be compelled to enter the inn, the more especially as old Mr. Percy was complaining bitterly of the cold, when, to her joy, she heard the voice of Jones, as he and Ned Witlet entered the archway leading to the inn-yard.

"You'll find her here," said Jones, "to a certainty ; she wont stray from the waggon, it puts up in this yard.

"I am here, I am here," said Miranda, rushing forward.

"And well, I hope, Miranda Rankley?" said Ned Witlet.

"You here, my good friend?" said Miranda, and then a sudden flush of terror came across her, as she thought that something surely must have happened to Rowland Percy, to account for the appearance of his generous protector without him ; an inquiry which she dreaded to make, trembled upon her lips, and it was some moments before she could muster courage enough to say,—

"Rowland—Rowland Percy—what has happened to him ? Oh, tell me, is he safe?"

"Quite so, I trust and expect," said Witlet ; "do not be alarmed at seeing me without him. We have met with some little accidents and difficulties upon our road, but nothing of half so serious a character as might fairly have been expected. He is in good hands now, and it was only as a measure of precaution for a short time that he and I separated."

"Thank Heaven, then," said Miranda. "Then all is well ; your appearance alone did certainly give me a pang of uneasiness, but I am amply repaid by the assurance that you have afforded me."

"Miranda, Miranda," said Witlet, in a tone of sorrowful expostulation, and forgetting for a moment the promise he had given to Jones, not to annoy her by any strictures upon her conduct. "Miranda, Miranda—I implore you to think calmly and dispassionately of the circumstances by which you are surrounded. Let me beg of you to return to York, to remain with those friends to whom it would be a pride as well as a pleasure to give you a welcome."

"Hush ! hush !" said Miranda ; "I implore you upon that point not to urge me ; do not, I pray you—my mind is fixed, and it is ever grievous to hear censure from those we esteem."

"I will say no more—I will say no more. Heaven help both you and Mr. Percy—he is not in London yet, but awaiting me at a very short distance from this place. If you will see him, let it be but a short interview, for I must urge you by every feeling of reason and reflection to abandon the intention, if you ever had such, of proceeding to London with him."

"Except as regards my return to York," said Miranda, "I will follow your advice most implicitly; I fear, that in this world it will never be in my power to repay you, for that is impossible altogether;—but even to give sufficient expression to my gratitude for the great service you have done to me and to Rowland."

"Oh, that's all gammon," said Jones; I doesn't like to hear nothing about gratitude, it's out-an'-out affecting, and if I wants to cry, I can always buy an ingon."

"Rowland Percy," said Ned Witlet, " is at an old roadside-inn called the Old Moon, some distance further on the road to London, He is awaiting my coming with no little anxiety, I believe. My counsel to you is this—to get forward on your road to-morrow as quickly at you can, while Rowland and I will make a return of a few miles, in order to meet you—have then, Miss Miranda, a brief interview with him. I know it will be a great pleasure to you both, and I would not baulk it for a thousand pounds. After that you can still proceed under the protection of Jones, while Rowland and I of course push on at a quicker rate towards the metropolis."

"It shall be so," said Miranda; "I will implicitly follow your directions, You know, Witlet, I have not seen him since that dreadful night when he left me a prisoner in the condemned cell at York."

"I know it—I know it, and can well appreciate your feelings. Sleep at this inn to-night, and in the morning Jones will endeavour to get some conveyance that will bring you some distance on the London-road. Be assured you shall meet us; —but as we are surrounded by dangers, and I may be aware of circumstances that you are not, when you do meet us, wait for the first salutation to come from me—there may be strangers on the part of the road we meet at, or sufficiently near to make a sudden recognition dangerous. Jones, be cautious and discreet."

"Unkimmon," said Jones—" a weasel in a rat-hole shall be a fool to me."

"And now as to money," said Witlet : " my exchequer is not very well stocked at present, but I can supply you with some."

"Oh !" said Jones, " we've been doing the rig as we com'd along, and we can lend you a few pounds if you want it, Neddy."

"No, no. I will be off, for it is dangerous for us even to be seen conversing together. We shall meet to morrow. Adieu, Miss Miranda, and Heaven bless you !"

"There's a fellow for you," said Jones, when Witlet was gone—" an out-an'-out natural philosopher. Lord bless you, that fellow tried to be honest for a matter of ten or a dozen years afore he found out what the world was, rayther, and then he seed the error of his ways, and became the owdacious family cove he is. He's made up of feeling, and he never robs nobody as can't spare it—and that's more than your moral-going coves does, for the only people they robs is the poor, as haven't the means of making head against such outrageous piety. Why, bless yer! I know'd a feller as let his own child, a girl of some seventeen years old—cos she'd gone a little astray, poor thing !—die in the streets ; and then he gave a thousand pounds to translate the blessed scriptures for the King of the Cannible Islands, or same such outrageous humbug. Piety wersus feeling !—cant wersus charity! Thank God ! I am a prig, and not a beast."   *   *   *   *

The police officer, who was left in so uncomfortable a position by Ned Witlet, was in too great a rage for a long while to reflect at all calmly upon his situation—but that first ebullition was sure to pass away ; and, when it did he assured himself, over and over again, thas he was most certainly on the right track for the discovery of his prisoner, or he never would have been handled in so systematic and rough a manner as he had been.

He therefore lay upon his back, muttering a great many curses, and resolved in his own mind, that the moment he got free of his present dilemma he would take up the pursuit, with still a hope of achieving something of a more satisfactory a character on the road between York and London.

It was after a great many ineffectual struggles and plunges that he at length got upon his feet, and, after that, liberation was not far distant, for he contrived to make himself seen by some of the labourers adjoining a farm; and, being freed from his bondage, he thought his safest and best way of getting back to York was to wait on the London-road for a coach, which he did, and in not many hours was once again set down in the ancient cathedral city.

We need not follow this worthy in the steps he took to get up a considerable force, with which he proposed to ride all the way from York to London, but, suffice it to say, that within six hours he again started on the same errand which had been before so full of peril and misadventure to him.

It was strange, thus, that all our characters should be upon the road; Bernard Varley was posting to London. The police-officers were riding at a hard pace; and our persecuted friends were, with deep anxiety, waiting the chance of events which should place them in a condition less full of moving accidents.

If Rowland Percy's mind had been disengaged, and if he could have got rid of the many deep anxieties, both for himself and others, that oppressed him, he could have much enjoyed his residence at that ancient and venerable hostel. It was just the place which at another time, and under happier circumstances, he would have gloried in visiting, and thoroughly exploring. The exquisite irregularity of its structure, and the constant surprises which awaited any one who might be rummaging over it in the shape of unexpected staircases, little odd quaint-looking rooms, and dark tortuous cupboards, in out of the way corners, was just the thing to keep the mind in a state of pleasurable occupation.

But poor Rowland had too many crowding cares and anxieties to give but a wasting meed of pleasurable admiration to the old house. He thought once or twice, with almost a smile of anticipated delight, how happy he should be to visit it some day with Miranda—some day, perhaps, after his innocence had become discovered, and admitted by all men, when he could point out to her with a sigh for the past, and paint to her in love's own glowing language, the mental suffering he endured upon his first visit beneath its romantic roof.

Such feelings as these were like glimpses of sunshine in November, beautiful, but oh, so transient that they made the gloom that had for the moment vanished, look doubly dark and mournful.

The landlord was extremely attentive to Rowland Percy, absolutely forcing him with rough hospitality to partake of many things, which he would have avoided. Then he amused him during the day by telling of some kindly acts of Ned Witlet, concluding, with a sigh that seemed to shake the whole of his ponderous bulk.

"Ah, sir, there's very few of the real knights of the road left now. Highway robbery, like everything else, has had its day, and gentlemen don't take to it now as they used to do, as a profession, without any malice or savageness at all. No, sir, it's only some rogue now and then who gets desperate, and tries to knock on the head a fat grazier or a commercial traveller. I look upon Ned Witlet, sir, as the last of his race—he's a real old English highwayman. One as ready to salute a fair lady, as rob a fat parson."

"Of course," said Rowland, with a smile, "you sink the morality of the thing."

"Morality," said the landlord, "is a very nice thing for nice independent people, who were born with silver spoons in their mouths, and continue to keep them there."

Rowland Percy was not anxious to prolong such discussions as these, for he was getting angry with himself, as he found himself now and then, in the free and easy manner of a Jones or a Witlet, making excuses in his own mind for lapses of integrity that he had always been taught to consider as great enormities.

"At all events," he thought, "I have learned one thing by my association with these men, and that is charity towards my fellow creatures, and a conviction that one departure from the strict line of moral rectitude by no means necessarily implies that he who so departs is a bad man or destitute of admirable feelings."

* * * *

The ancient inn looked more lonely and isolated than it really was; far behind and out of sight, unless the traveller looked for them out of the back windows, were some thriving pleasant little villages, some of the inhabitants of which made a regular practice of spending an hour or two in the evening, in the parlour of the Old Moon.

Rowland Percy was so vociferously requested to join these worthies by the landlord, that he could not resist, nor did he regret that he yielded, when he found himself within the sphere of the ruddy heat from a blazing fire, and surrounded by the hearty bronzed English faces of some of the neighbouring farmer's men, who seemed to enjoy life as a rich boon of itself, and to be so gloriously obtuse to all care, that Rowland Percy felt a most unchristian feeling of envy taking possesion of his bre   as he looked at them and listened to heir boisterous language.

CHAPTER LXXVI.

THE PARLOUR AT THE OLD MOON.—THE MYSTERIOUS TRAVELLER AND THE BLUE BED-ROOM.

ROWLAND PERCY had no reason to regret the good-tempered compulsion which had forced him into the parlour of the Old Moon ; for, although the hilarity and mirth was of rather a boisterous description, yet there was no mistake in it. It was real, genuine, hearty good humour, and more than once he envied those unrefined, but happy yeomen, who, alas ! are fast disappearing from the face of merry England, before the demon of manufacturing monopoly.

Heaven forbid that the selfish and infamous society of men, who have leagued themselves for the destruction of the hardy sons of agricultural labour, should succeed in their iniquitous design.

There were over a dozen guests in the old parlour ; and, although the conversation was not of the most refined order, it lacked neither energy nor sincerity ; if it wanted some of the courtesies of more elegant society, it escaped its duplicities, and both the novelty and nature of the talk amused Rowland amazingly.

The weather, of course, formed a principal topic for some time, and it was handled with great learning and vigour, as it related to agricultural produce, the only shadow of a difference of sentiment being between two extremely fat men, one of whom wanted it to rain, and the other didn't.

It seemed, too, as if the elements themselves were intent upon supplying matter for further conversation to the inmates of the parlour of the Old Moon ; for the wind was getting up, and beginning to sweep round the old house, rustling among the ivy, and shaking the ancient casements, as if anxious to find some place of ingress through which it might make its way, and blow about the tables and chairs in the Old Moon at its pleasure.

" The wind's a-blowing," said a little, hard featured old man, the skin of whose face appeared at one time to have been a great deal too large, and, rather than hang about in an unsightly manner, had done itself up into little crinkles. " The wind's a-blowing, and, for all the world, it reminds me of how I have been told it blowed when a circumstance took place at this here very inn a many years ago."

The little old man looked with such a solemn and fixed stare in the face of Rowland Percy, that the latter felt himself compelled to say something, if it were only, " Ay, indeed !"

" Oh, we know all about that," said the fat man, who wanted it to rain.

Upon this the little old man pointed triumphantly, with the stem of his pipe, to Rowland as much as to say, " he don't," and that being an unanswerable argument in favour of telling the story, the fat man who wanted rain, felt himself very small, and said no more about it.

The little old man then, having first taken a few whiffs from his pipe, gently tapped the bowl on the toe of his boot, and kicked the ashes into the fire in a manner that told he had done so before ; and, laying it down, he said, slightly elevating himself, to look on all around, to see that none were inattentive—

"You must know that this occurred in my father's time ; he was sexton, and buried him."

"Buried who ?" said one of the guests.

"You'll know all in good time," replied the old man ; "you must hear the beginning before you know the end.

"It was about fifty years since that my poor father—poor man, he's dead and gone—was sitting one night, as I am in this parlour ; it was a stormy night, I can tell you, for the wind howled and roared in the chimney of the Old Moon, while the rain beat against the outside with fury.

"It was growing late, too, and many of those that were sitting round the blazing

No. 53.

fire thought it was time they should return home; but the rain came down so heavily that they did not like to leave good shelter, good fire, and good liquo:, to encounter the inclemency without, when suddenly there was a sharp rap at the inner door as if with the butt-end of a riding-whip, and somebody called, in strange accents, 'House—house, here, house!'

"Well, they were all very much startled, not so much at the mere fact that a traveller desired shelter hastily—it was late and sudden, it was true,—but it was at the signular and almost painful tone in which the demand was made, and then a dead silence ensued. Each one looked at his neighbour, in doubt if he should break it, or was desirous of hearing somebody else's voice but his own.

While they were thus looking at each other in something more than mere amazement, the knocking was repeated, the same voice said, in louder but almost despairing accents, that rung in their ears,—

"'Hilloa, house! house! hilloa!'

The landlord then jumped up from his seat, for he was dozing by the fire when the first call was heard, and went to the door, and in a few moments returned with a traveller, who wore a horseman's cloak and slouched hat, sword and holster pistols, which he brought with him.

He drew off his cloak, and seated himself near the fire, as if to warm and dry himself.

The guests looked at him with much curiosity, not to say awe, for they knew not what to think of him. He was tall and well made, and scarce more than thirty years of age. But what interested them, was the peculiar air of melancholy that sat upon his strongly marked and handsome features, and he sat several minutes without uttering a word. This silence was particularly painful, and the landlord said respectfully,—

"'Your horse, your honour, is well taken care of—'tis a noble beast.'

"The stranger looked up as if he did not comprehend what was said.

"'I was saying,' repeated the landlord, 'that that's a handsome horse, sir, and well deserves to be taken care of; you could not come to a better inn, though I say it, to have your cattle better well after.'

"'Ay, that is right,' said the stranger, slowly. 'He has come far and quickly —see to him.'

"'I have, your honour.'

"''Tis well; can I have a bed here to-night! I would not travel further in such weather.'

"'You can, your honour—you can, and a better——'

" 'Hold,' said the stranger, 'I am content to take it, for what it is; and be it what it may, it will be all that I shall require.'

"'Won't you take any refreshments?' said the landlord, who began to think that his guest had been in long enough enjoying the warmth of the fire to order something without being spurred on.

"'No,' was the short reply; 'but you may draw what you like, and charge me with it.'

"'Well,' muttered the landlord, 'this beats Akibo, and he beat What-d'ye-callum.'

"There was now another long pause, during which no one spoke, though several had made up their minds to be easy, and converse about things; and yet, think as hard as they could, they could not find anything to say; sitting staring at each other in perfect silence, and stealing sidelong glances at the stranger, whose mind appeared to be ill at ease, for his breast now and then rose with a long inspiration, as if he were about to sigh heavily, and then recollecting himself, he would suppress it.

"He sat before the fire, leaning his head on his hand, with his elbow on the table, gazing with a vacant eye upon the blazing logs.

"'He is surely crazed,' said the landlord to my father.

"'Yes, and had you seen his eyes as I did when you spoke to him, you would have seen them like living fire—he must be mad.'

" ' God bless me !' said the landlord. ' What shall I do when I show him to his room ; he'll become outrageous, for there is no hangings to the bed.'

" ' Indeed,' said my father ; ' what room do you intend to show him into.'

" ' Why, the blue-room, to be sure.'

" ' The blue-room ? I have heard you say that nobody has slept in that old rambling room since the death of the squire, who broke his skull while taking a leap after the hounds.'

" ' Hush ! say nothing about that. That is one reason I want to have somebody to sleep in it, else the place will get a bad name, for nobody likes to sleep there ; besides, it's easiest got ready.'

" I have heard my father say," continued the little old man, " that he was upon the point of saying something by way of reply ; but the stranger suddenly turned to the landlord, and said,—

" ' Will you show me into my room ?'

" ' Yes, your honour, certainly. I have ordered a fire, and in a few minutes the room will be well aired. It will be warm and comfortable.'

" ' Never mind about that,' said the stranger, interrupting him. ' All I want is the room ; but if there be a fire there already, well and good—let it remain—but if not, you need not light one.'

" ' Not—not a fire—such a night as this, too,' said the landlord, very much bewildered.

" ' No,' said the stranger, in a sudden stern voice, so different from the painfully melancholy tones in which he had hitherto spoken, that the landlord gave a sudden start, in common with every one present.

" ' But—but there is one,' was the reply.

" ' Show me to the room at once,' said the stranger, who evidently neither liked company nor conversation, ' and I will thank you.'

" The landlord was much puzzled at the conduct of his guest, but led the way out of the room. The stranger rose and followed him with a faltering step, and disappeared from the parlour.

" In a few minutes the landlord returned into the room, and threw himself into a chair near the fire, drew a long breath, like a man who is suddenly relieved from some load of misery, and seizing the poker, began to stir the fire, as if actuated by an insane desire to destroy the fuel.

" ' What's the matter ?' said one. ' What have you seen !' said another. ' Who is it ?' said a third.

" ' I don't know. Nothing—nothing,' said the landlord ; ' but I never came near his like before—that's all. Why, hark how the wind howls, and how the rain beats, and he wants nothing—is that natural ?'

" There was a moment's pause before any one replied, during which the howling of the wind seemed to increase, and they thought it sounded more dismally in the old chimney, while the rain beat fearfully against the closed window,

" ' It is not natural,' said one of the guests, ' for any man—mind I said man—to be riding far in such weather, and on such a night as this, to go to bed supperless. I wouldn't do so."

" ' And I could not, if I would,' said another.

" ' No,' continued the landlord, ' I am sure I could not ; but I have left him in the blue-room—that's some satisfaction.'

" ' You don't mean that ?" said one.

" ' I do though, and it's quite good enough for the occasion. Moreover, it's the best room in the house.'

" ' How did you leave him ? What did he say ?' inquired one or two, in a breath.

" ' Nothing—nothing ; he walked in, just looked round the place, and took his hat off his head, and threw it on the bed ; he seems to have something that weighs heavy on his mind—some load of guilt, I am sure.'

" ' He is a very strange man,' said one ; ' but what makes you think that ?'

" ' Because he trembled, and clasped his hands together, and fell rather than sat down in a chair oppositethe firea if in great agony, exclaiming, in a dreaful whisper,—

" Oh, Agatha—Agatha, and has it come to this at last. Lost! lost!"

" ' Poor soul,' he is to be pitied.'

" ' I don't know that.' said the clerk. ' You know, neighbours, that a lost soul may not be deserving of pity. He may have sold himself, and now repents.'

" ' You don't think he has sold himself to the devil ?' said one, who was compelled to jerk the last word out, else it had remained unsaid, to the danger of choking the speaker.

" ' He may be the—the—the——'

" ' God bless me !' exclaimed the landlord, jumping up and over-turning his seat at the same time.

" This exclamation was called forth by the stunning report of a pistol which was discharged in the Old Moon. The sound found many echoes in the old rambling building, and to the fear or fancy of the guests, it seemed as if a regular discharge of small arms had taken place.

" Terror sat on every face—no one moved—they appeared like human beings turned by the wand of some demon enchanter into blocks of marble, so silent and so motionless they sat, with their eyes protruded with intense and fearful anxiety from their sockets."

CHAPTER CXI.

THE REMARKABLE DISAPPEARANCE.—A NEW ALARM.—THE ARRIVAL AT THE OLD MOON.

" How long this state of things might have lasted it is impossible to say; but after a while, before a syllable was uttered, they began to recover from the shock, and to think, but no sooner had their faculties become a little thawed than they were again driven to their wits' ends by a loud and continued knocking.

" It was long ere any one spoke, but all looked at the landlord, who was wiping the perspiration from his face, at length he said,—

" ' Will any one go to the door for me?'

" No one, however, stirred hand or foot, or offered a word in reply, and by the time the knocks had been repeated for about the fourteenth time, he rose to his feet, and, without saying a word, he slowly went to the door, and demanded who was there, and having received an answer from without, in a mortal voice, as they thought, of a woman, a horseman entered, dressed precisely as the former, but of a different form and feature. He was short and slim, his clothes loose, but with hat, cloak, sword, and pistols the same as the former horseman. The landlord recoiled in terror, when the traveller, said, seriously,—

" ' Are you deaf, that you keep me waiting outside on such a night as this? Why, what ails you ?—you look frightened.'

" ' The traveller—the pistol !'

" ' What does all this mean ?' said the stranger, turning to the guests.

" ' Somebody fired a pistol up stairs.'

" ' Indeed ! then why not go up stairs and see who it is?'

" The guests all shook their heads, and the landlord evinced no desire to do so, when the stranger inquired further about the occurrence, and appeared deeply interested, and at length offered to go up to the blue room, and asked if any one would accompany him, but one and all refused. The traveller then took a light, and, being directed by the landlord, walked up stairs.

"During the traveller's absence not a sound was uttered, for all were too deeply engaged in speculating upon the result of the stranger's search, and their expectation was painfully wrought by the time he remained above, but presently they heard him descending the stairs slowly, and then enter the room. Every eye was fixed upon his features, which were, though beautiful, deathly pale, and his lips of an ashy hue. He slowly turned to the landlord, saying,—

"' There is no one there.'

"' No one there !' shouted the landlord, surprise getting the best of his terror for the moment.

"' No one,' replied the stranger, with a sad and sorrowful accent, as he turned on his heel and left the house.

"When they heard the clatter of his horse's hoofs die away in the distance, the landlord said,—

"' A pretty pass things have come to, indeed. He was certainly the devil. I shall not go to see till to-morrow, nor shall I go to bed while I have a good fire; and if you'll all stop and keep me company till morning, you shall have what you like, free of all charges.'

"This was agreed to, and they sat up all night, and in the morning they went to the blue bed-room; but there was no one there, and traces of blood were seen plainly.

"This was a most mysterious affair—but the strangest part of all was, perhaps the existence of a most abominable odour that was ever after smelt in that room, though the windows were always open, and its cause could never be ascertained.

"Ever after, on that day twelvemonths, noises were heard in the blue-chamber, and it has been said that a figure appears, but its features are always smeared so with blood, as not to be seen, and the knocking at the outer door always continues for some time.

"Some years after this, my father got me a place in London—to attend on a lady. I was a page, you must know, and seldom had come to these parts, save once in a year or two, to see my father, and of course knew but little of what occurred.

"I was one day attending upon the lady in the drawing-room, when my master drew his lady's attention to a paragraph in a paper, which related how a dead body had been found in a concealed cupboard of an old inn—it had lain there for many years, and was discovered in consequence of some repairs, when it fell forwards, a mass of bones and festering flesh. That was the body found here in the Old Moon —the missing traveller.

"It then said that there was merely a letter addressed to the unfortunate man by his unfaithful wife. According to the letter, his name was Walter Montrose, and the letter was signed Agatha.

"My mistress no sooner read it, than she sprang to her feet, clapping her hands, and shrieking —

"' I dragged him there—I dragged him—God forgive me—God forgive me !' and then fell dead on the carpet.

"From all I could learn, she had been living. and was then, with her seducer who had been her first lover. She had followed her husband, with the hope of making peace, or obtaining his forgiveness, but he had committed the rash act that placed it beyond his power to do so. She found him as I have told you, and being desirous of saving his body from the suicide's dishonoured grave, exerted her strength to conceal the body, which she did, and then left the house.

"A fit of illness afterwards occurring, she lay bereft of reflection for many months, and then upon the solicitation of her lover and tempter, she returned to his arms. But the occurrence was only known to herself and maid, who attended her through her illness, and from whom I learned all."

"I suppose the ghost was laid, and the knocking discontinued after that ?" said one, inquiringly.

"I believe not," said the narrator, solemnly; "for I have heard that to this day no one will venture to sleep there, at least on that night twelvemonth, for strange unearthly voices have been heard, and it is said that the spirit of the man still haunts the place, and will do so until a hundred years have expired,"

"And the knocking, does that continue too?" said one, who was determined to obtain all the information he could upon so interesting a matter.

"Yes and the—',

Here the speaker paused suddenly, for just as he was about to say something more, a tremendous rapping was heard at the old inn door, and a voice crying out with stentorian lungs,—

"Hilloa! house! house, here, hilloa!"

The sounds acted like an electric shock upon those present, including the narrator. None dared move, or so much as breath, and an universal panic pervaded every mind.

The greatest effect, however, seemed to be upon the fat man who wanted rain, for he slipped off his chair with a great dab on the floor, and in doing so, tilted it forward in such a manner, that the back of it gave him naturally a blow on the head, and not being quick at ascertaining cause and effect, the fat man who wanted rain bellowed murder most lustily, and ever afterwards believed that the fat man who didn't want rain had done it.

As for the landlord, he certainly made an effort to move from the great arm chair in which he sat, but it was only a preliminary one, consisting of a sort of convulsive movement of his fat, which like a piece of *blanc mange* in a state of agitation, gradually again subsided.

Again the tremendous knocking came at the inn door, and the voice in still louder accents, cried,—

"House! house! Are you all asleep? Hilloa! It's trouble enough the Moon, and one might as well be let in at once.—Come, old guts and gaiters open the door."

"He means me," gasped the landlord; "he means me," and he gave himself a terrible wrench, which brought him to his feet.

"Don't—don't!" cried four or five of the guests at once; "don't let him in; it's the ghost of the blue chamber."

"If it is," said the landlord, "I can't have the door of the Old Moon knocked in."

He made a movement towards the door, but the fat man who didn't want rain interposed, and the greatest confusion prevailed in the room; every one spoke at once, which certainly saved time though it did not add to the general clearness of the affair, while the knocking at the inn door sounded like an accompaniment on a cracked drum to the tumult within.

Suddenly, then, the knocking ceased, and a rush of cold air, accompanied by a general slamming of doors in the upper part of the house, proclaimed that the outer door was open, and that the ghost, if such he was, [accompanied by a great gust of wind had found his way into the house.

Some then sat down behind chairs; one tried to clamber up the chimney, and four or five more made a rush to get under the table, which at once upset it, together with the lights and everything that was upon it.

The scene of riot and confusion was at its height, when the parlour door was dashed open, and the gleam of a lantern, carried by the hostler, shone into the room. Behind him was a tall man, enveloped in a riding cloak, who, after looking about him for a moment in surprise, said,

"Why—what on earth's the matter? Have you all gone crazy?"

"Gracious!" said the landlord, "it's the squire;" and snatching the lantern from the hostler, he held it up to the face of the new arrival, and discovered the well-known features of Ned Witlet, who so unconsciously had created such an alarm at the Old Moon.

"Why, Neddy, is it you, after all?" said the landlord; "who would have thought it? Here's been a skrimmage about nothing. I tell you what it is, Peter Smuggs if ever you tells that story here again, I'll take an opportunity of treading on yer some day, and smashing of yer, and at the crowner's quest, I'll purtend as I mistook you for a black-beetle which we is haunted with, as will be well known to the blessed jewry, no doubt, seeing as they have all on 'em found 'em occasionally in their ale."

Ned Witlet cast an anxious glance around him; it was in search of Rowland Percy, and when his eye fell on him, he held out his hand, saying,

"I am glad to see you; the Old Moon has done you good; you are looking a thousand times better than when last we parted. Come this way."

So saying, he took Rowland by the arm, and led him from the oaken parlour, leaving the guests to recover from their consternation as best they might, and to alarm themselves, which they did, by ghost stories for the rest of the evening.

CHAPTER CX.

THE NIGHT AT THE OLD MOON.—THE MORNING.—THE EXPEDITION TO MEET MIRANDA.

THE fat landlord followed Rowland and Ned Witlet from the parlour, and the three were soon together in a room on the first floor of the old inn, which, although it had none of the comforts of the oaken parlour they had just left, was still much better calculated for a private conference.

"Well, Mr. Percy," said Ned Witlet, "we've been much longer on the road from York to London than I could have wished, and I think we've been the victims of as many accidents and crosses as could possibly be crowded into a small space of time."

"We have, indeed," said Rowland, "and most certainly should I by this time been in the hands of my enemies had it not been for the advice and assistance I have received from you. I hope now, however, we may continue our course uninterrupted; and believe me, I hope it for your sake, as much as my own, being far from unconscious what a troublesome acquaintance I must be."

"Ah, well, well," cried the fat landlord; "we all have our ups and downs in this ere world. Human nature is a good 'un to look at, but a rum 'un to go. I suppose you've been on the roadside, and met with some ugly mischance; when I was young, and not quite so stout as I am, for you see I'm rather inclined that way, I used to do a little business on the highway myself. It was an active, stirring sort of life, and suited me well, till I became not quite so active as I ought to be, and I was thinking of some genteel retirement, when my uncle, who kept the Old Moon here, died, leaving me all his sticks; so, as the things fitted the house, I thought I had better rent it as well, and here I is."

"You are mistaken in me," said Rowland Percy. "I am not flying from justice, I am endeavouring to save my life from the cruellest persecution that ever man endured; accused and convicted of a murder, of which I am entirely innocent—even in thought: by rare good fortune, I have thus far escaped the malice of my enemies, and the ill-directed vengeance of the laws. My name is Rowland Percy."

The landlord gave a loud whistle, and then said,—

"Oh! oh! you're the chap there's been all the riot about in York. I've heard of you; but, howsomd'ever, you are quite as welcome as if you'd been the most dashing cracksman that ever stepped."

"I am obliged to you for the compliment," said Rowland, with a smile; "and I presume, Witlet, we shall now start at once."

"No," said Witlet, "another delay has interposed itself; we cannot start till to-morrow morning, and then it must be towards York."

"Towards York?" cried Rowland, in surprise.

"Yes, to meet Miranda, who is on her journey hither."

"Miranda! to meet Miranda. Can it be possible that she is on the road, trusting herself to all its chances and disagreeables for my sake?"

"It's not only possible but true," said Witlet; "she has forsaken every friend she had at York, she has rejected the friendship and offers of assistance from those who would have felt a pride in rendering it; and with a noble heroism, the discretion of which I cannot praise, but which, at the same time, I cannot help honouring greatly, she has resolved to join her fortunes, and to share with you in London whatever fate may have in store for you."

"Noble, generous girl," said Rowland. "Oh, how richly has Heaven repaid me in the possession of such a heart as Miranda's, for all my sufferings. I should be insensible indeed did I not feel conscious from the very bottom of my heart of the value of the richest treasure which is mine."

Ned Witlet then explained to Percy the arrangement he had made with Miranda as to meeting them on the road, as well as informing him of the events which had occurred during their separation, concluding by saying, that he himself would take at the Old Moon what he was in so much need of, namely, a night's rest, advising Percy to do the same; when, early in the morning, he would move slowly down the road to meet Miranda and his father.

As the hour was getting late, Percy and Witlet each retired to a well appointed chamber in the Old Moon. The latter to sleep away his fatigues, and the former to lay long in thought upon the beauty and excellence of Miranda, and when fairly exhausted and overcome by sleep, to dream of her, and happy days which were in store for them both.

Time wears on and another night is near its termination, and the pure light of the sun will soon be seen peeping over the distant woods in the east, whose dark frowning masses can be traced even by the fast dimming light of the moon.

The quiet hour of morning, that which precedes the earliest dawn, is one which seldom is chosen by man for a ramble, and yet it is not without its beauties, and they are peculiar; the death-like stillness of all around, the absence of aught that has life save the few large moths that flit about uneasily, as if they knew their time was drawing to a close. The owl has retired to his hollow tree, and only the noxious bat prowls about till the sun's rays shall drive him to seek shelter from the daylight, and hide his misshapen form from a contrast with the more favoured denizens of the air or earth.

And yet why should the poor bat be derided—why hated—why condemned, and despised? And yet it is so, and no reason given, save that it is so. Providence permits him to bear, or gives him that form, and those who rail at the bat or shudder at its form and singular motions to escape its persecutors; and he or she who does this shudders at the works of Providence, and even casts blame on the divine wisdom it has displayed in its works.

But enough of this; see yonder the white streak in the east speaks of another day. The night clouds are losing their density already, and appear to rise higher in the air, while the advancing luminary throws his warm tints through the sky, gladdening the heart and gratifying the sight.

The sun-rise, when the night clouds and vapours are disturbed in varying masses, forms a pleasing and imposing spectacle; not a cloud that can be seen but has its own peculiar hue and colour, its density, or its lightness—its masses or isolated state, all reflect different colours, thus rendering the sky a most gorgeous and brilliant spectacle.

The first sound you hear is that of the lark, who, notwithstanding all that has been said of the rook, rises and mounts the aerial regions, before the black feathered tribe have left their abodes, and pouring forth in the fullness of his song the sweetest melody that ever sounded in the wide fields,

> "Hark! the lark at Heaven's gate sings,
> And Phœbus 'gins to rise."

Indeed the day has broken, and now the heavens and earth once more display the signs of life and mobility. The pretty reed sparrows as they skim along the surface of the river, give forth their lively notes, and their varied plumage adds to the gaiety of the scene.

It is early morn, and few, if any, signs of human life can be seen or heard, for though a solitary figure may be seen, it is that of some benighted toper, or some labourer who is proceeding with steady step towards a distant scene of labour.

JONES LEAVES THE TRAVELLERS TO SEARCH FOR IKEY SAMUELS.—PAGE 402.

Then the note of chanticleer comes across the meadow as loud and full as if heard in the farm-yard; and behold him with flapping wings, how he struts and marches out to the field at the head of the flock, as if to face any sudden danger that might be lurking near.

The warm rays of the sun rapidly draw off the vapour that the night engendered, and dew-spangled bushes are fast losing their lustrous and sparkling pendants deposited by the fleeting mist : nature has resumed her wonted hue, and the broad shadows of night have been replaced by the sunny beams of the rising sun.

The cool morning air now becomes congenial and very pleasant, laden with fragrant odours from many a flower and shrub ; but few things equal the sweet scents of the meadows in which the primrose, cowslip, and the blue-bell grow ; there the lover of beauty and sweet odours will find a treat of which he can never pall.

Rowland Percy was startled by a hand that was laid upon his shoulder. It was Ned Witlet's.

" Up ! up !" he cried, " we shall have just time to do some justice to the morning cheer of the Old Moon, and then start on our expedition."

" I shall be ready in a moment," cried Rowland, springing to his feet, for he had only taken off some of his outer garments, for the feeling that he was surrounded by danger, prevented him from lying down with that feeling of security which is so delightful, and which people never estimate fully, unless by some untoward circumstances they are deprived of it.

A substantial breakfast awaited them in the room below, and after partaking of it, and shaking hands heartily with the fat landlord, they repaired to the inn door, where were Witlet's own horse and another which he had borrowed of the landlord for Rowland's use.

" I regret," said Witlet, " that I could not provide you with a better steed than this ; in the event of a close chase, he will be of very little service to you ; I do not, however, anticipate further disagreeables on our road, and, in that case, we shall do very well, for I can accommodate my horse to the speed of yours."

" At all events," said Rowland, as he mounted, " I shall feel myself far more secure and capable of resistance now, than before."

They went down the road from the inn door at an easy trot, and, absorbed as he was with many painful reflections, still Rowland could not be entirely dead to the beauties of the scenery through which he was passing ; and although, in his conversation, he kept continually reverting to Miranda, and the probability of soon meeting her, he showed himself fully alive to the varied charms of the sylvan scene that greeted them on every side.

Rowland pictured to himself what was Miranda's state of mind on that eventful morning, and in doing so, he was very far from exaggerating the state of anxious suspense she must be in ; she obeyed Witlet's directions faithfully, and at very nearly the same hour which witnessed the departure of Rowland from the door of the Old Moon, she started with Mr. Percy and Jones from the place where they had succeeded in obtaining shelter for the night.

Miranda thought it would be imprudent to say anything to Mr. Percy in his peculiar state of mind, with regard to the probable immediate meeting with Rowland ; she knew not what enemies they might still encounter before that meeting took place, in which case, an imprudent word or two from the old man might be productive of the most fatal consequences to him, who held existence upon so frail a tenure as his escape, day by day, from the dread ministers of the law. Both Miranda and Mr. Percy felt much invigorated by the comparatively quiet night's repose they had had ; and although the road seemed long to that tenderly matured girl, that feeling arose from the state of anxious expectation, for, if anything, she felt herself more capable of undergoing the fatigue of walking then than on the preceding days of her pilgrimage.

As for Mr. Jones, he now and then amused himself with a song, interspersed occasionally with scraps of his own peculiar philosophy, and many curious remarks concerning Ikey Samuels, and the peculiar interview he recently had with him.

There were but few pasengers on the road, and although the actual distance when they both first started, between Miranda and Percy, exceeded five or six miles, yet it must be recollected that that distance was being decreased in a double ratio, so that something very far short of an hour would abundantly suffice to bring them together ; but, oh, on what leaden pinions the moments move, when expectation is at its height, and some event is looked forward to, which engrosses the whole heart and soul of its anxious expectants. Miranda had never felt a short distance so long, so weary, and so monotonous.

As for Mr. Percy he walked on listlessly, now and then muttering to himself some surmises or expressions little in accordance with his real situation.

Miranda saw that, about half a mile in advance of where she was, there was a sudden turn in the road ; and a fluttering sensation at her heart led her to suspect, she knew not why, that, at that turn, she should surely meet with Rowland Percy. She had no particular reason for so thinking, but a kind of perception came over her that such would be the case.

" He will be there, he will be there," she said to herself, " I feel that he will be there—I shall see him again, free from the terrors that surrounded him in that dungeon—that frightful condemned cell, to enter which was sufficient to cast a deadly gloom over any mind. Whatever dangers—whatever perils, I pray to Heaven, we may be permitted to suffer them together, and not left to conjecture of each other's sorrows and dangers. Rowland !—Rowland !—I shall surely know a moment of exquisite joy, when I look upon your face again."

The sound of horses' feet came upon their ears, and now that she thought she was surely about to meet with Rowland Percy, all her courage, all her fortitude forsook her, and, but she clung to the arm of Mr. Percy, she thought she must have fallen to the earth. She could not proceed another step, but with her eyes rivetted upon the turn of the road, she waited until two horsemen came in sight.

With a cry of joy, she uttered the name of Rowland, and then stood as pale as a marble statue awaiting his advance.

CHAPTER CXI.

THE MEETING.—A SCENE OF PURE AFFECTION.—THE ALARM.—THE DANGER OF THE FUGITIVES.

THE recognition between Rowland and Miranda was simultaneous. Not less intent was he, at that turn of the road, of catching a glimpse of her than she had been of him, although he had scarcely expected to find her so very short a distance from him.

" 'Tis she, 'tis she," he cried, and he urged his horse to its utmost speed. Then by a sudden impulse, he drew up, and hurriedly dismounted, preferring to rush forward on foot, to meet her who was the great object now of his existence. Two or three minutes brought him to her side. Pleasure beamed from his eyes, and heedless of the presence of others, forgetting everything but that he saw again the dear object of his heart's idolatry, he clasped her to his breast.

Let those who prefer the cold proprieties of existence to its most exquisite feelings, censure that embrace. It was one of the purest and tenderest affection, unalloyed by a single thought on the dreamiest aspiration of evil.

An exclamation of joy escaped old Mr. Percy, and he clasped one of the hands of Rowland, while the tears fell fast down his furrowed cheeks.

" Found—found !" he cried. " My boy Rowland—he is found at last—long sought for—long sought for as he has been. We shall all be happy now, for he is found at last. His enemies could not slay him. See, Miranda, he is unhurt. He is saved—he is saved !"

" Father—Miranda !" was all that Rowland could utter at the moment in the excitement of his feelings, and had not a few tears come to his relief, he felt that he should almost have been choked by his emotions.

Any stranger would have wondered what could have been the circumstances under which this party met. There was so little for some time said, and yet such evidently deep emotion in the hearts of them all. Under such circumstances, words seemed so very weak to give expression to the feelings that filled the heart, and their first gush must in some measure subside, before language can step in to the aid of the excited spirit.

How long Miranda and Rowland Percy would have continued gazing at each other, unheedful of everything but the intense pleasure they derived from such a process, it is hard to say, for a warning intimation was given to them by Witlet, that time was on the wing.

Being on horseback, he commanded a view to a considerable distance on the road towards London, whither he kept his eyes fixed , while, agreeably to his directions, Jones had mounted a high bank in the immediate vicinity of the place of meeting, and kept a good watch in the direction towards York.

"Mr. Percy," cried Witlet, " I am sure I need not warn you that this interview must needs be brief. Part soon, with a better hope of meeting again soon."

Both Rowland and Miranda started at the warning voice, and the former said,—

"Yes, Miranda, it is even as he says. We meet in difficulty and in danger, to part only with a hope of happier days, and we must part so very soon, that this meeting will appear to me like a glimpse of heaven in a dream."

"But the time will come, Rowland," whispered Miranda, "I feel assured it will, when we shall meet to part no more. When danger and suspicion will no longer hover over you, and when you will be free and honoured as you so amply deserve to be."

"My own Miranda, it rejoices me to find you so hopeful. If from any source I can derive pleasurable feelings in my calamitous condition, it must be from your lips !"

"Then be assured, dear Rowland, that I am full of hope. Does not everything which has occurred tend to the creation of such a feeling ? Have you not escaped almost miraculously from death, and has not Heaven shown its care of you, by giving me, a weak girl, power to snatch you from a prison, surrounded by all the care, and caution, and strength, which could be expended upon its defence ? Let us be full of hope, Rowland, and derive even from the calamitous circumstances you think of, holy and cheering consolation. Your accusation, your condemnation, and the ultimate triumph of your innocence—for that it will ultimately triumph I feel most certain—will be a graet practical lesson to mankind, and induce judges to be careful how they sacrifice a human life to the evidence of an act, wh'ch is in direct contradiction to all its former tenor. Moreover, Rowland, could any circumstances of prosperity have bound us to each other, as we are now bound to each other by misfortune? could any other circumstances have shewn to us each other's hearts as we now see them? none, Rowland, none. Let us then from out of this calamity extract some good, and while we have a hope of extrication from circumstances that cannot be otherwise than deeply painful, let us assure ourselves that the evil is not unmixed, but that when the day of tribulation shall have passed away, we shall find that we have not suffered altogether in vain."

It was soothing and delightful to Rowland Percy's heart—it must have been pleasing in the eyes of Heaven, to hear that young and innocent girl breathing such pure piety, and uttering such sentences of firm reliance on the even-handed justice of that Providence, which can turn afflictions to blessings, and make the wounded heart radiant with joy.

"Let us go home, let us go home," cried Mr. Percy; "we have surely now wandered far enough from York. Rowland is saved. What more have we to do ?"

"Much, much," said Miranda; "leave him to me, Rowland, he attends greatly to my words. We have much yet to do, Mr. Percy; Rowland, although safe at present, cannot be called saved. He is still environed by snares for his destruction; and although I have a fervent hope, amounting to a conviction, that he will be saved, we have yet still much to do. We must go to London, and Rowland must precede us. You know that when I say so, Mr. Percy, there are ample reasons for the act."

"Ample, ample," said the old man ; "you are always right. Can an angel err ?"

"You hear," said Miranda to Rowland; "he will accompany me cheerfully. We will submit ourselves entirely to the counsel of our best friend, Witlet, and as he considers that we had better not proceed to London together, we will satisfy ourselves with this brief interview, in the hope that a more lasting one awaits us when we meet again."

"You are right, Miranda," said Rowland; "you are right. Life and liberty to me now are ten times more precious than they could be under any other circumstances; when I see you, Miranda, full of hope and expectation, that a period will be put to our calamities, I ought to be the last to despair. You have ever been, and ever will be, dearest, my guardian angel; one who not only finds power to step between me and my enemies, but who likewise weans me from my own sad and sinful thoughts, winning me back again by your own gentleness and goodness to a better frame of mind. Ah, Miranda, Miranda, amid all these circumstances of pain, and toil, and trouble, what should I have been without thee?"

"And what," said Miranda, in a whisper, "what other feeling than that I have for you, Rowland, could have nerved me to do what I have done? we will mutually assist and support each other, trusting the while to Heaven to help us both."

"Mr. Percy, Mr. Percy," cried Witlet; "for God sake be brief. We know not even now what danger may come upon us."

"I will," said Rowland; "I will, but spare me yet a moment."

"Don't you wish you may get it," said Jones; "I expects as how we shall be in a out-an-out fix in a little while."

"What do you mean, Jones?" cried Witlet; "is any one coming?"

"I wish it was one as is coming," said Jones: "but it seems to me somewhere about thirteen to the dozen. There'll be a spree, as sure as my name's Jones. They are coming."

"But who are they?" said Witlet; "for Heaven sake be more explicit, Jones."

"More 'plicit—the only 'plicit as I knows is, I'm more elevated than you is, and sees 'em when you doesn't. There's a lot of fellows on horses; they've just turned the top of one of the hills, and all I can say is they're a-coming."

Witlet immediately dismounted from his horse, which stood as quiet as possible while he left it; then springing up the bank upon which Jones stood, with such suddenness as to disturb the latter's centre of gravity, and caused him to roll down it into the roadway, he took a searching and anxious glance towards York.

"Enemies," he exclaimed, "they are enemies. By Heavens, Jones, they are coming."

"I told you so," said Jones, "and you might just as well have said as you was a-coming just now, and not make a fellow fall down, with the hind part of him in a ditch. But what's to be done, Neddy? I forgives you, but what's to be done."

"I know not—I know not," said Witlet, "the danger is great; I could swear to those men being officers from York; and what fresh information has induced them again to take to the road I know not. Our danger was never so great as now. They'll be upon us in ten minutes."

"Farewell Miranda," said Percy, who had paid but little or no attention to what was passing between Jones and Witlet, "farewell, dearest; but, I pray Heaven we may soon meet again."

"There is little utility in parting now," said Witlet, "danger thickens; and there are now on the road twelve or thirteen officers from York, no doubt bent upon your capture. They are not riding fast, still something less than ten minutes must bring them to this spot."

A flush of colour came over Rowland Percy's face as he said,—

"Is the danger indeed so near? Alas! Miranda, there may even yet be more sorrow in store for us. But now do not mourn for me. I will die, contesting for my life with those who would deprive me of it, rather than be dragged back again to that cell from which you rescued me."

" Then, Rowland, we will live and die together," said Miranda.

" Who talks of dying," said old Mr. Percy ; " who talks of danger to you, Rowland and Miranda ? Fools ! do they know what it is to face desperation itself ? Unarmed, though I am, they shall find me more than their equal. Heed them not —heed them not. You shall see this roadway dyed with their blood. Let them come—let them come."

" That's all very fine old gentleman," said Jones, " and I haven't no doubt you means the pleasant little theatrical performance] as you mentions, only some peoples bow-wow is never such a lot worser than their bite, no exparagement to you, old gentleman ; but I'd rather not put you to the inconvenience o' eating all these ere dozen officers as is coming."

" I do not understand you," said old Percy.

" Oh, it's all the same. Now, Neddy, I tell you what, it strikes me we must come the artful."

" How do you mean ?" said Witlet.

" Why, there's a ditch on the other side of that ere hedge, and I moves as we all lays down on the bottom of it, and trust to Providence and quickset."

" But the horses," said Witlet, " the horses."

" Why, your own will lay on his back just whensoever he's axed ; and, as for the t'other one, I moves as we gives him a whack, as'll start him off at a devil of a rate."

" Ay, and so excite suspicion that his rider has hidden himself close at hand," cried Witlet. " That will not do, and you must bear in mind, likewise, Jones that you and I are always obnoxious to the officers, and they would not scruple an instant in arresting us, and lodging us in the gaol in the next market-town. However, your plan I fear, is the only one which presents the least chance of escape. But Mr. Percy's hack must learn a lesson in training on the spur of the moment, and he must hide himself, whether he likes it or not. Come on, to the hedge—to the hedge."

CHAPTER CXII.

THE CONCEALMENT FROM THE OFFICERS.—THE PURSUERS OUTWITTED.—THE CON-
TINUED JOURNEY.

ALL but old Mr. Percy followed Witlet to a high gate, which led into a meadow adjoining the road side, which otherwise was skirted by an impervious hedge, at the foot of which was the ditch Jones had mentioned as likely to afford a shelter to those who were anxious to conceal themselves from the approaching horsemen.

The plan seemed feasible enough, had it not been for the horses, whose bulk it was difficult to conceal, and whose discretion could not altogether be relied upon.

" We could hide in the ditch, for it is nearly dry," said Witlet, " with every chance of escape ; but, for the horses, there, I think, is an insurmountable difficulty."

" Why not," said Miranda, " strip them of their bridles and saddles, and turn Them into the meadow ? It is no extraordinary thing to see two horses grazing in a road-side field."

Witlet and Jones looked at each other for some moments in silence, and then the latter said,—

" You punch my head, and I'll punch your's ; then we shall both be properly served out for being two such fools as never to think of that afore ; to be sure, that's the very plan, Miss Miranda. I beg to remark, as in some things you is as green as possible, while in t'others you is positively downy; in course it ain't extra-ordinary to see horses a grazing. Neddy, what two spoons we is. Hilloa—how he's a-working!"

Ned Witlet was busy unlocking a padlock, which fastened a gate, with a false key, which, when he had accomplished, he led in both the horses, and commenced hastily divesting them of their harness, in which he was assisted by Jones and Percy. In a few moments the horses turned upon the meadow began, as Mr. Jones re-marked, in the most natural manner in the world, to crop the sweet herbage that grew in abundance at their feet,

"Now to the ditch—now to the ditch!—we've not a moment to lose!"

Even as he spoke, the sound of horses' feet, and even the voices of their pursuers, came with painful distinctness upon their ears. Miranda took old Mr. Percy by the arm, saying to him,—"Follow me, and do as I do," Then she crept close to the edge, and lay nearly completely hidden among the brushwood and mass of decayed leaves that formed the base of the ditch.

In an instant they were all concealed in a similar manner.

"Hush—hush," cried Witlet; "now, not another word."

"Mute as a coffin," murmured Jones, and then all was silent.

On came the horsemen, not at any extraordinary pace, but at one which, with-out distressing their horses, would carry them over a great quantity of ground in a few hours. Several of them were talking loudly; and so near were they now, that their words sounded plainly and distinctly upon the ears of those who were so anx-ious to escape their observation.

"Well, if we don't come up with him," said one, "or, if he takes any of the cross roads, instead of keeping to this one, we shall at least reach London time enough to raise a pretty hue and cry about him."

"We shall—I must have him!" cried the leader; "and, if Rowland Percy escapes us, I shall think myself well paid if I catch the scoundrel who took me so much unawares yesterday. Mind, I stand twenty pounds out of my own pocket to any one of you that places a pair of handcuffs on him; he is a tall, thinnish, sinewy looking man, with a slightly aquiline nose.

"By-the-bye," said another, "didn't you say, Viggers, when we were on the brow of the hill, that you saw some people hereabouts?"

"Upon my soul, I did," said the officer, suddenly checking his horse, and wheel-ing round to his companions; "I certainly did see four or five people hereabouts but how they have disappeared I can't think, for theres no house about."

"Oh!" cried another, "don't you see what a twist there is in the road They've gone on, of course, whoever they were, and, to set that question at rest, we'd better push after them."

"I say, one of those horses in yon field is a good 'un," remarked one of the officers to his companion.

"Yes, a beauty," was the reply; "come on—I only wish I had him instead of the beast I am upon."

This short colloquy took place exactly opposite to where the party lay concealed, and there can be no question but that it was listened to by them with an interest amounting to the deepest anxiety, particularly when Witlet's horse became a sub-ject of remark; for, if Viggers the constable had looked at it, which he did not, there was every probability of his knowing it again, and at once suspecting that its rider, against whom he felt so much animosity, could not be far off; in such an event, detection would have been almost certain, and through Rowlands determi-nation not to give himself up to his enémies alive, blood would have, in all proba-bility, been shed in the scene of violence that must have ensued.

Such, however, happily was not the case; and the ears of our friends were in a few moments blessed by the sound of the retreating footsteps of those who, by their superiority of numbers, must have been victorious over them, however gallant the resistance might have been.

"They are gone—they are gone," said old Mr. Percy.

"Stow that ere gab," muttered Jones.

"Hush, for God's sake, hush," said Witlet.

"Nay, I will rise and go after them," said old Mr. Percy. "I wish them to know how dangerous it is to become enemies of my son Rowland. I will go after them and slay them. Nay, Miranda, stay me not. It is my duty—a sacred duty. Rowland will always have enemies, unless I slay them ; the dead can do no injury—therefore I must kill them. Let me go—let me go. Do not attempt to stay me from my just revenge."

"Mr. Percy, Mr. Percy, I charge you to remain where you are ; believe me, you are doing more for Rowland by quietness now than by violence."

"Ah, say you so? Yes, yes, Hush, not a word—not a word."

"They are far enough off, now," said Jones; "and I don't see as we need be so particular about holding our tongues ; only it wouldn't be just the prudent thing for the old gentleman to go after them, and make a kick up; for he'd do himself harm, and us no good ; which I take it is somewhere about the same sort of thing."

"He will be still—he will be still,' said Miranda. "Thank Heaven, we have escaped!"

"Yet remain quiet awhile," said Witlet, "while I cautiously reconnoitre the road these horsemen have taken. Although the officers of York could not hold a prisoner when they had him, they seem determined to repair their error."

Ned Witlet crept along the hedge, until he came to a lower portion of it, and raising himself then only so high as his eyes, to obtain a clear view over its top, he gazed after the retreating horsemen, who little suspected that they were really exerting themselves to increase the distance between themselves and the object of their pursuit.

"'Tis well," muttered Witlet. "In the chances of escape, the greatest is always to be fully cognisant of the whereabouts of our enemies. Ride on to London, most sapient officers ; if you will, you shall have the road to yourselves, and no hindrance to its full enjoyment, if it can produce you any. This, I take it, is about the narrowest escape we have yet had—our danger being so much the greater, in consequence of the number of our party."

He waited until the officers were nearly hidden from his sight, and then abandoning the caution that was no longer necessary, he walked back to the ditch, saying,—

"The danger is passed ; and with a feeling of relief we can at least tell ourselves that we need not expect an enemy in every chance person that may cross our path. Out of the worst circumstances we may gather some good ; and the benefit we shall derive from this little dangerous rencontre is, that we know the tactics of our enemies."

"And I have one consolation," said Rowland Percy, "that if the worst comes to the worst, they would surely be satisfied with my destruction, as the principal party involved in these transactions."

"Indeed, Mr. Percy, I don't know that," said Witlet. "I think I may make common cause with you now most fairly ; for Viggers, the officer, seems as intent upon my capture as upon your's—nay, probably more so, for people's revenges are always more dear to them than their public duties. After what we heard Viggers say, I shall begin to think that he comes after me as much as you. Help me to saddle the horses, Jones ; and although I believe we are tolerably safe just now, yet I counsel an immediate separation."

The horses were soon in a fit state again for the road, and the whole party passed from the meadow which afforded them so timely a shelter—each with a feeling of thankfulness at the escape, with the exception of poor Mr. Percy, whose state of mind would not permit him fully to appreciate the circumstances.

Miranda and Rowland Percy looked in each other's faces with the greatest tenderness. Every new danger seemed to draw them closer together, and they felt as unwilling to part as they had been before. Stern necessity, however, admitted of no other choice ; and with a few hurried sentences of affection they bade each other farewell—that sort of painful indefinite farewell with which persons involved in difficulty and danger separate, when their meeting again is involved in doubt and uncertainty, and much misery may befal each ere they can look into the light of each other's eyes, and with a thrill of joy exclaim—" Thank Heaven we've met again !"

Witlet was standing with the bridle of his horse over his arm, while Jones held Rowland's steed ready for him to mount,

" Now, Miss Miranda," said Witlet, " do you keep the high road; for even if the officers should recognize you they have no power to molest you, or obstruct

THE LANDLORD OF THE OLD MOON SCRUTINISING ROWLAND.—PAGE 408.

your proceeding in any way. Nevertheless, I should say, keep out of the way, if you can, and if you should come across them, try, with the assistance of Jones, to puzzle them as to the track you are pursuing. I do not think that Mr. Percy and I will reach London much before you do yourself, for we shall take a course far out of the high road, unless at intervals we succeed in ascertaining exactly that the officers are many miles ahead of us. Do not forget the address in London, where you are to inquire for me."

" I'll see that that ere dodge is all right," said Jones. " We shall soon be at No. 55.

the Star and Tinder-box, in Steeple-court ; and when we does get there, we rayther knows what to say. I doesn't make no sort of doubt we shall get on uncommon well on the road.   I think as how we've got enough for our expenses in a moderate kind of way, and if we want any more, I ain't such a fool as not to know some-think about what people calls the rights of property, which means, in my very humble opinion, as you are to grab all you can, and d—n all the remainder."

"A comprehensive doctrine, truly," said Witlet, as he sprung upon his horse. "Ah, Jones, Jones ! I'm afraid you'll never mend your life."

"It ain't broke yet," said Jones ! "and if so be as there's anything wrong, there's two on us, you knows Neddy."

"Farewell, farewell," said Rowland to Miranda.   "May Heaven have you in its choicest keeping !"

"And you," said Miranda, "if you are well all is well."

There was a silent pressure, and then Rowland turned to his father.

"We shall meet again soon," he said ; "but, in the meantime, I must leave you with my heart's best treasure, Miranda."

"What," said the old man, as a tear sprung to his eye, "will you leave us so soon, Rowland ? Oh ! come home ! It seems to me that we are far from York —the pleasant meadows and the little wooded park, which is all our own—which will all be yours, Rowland, when death has taken me from you, and I can no longer love you with the love of a mortal heart—a heart which, until it ceases its painful pulsations, is all your own and Miranda's. I have hopes, Rowland, great hopes, of procuring the full and entire consent of Sir George Rankley to your marriage."

"Father—father ! think again," said Rowland, "and you will surely remember that he is dead ?"

"That is a delusion," said Mr. Percy, quickly—" a delusion which the whole world is labouring under, except myself. Leave all that to me, Rowland, and in the meantime come home. Why, you were born in the old house and passed your happiest days in it, Why, then—why, then, should you wander from it now ?"

"I have no choice, father—I have no choice. Even now, moments may be precious ; and although in the wide world there is but yourself and Miranda for whom my heart feels most specially, yet must I leave you, although with greater ease and confidence, because you have with you the angelic spirit, which surely must be under Heaven's especial care,"

"You mean Miranda ?"

"I do, father—I do. Remain with her, and be all that kindness can dictate ; but as you love her and myself, do not mention to her Sir George Rankley, for indeed he is dead. Farewell—farewell."

Rowland then mounted his horse, and he and Witlet were ready again to pro-ceed on their toilsome and dangerous journey. He waved his hand again to Miranda but could not trust himself to speak.

"On—on," said Witlet, and in another moment they were going at a sharp trot up the road.

Poor Miranda felt as if a sudden change had come over the face of nature, when Rowland Percy was gone. She had felt a sense of security and freedom from harm when he was by, which seemed now to desert her. It required all the really strong mind she possessed to be able to bear, with even outward composure, the parting, and it was only by reflecting upon the important trust she had in the protection of him whose wandering intellect forbade him to control his own actions, that nerved her to undergo whatever further trials might be in store for her.

Jones first broke the silence, by saying,—

"Miss Miranda, I have got a scheme of my own, which I didn't say nothing of to Neddy, cause he, perhaps, would have kicked at the way in which I wanted to compass the browns. It appears to me as we should run a much better chance of getting to London quick and easy by coming the bold caper."

"What do you mean, Jones?"

"Why, I means this ere, Miss Miranda. I takes it we are a third of the way between York and London, that is to say, we haven't much above a hundred miles to go; but that is a tolerable long way to foot it, with only the chance of a waggon, or something of that ere sort, to give us a lift. Now I propose we go to the next town and waits comfortably for the mail or coach, when we can get a lift as far as we like, or all the way, for a matter of that ere; or, if you likes it better, Miss Miranda, we'll come it more out-and-out, and take a chaise, only, as I haven't got quite tin enough for that caper, I should be obligated to borrow some of a gentleman afore we could come it, cause we mustn't be in London without no tin for a start."

"I can really see no objection," said Miranda, "to our taking a coach, except the one which would most likely occur even under any circumstances, that is the meeting with those whom we would fain avoid, and their consequent discovery that I was bound to the metropolis, from which they would infer that Rowland was there likewise."

"If you and the old gentleman can get inside places, it seems to me as there isn't much to be feared. I'll warrant they sha'n't know me on the roof. To be sure, we should get to London before Neddy and Mr. Percy, but where's the odds, you can make yourself comfortable when they comes."

"True," said Miranda, "and, after all, in London we may succeed in hiding ourselves from any spies that might be set to watch us, for the great object, of course, will be to avoid being dangerous to Rowland in consequence of making inquiry for him, and being traced to the house where we are to hear news of Witlet."

"The very ticket," said Jones, "leave me to arrange all that; they'll be rum'uns if they finds me out in going backwards and forwards in London. I knows too many ins and outs there to be easy tooked in, and if they tries to follow me, I'd lead 'em a dance they'd be sick on before they'd done with it."

"Then let us at once resolve," said Miranda, "upon that course of action. I am willing to risk it, if there be any risk in it."

"Kim on then," said Jones, "and I hopes we shall have the pleasure of seeing the most beautifulest and most romantic spot in all London afore we is twenty-four hours older."

"What spot is that?"

"Dury-lane, especially on a wet day. You should see the ins and outs as is there, Miss Miranda—nothing werdent, and no mistake—lots of conweniences of all sorts and descriptions. Hot saveloys at a ha'penny a piece, and baked 'taters for nothink, only you must be up to the doge of grabbing of them when the fellow's looking another way in a fit of confidence. Then it's not like here, where you may go never so many miles without so much as seeing of a public-house—for, no, it's quite the rewerse—if you wants a glass of gin, you've nothing to say but 'give us a penn'orth.' What do you think of all that, old gentleman?"

"I am thinking of the stars," said Percy.

"Do you mean the Seven Stars in Russell-court?"

"No, no—the heavenly bodies."

"Oh! that's another thing—they is all earthly bodies as is there—the only thing as is heavenly is the gin, and that is out-an-out.'

CHAPTER CXIII.

THE PLAN OF THE OFFICERS.—MR. JONES'S DISGUISE, AND THE COACH FROM
YORK.

WITLET explained to Rowland Percy his plan of reaching London without
encountering the officers, by taking cross-roads, and out-of-the-way bridle-paths,
with which he, Witlet, was familiar, and although such a mode of operation must
necessarily consume considerable time, yet itpresented such great chances of safety,
that they both determined to adopt it, and accordingly started off at the first
turning they came to with the resolution to go near the high-road as little as possible, and to obtain what refreshments they required, if it could be so managed, at
cottages by the road-side, instead of at inns or public-houses.

Witlet could not but perceive Rowland's intense anxiety as regarded Miranda,
and he took occasion to assure him that she could not possibly come to any harm.

"Jones," he said, "with all his peculiarities, is courageous and full of ex-
pedients. He is tolerably well known on the road, and liked for a certain rough
humour that characterises his sayings and doings. I have every expectation that
he will bring Miranda to London in perfect safety, and although I have warned him
as you heard to be particularly careful not to involve her in any of his peculations
on the road, I believe such warning was not required."

"I am rejoiced," replied Rowland, "to hear you talk so cheeringly upon the
subject, which of course must be uppermost in my heart. Heaven knows what
may eventually become of me, or whether my innocence will ever become apparent
to the minds of men! I hope it will, or I shall soon die, for I should be even in
London like a man sent to seek his bread manacled. I dare not even shew myself
to those who would purchase the labour of my hands, or my head."

"Sufficient for the day," said Ned Witlet, "is the evil thereof. We will think
of all that when we get to London. Your escape is now the one great object in
view."

The plan of the officers, who were so anxious to recapture the convicted
murderer, as they called poor Rowland, was not a bad one. They rightly enough
conjectured that his progress would be slow, on account of the many shifts and
manœuvres he would be compelled to resort to, to escape recognition, and consequent capture. They, therefore, considered that their safest way would be to
take the high road to London as quickly as possible, with the remote chance of
finding him they sought on the road, but the greater probability of leaving him
on it.

Viggers then intended to make arrangements with the London police, so that
every avenue to the metropolis would be watched for a few days, and then his
party, being a powerful one, could separate itself, and taking different routes back
again, stand possibly a chance of meeting Rowland.

How they sped upon their errand, our readers will discover as we proceed, for a
very short time must now suffice, to bring those in whose fate we are so much
interested, as well as their enemies, to the metropolis.

In fact, the road was clear, and it would have required some out-of-the-way
accident, to involve Rowland in such danger, now that the York officers were some
miles ahead of him on the high road, while he was making various divarications
from his course, each of which enabled them to gain a still greater distance in
advance.

As for Miranda, she had not to go above three or four miles at the very utmost,
before reaching a straggling village, through which, Jones ascertained, all the
coaches between York and London must necessarily pass; and there they resolved
to wait, as they were told one would be by the course of an hour and a half, which
had started at a very early hour from York.

In the neat, sanded parlour of the half-farm, half-inn, at which they had made the inquiries, Miranda and old Mr. Percy rested themselves from the fatigue of the morning, while Jones went through the village until he came to the barber's shop, into which he entered with an air of great familiarity, saying,—

"How is yer? How do you find business?"

"Really, sir, upon my honour and conscience," said the barber, "you have the advantage of me."

"Lor," said Jones," you don't mean to say that! why, I had my hair cut here seven years ago. What a memory you must have to be sure."

"Ah, my dear sir," said the barber, "seven years, you know, is a long time; we can't remember every gentleman who does us the honour of having his hair cut here; but, perhaps, you will like to do so now sir?"

"No, I wants a wig."

"A wig, sir; certainly, sir, I believe, sir, my stock of wigs, consisting of seven, to be the finest in this part of the country; and I have got one, sir, that will match the colour of your hair to a T."

"Thank you for nothing," said Jones; "that's just what I don't want; I am tired of my own head of hair, and wants a change."

The barber produced his stock of wigs, and Jones chose one which differed as materially as possible from the colour of his own hair; then, borrowing the barber's scissors, he, to the astonishment of that functionary, cut his hair off in great masses, so that, when the wig was on his head, no traces of it could be seen.

Having honestly, then, paid for his purchase—for Mr. Jones, in his refinements upon philosophy, would have thought it a very low thing indeed, not to pay for anything he had fairly offered to buy—he hastened back to Miranda, to show her the effect the singular coloured wig produced upon his physiognomical expression.

"I don't mean to say for sartin, Miss Miranda," he remarked, "that I should be tooked up even if they was to see me, only you see, it's just possible, as I had rayther a scrimmage¹ with one of the magistrates when you was in quod, about what they called the Riot Act, which you may have heard as I boned, he may have turned wicious, and offer the officers something to lay¹ hands on me, so I wishes to keep myself snug and quiet, rayther than trouble him, which is the reason of this ere wig. Now, if there's room inside, when the coach does come, you and the old gentleman shall get there, and I'll take care of myself on the roof; and pervided there should be a scrimmage of any kind, I can always get down, and put my spoke in the wheel. What have yer had to drink?"

"This ale," said Miranda, "suits my appetite well, though it may not your's. You will, doubtless, call it weak."

Mr. Jones tasted the ale, and then made a hideous face.

"Weak be blowed," he said, "I calls it strong, only it's strong of the wrong thing—the water, I mean. This ere ale has a very slight acquaintance with malt and hops."

Mr Jones then went and made such a clatter in the house respecting the quality of the beverage which had been supplied, that, as is almost always the case in public-houses, large or small, a better article was produced, an article usually kept for guests who make a disturbance, and who will not be put off with inferior commodities.

The coach came pretty nearly about the time which had been mentioned, and, upon hailing it, Mr. Jones found that there were two inside places, and only two, vacant. Mr. Percy and Miranda were soon installed into the vehicle; and Jones, by the special invitation of the coachman, had the box seat, which gave him an opportunity of discoursing with that worthy, and beguiling the tedium of the way wonderfully.

In fact, the coachman thought Jones so extraordinary a person, that he treated him wherever they changed horses, and listened to the outrageous inventions with which he was amused, with the fullest belief, and the most unbounded satis-faction.

Thus are all our dramatis personæ fairly without let or hindrance on the road to London, where, let us hope, though it may be after many changing scenes and vicissitudes of fortune, Rowland Percy, with his faithful and beautiful Miranda, may meet the reward of their innocence, their rare fidelity, and their many trials of fortitude, by being blessed with the society of each other, never again to part, until death shall prepare them for a meeting of an eternal charcter, in those realms where the judgment of the judge is infallible, and sorrow is a thing unknown.

CHAPTER CXIV

THE ARRIVAL IN LONDON.—EVENING IN THE METROPOLIS.—THE INN YARD.

OF the four separate parties—some of whom were so anxious to meet each other, others to avoid a collision—that were proceeding towards the metropolis, the one which comprised Bernard Varley and Samuel Twitter was the first to arrive at its journey's end.

Regardless of expense, Varley travelled post, and, of course, secured the best relays of horses that could be had on the road ; the consequence of which was, that he reached the metropolis in an exceedingly short space of time, considering the distance he had to traverse. Twitter sat with him ; for although Varley took good care to let him know and thoroughly feel the difference in their positions, yet, like most men with an overburdened conscience, he would consent to any compan-ionship, rather than be alone, and, therefore, he admitted Twitter to a seat inside the carriage, with a view of conversing with him, when dark and desperate thoughts should come crowding on his brain, and he should feel the want of some human companionship, even if it were that of the man whom he most hated and abhorred.

After their recent quarrel, the reader is aware that a better understanding existed between these worthies, or, at all events, the semblance of one, which answered the same purpose, so far as they were mutually concerned. It was upon the strength of this, and the elation of mind, arising from the possession of a hun-dred pound note, that Twitter, during the journey, sought several times to wean Varley from the desperate pursuit in whch he was egaged, and to lead him to more rational resolutions as concerned his future life.

It was curious to note how the half imbecile, weak-minded man rose, under the peculiar circumstances, far above him of an acuter-intellect, in, at all events, the one quality—discretion.

Samuel Twitter had not the mind to be diverted from his own petty avarice and considerations for his personal safety by any such passion as that which inflamed the breast of Bernard Varley. Miranda might have been more beautiful, more innocent, more full of angelic qualities than she really was, without disturbing the mind of Samuel Twitter from its deep selfishness ; but Bernard Varley was com-posed of more penetrable stuff ; and, hardened villain as he was, he had a perception of the good and beautiful, which induced him to covet the possession of the beau-tiful being whom he had deprived of fortune and friends, and from whose very destitution he had gathered his greatest hopes of a successful result to his wild passion.

We cannot but believe, likewise, that Heaven's atoning justice shone conspicu-ously in the person of Bernard Varley, and that a part of his punishment in this wor for the frightful and ungrateful murder of the father, was a soul-consuming and hopeless passion for the child.

But be this as it may, not a day, not an hour, not a minute passed over the head of Bernard Varley, without adding fresh fuel from the depths of his own reflections to that master feeling of his mind which Samuel Twitter, with a groaning horror, foretold would be his ultimate destruction.

Ever dreading Varley's violence as he did, and knowing that he was about to touch upon a topic that would influence his fiercest passions, they had not proceeded twenty miles upon their journey, when, with cringing accents, Twitter aglan implored him to reconsider the labyrinth of chances into which he was about to plunge himself.

"Rememeber, Varley," he said, "you have gained all, ay, more than all you ever expected. Let your exertions be for the death of Rowland Percy, but leave Miranda. I pray you leave her to whatever fate that may await her. Can you indulge even the faintest shadow of a hope that she will ever be yours?"

"I have three means before me," said Varley, gloomily—"entreaty, fraud, and force. I have placed them in their proper order. If one will not succeed, another shall."

"But neither will—neither can; and I repeat what I have before urged, that in some of your wild and lost appeals to Miranda, you will say something that will bring us both to—"

"To what?"

"To a scaffold. Hush!—speak low, Oh! Varley, think of what you might be, and what you are risking to become. Suppose the Grange estates will not be purchased by any one, is not the income derivable from them most ample and satisfactory—satisfactory alike to you as to me; for, upon mature reflection, I believe, Varley, you were only joking when you talked of not giving me my full share of the proceeds; I am confident you were only joking."

"Samuel Twitter," said Varley, putting his hand into his pocket, and drawing it out again very slowly, with a pistol, "there are two things, it appears to me, that step between you and your wits; the one is a love of money; the other, a horror of my pursuit of Miranda Rankley. I have warned you often before; now be warned again, and let me tell you that in some unhappy hour you will say too much upon those subjects, and I shall be compelled to blow your brains out. After which I will place the weapon with which the deed was accomplished in your dead hand, so that before the muscles become rigid you shall grasp it tightly, and be deemed the author of your own death."

"Gracious powers!" cried Twitter, "what a horrible plan! I will be silen since it is no use to speak; it was for your own good I addressed you; but I will be silent—I will be silent."

"When we arrive in London," added Varley, "you will want for nothing; but unless you fully aid and assist me in my pursuit of Miranda, I shall be apt to consider you an incumbrance, and such a thought on my part might be dangerous. You understand me, Samuel Twitter?"

Twitter only replied by a groan; and the subject was not renewed during the remainder of the rapid journey which ushered them into London.

The coach which conveyed Miranda and her two companions was not very far behind the post chaise, which carried him who had worked her so much woe and wretchedness, and Mr. Jones hailed with no little pleasure distant glimpses of the great city, which to him contained all human enjoyments, and in which he had passed most certainly his happiest days; but it was not until he came considerably nearer that he thought proper, by tapping on the glass of the coach, to give Miranda an intimation that they were so near their journey's end.

"Hilloa!" he cried, "we ain't far off now; we've come it out-and-out, miss— mum, I mean—and take a look at the jolly great hive."

'Twas towards the close of a fine, though wintry day, that our travellers neared the great metropolis, such a day that brings to our minds spring and its gaily clothed hedge rows and gardens. The air was keen, and the wind blew coldly, yet the sun, for a few short hours, cast a gleam of gladness upon the country round within the reach of vision; but the sunshine of autumn and winter has but little effect upon the cold earth in comparison to the cheering effect upon the mind.

The clearness of the weather enabled the observer to obtain a better and more extended view than is often obtained at the decline of day, when the mists rise from the low grounds, dimly obscuring those objects that are situated at but short distances from the main road, which were now interesting, and of a character that indicated the near approach to an important city.

Detached villas, standing in the midst of high walls and costly fencing, and usually surrounded by ornamental shrubberies, lawns, and flower gardens, while the spotless white of the walls was relieved by the carefully painted verandahs, doors, and other parts. The cottages of the poor—the alms houses—the very roads, indicated the approach to a spot where numbers and opulence dwelt.

The approach to the metropolis is more or less hilly, though it lies in a kind of amphitheatre, surrounded by bold hills, whose heights and sides are at these days crowned with many of the most beautiful residences the country can boast of. The many vehicles that were passing to and from the place they were approaching, their number, miscellaneous character, some of them of superior descriptions, both public and private, drawn, in many instances, by superb cattle, were such as can nowhere be met with in such numbers as in London or near it.

The roads were dry, and hard, well kept, while the frequency of the turnpikes was such that those who travelled frequently found this necessary tax heavy,

Within a few miles of the great metropolis how the scene changed, from the purely agricultural country, that at a greater distance it is, to one of ornamental and even business appearance.

Much of the land is occupied as dairy-farms, and much of it belongs to market-gardeners, whose constant care and busy labour are well repaid by the return they receive for their goods. The daily supply these men bring to the great mart or emporium of animal and vegetable matter is enormous, and this supply is voluntary, depending entirely upon the wants of both purchaser and vender.

The sun was descending towards the west, his pale faint gleams were of a ruddier hue than usual, and in his declension exhibited a dense vapour, that rose strangely towards the heavens at a short distance. To describe this appearance is almost impossible, for the vapour did not rise equally. Many persons may have noticed the rugged form of the clouds after a heavy rain, at some distant spot, as the winds drive them onward; they hang as if partially discharging, or continuing to discharge, aqueous vapour, and some contain a greater weight, so these parts hang lower than those which have become lightened.

'Twas thus the vapour rose from "the great wen," the metropolis; in parts it rose rapidly and high, in others it ascended more slowly; in some places it was of a lighter, and in others of a deeper hue. To the stranger approaching London the appearance of the vapour arising from this vast city has a singular and strange effect, many thinking it must be a fog; but, though at first glance it may be eemed such, yet it has not the opacity of either fog or mists.

Great, indeed, is the change between town and country, but not in many towns is this change very perceptible, for they are immediately environed by the country, the open and bona fide rural districts. Not so is the vicinity of London; it has as distinct a character as the metropolis itself; it is quite a different thing to the country, where the pigs and the peasants luxuriate in all their pristine glory and character.

It would appear that everything seemed of a higher, or perhaps, more expansive character; more money seemed to circulate, and more earned, for large houses and small seemed to increase at a rapid rate. Men and women were better clothed, and those clothes of a more modern cut; children were the same, and had contracted a much shrewder, or more knowing look; houses and lodgings appeared better furnished, while public houses multiplied most amazingly, in a manner perfectly unaccountable, if they were presumed to make a living from the custom of those who lived in their immediate vicinity.

The scene now became of great interest; long rows of houses, before which grew stunted pollards or elms; long rows of iron railings; again these would be supplanted by perhaps smaller houses, whose lower apartments were converted into shops of all kinds. Vehicles passed to and fro; sometimes, indeed, a not of idlers would gather here or there, while some would gather round some shop to examine the goods, not with the remotest idea of becoming purchasers, but from mere habitual curiosity.

The entrances to London—that is the extremities that have grown out of it are, in all cases, meaner looking than the metropolis itself, and so it was here; men and women were crying their wares and offering them for sale in baskets in the open air; the houses now were nearly all shops, while the side streets alone contained private houses.

Upon this scene of busy confusion, which is perfectly incomprehensible to a stranger, who is bewildered with the quantity of what he sees, and the rapid motion of every living creature around him, the sun was rapidly setting, just illumining

No. 56.

the higher portions of the houses, and the great and well-known public edifices at the east end of the metropolis were yet seen in the full light of departing day.

Proceeding further towards the quarter in which the city was situated, the houses became more dense, private dwellings disappeared, and, turn which way you would, shops and nothing but shops met your gaze.

The coach proceeded to one of the oldest and best inns in London, where Miranda alighted, not a little surprised at the intense bustle around her, and had her mind been free from anxieties, she would have derived from the new scene into which she was plunged, much food for amusing speculation.

CHAPTER CXV.

THE ILLNESS OF MR. PERCY.—THE HOSPITAL.—VARLEY AND TWITTER IN SMITHFIELD.

"WELL," said Jones, when he had paid the fare, and Miranda and old Mr. Percy were standing by him, as little regarded in the inn-yard as if they had been two chests of goods,—"well, here we is at last. Isn't it pleasant? There's a constant scrimmage going on in London, which you can't get at no how in the country. There's something for everybody to do, and you'd open your eyes, Miss Miranda, if you know'd what a precious sight of cribs as was cracked in one night in this ere city."

"Surely," said Miss Miranda, "there is some universal tumult in the streets. Let us wait until it has passed away before we venture forth from this shelter."

"A row, do you mean? Lor' bless you, there's nothing of the kind, the sort of imitation of a shindy as you now sees goes on all day without never a stop; but what's the matter with the old gentleman, he dosen't seem altogether the thing?"

Miranda turned hastily, and looked in the face of old Mr. Percy, in which she was shocked to observe a change as sudden as it was unexpected. A death-like paleness was spreading itself over his countenance. It seemed as if the very air of London was inimical to his existence, and that he could not breath freely in the pent-up atmosphere of the great city.

"He is ill—he is ill!" said Miranda. "What shall we do now? Ah! this is a new calamity I did not expect. Mr. Percy, speak to me; you are not well."

"Not well," he said, "and yet scarcely ill. My strength seems to have given way for several hours—where— where is Rowland?—my boy, Rowland?"

His languor seemed to increase each moment, and but for the timely interposition of Jones, it is probable he would have fainted upon the spot.

"Hilloa, old gentleman," said Jones. "Take things easy—what's the dodge?"

"I fear I am not well," he said. "Miranda—Miranda—how came we here?"

Miranda bent eagerly over him, watching every change in his countenance, while a throng of idlers began to gather around the little anxious group.

"Can't you keep out of the way?" said Jones. "I'm blessed if that isn't always the way; if anybody feels a little faint, he's a most smothered outright by a crowd of fools as seem to want to get down his very throat. Come now, you with the fur cap and the cribbage-board countenance, just be so good as to draw a jug of water from that ere pump, and make yourself useful, as nature won't let you be an ornament."

The man thus appealed to stared at Jones in astonishment, and then went with some alacrity to do as he was bidden, apparently quite amused at the jest which had been made at his own personal appearance.

A draught of water seemed to revive Mr. Percy, at least, so far as his fainting was concerned; but an occasional shiver would pass across his frame, which alarmed Miranda, and induced her to press Jones to let a medical man see him.

"Wery good," said Jones, "there's no want o' doctors in London; d—n it, you might walk on their werry heads. The old gentleman had better go inside the house, while I goes and fetches one; but, between you and me, Miss Miranda, I'll have a wetter-and-hairy."

"A what?" said Miranda, in some surprise.

"I means a doctor as is used to horses. I never was outrageous ill but once; and then the doctors all guved me up, and said as how I was going to assault the bucket; but arter that, just as I was really beginning to think o' croaking, there comes a wetter-and-hairy chap, as knowed me many years ago, and he says to me,—

"'Do you recollect that ere mare as I had once—she with a white spot on her nose, as won the silver cup and the kiver?'"

"Oh! go at once," said Miranda. "I fear he is getting worse; I will see that he is assisted into the house while you are gone."

"Wery good," said Jones; "recollect, I left off at kiver. I'll tell you the rest at another time."

Jones was right enough when he alluded to the number of medical men, for there were three or four within a stone's throw of the inn, and he soon returned with a sensible-looking middle-aged man, who, by great good luck, was a clever practitioner as well as one above making a patient.

Mr. Percy had been kindly helped into a spare room, adjoining the parlour of the inn, and the medical man, after an examination of the symptoms that oppressed him, said—

"I would advise you, miss, to get the gentleman home as quickly as possible; there are signs of fever about him which, if not checked, may do serious mischief. Pray get him home immediately."

"Home!" said Miranda, rather impulsively than from reflection. "Home!— we have no home."

"No home?" said the surgeon, looking with surprise at the party.

"Why, we've just come from the country," said Jones, "and our town-house ain't quite ready. We likes it to be well whitewashed, you see sir, before we goes into it. Servants is nasty beasts, unless one is always abusing 'em."

"If you've not a comfortable place immediately to take him to," said the surgeon, "I would strongly advise you to try one of the hospitals."

Miranda shrunk from the name of a hospital, and the surgeon, observing it, added,—

"I can see such a course is repugnant to your feelings, and although I admit all the abuses of the hospital system, yet I must repeat my advice. You had better let your father be taken there at once."

"He's not my father," said Miranda, "except by adoption."

"Then I the more strenuously urge my advice."

"And wery good adwice, too," said Jones. "What do you say to it, old gentleman?"

"Miranda," said Mr. Percy, "it seems to me that I have been in a dream for some time, and knew not my real situation. I am willing to go, for I feel sickness coming fast upon me."

"His reason has returned again," exclaimed Miranda; "that look and tone assure me of it. Thank Heaven for its mercies! I know nothing of hospitals, further than they are medical institutions for the relief of the necessitous; but Heaven forbid that I should stand in the way, from, perhaps, false feeling, of anything which is for the benefit of Mr. Percy."

"Ahem!" said Jones, with a warning look not to pronounce the name again. "I'll get a coach. What's to pay, sir?"

"Oh! there's nothing to pay," said the medical man, "I have done nothing; but you must come to my house again, to get a letter, without which the patient will not be admitted."

This was done, and nearly an hour of painful anxiety passed, before poor Mr. Percy, whose mind was still weak, although the sudden accesssion of physical indisposition seemed to have restored it in a measure, was placed in Saint Bartholomew's Hospital, which, as well as other similar metropolitan institutions, would be much more estimable if the medical men would consider the patients as human beings, possessed of human feelings and affections, and if the nurses of the sick did not belong to the dregs of society.

    *   *   *   *   *

Poor Miranda felt as if her misfortunes were thickening around her, for wearisome as would have been to any one but herself the close attendance that was necessary upon old Mr. Percy, still for Rowland's sake she could endure it cheerfully, and without a murmur bend her energies to the service of him whose mind misfortune had stricken, but who was dear to her from the very name he bore.

She stood in Smithfield, along with her strange companion, Jones, and it would almost seem as if he guessed the purport of the thoughts that were crowding round her heart.

"Miss Miranda," he said, "I dare say the old gentleman will get better, and if he don't, don't you be taking on about it, for, sooner or later, you know, we must all give in to the enemy; and it's natural that the old should go first, to make way for the young 'uns as is to come; so pluck up a good heart, Miss Miranda; laugh at care, and it's ten to one but he gets so indignant that he cuts away."

"It's good philosophy, but the saddened bosom recognises nothing but it's own griefs. What, oh, what now will become of me in this labyrinth of streets and houses, until Rowland shall arrive! Methinks it would have been almost better to have lingered on the road."

At this moment Miranda was surprised at Jones suddenly seizing her by the arm, and whispering in eager tones,—

"Back, Miss Miranda—back, back. Here's a go, here's a go! Don't speak now, miss. Don't think or move for a minute, till he's gone past. Well, I never, What an ugly-looking thief, to be sure. Who'd a thought it. There's a phisigogonemy."

Miranda retreated into a door-way, which was very dark, and in the next moment she saw Bernard Varley pace slowly by, with a melancholy and abstracted air. He was enveloped in a long brown cloak, which made him look even taller than usual, and his face was cadaverous and ghastly in the extreme. He seemed like a man soul-stricken by misfortunes, one on whom the hand of Heaven had pressed heavily, and who had almost lost hope, from the dull weight of afflictions.

"There, there," said Jones, as he looked after the retreating figure. "Talk of people being misfortunate, and all that kind of thing! There's a wretch for you. I wouldn't be him for a guinea and a clean shirt a day."

"Hush, hush," said Miranda; "look again, look again."

"Gracious preserve us," said Jones, as he drew back, and nearly fell over the scraper.

Creeping along in a stooping posture, as if he would willingly have made his way under the pavement, instead of over it, provided a passage had been practicable, came Samuel Twitter. His eyes were fixed upon Varley's movements, whom he was evidently dogging, with all the suspicions and alarm that were characteristics of his nature. Had Miranda stood fully in his way, he would scarcely have seen her, so absorbed was he in his feeling of necessity of watching his companion in guilt, to see if he were bent on any desperate means prejudicial to the safety of both.

It was quite a study to see how Twitter glided along with his body bent, and his eyes so fixed upon the tall dark figure which preceded him. In fact, full of ample food for philosophical reflection, was the mere appearance of those two men, one of whom, at least, had reaped the full fruits of his villany, but who was yet as unhappy, if not more so—as intolerably wretched as he who fancied then that his chiefest cause and anxiety was to possess himself of money, that he might fly from possible dangers to his personal safety.

"There's a couple of tidy nuts for the devil to crack," said Jones. "We needn't ax for no vengeance against them, Miss Miranda, for, as the man said in the play I seed one night, they've got that there inside which isn't out. There they goes— what a kipple. I should like to drive 'em in a tandem to the gallows."

A deep sigh escaped Miranda, as she said,—

"So, even here I am to be haunted by that fearful man; even here, nearly two hundred miles from where he first commenced his persecutions, I am still to feel the consciousness of his dreadful presence, and to look for fresh evils at his hands. Heaven help me! I will endeavour to submit myself to thy holy will, but forgive me if I am impatient of much misery, and implore in the bitterness of my heart, for mercy—mercy."

"Werry good," said Jones, looking intently at the sky, just above Giltspur-street Compter.

CHAPTER CXVI.

MIRANDA IN SEARCH OF A LODGING.—A FEW WORDS ABOUT GENTEEL PEOPLE, AND THE MANNERS AND CUSTOMS OF SUCH TRIBES.

THE evening was rapidly advancing, and of course Miranda's first object was to secure some respectable lodging, where she could remain until there was a chance of Rowland Percy's arrival.

Turning to Jones, she said,—

"What will become of me now? notwithstanding the heavy charge which Mr. Percy in his afflicted state was to me, I feel ten times more lonely now, and desolate at my heart, than I did when he was my companion."

"Why, Miss Miranda," replied Jones, "what's the use of grieving, as the song says; just you make yourself comfortable till Mr. Percy and Neddy shows themselves in Drury lane. There's a few pounds yet left, and if there wasn't why there's ways and means of getting more. Now my advice is, that you becomes Miss Jones."

"How do you mean?"

"Why just tuck your arm under mine, and we'll go and look for a lodging; I'll say as you're my sister, and that I'll pay the blessed rent; but, being myself a traveller in the hardware line,—and gracious knows, precious hard wear it is, sometimes—I can only come to see you now and then; when they axes us for a reference, we can tell 'em to go to blazes, and we'll pay a week's rent in advance, which is something ekal to being seven days afoae the rest of the world in honesty."

"I think," said Miranda, "the plan seems feasible; my own name I certainly object to using, as it has become unhappily too notorious through the public press, in consequence of the unhappy circumstances in which I have been involved."

"Call yourself Miss Jones, mum, it's a out-an-out good travelling name. I sometimes waries it myself, by being Smith for a year or two; but I never troubles my real name if I can help it. I am afeard as my relations would be continually inwiting of me, and axing on me to be godfather to babbies, when I'd quite as leave be the real father on 'em,"

"I would," said Miranda, "that I knew in what part of London Bernard Varley resides, in order that I might keep at as great a distance from his locality as possible."

"I'll find out the warmint," said Jones. "You make yourself as comfortable as possible to-night. Think o' nothing but snoozing, and depend upon it everything will be as right as ninepence."

Mr. Jones, with his peculiarity of apparel, was not the most pleasant figure to parade the streets of London with ; but Miranda was far from being hypercritical about the appearance of any one whose heart she knew to be in the right place ; and of the purity and kindness of Mr. Jones's intentions towards herself, she felt she should be doing him the greatest injustice for a moment o doubt. Therefore, arm-in-arm this strangely assorted couple proceeded through Smithfield towards the dense mass of houses lying about the neighbourhood of the City-road—a complete town in itself, where any one might remain concealed for years amid the intricacies of hundreds of streets.

The first house to which they applied for a lodging was in a street which came fully up to the popular notion of the shabby-genteel, and that particular house by no means set itself up as a contrast to its neighbours.

It was one of those streets which, in the most disgusting manner, is always affecting to be what it never can be, namely, quite noble, while its inherent meanness can never be got rid of. The houses were inhabited by persons who affected thorough gentility upon extremely limited resources, who hated everything low with a violent hatred ; of people who were up to their necks in shabbiness, and who, avoiding the onus of a really large respectable house, as much as they shrunk from the little residence consonant with their means, plunged into a genteel street, and let lodgings.

There is an enormous quantity of eight-roomed houses in London, with little kitchens and a little yard, and a little front parlour, and a little back parlour, and a little drawing room, and a little back drawing room, and two little attics, into which genteel people rush with a sort of frantic zeal as if they were achieving something astonishing, and establishing quite a wonderful station in society, by putting an embossed card in the parlour window announcing "furnished apartments."

Oh, spirit of enterprise, where are you hidden, that you allow petty gentility to crow over you, and assume your form and likeness?

A man may take a large respectable house, and speculate in letting a portion of it furnished ; but, to luxuriate in one of the eight-roomed abortions, is equivalent to the most despicable confession of want of means, that a very genteel family can make.

We do not quarrel with them for so acting, if they did it in a proper spirit ; but we do, most certainly, laugh at the notion of their pretending that it is "uppish," "stylish," and "genteel;" and yet, such is quite a prevalent opinion ; and people actually do not consider it as a candid confession of the most audacious attempts to do something which they cannot accomplish, when they recklessly make themselves amenable for the rent and taxes of a house in a very genteel street, and immediately announce furnished apartments.

The curse of a once bachelor, who has lived in many such furnished apartments, light upon them ; and let them be shunned by all persons with more brains than can be put in some one else's eye, without injuring the vision. Oh, the discomfits and the horrors of such nice, clean, and very genteel houses, where everything is pretty, cheap, flimsy, and trumpery, and yet set a great store by, as if they were efforts of human ingenuity, after accomplishing which, the superhuman workman had died, taking his mantle to the grave with him.

You mustn't bring in any dirt upon your shoes, nor must you rub them too hard upon the mat, least you wear it out prematurely. Woe be to you, if you lay hold of the bannisters in ascending to your room, for, by so doing, you will remove some of the bees'-wax and turpentine, which makes the stained wood look almost like mahogany.

Then, don't lean on your tables, or they will break down with you. Don't walk across your room with a heavier footstep than a cat, or you disturb Mr. Somebody below ; and, oh, gracious ! don't lie down on the sofa, or it will give an ominous creak, and you will leave the indentation of your person in the straw stuffing.

By-the-by, ingenious upholsterers have recently made very genteel lodging-house sofas in such a manner, that it is impracticable to lie down on them at all, inasmuch, as they resemble a very narrow shelf, considerably off the level, with a hard projection at each end. But then, lodging-house sofas are emphatically to be looked at, and not plumped down upon, gracious Heavens! the very reverse of genteel.

Then, good God! whatever you do, don't put your feet on the fender, nor, indeed, poke the fire too often, or ring the bell too often, or do anything, or imagine anything, that is not very genteel.

The very genteel people, generally keep the parlour to themselves; but they never go into it except when a visitor comes. Good gracious! no, they live in a kitchen, and that, as the very genteel lady of the house would remark, keeps the muck all in one place.

Another remarkable peculiarity of the very genteel people, consists in the covering up of every article, by some other article, of a supposed cheaper or durable texture, so that, picture frames are defended by gauze, stair-carpets by brown Holland, carpets by sad-coloured drugget, until, in fact, the whole house, from top to toe, looks as if it had packed itself up to go on some extremely dusty country excursion.

One more word about the shabby-genteel people, and we are done,—they have a gilt edged prayer-book, which they never open, for fear of staining the binding; but which they carry to church or chapel, every Sunday morning, with a white pocket-handkerchief, nearly folded on the top of it, for the purpose, we humbly presume, of catching devotional tears, which else might fall, with an evangelical dab, upon the binding.

"I doesn't like this here house," said Jones, before he knocked at the door of the first one they came to, in which was the announcement of "Apartments Furnished." "I dosen't much like this ere house, Miss Miranda; it's like trying to make the condemned cell look cheerful; it's so outrageous nice, and there's such a blessed air of propriety about it."

"We must not always," said Miranda, "judge by appearances; kindly people may be living here."

"Oh, as for that," said Jones, "it's very much the same, so long as we pays 'em, and doesn't give them much trouble, and puts up with all sorts of impositions; it will be very well, and nothing the matter; howsomedever, here goes, we'll let 'em see as we knows what's what, and is quite as genteel as they is."

Mr. Jones then perpetrated what he considered a genteel knock, which, first of all, consisted of a couple of postman's peals, then a running fire of small knocks, and then a dab at their end, which alarmed the whole street.

In a few moments the door was opened by the usual dirty servant, who is found in all lodging-houses; and why? because the mistress being only a degree cleaner herself during the morning, wishes to keep up the proper distinction of ranks.

"We wants to look at the cribs," said Jones. "What's the damage?"

"The apartments," said Miranda.

"Please to walk in," said the girl, "and I'll call Mrs. Flint."

"Flint," said Jones, when they were ushered into the little parlour; "what a name for one of the soft sex. I thinks I sees her, just like a bundle of tangled wire, set up on end."

"Hush! hush!" said Miranda, "pray allow me to speak, for they will scarcely understand your meaning."

"Wery good," said Jones, "I'll make my own observations, while you converses with the Flint."

The door opened, and a very genteel-looking female entered the room. Her thin lips were compressed as closely as if she suspected the visitors of a design to purloin her teeth ; and there was that air of general suspicion about her, which is a characteristic of genteel people.

"We have come," said Miranda, "to inquire concerning the apartments you have to let. I want accommodation for myself alone."

"Oh," said Mrs. Flint, "of course, we exchange references, always."

"Oh, mum," said Jones, "we couldn't think of doing that ere ; we think so much of our references, we couldn't change 'em for nobody's. We pays our tin like bricks, and, if anybody objects, we tells 'em to take it out of that."

Mr. Jones tapped his elbow a great many times, to the unspeakable horror of Mrs. Flint, who nearly sat down on one of the impracticable sofas in her surprise.

"We've come far from the country," said Miranda; "if I can find a suitable home here, rent will be paid in advance, as I have no friends or connexions in London."

"We have a first floor," said Mrs. Flint ; "the front room is very genteel, and the rent is eight-and-twenty shillings a-week."

"We'll see it, old lady," said Jones. "We doesn't mind the tin ; but, as you sees, we's out-an'-out genteel people, we ain't a-going to put up with nothing rummy."

"Gracious powers !" thought Mrs. Flint, "this must be some country gentleman unused to the ways of London. Why didn't I say thirty shillings ; but I can make it up in extras."

The first floor was a very pattern of gentility; everything was so abominably small, and so frightfully clean ; then there were little ornaments here and there, and everywhere, such as muscle-shells, and watch-pockets, and little pincushions, and artificial flowers, and two or three nice little evangelical books, the very covers of which looked like a reproof to sinners, they wore so nice and stainless an aspect ; moreover, nothing was covered up. Oh, no, that process was gone through after the victim had been entrapped.

The bed-room was adjoining, and into that Miranda just looked, sufficiently to see that it was very small, but clean.

"I think this will do," she said, appealing to Jones.

"Wery good," was the reply. "I suppose, mum, there's no d—d bugs here ?"

"Bugs !" shrieked Mrs. Flint. "Good God, sir !"

"Well, they're bad enough," said Jones; "but you needn't swear about it. I tells you what, mum, if ever you finds any, what you've to do. Just you get under the bed, and smoke a short pipe for an hour or two, they'll never come no more that night. It's not a bad plan either, to chew a bit of pig-tail, and if you sees one on the roof or the wall, jest spit in his eye ; and, if that don't astonish him, I'm a hass."

There's no knowing what effect this speech might have had on Mrs. Flint, if Jones had not, at the moment, produced a couple of sovereigns, which acted as such a balm to the wounded feelings of Mrs. Flint, that she very nearly smiled, and immediately made up her mind that Mr. Jones was only a little eccentric ; but, taking everything into consideration, quite the gentleman.

The negotiation now proceeded without any hindrance, and Miranda, with some pounds in her pocket, found herself fairly installed in her new home.

CHAPTER CXVII.

THE ARRIVAL OF ROWLAND PERCY IN LONDON.—THE STAR AND TINDER-BOX IN
STEEPLE-COURT.—THE REWARD FOR ROWLAND'S APPREHENSION.

NED WITLET's intimate acquaintance with the topography of the country, saved
him and Rowland Percy from traversing many an useless bit of road, so that, after
all, their progress, although certainly, considerably slower towards London, than
if they had been at liberty to take the high road, did not throw them above a day

behindhand; and at although a somewhat later hour than Miranda, on the preceding evening, had reached the metropolis, Rowland and his friend looked upon the
glancing lights of London.

It was only now and then, by turns in the road, that the distant glitter of the gas
lamps was visible, and ere they had proceeded much nearer, Ned Witlet turned his
horse's head down a narrow green lane, saying to Percy,—

We must do the remainder of our journey on foot, as well as making some alteration in our appearance, for we must not forget that our enemies are already in
No. 57.

London, and have, of course, taken care accurately to describe us to the metropolitan police. I know a house at the bottom of the lane, where we can receive a temporary accommodation, althought it would not be safe for us to remain there for any length of time."

" Heaven be thanked !" said Rowland, " we are so near our journey's end. I shall feel a sense of security amid the mass of humanity in London, which I could nowhere feel but in a large capital."

The house to which Ned alluded, had once been a flourishing one ; but its fortunes had been sadly changed ; and it was now unfrequented ; and, but for a peculiar connexion, scarcely worth keeping open. In its ample stables they left the horses, and, from a miscellaneous collection of wearing apparel, which was freely offered to their selection, they both succeeded in equipping themselves as decent-looking mechanics, and then hurried on towards London, of which so much has been said and sung, and which has been so strangely chronicled by so many persons who know nothing about it ; Grant, the Scotch literary imposter, for example.

As the sun declines, and day is merged to eve, a sudden change comes over this great city, as remarkable, perhaps, as any that was ever fabled to follow the waving of the enchanter's magic wand, for who can say that he has seen London, when his hours have been but those of daylight.

To see London, then, in all its glory, and, perhaps, in its most interesting point of view, when most can be seen and heard, you must see it after sunset, when it is lighted up by the artificial light carried along the streets in pipes as if it were water. Then, indeed, London shines.

The long regular rows of lamps cast a broad light upon all objects, below, and to certain distance beyond each individual light, and before this has lost its influence by distance, another is placed, and thus it is continued for miles along streets in the most regular manner imaginable ; but, as we know well enough, this is not confined to the main streets, but every branch, right and left, court, or alley, however poor and insignificant it may be.

This has a singular effect when viewed from a high spot ; for instance, stand upon Ludgate-hill, and look towards Fleet-street. The rows of light on either side present a striking scene. The same may be seen to a greater extent in the City-road, or the New-road ; but in the city, the strangely reflected lights in the various shops, throw much more light in the various thoroughfares than even the lamps.

Here is, indeed, a busy scene. Countless numbers of men and women hurrying backwards and forwards, and no sooner is one gone than his or her place is supplied instantaneously by others, who are, in like manner, followed again by more, and thus they go on, until the sight dims, and the head becomes giddy with watching.

Where can this stream of human beings come from or go to, for it is nearly certain that such a flow of human beings continues for sixteen or seventeen hours daily, and yet it is more than likely that barely any two are going to precisely the same spot, or come from the same quarter.

The shops of London naturally attract the attention of the stranger. Their expensive fittings up—their elegant appearance—their strong lights—their diversity—and the costly quality of the goods that are displayed in them. London is, indeed, a city of riches and merchandize ; for here, indeed, are collected materials from all quarters of the known world ; here meet the greatest extremes. Things which are rich, rare, and curious—things that are costly, beautiful, and splendid —all things that can be desired to adorn the human body—those which elevate and amuse the mind—with the greatest delicacies and dainties that the pampered appetite can require—as well as the productions of man's labour, corporeal and mental.

Who could then pass along our principal streets, and not be struck by the concentration of the whole world.

Great and various must the industry of man be ; his habits and tastes—his desires and his wants—all are ministered to ; the gratification of sense, and the enlargement of the mind, are all amply provided for.

With all these things on either side of him, the stranger, on his first entrance into this leviathan city, is naturally lost in wonder, and unable to comprehend, at his first glance, the nature of what he sees ; his mind is in a state of abeyance. Little is to be wondered at, then, that he is frequently a prey to the dishonest and designing ; his faculties have lost their power, and he sees not things in their true light ; and in consequence, becomes a victim, and hence, he who speaks of coming to this city for the first time in his life, is gravely cautioned, to an excess, against the tricks of town, till he becomes impressed with the belief that it is the abode only of men who prey on the simple and unsuspecting stranger ; but he, nevertheless, suffers—usually—and the " why" is—that the cautions so freely given have not prepared his mind to understand all he sees, to make him look on wonders without amazement, and see sights without astonishment.

The constant din and rattle of passing and repassing vehicles which appear literally to have choked up the thoroughfare, and yet they move on, and are followed by more ; and so long as there is a human being afoot in London, so long are there carriages of nearly all kinds passing and repassing, presenting such an inextricable maze, that none but a Londoner would ever venture into the throng, and if, by chance, the stranger becomes involved in this vortex of vehicles, he despairs of ever extricating himself.

Rowland Percy had never before visited the great city ; and consequently, everything was new and strange to him. Had his mind been disentangled from the circumstances which clung to it with such a withering blight, he would have experienced the most intense pleasure in watching the great human movement which was taking place in the vast city, in the midst of which his evil fortune had thrown him.

Ned Witlet guessed his thoughts, and said, in a kindly tone of voice, " Mr. Percy, there will come a time, as I confidently trust and hope, when you will be able, as a free and acknowledged innocent man, to traverse the streets of London, and visit its extraordinary buildings and monuments ; till then, I fear you must be satisfied with but a transient glimpse of the great world into which you are thrown."

" I will live on," said Rowland, " with a fervent hope that some day I will take my place among my fellow-men, without a price being set upon my head, and without my name awakening the indignation of that society which Heaven truly knows I have never outraged ; when that shall happen, I have another hope, which has been latterly, day by day, growing stronger in my breast, the realisation of which will give me as great a satisfaction as could possibly confer any personal benefit to myself."

" Indeed," said Witlet, " and what hope is that ?"

" It is the hope that ample opportunity may be afforded you of embracing a different course of life, and that in a new arena, which will bring you ample honour and reward, you will exercise those abilities of intellect, and those excellences of heart, for which you are conspicuous."

Ned Witlet was silent for a moment, and then it was in a tone of emotion that he replied,—

" Mr. Percy, for your kind words I give you my warmest thanks ; and the more so, because I am really unused to such from any one ; but my day is passed, and I have no hope of being other than what I am. The circumstances that have driven me to my present course of life lie buried in my heart. There may come a day when I shall not shrink from communicating them to you, but I think when I do so, I shall be near quitting a world, which, perhaps, after all, I wrongly accuse of not using me well. I dread every moment that you are in the open streets. Let us hasten, at once, to Drury-lane, where, I have every reason on earth to believe, I can procure you a safe asylum."

The Star and Tinder-box, in Steeple-court, Drury-lane, was a very famous house. Indeed, some malicious people made the adjective a letter longer, and called it an infamous house; but those were what Mr. Jones would call straight-laced people, who did their thieving all on the sly, and hadn't pluck enough to go on the high. way, like reputable folks.

The court in which it was situated, was sufficiently narrow to be called a passage; and the Star and Tinder-box was down a narrow entry out of that again, so that it could scarcely be said to be in Steeple-court, although the passage, which abutted upon that beautiful locality, was the exclusive property of the Star and Tinder-box to all intents and purposes, and an admirable place for concealment and secresy was that Star and Tinder-box, for so dark and dingy was it, that one might well assimilate it to the Tinder-box, without troubling the Star at all about the matter.

"You will find this rather different," whispered Witlet, as they dived down the dark entry, "to the free, open meadows of your father's estate at York."

"Indeed," said Percy, "I do not compare it with them; in my mind, it only contrasts most favourably with the condemned cell in York Castle."

In another moment they were standing at the bar of the public-house, and Witlet leaning over, looked into a little parlour beyond, where a man sat either in deep thought, or half asleep, and cried,—

"Bill! Bill!—what's the dodge?"

"Eh!—Eh!" cried the man, starting up, and rubbing his eyes. "The old caper, to be sure. Who the deuce are you?"

"Look again," said Witlet. "How's the old woman?"

"D—n me up in heaps," said the man, "that I shouldn't know you. Come in —come in. Bless us, where have you been? Split me into gold-leaf, if I've seen you for two months. I was afeared you were nabbed, and had come an alias over the grabs. My eye and Elizabeth Martin, I supposes as you've been the grand tower, as they calls it? Strike me unfortunate, and kick me into the middle of the new moon, if I know'd yer at the very first glance. Hilloa! who's that?"

"A friend of mine," said Ned Witlet, as he took Rowland by the arm, and ushered him into the parlour, at the back of the bar.

"Oh, well, if he's a friend of yourn, it's all right. Has he been on the moonlight lay?"

"For aught I know, Bill," said Witlet, "time may be precious, and you may as well know at once that this is Mr. Rowland Percy, who was convicted at York for murder; but who, I pledge you my word, is innocent. He has escaped almost by a miracle; but, of course, for a time, there'll be a hue and cry, and, in one word, I have brought him here for safety."

The landlord walked into the bar without a word, and called loudly to somebody of the name of Joe, to look to it. He then returned to the parlour, and locked the door on the inside, after which he drew a curtain across the upper part, which was glass, and turning to Witlet, said,—

"It's no go. Not the remotest insignification of a go; and I'll tell you why. First of all, look here."

He took from behind the looking-glass a printed bill, which he handed to Witlet, which was headed with the ominous words of "Five hundred pounds reward!"

Witlet handed it in silence to Rowland Percy, who read the following words:—

"Five hundred pounds reward! Whereas, one Rowland Percy, convicted of murder at the last York assizes, escaped from custody on the eve of his execution. This is to give notice, that the above reward will be paid to any one who will lodge him in any one of his Majesty's gaols. The said Rowland Percy is——"

Here followed an accurate description of his person; and the paper dropped from Rowland's hands.

CHAPTER CXVIII.

THE OFFICER IN PURSUIT OF ROWLAND.—THE ESCAPE FROM THE PUBLIC-HOUSE
—THE DRIVE TO SOMERS-TOWN.—THE SECRET PANEL IN THE WIDOW'S
HOUSE.

NED WITLET picked up the handbill which Rowland had dropped, and read it attentively ; after which he said,—

"Mr. Percy, you need not be surprised at this. Your enemies are sure to be active for some time to come. You must recollect that private hatred is leagued against you along with the law ; but this virulence of pursuit will wear itself out ; and if we can but keep you concealed until such is the case, you will be safe from further interruption."

"Listen to me, Neddy," said the landlord. "I don't know why it is so, but my house has been regularly set upon about this matter. I rather think the police must have an inkling that you have an hand in it, and it's my decided opinion that there are spies lodging here at the preset time, with the hope that Mr. Percy will make this his home."

"Lodging here ?" said Witlet, in surprise.

"Yes, and I can't help it. We've beds to let, and it is impossible for me to pick and choose my customers, for sometimes I almost feel convinced they are set on me by the police. All I can do is to let them come, and warn other parties, as I now warn you, and I candidly say I think a more unsafe place than the Star and Tinder-box for you isn't in London."

"When you say so much," said Witlet, "I know it can be relied upon. Mr. Percy, we must seek some other shelter. I had hoped that you would have remained here with security ; but as such is not the case, the sooner we decamp the better."

"I should say so," remarked the landlord ; "and all the good I can do you is to offer you any assistance in the way of money you may want, so don't scruple to ask me for it if it should be sarviceable. Take a glass of something with me, Percy, and be off with you, in Heaven's name, for I assure you, you can't be in a worse place than this."

Rowland Percy declined the something to drink, but intimated that he was quite ready to go.

"Very well, then," said Witlet, "I know well, Bill, you are not the one to make the most of danger, and a hint from you is as good as a long speech from any one else."

"Hush !" said the landlord ;—"hush ! Do you hear that ?"

As he spoke, the sound of a man's voice was heard from the outer side of the bar, and Ned Witlet immediately said,—

"Indeed, I do hear it ; it's Fletcher, the Bow-street officer."

The landlord opened another door in the little parlour, beyond which all appeared darkness.

"You can get out that way," he said, "which will take you into the court. I will keep Fletcher in talk till you are clean off."

He, then, himself, passed into the bar ; and Witlet, placing his hand upon Percy's arm, said,—

"Wait a moment ; there can be no danger, and there may be some good in hearing what the officer says."

Percy assented, and in a moment the landlord's voice was heard.

"Well, Fletcher," he said, "what's the news ?"

"Once for all, Bill," said the voice of the officer, "don't be a fool, but look to your own interest. Among your set you are sure to find out something of the fellow that we want, and when I tell you I want him very particularly indeed, you may guess there's something to be made by the affair past common, and, of course I can afford to be liberal to you."

" I tell, yer," said the landlord. " I knows nothing about it, if so be as it's the young chap about the murder at York."

" Oh, nonsense !" said the officer. " We are quite sure that some of the knowing ones from London must have helped him out of the scrape."

" I tell you, Fletcher, I knows nothing about it, and you needn't bother me."

" You shall have a hundred pounds down to-morrow morning, if you promise to assist. Mr. Varley, the prosecutor, is red-hot about it, and will stand any sum in reason."

" That is enough," whispered Witlet to Rowland Percy, " Let us go now."

He took Rowland by the arm, and led him through the dark doorway, down a long narrow passage, which then took an abrupt turn that brought them within view of a glare of light, and in another moment they emerged into the upper part of the court, close by the flare of a gas-lamp in Drury-lane.

" I must house you somewhere," said Witlet ; " but really where I can scarcely at present determine. There are, certainly, persons in London who are under sufficient obligations to me, but in such a matter as this I know not in whom I can trust ; yet now, I bethink, there is one who has ever expressed so anxious a wish to repay the deep obligation under which I was enabled at one time to lay her, that I think I may be safe to take you there. However, we will get into a coach, and drive to the locality. While we are so doing, I can explain some necessary particulars."

A coach was quickly procured, and Witlet desired to be driven to the end of Chalton-street, in the New-road.

" The street I have named," he said, to Rowland Percy, " leads into a densely populated district, called Somers Town, which, although I cannot recommend it for salubrity or beauty, may answer your purpose very well as a place of concealment, if everything has gone on smoothly with the person to whom I wish to introduce you."

" Of the two," said Rowland, " I should, certainly, prefer a refuge in some private dwelling to one in some public-house ; but I implore you to take two steps so that Miranda may not be disappointed when she makes inquiry for me."

" Leave that all to me," said Witlet ; " it shall be arranged properly. The person I am now taking you to is a Mrs. Howell, whose son fell into unhappy circumstances, although innocent, the particulars of which I shall get her to relate to you the first thing, in order to give you the consolation of knowing that there are others who are quite as misused as yourself."

When they alighted from the coach, Witlet led Percy through a number of intricate streets, until they came to one branching off to the northward of the Polygon. He knocked at the door of a small but neat house, and inquired of the girl who presented herself if Mrs. Howell was within.

The answer was in the affirmative ; and an elderly lady with a widow's cap, made her appearance, who greeted Witlet in as affectionate terms as if he had been her own son, and immediately ushered him into her parlour, where the tea things were all laid, preparatory to the evening meal.

" You have just come at the right moment, Mr. Witlet," said Mrs. Howell. " Sit down, and this gentleman, too. You appear tired, and will have some tea with me."

" I will, Mrs. Howell, but, first, this gentleman is Mr. Percy ; he has many troubles to content against. You know what misfortune is, and, to give him some hope, you will be pleased to relate the affair of your son, who was so full of hope, but suffered so great a reverse, while we solace ourselves with your tea."

" That I will : pray be seated ; but I am always sorry to hear of any one's misfortunes."

"And mine are of no ordinary character, I assure you, madam," said Percy, as he took the cup that was offered him.

"Ah, well, Mr. Percy," said the widow, "we've all our troubles, there are none of us without them, and they are best off who have the fewest."

"It certainly is so, Mrs. Howell, though I must confess that I am sometimes impatient of mine," replied Percy, setting down his tea-cup, and looking at the blazing fire, which threw a bright reflection over the room.

The apartment was a small one, possessing more furniture than was necessary, and that not of the most modern description; but there was an air of humbleness and comfort thrown over all that insensibly imparted similar feelings to Rowland Percy.

The widow herself had been a pains-taking, hard-working woman in her time, though for the latter quality she had no present necessity, yet, from acquired habit, she busied herself in all matters connected with her house. She was past the middle age of life; indeed, she must have been over fifty, tolerably stout, at one time pretty and attractive, and the fire of her eye was sobered down to an occasional twinkle of satisfaction. She supped her tea and ate her toast with a pleasure so evident, that Percy, as he looked at her, could not forbear a smile.

"You have been many years here?" said Percy, inquiringly, after a long pause by way of breaking silence.

"Yes, sir. It's twenty years ago since I first came here, sir. Ah, this place is not what it was, I assure you: there were but very few houses in these parts; we were quite in the fields. My husband that's dead and gone, bought it, saying he would have a house to live in without paying rent for, and the little money he had should not be thrown away in business, more especially as he was only at home once in a way."

"What was your husband's employment then?" inquired Percy.

"He was a sailor many years, and at last he was made a boatswain. Ah, Mr. Percy, I was a lone woman then. I was left with only one child, and he, poor fellow, is not here."

"Ah," said Percy, "I have heard Witlet speak of him. He, like myself, has suffered from the deep-laid villany of others, and obliged to fly for his life."

"Yes," replied the widow, with a sigh; "he was indeed the object of another man's hatred; he stood in his way, and my poor boy was ruined—totally ruined. I fear I shall never see him again, and he's the only relation I have living, and the only tie that binds me to earth."

The poor woman took the corner of her apron to wipe away the starting tear, which had risen unbidden to her cheek.

"Be comforted, Mrs. Howell," said Percy, in a kind, though saddened tone, for his own unhappy fate rushed across his mind. "He may yet come back to you, when there will no longer be any danger. I did not hear the particulars from Ned Witlet, and should like to hear them, if the subject be not a painful one."

"It is painful, sir; but not more so to repeat the story to you, than to think of it in my own mind," said the widow, who dearly loved to talk of her son, though it occasionally cost her a tear; and her lodger was so kind, and an ill-used man himself, that she longed for an opportunity to unburthen her mind of her load of grief to one who was by his own unfortunate situation in a position well calculated to enable him to appreciate them justly.

"My Henry, sir, was my only child. He was young when his father died, and I kept him to school, though many said that I ought to put him out to place, where he would, at least, be earning something towards his own support; but I said that I would keep him to school, and then he would be better able to get on in life afterwards, if he acted properly, than if I made an errand-boy of him when very young. Besides, he was not so strong and robust a lad as many are, and for that reason alone, I was afraid to let him go anywhere where his strength would have been tried. He was a good boy, and a quick one at his letters, which repaid me.

"When he was fourteen, a gentleman who lodged in this house said he could likely enough, hear of something in a counting-house that would suit him, if I would like to let him go.

"Of course I was very glad, and said I should be very much obliged to him if he would get any employment that way for him, which would be an opening in life for him. This he promised to do, and before a month had passed over, the gentleman called me up stairs, and said :—

"'Mrs. Howell, if your son Henry will go with me to the city to-morrow, I will take him to some gentlemen, who will most probably take him into their counting-house, where, if he minds what he is about, he may stay all his life, and be very comfortable.'

"Of course, sir, I was well pleased at such a chance as this, one that I could not hope for from myself, for I had no connexions that way.

"I sent him in the morning—I remember it as if it were only yesterday ; he had a new suit of clothes on, and he looked very well. I was all anxiety for the return of night, until my lodger should return, for he would keep him until he came home at night. When evening came I knew hardly how to await their arrival with patience. I listened to every footfall as they came past the door, and felt disappointed at every one that died away in the distance.

"At length they did come ; no sooner did I hear them on the step than I had the door open to receive them, and by my Henry's sparkling eyes I knew that he must have succeeded, for he had often talked of being able to earn me money, so that I should not be obliged to work so hard.

"'We have succeeded, Mrs. Howell,' said my lodger good-naturedly, as he entered the house ; 'Henry is bursting to tell you all about it, so when you have heard all that he has to tell you, I'll give you any information you may want.'

"I thanked him for his goodness, and brought my son into my room, when he related to me all that had happened. The gentlemen seemed so pleased with his appearance, and the manner in which he answered the questions they put to him, that they at once agreed to take him into their counting-house—of course in the lowest capacity, as he was the youngest, and last there ; but still he would rise in rotation with the rest.

"He had to go next day, for they took him from the first day of his appearance at the office.

"It was a happy time that, for me, Mr. Percy. He was my only hope—the only being I had to look to for love and affection, and his conduct deserved all that I did for him, for as regularly as he received his money, so regularly did he bring the whole of it to me. He never stayed out with companions at any time, but always came home direct to me.

"This went on for several years ; till, indeed, he was between nineteen and twenty.

"One day he came home in a very thoughtful manner—a very unusual thing with him ; he looked very serious and sad. I could not bear this, and at once inquired what was the cause of his thoughtful and melancholy look. At first he evaded me, but at length he said,—

"'I am afraid all is not right with our head clerk, mother, and I don't know what to do about it.'

"'All right, Henry,' said I. 'What do you mean?'

"'I think our head clerk's accounts are not right, or that he has appropriated money to his own use that he ought not to have touched, but which belongs to his employers.'

"'Are you sure of it?' I inquired.

"'Not so sure of it,' he replied ; 'but that I may be mistaken, and therefore I do not like to make any accusation against him.'

"'Certainly not,' I replied, 'for by that you may make many enemies, and no friends.'

"'I know that,' he replied, 'but there can be no harm in my drawing his attention to it, and by that means, if it be merely an error, he can correct it, and if not, he will use what exertion he can to make good any defalcation into which he may have fallen.'

"'That will undoubtedly be the best course,' I replied, 'for it will give him a chance of retrieving himself before he is utterly lost.'

"Having made up his mind to this course, he promised to do so the next day. and it was with a sense of sadness that made me feel impatient for his return. I began to feel sorry that I had given him the counsel I had. I regretted I had not begged him to leave the affair alone, and let the whole thing take its own course.

Some undefined notion of what was to follow appeared to depress my mind, and I was only relieved from it by hearing his step at the door, and when I let him in, I saw he was vexed about something; but I said nothing until he had had his tea, and I then inquired how he had got on with the affair he had been speaking about the day before.'

"'Rather badly,' was his reply; Mr Crosby, the head clerk, has taken it all in bad part, and we have had a quarrel.'

"'I am sorry for that, Henry,' was my answer, 'for I fear that it will make you uncomfortable.'

No. 58.

"' Oh ! no,' he replied, 'I have nothing to fear on that score—he cannot prejudice me, or hurt me in any way, though he as good as said he would do both.'

"' Indeed, tell me what he did say,' I asked.

"' Do not be alarmed, mother—you look serious, and there is no need of your doing so. I showed Mr. Crosby what I believed to be errors, and he flew into a great rage about my meddling with things that did not concern me, though at first he trembled in every limb, and was as pale as the paper upon which he was writing. I merely replied that thinking there was something wrong, I thought it better to name it first to him. I shall not forget easily the expression of his face when I said this, and he answered me by saying, that I should know what it was to interfere with him, and that, too, upon such a subject—he understood his business, and begged me to keep a strict eye upon my own accounts, as it was possible I might find errors there."

"' What does he mean, Henry ?' said I.

"' I know not,' he replied, ' nor do I much care, as I have nothing to fear, and so I told him ; and he said to me, that my impertinence would cost me dear,—there would be a day when I should remember this. I was then called away, and nothing more has been said.'

"' Be careful, my dear boy,' said I, ' lest he should have it in his power to do you an injury.'

"This was all that passed, and no more was heard about the matter, save that my son and Mr. Crosby were ill friends, and Henry was determined to keep a strict eye on the other's motions, and also the accounts, at which he seemed much annoyed.'

"Some months after this, my Henry returned home much earlier than usual; he entered the house without saying a word, which was unusual with him ; it was dark, and I had no light with me, and did not see his face, but when I did see it I was much shocked at the sudden alteration that had taken place in his features.

"He was dreadfully pale and haggard—his eyes almost fixed, while his whole frame seemed agitated by something very dreadful. I was so alarmed, that I could not muster courage to speak for several seconds ; at length I did contrive to say,—

"' Henry—Henry—what can be the matter ? Are you ill ;—pray, pray speak to me.'

"' Oh mother,' he said, but in such an altered voice, ' I am ruined—lost, quite lost.'

"' Ruined !—how, tell me all, Henry—tell me all ; keep nothing from me, I command you.'

"' It is all true, I am ruined—entirely ruined ; that Crosby has kept his word. It is his devilish malice that has caused all this. I saw him smile horribly, as if he felt all the pleasure of a demon at my early downfall.'

"' What is all this about, my dear Henry—you talk of ruin and downfall ? What does it all mean ?'

"' Why this, mother—I am accused of forgery, and appropriation of mn y so obtained to my own use."

"' Good God, my son, you—you have not done this—tell me you are innocent.'

"' Yes, I am innocent, as I hope for Heaven's grace. I am indeed innocent, but I am accused, and shall not be able to prove that I am so, I know, for a most cunning device has been laid to entrap me, and it has proved successful; I will tell you all about it.

"' About two months back, I was desired by Mr. Crosby to take a bill to a certain party and get it cashed, and bring the money to him, less the discount. This was an ordinary occurrence, and I did as I was desired, without any hesitation whatever, and thought no more of the matter ; I acted merely the part of a messenger on the occasion, and, therefore, I made no entry of the transaction, but delivered the money to Mr. Crosby, who received it, and appeared to me to enter it.

"'To-day a bill was presented at the house—it was the same one that I had carried to the holder, and obtained the cash for; for two hundred pounds, and payment demanded. The gentlemen were much surprised, and knew nothing of it, and declared it to be a forgery.

"'That must be a mistake,' was the reply, 'because one of your own clerks came and cashed it at our office.'

"'Mr. Crosby was called, but he declared he had never seen the bill before, and had no note of it, or entry of any kind; and more, he declared he believed that the signature was forged.

"'The person who came was desired to point out the clerk who came to him, and I just entered the place.

"'That is the young man,' was his immediate answer. 'Don't you remember coming to me to get a bill cashed about two months since?'

"'Yes,' I replied.

"'Then where is the money?'

"'I gave it to Mr. Crosby.'

"'I never received any such money,' replied Crosby, coolly. 'It is a wicked falsehood.'

"'I not only gave it to you, but I received the bill from you in the usual course of business.'

"'That is too gross and improbable,' replied Crosby. 'I believe the bill to be a forgery, and the more I look upon the signature the more I am inclined to think that Henry Howell is the man who forge d it.'

"'Several specimens of my handwriting were immediately procured, and they were compared, when they all concurred in the opinion that I had done the deed. The holder of the bill demanded the money—my employers refused to pay what they did not owe, and then they all turned upon me, saying, that if I would produce the money by to-morrow, I should escape with life, but if not, I must expect the worst.'

"Picture to yourself, Mr. Percy, what were my feelings when my son related all this to me. I was more dead than alive, and I knew not what to do or what to advise. The money I knew I could not obtain, nor a tithe of it, and even that small sum I could not get until I had sold all that I had.

"There was no resource left except that of waiting till time should establish his innocence, and in the meanwhile he must hide from the officers of justice. It was a terrible time for me. The officers came next day and searched my house, and all around; but Henry had gone away for a few weeks, with what little money I could spare, until the heat of the affair had blown off.

"About six weeks after, and late one night, he came back to me, and for a few days was hidden up stairs, and during this time he contrived to move some paneling, which exposed a large recess in one corner of the room which was not observed elsewhere. This he caused to slide backwards and forwards, so that he could easily go in or out as he pleased, and, if need be, he could stay in for a day or two, having food put in for his use.

"It was lucky that this was done, for it seems the officers had some notion of his being about the house. They came in one day, and, before I was aware of it, commenced a search for him. However, Henry caught sight of them without being seen, and escaped to his place of concealment, where he remained till they had gone. This happened several times, but they never discoverd the secret hiding-place.

"He remained at home for more than two years, when, finding all chance of establishing his innocence to be distant, or very improbable, he quitted this country for America, where he is doing very well; but I shall never see him more; I fear I shall never see his face again."

"And that place of concealment, which served so well for Henry, is still in existence, Mrs. Howell?"

"It is," she said. "I would never have it altered, though the sight of it always produces a sad feeling in my mind, when I reflect how hardly used was my poor boy, Henry."

"Mrs. Howell," said Witlet, "this gentleman has been accused, convicted, and actually condemned to death, for a murder of which he is as innocent as you are."

"A murder !" exclaimed Mrs. Howell.

"Yes, and he requires, until the eagerness of pursuit has abated, just such a place of concealment as that you have in your house."

"Heaven forbid that I should refuse to succour him in his misfortunes," said the widow. "What would have been my feelings if my poor boy had appealed to any one in vain ?"

"Then, Mr. Percy," said Witlet, rising, "I feel confident I leave you in safe hands. Expect to see me to-morrow, and now I shall hasten back to the Star and Tinder-box, to make arrangements concerning Miss Miranda."

"Heaven bless you !" said Mrs. Howell, as she rose to light him from the room. "To you, mainly, I owe the safety of Henry, and Heaven forbid that I should not do my duty by a friend of yours. It seems like paying a small portion of the debt I owe you."

CHAPTER CXIX.

TWITTER'S DEMAND UPON VARLEY.—AN UNEXPECTED CHANGE OF DEMEANOUR.— MUTUAL DISTRUST.

BERNARD VARLEY had put up at one of the most expensive and magnificent hotels he could think of in London. He could not get rid of the idea that, by surrounding himself with the magnificent and the beautiful, he should, to a certain extent, succeed in stilling those pangs of conscience which would ever make themselves felt in such a breast as his. He fancied that the glitter of decoration around him would war successfully with the dungeon-like gloom of his own heart. How vain an idea ! The more of elegance, the more of beauty he saw around him, the more dark and wretched by contrast did his own feelings appear ; and any momentary feeling of satisfaction was but the precursor of an acute pang, and the forerunner of much greater misery than could be repaid to him by the greatest gleam of sunlight that had danced upon his spirits.

When he had made all the arrangements in his power with the police, and had done all that he could possibly think of to ensure the capture of Rowland Percy, he turned the whole attention of his mind to the pursuit of Miranda, and although he had no clue whatever to her place of concealment, yet he thought that, with his great resources, he should surely be able to ferret out one who would be compelled for the sake of an existence to mingle with the world and make herself known to many persons.

"She has not yet," he said, "felt the acute sting of poverty ; cradled in the lap of luxury in early life, and then when misfortune came upon her, surrounded by sympathising friends, she has not yet endured that poverty, that destitution which, like mental poison, preys upon the intellect, destroying its best energies, and fitting it for the reception of thoughts, that in a more easy and pleasant state of existence it would have scorned as far beneath it. The sympathies of friends soon wear out, or become cold, and Miranda will be left to her own resources. Her pride too will step in to consummate such a result, and then in some sad hour, when her experience in the world has deepened into terror, I shall come to her with an offer of wealth and an unvarying round of pleasures. Surely she will then be mine, and shrinking from an abyss of poverty into which she had plunged, would be glad again to ascend the height of prosperity. Yes, she must be mine, or I must perish in th pursuit of so much beauty. Whether Rowland Percy live or die, Miranda sha be mine, and in the pursuit of her, too, will I pursue him. I have now a fixed determination, that let me but catch a glimpse of his person, I'll kill him, and plead as my justification for the act, that my own life was in jeopardy on account of his resistance to being captured. Always armed as I am with weapons upon which I can depend, his death, should we chance to meet, shall be certain. Well, Twitter, what now?"

With the usual snake-like movement that characterised his steps, Twitter had glided into the room, and stood peering at Varley out of his small eyes as if he had something to say which he yet could scarcely give utterance to.

"Well, Twitter," added Varley, "I did not ring for you."

"You're considerate," said Twitter, "and you ring for me so seldom that I do not feel my servitude very heavy, although you have compelled me to become your valet. I almost think, Varley, sometimes, that you would quite as soon be without me altogether."

"Indeed!" sneered Varley.

"Yes; and you would scarcely regret if I were to remove myself."

"Not at all, not at all—far from it, Samuel Twitter; only I wish to dictate the place to which you remove if you leave me; that is a point I must reserve to myself."

"And where should that be?"

"Into your grave, Samuel Twitter: remove there when you please, and I will bid you adieu upon its brink. You understand me, Twitter? No more of these attacks upon my purse, for such they are."

"But you promised me."

"Pshaw! promises to you! Why do men keep promises but for special reasons which can never exist between us. Some will keep a promise for what they call character sake; others, to beget confidence which will unable them to break one of more importance at another opportunity; but, Twitter, we have no such motives, and I can make and break promises to you at my own good pleasure."

"Cursed thief!" muttered Twitter, in too low a tone to be heard; and then he added aloud,—"Well—well, I came to make a trifling request. As we are now in London, Mr. Varley, I would fain see some old friends that I have not visited for many a year, and as I would wish to make a liberal appearance, and be very gracious to them, lend me a hundred pounds."

"Lend you a hundred pounds!"

"Yes, I say lend, because you can pay yourself out of my share of the Grange estates whenever you like."

"Are you tired of your life, said Varley, "that you insult me with such propositions?"

"Nearly," said Twitter; "ain't you?"

"Now, by heavens!" said Varley, rising, "this insolence shall not go u i n d Samuel Twitter, if you have taken the absurd notion into your head that you can acquire any mastery over me by intimidation, or threats, or coarse insolence of conduct, you shall find yourself most wofully mistaken."

"I threaten nothing," said Twitter, who, certainly, since the quarrel when he had called for assistance, had presumed upon Varley's fears, and with a dogged kind of resolution not given way so completely to the other's threats. "I threaten nothing, and know not what you mean. I only ask for a hundred pounds on account, Mr. Varley; surely that is moderate out of I know not how many thousands which are my due. As for threatening, we neither of us can threaten the other. The fact is, when there are two men who can——" Twitter walked to the door, and looked out to assure himself that no one was listening, then coming back, he added,—"hang each other, it behoves them to be civil."

Varley felt annoyed, for Twitter had never ventured upon quite so much boldness before, and was looking anxiously in his face to see how it was received.

"Samuel Twitter," said Varley, "have you totally forgotten the desperate man you have to deal with?"

"I am more desperate still," said Twitter. "Try you and be my valet for a month, and let me have the disposal of the whole of the Grange revenues; you will then be able better to speak of what it is to be a desperate man."

"Did you say a hundred pounds?" said Varley, with a calmness that made Twitter give a jump towards the door, for it alarmed him much more than any ebullition of rage would have done, on the principle that a violent man is always more dangerous when he thinks proper to smother his passion for a time.

"Did you say a hundred pounds, Samuel Twitter?"

"Yes, I do. Come now, Mr. Varley—no—no outbreak. We—we are bound together by mutual interest; danger to one of us is danger to the other. Only a hundred. I am sure my request is reasonable. I threaten nothing, and never attempted to threaten anything. I only wished that we should mutually have a good understanding."

"Oh! certainly—certainly," said Varley. "I dare say you are quite right. When you have expended the hundred pounds I shall now give you, pray come to me for another. I begin to feel, Samuel Twitter, that my conduct must have been faulty towards you, and that you have a claim which must be satisfied."

"You—you ain't joking, Varley?" said Twitter.

"Joking! Heaven forbid. You'll find by the result, that there isn't the shadow of a jest lurking in the whole affair. I am extremely serious."

Twitter looked anxiously into the countenance of his associate in crime, but he could detect nothing but cold austerity, and he was puzzled as well as alarmed at the remarkable change in Varley's manner towards him.

"I do not wish to annoy you, Varley," he said, "very far from it. You know I would do anything for you, and in fact, as I have remarked, our interests are identified."

"Admirably reasoned," said Varley; "but it is a work of supererogation, for I am already convinced that I have been proceeding upon a mistake. I am quite clear now with respect to the claim you have upon me, and be assured upon the first convenient opportunity, you shall be settled with in full; but the complete wind up of an account, you know, Samuel Twitter, requires some little careful consideration of one's ways and means, even after the act itself is quite determined upon. Is a hundred pounds quite enough for the present?"

Twitter was getting in a perspiration at this unexpected change in Varley's manner. It was something out of all calculation; a state of things for which he was not prepared, and made him full of suspicion, although he could not tell in which way his danger lay. If Varley had but got into a great passion, Twitter could have understood him, and all would have been well; but that he should so suddenly become polite, civil, and considerate, was perfectly horrible, and put him in a state of alarm that almost took away his breath.

"Varley—Varley," he gasped, "what on earth do you mean? Why ain't you in one of your furies. Explain your meaning, Varley, by this unnatural calmness—it—it is terrifying."

"Nay, now," said Varley, "what a hard matter it is to please you. If I storm at you and get angry, you think yourself mightily ill-used, and wonder that I should so treat you. Then, again, now that I am calm and considerate towards you, and candidly confess that I have treated you in a mistaken way, which shall be amended for the future, you are angry because I am not angry. Really, Samuel Twitter, you are a most inconsistent person."

"Nay, but Varley, do you really mean what you say? or are you with a frightful irony, deceiving me?"

"I never was so clear in my intentions regarding you," said Varley; "if you doubt my words, time alone can show my deep sincerity."

Twitter gave a deep groan, as he folded up the hundred pound note which Varley handed him.

"Well, Varley," he said, "I hope that for the future no harsh words need ever pass between us. You will do me justice—I feel assured you will do me justice."

"Most ample—most ample, you may feel assured. I will not deny that at times your principal claim upon me has come forcibly upon my mind ; but I never felt so thoroughly convinced that it ought to be paid in full as now ; but then, as I said before, Twitter, one must take one's opportunity. Good morning to you ; a pleasant day with your friends, Samuel Twitter?"

Twitter shrunk to the door, and trembling in every limb, passed out of the room.

"Yes," said Varley, stamping vehemently, when Twitter was out of the room. "By Heaven! he shall have his claim—he shall."

"Eh?" said Twitter, putting in his head at the door.

"What now?" said Varley, suddenly dropping his voice.

"Nothing," said Twitter; "only I thought you spoke."

"No—no—you are a man of imagination, and fancied it."

"Oh!" said Twitter. "Good morning."

This time Varley held the door in his hand, while Twitter descended the staircase, after which he closed it, muttering to himself,—

"He covets death at my hands, and he shall receive it. While he continued the low, cringing villain, upon whose neck I could place my feet, I was content to let him live ; but now he has begun to resist, he is finding out his real strength, and like all cowards, under such circumstances he will use it recklessly. I am decided upon his death. The manner of its execution I must think upon. The means must be safe, and certain, and noiseless—yes, noiseless, if possible."

He sat down, and fell into a long train of thought with regard to the means of taking the life of his associate in crime. As for Twitter himself, no course of conduct which Varley could possibly have pursued, would have entailed upon him such absolute misery as that he now suffered from the mass of conjectures that rose upon his mind, in consequence of the sudden alteration in the conduct of him who had always shown himself to be of the most violent disposition, and ever ready, at a moment, to break out into the most angry denunciations.

The real truth did certainly cross Twitter's mind more than once, but, strange to say, he discarded the supposition, more than any other, that Varley intended to murder him. First of all he shrunk from it, and strove to shake it off, as weak-minded people commonly do, any idea that is of an extremely distressing nature to them. Then he thought of what great difficulties Varley would have to encounter in the accomplishment of such a purpose—difficulties nearly insurmountable—for would he, Twitter, be so foolish, as to trust himself with Varley under any circumstances which would give him a fair opportunity of executing so terrible a purpose.

"No, surely," he muttered, "he cannot mean my murder. To put me to a violent death he shall have no chance, for I will never meet him but in the populous haunts of men, where his instant apprehension for the deed, or the attempted deed, would be certain. Dare he poison me? No; for what poison is there that he could administer, so quick in its effects, that it would not leave me time, ere I died, to denounce him as the murderer of Sir George Rankley? No, I do not—cannot think he means to take my life."

Having, as he thought, disposed of this conjecture, another rose up in Samuel Twitter's mind, which, bad as was the former, was of a still more agonizing description. That was, that Bernard Varley was maturing some scheme for escaping from England, and leaving him, Twitter, to take the consequences of the crime they had mutually committed.

From the moment this idea suggested itself to the mind of Twitter, the stronger and more feasible it grew, and he fancied he saw confirmatory reasons in every word which had fallen from Varley's lips.

"His first wild excitement," he thought, "has died away, and no doubt he has resolved to give up the mad pursuit of Miranda ; he has probably got some offer for the Grange estates, which he will close with ; and then, repairing to the yacht which he has purchased, the existence of which I became aware of by so strange a chance, he will sail, Heaven only knows whither, denouncing me, in the meantime, for my share in his crime, and so, in his own language, pay me the debt he owes me."

Samuel Twitter quite satisfied himself that he had found out Varley's real meaning, and the course of conduct he pursued thereon will be quickly made manifest, a course of conduct eminently calculated to ensure the destruction of both of those men, who, had they but held together in their iniquities, deeply dyed with guilt as they were, might have defied the hand of justice; but, how true is it, that great criminals are their own greatest enemies, and that a chain of union, forged in iniquity, has not the strength of a hair to hold them together.

CHAPTER CXX.

THE DELIGHTS OF DRURY-LANE.—THE SPY.—THE MEETING BETWEEN WITLET AND JONES.

The large rewards which had accumulated upon the head of the unfortunate Rowland Percy, induced an unprecedented activity among the London police for his detection.

The government had offered five hundred pounds for his capture; Bernard Varley five hundred more.; and the magistracy of York, feeling themselves in a very peculiar situation, in consequence of letting slip the only great criminal that had been in their hands for the last four or five assizes, offered three hundred ; so the total rewards for the recapture of the innocent Rowland Percy amounted to the large sum of thirteen hundred pounds, and, it will be recollected, that this sum was only for the seizure of his person, and not, as is ordinarily the case in such money matters, contingent upon the conviction of the party, for Rowland had bt to be identified, in order to make him again amenable immediately to the sentence of the law.

The most incredible exertions were made to secure him ; and, had he not been in the extremely unsuspicious place he was, in the first flush of the active search, he surely would have fallen into the hands of his enemies; the avenues of London were well watched; the passengers on every coach coming from York, or its direction, scrutinised ; and persons, having the appearance of quiet, harmless sojourners in the metropolis, were placed as lodgers in those public-houses where it was well known to the police any criminal, however grave his offence might be, would obtain shelter and assistance.

The metropolis swarmed with bills, giving a description of Rowland Percy, and detailing the rewards offered for his apprehension ; while the newspaper press of course was added to the hue and cry which was raised against him.

Happily, perhaps, for his peace, Rowland knew not of the extensive arrangements that were made for his apprehension ; true he saw the newspapers, but their information being notoriously defective, they contradicted each other so completely that he placed no reliance upon any of their statements. Indeed, the *Times* announced his capture in large letters one day, and boasted largely of the exclusive information they had obtained from " our own correspondent," at an immense expense, and most wonderful and exclusive was the information, since it preceded the fact.

But how, says the reader, did they get out of the scrape the next day ? Why, they said, from exclusive sources, they knew he had been caught, but got away again just after their second edition had been sold, and they defied the whole world to prove the contrary, appealing triumphantly to two long letters, one signed " A

Magistrate," and another signed "A reader of the the *Times* for thirty years," both of which declared it quite swayed the destinies of the world, and was the most valuable in Europe, the editor quite forgetting to add that both the letters were written in Printing-house-square, by an odd man on the establishment.

But to return from this digression—the Star and Tinder-box was more watched by the police than any other house in the metropolis; and had Net Witlet been thoroughly aware of the great exertions that would have been made for the recapture of Rowland Percy, he would have quite altered his mind as to the propriety

of taking him to Drury-lane; for not only was the house what is termed a flash one, but the landlord, being a Yorkshireman himself, was well known to the police for his sympathy with offenders from that part of the country.

He was quite right in the information he had given to Witlet and Rowland, that parties came to his house on the look-out for the latter, and it was fortunate that the persecuted young man and his friend, the highwayman, left as early as they did.

Mr. Jones, upon leaving Miranda in the genteel establishment which we have taken some pains to describe, hastened to the Star and Tinder-box, a house much

No. 59.

more congenial to his tastes and habits. A sort of cheerful expansion came over Jones's face as he neared the purlieus of Drury-lane, spots as dear and hallowed to his memory as are the arcadian groves of Italy to the worshipper of classicality and romantic beauty.

"Drury-lane!" cried Mr. Jones, when he arrived at the corner of Broad-street. "Here yer is, bless yer. Talk o' streets, and squares, and willas, and all them ere things, they're none on 'em ekal to Drury-lane. If I was ever to retire from business, I should just like a willa up some of them ere courts. There's no air as comes near the air of Drury-lane. Sometimes its pork sassengers, then there's a wariation of skinned eels and calfs' foots, and, above all, there's a aromatic odour, as people calls it; and nothing disagrees with nobody, cause of the particles of gin as is floating in the air. Then what's to come near them courts and alleys, running quite beautiful into St. Giles's, and out on it again, quite natural, where a fellow might dodge the grabs for a month, and dodge in and out like a dog in the fair. Then there's the fences and the flash kens. Drury-lane, you is a beauty! Some people says the smell on yer is rather strong, but it's wery pleasant for all that; and here's Steeple-court, too. Was there ever such an out-an'-out rummy, little, dark, down-hill alley as this here; it's quite romantic and lovely. If I was a great monarch, I'd have that ere Star and Tinder-box as one of my royal residences, that I would. Why, there's baccy smoke in every room on it, 'cause it creeps up the staircases just like a living creature."

By this time Mr. Jones had arrived at the Star and Tinder-box, where the landlord was not visible; but he quickly summoned him by leaning over the bar with an air of great familiarity, and shouting "Vell" in a voice that quickly reached mine host.

"Lord love us," said the landlord, "is it you? you are an inch too late."

"Give us six foot of explanation," said Jones. What sing'lar noise is that ere?"

"D——d if somebody hasn't left the Old Tom tap running," said the landlord, in a rage, not at all suspecting that Jones, by way of practical joke, had just accomplished that feat.

"That ere was wilful waste," said Jones. "Guv us half a pint to begin with. Have you seen Neddy? How does times go? York, eh? Tow-row. All right —somewhere up stairs?"

The landlord placed his finger mysteriously by the side of his nose, and said, "Hush!"

Behind mine host was a looking-glass, which reflected a good view of the parlour-door, which by that means Jones saw slowly open, and a head protruded, in the act of listening.

"Sneaks about," inquired Jones.

"Werry," said the landlord.

By a dextrous fling of his hand, then, Jones threw the whole half pint of gin over his shoulders, exactly into the eyes of the prying listener, who immediately disappeared into the parlour with a howl of pain, and such a volley of curses, as quite delighted Mr. Jones, some of them being of a very original character.

As for the landlord, he sat down in his little parlour, and roared again with laughter. After which he upset several glasses, and leaning over the beer-engine to touch Mr. Jones on the back in token of his high approbation of his conduct,—

"Bless yer," he cried, "I always said you was a ornament to society, and so you is. That feller's been here for a week a prying and poking about. Come in, yer amusing wretch; I could swaller yer."

The feelings of the gentleman who had had the gin thrown in his eyes appeared to have been rather excited by the circumstance—an excitement which was most probably added to by the roar of laughter with which he was greeted in the parlour; for after executing a grotesque dance, in great agony, from the gin in his eyes, he rushed to the bar, looking as if he had been crying for a week, and, in a voice compounded of rage, fear, and pain, he shouted,—

"What villain did that?—what infernal scoundrel did that? D——me, I can hardly see. Who threw gin in my face? Who dared to half-blind me in this way? D—me, I'll be the death of him."

"Why, you're drunk," said Jones. "What do you mean, poor cretur? You've had so much gin, that it's running out of your eyes."

"Was it you threw gin at me?" shouted the man.

"Over the left," said Jones.

"Well, d—n it, it was over the left," cried the man.

"Hark yer, my friend," said the landlord; "I know yer. They say listeners never hear no good of themselves; but you've done better, for you've had half a pint of gin for nothing; I shan't charge yer for it. Now mizzle. A spy's business is over when he's found out. Take a hint; it wouldn't be good for your health to stay here to-night."

"Exactly," said Jones. "Something might happen uncomfortable in the night."

"Curse you all!" said the man; "you'll do yourself a deal of good by all this, I'll give a report of the house, that you may hear of next licensing day."

He then rushed into the street, with a very despairing look, feeling, indeed, according to the landlord's dictum, that his occupation was over.

"What is the news?" said Jones to the landlord. "Is Percy here with you as escaped from York scragging?"

"He's been here, but he ain't here now. I advised Neddy to take him away, as I knew there was a dead set made here for him; and so, you see, Neddy knows when I adwises anything I means it. He took him away, and where he's stowed him I can't say."

"Safe and sound somewhere, I'll be bound."

"Why, Neddy isn't the man exactly to do things half ways. I'd say as much of him behind his back as I would before his face, that a better fellow never stepped in shoe leather; he's too good for this ere world, Mr. Jones. I respects him as if he was my own babby; and come what may, I'll stick to him like bricks through thick and thin, odd or even, and all sorts of luck; I'm not the man to turn tail on an old acquaintance; and as long as the Star and Tinder-box has a bit of flint in its lockers, hurrah for Neddy!"

'Thank you," said Witlet, who at that moment appeared in front of the bar; "I owe you one for that. Jones, is she all safe?"

"I should think so," said Jones; "and snug as a domestic warment in a rug."

"Thank Heaven!" said Witlet, as he walked inside the bar; "I think, then, there is a prospect of holding out until the ardour of pursuit is abated—a pursuit which I never could have believed would have been carried on with the rancour it is. The aggregate rewards offered for the apprehension of poor Rowland Percy this day amount to thirteen hundred pounds."

"He may thank his stars he's not here then," said the landlord, "for we have fellers come into this crib as would make their own mothers into sassages, fry, and eat 'em, for half the sum."

"Thirteen hundred," said Jones. "I should just like to meet the kiddy as was walking away with that ere sum in a rayther lonely place."

"Some of the rale," said the landlord, handing a glass to Witlet. "Drink it, my boy. Here's better luck, more friends, and less need of them. Lor bless yer, beaks and officers are but human beins after all. Some on 'em has a little cleverness, and some on 'em hasn't; but take 'em at the best, we generally gets the better on 'em; so never fear, all will be right, and the young chap will give 'em the double. Here's luck to him; and may willany meet with its just reward."

"I trust it may," said Witlet. "I have heard, during my brief life, many instances of oppression and false accusation, but I never even in a romance could have expected to meet with such a systematic course of villany as that which consigned Rowland Percy to a dungeon, and precipitated one of the most beautiful and innocent of her sex from the very height of prosperity to the lowest depths of despair and destitution. Heaven cannot, will not, look calmly on such frightful wrongs ; and the day must soon come when the oppressor shall fall, and innocence rise more triumphant still upon the ashes of its former glory."

"Knock my back, " said Jones to the landlord ; "thank yer, I've swallowed it now. Give us that another time, Neddy, in little pieces, and lend us a dictionary as it goes on. Blessed if ever I heared anything so strong in my life. One's forced to swallow it all at once, for fear it should evaporate."

CHAPTER CXXI.

THE ATTEMPTED CAPTURE.—THE SEARCH BY THE OFFICERS AND THE DREADFUL DISAPPOINTMENT.

IN a few minutes the discourse changed to a much more serious aspect between Jones and Witlet, and they mutually communicated to each other the particulars concerning Rowland Percy and Miranda, with the urgently expressed desire of each of those persons to have an interview with each other.

"Mr. Percy, I believe," said Witlet, "is perfectly safe for the present, in fact, I feel quite sure that no inducement upon earth would get the person he is with to betray him. His subsistence must be my care, and I must as well do what I can for Miranda, who must surely claim the tenderest sympathy of every man of true feeling. She has borne herself most nobly under the acutest trials, and one cannot but respect the fortitude and courage which has raised that young, shrinking and timid girl, to be a perfect heroine."

"Werry good, Neddy," said Jones ; " werry good. All I can say is, as she is in a werry genteel house, in a werry genteel street. I never was genteel, thank God, and never shall be. Blessed if I don't think it's another name for being uncomfortable Howsomdever, you know, Neddy, she may like it, as she's been brought up in the young-lady way, which I wasn't. Now and then she takes on a little melancholy, and then she picks up a bit, and she wants to see that sweetheart of hers, young Mr. Percy ; and as it's a werry genteel house she lives in, and nobody would suspect as anybody worth a curse would live in it, or wisited at it, I don't see why he shouldn't go and see her. It 'll make 'em both very comfortable. What do you think of it, Neddy ?"

" I would gladly," said Witlet, "assist in procuring an interview between them ; but you've really no notion, Jones, of the hot pursuit that's made after him. Believe me, he cannot, for a short time, leave the widow's house with any degree of safety, and, when they meet, I should advise that she should go to him, instead of his visiting her."

"Werry good," said Jones ; " but I should like you to see that ere genteel house. It's out-and-out nobby in its way. I wouldn't live in it if you'd give me never so much. Talk of comfort—oh, lawks ! I dare say, if you and me were to smoke a pipe on the roof, they'd think themselves ruined for ever."

"With Miss Miranda's permission," said Witlet, "I shall certainly call and see her ; and certainly the danger of her visiting Mr. Percy at the widow's is not near so great as his visiting her, for even—which is very unlikely—if she should be seen and followed, still the discovery of his hiding place is not a necessary consequence."

" Sartenly not."

" Yet, Jones, I should advise, that a day or two be allowed to elapse. We cannot be too prudent. Only consider the dangers we have already passed through, and the great hopes that Mr. Percy still has of some circumstance happening to prove his innocence. Were he really a guilty man, I own the case would be widely different, even if we wished to save him."

"That's all werry true," said Jones, "and I needn't say, Neddy, that I leaves the affair in your hands , and now as to the keep of these ere unfortunate creters as can't keep themselves. You knows my business as you knows your own. There's a little unsartenty in all speculations; I may crack a crib as is worth the cracking, or I mayn't. I tell you what we'll do, Neddy, we'll meet once a blessed week, and calculate what's wanted. If you havn't got, perhaps I shall; if I havn't it perhaps you may. I think that ere'll be the way to work the oracle, Neddy?"

"I see no objection to the plan," said Witlet; "but mind, Jones, I implore you to be careful not to bring suspicion on the innocent Miranda, by visiting her after any of your professional avocations. You know not what might result from one such act of imprudence."

"Leave me alone; I'll be as prudent as the Lord Chancellor when he won't decide a case, because he don't know what to think of it. When I think all isn't right, when I want to send her any blunt, I'll pop it in a letter, and she'll get it, and nobody suspect it nohow."

"Hilloa !" said the landlord, "visitors;" and in another moment three men lounged to the front of the bar.

"Your sarvant, gentlemen," said the landlord, who knew them at once as Bow-street officers. "What's the row?"

"Game's up," said one of the officers. "We must have him—it's a serious case —so make no bones about it."

"Have who?" said the landlord. "I never was good at riddles; if my grandmother had been alive, she'd have given you an answer quite pat."

"Come, come, no nonsense," said the spokesman of the party. "Rowland Percy, the murderer from York, has been traced here. We have a warrant, and it includes the Slashing Squire, for aiding and abetting. Come, now, don't put on such a phiz as that, it won't do any longer; we must have both on 'em. As for the Slashing Squire, he's booked too; for there are two or three highway robberies waiting to be down upon him as soon as he's nabbed."

"Perhaps you'd like to get me first?" said Witlet, making his appearance from behind the landlord and Jones.

"Here goes for a try," said the officer, as he stretched his hand over the bar, in which was his little brass staff, and made an attempt to seize Witlet. The latter, however, struck up his arm, and wrenching the staff from his hand at the same moment, he disappeared through the door leading into the back-alley, by which he and Rowland had made their exit from the Star and Tinder-box.

"It's no matter—it's no matter," cried the discomfitted officer, as he tried to scramble over the bar. "He'll be nabbed at the end of the alley."

"In the meantime," said the landlord, taking up a large toasting-fork," there is no occasion for you to come into my bar. I haven't seen your search warrant, and I don't mean to take your word for it."

Several vigorous thrusts of the toasting-fork, induced the officer to withdraw his leg.

"Where's the warrant—where's the warrant? Show this fellow the warrant, and then let him resist if he dares."

While the landlord affected to be very seriously looking at the warrant, Ned Witlet walked hastily down the dark passage, until he was suddenly seized by some one, who cried,—"Hold! not so fast" and the gleam of a dark lantern immediately illuminated the place.

Witlet saw in a moment that the officer was a new hand, and did not know him.

"My good fellow," he said, "are you an officer? because if you are, I am one of the York police, and am come to tell you you are particularly wanted in the house; we've nabbed our men, but there's something of a row going on."

Witlet showed him the officer's staff as he spoke, which completely silenced his scruples, and exclaiming—"The deuce there is," he rushed up the alley, leaving Witlet at perfect liberty, who, darting into Drury-lane, crossed it, and was soon lost in the intricacies of a maze of courts which branched from its opposite side.

The officer who had been so outwitted, rushed breathlessly into the bar, exclaiming,—

"Here I am—here I am—what's the matter?"

"The matter!" cried the others. "Where's your prisoner?"

"Prisoner! I've seen nobody but the York officer, a big fellow, with his staff. He told me you wanted me."

"Done," said the officers, looking at each other. "You're an ass, Fredericks; one of the birds has flown."

"Yes, but we'll have the other and the principal one," exclaimed one of the officers. "The front door is well guarded; and now, Fredericks, do you stick your d—d broad back against the one you have just come through. Let this be a lesson to you, and don't let a prisoner go, because he happens to show you a constable's staff."

"What a skrimmage!" said Jones. "Really, gentlemen, you turned all my milk. Do you want to take anybody up, or are you only in joke?"

"You mind your own business," said the senior officer, "when we want you, we'll call for you."

"Oh, thank you," said Jones. "If I shouldn't happen to be at home, you can leave your card, you know. You won't take anything to drink now, I suppose, as you're rayther in a hurry?"

The officers disdained to make any reply to this observation, but commenced a vigorous search through the house, with, as they thought, the certainty of finding him they sought, and, indeed, they had taken their measures very well for the accomplishment of that result, had Rowland Percy been so unfortunate and ill-advised as really to have taken up his abode at the Star and Tinder-box.

They had placed the man Fredericks, who, although but a young officer, possessed remarkable muscular power, in the narrow passage by the back alley, with instructions to make prisoner any one who attempted to pass from the public-house. How he acquitted himself we have seen.

Then, at the front door an officer was stationed, and another one on the roof of the opposite house, in order to watch if any attempts were made by Rowland Percy to escape over the roof of the Star and Tinder-box. From the description of the York officers, they had been quite able to identify Ned Witlet as the person who appeared to have assisted Rowland Percy in his flight; hence was it that his name was included in the warrant.

From a woman, who kept a mean shop opposite to the Star and Tinder-box, they had been told that two persons answering the description of Percy and Witlet, had been seen to enter the public-house, but not to leave it. This was the whole of their information; but, coupled with their previous suspicions, it was amply sufficient to obtain a warrant upon, and to serve as a foundation for a tolerably well-grounded belief that an active search in the Star and Tinder-box would discover Rowland Percy.

The landlord, feeling so very conscious as he was that the search throughout his house would be just nothing, had the malice to amuse himself at the officers' expence, by expressing great fear and anxiety, as they entered into every room, calling frequently upon his lucky stars to save him from the consequences, if he looked into this cupboard or that, so that he kept the officers in a perpetual state of fidget during the whole time of the search, they being always expecting something, and finding nothing to repay them for their labours.

It took a long while to go over the Star and Tinder-box, for it was an old rambling house, with a great variety of odd nooks and curious corners. There were deep, out-of-the-way cupboards here and there, where they would have been least expected, so that to perform the search thoroughly, even to those practised men, occupied much time.

Doubly toilsome, too, did it become, as floor after floor, room after room, cupboard after cupboard were searched in vain, and at the end of about an hour they stood in the attic, weary and discomfited. The last attic, too, they had to search —and Heaven knows that was done easily enough—it presented nothing to their gaze but four bare white-washed walls, not even relieved by the wretchedest skeleton grate.

They were begrimed with dust and dirt, for such a rout out of all the old holes and corners in the Star and Tinder-box had not taken place for many years ; in fact, as the landlord himself emphatically declared, he was'nt aware of half the conveniences of the ancient house, until they were so kindly pointed out to him by the officers.

"Well, gentlemen," he said, when they took a despairing look round the miserable attic, "you would take all this trouble, you know, and its no fault of mine ; you would not be satisfied without poking your noses into every hole and corner in the old house, and making yourselves more like a set of chimney sweeps than respected Bow-street runners."

"D—n him, he is'nt here," said the senior officer, "unless there's some hiding place we can't find out. Now remember," turning to the landlord, "this is a serious affair, and one which may do you a good deal of good or a good deal of harm. You know we don't trouble your house oftener than we can help it ; but when we do it must be to some purpose. A poor devil of a house-breaker is one thing, and a fellow convicted of murder is another ; besides, here's thirteen hundred pounds reward. Come, now, say the word of where he is, and you shall have the odd money—the three hundred, I mean."

"You must think me a precious ass," said the landlord, "to hand over to you a thousand pounds, if I had the means and inclination to pitch upon a poor devil who was playing at hide-and-seek with the law. I tell you, as I told you before, he ain't here, if he was, and I wished to do the sneak, do you think I'd do it for three hundred pounds, when I could get thirteen for the job. Bah ! you've gone to sleep."

"Oh, that's all very well," said the senior officer ; "but you know what I mean as well as I do myself ; it isn't three hundred pounds, or thirteen either that would pay you for losing the confidence of the *family*, you know that as well as I. When I spoke of the three hundred, I meant that I'd hold you harmless in the affair, and nobody would know that you had given us the office."

"Lor bless me," said the landlord, "how some people make money like dirt. You may depend upon it, gentlemen, I'll look for him high and low, and if I should find him, I'll come to you for the three hundred, never fear, it's so very kind of you to hold me harmless. It's enough to bring tears into my eyes."

"Come along," said the officer to his companions "its no go ; if he's been here he's gone again ; but hark ye, master landlord, when it comes to light, which it will some day that you know more of this matter than you'd tell, look out for squalls, that's all."

"Certainly, Gentlemen, I'll look out for anything you like to mention. Mind how you go down the stairs, if one of you were to slip and break his neck, what a thing it would be. I think I should never look up again,"

The officers went down the stairs, muttering curses to themselves. At the bottom of the first flight was an old cupboard, which wound a good deal under the staircase, and which they had been at great pains thoroughly to explore ; now, however, as they came opposite to it, they all made a dead stand, for the door moved perceptibly, though slightly.

"Ah!" said the senior officer as he folded his arms, and placed his back against it, "will you take the three hundred now, landlord? Come say the word."

"Ah," said the landlord, "its better to be born lucky than rich. Its a great offer, gentlemen, and when I find him I'll run and let you know, without my hat."

"Then my man," said the officer, "I strongly suspect you're a fool."

"Do you indeed ! I suspected that of you when you first showed your nose here to-day, but now it's come to a dead certainty."

"Very good—very good, have your grin ; perhaps it will change to the other side of your mouth in a little while. You won't take the three hundred now, and tell us where he is, candidly?"

"There you go," said the landlord, "poking your fun at a poor fellow ; upon my soul, it's aggravating."

The officer laughed, and rubbed his hands together, and then he laughed again, in the most joyous manner imaginable. Altogether a more happy-looking man could not be found within the bills of mortality.

Various smiles passed across the faces of his companions, and they winked at each other, as much as to say that their chief was a wonderful clever fellow, and was quizzing the landlord amazingly.

"Upon my life," said the senior officer to the landlord, "you carry it off d—d well.—Ah! ah! ah! I never saw such a face in my life, its positively quite rich, but it wont do; oh dear no, not at all. It's a lot of cleverness all thrown away—an amazing lot of cleverness.—Ah! ah! ah!"

The other officers laughed as in duty bound, and altogether the landlord was made quite a butt among them. It seemed cruel and heartless, but such was the fact.

"Now," said the senior officer drawing out his staff; "hocus pocus. I'm a conjuror; stand off a moment; now, in upon him—hold him—hold him—that's the ticket."

Uttering these, and such warlike expressions, he pulled open the cupboard door, and discovered——Mr. Jones sitting very composedly, smoking a pipe in a chair, with a spittoon before him.

"What's all that blessed talking been about?" said Jones. "What an out-an'-out sanguinary disturbance."

"You d—d scoundrel!" said the enraged officer.

"Hi—hi!" said Jones, "fetch us a straight waistcoat; there's a skrimmage."

The officer, stamping and swearing for a few moments, rushed down the remainder of the staircase, nor paused in his speed till he had gained the open street. After which, with a volley of abuse against the Star and Tinder-box, he walked in a very melo-dramatic manner to the Bow-street police office.

CHAPTER CXXII.

MIRANDA AT HOME.—HOW TO GET FOUND IN LONDON LODGINGS.—NIGHT AND MORNING.

MIRANDA felt very sad and lonely in her new home, situated as she was. It was cheerless and wretched in the extreme, to have no one who would address to her a kind word, or to whom she could discourse upon those subjects nearest and dearest to her heart.

Even the rough kindness and strange courtesies of Jones would have been very acceptable to her in her isolated condition, but he was gone, and she felt herself truly and sadly alone in every sense of the word; moreover, there was nothing cheering in the place which she felt compelled to make her temporary home, and it was with a sigh of regret that she told herself that she would much rather have taken up her abode in some more homely and domesticated place, but she soon checked these mental aspirations, by exclaiming,—

"Ought I not to be thankful, most thankful, for any home, situate as I am in such melancholy circumstances, and not critical as to its advantages and disadvantages? If I have much to sigh for, at least I have much to be thankful for; Heaven forgive me for repining for a moment."

But if poor Miranda thus early found her home in the lodging-house, cold, selfish, and disagreeable, what would be her feelings when she should eventually discover the heartless selfishness that would dictate every word that was spoken to her, and influence every action that was done, that was in relation to her.

She little imagined that the lodging-house keeper's creed was to look upon every one who by evil destiny came to reside on the genteel premises, a special victim to the altar of avarice. One who is to be robbed, annoyed, unsettled, victimized in every possible manner, until driven out of the place to make way for some new comer, who might not be fully aware of the region of rascality into which he or she was plunged.

Jones had not left many minutes, when the the the landlady made her appearance on a voyage of discovery, to ascertain to what extent her new lodger would submit to be fleeced.

THE DISCOVERY OF THE SKELETON AT THE OLD MOON.

Upon Miranda's saying "come in," in answer to a knock, she entered with the true lodging-housekeeper's hypocritical smile.

"Miss Jones," she said, " I have just taken the liberty to come to know if you mean to find yourself or not. I generally find my lodgers, particularly the first floor. By-the-bye, you'll find the parlour very quiet—the second floor back is out of town, and we never allow keys, ever since we had a first-floor come home drunk."

"I do not understand you," said Miranda, " when you talk of finding me. If you'll have the kindness to explain your meaning, I shall be obliged to you."

No. 60.

"Oh, very good," thought the landlady; then she added aloud, "perhaps you never were in a lodging-house before?"

"Once, and but for a very short time," said Miranda, as she thought of her humble abode in York, with old Mr. Percy; "but it was far away from here, and the same usages may not exist in London."

"Why, finding you," said the landlady, looking very benign, "means saving you a deal of trouble in buying little odd matters, such as candles, and coals, and wood, and soap, and blacking, and so on, which can all be done up in a little weekly bill."

"You're very kind," said Miranda; "but it would be giving you a deal of trouble, to spare me some."

"Oh, not at all, not at all; of course I must buy these little things for myself, and I can oblige you at the same time. I have no objection to finding respectable lodgers."

"Very well," said Miranda; "if you will do so much for me, I am greatly beholden to you."

"Perhaps I had better find you everything else besides? because I am sure, when I go and buy my own tea and sugar, it will be no trouble to buy you some; as I say, I generally find the first-floor."

"If you please," said Miranda, "I will leave all those matters to your kind superintendence."

The landlady was amazed, and went down into the kitchen with the firm conviction that Miranda was a fool, and certainly had never been found in a London lodging before.

Great fatigue as the persecuted girl had suffered, it is no wonder she slept soundly, even under the cold and cheerless roof of the lodging-house, and with a prayer for the safety of him who had already escaped so much danger, upon whose head the error of human judgment had put a price, she laid down in all her innocence and virtue, and all her troubles, to enjoy a purer and more refreshing sleep than would visit the couch of luxury or the tapestried beds of the great.

It is true that some faint visions crossed her gentle slumbers; she thought she was again in her sweet little chamber in the Old Grange. The sweet odours of the honeysuckles that twined around the window, came upon her senses. She heard the well-known songs of the birds that used to welcome her to morning, to joy, and hours of quiet happiness—to such as she had not known for many a weary day.

Then she would be wandering with Rowland Percy in deep wildernesses, made beautiful and full of life-like beauty by the presence of him she loved.

It was from such soft visions that Miranda, at a very early hour, awoke in the lodging-house; but little knew she of the great change which morning produces in the gigantic metropolis.

The inhabitants of this leviathan city still lay wrapped in slumber; the streets were empty, and none but the solitary watch could be seen to perambulate the deserted thoroughfares. The hour chimed from the many steeples, and echoed each other from one extreme end to the other, and announced the hour of early morn. Even those whose revels lasted nearly the live-long night, had now found their home, endeavouring to sleep off the effects of late hours and excess.

Hitherto the sky had shewn no signs of day—the stars continued to shine brightly, though the moon was fast fading from the sight.

A dim light in the eastern sky now began to shew itself, and proclaim the coming of the great luminary. At first it barely discovered the form of the heavy masses of clouds that hung in the east, but presently it grew stronger and stronger, peeping from among the aerial masses, which took all kinds of fantastic shapes, until at length the grey of morning reached the zenith.

The sun now just peeped up from beneath the dark mass, and shed a long, bright, golden ray along the clouds, that had a most striking and beautiful appearance, for it was reflected back by a hundred colours, which increased in quantity and beauty, as the sun slowly emerged from beneath the horizo

The tall spires of the different churches, the golden cross of St. Paul's, and the cupola of the Monument, caught the sun's earliest rays, while the long tapering masses shone well in the skyey relief.

An observer who might have been placed on some elevated spot, would have seen a glorious spectacle. From a dark and obscure mass, he would have seen arising gradually a great and glorious city. Public buildings and great edifices would at first attract his attention, and then as the daylight grew stronger he could note the smaller buildings, and more minute parts of others, forming a great and wonderful structure.

The streets might be traced by the house-tops, while in the centre of all this might be seen the silvery Thames, flowing through a mass of habitations on either side, bringing wealth and luxuries to the rich, labour and necessaries for the poor.

The cool, clear air, hovered over this immense mass of buildings, the only time that it is pure. The clear sunlight was now gradually falling upon its different quarters, and no spot escaped, save such as were thrown into shade by a neighbouring structure, and more of London could now be seen, than at any other hour of the day, for the vision is obscured in the finest weather, by the volumes of smoke that rise from the thousands upon thousands of fires which are daily lit by the inhabitants.

Even at this moment, thus early, a few chimneys are smoking, a white, curling wreath of mist rising slowly into the air, rising higher and higher, until it becomes so attenuated, as to be invisible to the naked eye. These are soon joined by others of the more early inhabitants, those whose daily labours commence with the dawn ; these are followed by others, and others still, till not a house but has its lighted fire, and reeking chimney, as if all were compelled to furnish their quota of vapour, to shield this great mart from the unmixed rays of the sun, or the pure air of the open country.

London was now alive. The inhabitants of many parts were seen hurrying busily to and fro ; markets were full and busy ; while all who had the bread of life to earn, were busily enough employed either in the actual labour of the day, or those which precede, or are preparatory to it.

The sun is now fairly in the heavens, and the splendour of a lovely morn promising a fair and a sunny day, is seen in all its beauty, by the thronging thousands. Still in some parts of this vast metropolis, considerably west of Temple-bar, are spots deemed fashionable, and where the inhabitants never see the sun rise, save when it accidentally overtakes them after a night's revel, as they proceed towards their homes, and who, but they know there is a sunset, would never know there was a sunrise.

To such as these the morning's beauty is an entire stranger—the sun has often passed the meridian ere their eyes are open to his rays, pressing the soft couch, while those hours of life and healthy joy are lost to them for ever.

A bright gleam of sunshine stole into Miranda's room, playing sweetly upon her innocent face.

"Thank Heaven," she cried, "for, amidst all my other troubles, yet another day of health and life."

CHAPTER CXXIII.

WITLET'S INTERVIEW WITH MIRANDA AT THE GENTEEL LODGINGS.—THE SPY, AND THE CONSEQUENCES OF LISTENING AT A KEY-HOLE.

A STRANGER as she was in London, poor Miranda felt the painful consciousness, that were she to leave her temporary abode alone, she would not be able to fulfil her first intention, namely, that of seeing old Mr. Percy, and ascertaining the state of his health.

In the whirl of events of the preceding day, she had forgotten to ask for a particular direction to the hospital whither he had been conveyed. Indeed, she did not even know it by name, so that she was not in a condition even to ask her way, had she chosen to risk wandering about the great metropolis alone.

But still she thought there could not be many institutions of the kind, to one of which Mr. Percy had been conveyed, even in London, and had it not been for the dread of encountering Bernard Varley, and affording him perhaps a clue to her own place of abode, which might ultimately lead to a discovery of Rowland, she would have ventured, ignorant as she was of the localities of the city, alone into its streets, in search of the afflicted old man, who had been, by so strange a combination of circumstances, committed to her care.

In the present state of things then, she felt that prudence, if not downright necessity, compelled her to await for another visit from Jones, ere she should stir from the lodging-house; and more strongly than ever came over her mind, the wish for some domestic companionship, which would have beguiled the tedious hours of what might have been called her imprisonment.

Such, however, was not to be had, and poor Miranda, after partaking of a lonely and cheerless breakfast, which was found her by the landlady, with only the trifling addition of about a hundred and twenty per cent. for so doing, sat with a forlorn feeling by the window, with no other amusement than that of looking into the genteel street, and seeing the occasional visiters that knocked at the highly respectable houses.

She asked her landlady for the loan of some books, but genteel people never have any light or profane literature by them; and even had the gilt-edged prayer-book been offered, which it certainly was not, Miranda was certainly not in that frame of mind which would have enabled her to sit down and peruse it with the purpose of wiling away a few tedious hours, so that she had no resource eventually but to sit brooding over her own sorrows, a sad employment, for there were but a few faint streaks of light in the gloom that surrounded her.

It was ten o'clock in the day when the first application was made to the knocker of the genteel house, and startled Miranda from her meditations. Her heart beat quickly with pleasurable emotion at the thought that it might possibly be one or other of her friends, come to speak comfort to her, and to take her not only to see old Mr. Percy, but perchance to Rowland, whom she longed to see, now that the great dangers on the road from York to London were over.

The suspense of the next few minutes was painful in the extreme, and when the door of her room was opened, she could scarcely speak, from eagerness, to inquire who it was that wished to see her.

"Here's a gentleman, mum," said the dirty servant.

"And his name?" said Miranda.

"I don't know his name, mum."

It is not one lodging-house servant in a hundred that can be drilled into asking the name of a visitor, and this one thought Miranda mighty particular in asking such a question—a question, however, which was speedily set at rest, by Miranda observing the friendly face of Witlet, as he ascended the staircase. With a flush of pleasure mantling in her cheeks, she advanced to meet him, shaking hands with the lawless highwayman more cordially than she would with the first nobleman in the land; but then Miranda's mind was unsophisticated and natural, she credited people for their good actions, feeling more pleasure in so doing, than in censuring those faults which, in many cases, circumstances have forced them to.

Far be it from us to insinuate a defence of Witlet's predatory mode of life. We wish to represent human nature as it is, and in so doing, we must not assume, because a man is a highwayman, that he is destitute of every better feeling of humanity. Moreover, vice is divided into two great classes in this country, namely, that which is made punishable by law, and that which is not—the latter, in our opinion, far exceeding in atrocity the former.

Is the guardian, to whom is entrusted the solemn charge of protecting the interests, and watching the mental formation of young children committed to his care, but who robs them of their substance, and neglects their culture, not a far worse member of society than he who stops you on a common, taking from you the few guineas that may chance to be in your purse.

Is the reckless mother, who, to gratify vanity, pride, or passion, contracts a second marriage, and allows the young children of her first connexion to be turned adrift into the streets, a more pleasant or reputable character than the poor wretch who steals your silver spoons?

We mention these cases, because we know them to have been of actual occurrence; and without defending Ned Witlet, or casting anything like a halo about highway robbery, we certainly look upon him as an angel of light, when compared to that guardian, and that mother, and yet what very respectable people are they. The guardian who robs rides in his carriage, and like Alderman Gibbs, it's difficult to get an account out of him. The heartless mother is again a widow, two of her sacrificed children have died at sea, the third has met the fate of a felon, and in the most becoming weeds possible, she is driving round the park every day in a pony phaeton, looking out for a third match.

Verily, Ned Witlet, we will shake hands with thee, for in point of purity of act and intention, well might thou sit in judgment upon these people.

"Miranda," said Witlet, "I should have been with you earlier, but, to tell the truth, I am not so well acquainted with London as to have found out this street very easily."

"You're very welcome," said Miranda; "I feel myself very solitary and prisoner-like in this place. I have been for some hours longing for some friendly face to make it look home like. Is Rowland safe?"

"I think I may say quite safe from all ordinary accidents. It must be something very far out of the usual course that can bring him to any danger, situated as he is at present; that he suffers much mental anxiety cannot be denied, and chiefly, too, Miranda, on your account, for the more he feels that you have done for him, the more uneasiness seems to mingle with his thankfulness to Heaven for bestowing upon him so pure a gift as your own spotless heart."

"Alas!" said Miranda, "we seem both the children of misfortune; but if, by aiding each other, we can ward off some of the bitterest blows of fate, we should be thankful to Heaven for permitting us."

"I have seen our friend Jones," said Witlet, "and he has possessed me of all the circumstances that have occurred since last I saw you."

"And Mr. Percy," inquired Miranda, "have you ascertained his condition?"

"I have, and I am sorry the report I have to give is not a favourable one. It is the opinion of the medical men at the hospital that a complete break up of the physical powers is taking place."

"Alas—alas!" said Miranda, "this will be another severe blow to poor Rowland."

"Nay, Miss Miranda," said Witlet, "death has ever appeared to me an evil that ought to be borne with greater fortitude than many which afflict us during life. It is the end of all sorrows, instead of being, as is too generally supposed, the greatest sorrow."

"You are right," said Miranda. "What thinking mind could say otherwise? But when did philosophy ever yet succeed in successfully combating the feelings?"

"Never, indeed—never, indeed. And now, Miranda, I have called to make with you some definitive arrangements for the future. I have great hope that the time is not far distant when the innocence of Mr. Percy will be established, and you and he will be placed in a far higher position than to require any advice or assistance from poor Ned Witlet, but till then I beg you to relieve your mind from all anxiety with regard to the means of living. Rowland shall want for nothing; and I will likewise take care that no claim upon you shall be unsatisfied. I rather question Jones's discretion in bringing you here; there is an appearance of very cold comfort about this place that does not assimilate to my ideas of even a temporary home for you. I think you would have been happier in some quiet, pleasant, domestic circle, instead of being shut up here with such very few real comforts about you."

"I cannot say I much like the place," said Miranda, " nor the people."

" Very well, then," said Witlet; "that being conceded, I will look out for a more comfortable home for you! this can be left at any moment."

" Would there be danger," said Miranda, "in my seeing Rowland?"

" I cannot say that your visiting him in his place of concealment would be entirely destitute of risks; and yet when I come to consider how very safely he is housed, and how unlikely it is that any one who knew you should see you and follow you, I am tempted to make arrangements between you this very evening. I have combatted with Jones the notion of your meeting for some time; but upon reconsidering, I cannot say the danger is greater now than it would be a few days hence."

Miranda's eyes sparkled with pleasure at the near prospect of once again holding communion with him she loved, and who had become far more dear to her for the disasters and dangers they had passed through.

" This evening, then," she said, "I will expect you; Witlet you—you, will not disappoint me?"

" On my sacred word," said Witlet; " expect me here, and we will walk quietly together to the house in which Rowland is concealed. The distance is but short, and there is one desirable feature in the circumstances—namely, that both your own situation and Rowland's are known, and probably sympathised with by the party in whose house he has taken refuge, so that when there, there will be no need of concealment, or terror of being overheard."

These words had scarcely escaped from Witlet's lips when a sudden thought seemed to strike him, and rising so as not to make the least noise, he approached the door of the room, which he suddenly flung wide open.

The landlady, who had been surreptitiously listening at the keyhole, rolled into the room on the floor, uttering a loud scream.

" Oh, indeed," said Witlet, as he strode over her, and locked the door on the inside; " you are a nice article, madam. I have a trowel in one pocket, and a double-barrelled pistol in the other, and if you attempt to say one word, or raise the least alarm, I'll blow out your brains with the pistol, and plaster them up against yon wall with the trowel, as an example for the future to all prying lodging-house listeners. I am a man of my word, and one cry will be equivalent to sentence of death upon you."

The word murder died away on the landlady's lips into an indistinct whisper, and she glanced at Witlet with frantic dismay, as she pictured to herself the process of plastering the wall with her brains, and for ever ruining the paper.

" 'Tis hard, indeed," said Witlet, "that persons cannot freely converse in rooms, for which I have no doubt they have well paid, without being subject to the prying curiosity of those who should be the last to practice such meannesss. Miranda, I advise you at once to leave this place with me."

" I must have a proper warning," said the landlady. "I'm not going to be imposed upon because I am a lone woman. I insist upon a proper warning, or——"

" Hush—hush!" interrupted Witlet. " I mean you to have a proper warning, and one which I hope you will never forget. I only wish you were a man, for in that case the proper warning should partake of a more violent character than you would consider at all pleasant. As it is, however, madam, you have placed both yourself and me in a disagreeable situation. Speaking very candidly, as I have been, I don't know exactly that I have said much that I would care to hear repeated; but in case I should, and by way of giving you the proper warning you require, I shall just trouble you to remain in this apartment for one hour from this time, during which hour, if you move or speak in the slightest, I shall feel it quite a duty I owe myself and society to take your life. I am perfectly serious, madam.

As a convincing proof to the landlady that her danger was great, Witlet produced a horseman's pistol from his coat pocket, the sight of which put her in a perfect agony: for although Witlet held the butt end of it towards her, but it was still a pistol, and, to her mind, an equally dangerous weapon as it turned into her mouth.

"Oh! have mercy upon me!" she said. "I didn't hear anything, sir. I was only passing the door accidentally, and my foot slipped as you opened it. Besides the man you was speaking of may'nt be the York murderer after all, although it is the same name as we have all of us read in the newspapers."

Witlet looked much vexed as he said, in a low tone to Miranda—

"You will scarcely forgive me for the folly I have been guilty of, in talking so freely in a strange house. I will do, however, my best to repair my error, and in the meantime attire yourself for the streets, for you must leave this place immediately. Another hour would be fraught with danger."

Miranda, without another word, entered the inner room, and began hastily putting on her cloak and bonnet, in order to accompany the friendly highwayman.

Witlet then, in a low but serious tone, said to the landlady,—

"If you do not in all respects conform yourself to the directions I shall give you, be assured you had better have had your winding sheet ready, for you'll be a dead woman before an hour shall have elapsed."

"Oh, Lord, have mercy upon us, miserable sinners! Amen!"

Witlet placed an arm-chair close to one of the walls, and then added,—

"You will sit in that chair, in which I shall bind you, and not dare to speak or turn your head for the next hour. I shall be in waiting myself at the head of the staircase, and should assuredly hear you, when it will become my duty to myself and others to put my threat into instant execution."

If avarice be a master-passion, strong even in death, or with the prospect of decease, it is to be found in all its strength and mastership in a genteel lodging-house-keeper.

"I—I found the young lady," she gasped, even in the midst of her fears; "I've only been paid a week's rent. I found the young lady, and that, with a week's warning, makes three pounds seventeen and twopence."

Witlet made no answer, but, getting upon a chair, took down the bell-ropes, and the terrified landlady, being already seated in the arm-chair, as he had directed, he proceeded to bind her therein with the cords he had obtained. One he tied round her neck, and then secured it in an elaborate manner to the legs of the chair, intimating to her at the same time that even when the hour had expired, if she made much effort at liberation, she would, in all probability, hang herself—a consummation which, he said, for his part, he devoutly wished.

The other rope he tied first of all round her ankles, and then passing it under the chair, he secured it to the back, so that it would require a great deal more ingenuity than the genteel landlady possessed to have liberated any one else under such circumstances, had she herself been free.

Miranda was by this time ready to depart, and made her appearance in the front room.

"Now, madam," said Witlet, "this lady will leave your house, and I shalll keep guard at the head of the stairs—move or speak at your peril."

A half stifled groan came from the terrified woman, and then Witlet and Miranda left the room—the former locking the door on the outside, and putting the key into his pocket.

In a few moments they were in the street, when Witlet said,

"Miranda, I was nearly leading you into a great danger, but I hope, however, I have now rescued you from it. Here is money; go into the first shop you come to, and purchase some shawl or other article of wearing apparel, which shall be different from what you have on, for no doubt your dress has been accurately described by Varley to his numerous spies, who, I believe, are hunting London in all directions."

As he spoke, he placed some gold in Miranda's hands. She was only able to thank him with an expressive glance, and a draper's shop being near at hand, she made purchase of a large shawl, which, although far from being to her own taste, was probably far better calculated for the purpose of concealment.

"As we are in the streets, we will take a coach, and go and see Rowland Percy at once."

"Oh, I am thankful," said Miranda, with fervour, "for the slight mischance that has happened to procure me so much happiness. I shall see Rowland once again out of the gloom of a prison."

CHAPTER CXXIV.

THE VISIT TO ROWLAND PERCY.—THE WIDOW'S HOUSE.—AN UNEXPECTED AND AWFUL DENOUEMENT.

THE street in which the kind-hearted widow, Mrs. Howell, lived—she with whom Rowland Percy found refuge—although not a very secluded one, was still sufficiently quiet for any unusual circumstance in it to create a considerable degree of attention on the part of its inhabitants, who were ever ready, as is so generally the case in such localities, to pop their heads out of windows on a very slight provocation.

Ned Witlet was aware of this amiable peculiarity on the part of the dwellers in narrow streets towards the suburbs of the metropolis, so he would not, on any account, allow the coach, into which he had handed Miranda, to be driven to Mrs. Howell's door; but he ordered the driver to stop at the Catholic chapel in the Polygon, where he paid him, and saw him out of sight before he would walk with Miranda direct to Mrs Howell's.

"You see, Miss Rankley," he remarked, "that considering the vast size of London, you were not so very far from Mr. Percy. His place of concealment is in a street but a very short distance from where we now are. On any other occasion I should, perhaps, have cautioned you that the visit should be brief, but now, as you have come here in daylight, I think it would be more prudent for you to remain till the dusk of evening."

This was a pleasant and welcome piece of advice to Miranda. She knew that it was dictated by sincerity, and consequently, she felt doubly grateful to find that it accorded so well with her heart's first wishes.

A long and confidential conversation with Rowland Percy was what she most ardently desired, as not once since her father's death had she been able to talk, particularly at large, of the various circumstances that had occurred to separate them. The longest interviews she had had with him were during his confinement at York, and then so many hopes and fears connected with his own actual position had pressed upon their attention, that no time had been spared for retrospective glances or anticipation of the future; but now, in her great faith in Witlet's skill and management, the present did not appear to her mind so engrossing, and she wished to compare her own hopes of the future with those of Percy, from which free communion, perhaps, both of them might gather fresh courage and hopes for the time to come.

Miranda trembled, and leant more heavily upon the arm of Ned Witlet, as she felt that each step drew her nearer to her heart's only treasure—for since her father's death there had been no one on whom she could expend any portion of her affection but Rowland Percy; he was the one sole tie that bound her to existence; it was the love of him that armed her with fortitude to bear the heavy trials she had passed through, and which had changed her, as Witlet had truly remarked, from a timid, shrinking girl to a heroine of romance—a heroine not surpassed in fortitude and noble courage by any that have figured in the world's great history.

"While you remain here," said Witlet, as they neared the door, "I will find some other home for you of, I hope, a more agreeable nature than the one you so recently left. If it were prudent for you, under the circumstances, to become an inmate of this house, I should rejoice exceedingly; but, believe me, it is not. By you and Rowland living separately until the ardour of pursuit is abated, his danger is considerably lessened. There are means of concealment for him, which

THE INTERVIEW OF ROWLAND AND MIRANDA ON THE ROAD TO LONDON.

could not be available for both of you; and although, if your residence in London was known to the whole world, no one could interfere with you, yet it might, you see, if you resided here, afford a dangerous clue to Mr. Percy."

"The idea," said Miranda, "did rise in my mind of how pleased I should be to be an inmate of the same house with him; but I have dismissed it for the same reasons you have yourself urged to me."

Witlet cast a hasty glance about the street to see if they were observed, and then he knocked lightly at the widow's door.

No 61.

Mrs. Howell herself admitted him, and guessing in a moment who was his companion, took Miranda affectionately by the hand, and led her into the homely little parlour.

Oh, how delightful and full of excellence did that humble home seem to Miranda, since, beneath its roof was sheltered her lover, who had passed through so many dangers and vicissitudes of evil fortune.

We have always thought there is something in keeping between people and their houses, and that the one might be judged of by the other quite separately. It was particularly so with regard to Miranda's last place of abode, the mean gentility of which seemed only equalled by that of its landlady.

If Miranda was not struck by such a coincidence, then she was wonderfully so with it at Mrs. Howell's. The poor widow and her little neat parlour, about which there was no vain parade, seemed quite to be made for each other; there was none of the flimsy striving for effect and flourish upon scanty means that had characterized everything at the genteel house; but, oh! what a world of comfort and homely fire-side enjoyment were there, instead of that cold attempt to be something for which there were neither the means nor the mind.

The little parlour might be a trifle overstocked with its old and well-kept furniture; the ancient prints that hung upon the walls were not of the modern flimsy character, nor had the widow been indebted for them to an art union, which crams down the throats of people unfathomable subjects, so that the artistical display upon a person's walls may be in direct violation of his or her taste.

Even the old eight-day clock seemed to tick in the corner with a deliberation that promised a great deal more steadiness, and to-be-depended-upon works within, than many modern specimens of its class, which, like Master Humphrey's clock, notwithstanding all the winding up in the world, and the wheels within wheels, play the Dickins with the purchaser, and turn out no go.

Then, upon the mantelshelf, was a piece of real coral, instead of the piece of petrified sponge which did duty at the genteel house, together with some new and costly shells, which poor Mrs. Howell set great store by, and upon the beauties of which she would sometimes expatiate with tears, for they had been gathered by her lost husband's own hands from the shores of the Indian seas.

The very fire threw out a warmer and kindlier beam than it did at the shabby-genteel lodging-house, over everything connected with which a moral winter seemed to reign, rendering what otherwise would have been cheering and pleasant, cold and drear.

And in what admirable keeping was the widow Howell herself with her home! You might look at her, and then, casting your eyes around, you felt assured that the parlour was hers, and that she had long had the management and ordering of its contents.

A place altogether more consonant to Miranda's chastened feelings her friend Witlet could scarcely have taken her to. It was a home which had kindly and gentle effects upon the saddened mind of Rowland Percy, for it is not to be supposed that there always existed a necessity for his continuing in the place of concealment which had proved of such service to the widow's son. Mrs. Howell's household consisted but of herself and a young girl, the daughter of a poorer neighbour, who was in the habit of coming the morning as a domestic assistant, and going to her home at night, so that, by a little management on the part of Mrs. Howell, the girl was got rid of at a much earlier hour than usual, when Rowland could emerge from his place of concealment, and sit down by the fireside, in the old-fashioned, but comfortable, fireside in the little parlour.

Upon the whole, therefore, his abode at the widow's promised to be far less irksome than it would at first appear; besides, she reasoned rationally enough, that he might enjoy considerable personal liberty in the house without great fear for his safety, for she would say,—

"You are much safer here, Mr. Percy, than was my poor boy; there was no place where a search would more naturally be made for him, than in his mother's house; so that I was kept, and he, too, poor fellow, in a constant state of alarm; but it is different with you, you see, Mr. Percy, for there is notthing to point out my house as your hiding-place more than any one of the many thousands of London."

Rowland could not but assent to the justness of this reasoning; and although he made up his mind always to retire to his place of concealment when a knock came at the door, yet he did so without any great nervousness as to the result.

Then, it was soothing and pleasant to him to have such a one as Mrs. Howell to whom he could speak of Miranda, and who, kind soul, quite agreed, although she had never seen her, in every word Rowland uttered in praise of her.

"Oh, Mrs. Howell," he would say, " many and many a time I could have given up all human hope, and let them, innocent as I was, drag me to an instant and ignominious death, had it not been for that dear better angel, who stepped between me and my rash resolves, winning me back by her beauty and innocence, to better hopes and a firmer reliance upon that Providence it was sinful to doubt."

    *   *   *   *   *

It is not to be supposed that poor Miranda, oppressed with so many hopes and so many fears, could take the notice we have done of the widow and her home, but we like ourselves the picture of humble and cheerful poverty, as a contrast to the detestable shabby gentility of the house from which Miranda had just escaped so strangely.

"Cheer up, cheer up," whispered Ned Witlet to Miranda; "you're looking pale and ill."

A languid smile played across Miranda's beautiful features, as she replied faintly,—

"I believe it is the fault of my nature never to feel bold and confident, unless I am oppressed, or at war with some one. Surround me by friendly faces, let me hear kind voices making sweet music to my heart, and I know not why it is, but I then always wish for tears to relieve my sinking spirits."

"The feeling is natural."

"And yet I ought to be happy now—very, very happy."

"And I too," said Witlet, " for at a public part of the day, when I should not have advised your coming through the streets, I think we have scccceeded in doing so in perfect safety."

This short conversation, spoken in a gentle voice, took place in far less time than it takes us to record it, and it was uninterrupted by Mrs. Howell, who was too intent upon gazing upon the beautiful face of Miranda, to attend to anything Witlet might be saying.

The widow was one of those rare females who can bear to look on female loveliness without a pang of envy, and she received real pleasure from the contemplation of the child-like beauty of Miranda, mingled as it was with an expression of nobility of soul as rare as it is admirable.

"My dear young lady," she said, " you're Miss Rankley. I have heard sufficient of you, to have got up a notion of you in my own mind, and you are very much like that notion, only much more beautiful. Trust all to Heaven, my dear young lady, and in the end, innocence must prevail."

"There was a time," said Miranda, " when to have heard words of kindness such as these being spoken to me in my forlorn and calamitous state would have brought the ready tears to my eyes; but I have not wept since—since—my poor father became no more."

"Now, my dear girl," said the widow, " do not distress yourself by mournful recollections. You have come here to have an uninterrupted and happy interview with one, of whom it is no slight praise to say, I think him deserving of you."

"Mrs. Howell," said Witlet, for he saw that Miranda was distressed, and scarcely knew what to reply, " Mrs. Howell, I will leave Miss Rankley here until sunset, if you please, for it has become necessary for me to seek another lodging for her."

"Would to Heaven," said Mrs. Howell, " she could stay here altogether, but I quite understand how dangerous it would be. Why, bless you, my dear, with your sweet innocent face, you would soon be the talk of the whole street, and then it might get to ears that we specially wish to keep it from."

"I am quite convinced," said Miranda; "quite—quite—and very thankful for all the kindness which is being shewn me."

"Miss Rankley," said Ned Witlet, " by Heavens, if I thought the world was so bad, as not to contain many hearts that would truly sympathise with you, and admire your courageous conduct, I would not care how soon I left it. I will anticipate no danger while I am gone ; farewell, and Heaven protect you."

Ned Witlet left the house, and Mrs. Howell, after kindly assisting Miranda to take off her bonnet and shawl, seated her upon a sofa, and after a few more gentle words, left the room. Miranda's heart told her it was to fetch Percy, and such was the excitement of her feelings, that for a moment every object swam before her. Her heart beat with tumultuous emotion, as she sat with her eyes fixed on the door, in a state of breathless agitation.

The door opened, and Bernard Varley, the author of all her misfortunes, stood with the smile of a fiend upon the threshold.

CHAPTER CXXV.

VARLEY'S PROPOSAL.—DANGER THICKENS.—THE MELLEE AND THE SEARCH FOR ROWLAND.

To describe the surprise, mingled with terror, of Miranda, at the sudden and inexplicable appearance of Bernard Varley in the parlour of the widow, would be a hopeless task ; for a moment she actually doubted the evidence of her own senses, and she would have as little expected to have seen the apparition of some one who had been in life a thousand years before, at that moment, and in that place, as the man who had wrought her so much woe, and who still seemed following her with a determination and malice perfectly fiend-like.

An utter prostration of strength came over her. She felt like one afflicted by a night-mare, who tries to scream, but finds scarcely voice enough to utter the faintest sigh. The various objects in the parlour seemed to whirl before her eyes, as if instinct with life ; by a strong effort, however, she kept herself from fainting, and then her frame slowly recovered from the shock it had received, and she became assured of the reality of the appearance before her.

It was Bernard Varley; there could be no mistaking that ferocious, yet pale and haggard countenance, and those dark lustrous eyes that were bent upon her with a wild and fearful gaze, that seemed not of the earth.

Slowly he paced into the room, closing the door behind him, and turning the key in the lock. He stood within a few paces of her, but still he spoke not, nor could she command voice enough to call for help in that frightful emergency. He folded his arms across his breast, and gazed with a deep earnestness in her face, as if it were a feast even to his eyes, to look again upon so much loveliness.

When he did speak, it was in hoarse, low, guttural tones, as if he were making an effort to be calm, whilst a tempest of passion was raging in his breast.

"Miranda Rankley," he said, and slowly drawing the watch from his pocket, he held the dial before her face; "Miranda Rankley, do you note the hour."

He pressed a spring, and with a sweet silvery tone, so much at variance with his own voice, and the harshness of his general demeanour, that Miranda might well shudder and start at the contrast, the repeater struck twelve, then the three-quarters past were proclaimed by the fairy-like bell within that rich encasement.

"Do you note the hour?" said Bernard Varley. "Miranda Rankley, do you note the hour?"

A cold chill struck to the heart of Miranda ; she felt as if something was about to happen, yet transcending all the miseries she had already gone through, a blight seemed to have fallen upon her mind—she could see nothing but the dial of that watch—hear nothing but the echo of soft sounds, that had proclaimed the lapse of time.

" 'Tis well," said Bernard Varley, " you feel my power ; that power you have mocked at, Miranda Rankley—'tis reached a fearful height, a height only equalled by yours—the life of Rowland Percy is in my hands. Miranda Rankley, it is likewise in yours ; we two can only save or destroy him."

Miranda sprung to her feet, the spell that entranced her faculties seemed broken.

" Help, help !" she cried. " Rowland, Rowland, help !"

" Ah, ah !" laughed Bernard Varley ; " you but expedite the doom you may avert. This is no child's play, no affectation of doing something which will fail in its execution, Miranda Rankley ; my information is ample—Rowland Percy is concealed in this house, the door is watched by an emissary of mine. At one o'clock, officers will be prepared for his apprehension ; he cannot, cannot escape, unless—aye, unless—do you note the time, Miranda Rankley? do you note the time ?"

A fearful thought rushed across Miranda's mind ; it was, that poor Rowland had been betrayed by the widow, and that, innocent though he was, that he had been sacrificed for money. Hope seemed extinguished for ever, and the appalling power of Bernard Varley rose giant-like before her imagination, blasting, for a time, her faculties by its greatness. With frightful rapidity her mind ran over all the circumstances of her position, and that process only served to augment her despair, which was sufficently depicted in her countenance.

" Monster," she gasped, " is your soul dead to every spark of feeling ? Bernard Varley, have you no compunctions for the past, that will stay now your murderous hand ?"

" But ten minutes remain," said Bernard Varley. " Do you note the hour ? I tell you again his life is in my own hands. Give me, even now, your sacred promise, in the name of that Heaven which I know you hold so sacred, to become my wife, and I myself will open the door of this house, allowing Rowland Percy freely to walk forth, as well as providing him with ample means—carriages— horses, and faithful attendants, to convey him to the-sea coast, where he may embark on board a vessel of my own, and ensure his safety. On the other hand there is an ignominious death, the writhings of a criminal at his execution, and he will be heralded to another world amid the shouts and execrations of all who witness the painful and horrible death of the murderer ! Miranda Rankley do you note the time ? "

Miranda clasped her hands.

" Heaven," she said, " has boundless mercy yet."

" You consent ? " cried Varley, " you consent ? "

" Never ! "

The handle of the door was now turned by some one from without, and the voice of Rowland cried :—

" Miranda—Miranda ! "

" Rowland ! " she cried, " save yourself ! Fly—fly—fly—Rowland—fly "

" Ah ! ah ! ah ! " said Varley, " for but one kiss from those pouting lips I will give him a chance even to the street, and yet not fear to hunt him down. Miranda Rankley, are you mad in your wild obstinacy ? his death and the last shriek of his agony lie heavy upon your head."

" Fly—Rowland—fly ! "

A heavy knock on the street-door at this moment resounded through the passage.

" You note the time—you note the time ! " cried Bernard Varley. Truly, they are more than punctual. You might have saved him, Miranda, but now—"

" Miranda—Miranda," cried the voice of Rowland again ; " what is the meaning of this ? Who is with you ? "

" Ask not, but fly, Rowland, fly !" shrieked Miranda."

"'Tis I, Varley," cried the villain, in a deep hoarse tone.

Bang went the knocker again, at the same moment that Rowland made a violent but ineffectual effort to burst open the door of the room.

"Even yet—even yet," said Varley, seizing Miranda so forcibly by the wrist that he left the mark of his fingers upon her fair skin ; "even yet I can save him, if you consent. These are London officers, who know him not—and there is no one who can identify him but myself. Will you swear, by all that you hold sacred, to be mine?"

Bang went the parlour door into fragments, and Mr. Jones rolled on to the floor as if he were performing a somerset, by the suddenness of his entrance.

"Wery good," he said, as, without rising, he took hold of Varley by the ankles, and brought him down on his back, with such a smack that it was enough to dislocate every bone in his body, not to speak of his head coming in contact with the fender, which it actually bent.

"Rowland!" cried Miranda, and in another moment she was in her lover's arms ; tearing herself then from his embrace, she cried, in almost inarticulate accents:—

"Save yourself, save yourself, Rowland ! Fly—fly—lose not a moment ! They—they are coming—the officers—the officers. Fly, Rowland, fly ! I implore—I entreat—God of Heaven, Rowland. Fly,—fly ! "

"Wery good advice," said Jones, "but don't think of flying by the front door, for I'm blest if there isn't that immortal thief Twitter on the spy, and any fool can cry ' stop him.' Be quiet, will yer?"

This last remark was addressed to Varley, and accompanied by such a punch on the jaw, that, added to the blow he had received on the back of the head it quite bewildered him. "Cuss you," added Jones, " I've thought of a scheme."

Turning Varley upon his face, he sat down on the middle of his back, and Mr. Jones being no trifling weight, Varley was as effectually pinned down as a grasshopper, with a pin through his entrails, in the cabinet of an entomologist.

"Rowland, why delay a moment?" still cried Miranda. "Surely there must be some means of escape, so that you may fly from here. You've been betrayed—you've been betrayed."

"As Heaven is my judge, not by me," said Mrs. Howell, wringing her hands, and weeping bitterly.

"Gracious Heavens!" cried Rowland, "what can I do? I am helpless, save this last, only friend ; in life they shall not take me."

He drew a pistol from his pocket, and at the same moment a voice shouted through the key-hole of the door:—

"Open, open; 'tis I, Ned Witlet. For God's sake open."

Rowland himslef opened the door, and Ned Witlet, without a moment's pause, dragged his arm within his, saying:

"Away—away; come with me this instant. This house is watched, but I believe by but one spy. I have just knocked down Samuel Twitter, on the other side of the way, and while he lies insensible you may escape."

"Bravo !" said Jones, "here's t'other beauty ; he's wriggling about like a blessed old snake, but it's no go. Be quiet, will yer? "

Jones took hold of the hair of Varley's head behind, and gave his nose two hard jobs against the floor, which appeared to have the desired effect, for Varley became quite quiet, and, in fact, he was insensible for some short time.

Ned Witlet's conduct now became rather of a contradictory character, for after dragging Rowland Percy on to the step in the manner we have described, he as suddenly pulled him into the house again, banged the door shut, put up the chain, and bolted the two bolts with marvellous rapidity.

"You've been betrayed, Mr. Percy," he said. "Four Bow-street officers have but this moment turned the corner of the street. God help you, sir."

"Rowland—Rowland, my Rowland !" cried Miranda, as she flung herself upon his neck.

"If my last hour has come," said Rowland Percy, "I will meet it like a man. Farewell Miranda ; the Almighty shower his blessings on you. They may take me, but their triumph shall be a poor one, for it shall be over the lifeless, and not over the living."

"Walker," said Jones, "never say die. You are worth a dozen stiff 'uns yet. I say, Mother What'soname, don't be wringing your hands and turning on the main there; come and sit on this gentleman's back, while I makes myself a little more active, and if you've got such a thing as a carving fork, just hold that in your hand, and job it into him if he gets obstropulous. Is there a sky peeper atop of your roof."

"He means a trap-door;" said Witlet, "it is the only chance, poor though it be. We must not trust to the place of concealment you have in this house, Mrs. Howell; whoever has betrayed Mr. Percy's residence here, is most probably aware of that likewise—there—"

A loud rat-tat at the door announced the arrival of the officers.

"Vy don't yer ring?" said Jones, "we never hears knocks here. Neddy, look arter affairs down here, while Mr. Percy and me tries what we can do through the trap."

"There is one," said Mrs. Howell. "Heaven speed you."

"Then go Jones," said Witlet; "do the best you can, and I will keep the officers out of the house for some time at least."

Jones sprung to his feet; and Varley, with a deep groan, rolled over on to his back, but Witlet took some cord from his pocket, and tied his hands, so that he could make no use of them; and from the shock that he had received in his fall, he was too confused to feel the necessity for calling out for help.

Another loud appeal to the knocker, announced the impatience of the officers; and, after a few kind words, Miranda and Rowland parted again, in circumstances of greater trouble and danger, probably, than they had ever experienced before.

"Come all into the parlour," said Witlet, "and we will leave these gentlemen to get in outside as best they may. You, Miss Miranda, they will not interfere with. If I escape, which I intend trying, although the chance is small, I will meet you to-night, at nine o'clock, in Whitehall, opposite the Horse Guards; you can easily inquire your way, but on your road there, be careful you are not watched. Go down some of the streets in the Strand, get in to a boat and cross the river; take a coach, then, on the other side, and drive to Whitehall, and be sure you are not observed. Here is money. And now, Mrs. Howell, remember you know nothing about Mr. Percy, but merely had a young man lodging here, whose name you believe to be Smith, and that just now you can't open the door to the officers because you are coerced by me."

The knocking at the door now became perfectly furious; so noisy, in fact, as to drown all further conversation. Poor Miranda sat down, looking as pale as one newly risen from the dead, while Bernard Varley looked vacantly around him like a man half asleep, and not able to distinguish realities from the visions of his sleep.

With amazing strength and quickness Ned Witlet drew some heavy pieces of furniture to block up the doorway, and constructed a very tolerable barricade. He then darkened the room by drawing the curtains close; and scarcely were these completed, when a harsh grating noise at the outer door proclaimed that it was being forced from its hinges.

"They are using crow-bars," said Ned Witlet; "but yet it will be some time before they can gain an entrance, and moments are like drops of blood to Mr. Percy."

CHAPTER CXXVI.

THE ESCAPE OF WITLET.—THE TRAP-DOOR IN THE ROOF.—JONES'S ADMIRABLE
SCHEME, AND TOTAL DEFEAT OF THE OFFICERS.

THE officers worked might and main to gain an entrance into the widow's house, for visions of the thirteen hundred pounds reward were floating across their imaginations, and they were not very scrupulous about breaking through a door, provided they could share so very desirable an amount among them.

The alarm in the street was tremendous, and a dense crowd was rapidly collecting. The rumour ran from mouth to mouth that a dreadful murder had been committed at the widow's, and the excitement was each moment on the increase, when the officers succeeded in dashing open the door and rushing into the passage.

The moment they did so Ned Witlet, without much noise, opened one of the parlour windows as far as it would go, and stood upon the ledge, in a crouching attitude ; it looked a fearful leap to clear the area-rails, but to hesitate was not a part of Witlet's nature, and before a cry of alarm could arise from the multitude, he took the spring, and alighted safely upon the pavement.

His danger, however, was not over ; for, before he could advance above half-a-dozen steps, he was collared by several of the mob, who, seeing him make such a singular exit from the house, at once believed him to be the person whom the officers were in pursuit of.

"Thank you," said Witlet, calmly, "but you are mistaken, friends. Catch the real man, if you please, but don't impede me. We want more force, and I must be off to Bow-street as fast as possible."

As he spoke he took from his pocket the constable's staff he had wrested from the officer in the back passage in the Star and Tinder-box.

"Hurrah !" shouted the mob, as they let him go. "Be off with yer. We'll take care nobody gets out. Who's murdered ?"

"A woman and six children," said Witlet ; "and added to it, is the most desperate swindle ever conceived."

In a moment or two he was out of sight, and the officers, little suspecting that both their victims had escaped them, placed one of them as a sentinel upon the door-mat, whilst the others commenced busily removing the articles of furniture with which Witlet had barricaded the parlour.

This was soon accomplished, as, of course, there was no resistance offered from the inside, and, to the disappointment of the officers, they at first saw no persons but Mrs. Howell and Miranda. In a moment, however, they pounced upon Varley, who, having a chair overturned upon him, they thought was one of their prisoners, making an insane and stupid attempt to conceal himself.

He was recognized, however, the moment they had raised him to his feet, for there was not one of the principal officers of Bow-street that Varley had not himself seen and conversed with upon the subject of Rowland Percy's apprehension.

"Mr. Varley," cried one, "is it you, sir ?"

Varley glared about him like a madman, and then espying Miranda, he cried, in hoarse and terrible accents—

"Tremble, Miranda Rankley, for this day's work shall be at your door, you are in my power, if others have escaped. Search the house—d————n ! Search the house. Leave not a hole or corner unexplored. A hundred pounds on the spot to him who first lays hands on the convicted murderer, or any of his associates. I—I—I—curses on them all—they've nearly killed me !"

He reeled and sunk into a chair as he spoke, for his brain was much bewildered by the usage he had received ; and his sudden energy was but the result of a burst of passion, which had lent him a momentary strength.

"You hear that man ?" said Miranda Rankley, appealing to the officers. "I charge you to take notice of the threats he makes use of towards me, as I may choose to make them a subject of inquiry. Bernard Varley, with indignation and contempt I defy you! Heaven preserve Rowland Percy from your machinations."

The officers knew not what to make of this strangely recriminatory conversation; and having satisfied themselves that neither of the men they came to seek were then in the parlour, they hastily proceeded to search the house; and their information must have been tolerably correct, for they at once proceeded to the part of

ROWLAND AND WITLET INFORMED OF THE REWARD BY THE LANDLORD.

the room above them where was the sliding panel, which, after some difficulty they succeeded in opening, although, to their great chagrin, they found nothing but one old chair, which just fitted into the narrow space between the two walls.

"Here's the nest," said one, "but the bird's flown—we are done as safe as ninepence, and I'll be hanged if I didn't think we should be, whenever I heard the Slashing Squire had anything to do with the business—he's an out-and-out fellow that—I've often told Sir Richard that he'd make a charming officer."

No 62.

"Never despair," said another; "let's search the house thoroughly; hilloa what the devil 's this ?'"

Lying upon the stairs leading to the upper story, was a small step-ladder, and the officers were too used to escapes of all kinds not to feel at once assured that it had been used in reaching a trap-door at the top of the house.

"We have him now—we have him now," they cried, and upon arriving at the head of the staircase, they saw that the trap-door admitted a beam of light, bearing every evidence of having been recently disturbed. They immediately placed the step-ladder against the opening, and felt quite certain they should find those they sought on the roof of the house. They all three ascended with great rapidity.

No sooner had the last man disappeared through the narrow opening, than Jones walked out from the front attic, and ascending the ladder, he, without a word, shut the trap-door, and firmly bolted it within.

"Just wait there till you are wanted, my tulips," he remarked ; "it's a fine airy situation, and will do you a vorld of good—you can make speeches to the mob from the blessed parapet, for as these ere houses are built, blow me if you can get into any of the attic windows—out-an-out knowing blades these ere officers is, to be sure. Come along, Mr. Percy, but mind your eye, for there's one on 'em down stairs, seeing as there's only three been so obliging as to get on to the roof."

Rowland Percy, with a pistol in his hand, appeared from the attic.

"Escape must be impossible—save yourself, Jones, and risk no more on my account."

"Gammon," said Jones. "Stow that ere guffery and foller on—never say die —I tells yer what you do, Mr. Percy ; walk down to the first floor, and just stay in the room till we sees what will happen next."

"I will obey your directions, although hopeless ;" and the two descended the staircase together.

The street-door was not broken entirely off its hinges, and the officer who was left in guard of it thought it his wisest plan to shut it as close as he could, so that if any one was to attempt to rush past him, their manœuvre would be foiled, and there he stood with his staff in his hand looking as vigilant as half a dozen officers rolled into one, reckoning up in his own mind what a windfall his share in the rewards would be, and cursing his luck for not having a chance of the hundred pounds down upon the nail in addition.

Mr. Jones and Percy of course reached the landing without any hindrance.

"Just step into the back-room for a moment," said Jones, " it's hit, or miss."

Rowland obeyed him, and then Jones took a sudden run about half way down the staircase, when he pretended to see the officer for the first time, and exclaiming, "Lor, I'm nabbed !" he ran up again.

Now, if Bernard Varley had not been so ready with the offer of his hundred pounds, in addition to the high rewards already heaped upon poor Rowland Percy's head, the officer would in all likelihood have remained where he was, with a perfect confidence of his companions above stairs catching the man who had so suddenly appeared, and run off again ; but that hundred pounds did the business, and he darted up the stairs after Jones like lightning, a measure which Mr. Jones was in his own mind devoutly wishing and expecting.

"Come, my fine fellow," cried the officer, rushing into the room after him, "no nonsense."

"Devil a bit," said Jones, as, stepping from behind the door he dealt him such a tremendous facer, that the officer reeled again. The advantage of a first blow between two strong men is immense, and in this case it was everything, for Jones took care to follow it up by another, which he denominated "a stunner," that sent the officer sprawling, and deprived him of all sense and consciousness.

"That'll do," said Jones ; "there's a muff ; Mr. Percy, now for it—a clear stage and no favour. I think we've nothing to do but to walk out, take it easy, and nobody will suspect us—where the deuce is your hat ?"

"I really don't know," said Rowland.

"Then take this ere," remarked Jones, pointing to the officer's, which had rolled into the landing. "Yet, stop a minute, there's such a blessed crowd in the street, that some officious fellow will be stopping us—I have thought of a move."

He possessed himself in a moment of the officer's staff, and taking Rowland in a very scientific manner by the collar, he added,—

"Now, come on—mind, you are in custody."

When they reached the door in this manner, there was such a shout from the crowd, that Rowland involuntarily shrunk back for a moment, but Jones pulled him down the steps, saying,—"Kim on, yer warmint, no shying," and he held the staff in a very threatening manner close to Rowland's nose, to the immense delight of the mob, who cheered again vociferously.

It was pleasant to see the three officers on the roof making what appeared to be from their gestures highly inflammatory speeches to the mob, scarcely a word of which, however, was heard by those below, in consequence of the noise in the street.

"A coach—a coach!" cried Jones; "a tanner for a coach—now, yer cripples."

Nearly one-half of the mob ran for a coach, while the remainder set up a tremendious hoot of execration at Rowland, the supposed murderer of the woman and six children, and Jones kept making him wink again by flourishing the constable's staff in his face.

Before the coach arrived, a very fat man, in a copious prespiration, bustled on to the step of the door, carrying in his hand a huge painted constable's staff.

"Hilloa! have you caught the willain? I'm a constable in my own right, and landlord of the Magpie and stump. Have yer cotched the willain?"

"Yes, little 'un," said Jones; "will you lend us your vescoat for a great coat—how are you off for tallow—do you spit on 'em when you wants to greese yer hinges?"

The constable in his own right looked rather amazed at this sally, which greatly amused the mob, who thought Jones a most capital fellow and most enterprising officer.

One of the officers on the roof now raised his voice to an extraordinary pitch, so that the people below heard the words,—"Somebody's bolted——" but nothing else.

"Well," said Jones, looking up, "why don't you bolt arter 'em instead of speechifying up there. Pretty gem'mens you is. Just stoop over, and I'll give you a leg down."

"The trap!" shouted one of the officers, swinging his arms about like the sails of a windmill.

"Wery good," said Jones; "they've found a trap up there—there's a discovery; they only want a bat, and either of them's capable of getting up a ball at a moment's notice."

At this moment, escorted by an immense crowd, as if it had been some wonderful natural curiosity, the hackney-coach arrived.

"Now, Jarvy," said Jones, "just crawl down with all them ere wonderful coats of yourn, and open the door—this chap's like an eel as I've got hold on."

"Stop the murderer!" shouted one of the officers from the roof of the house, getting very red in the face from the exertion, and to which Mr. Jones replied with such an admirable imitation of the braying of an ass, that the mob would have let off any murderer whatever in its intense satisfaction.

In their rage, the officers took the ill-advised step of throwing their hats upon the heads of the mob, which of course produced a retaliation in the shape of stones, so that in a few moments they were forced to disappear altogether, two of the hiding behind the chimney-pots, and the third lying flat in the gutter.

"Vere to?" said the coachman, as he banged the door.

"To Bow-street," said Jones, and off they went amid the cheers of the assembled multitude.

CHAPTER CXXVII.

ROWLAND PERCY'S PLACE OF REFUGE.—THE SECOND FLOOR OF THE STAR AND
TINDER-BOX, DRURY-LANE.

WHEN the hackney-coach containing Percy and Jones had got thoroughly clear
of the mob, and about half way to Bow-street, the latter pulled the check-string,
and when the coachman stopped and looked inquiringly through one of the glasses,
Jones said,—

"We won't trouble you to go quite so far, old brick. Charge your full fare,
and we'll get out here."

This was an arrangement the coachman was not at all likely to object to, and
he accordingly rolled off his box and opened the coach-door, permitting, if he had
but known it, thirteen hundred pounds to slip through his fingers as comfortable
as possible; but Providence was merciful, and the jarvey never did know it, or,
Heaven knows what desperate act he might have committed upon the horror of
achieving such a loss.

Thus, then, was the hunted and persecuted Percy in the streets of London—
free, certainly, but still surrounded by dangers—dependent for food, and shelter,
and sympathy, upon strangers, and such a price set upon his capture, that it would
have tempted many a sleek, well-fed highly moral man in the world's opinion, to
have surrendered him to death. But such men as Jones and Witlet certainly do
not set that high and startling value upon money that many persons do. They
are accustomed to the extremes of affluence and poverty; they make no calculations for the future; they are not hoarding for this or that particular object, and
the temptation to betray such a man for money certainly did not present itself
very strongly to either of them, for, with much less violence to their feelings, they
knew not the hour that they might possess themselves of a much larger sum in
what they considered quite a legitimate way,

"Vell," said Jones, "here we is. Now I tells you what, Mr. Percy, it strikes
me as the safest place you can go to now, is the Star and Tinder-box. It's
been out-and-out rummaged by the officers, and they have made up their minds
that you are not there. Give them the double, say I, and go there now. The
nearer to the church, they say, the further from the great Being what rules
everything; and if a gentleman of the road, or a cracksman wants to hide, I am
convinced it ought to be very near Bow-street."

"Ignorant of London, as I am," said Rowland Percy, "and utterly
destitute of resources, I am but too thankful to you that you will guide my
steps."

"Werry good," said Jones; "but don't guve up just yet. It's a werry extensive out of town thoroughfare as hasn't a turning; and some of these ere days it
will be Percy's riz and Varley's fell."

"This is but a sad life to lead," said Rowland, mournfully. "If poor Miranda
and I could leave England, perhaps, after all, it would be our best plan. By
the exercise of our unfettered industry in some foreign land, we should no
longer be a burden upon those kind friends who have already done so much
for us."

"Burden be bothered," said Jones. "This here's the state of the case.
Society sarves you out, and hunts you about, here and there, and around
and about, just like a dog in a fair, because they fell into a mistake that you
smothered an old gentleman. Now that ere is a blunder of society, 'cause you
knows you didn't."

"As Heaven is my judge, I am innocent."

"Stow that, I knows it. Well, in course, if individuals makes blunders, they
has to pay for 'em; so as society won't let you get your living, Neddy and I mean
to make 'em keep you. Lor bless you, two or three good family jobs will keep

us all like game cocks for a twelvemonth ; but here we are in Holborn. Just step out, and we'll be housed in the Star and Tinder-box in something under ten minutes."

How would Rowland Percy, a few short years before, have scorned, as an affront upon his understanding, a prophecy that he would have been indebted for his means of existence to the indiscriminate depredations of a housebreaker or a highwayman ; and yet circumstances were now such, that he could almost invent excuses to himself for so doing : and, at all events, if he had rejected such aid, he must have become a beggar in the public streets, and, most probably, a far greater social evil would have been perpetrated by his apprehension and execution upon a charge of which he was innocent.

Unwelcome to his mind, and startling to all his previous notions as was the proposition, he began almost to think with Jones and Witlet, that criminality was scarcely anything of itself, but a circumstance altogether dependent upon other circumstances for its complexion.

Rowland Percy, however, required the lesson he was receiving in the rude school of adversity before such a sentiment could have entered into his brain ; but now he said to himself,—

"If once the cloud which hangs over me and my fortunes should dissipate, and I should once more attain that level in society from which I have been so roughly driven, I shall look with a kindlier eye upon human frailties, and that sad class of humanity called criminal by its fellows ; I shall ever be tempted to look deeper than the act itself, and endeavour to ascertain what circumstances have given rise to it, always remembering that in my own misfortunes the principal sympathy I ever met with was from persons amenable to the laws, and that every piece of bread I put into my mouth was part of the produce of a robbery."

The Star and Tinder-box was reached some minutes before the time Jones had mentioned, and Jones conducted Rowland Percy through the narrow back entrance which terminated at the door leading into the landlord's little private room behind the bar, at which he gave a peculiar knock, which was immediately answered with the loudly expressed question of,—

"Hilloa ! what's the dodge ?"

"The old caper," said Jones.

"I have a gentleman's fancy, fair and free ;
The Star and Tinder-box does for me,
When I'm out on a rollicking, roaring spree.
Tooraloo, slash away."

The door was opened, and the landlord, shading his eyes with his hands said,—

"Walker's the dodge for five minutes."

"Scooped out ?" said Jones.

"Tow-row," said the landlord, and the door was immediately shut.

"Will he not admit us ?" whispered Rowland.

"Yes, suttenly ; but did'nt you hear him? He said it wasn't safe for five minutes, cos somebody was lounging about the bar as he did'nt know, but rather suspected."

"Oh," said Rowland, "I certainly did not understand the singular little bit of dialogue in which you have been indulging."

"Defects in the edication," said Jones, "isn't people's own faults. If you doesn't understand all that the English langivedge can do, it's yer broughtins up, and not you, that should have a hit in the eye for that ere neglect."

"Flicks, away," said the landlord, opening the door.

"Crush the downy," said Jones, and taking hold of Rowland by the arm, he led him into the little bar parlour, from which the landlord immediately opened another door, leading to a further room, of tolerably ample dimensions, which from the general decorations and furniture, was evidently used for what are called convivial purposes, although at that time of the day it was completely empty, and the landlord further secured it from interruption by locking a door on the inside, which led into the passage, and was the usual entrance; after which, turning to Jones and Percy, he said,—

"What's the row now?"

" You knows him?" said Jones, pointing to Percy.

" I does," said the landlord. " That is Mr. Percy. They've put a good price upon you, sir, and, upon my word, I think it's imprudent of you to be walking about in this way."

"In course it is," said Jones; " but what's a chap to do when he's bowled out? The hawks have been down upon him ; he was as near nabbed as possible, and the last nest is a d—d deal too hot to hold him. Now, there's been a thorough hunt in every hole and corner of the Star and Tinder-box, so it strikes me now outrageous forcible, that this is his safest place."

" It's hard to say," replied the landlord , but if you like to stay here, we'll do the best we can for you, and, for Ned Witlet's sake, you shall be as welcome as flowers in May."

"Hasn't Neddy been here?"

" No."

" Then he will be soon, for he's had to make an extraordinary cut of it himself. The grabs are sharp after him, and he'll have to make up his mind uncommon clear what he's going to do next."

"In truth as far as I am concerned," answered Percy, in answer to the land-lord, " I'm thankful for any shelter, proscribed and hunted as I am. If you'll permit me to remain here until I decide upon some line of conduct, I shall be your debtor for a great kindness."

- " Oh, never think of that," said the landlord; " it's quite understood among all of us that you didn't do the murder. We decide upon those things much better than juries, and we all of us feel as certain that Bernard Varley murdered Sir George Rankley, as if we had seen him do it."

"In truth, your opinion coincides with my own," said Percy, " and I am scarcely more assured of my own innocence, than I am of his guilt. Heaven help the innocent Miranda, and save her from his machinations."

" Werry good," said Jones ; " and now let's come up stairs, for that's the place to hide in."

The second floor of the Star and Tinder-box consisted of a number of rooms connected with each other by such a quantity of doors, that had it not possessed numerous hiding-places, in the shape of curious closets and cupboards, a more admirable place to play at hide-and seek could scarcely have been found ; and it would require some one exceedingly intimate with the localities, to run the slightest chance of successfully pursuing any one through such a labyrinth.

" Now," said the landlord, turning to Rowland, " we've been searched here once, and we may be again. I can't put you into a hiding-place where you can lay down on your back, and take your chance to see if you are found. We never tried to get up such a thing here, and if we had I don't think we could have done it ; yet, notwithstanding all that, many a chap that's been hard pushed has held out for weeks together in this second floor."

" Ah, I knows it," said Jones ; " there was Conkey Joe as stopped some-where by Kennington, a parson feller, as they calls a wicker, and took nigh a thousand pounds out of his pocket, besides putting him in what they call bodily fear. Well, Mr. Percy, this here wicker got wicious, and arter cussing Conkey Joe as none but a wicker could cuss him, he offers five hundred pound to any one who could grab him. Well, Conkey Joe was hard pushed, and he comes here, and the grabs searched this here floor three times, and went into every hole and corner of it, but Conkey Joe gave them the go-by."

" So he did !" said the landlord ; " so he did ; and you must do it the same way, or no ways at all, Mr. Percy."

" What way's that ?"

" Why, the rooms go in and out of each other curious, and the only way was first of all, to get into a cupboard of one of the further ones, and wait there till they have poked their noses into some of the outer ones; the caper then is, to know the rooms well, and double upon the officers as they are going through them, by which means you get into one of the cupboards they have searched, where they are not likely to look again."

"That's the way Conkey Joe did it," said Jones; "three times the officers passed him in a cupboard at the head of the stairs, the door of which he left ajar, but then they knowed they looked into it afore, and never dreamed of wasting time by a second search."

".Then," said Rowland, " I must run that risk at present, or at all events until I see my friend Witlet, under whose guidance I have placed myself, and upon whose judgment I have so firm and entire reliance."

."Come on then," said the landlord; " keep your eyes about you, and I'll walk you through the rooms to show you how you may manage the matter should there be occasion for it."

Rowland saw that the scheme was practicable, although certainly attended with great risks. He followed the landlord through the various apartments, taking the most careful notice of each, and as he did so, he was perfectly amazed at the multitude of cupboards and little secret places with which that floor abounded.

"No one comes up here," said the landlord, "and although there are several bed-rooms here, as you perceive, we do not let any of them. This floor is especially kept for private use, and I only hope it may serve your turn as well as it has others."

"Mind," said Jones, "if you should be forced to come the double upon the grabs here, take off your shoes, and slip along without them, for the least sound would be ekal to your death-warrant."

" I shall be very cautious," replied Rowland, " but I do not believe I shall be here long. It seems to be my fate to be hunted from place to place; and since I have left York I have had so many hair-breadth escapes that I believe I am almost getting reckless, and care not what I do."

"Reckless—nonsense," cried Jones; " recollect your young woman, and if you don't care for yourself, keep up a stout heart for her sake."

"Bah," said the landlord, " people with ropes round their necks shouldn't think about young women."

"Don't be making yourself a ass now," said Jones, "by talking about what you don't understand. You knows nothing about it, so jest hold yer mag. As for me, I shall wait here till Neddy Witlet comes, which won't be long, I guess. I do long to know from somebody how them ere fellows got off the roof, and I believe I must make an expedition to-night to Somers-town to find out the {blessed particulars. Oh, that was a go! I think I sees 'em now a preaching from that ere blessed parapet, and the out an-out congregation pelting them with stones like mad. Then there was the feller, too, that took care of the street-door, and thought himself so cunning.—Lor bless us, some people is so very green!"

The tinkling of a little bell on the landing stopped Mr. Jones in his felicitations, and the landlord immediately said,—

" I am wanted below. Mr. Percy, I must leave you to take care of yourself; only if you should have any unwelcome visitors, I'll take good care to let you know in time."

CHAPTER CXXVIII.

MIRANDA'S ESCAPE FROM VARLEY.—MOB SYMPATHIES AND THEIR RESULTS.—A DSEPERATE CONFLICT

IT was some time after Jones and Percy had left Mrs. Howell's house that the officers got liberated from their disagreeable position on the roof, which chivalrous feat was executed by the fat landlord of the Magpie and Stump, who boasted so much of being a constable in his own right, and who had been so very unceremoniously put down by Jones; they then pretty accurately guessed the state of things below, and having learned from their stupified comrade, who was lying with a most dolorous aspect where Jones had thrown him, what had happened, as far as he was concerned, they gave up the affair, for the time being, as hopeless, feeling all the intense mortification of men who have allowed themselves to be thoroughly outwitted in quite a professional matter, and with the additional aggravation, as in the present case, that the reward of success would have been so great.

They looked at each other with the most ludicrous and dolorous expression.

"Well," said one, "we three have lost our hats, which I don't know what the devil induced us to throw among the mob; but we are better off than Godfrey, for he seems to have lost his nose, at least it won't be near the feature it was."

"D———n!" said Godfrey; "and my staff, too, for I can't find it anywhere; but we will have up the woman of the house as an accessory to the escape of our prisoners."

"There now, you spoke in a hurry," said the oldest and most experienced of the party; "if anybody had told me as I should have been such an ass as to get on the roof of a house without securing my retreat back again, I shouldn't have believed him. I did it, though, and there's an end of it. I knew we were done the moment I heard the bolt shot underneath. Now, take my advice; come away and don't say anything about the affair. We can plant a spy upon this house, and it's odd to me but something will come of it; but for my sake don't let it get wind that there's been such a regular do."

A moment's consideration convinced the others that that was the proper view of the subject, and although it diminished not a bit of their vexation, they acceded to the proposition, and walked in a body down the staircase, in order to put it in immediate execution.

It was some few minutes before the officers arrived at this sage conclusion, that Miranda thought she would leave the house, for the presence of Bernard Varley was a source of great annoyance to her; and although she despised him as much as her gentle heart could despise any one, yet she could not but look with fear upon the dark scowling countenance, and the wild, glaring eyes that were fixed upon her face.

Her slight movement towards the door, however, seemed to rouse Varley from the moody reverie into which he had fallen, and springing to his feet, he opposed her passage, saying,—

"No, Miranda; with pain, toil, trouble, and expense, I have sought you, and found you—we part not again thus easily."

"Murderer of my father!" cried Miranda, "what right have you to bar my progress?"

"Call me what you will," cried Varley, "heap whatever charges on my head your imagination may suggest to you—I have found you, Miranda, and I will cling to your footsteps as your very shadow."

"Villain!" said Miranda, "you dare not. I will pass, were you ten times the monster you are—raise against me your guilty hands if you dare."

"Hold!" cried Varley, "another step, and you are in my arms. Ah! ah! ah! Ample payment for all that I have suffered, to grasp, even for a moment, such peerless charms—advance, Miranda, advance. Welcome, welcome."

Miranda shrunk back instinctively, and at that moment the officers appeared in the passage.

"What's this?" cried one; "what's this?"

"I claim protection," cried Miranda, "against this man—this villain—Bernard Varley. You are men, and be you who or what you may, you cannot have such hearts as his. I claim your protection from him—why should he prevent me going forth?"

THE ARRIVAL OF THE MYSTERIOUS STRANGER AT THE OLD MOON.

"Oh, Mr. Varley, is it you?" said the senior officer. "What's the young woman done?"

"I answer no questions," answered Varley, furiously, "and ask them at your peril."

"Come, come," said the landlord of the Magpie and Stump, "what's the row, Mrs. Howell, what's the matter? You have your beer of me, Mrs. Howell, and I am sure you are quite a respectable woman,—ahem!—What's the matter, ma'am?"

No. 63.

"This young lady," said Mrs. Howell, "is a friend of mine, and on a visit to me; how this man," pointing to Varley, "came into my house, I know not, but surely I can make him leave it?"

"Ah! to be sure," said the landlord, "not a doubt—not a doubt. What a thing it is to have a constable in his own right in the street. A precious vagabond he looks—there's not a jury in England, Mrs. Howell, that wouldn't have him hung on the least suspicion. Count your silver spoons, Mrs. Howell, and if you find one missing, I'll take him into custody directly. Hilloa! hilloa!—no resistance —hilloa! hilloa!—somebody outside there, run to the Magpie and Stump, and tell my big pot-boy, Tom, to run here; he'll collar the warmint, while I make the end of my staff acquainted with his ribs."

"Miranda Rankley," said Varley, "while you stay here, I stay here— there," stepping aside, "your passage out is free, and I will follow you closely as your shadow."

"Gracious Heavens!" cried Miranda, "can I have no protection from this man?"

"Lots—lots," cried the constable in his own right, "we've no half measures here—everything tip-top with a head on it."

"Mr. Varley," said one of the officers, "I think you had better leave the young lady alone."

"You think," said Varley, with ineffable scorn, and crossing his arms upon his breast, he leaned back against the door-post with apparently quite a fixed determination of carrying out his declared intention.

"Come, toddle," cried the constable in his own right, flourishing his staff; "just move your long legs out of this place; we can't have you here, you know. Come, make a virtue of necessity, and go before my great pot-boy, Tom, comes. There's the Magpie and Stump at the end of the street—you look thirsty, why don't you go and stay there—Barclay and Perkins entire? Genuine wines, and neat compounds—the celebrated house for a glass of stout, and fine cordial gin— come, don't be a fool."

"You'll get yourself into a mess, master constable," said one of the officers; "you can't turn him out unless he's given in charge to you on suspicion of being here to commit a felony, or the occupier of the house attempts to do it, and he resists—that's the law."

"D—n the law," said the landlord; "what's the use of a constable?"

"None at all when he's such an overgrown porpoise as you are."

"Great God! where's my pot-boy, Tom?"

"And do you mean to tell me," said Mrs. Howell, "that I, a weak woman, am to risk a blow from that ruffian, in an attempt to put him from my house, while all you men stand by, and lend me no assistance?"

The officers looked at each other rather curiously at this appeal, and Miranda stepping forward, said firmly,—

"I will end this difficulty; I have heard that the slightest touch is sufficient to constitute an assault in law."

"Certainly," said the officers, "if Mr. Varley touches you, miss, you can give him in custody."

Miranda stepped boldly forward, and he shrunk back, and allowed her to pass. Varley then darted after her, and reached the step of the door at the same moment. Miranda was in despair; where to go, or what to do, she knew not; and there stood Varley, with his fierce sparkling eyes fixed upon her face, as if he would read her very soul, while a triumphant expression spread itself over his features, as he remarked the dilemma in which she was.

The crowd in the street was still very great, and Miranda's beauty became in a moment the theme of universal admiration. A sudden thought struck her that she might succeed in ridding herself of Varley by throwing herself upon public sympathy. A flush of colour gradually spread itself over her pale countenance, and her agitation as she began to speak, was painfully observable. The mob seemed intently interested in what she was about to say, and a dead silence ensued while she spoke the following words,—

"I am an orphan, and at this moment friendless; this man," pointing to Varley, "whom I believe, from my heart, to be the murderer of my father, threatens to pursue me wheresoever I may go, because I will not receive his fulsome addresses. Is there a father, a brother, or a pitying heart, in this crowd, that will step between me and this dreadful oppression?"

A great shout arose from the crowd, and Miranda descended on to the pavement. Varley made an effort to follow her, and then a tremendous rush took place, aided by a gigantic dustman, with a short pipe in his mouth, who pushed himself between Varley and Miranda, crying,—

"Take it easy, my little wench, take it easy; we'll soon clear out this ere bin. Well, my grand Turk, what now?"

Varley tried to dodge him, but the effort was in vain, and he only got his toes desperately trodden on by the dustman, while Miranda was each moment increasing her distance from the house, pushing through a lane of the people, who were cheering vociferously, while the constable in his own right was standing on his tip-toes, making a very elegant harangue, which nobody heard a word of, and getting dreadfully red in the face, from the stunning depth of the sentiments he was uttering.

Rage got the better of all discretion in the breast of Varley, and he seized the collar of the dustman with both hands, dashing the pipe out of his mouth in the effort. He might, however, as well have tried to shake a great tree by laying hold of its trunk, as to move the mass of bone and muscle he was opposed to; and he became soon painfully aware that dustmen wore dreadfully heavy shoes, for he received a kick on the shins that made him release his hold in a moment, and execute quite a dance in his agony, to, of course, the intense gratification of the mob, which unfeelingly laughed, like a great hyena.

Then the fat landlord, having arrived at a climax in his discourse, which might possibly call for such a movement, gave Varley a push behind, which sent him right among the mob, and then one bonnetted him, another kicked him, and another cuffed him. Several women, of more energy than gentility, scratched his face, and he was hustled about so dreadfully, that in the course of five minutes he had but half a coat and no cravat, and was in such a state of rags and bewilderment, that, although he fought like a maniac, he must soon have dropped from sheer exhaustion, had not the officers rushed to his rescue.

Four men acting together will do wonders, even in a crowd, which is always a disorganised body; and the officers succeeded in a very few minutes in reaching Bernard Varley; who, more dead than alive, fell into their arms, and was conveyed into the very Magpie and Stump he had been advised originally to go to by the fat landlord; an advice, could he have foreseen what was to have occurred, it would have been so much better to have followed than resisted.

As for the fat landlord himself, he was perfectly in his glory, and, assisted by the dustman, he scrambled on the top of a beer-barrel, and commenced a speech to the multitude, which would have done him very great credit any Wednesday evening at Conciliation Hall, just at present; only the landlord of the Magpie and Stump, was really not a long-headed selfish knave, but said what he said without attaching any particular meaning to it whatever.

CHAPTER CXXIX.

THE DEATH OF MR. PERCY.—OFFICIAL INDIFFERENCE, AND MIRANDA'S DESPAIR.

FOR the first time, Miranda found herself utterly alone in the streets of the mighty city, whither she had come so far for refuge from a series of persecutions unparalleled in private life, and the endurance of which, as she had endured them, should certainly make her a heroine of no ordinary character.

At first, of course, her feelings were of a pleasurable character, because sl was hastening away from the dreaded presence of Bernard Varley; and she h seen him in whose safety she was so deeply interested, escape from, perhaps tl greatest danger to which he had hitherto been exposed.

A pleasurable feeling of excitement pervaded her frame as she walked rapid through the streets, heedless of what direction she was taking, so long as sl increased her distance from Varley, who, she little suspected was receiving suc rough usage at the hands of the mob on which she had called for sympathy.

She walked onwards for about an hour, and then feeling wearied and exhauste she slackened her pace, and stood gazing with admiration not unmingled with aw at a massive and splendid cathedral, which spread itself out far and wide befoi her eyes.

To her left she saw, what she supposed to be, the river Thames, spanned by a ancient bridge, on which was such a mass of people and carriages, moving alon in regular order, that she could not but believe that some extraordinary circum stance had just occurred or was about to occur.

But most of all did that venerable pile with its splendid architecture attrac her steadfast gaze; and so little acquainted with London was Miranda Rankle that she could but hazard a guess that it was the ancient and noble Abbey c Westminster upon which she gazed.

A clock at the moment struck three, and with a sigh, she asked herself wha she was to do with herself for the six hours that were to intervene before sh could meet Witlet according to the appointment that he had made with her; the a sudden thought struck her, and she said,—

"Alas, alas! how one great anxiety blots out another from the memory. Ii all this terror and tumult connected with Rowland's escape, I had for a momen forgotten that there was one who claimed my tenderest sympathy. Poor Mr Percy is pining alone, sick and wretched, with none to whisper a word of consola tion to him, surrounded by strangers, whose attentions are those of cold custom I had nigh forgotten him, be it my task now, hopeless though it may appear, tc seek him in this gigantic city, and ascertain his true state; even now he may be accusing me of breaking the pledge which I had given to consider him as my second father, and to cling to him in sickness and in sorrow."

It was easy, however, to make a determination, whilst standing by Westmin· ster Abbey, to visit Mr. Percy, but not at all so easy to carry it into effect; and a moment's thought convinced Miranda that a hospital in London was rather a vague address, when so many of those establishments existed, and she blamed hersell much for not procuring the requisite information with regard to the precise name of the establishment to which he had been conveyed, of Witlet or Jones, at the widow's house; but then her mind had been so intensely occupied during that period, that indeed it was next to impossible she should be able to think of any· thing but Rowland Percy's excessive danger.

"Surely, however," she said to herself, "there cannot be so many hospitals in London, but what I may make a tour of them in the time I yet have, before it is necessary that I inquire my way to the place of meeting with Witlet."

The money which Witlet had handed to her she felt conscious would be more than sufficient to carry such an intention into effect; and her object now was to hire a coach, and desire to be driven to the nearest hospital, where, if unsuc· cessful, she could repair to another and another, until she found the object of her search.

There was a stand of vehicles where she paused to consider the solemn and beautiful abbey, so that she had no difficulty in procuring a hackney-coach; in fact, the difficulty was only to procure one, for there ensued quite a contest be· tween some half dozen, as to which should have the job, so that Miranda ran a risk of being almost torn to pieces by the rival candidates.

"Don't go into his wehicle, mum," said one; "it's quite celebrated for carry· ing corpses. Von of the cushings has the small-pox, and t'other the measles, mum. There's typhus fever among the straw."

"Oh, you're a nice warmint," said the man whose carriage was thus libelled "to begin to talk of coaches; yer knows quite well that the last lady as had the misfortune to get into your vehicle was eat up by fleas, and when yer came to open the door yer found nothing but her teeth, vich they couldn't bolt nohow."

A third candidate for Miranda's patronage succeeded in getting it, for he had the wisdom to say nothing, preferring deeds to words, and seizing Miranda by the arm, he pushed her into his coach before she was aware of where she was going.

"Vhere to, mum?" said a singular-looking man, with a wisp of straw round his hat, and attired in so strange a collection of cast off garments, most of which were too long for him, that he seemed as if he could have withdrawn his face at any time altogether, and hidden it among the mass of clothing, "vere to, mum? Please to remember the vaterman."

"Certainly," said Miranda. "I want to go to the nearest hospital. I want to discover some one who has been taken to an hospital."

"Yes, mum—remember the waterman."

"Certainly—certainly."

"Done again," said the man, as he slammed the door. "It's bad enough to be refused a copper, and not be made fun on into the bargain. Bill, you've got to go on your travels, a grand tour to the hospitals, in search of some sanguinary humbug, and it strikes me you've got a fat customer inside. I've had some gammon pushed down my throat instead of a copper. Suttenly be blowed! Some people's mean and wicious too. Suttenly—suttenly! Oh, cus yer, why didn't yer say yer would see me d—d first!"

The hackney-coach now made a violent demonstration of an intention to proceed, and after some formidable oscillations, it proceeded at a very leisurely pace up Parliament-street, the coachman fully making up his mind to visit the metropolitan hospitals in such order as should cover the greatest quantity of ground; but the schemes of mankind are sadly liable to derangement; and while he was congratulating himself upon nearly a day's work, the fates were so ordering it, that he should in the first instance proceed to St. Bartholomew's Hospital, where Mr. Percy really lay; and so great was his disappointment, when in answer to Miranda's inquiry of the porter, she was informed there was such a person in the establishment as Mr. Percy, that in a fit of absence of mind, he charged only his proper fare; and upon discovering how frightfully honest he had been, he drove to the next public house, and got drunk instanter, all of which terminated in the coach being taken to an uncomfortable place called the green-yard, because there's nothing green about it, and the coachman himself being provided for till next morning in the nearest watch-house.

The officials at hospitals are something like those at the War-office, of whom it is related, that during the long war with Buonaparte, they were so pestered with applications from the friends of soldiers, to learn what had become of them, that in some measure to stop the frighful increase of family sympathy, a shilling was charged for searching the return of killed and wounded, and the answer of the clerk, when the subject of inquiry happened to be in the former list, ran without the slightest variation of tone, or effort at punctuation, as follows—

"Dead a shilling no crying here."

The porter could give Miranda no information with respect to the condition of Mr. Percy. All he knew was from the list he had, that such a person had been received; but he told her she would soon find which ward he was in by walking into the building, and making inquiries of some of the nurses.

Miranda obeyed his directions, and meeting an elderly female, she inquired of her in which ward was placed Mr. Percy, an elderly gentleman, who had been recently brought into the hospital.

"Percy—Percy!" said the woman, "Oh, I recollect. Go through that door, and you will find him at the further end."

Miranda slightly paused at the door, but duty conquered her repugnance to enter that long apartment, where so many strange eyes from the occupants of various little truckle-beds were gazing upon her.

"This is not a time," she said, "for idle scruples. I have a duty to perform, and it shall be done."

At the further end of the room a screen was placed round a particular bed, and a chilly sensation came over the heart of Miranda. She knew not why, for she was new to the habits and customs of such a place. She could see Mr. Percy nowhere ; and accosting another female, she said, in tremulous accents—

"I have come to see Mr. Percy, who, I understand, is in this apartment."

"Oh ! a tall, elderly gentleman ?"

"Yes—yes."

"Really, I don't know, but I dare say he's dead."

"Dead !" cried Miranda, clasping her hands.

"Yes, Mr. Furgusson's just felt his feet, and says they are getting colder. He's behind that screen."

Miranda looked for a moment in the calm undisturbed countenance of the woman, and wondered at the want of feeling, that could so speak of a fellow-creature in his last moments. She then tottered to the bed, which was enclosed by what might appropriately be called "the death screen." She passed round it, and in another moment gazed on the pale and ghastly features of Mr. Percy.

"Speak, oh, speak," she said, " I am here—Miranda is here."

There was a strange noise in the throat of the dying man. He made a painful effort to articulate, pronounced the one word " God !" and instantly expired.

"I think he's gone," said the nurse, peeping round the corner of the screen with a shovelfull of coals in her hand. " Isn't he gone ?"

Miranda felt for a moment as if she could scarcely stand. She spoke not, but tottering down the ward with a face as pale as one newly risen from the grave, she reached the door. All strength then deserted her ; she could just say help, and then fainted upon the threshold.

"Well, I am sure," said the nurse, as she flung the coals on the fire, " fine feelings are all very well in their way, but they don't do in hospitals."

CHAPTER CXXX.

VARLEY'S LEVEE.— THE FALSE STAIR, AND THE CAPTURE.

VARLEY had held quite a levee of spies, police-officers, and informers every morning since his arrival in London ; but on the morning following his disagreeable adventure in Somer's-town, he was by far too ill and exhausted to give so early a reception to that class of visitors as he had been accustomed to do. The consequence was, that they all dropped off, with the exception of t o of the officers, who had made so unsuccessful an attempt to capture Rowland Percy, and these remained, being resolved to see Bernard Varley, in order to get his sanction for the employment of more spies, and an advance of money to pay them, for they were not the sort of gentry to give long credit, or, in fact, any at all ; so they exerted what patience was in them, until their dastardly employer should be visible.

It was early, and Bernard Varley was not yet up, and the two officers were shown into a small waiting room. It was just such a room as is usually set apart for the reception of strangers, until they can be otherwise disposed of. In form it came as near a parallelogram as possible, with two long windows on one side, a bare wall, garnished with two maps—the one of London, and the other of the country a few miles round it, varnished in black frames—a door at one end, and a fire-place at the other.

It had, besides, a table, on which were placed writing materials of not the best order ; several chairs, with uncomfortably hard seats, a carpet, the pattern of which had long since departed, and a hearth-rug, on which the two ears, tail, and hind leg of a leopard were still visible.

"Well," said the senior officer to his companion, "I suppose we must wait his leisure, though, having appointed the time himself, he ought to have kept his appointment, for he must know that our time is valuable, or it can be spent to more advantage than being cooped up in this place."

"Why, yes," replied his companion, "it may be a grand and a respectable place, but this room is not comfortable, anyhow. It strikes me that it takes but little to make a place respectable, and uncomfortable too, eh ?"

"Yes ; but we can make ourselves tolerably easy, I dare say ; here's a fire and a seat. We are by ourselves, and can chat for half an hour, and so pass the time."

"With all my heart ; anything for a quiet life, as the man said when his wife made him get up to nurse the baby in his shirt. What do you think of this affair we have on hand ?"

"It's no matter of ours, that we should think at all about it," replied the first ; "but Mr. Varley seems bent upon the recapture of this young fellow. I can't understand it, but that he bears great ill-will towards him, because he is a successful lover of the girl. Jealousy may aid his desire for public justice, you know."

"Ay, I think it does ; though, if that be the case, it would go far to render his evidence suspicious."

"Oh, no—he's a gentleman, and would hardly go to such lengths as perjury—besides, the jury on the spot did not hesitate in returning their verdict."

"No, but it was a strange escape, not only from York gaol, but from York too —indeed, the whole route must have been cleverly conducted."

"You may say that ; there are old hands engaged upon it ; but much depended upon accident in such a protracted affair ; but that was an unlucky escape from the Star and Tinder-box, last night."

"There may be more chances yet."

"No doubt. I have spoiled better laid plans than even theirs, I can tell you. I've ferretted men out of strange holes and corners, such as you would hardly ever dream of, and such as I should never have thought of, but for some trifling thing or event, which no one could calculate upon happening."

"Well, you may as well relate one or two, you know, for we have time, and it may be useful to learn a little, for a stale trick may some day be repeated."

"True, true," replied the senior officer, pleased with the attention of his junior. "Well it's not many years ago that a desperate gang of house breakers infested London and the country many miles round. At first they spread great terror through the whole metropolis, and many complaints were lodged at Bow-street ; but there was no great stir about them, though the men were pretty well known, who were suspected of forming the gang. There were five of them, as resolute and desperate a set of men you would wish to meet with ; they were all young and strong fellows, so that resistance was vain, and never attempted, or murder would no doubt have been the result, as indeed it was in the end.

"At first we did not make much stir after them, for there was no great temptation, till so many daring robberies had been committed with impunity, that it began to reflect upon the office, and a search was ordered to be made.

"Well, we did look out pretty sharp. I had my eye on one of the gang ; I was but lately in the line then—I had my eye on one of them, the head man of the gang, a carpenter by trade, a clever fellow ; his name was Charles Hardman, or Hammering, as he was nicknamed, from his desperate fighting qualities ; but I could catch him at nothing—the whole of them were so wary and watchful, that you might as well have tried to catch a weazle asleep, as to trap them. No, no; they were knowing coves, and not to be had for a trifle.

" Soon after this a desperate robbery took place at Sir Philip Heatheridge's, near the New-road, and the Adam and Eve in St. Pancras-fields. Well the old knight, having served in the wars, I suppose, and having been a soldier, could not bring his mind to be quiet; but, rising hastily, he seized his sword which hung by his bed; he drew it, and attempted to make a stand against the thieves, who, not used to this kind of reception, at first knew not what to make of it; but he gave them no time to consider, for he, seeing them move, rushed at them, brandishing his sword, would have cut one, at least, down, but he was shot dead through the heart by, it was supposed, Hammering Charlie.

" This, as you may imagine, created a devil of a row. The people were up in arms about it, and the Secretary of State offered a reward of three hundred pounds, and his family a further reward of two hundred pounds, for the apprehension and conviction of the murderers.

" You may be sure we went to work in earnest now, and, notwithstanding the carefulness of the gang, they had been seen and recognized in the house, especially Charlie, who had been at work there some time previously as a carpenter, and hence how he came to plan the attack upon the house, knowing the quantity of plate, jewels, and money they kept in it.

" He was advertised for by name and description, but he appeared to have vanished, for no one could tell of his whereabouts. I knew his haunts well, for I had my eye upon him, thinking that some day he would be worth a heavy sum to the public; and now he was, and I set about capturing him if I could; but this was a matter more easily thought of and said than done.

" I am no chicken, and then I was in the pride of my strength, as they say in the plays; but I felt that if we ever did meet, and a scrimmage was to ensue, and that Charlie would not be taken (and I could not expect he would, for the charge affected his life, and hanged he would be), I felt it would be a doubtful and desperate affair; but I cared for nothing, but determined to brave all for such a sum.

" Several of his companions had been taken, and one had been fortunate enough to escape from the country; but not so Charlie. We knew that he was in London, and from information that I had received, and several hints I had heard among his own friends, I felt convinced that he was near his old haunt in St. Giles's rookery.

" I told you he was a carpenter, and a clever one. This made me feel convinced that he was secreted in the house where he usually lived; but I could see no trace of it; however I mentioned my suspicions to the magistrate, and got a search-warrant immediately, and with two more I determined to make a sudden rush into the house when least expected by the inmates, and, if possible, secure my prisoner.

" Well then, I thought it of no use to pounce upon them either in the day time or night; Charlie would be too wide awake for that, and I determined to go before daybreak one bleak cold morning. I did so, and got into the house readily enough, and searched over every room, every cupboard, and every nook and corner of it that you could think big enough to conceal a cat; but, no, he was not there.

" We stood staring at each other in vexation and shame, for we could easily perceive the anxious faces of some of the inmates were bent upon us, while others jeered at us for our non-success, and we were compelled reluctantly to quit the premises. Having got into the street, I said to one of my mates who was with me,—

" It strikes me that our man is in that house now, notwithstanding we have not been able to find his-hiding place."

" 'He must have doubled himself up into an uncommon small compass then; for we have not left a place unexplored into which I could find room for my hat,' said he; 'but yet some of the women looked plaguy anxious and troubled.'

" 'They did,' I replied, 'and that's what makes me pretty sure that he was there, and I have a great mind to return to them and make another search all over it."

" 'I think it would be useless,' he replied.

" 'Why useless? they think we are gone, and will not expect us now.'

" 'No such thing; we are watched now,' he said, ' there can be no doubt; but we can return at another time, setting a watch upon the door, to see who and what goes in and out.'

" 'That's very good advice,' I replied; ' but yet he may be carried out in some

piece of furniture, or some such scheme as that. Well, I suppose it can't be helped, but I'll have another rummage over that house before long.'

" Well, that passed over, and I was then engaged in tracing the stolen property. The plate was no doubt melted soon after the robbery was committed, and turned into cash ; but not so the jewellery—that, I believed, had not been touched, for its value would be much lessened.

" I made careful inquiries among the Jews, but could learn nothing. These people have great advantages in the disposal of stolen property—they have so large

No. 64.

and confident a connection, that what they do seldom or ever transpires. My own belief was, that they had been turned into money, and at once sent from the country, safe, and beyond my reach.

"I had placed a man to keep watch near the house in which I suspected that he was concealed, to keep a good look-out, and inform me of whatever he saw of a suspicious tendency; and from him I learned that the family, though very poor, were doing extremely well, and none of them had any kind of work; they paid for all they got, he found, upon making enquiries, and, besides, they had all got new clothing.

"I had myself learned that Charlie had been among the Jews lately, and he had received large sums of money, and I had no doubt was laying by until a safe opportunity occurred of allowing him to escape to France or America.

"Taking all these things together, I determined to make another attempt to catch him.

"It was about midnight that I and two more once again sought the house with this intention. We gained admittance after some little delay and wrangle.

"We commenced our search carefully from the kitchens upwards. We proceeded slowly and with great care, not missing a square foot of either brick-work or woodwork; but all to no purpose. I could not see anything that would lead me to a conclusion that he was present in the house, and yet I felt certain that he was.

"It was vexatious enough to be thus foiled a second time, more especially as everything tended to increase my suspicion that he was there, the whole family, the female he lived with, his own relations, his clothes, some of which appeared to be recently worn, and had marks or stains on them as if they had been near bricks or mortar.

"This made me positive of his presence, and I remarked the appearance to my companions, who thought as I did. The family did not like it, but began to grow serious and angry. They complained of my presence. I showed them my search warrant. They admitted my right, but added that I was wantonly breaking in upon and destroying the liberty of the subject by my intrusion into their house.

"'That is my object,' said I. 'I do wish to abridge liberties such as these, hang them. It's too great a liberty in one man to take the life of another. But he's not here, and I'll leave you now; but you may be sure we'll have him despite of all he can do.'

"'You have tried,' said one of his family, 'and had better try again.'

"'I will,' said I, 'but not just now; I shall see you on another occasion.'

"So saying I walked down the stairs. I was in no good humour, but I strode down the stairs in anger. When I got to a very dark part, I thought I felt the stairs spring, as if they were supported on some soft body.

"'Hilloa!' said I, 'what is the matter now?' and on examining the spot, I could see that the top of the landing did not consist of boards that ran from side to side and under the skirting, but there was a clean cut all along. I instantly lifted it up; it came easily enough, and there lay my prisoner. The hollow place in which he lay was scarcely deep enough for his body, which would scarcely admit of its shutting flat down, and having been seized with the cramp during our search, he was forced to turn his body, and hence the discovery.

"No sooner was he conscious of his being detected, than he sprang up and attempted to escape; but I seized him, and a desperate struggle ensued, for the rest of the people took his part, and we were terribly beaten and thrust from the house; but yet I still retained my grasp of my man.

"Outside the struggle was renewed with greater desperation than ever, for he was assisted by some more of his people, and I had more than one chance of my life. During all this, Charlie kept biting and kicking most violently, I was losing strength, and soon I should have been overpowered, and to add to my distress, I could not get the handcuffs on. I had him fast by one hand, but the shower of blows I was enduring would I knew soon disable me, and, with a last effort, I fastened the other half of the handcuff to an iron staple by the railings, and at once secured him.

"I then got up with some difficulty, and sprang my rattle, and soon assistance arrived. My man was safe; but I fainted when I saw him housed, and I was on the sick-list for a long time after. But I got the rewards, which made the matter not so bad after all."

"No; but it would not do to have such often repeated," replied his companion, who had been listening attentively.

"It would not; but it was a feather in my cap, and my promotion was sure."

* * * * * * *

A waiter at this moment summoned them into the presence of Varley, who spoke with great pain and difficulty, for although he had received no one serious injury from the mob, he had been terribly shaken by the rough treatment he had received.

CHAPTER CXXXI.

TWITTER AND VARLEY.—THE PLOT FOR THE MURDER.—TWITTER IN TWO MINDS. —THE CONSENT.

THE interview between Bernard Varley and the officers was very brief; it consisted of a wild kind of harangue upon his part, the purport of which was, to authorise them to go to any expense whatever, provided it presented them with a good chance of apprehending either Rowland Percy, Witlet, or the third person, who was evidently rendering assistance to the fugitives—Mr. Jones to wit, whose name, however, was unknown to the officers, although they declared they could readily recognise him again, from the view they had of him during the recent proceedings; and they would take care to have him included in a warrant, which they would immediately apply for.

So far all was satisfactory to the officers, for they were making immediate cash by the transaction, as well as chancing the large reward that was offered for Rowland's apprehension.

Very far, though, was Bernard Varley from sharing in that satisfaction, for he could not conceal from himself, that hitherto he had been signally unsuccessful in his pursuit of the innocent parties, whom he hated the much more for their innocence than if they had been guilty, since all his endeavours had resulted in nothing but derision, annoyance, vexation, and personal injury. He was suffering too, considerable bodily pain during the interview with the officers; and that circumstance imparted an ascerbity to his tone, which made them think that his reason was certainly a little deranged, and gave rise to many grave suspicions among themselves, as to his real connection with the events which had produced so much troublesome excitement.

But this they wisely considered was no business of theirs; and although they had made the matter a subject of free discourse among themselves, their doubts of Rowland Percy's guilt made them not a whit the less anxious for his apprehension, the effecting of which they looked upon quite as a matter of business, his guilt or innocence having nothing whatever to do with their part of the work.

With full instructions, then, to spare no expense, and to leave no means untried for the destruction of Rowland, the officers left Bernard Varley, whose passions had reached a fearful height, that quite threatened his mental alienation. With a deep groan, then he threw himself upon a sofa, and tortured by the pain, he interspersed with groans, gave utterance to the agonising thoughts of his half-distracted mind.

"Fate seems to fight against me," he muttered. "Miranda! Miranda! I have seen you once again; and then you have been snatched from me at a moment when I thought it impossible you could escape me. Some accursed train of circumstances seems ever to step in between me and the accomplishment of the fixed purposes of my soul; the nearer I seem to approach the full accomplishment of my wishes, the further I may calculate, by some unlucky movement, to be hurled to a distance off, enough to deprive me of all hope of future success;—foiled—foiled—for ever; but I will live alone now for those two great objects of my soul—revenge on Rowland Percy, and the love of Miranda. There shall interpose nothing to prevent my continuing those two pursuits to their successful accomplishment; I will devote the large fortune that has come into my hands, as well as my life. Oppression may depress me, but shall not daunt me. I will either live to accomplish my desires, or not live at all. Death were a thousand times more welcome than this frightful state of painful expectation, and still more painful disappointment.

With a noiseless tread, Samuel Twitter glided into the apartment.

"Oh, good morning," said Varley, in a bland tone, much at variance with that in which he had been muttering the resolves of his dark and troubled spirit. "Good morning, friend Twitter, I regret—very much regret, that you did not escape scathless yesterday."

"Scathless," said Twitter, as he lifted up a green shade that was over one eye, and exhibited that organ of a variety of colours.

"Ay, I perceive, my good Twitter," said Varley, "some one has struck you in the eye; you have my most poignant regrets and deep commiseration. We are assailed by terrible ruffians, Samuel Twitter, persons quite destitute of humanity and conscience."

"For Heaven's sake," said Twitter, with a prefatory groan, "don't speak in that way, Mr. Varley; I would rather, ten times, that you abused me, as you used to do, than speak to me in that tone of mock civility and consideration, which makes me almost think—that—that ——"

"That what?"

"That some day you would take my life!"

"Oh, what a libel," said Varley, holding up his hands.

"The truth's a libel," remarked Twitter, with an uneasy shuffle in the chair. "You know the truth's a libel, Varley, in this country. Do you mean that?"

"Really, now, my dear friend, you allow your perverted imagination to picture to you evils that have no foundation."

"Dear friend!" ejaculated Twitter, with a tone of surprise. "Don't—oh, don't——"

"Do you want any money?" said Varley. "Pray draw upon me for as much as your necessities require. Between friends what are a few pounds?"

"I should like to have fifty," said Twitter, "if quite convenient."

"My dear Samuel, take a hundred," said Varley; "you find me in an agreeable mood this morning; and I confess, my mind is rather elated by some agreeable intelligence that I have received."

"Indeed?"

"Yes, the principal drawback upon my satisfaction, in fact, is that blow you have on you eye."

"D—d hypocrite!" said Twitter, jumping up, and making for the door.

"Nay," said Varley, "my dear Twitter, lend me your attention for a brief space while I explain to you that I have this morning, received intelligence that Rowland Percy and Miranda have found refuge in a house some distance from a place called Richmond, on the banks of the river. I have made an agreement with a strong posse of officers to meet us at a particular landing-place, about half a mile from the house. The shortest route is unquestionably by water, so you and I, Twitter, will take a boat, and row ourselves up to where we are to meet the officers. I have thought over the matter well, Twitter, and I have quite convinced myself that the shortest route, as well as the easiest, is by water—to your grave," he added, to himself.

"Oh," remarked Twitter; "did you say a boat on the water?"

"Yes," said Varley, unconcernedly fixing his eyes upon the ceiling.

"Don't you think that rather dangerous?"

"I don't see any danger if the thing is properly managed."

"Then I tell you what," said Twitter. "Bernard Varley, you may be as civil and pleasant-spoken as you like; but, before I trust myself with you in a boat on the river, I'll see you d—d first."

"Not trust yourself with me, Samuel Twitter, your old friend—your well-tried, old, faithful friend and confidant. How is it that you have given yourself up to such degrading suspicions? Oh, Twitter—Twitter, am I deceived in you?—and are you not the open-hearted, candid character I took you for?"

"Give me the money," said Twitter, "and let me go. You want to drive me mad, I know you do."

"Well, well, I will have no more suspicions," said Varley. "We will meet at Blackfriars-bridge."

"We will do no such thing."

"At the stairs to the right hand."

"No—no—no."

"At half-past eight o'clock this evening, when the silver moon is rising, and shedding its refulgent light upon the waters. 'Tis pleasant to be at such a time in an open boat, with an attached friend, from whom one has no secrets."

"I won't come—I won't come," cried Twitter, knocking the table with his knuckles vehemently. "It's no use tormenting me, Varley. I won't, and there's an end of it."

"Nay, now, but you will. Will you force me to the disagreeable alternative of saying that you shall? for if you do not, I shall stop the supplies, Samuel Twitter, and not another farthing do you procure from me."

"Reduce me to destitution," said Twitter, "and I confess the murder at York."

"Indeed!" said Varley, in the same bland tone he had used throughout the interview. "Then, it becomes me, in a friendly way, to save you from that inconvenience."

"Save me! How?"

"By blowing your brains out before you could carry that pleasant little intention into effect."

"Murder! murder!" said Twitter, as Varley upon the moment snatched a pistol from his pocket, and held it within an inch of his head.

"Will you come?"

"You—you dare not kill me here! The noise—the excitement—suspicions would be sure to be directed against you. You dare not kill me here, Varley!"

"Nay, do not make too sure; but, to convince you that your suspicions are groundless, I will excuse your attendance upon the occasion I have hinted to you; but by so doing, you force me to an alternative I would gladly have avoided—you will no longer be useful in bringing Rowland Percy to a scaffold, and so quieting suspicion once and for ever of the murderer of Sir George Rankley. I shall be compelled to make a confidant of some other person, Twitter, a measure fraught with frightful danger to us both, for I must have somebody to assist me in my schemes; that somebody should be you, but since you refuse, I am thrown upon the consideration of strangers, and our danger will be not a little increased by my taking to myself, into my full and free confidence—for full and free it must be, or not at all——"

"Varley—Varley," said Twitter, "you cannot mean to be so mad.

"The result must speak for my sincerity."

"In town, and where there are people about, I don't mind going with you, but, in lonely situations, I confess I always feel unhappy, and I cannot bear them, so do not ask me, Varley."

" Twitter, your services to me—in fact I may say, our mutual services to each other,—must be unfettered by foolish conditions. You fancy I have a design upon your life. What folly is that, when I have so much need of a confidant, and have in you a perfectly safe one, because implicated, ready to my hand. What one object on earth would your death avail me, especially that now we are upon such civil and very pleasant terms, and understand each other so fully and so completely?"

" I know not, I know not," said Twitter; "but I have horrid snspicions. To speak candidly, Varley, I am very—very much afraid that you thirst for my death."

" Twitter, Twitter, such a thought is quite unworthy of you. It is foolish; because not based upon reason. Ask yourself for a moment, what advantage could accrue to me from your decease. What possible good could it do me, if by a word I could hurry you to eternity? On the contrary, Twitter, you have been very useful to me, and you may, in all human probability, be more useful still. You fancy me mad in my passion for Miranda, but I am not so mad, Samuel Twitter, as not to know what I am about. Do not expose me to the danger of employing strangers, and I promise you that if Rowland Percy be brought to a scaffold, as I think he may, by your assistance to me, that I will sell the Grange by auction in London here, and give you a large sum from the proceeds,—a sum that shall at once enable you to take what course you please, and place you far above the reach of pecuniary difficulties."

" Oh if I could but trust you—oh, if I could but trust you!" said Twitter; "but I cannot, Varley—you know I cannot—you know I dare not."

" Twitter, Twitter," said Varley, "we have so long, figuratively speaking, rowed in the same boat together, and now you shrink from doing so actually for the space of about an hour. Excuse me for saying, Twitter, that such a course of conduct is quite unworthy your high reputation for sagacity and courage."

" My reputation!" said Twitter. " Oh, dear, Varley, Varley, if you would not say such things as that I might almost believe you, but how can I when you talk in such a strain? I repeat, how can I? You know well that your conviction goes not with your words, and that were you to speak what you would consider the truth, you would absolutely deny me the possession of any of the qualities you mention. I would go with you freely, if I could really trust you—if I could really rid myself of the frightful supposition that you seek my life."

" Rid yourself of it, Samuel Twitter, once and for ever," said Varley, with such an air of sincerity that Twitter was absolutely staggered, and half believed him. " Accompany me this evening upon the expedition I mention, and which I honestly believe will be crowned with the most perfect success, then the other occurrence such as the sale of the Grange and the possession by you of a large portion of the proceeds, would follow as things of course, and you would reach the ultimatum of your wishes, without any further doubt, danger, or difficulty."

" 1—I think," said Twitter," I will venture—I think I will try to venture. At half past eight, you say, Varley?"

" At half-past eight," said Varley, in an indifferent tone. " On the steps by the left-hand side of Blackfriars bridge."

" I will think between this and then."

" No," said Varley, " you must decide now, for between this and then I must procure some one to accompany me, in case of failing meeting with the officers, or any other accident which should leave me alone otherwise."

" I—I will come—I will meet you, Varley. You will really sell the Grange estate, and let me have my share?"

" I will; but, of course, you know, it must be subject to the deduction of what you have already received. That must be considered, you know, Samuel Twitter."

" Certainly—oh, yes, certainly."

This seeming urgency in the reduction of his demand by the amount he had already received, went a long way with Twitter in convincing him of the sincerity of Bernard Varley. He thought to himself " he surely would not be so anxious in making such a condition, if he intended any foul play, for he would be too ready to promise me anything, rather than that I should refuse to accompany him on this expedition, which after all may be, as he says, a means of ridding us entirely of Rowland Percy, who, while he lives, will ever be to us the greatest possible enemy, because, if his innocence should become apparent, guilt must be sought for elsewhere."

Alike fearful of refusing, and of going to meet Varley, Samuel Twitter at length gave a reluctant consent, and advancing his claim upon Varley from fifty to a hundred pounds, he left the hotel, scarcely quite clear in his own mind whether he meant to keep his own word or not.

CHAPTER CXXXII.

MIRANDA'S ADVENTURES IN THE STREETS OF LONDON.—THE HOSPITAL.—THE MEETING WITH NED WITLET AT WHITEHALL.

WHEN Miranda recovered after fainting at the door of the hospital ward, in which poor Percy lay a corpse, she found herself in a little dingy apartment, surrounded by several persons. It was some moments before she recovered consciousness sufficient to remember what had occurred to her, but when once the memory again asserted its power, nothing was forgotten, but, like a flash of lightning illumining a dreary waste, her mind became at once full of the consciousness of her painful situation.

"Ah!" she heard some one say, "it's over now!"

She tried to rise from her seat, but found herself almost inadequate to the task.

"You had better remain here for some time," said a gentlemanly-looking man. "Here, drink this."

Miranda instinctively drank the contents of a small glass that was placed to her lips, and almost instantly she felt the reviving effects of the stimulant that had been administered to her.

"Alas! alas!" she said, "he's dead! he's dead!"

"Ah, you mean the old gentleman in the ward," said the same person who had addressed her; "there wasn't a chance for him from the first; he was sinking when he came in, and never rallied."

"Perhaps it is a great mercy," added Miranda, clasping her hands. "Heaven only knows what he might yet have had to struggle with!"

"About the body," said another person; "do you mean to claim it?"

"Claim it!" said Miranda. "What mean you?"

"Oh, nothing particular; but we'll take the trouble off your hands of the funeral, and that kind of thing, provided you have no particular objection to a slight, nay, almost nominal post mortem examination, for the purposes of science."

"The body," said Miranda, as she rose, and moved towards the door, "will be claimed, and not left for the purposes of dissection. I quite understand you, sir."

"Oh, very well, very well; but mind it must be done within four-and-twenty hours. Curse people's infernal prejudices! D—d a chance of meat and bone have we had this fortnight! It's enough to make a fellow swear by jingo and the holy fire-irons! and upon my soul there isn't a case worth a curse in the hospital! The only fellow, and be d—d to him, that was worth looking at,—because, if you recollect there was a complication of, as we thought, a fracture of the occipital bone, with two or three luxations; a crushed pelvis, and a displacement of the vertebral column; and after all it turns out to be no go, for the luxations have been successfully reduced, and the d—d fellow is getting well."

"Then there's the other thief," remarked another, "who fell from the scaffold in Newgate-street—sixty-five feet, by Jove. Jinks, the porter, of course sent for me. I got here out of breath, and nearly in a state of collapse with hurry, and the infernal strutting thief had only a few contusions, and an abrasion of the cuticle on the left temple. I could have kicked him out of the hospital, I could."

"Ah! so could I. You heard what Green said, didn't you?"

"No, what?"

"Why, when he found that he was not the mass of broken bones and dislocations that he expected, he said to him, 'You d—d calf-like vagabond, what do you mean by falling sixty-five feet, and only getting a few bruises? I tell you what, my fine fellow, you are a swindler—an infernal swindler! You ought to have broken every bone in your body!'"

"Very true—very true."

While these professional remarks were being made in the surgery of Bartholomew's Hospital, poor, sorrow-stricken Miranda found her way to the outer gates, and emerged into Smithfield.

She was pleased to see by the lengthening shadows, and the dim evenness of colour that pervaded all objects, that the evening was rapidly approaching. Still, however, it wanted some hours to the time of meeting with Witlet, and she felt herself greatly in need of some bodily refreshment, in order to sustain her exhausted steps; where or how safely to procure such she knew not, but her increasing faintness warned her that she would be exposing herself to the absolute peril of again fainting, if she did not hasten to procure food of some description.

She turned down a narrow street in the immediate vicinity of the hospital, and soon observed a small shop, into which she was encouraged to enter, because she saw no person but a woman in it, although the display of eatables of all kinds and descriptions was not of the most inviting character.

There were pickled herrings, Flanders bricks, butter, soap, kitchen-stuff, tocacco, hearth-stone, split-peas, snuff, cabbages, sugar, birch-brooms, soda, starch, table-beer, and blacking, candles, tea, and the best white linen rags, &c., &c.

Into this *olla podrida* of a shop Miranda, with some reluctance, entered, and inquired if she could have some bread, when to her surprise the woman replied,—

"Certainly; would you like a Frenchman, or a buster?"

"I really don't know," said Miranda. "A small one will suffice."

A twopenny loaf was handed to her, and the woman stared when she asked leave to eat some of it in the shop.

"We've small-beer at a penny a pint."

"Have you any milk?" said Miranda. "I should prefer it."

"Yes," was the reply; "we are forced to sell everything to get a living in this world."

A suspicious looking liquid, which, from the courtesy of the inhabitants of London, is usually considered to be milk, was handed to Miranda in a cracked mug, and having partaken of some of it, and eaten a small portion of the bread, she paid threepence for her frugal repast, and left the shop.

As she did so she heard seven o'clock striking from some neighbouring church turret, and not knowing how great a space she might have to traverse in order to obey the injunctions of Witlet, before meeting him, she resolved at once to start on the undertaking, and as a preparatory step, she called a hackney-coach, and desired to be driven to the Strand, to which the reader will recollect that Witlet had told her to go, for the purpose of procuring a boat at some of the stairs at the bottom of the numerous streets running from its southern side towards the river. A very short drive sufficed to place Miranda in that bustling thoroughfare, and she required not to make many inquiries before she found herself on the banks of the river, at the bottom of a flight of wooden stairs, where a number of wherries lay moored, ready for hire.

In answer to the repeated inquiries of "Boat, mum?—boat, mum?" from a lot of idlers on the stairs, she desired to be conveyed across the river, and after agreeing, to the great surprise of the waterman, to pay sixpence for the accommodation, she stepped into a wherry, which was soon gliding along on the surface of the waters with that pleasant, easy motion which is so delightfully superior to every other artificial mode of progression, and which, were it not for the mass of sputtering, fumigating steamers that make the Thames a highway, would form one of the most agreeable pleasures in the summer season which London could present to its inhabitants.

A very few minutes sufficed to land Miranda on the opposite side of the stream, and she ascended some steps very similar to those she had descended on the Middlesex shore—finding herself in a dirty narrow street, which, after pursuing some time, conducted her into a large rambling thoroughfare, where the houses

(Miranda at the bar of the star and tinder box)

were quite of a miscellaneous character; shops, of all kinds and descriptions, and private dwellings, being jumbled together in the wildest disorder.

To procure a coach in such a thoroughfare was by no means a difficult matter; and Miranda directed that she should be driven to Whitehall, looking carefully about her previously to stepping into the vehicle, and being quite assured she was unwatched. Indeed, the mere fact of crossing the river alone was a sufficient guarantee that no one was upon her track; and in the midst of all her misery, she felt a glow of satisfaction pervade her frame at the thought that she should soon.

No. 65.

meet a friend, even although that friend was of so doubtful a social cast as Ned Witlet, the professed highwayman.

She ascertained when she reached Whitehall that she would have still very nearly an hour to wait for the time of Witlet's appointed arrival. She asked the name of the large building opposite to where she had alighted from the coach, and being informed it was called the Horse Guards, leading into St. James's Park, she thought that in preference to loitering about in the open streets, she would walk into the park, of which she had read a great deal, and which, to her mind, was full of historical recollections.

In a few moments she was standing in the broad expanse opposite the park front of the Horse Guards, but the darkness had increased greatly, and she could but faintly see around her those objects which would have been of great interest in consequence of their being mingled with memorable realities.

Here she lingered until half-past eight was chimed from the Horse Guards' clock. Then she passed again through the gloomy-looking archway, and crossing the road, stood close to that building which had been the prison, and witnessed the execution of Charles the First, who allowed his resources to get weaker while his enemies were gaining strength, instead of crushing, as he should have done in the germ, a political movement which brought years of distress.

"Miranda," said a voice behind her, while a slight touch caused her to start suddenly, and she beheld the friendly face of Witlet a few paces from her.

"Thank Heaven," cried Miranda, "you have come. Oh, what a weary day I have passed; I seem to live again now that I have met you. Tell me of Rowland. Is he well?—is he well?"

"Yes, Miss Rankley, he is well, and he is as happy as circumstances will permit him to be. He wished me particularly to inquire of you concerning his father."

A grief-like shadow passed over the countenance of Miranda, and, shaking her head, she said, sadly,

"Alas! he is gone—gone!"

"Dead!" exclaimed Witlet; "can it be possible!"

"It is true the satisfaction was a melancholy one of being with him at his death, but such as it was I had it. He is now far removed from earthly cares and earthly miseries. Heaven receive him."

"Amen!" said Witlet. "This will be a sad blow to poor Rowland Percy, for he never believed his father in any danger. Well—well, we must reason with him upon the subject, and endeavour to convince him that all is for the best, for that is a philosophy that is very difficult to convince people of when suffering from the severe hand of misfortune."

"That is too true," said Miranda; "it is the wealthy alone that, in the midst of their luxuries and socialities, can treat misfortune as an abstraction, reasoning calmly and dispassionately upon it; but let those same persons feel the biting of real sorrow, and they shall be the first to shrink aghast from its presence."

"You have learned some home truths early in life, Miss Rankley," remarked Witlet. "Heaven send they may conduce to your future happiness; but now tell me, are you quite certain that throughout the day no one has dogged your footsteps?"

"Quite—quite," said Miranda. "I escaped from Bernard Varley by a miracle."

"You shall tell me all particulars as we proceed to where I hope you will enjoy a most uninterrupted interview with Rowland Percy; but we must be perfectly sure we are not followed; if any one is watching me now, I shall be pounced upon before I can get into a hackney-coach."

As he spoke he beckoned one from a stand which was near, and, handing Miranda into the vehicle, he himself followed, desiring the coachman to drive to St. Paul's Cathedral.

"I think we are safe," he said; "but, in order to make assurance doubly sure, we will ride about a little in an opposite direction to that in which we really wish to go."

The coach started, and during the drive Miranda related to Ned Witlet the daring attempt Varley had made to stay her, and the very singular manner in which it had been frustrated.

CHAPTER CXXXIII.

THE SPY AND THE LETTER.—MIRANDA AND THE LANDLORD OF THE STAR AND TINDER-BOX.—THE MEETING.

In St. Paul's churchyard Witlet and Miranda alighted from the hackney-coach, and after the coachman was paid, the former said to the latter.

"If we were being watched at all, the number of this coach would have been taken, because it would be a greater object, of course, to follow me to Mr. Percy's place of concealment, than to effect my apprehension in the street. I feel quite assured that we have not been followed, for if so, it must have been in a vehicle, and now let us walk round the cathedral, and make sure that our late coachman does not see the number of the next vehicle we get into."

This was easily accomplished. for the coachman evidently took no notice of them whatever, and stepping into another vehicle, which was plying for hire at the top of Cheapside, Ned Witlet at once desired to be driven to Holborn, and he drew the check-string within about a hundred paces of the top of Drury-lane.

"Now," he said to Miranda, when they were in the street, "comes our great peril; we must walk down Drury-lane, and of course it is just possible it may be well watched. A few moments, however, must decide that question, and I only speak to you now, in case it should be necessary for us to part company, which I beg of you to do without ceremony, should I see occasion to give you such a hint. Rowland Percy is at the house I mentioned to you. Should I be apprehended, you will be untouched, and when the row and excitement has subsided, you can proceed quietly and ask for him of the landlord."

"Do not run the risk," said Miranda. "Why, walk down this dread thoroughfore at all. Let me proceed alone."

"Nay," replied Witlet; "I want a day and night's rest at the Star and Tinder-box. I think if I can once get into the house undiscovered, I shall be comparatively safe. It is in the passage to it which alone is dangerous. Let us hope for the best."

With Miranda Rankley upon his arm, Ned Witlet walked boldly down Drury-lane. The night was dark, and, consequently, he was so far favoured by circumstances, and when he and the beautiful being who accompanied him turned into Steeple-court, he remarked—

"I think, Miss Rankley, we have performed the perilous voyage with safety; but let us pause in this old doorway, a little while; if we have been dogged hither, the party or parties so doing will soon appear."

Some minutes of very anxious suspense passed to Miranda, but all was still, the only person passing up Steeple-court, being a slip-shod girl with a mug for some beer, who was as unlike a policy spy as could well be imagined.

"We are surely safe," whispered Miranda.

"Yes I think so. Do you go to the bar, and ask for the landlord. He's a stout rather rough-featured man, but good humoured withal. Say to him when you see him, 'Is there a loose box for a hunter in the Star and Tinder-box?' If he says yes, and there's nobody by, you can come and tell me directly; but should there be persons about when he says yes, just add, 'He's nearly beat and shy of the crows.' He will understand you, and get rid of any obnoxious personages if they be loitering about."

"I will recollect," said Miranda ; "depend upon my doing your bidding carefully."

Poor Miranda stepped on towards the public-house. When she reached the bar there were two persons standing ; one was the girl who had recently passed her and Witlet in the narrow passage—the other was a young man of the class denominated "shabby-genteel," and he was smoking a cigar with an air of great nonchalance, as he leaned idly against the bar, with his hands in his pockets. After a hard stare at Miranda, he continued apparently some remarks that he had been before making, for he said—

"Yes, it's my decided opinion that the laws are often and often too hard upon a fellow, and don't take into consideration that one chap must live as well as another."

"Oh, sir," said the landlord, "I do know that dishonesty's a dreadful vice, and I really think thieves and vagabonds ought to be punished quite dreadfully."

"Oh, pho—pho—pho !" cried the man. "Come, now, no reserve with me : I'm on the lay myself. How is business ?"

"Why, we've drawn half a butt to-day," said the landlord, considering ; "but really, sir, if you begin talking slang to me, you'll puzzle me completely, and if you mean to insinuate that you are not strictly honest and honourable, I must beg that you will leave my house."

Miranda was quite delighted to hear such a sentiment, but she little suspected the shabby-genteel man was strongly suspected by the landlord of being what is called a plant upon him, and that the landlord himself was the greatest proficient in slang, London could produce. She was now about to speak, when the little girl, poking a jug upon the bar, said,—

"A pint and a half of the sixpenny ale, and mother says please draw it mild. A gentleman in the street's given me this letter to bring here ; it's all right, sir, cos he guved me twopence for bringing it."

The landlord took the letter, and read aloud the address as follows :—"Mr. Rowland Percy, care of George Frith, landlord of the Star and Tinder-box, Drury-lane."

"What !" cried Miranda, stepping forward, hurriedly ; "did you say Rowland Percy ?"

"Eh !" said the shabby-genteel man, taking the cigar out of his mouth, and looking deeply interested.

"Yes, I did," said the landlord, loudly ; "but as I don't happen to know the gentleman, I think, my little girl, you had better take the letter back to the d—d fool that gave it to you, or swallow it, as you think proper."

"Oh !" said the little girl, as she took the letter again.

"Rowland Percy—Rowland Percy !" remarked the shabby-genteel man ; "why, that's the same name as the murderer from York—ain't it ?"

"I dare say you know best," said the landlord ; "perhaps you had better take the note ; you might find him him out before I do."

"Oh, I—I have nothing to do with it," said the man.

"Pshaw !" said the landlord ; "you are as shallow as a saucer. Go and tell your employers that I have nothing to do with Rowland Percy, and don't mean. You may say, too, it's no use sending every hour in the day a fool like yourself on the spy ; there, now go away, my good man, the little girl's waiting outside with the sham note. I tell you Percy is not one of my sort, from all I can hear of him, and if he was to come in here, I should just say, my good fellow, bolt— this house is too hot to hold you, for I've been doing a roaring trade this last week, among spies and informers. Now will that do, or must you have a kick ?"

"Really," said the shabby-genteel man, "I don't know what you mean ; and as for Godfrey employing me, I don't even know him by sight."

"Ah," remarked the landlord. "you may know a goose by its gabble. Who spoke of Godfrey but yourself, spooney? I do think when the police want a spy, they go through London for an idiot."

The shabby-genteel muttered something that was quite unintelligible except to himself, and then sneaked out of the house like a cur that has been unexpectedly found under a dining-room table.

"Well," remarked the landlord, "I can forgive a rogue, but I've no patience with a fool; here's that fellow drunk four shillings' worth of mulled port, and smoked three cigars, just to expose his own want of the common assortment of brains. Well, hurrah's all I have to say."

"Are you the landlord," said Miranda, " of this house?"

"So they say."

"Then have you a loose box for a hunter in the Star and Tinder-box?"

The landlord placed his elbows on the bar, and looked long and steadfastly in the face of his fair questioner.

"I don't know you, my dear," he said; "but you've as pretty a face, for all that, as I've seen for many a year. Yes, I have got a loose box for a hunter in the Star and Tinder-box, and for your sake, it shall be a snug one. Now tell me, as there's nobody here, who is the out-of-the-way lucky dog to own you."

Miranda shrunk a little from the familiarity of this address, and then said in a low voice,—

"I have been told I might trust you; my name is Miranda Rankley. I am the daughter of Sir George Rankley, who was basely murdered. My errand here is to see the innocent Rowland Percy. My companion, now waiting in the court is named Witlet."

The landlord gave a long whistle, and then opening the little wicket, that led into the bar, he said,—

"Come in, Miss Rankley. Of course, I couldn't know you. Excuse me and my odd manner; I am rough and ready, like a Scotch terrier."

"Nay," she said, " I must go back with the news that all is safe."

"Leave that to me; I'll fetch Witlet in: walk in here yourself, for it's seldom that the bar of the Star and Tinder-box is as it is now. We don't know a minute but that we may have some ugly customers walk in."

Miranda no longer hesitated, but passing the little bar, she accepted a proffered seat in the parlour beyond it, with a feeling of great relief. A glance around her let her see that Rowland Percy was not in the apartment; but she could scarcely be said to be disappointed, for a moment's reflection told her how unlikely it was that he should be so readily accessible in his place of concealment. She heard the boisterous mirth of some topers who were making merry in the parlour in the ancient hostel, and rude and coarse as those sounds were, they came with a chastened effect upon her ear, because she felt that she was under the same roof with Rowland Percy—a conviction which gave beauty to every object around her, and made that house of entertainment an object in her eyes dearer than a palace.

"Now, at least," she thought, "we shall meet without the accompaniment of those calamitous circumstances which followed so hard on our last attempt at a conference. Oh, Rowland—Rowland, surely some day the clouds of misfortune which now environ us will separate, and we shall see the future more clear and bright, perhaps, than ever was the past. While I have faith in Heaven and its justice, I will not desert hope—a hope of happier times, which will yet dawn upon us when we least expect it. We shall yet live, I feel a conviction, to look back upon the past as the troubled phantasma of a dream, from, which we have escaped, but which has not been altogether full of evil, inasmuch as while it has chastened us it has taught us the true value of many things and many persons which, in the palmy days of prosperity, we could never have arrived at."

Minute after minute passed slowly, and no one came to her in her solitude. An irrepressible feeling of loneliness began to oppress her, and she exhausted her mind in endless conjectures as to what could be the occasion of the long delay. Suddenly, then, she heard a door slightly creak upon its hinges, and turning hastily to where the sound proceeded from, with a cry of joy she recognised Rowland Percy, who in a moment sprung towards and clasped her in his arms.

"Once again—yet once again, my noble—my heroic Miranda," he said; "once again we have met; fate persecutes us, dearest, but it leaves our own hearts untouched."

"Ah, Rowland," replied Miranda, "misfortune is real love's only test: we will have faith in each other, and stand it bravely. You are looking wearied and ill, Rowland. Oh, that this life of incessant disquietude and harrassment would cease."

"We will bear it, Miranda, as best we may, gazing upon the future as upon some bright particular star, dearest, which we may hope to reach in the fulness of time; but the roses have deserted your cheek, Miranda, and I feel myself too much the cause."

"No, no, Rowland; do not add any self-accusation to the already more than sufficient oppression that must have been upon your mind. Trains of circumstances, as unprecedented as terrible, have given us much suffering, and may give us much more; but always remember, Rowland, we are but passive instruments in the hands of that Providence which, in its own good time, will release us from our thraldoms, and permit us, dear Rowland——"

"To live and love together," added Percy. "To be all the world to each other, my Miranda."

"As we are now, Rowland. We are both orphans, and our hopes in this world must be centered in each other."

"Both orphans!" exclaimed Rowland; "my—my father——"

"Is in Heaven."

Rowland Percy clasped his hands, and tears glistened in his eyes, and then, by a great effort, he in part controlled his feelings, saying in a voice of emotion :—

"I will not weep—I will not weep : he is the happiest. But, tell me, Miranda, how happened this ?"

"His end was peaceful," said Miranda; "ask no more."

"I will strive to be content," said Rowland, with a deep sigh; "but this is a blow I did not look for. I—I—I thought—but no matter, Heaven's will be done."

"Yes Rowland; let us now look to the future. Tell me what is to be done, and how you are to free yourself from the frightful entanglements that surround you ?"

"I am helpless, Miranda, as an infant, and the few energies I possess are all locked up in that one deadly circumstance that a price is set upon my head by my accusers, and, innocent though I am, I dare not show myself in the face of day, for my very life's sake. Thus you see, dearest, I have become dependent upon those I would fain not hamper with such a charge."

"And yet," said Miranda, "amid all our misfortunes, all the false accusations that have been heaped upon you, and all the malignant persecutions we have endured, how wonderfully and strangely have friends sprung up around us! and even among those, where perhaps, we should have at most looked for sympathy and sorrow, we have found such warm hearts, that they are sufficient to redeem human nature from any stigma of universal selfishness that might be cast upon it."

"True, true; in the darkest storms of fate there are some rays of light, bright and beautiful, that bring comfort to the distressed soul, and bid the aching heart not to quake in despair."

At this moment the door of the room leading from the little bar was flung open and Ned Witlet, with the landlord, entered the apartment.

"There is danger, Mr. Percy," cried Witlet, "immediate danger, though what may be its extent I know not."

"The old Star and Tinder-box," said the landlord, "is teleagured at last, and, for once in a way, I'm nearly at my wit's end."

"Rowland—Rowland," cried Miranda, as she flung herself upon his neck in a paroxysm of apprehension ; "I am doomed ever to be to you the harbinger of danger."

"Hush! hush!" said Rowland ; "my only hope, my only joy."

CHAPTER CXXXIV.

THE INTERRUPTION, AND ARRIVAL OF MR. JONES.—MEDITATED SACRIFICE, AND ESCAPE.—DESPERATE CONFLICT WITH THE OFFICERS.

SCARCELY ever had Witlet worn such a face of alarm as he did upon the present occasion, or, rather, it should be called excitement, instead of alarm, for there was not the remotest trait of timidity in his words, looks, or actions ; the landlord, too, seemed quite possessed with the idea that no common danger was a-foot and locked the door through which he and Witlet had passed, as well as the one at which Rowland had entered, and said :—

"Now, some of you just have the goodness to tell me what I am to do. I'm stumped for an idea, and don't know which way to turn myself. It seems to me that we are all rather in for it."

"Affairs are desperate," said Witlet ; "and yet not quite so bad but they might be worse. I do not think, Mr. Percy, that we can both save ourselves ; the house is guarded at every available point of egress by officers ; nevertheless, I do think that by making up my own mind to be taken, I can make an outlet for you."

"Never," cried Rowland, "never, let the consequences be what they may. I never can permit such a self-sacrifice upon your part ; I will stand or fall by my own evil destiny. Accept the thanks and admiration of my heart. I should despise myself, as well as he despised by all of you, were I to accept safety upon such terms."

"Right, Rowland, right," cried Miranda, with a firmness that perfectly astonished Witlet and the landlord ; "We may suffer, but it shall be with clear breasts. Never shall it be said that, even in the greatest extremity of evil fortune, you consented to the sacrifice of another to save yourself ; death with honour is more noble, more glorious, than life with infamy. Rowland Percy, dearly as I love you I would stand by your grave rather than purchase your safety with one act that you could look back upon with the burning blush of shame!"

The landlord opened his eyes and mouth so wide that it seemed doubtful if they would ever close again, and as for Witlet, such a glow of pleasurable admiration shone upon his face, that any one would have thought him a man just apprised of some bright and pleasant destiny, instead of one on the brink of capture for infringing laws that would show him but little mercy.

"Mum—miss," said the landlord, when he recovered his speech, "all I have got to say is this ere—you are the out-and-outest female trump as ever I heard on, and afore anybody should so much as wag a little finger at you, they should walk bang over my carcass with rough nailed shoes. I'd guve myself up—I'd guve up the Star and Tinder-box—I'd guve up everybody, d——e, rather than a hair of your head should be placed awry. I've been married once, and, consequently, always misdoubted such things as female trumps ; but now I'm convinced."

"My heart's best treasure!" cried Rowland, "how admirably have you spoken for me that which I feel, and should myself have said."

"For the love of right, justice, mercy, and Heaven," said Witlet, "hear me. You take a wrong view of this case ; the sacrifice on my part is nothing near the sacrifice on yours. I am hunted by the officers of the law for what I have done, you for that of which you are entirely innocent. Sooner or later I must be taken. Moreover, if I am, there are a great many chances in my favour, and not one in yours; for what I am known to be guilty of is of far less importance than that of which you are so wrongfully accused. For Heaven's sake, Miss Miranda, listen to reason, and allow me to act as I propose."

" I cannot—I cannot," said Miranda.

" "Moments are precious—I have means of escape, Rowland Percy has none. The narrow back passage of this house is guarded by officers; If I make a rush through them they will pursue me, which is his only chance, for so strong a party of your enemies will take possession of the house, that I fear the up-stairs rooms will be of no avail, however skilfully they might be used."

A loud knocking at the bar now attracted their attention, and the landlord, with a sort of half-groan, said :—

" There, it's all up now—we are done. They've taken their measures, and won't wait any longer, so there's an end of that caper."

The knocking continued furiously; and while Witlet laid his hand upon Miranda's arm, and earnestly besought her to reason with Percy, and induce him to act as he advised, the landlord left the room to see who the impatient person was that seemed so intent on attracting attention at the bar.

" Once for all," cried Witlet, " I tell you you will be sacrificing yourself for no earthly object; one of us must be taken, and you could only save me by the same manœuvre that I propose for your benefit; you must recollect, too, Mr. Percy, that, without any disparagement to you, you are not so capable of executing that manœuvre as I am; my firm conviction is, that you are throwing away your only chance of escape for a mere chimera; for, if you do not accept of my proposition, we must both inevitably be taken."

" Witlet, Witlet," said Miranda, " on your soul, tell me, do you speak from your true conviction, or from your noble and disinterested desire to serve the unfortunate ?"

"From my true conviction, as I am a living man, Miss Rankley," exclaimed Witlet.

The door of the apartment was opened, and the landlord entered with Jones, who was carrying a bundle, and who without a word went up to Rowland, and began hauling off his coat.

" Good Heavens!" said Percy, " what's the meaning of this ?"

" Hold your gab," said Jones; " I'm a-going to try to make a honest woman of yer; all the fat's in the fire, and we shall have a scrimmage here as 'll beat the battle of Waterloo into fits; just open that ere bundle for me, Neddy; you'll find a gown and a cap there. Mind, Mr. Percy, you are to be for the future a respectable young woman, in search of a place; dont speak to the fellows, and mind yer sanguinary eye. Miss Miranda, mum, just give us a help."

" Jones, Jones," said Witlet, shaking his head, " I fear such a disguise will not evade the eager eyes of Bow-street runners."

" Neddy, Neddy," said Jones, " Bow-street runners is human beings, and they is do-able as well as other people. Have you got any hot water, landlord ?"

" Ah! to be sure."

"Then I tells you what, Mr. Percy; when you have got on these ere female togs, just you go into the wash-house, and we'll bring you a tub of hot water and some clothes, and do you pretend to be washing away like a brick. As for you, Neddy, I shall make a diwershun in your favour; there's no warrant agin me as yet. Just lend me that ere swell tile of yours, and out-an'-out cut away coat, and I'll try and bother them ere officers' notions of 'dentity."

A tremendous smash at this moment occurred at the bar; it seemed as if every bottle and glass had made up their minds at one instant to commit suicide, and the little party in the inner parlour looked at each other speechless and aghast.

"They are coming it now," said the landlord, and he placed his back against the door as he spoke.

Mr. Jones began whistling a popular air, and at the same time turning up his cuffs very deliberately.

"Lots o' work," he said; "jist say what's to be done, and then a fellow has a chance of doing it; this ere wash-tub business as I was a speaking of looks now remarkably like no go."

Such a drive came at the door, against which was the landlord's back, that, had he not been of a tolerable, or, rather, an intolerable weight, it must have been burst open.

"Now, Mr. Percy," said Ned Witlet, "can you hesitate? Clear the doorway, and, while I am in the midst of them, by a little activity you may get clear of the house."

The landlord moved from the door, keeping his hand upon the key.

"Are you ready, Ned?" he said.

"Quite."

"And," said Rowland, we will both attempt this desperate adventure, and let

No. 66.

either of us escape, as chances may direct.   Miranda, farewell! something at my heart tells me we shall meet again."

" Open this door, or we force it," cried a voice from without.

" Oh! the door," said the landlord, "certainly," and he turned the key, and flung it wide open.

Three stout men made a rush into the room, but they were met on the threshold by Rowland Percy, Jones, and Ned Witlet.   Not a word was spoken, but a desperate struggle ensued for several minutes.   The critical nature of his situation, and the awful consequences of being captured, armed Rowland Percy with preternatural strength; so that, although the man he had to contend with, was his superior in weight and strength, he fought with a desperation that the officer could make no head against; they fell heavily to the floor together, but Rowland Percy was uppermost, holding the officer's throat with such a grasp that his strength was evidently fast failing, and a blueish hue began to spread over his face.

In the meantime Witlet had given his antagonist a heavy fall, which brought him on his head with one of those frightful dabs, which experienced wrestlers know how to present to those who are opposed to them.

The third officer who had come into collision with Mr. Jones seemed not to like the turn events were taking; and, drawing a small pistol from his pocket, he placed the muzzle within half an inch of Jones's ear, and pulled the trigger; the weapon missed fire, or his destruction must have been certain.

" Thank you all the same," said Jones; and, taking the opportunity of the moment, he drew back his left hand, and gave the officer a frightful crashing blow on the jaw.

It would appear that the officers had made some arrangements with their companions concerning an accession of force, in case any disturbance should be made, for two more of the Bow-street runners made their appearance, at this identical moment, at the door of the room.

" Help!" gurgled the man who was held in such an iron grip by Rowland Percy, and in a moment the two fresh arrivals threw themselves upon Rowland, and his capture seemed certain; a second blow, however, on the stomach of the man who had attempted to shoot Jones put him *hors de combat*, and in an instant Witlet and he threw themselves upon the fresh arrivals, with the view of rescuing Percy from them, and giving him a chance of a rush from the house.   The struggle was a terrible one between those five men; but, as Witlet's object was to free Percy from the entanglements of the fight, and not himself, he was more likely to succeed than if his own safety had been his sole object.

At the expence of a considerable portion of Rowland's coat, and the whole of his cravat, the officers were dragged from him.

" Now, now," shouted Witlet; "scruples are madness; fly—fly—fly!"

This was not so easy, however, as it appeared, for the half strangled officer had recovered his faculties, and was just scrambling to his feet with an exclamation of,—

" Not so fast, young fellow; you must get yourself some better wings before you can fly yet—you are a prisoner."

Poor Miranda, who had been an agonised spectator of the fray, saw that now all was lost, unless she could do something more than sympathise with the unfortunate Rowland Percy; there was no time for hesitation, and, on the impulse of the moment, seizing the poker from the fire-place, she dealt the officer, who was scrambling to his feet, a blow on the head that laid him flat again in an instant.

With one bound Rowland was over the bar; a few moments brought him into Drury-lane, which he immediately crossed, and, diving into a mass of courts on the opposite side of the way, disappeared from the astonished gaze of the passengers, who took him for a madman by his disordered appearance and torn apparel.

CHAPTER CXXXV.

THE APPOINTMENT BETWEEN TWITTER AND VARLEY.—THE THAMES AT NIGHT.—
THE LONELY SPOT.

THE season now was far advanced, the sun sank dimly beneath the horizon, and day closed early; the long evenings were now setting in—lights and lamps were now the glory and pride of London.

The long avenue of lamps that now held an unbroken course from Holborn, down Fleet-market, Bridge-street, and Blackfriars-bridge, and thence all the way down the road till it terminated in a circle, from which ran several roads, seeing a magic line, giving forth light and animation to a scene that would otherwise have been dark and possessed of no charms to the many busy men who perambulated about as if they never tired or thought of rest.

To these might be added, and no insignificant addition either, the many strong lights thrown from the shop-windows, whose owners had arranged their goods and lights in the most attractive form, and which, consequently, threw a broad, glare of light often, at least, half across the roads, and far on either side, which being met by the light from other shops fomed a goodly stream of light, and when viewed from the bridge, gave a rich and warm appearance to the otherwise blackened view.

It was like looking into "blackest midnight" and beholding the eccentricities of a world of beings living by artifical light—some of the old tales of dwarfs and brownies would recur to the mind and become realities, and the busy beings below would appear like the "little men" who are doomed to be ever toiling not for their own good or of their free wills, but for the benefit, and under the surveillance of some capricious and hard-to-be-pleased giant.

All things and everybody bore a midnight and secret air about; them you could scarcely know your most intimate friend—especially as they, that is all that could —were wrapped and buttoned up in such guise that they might escape the keen and cold air of the night.

The clock of St. Paul's boomed forth the hour of eight, its dull, heavy, but sonorous sound vibrated long on the night air, and could be sensibly felt long after the last stroke had been dealt by the hammer. The clocks of various churches chimed forth the hour in shriller and more acute tones, and then died upon the air; but the vibration of St. Paul's clock remained long after the sounds of the metropolitan churches had ceased; its majesty of tone was unrivalled, and the tremulous ring in the air was borne away by the light breeze that swept through the city.

Blackfriars-bridge, on a dark night, when the air is cold and thin, and when a light east wind springs up and sweeps the principal thorougfares and the river for its whole length, is not the warmest or the most comfortable spots in which to await, or to stroll about in; but yet, up to this time, there had been waiting near the centre of the bridge, a tall, gaunt man, wrapped in a cloak, and soon after the hour had spoken out of so many months, slowly left the spots and descended the stairs leading to the water's edge, but standing on the first landing about half-way down.

There he mused for a time, and a dark smile crossed the sallow features, and an impression shot from his eye that would have appalled the soul of any man who had suddenly witnessed it for a moment.

This was Bernard Varley, who, not knowing well what moment Samuel Twitter might, in the agony of his spirit, arrive at the appointed place, came much before the time in order to prevent his cooling over his half-made promise; and the untempting appearance of the night and water, he thought might induce him, Twitter, to repent, and quit the spot, which if he, Varley, were present, might possibly be prevented.

Twitter was not yet come, and Bernard Varley paced the few yards backwards and forwards for some time in deep thought, and then he leaned with his back against the bridge, and was lost in the deep contemplation of the dim obscurity that enveloped the river.

"The night is dark and cold," he muttered; "so much the better—we shall meet with fewer obstacles—fewer craft will be on the river, and the gloom that shrouds everything around will strike terror to the heart of the cowardly wretch, and he will be an easier victim than I expected to find even him. The tide running up, and the wind blows up the river—it will be easy work—a sail—ay, that must be it—oars will not do, I will steer the boat, and Master Samuel Twitter shall mind the sails—yes, he can trim a sail doubtless. This night appears as if especially appointed for such purposes as that which I have in hand."

He walked down to the water's edge, and looked on the stream as it silently glided by, its deep calm bosom here and there slightly ruffled as the waters struck against some impediment in their course, such as the arches of the bridge, a moored boat, or lighter ; but passing these they again flowed swiftly and silently by.

"Yes," resumed Varley; "a better night for such a work could scarce be found. I trust he will not fail—it is a pity he should miss so fair an opportunity of quieting all his fears and troubles for the future."

Varley turned towards the stairs and ascended them to the top, and then he gazed around him. The distant lights appeared to burn more brightly, and seemed to throw out a ruddier glare of light since he looked upon the dark and silent stream below.

"He comes—he comes!" he muttered to himself, but in such a tone of inward satisfaction, that at once betrayed the deep-set resolution of his heart, and a brighter gleam of fiendish gladness shot from his eyes, and he crept close beneath the shadow of the balustrades.

At some distance was the figure of a man, whose irresolution was apparent from the very mode in which he made his way towards the spot where Varley stood, but where he was not seen. He walked forward for a few yards, but at a slow, varying pace, and ever and anon he would come to a halt, as if he debated in his own mind the propriety of returning.

But again he would move forward, and again the same process would be gone through ere he would advance many paces, and all this was done with such an air of secrecy, as if he were fearful lest he should be seen, which induced many persons to look after him with curiosity, to know what a man so acting could mean.

At length, however, Samuel Twitter arrived at the head of the stairs, and peering down towards the water and seeing no one, he said,—

"I wonder if Varley will come; he's not here. Well, I'm glad of it; I have kept my promise, and he cannot complain if I refuse to come again, since he keeps not his time. It is dark, cold, and gloomy ; I am very glad he is not come."

"But I am come, Samuel Twitter," said Varley, stepping out from his place of concealment.

Twitter started back with a half-scream, and showed an inclination to quit the spot with much precipitation ; but Varley said,—

"I am glad too to see that you are so punctual and ready, Samuel Twitter ; it will be a matter of congratulation to yourself at a future time if you ever think of this night again, to know it was the means of rescuing us both from many difficulties and dangers, and that this night's work enabled me to settle definitively with you."

"True, Varley, very true;" replied Twitter, whose teeth chattered with cold and fear ; "but do you intend to go on the river such a night as this—so cold, so dark, and so severe ?"

"Yes, Samuel Twitter; do you think that Rowland Percy would wait where he is as if he had to keep an appointment with me for his own benefit, instead of being hanged, as he assuredly will, if, with your assistance, I can secure him, and safely bring him to town ?"

"With my assistance, Varley? I cannot do much, and it's so cold that I can scarce stand. Think better of it, and let the officers take him themselves—it is their business, and not ours; what else are they for?"

"Samuel Twitter, do you not know that so long as Rowland Percy is at large so long are we in danger of being hanged,—ay, hanged—would that have any charms for your mind, Samuel Twitter?"

Twitter shook his head with a groan, and Varley then went on,—

"Besides, were he safely disposed of, I tell you again, that the Grange estate shall be sold for what it will fetch, and then I shall settle my account with you, which you know, Samuel Twitter, I could not do else."

"But will you really sell the Grange estate? If I could believe that you meant me fairly, Varley, with what pleasure could I go with you? I fear—I fear——"

"What can you possibly fear from me, Samuel Twitter—are we not as brothers?"

"Brothers, Varley, brothers?"

"Ay, brothers in crime, you know at least."

"I didn't do the—the ——"

"Murder," added Varley, "no—I know you did not; but you could not well tell what my share was, save at the expense of your life or liberty, which would be the same in a short time; we are both, therefore, deep enough in this affair to make it desirable that we should act fairly to each other, so that we may, if we choose, part from each other, and have the choice of living in separate countries, and thus put it out of the power of either to injure the other by accident or design. This, I believe, is for the good of us both. Your intellect, Samuel Twitter, must surely at once, and in strong colours, show you that I am acting for your benefit, equally with my own."

"Well," said Twitter, "when shall we go? but you are sure that you will sell the Grange, and give me my share of the produce?"

"I will—I will, by all that I hold, or ever did hold sacred, do as I promised you, if you fairly assist me as I require of you."

They turned down the steps and proceeded to the foot of the stairs, and getting into a boat, desired to be taken to Searle's boat-house, Lambeth.

They now silently glided over the bosom of the Thames towards their destination, which they were not long in reaching, as the tide went with them.

"Now," said Varley to Twitter, as they quitted the boat, "we will have a sail, you can manage that very well, and I will steer; there is only a light breeze which will render it perfectly safe."

To this arrangement Twitter proposed no objection—indeed, he would rather it were so, since the labour was less, and Samuel Twitter hated labour. Ere long, they were suited, and a sail was hoisted for them. Twitter stepped into the boat, and Varley followed, seating himself in the stern to take the helm. In a few moments more they had gained the stream, and the light wind filled the sail, and away they went towards Richmond.

The night was very cold and dark, the red glare of the buoys, and the light from the shore looked dim and distant, which seemed to make their position the moae lonely and cheerless.

There were but few craft on the water, and after they had passed Vauxhall bridge, they met with scarcely a boat of any denomination.

Twitter's mind was a prey to a thousand torturing reflections; he noted all that would conduce or assist in the commission of such a crime as that which Varley meditated, while Varley himself was well noting all that passed around—the position he occupied on the river—the spot—the lamps—and, lastly, Twitter himself, occupied no small share of his thoughts; for he had seen, by the light at the boat-house, the stock of a pistol protruding from under his waistcoat; of this, however, he took no notice whatever.

They now passed Battersea bridge—here the river was very wide, and not a boat was to be seen. On the right lay a piece of low, swampy ground, on which grew tall trees, and in the summer, parts were cultivated with vegetables, but which was now scarcely to be approached. On this spot Varley fixed his eyes, and calculated chances.

CHAPTER CXXXVI.

THE ATTEMPTED MURDER.—THE DEATH STRUGGLE.—THE LAST SHRIEK.

TWITTER's uneasiness had evidently been on the increase from the moment of starting until the present time ; he each moment more and more in his own heart cursed his folly for trusting himself to Bernard Varley, and under such favourable circumstances for the commission of some act of desperation, which should at once hurry him from the world and all its anxieties, a consummation which Twitter by no means devoutly wished ; for, like most men, who have perpetrated, or assisted in the perpetration of great crimes, he shrunk from death as the greatest of all possible evils.

Moreover there was, or he thought there was, which was quite sufficient, a lurking mysterious meaning in every word Varley uttered. Once or twice, too, he caught the dark flashing eye of his master in iniquity glaring upon him, so that, altogether, Samuel Twitter was about as uncomfortable during his aquatic excursion, as any one could very well be under any such circumstances whatever, and most devoutly did he wish it over.

The part of the river they were at was not overburdened with houses on its brinks, so that it was only occasionally that a gleam of light shone upon the water and gave poor Twitter a ray of comfort, for he thought that Varley would surely attempt nothing while there were human beings sufficiently near to be cognisant of the cry of distress.

" This is rather a lonely spot," remarked Twitter. " Are we near the place of of our destination ?"

" I trust so," was the reply. " The inquiry, Twitter, is a more profound one than you intended it."

" Profound !"

" Yes, Samuel Twitter ; for putting aside the fact, that we are all near our destination—I mean the grave—some of us may be much nearer it than others. The most cunning of us, Samuel Twitter, in a moment of incaution, will do things that life would be too short to repent of."

" Yes," groaned Twitter ; " you've grown quite metaphysical lately, it's not a pleasant subject."

" And yet," said Varley, as if pursuing quite an abstract chain of reasoning.— " what is death but a release from wordly troubles,—and which of us are without troubles ?"

" Very true," said Twitter, trembling so violently that he shook the sail. " I don't mind putting up with my troubles though a little longer ; besides, you know, Varley, it's very unmanly indeed, to fly from one's troubles."

" Ay, true—but why do you keep your hand so constantly in the breast of your coat ?"

" My hand—the breast of my coat ? Oh, oh ! for nothing."

" You look suspicious, Samuel Twitter. What a curious calculation it would be to consider if you could gain most by murdering me, or I the most by murdering you."

" Very," cried Twitter, with a deep groan ; " more curious than pleasant a great deal."

" Indeed !

" Why—why—where are you going, Varley ; why—why don't you keep the middle of the river ? Good gracious ! where are you steering ?"

" I like this side of the river, especially in a quiet spot like this, where one can indulge in pleasant imaginations without interruption."

The boat now moved slowly and languidly through the tangled weeds, among which Varley had steered it, and Twitter half drew the pistol from his bosom as if he expected each moment that a desperate attempt was about to be made against his life. The spot was very dark, but the distance between those two guilty men in the boat was so short, that Varley could easily perceive the action of Twitter, and if he persevered in his intention of attempting his destruction, he felt the necessity of securing the weapon with which Twitter was armed, as a preface to any other hostile movement.

" Nay, now," he said, " I was foolish to steer in here, for we have got entangled among the weeds, and I must use the skulls with which we are happily provided, to row us out. Step over here and do you take the helm."

" Eh ? step over there ? I'm rather nervous, and think I can't."

" You think you cannot ?"

" Ye—yes, Varley ; just manage the helm yourself ; I am so cold I couldn't move on any account, besides you are——that is, nothing.'

By what he thought a very dexterous movement, Twitter, got the pistol completely from his breast, and hid it beneath the skirts of his coat, but the manœuvre was not executed so quickly as to escape Varley's notice, and he said—

" Well, Twitter, at least the sail must come down, so let us see your seamanship in accomplishing that."

Twitter looked up hopelessly at the sail, for he had about as much an idea of how to pull it down, as how to manage a man-of-war.

" Ah, now, Twitter," said Varley, as by a movement of one of the skulls he hit him a great rap on one side of the head. " You're but a clumsy sailor, but perhaps you think life is too short to make it worth while to learn everything."

" Keep off—keep off," cried Twitter, in an agony of terror and pain ; " keep off, Bernard Varley, d—n it ! keep off. I may be a fool for trusting myself here with you, but I am a desperate and dangerous one. Keep off, I say, keep off."

He held out the pistol as he spoke, steadying it with both hands, and pointing it as correctly at Bernard Varley's head as his nerves, and the little light there was would permit him.

" Why, Twitter," said Varley, " are you mad, what is the meaning of all this show of violence ?"

" It's loaded to the brim," said Twitter ; " get out of the weeds—go home, no nonsense, Varley : I tell you it's loaded to the brim."

" This is strange conduct," added Varley, as he pretended to make great efforts to get out of the side of the river, " this is very strange and ungrateful conduct, I really ——"

While he spoke, Varley had been artfully getting one of the skulls in a position for effective use, and at this moment, with a sudden swing of it, he struck Twitter's arm, throwing himself back in the boat, simultaneously, or rather a little before the blow. Partly with the sudden fright, and partly under the influence of pain, for the edge of the skull had struck his wrist very sharply, Twitter pulled the trigger of the pistol, a tremendous report followed, and a strange shower of some sort of missiles from the weapon, for Twitter had really loaded it to the muzzle, passed over Varley's face, within an inch of his most prominent feature.

This was just what Varley wanted ; that is to say, that Twitter's pistol should be discharged, and harmlessly. It screwed up his courage to the sticking-place, and it took away, too, from the murder he contemplated, much, if not all, of its cold-blooded atrocity, since he could now almost persuade himself that Twitter was the aggressor, and had tried first to take his life before he, Varley, made any hostile movement whatever.

Abandoning rudder and skulls, with an oath, he rushed upon Twitter, and in an instant had him by the throat.

" Villain !" he cried ; " no power on earth or hell shall save you ; you are a dead man."

"Help! help! murder," shrieked Twitter. His voice rung over the water wildly and fearfully, but no help was near, and Varley laughed aloud at the impotence of his rage.

"Ay, shriek on," he cried, "Samuel Twitter, shriek on; your cries are music to my ears. Wretch, did you think for one moment you had subdued such a man as I am; you have courted your own destruction and nothing now can save you."

He tightened his grasp upon the throat of the terrified wretch. Twitter felt indeed, that his last moments had come, and yet, with what little breath was left him by Varley's tightening grasp, he shrieked for mercy, that mercy which he would not have shown himself, and which was equally a stranger to the breast of his ruthless companion in guilt.

"Varley—Varley!" he cried; "you would not kill me; you cannot, would not kill me; I will be your slave, your abject slave; I will ask for no money, and desire none; you shall command me to what you please, direct me to what you please, and I will not demur. Varley, you do not mean it: tell me you do not mean to kill me. Mercy—mercy—let me live! I ask but for life—life?"

"And you ask in vain," growled Varley, as he tightened his hold, and dashed his victim's head against the gunwale of the boat. "You ask in vain; I have made myself a promise that this night shall be your last, and I will keep my word."

"No, no—mercy! mercy!"

"Have you no prayer, Samuel Twitter—no last wish—no hope?"

"Yes; a prayer for mercy—mercy!"

"None other?"

"Give me life and I will pray for you."

"Ah! ah! ah!" laughed Varley; "I am past praying for."

There came over the surface of the water at this moment the sound of a distant voice chaunting some merry air, which, after a moment, had its burden taken up by others; and then there was a wild and merry shout of laughter, which came strangely and discordantly upon the ears of that terrified man, who believed himself, correctly enough, at his last gasp, for never had mortal man so determined upon a fiend-like act with more resolution than had Bernard Varley made up his mind to the death of Samuel Twitter.

The voices were far distant. "But still," he thought, "if I can hear them, they may hear Twitter—no time is to be lost."

Placing his other hand upon his throat, so as to have a desperate clutch of his throat, he struck his head against the side of the boat again, with the hope of producing immediate insensibility; but such was not the case, for Twitter raised another shriek of such an intensity, that it alarmed Varley beyond measure, and he dashed down the head of his victim twice more with fearful violence; to cast him over the boat's side was the work of a moment, and Varley believed then that he had got rid of, once and for ever, the greatest enemy to his peace.

Such, however, was not at once the fact? it might have been the sudden immersion into the cold water, or it might have been that nature herself rallied at the moment with one desperate effort to cling to life; for Twitter, although he was immersed completely in the river, clung with a desperate energy, by both hands, to the side of the boat, near the stern.

His faculties seemed too confused to allow him to speak; but by the dim light that came from the heavens, Varley could see the horrible countenance of his victim, white and awful, with here and there a spot of blood upon it, and the eyes bent upon him with so wild and frantic a glare, that even he, heartless ruffian as he was, shrunk for a moment aghast from the horrible apparition.

It was though but for a moment; a fear came over him that Twitter would find voice to cry for help, and that the persons he had heard singing might hear him, and come to his assistance. He sprung upon him, and strove to force him to disengage his hold; this, however, was more difficult to accomplish than he imagined, for even the most savage blows would not suffice, and what he apprehended did take place ; for, while he still clung with desperate energy to the boat, Twitter again found voice to speak.

"Heaven have mercy upon me !" he said, "I am guilty—guilty !"

"Down—down !" shrieked Varley ; "d———n !—down."

He struck the hands of the wretched man violently with the moveable seat of the boat ; they were crushed and bleeding, but still he kept a desperate hold ; it

seemed that only with life itself would he part from that one poor chance of yet saving himself.

Then Varley suddenly thought of an expedient as ferocious as it was effective. Taking a clasp-knife from his pocket, he opened its largest blade, and commenced drawing it across the fingers of Twitter until he severed the tendons, when, with one loud gurgling shriek, the unhappy wretch fell backward into the stream.

No. 67.

CHAPTER CXXXVII.

TEMPORARY TRIUMPH OF VARLEY.—THE NEWSPAPER PARAGRAPH.—TWITTER'S
SCHEME OF REVENGE.

THE perspiration stood upon the brow of Bernard Varley, as he plied his oars
with desperate energy, and rowed from that spot which would ever be frightful to
his imagination, fancying as his one only source of satisfaction, that now indeed,
he was a free man, and that the only secret that could consign him to the gallows
was locked in his own breast.

The thought struck him that it would be imprudent to return to the stairs with
the wherry, as it would afford another opportunity of identifying him, and likewise excite some observations, from the fact that he had gone out in company
with another, and come back alone. He managed therefore to get to land by
means of clambering over some coal-barges, and left the wherry adrift. He then
made his way to his hotel, which he succeeded in entering, as he thought, unseen
by any one.

When he rose the next morning, Varley eagerly ran his eye over the newspaper
which lay upon the breakfast-table, and with a flashing eye and burning cheek he
read the following paragraph :—

"ATTEMPTED MURDER ON THE RIVER.—Last night the attention of a party
on the river was attracted by cries of ' Help,' arising from some one apparently
suffering violence, but before they could reach the spot from whence the sounds
proceeded, all was still. Some time afterwards, however, the Thames, the shot-
tower by Waterloo bridge, and the coal-barges were thrown into a state of indes-
cribable consternation by the finding of the bleeding and inanimate form of a
man in the water. The vital spark was not quite extinct ; and by the praise-
worthy and active exertions of Mr. Mac Fudge, a medical practitioner in
extensive practice, he was restored.—We have ascertained from the very best
authority, that his name is Twitter, and the first word he uttered when he recovered
consciousness was Harley, and something about the Mange at York. At present
the affair is involved in considerable mystery, and a great number of rumours
keep perpetually floating about concerning it. The active inspector, Gobbles,
assisted by the enterprising officer, A 227, who is further associated with B 122,
will no doubt, ascertain some interesting particulars in time for our next
impression."

"Alive, alive," groaned Varley. "Curses on him, water will not drown him ;
he is born to be hanged."

He then again and again read the paragraph, and spent hours in calcula-
ting what Twitter would do, and what he could himself do, in the way of precaution.

Meanwhile Twitter remained at a little public-house, whither he had been
taken after his rescue from the river. It was not until he had awaked from a
long deep sleep that he became aware of what had occurred to him, and could
trace circumstance upon circumstance, until he found himself rescued from a
death which seemed inevitable.

"The villain Varley would have murdered me," he thought. "Oh what an
escape I have had. Oh, if I only dared accuse him! If I only dared to have
him put in gaol and hung afterwards ; but I dare not, I dare not ; he might keep
the secret till the morning of his execution, till he saw that there was no hope, and
then he would tell all about the murder at the Grange, and I should be hung too!
Revenge is sweet, but sometimes too expensive."

When the active inspector Gobbles called again at the public-house, in order to
get the full and interesting particulars of the attempted murder from the mouth
of the rescued victim, he was amazed to find that victim most unwilling to hold
any communication on the subject, and apparently as anxious to bury the whole

affair in oblivion, as if, instead of being the attacked party, he had compromised himself by a considerable amount of criminality.

The inspector was full of fury when he found that Twitter was resolute in his determination to render no further account of the affair, and at length left the house, defrauded, as he declared, of everlasting fame that would have attended him, had he succeeded in bringing to justice the perpetrator of so desperate an attempt at murder.

Twitter then fell into a sound sleep, and when he awoke felt himself so much refreshed in body and mind, as to be capable of forming some accurate conclusion as to his position and prospects.

"I must put," he said, "my long cherished scheme into operation, and take for myself advantage of the means which Varley has taken to secure his own safety. That yacht which he has purchased so wisely, and the particulars concerning which I so strangely, but fortunately became acquainted with, shall be put to my own use. When I am in some foreign land, then I can take active measures against him; nay, what is to hinder me writing a full statement of the murder at the Grange, and placing it in the Liverpool post-office before my departure, but only so short time before it, as shall ensure to me the advantage of many hours start before it can reach its destination. Yes, that will be a good scheme, a most admirable scheme, and one which surely cannot fail of success. All I require is a sum of money to support me abroad, and free me from the necessity of striving for a subsistence. I have before thought of a plan of procuring that—a plan, which under ordinary circumstances would be attended with much danger, but which, as I am situated, can do me no harm if it does me no good. I can commit a forgery upon Bernard Varley, and dare he accuse me of it? No; certainly if I am so situated with regard to him that I dare not accuse him of an attempt to murder me, he dare not accuse me of the crime of forgery—nay he must admit the signature to be his own. I have taken the opportunity of possessing myself of blank cheques from his cheque-book, and well I know his hand-writing—what is to hinder me from filling up one for a large sum?"

This was so pleasant an idea to Samuel Twitter that in the contemplation of it he almost forgot his numerous wounds. After much consideration he resolved that the cheque should be drawn for eight thousand pounds.

CHAPTER CXXXVIII.

THE FLIGHT OF ROWLAND.—CAPTURE OF JONES.—DEPARTURE OF MIRANDA FOR YORK.

ROWLAND PERCY no sooner got clear of the Star and Tinder-box than he rushed into a labyrinth of courts, on the opposite side of Drury-lane. Here he dashed from one part to the other, with a wild vehemence that excited the curiosity of the passengers. In this way, sometimes running, then pausing for a few moments to gain breath, and again rushing onwards, he proceeded till he had placed a very considerable distance between himself and the public-house whence he had been routed. He went on in spite of the rain which now fell in torrents, but at length he fancied he perceived some one following him, and, with a feeling of terror he rushed down a turning where a door stood invitingly open. What occurred there we shall leave untold for the present, while we glance at the other parties who were engaged in the scuffle at the Star and Tinder-box.

Several of the officers rushed into Drury-lane in pursuit of the fugitive, and those who remained were in such a state of confusion that Witlet contrived to effect his escape, but Jones was after a severe struggle secured, while the kind-hearted landlord took an opportunity of drawing Miranda into the bar where he caused her to sit quietly sheltered from observation by some tall hogsheads. The officers were not disposed to make any severe search for Miranda, notwithstanding her sharp attack on one of them, for they could not, rough beings as they were, forbear from admiring the bravery and constancy she had displayed. They were acquainted also with her history, and although they were well paid by Bernard Varley to attempt the capture of Rowland, they would one and all have scorned to join in his persecution of the orphan daughter of Sir George Rankley.

In about an hour afterwards a note was handed to the landlord by a man bearing the appearance of a ballad singer, it was addressed to Miranda, and was at once handed to her by the landlord. It contained these words.

" MISS RANKLEY—It will be impossible for me to return to the public-house where you now are for some days. My business will be to search for Rowland and give him all the aid I can. Meanwhile let me implore you for the present to return to York, for in London your footsteps will be constantly dogged by the emissaries of the villain Varley. At York you will find, as you know, dear friends who will kindly welcome you. Do not hesitate—The landlord will I am sure, on my account furnish you with the means. Do not I pray you sleep another night in London. God bless you, Miranda Rankley. Something even now tells me that happier days are in store for you, and that the clouds which have hitherto obscured your destiny will dissipate, leaving a brighter sun behind them than has ever yet shone upon your fortunes.   WITLET."

Miranda saw at once that the advice offered by Witlet was as rational as could be suggested under the circumstances, and the landlord when made aware of the contents of the note, lent his persuasions also, endeavouring to comfort her after his own fashion.

"Never mind what has happened my dear," he said; " Percy has got away again. It seems as if he was not to be nabbed no how. And if so be as you do wish to go to York, I'll put you in the coach and see you off to night."

" I will be guided by what you say," replied Miranda, " as I am sure your advice is the best, for you are well qualified to give it. I see I can be no longer useful here ; my presence but endangers him I would give my life to preserve."

" Exactly," replied the landlord, "and hope for the best. Stay at York till something happens that shall change the look of affairs. In my mind, Miss Rankley, there is no kind of doubt respecting the share those two men, Varley and Twitter had in the death of the unfortunate Sir George Rankley. They are guilty."

" They are, they are; and yet the one professed to be the bosom friend of my father, and the other was indebted to him on the score of gratitude, for Sir George was a kind and liberal master."

" Well, Miss Rankley," said the landlord, " I cannot pretend to fathom their motives, but the fact is evident to me, and will I trust one of these days be apparent to all the world."

Miranda soon completed her few preparations for travelling, and then set out with the landlord for the office from which the York coach would start that night.

It would have been a singular sight to any one who had known Miranda Rankley in her palmy days of wealth and happiness, when she had but to form a wish and it was gratified ; and who had been acquainted with the landlord of the Star and Tinder-box, with his mode of life and his associates, to have seen those two walking arm-in-arm through the streets of London, much in the guise of father and daughter.

And could Sir George Rankley have returned to life, he would indeed have been surprised at this association of his beautiful and dearly loved daughter with the companion of thieves and the worst characters that London abounds in.

But these men are not lost to all sense of justice, and it often happens that they display more untiring sympathy towards the oppressed than those who, from their wealth and station, are better qualified to afford, yet they lack the desire to do that good which they are so well able to give,

When the landlord and his fair charge arrived at the office, they found the coach just ready to start, and most fortunately one inside place not taken. This was speedily secured, and Miranda duly installed in it. The landlord at the same time gave her a small parcel which he told her to open on the road.

She had barely time to thank him and express a hope that Rowland Percy would be safe, when the coach began to move slowly away.

" Have no fear of that," replied the landlord, still holding by the door, and willing to give what comfort he could; " he shall not want a friend while I have it in my power to be one to him."

He could not hear the reply, for he was compelled to let go his hold of the door, and the coach drove off.

It was not until the first change of horses took place, that Miranda opened the small parcel the landlord of the Star and Tinder-box had given her, the contents of which she found to be a silk purse, somewhat [the worse for wear, well filled with cash.

Miranda looked at the purse and its contents; a tear of gratitude started to her eye as she thought of the sympathy and kindness she had experienced from people who could scarcely have been expected to show any. This last act of kindness from one whom she had never seen but once, and whom she should probably never see again, came forcibly to her mind.

The horses were quickly changed, and away went the coach at a rattling pace again on the way to York.

————

CHAPTER CXXXIX.

TWITTER'S RESOLVE.—THE FORGED CHECK AND THE DETECTION.—VARLEY'S ATTEMPT
TO POSSESS HIMSELF OF THE MONEY.

IT was in a perplexing and anxious state of mind that Samuel Twitter resolved the various modes of procedure over in his mind. Many things were desirable, he told himself, yet many were dubious or dangerous; the thing, therefore, that he endeavoured to encompass, was the most certain, and, at the same time, it involved the least possible amount of personal risk; for Samuel Twitter's recent adventure had but little tended to infuse a spirit of courage and adventure into his mind.

After much thought, he determined to provide against the next visit of the active and exemplary inspector, by decamping and leaving the nest empty. He, therefore, arose early while the people of the house were busily employed about ordinary affairs, dressed himself, and after assuring himself, by carefully listening at the head of the stairs, that no one was at hand, he quietly decended the stairs, peeping as he came down into every hole and corner, until he finally reached the door, which he opened and closed without disturbing any one of the household.

Twitter found that the exercise of walking was any thing but pleasant; his limbs were stiff and sore, while his bruises required some attention, and fearful of the consequences, he called a coach, and ordered the man to drive him to the hotel he had been living at, separately from Varley.

His appearance here was rather unexpected—at least, his personal appearance in such guise was scarcely looked for; and Twitter was much annoyed by being conscious that he was food for observation among the waiters. He, however, immediately retired to his own apartments, and drawing writing materials towards him, he began to practice on a sheet of paper the name of Bernard Varley, imitating signature he already possessed, written by Varley himself.

Many attempts were abortive, but at length he succeeded, and the signature was attached to the check, which was filled up with the demand of six thousand pounds. Twitter would have demanded more, but he feared that so much might not be there, and then he would get none. It was, however, much against his nature to seek a smaller sum, when he believed a larger one was to be obtained, even for safety's sake, but he did do it, and the check was accordingly drawn for the sum of six thousand pounds.

" Now," thought Twitter, " the next thing will be to present it and obtain the money."

So greatly was he elated that he ordered some refreshments to be brought him; then, after a time, he ordered a coach, into which he stepped, and ordered the coachman to drive to the bankers'.

Twitter was not in the most imperturbable mood as he was driven along; on the contraary, now that his scheme was so near completion, he became slightly nervous as to the result, though he felt conscious that if he were defeated, that Varley dared not do aught to injure him. Yet Varley was a desperate, bold, and bad man, altogether free from those fears which haunted his, Twittter's, imagination.

While these thoughts crossed his mind the coach stopped, and the coachman in another minute opened the door, saying:—

" This is the house, yer honner."

" Very well," said Twitter " Wait awhile till I return, as I shall want you to go back."

" Yes, yer honnor," said the coachman, with a touch of the brim of his hat.

Twitter entered the banking-house, and made strait for the desk where he saw checks were being cashed, and handed in his own. Twitter's manner betrayed embarrassment; indeed, he had scatce breath enough to speak, and he watched the expression of the clerk's countenance with a nervousness that was quite painful to himself.

The individual who took the check looked at the signature very hard, and then consulted a book, after which he left the room, and presently returned with another individual, who likewise consulted the book, and then they both came to Twitter.

" We cannot pay this check," said the clerk.

" Are there no funds?" inquired Twitter.

" Yes; but it does not appear genuine. The signature and filling up are different from what Mr. Varley usually adopts. I must detain it and yourself."

" Very well," replied Twitter, with more composure than he thought himself capable of, but which no doubt arose from his belief in the inability of Bernard Varley to do anything to his detriment. " You had better send for Mr. Varley, as my time is of consequence."

" Certainly, sir," said the clerk, somewhat staggered by the cool request; " have the kindness to walk this way, and we will immediately dispatch some one for Mr. Varley."

Twitter entered a small room, evidently used as a waiting-room, and seated himself before the fire, there to wait until Varley came.

It was some time ere he could arrive, and Twitter took up the morning paper, to amuse himself during the interval he had to wait, but, however well to appearance feigning he effected this, he felt but wretchedly at heart.

" I wonder what he will say," thought Twitter, with an uneasy shift in his chair: he cannot let me be taken for forgery, that's clear, because, though he would be very glad, indeed, to see me hanged, yet he would know very well that his fate would be similar to my own; for what motive should I have to keep the secret since my own life was no longer affected by it, and I could revenge myself upon him. " No, he must admit the writing as his; but should they make the inquiries without my being present, then I am lost," thought Twitter, with a groan.

There was a slight bustle, and one of the lerks uttered the name of Varley.

"Ah! he is come," thought Twitter, and, in another moment, Varley entered the room.

There was a strange mixture of malice and pleasure perceptible, as if he were glad that Samuel Twitter was thus safely lodged, and in his power. He looked more pleasantly than before, when he saw, too, the marks of violence he bore upon his person—evidence of his own brutality—which seemed to give him much delight.

"Ah! Samuel Twitter," he said, with a triumphant air, "I had not expected this interview. It is pleasant when friends meet unexpectedly, it brings joy to my heart, Samuel Twitter."

"Ah! you're very good—very," groaned Twitter, "and would, I dare say, be happy to have seen me at the bottom of the Thames."

Varley's colour changed for a moment as he met Twitter's eye during this reply; it brought with it a disagreeable reminiscence.

"Not at all," replied Varley; "not at all. You are here upon business I dare say; you did not desire my company, though, so much, perhaps, as I desired yours. Our meeting is unexpected, Samuel Twitter."

"Oh, yes, very; but the people here sent purposely for you upon business."

"What is it that you sent for me about?" he inquired of the clerk who was in attendance.

"A cheque has been presented to us, purporting to be drawn by you for six thousand pounds."

"Six thousand pounds!" echoed Varley, in a peculiar bland and subdued tone, that made Twitter groan internally.

"Yes, Mr. Varley; we were doubtful of the signature, and sent for you."

"You did very right," said Varley, in the same tone, but glancing at Twitter.

"Is it genuine?" inquired the clerk.

"Allow me to look at it," said Varley.

The clerk handed the check to him, and Varley carefully read it through, and after curiously and minutely examining it, he laid it down before him, and was about to speak when Twitter, fearful of the consequence, interfered, with the desperate attempt of silencing Varley, and even compelling him to acknowledge the signature, through fear of the consequence.

"Mr. Varley," he said, "knows that I would not commit such an act as your suspicions would imply; he knows, too, that I would not do anything that would cost me my life, especially as he is well aware that the existence of another person entirely depends upon my own."

This had all the effect it was intended for; Varley at once saw his imminent danger—he turned very sick—the room appeared to swim round, when he made an effort to speak and said, in a faint voice.—

"I recollect now—it is my signature. It is all right. You must cash it."

"Oh, certainly. Mr. Varley," replied the clerk, much puzzled by what occurred, for he could not understand what had happened; in his own mind the forgery was clear, and he thought Varley knew it; but why he should suddenly admit the cheque to be genuine was beyond his comprehension, but there was no room for hesitation, and he continued,—

"I am very sorry for having given you so much trouble, Mr. Varley, and must apologise to this gentleman for the unpleasant occurrence of his detention, but it was our duty to make sure where a doubt existed."

"Oh, don't name it," cried Twitter, delighted at the turn events had taken, but yet nervously apprehensive of Varley; "it couldn't be helped I dare say; but, as I have waited here long enough, perhaps you will have the goodness to give me the cash for this at once."

"Most certainly, sir," said the clerk; "step this way."

Twitter entered the public part of the bank, and once more stood at the corner, but closely followed by Bernard Varley, who watched every movement he made, and fixed his eyes upon Twitter, who felt as uncomfortable beneath his basilisk-like gaze, as it is possible to imagine, though he (Twitter) never once looked at Varley, or met his eyes. He hastily counted over the change for the cheque, and carefully secured it about his person, and then turned to leave the hall.

In this he was followed by Bernard Varley, who kept close to his heels, until he came into the street, when the latter seized hold of him with a nervous gripe of the throat, saying,—

" Samuel Twitter, the money—the money! I must have it. Give it up quietly, and save your life, or all the help you may call for shall not save you."

" Help—help! Murder! Police!" cried Twitter, as he felt Varley's grasp and his endeavours to possess himself of the booty he (Twitter) had about him, and a desperate struggle ensued between them.

———

CHAPTER CXL.

TWITTER'S ESCAPE.—VARLEY'S ANGER AND DESPERATION.

TWITTER'S cries for help soon brought a crowd of individuals around them, though no one seemed inclined to interfere between them—not knowing the nature of the quarrel, and, moreover, it appeared as if the superior had merely committed an assault on the inferior, which, as all the world knows, is a very venial offence; but just reverse the order of things, and the punishment is not yet invented that is sufficient, as a punishment, for the audacious inferior who may be goaded by provocation to inflict a merited chastisement on his superior in society.

Thus for some minutes they were left to themselves to fight it out as they could. Twitter's outcries could not long remain unheard by the police; and Varley's attempts to introduce his hands into Twitter's pockets became evident to all the spectators.

This being a point that touched them all very closely, they soon began to give vent to their horror at the idea of one man's putting his hands into another man's pocket, and Bernard Varley, instead of being popular in the affray, which he was nigh becoming at first, ran some danger of being maltreated.

" Murder! murder!—help!—police!" cried Twitter, as he writhed and twisted in Varley's grasp, at the same time he kicked and bit very hard.

" Do you want to murder the man ?" inquired one old gentleman, who was fat and short-winded. " Leave go his throat, you'll induce an apoplectic fit."

" Why, he's trying to pick the other's pocket," remarked the other ; " he deserves to be sent to the compter."

" Why don't you leave go, and fight it out like men ?" interposed a brewer's drayman, who looked on both Twitter and Varley with great contempt.

" Give up the money," exclaimed Varley.

" Murder !—police !" screamed Twitter.

" I'll kill you if you do not instantly give me the money you have robbed me off," exclaimed Bernard Varley.

" Murder !—police ! save me from this man, who has before tried to murder——"

Here his voice became drowned in the exclamations of several persons, who said,

" Here's the police !—here's the police !"

In another moment Bernard Varley was staved off Twitter by force of blows, and both combatants were secured by two stout city officers, either of whom would have made but little matter of a contention with the two belligerents at once.

" What's the matter ?—what's the row ?" exclaimed the officer who held Twitter.

"Come, sir, no violence—you must not resist the city police, or my lord mayor will have to deal with you," said the other to Varley, who made several demonstrations to renew the attack upon Twitter; but the policeman intinated that would not be allowed, by gently drawing him back by the collar, in a mode that rendered question as to the right of procedure useless.

"That man," cried Twitter, "he's nearly killed me."

"Why, you don't look as if he had used you gently. What's the meaning of this?"

VARLEY'S HORROR AT FINDING AN ACCOUNT OF TWITTER'S RESCUE.

"That scoundrel has robbed me."

"It is a lie," screamed Twitter, furiously; "he knows it's a lie."

"Do you give him into custody for robbery, sir?" exclaimed the officer to Varley.

"He dares not," vehemently exclaimed Twitter, though he trembled so violently in every limb from exertion and anxiety; "he dares not."

"I do; he knows he has robbed me."

N . 68.

" You know that you, Bernard Varley, are more likely to be hanged, than I am to commit a robbery, and that I see will be your fate before long."

" God bless me," exclaimed one of the officers ; " is this Mr. Varley from York ?"

Bernard Varley trembled in every limb with passion, but by a strong effort he subdued it, for the last sentence and Twitter's growing violence and audacity showed him the brink of the precipice on which he stood, and in reply to the officer's demand, if he should lock Samuel Twitter up, he replied,

" No, no—never mind now ; I have another way to deal with the scoundrel. Recollect, Samuel Twitter, life is short and uncertain—your new-found treasure may want an owner."

Though Twitter was nigh sinking when he met Bernard Varley's gaze, yet he replied,

" Remember, Bernard Varley, the slightest act of yours may bring ruin upon your own head, and then your long life of scheming becomes too short to enable you to enjoy the fruits of it."

" Farewell, Samuel Twitter," said Varley.

" Oh, don't trouble yourself about that," exclaimed Twitter ; " I suppose we love each other—eh ?"

Bernard Varley turned and left the spot. Calling a coach, he was quickly on his road to his hotel, and Twitter had followed his example, thinking it safest, and being desirous of digesting his other plans.

CHAPTER CL.

THE SINGULAR MEETING WITH ROWLAND PERCY.

One evening immediately succeeding the events we have just recorded, Varley passed out into the street, so absorbed in thought that he hardly noticed that a wretched night had set in.

At length the rain fell so thickly that he was fain to get into a doorway for refuge, where his reflections assumed as gloomy an aspect as the weather ; for towards the close of the day the wind, which had shifted round the entire compass now seemed to settle in the south, and blew with a freshness that many thought would carry rain, if any were likely to fall, off, though the clouds had been collecting fearfully for some hours.

The moon was near the wane, and her light was far from powerful, yet it was sufficient to show that there was a vast body of clouds passing beneath her ; they hurried onward with a speed that appeared astonishing, considering the heavy mass of aqueous vapour with which they were charged.

The wind came up with increased violence as the evening set in, and scarcely had the street lamps been lit when something like a falling mist was felt by those who were in the streets, and they hurried on with an increase of speed, having a wholesome dread of the heavy shower that threatened.

At such a moment when the wind howls and roars down the chimneys, those who sit anxiously by the small fire tremble with apprehension for the unfortunate member or members of the family who are likely to be exposed to its influence, for the poor and needy, the ill in health, the ill-clad, and ill-fed, are ever those who have to bear the greatest hardships, and bear the most frequent and the longest enduring exposures to the inclemency of the world.

'Tis then the passengers hurry onwards with hasty steps, in hopes to reach their estinations ere the wrath of the heavens shall fall upon them, and in hopes of getting through their daily toils and labours a little earlier, that they may change the discomfort of the streets for the warmth of the fireside at home.

The man of pleasure, the hunter after amusement, the mere perambulator, have now no inclination to indulge in their peculiar propensities, unless, indeed, they be housed at some midnight tavern, from which they find their way not until long after midnight, or nearer morning.

The rain, which was at first thought likely to discontinue, as the wind still blew fresh and hard, still continued, and, in fact, increased gradually, instead of abating.

The shops were now all lighted up, so that, notwithstanding the dark obscurity of the heavens, there was a certain life and gaiety in the principal thoroughfares, that contrasted strongly with the dripping forms of the unfortunate pedestrians who had been compelled to weather the storm.

Save these, the streets were deserted and bare, and the bye streets were dreary and dark also, for the few lamps that gave a dim light rendered them, if possible, more dreary and dark, and none passed through them save the wretched inhabitants.

There were but few vehicles of any description, and those public ones; and these dashed onwards with unusual speed, and each moment decreased in quantity, till at length the main streets alone presented the spectacle of a few breathing creatures, rational and irrational.

The howling of the wind still continued, and the rain, too, beat with force against the houses, rendering the contrast of within and without the greater; the sound of the heavy pattering and splashing of the rain was monotonous and dreary, and the shops were fast closing; for though not late, such was the general desertion of the streets that it was hopeless to keep them open any longer, and thus what was before dull and dreary now became very nearly dark.

The light of heaven was not to be seen, and the closed shops presented no brilliant glare of light; all that remained was the solitary spectacle of the distant lamps, whose very light gave the solemn stillness and deserted appearance a still more melancholy and dreary aspect.

Sure such a night as this was not fit for the traveller who desired to pursue his journey, but rather to stay by the ingle nook and listen to the pattering of the rain without.

In the course, then, of about half an hour the torrent of rain sensibly abated, and Varley was about to leave a place of shelter and hurry to his hotel, when some one turned into the door and commenced knocking the moisture from his clothes.

Varley made an effort to pass him. They met face to face. An exclamation simultaneously burst from each of them—Bernard Varley and the stranger.

"Rowland Percy!" shouted Varley.

CHAPTER CLI.

THE STRUGGLE FOR FREEDOM—THE PLACE OF REFUGE.—ROWLAND'S CRITICAL SITUATION.

PERHAPS in the whole of London no two men could have encountered with the same feelings towards each other as Rowland Percy and Bernard Varley. Feelings so very different in themselves, and yet so intense and vivid in their manifestation.

There was no man in the great city that Varley cared to meet but Rowland Percy There was scarcely one that Percy cared to avoid but Varley, and yet by one of those strange accidents which brings people together when such a circumstance might be least expected, here had they met, face to face, in a narrow doorway, as if by appointment.

After the first exclamations of surprise on each side, the energies of both seemed for a few moments paralysed by the intense surprise of the sudden encounter. Rowland was the first to recover himself, and feeling in its full force the critical nature of his situation, he drew back, determined to rely for safety upon his speed, for the thought occurred to him, that he might have been watched, and that, possibly, Varley had plenty of assistance at hand to ensure his capture.

"Villain! Heaven will save me yet!" he cried.

He, however, had to turn in the narrow doorway before he could fly from the spot, and before he could do so, Varley, with a cry of exultation, sprang upon him like an enraged tiger, and clasped him round the waist, shouting,—

"Help! help! help, to seize the murderer, Rowland Percy! Help—police! A murderer—a murderer! Ha, ha! caught at last! Triumph—triumph. Help! help! help!"

After a desperate struggle, Rowland Percy released himself from the iron grasp of Varley. He fled from the place, pursued by his enemy, who shouted for help to secure the murderer.

"Help! help!" he cried. "Murder—blood—blood! Hold him! See he flies—help! Secure the murderer, Rowland Percy, the murderer! A thousand pounds for him, alive or dead! Kill him! Help! help! Murder! murder!"

These cries brought many people from their houses, and quite appalled the few chance passengers who heard them. They could not but think that Bernard Varley was mad, or that the retreating man he pursued was some great criminal indeed. At least a dozen joined in the chace, and added their shouts to those of Varley.

"Stop him—stop him!" sounded from many throats, and poor innocent Rowland found himself thus fearfully hunted through the streets of London, as if he had been some wild beast that had suddenly made its appearance in the haunts of man.

Flushed, heated, and excited, he rushed on with amazing swiftness, he knew not whither. Down one street and up another, heedless of his course, so that he kept a-head of those who would have brought him to death and to despair. A narrow turning now presented itself to his view, which was very steep, but he would not swerve from it, as he had partially turned into it, and with increased speed, from the descent, he darted on. The place was of a dirty and squalid appearance, inhabited by low brokers, several of whom made a dart at the flying man, and in consequence of his speed, got rolled in the mud for their pains, or shot on one side with a great crash among their furniture and crockery which were exposed for sale.

But if Rowland had the advantage of increased rapidity in descending this thoroughfare, he soon found that he had an ascent before him of a steep character. He heard the loud shouts of his pursuers, and each moment he fancied those shouts came plainer to his ear, and that his capture was certain, although he was in reality increasing his distance from them by the tremendous speed with which he ran. Indeed, had he known the neighbourhood well, and all its resources of courts and alleys, there is no doubt he would soon have thrown those who were hunting him off the scent, but he was in such knowledge wofully deficient, and the consequence was that in taking a turning he was solely guided by the chance impulse of the moment.

When Rowland reached the summit of the hill he had been compelled to climb, he found a choice of several streets open to him, but being now alive to the danger of being pounced upon and captured, if he passed down a street of shops, he chose the quietest throughfare he could see, which happened to be Hatton-garden, and down that he darted at a tremendous rate.

He had got two thirds of the way towards Holborn before his pursuers arrived at the corner of Hatton-garden, but there they were informed by several officious persons which way the fugitive had gone, and the chase was joined by several constables from the police office near by, who, hearing the riot and alarm, eagerly took part in the business.

To reach Holborn did not take Rowland many minutes, and then when he saw the steep hill before him, he thought it prudent to dart across the carriage way into some obscurer street, which might lead him from so very public a place.

This plan he immediately adopted, but it appeared that the clamours of his pursuers in Hatton-garden had reached the ears of the people passing in Holborn and a little knot of persons had collected to see what was the matter.

None of them attempted to seize Rowland, and he got over the roadway in safety, but the moment he did so, a rush was made from the watch-house close to St. Andrew's church of several constables who tried to seize him. To escape them he diverged a little from his course, and stumbled over the steps of the church.

One man seized him, but Rowland shook him off, and with a feeling of desperation rushed up the steps, and finding the iron gates partially open, he went in, nor stopped till he reached the church-door.

A man was standing just within the porch with a lantern in one hand, and a large key in the other.

" Hilloa!" he said. " Who are you?"

" An innocent man," cried Rowland. " Aid me as you hope for Heaven's mercy."

" Hilloa! hilloa! You are a rogue—come, come, be off."

" Stop him—stop him!" cried dozens of voices. "Seize the murderer—seize him—the murderer!"

" Gracious!,' cried the man with the key; " my flesh creeps—they mean you. Here he is—come on—fire! murder! thieves! Here he is—come up. I've cotched him."

With one blow Rowland dashed the lantern from his hand, at the same moment that he wrested the key from him.

" I'm a dead man," cried the beadle, for it was no other than that functionary himself, who had been making some visit to the church in the course of his onerous duties. " I'm a dead man—save my soul."

He then threw himself down on his back and commenced kicking with his feet like a crab newly captured, and reciting the church catechism.

Rowland found the church door unlocked, for when he arrived so suddenly, the beadle had only just emerged, and had been on the point of locking it. In a moment Rowland passed into the sacred edifice, and locked the massive door on the inside.

Oh ! how sudden and how great was the transition from the noise and riot of the streets—the glare of the lights and the eager shouts of his pursuers—to the calm and beautiful stillness of the church. In an instant the very atmosphere of that place of holiness appeared to spread a delicious calm over the heart of the poor fugitive. There seemed to reign above, around, and about him, the spirit of gentleness and resignation. The air too was delightfully cool, and as it played sweetly upon the burning brow of the harassed Rowland, he could not help exclaiming,—

" Surely, surely, Heaven, which knows my innocence, has, in its mercy, sent me here for succour and assistance."

The busy hum of the city seemed completely shut out, or came in such indistinct murmurs as made that deep solitude more strikingly apparent. A dim light came in from the windows, just enabling him, after a few moments, to see the objects around him, and to guide his course down the aisle easily.

He had scarcely any notion of what next could or would happen. How to escape from where he now was, should a search be made through the sacred edifice, he had no idea ; and yet he felt a sense of security in that building devoted to God, which only his innocence could impart to him, and from that moment he told himself that come what would—let what apparent evil fortune environ him that might, Heaven, would not allow him to suffer the death which it was sought by his erring fellow creatures to inflict wrongfully upon him.

Impressed with the calm holiness of the place, and grateful for the relief it had afforded him, Rowland opened the little gate leading to the communion table, and there he knelt and offered up a prayer to Heaven—not a prayer of supplication for the future, but a pure and holy acknowledgement of his reliance upon God's mercy and justice—such a prayer as a thinking man may offer to his Creator in his humbleness before the Majesty of power, goodness, and intellect to which he is not arrogant enough to dictate.

The persecuted, Rowland rose chastened but happier in spirit, and better prepared for any fate than he had ever been since the commencement of his long career of trouble. As he did so he was astonished by hearing a solemn strain from the organ, which with its sweet sounds filled the whole church with a very atmosphere of melody. The organist, though Rowland knew it not, was practising a new anthem.

CHAPTER CLII.

THE ARREST.—THE CONVEYANCE TO YORK.

WITH surprise and and admiration Rowland Percy listened to the strains of music that came from the organ. For a moment a superstitious feeling crossed his mind that surely at such a time it was played by no mortal hand, but full of enthusiasm as was his mind at that moment, he quickly dismissed such a supposition, and scarcely had he done so, when he was rudely recalled to the world and its concerns—its hopes and fears—its few joys, and deep distress by a violent hammering against the church door, and the confused hum of voices in the porch.

"They come, they come," he said, " and I shall assuredly be taken here. What means have I of escape from this sacred edifice ? I am lost—lost."

Rowland crept as close to the church door as he could. It opened inwards, and should they force the lock, as doubtless they would, he thought there would be just a weak chance of escaping out of the building when, as was probable, his pursuers made a rush into it which would carry them past him. This was a very forlorn hope, but it was his only one, and a drowning man will eagerly snatch even at a straw.

As Rowland anticipated, a rush was made into the body of the church ; and that rush too, was the more vehement, because the figure of the organist was just dimly discerned coming slowly up the aisle. But there were more experienced officers now in pursuit of Rowland than those who went headlong into the church, and such remained at the door quite satisfied that the prisoner could not escape, and content to take him should he, as they thought highly probable, dodge those within, and attempt to leave the building.

Rowland waited but for an instant. He saw the organist seized, and then he thought himself in possession of a good chance of escape, and he made the rush he had projected.

Alas ! 'twas in vain ; in an instant he found himself seized by two powerful men, to shake off the hold of whom was a matter of impossibility.

With a deep sigh he surrendered himself to his fate, and made no useless struggle for release. He said but one word, and that was—

" Miranda !"

In another moment Bernard Varley pushed his way forward, and folding his arms across his chest, he stood within three paces of Rowland Percy with such a diabolical expression of exultation upon his face, that it was horrible to look upon. However, he was smeared with blood and dirt ; his apparel torn, and one side of his face, from the punishment Rowland had given him was frightfully swollen. A more awful-looking object could not be conceived.

" At last—at last !" he cried ; " at last hunted down, Rowland Percy !—murderer and my enemy ! Ha, ha, ha ! at last caught. Death, death ! Can you escape it now ? Dream of the scaffold, and all its frightful paraphernalia, until the reality bursts upon your sight. Die—die ! and carry with you to the grave my curse."

" Impious, wretched man," replied Rowland. " A thousand deaths, or a thousand scaffolds to the innocent man, could not make up the sum of the mental tortures which are yours now, which may be yours for all time to come. I am hunted down, Bernard Varley, and yet even now in this extremity of my fortunes, I can shudder and pity you."

The officers now interfered, and conveyed their prisoner in safety to the police-office, in the yard of which he was locked up in a cell.

The next day broke to poor Rowland Percy in the cell, with all the horrors of hopeless imprisonment.

His morning meal was coarse and disgusting to him, though had he been at liberty he could have eaten a much worse, but the knowledge that it was prison diet was poison.

However, Rowland Percy did eat; he knew on that day he should have to go through an ordeal that would, short as it was likely to be, require some little nerve to go through, for on that day he would be brought up for the purpose of being identified. The hour came round, and Percy was quickly placed at the bar.

One of the officers explained to the presiding magistrate the state of the case—that the prisoner, Rowland Percy, had been convicted of murder at the York assizes, and condemned to suffer death, but that he had escaped from the condemned cell, and was now recaptured.

"Have you evidence of his identy?" inquired the magistrate of the officer.

"Yes, your worship, Mr. Varley, the prosecutor in the case, is here to swear to the man."

"Then let him be sworn."

Varley, accordingly came forward, and, with a smile of fiendish malice, took his station in the witness-box.

"Do you know the prisoner, Mr. Varley?"

"Yes, I do. He is the same Rowland Percy who was condemned to death at York, and afterwards escaped from his prison."

"Well," said the magistrate, "then all I can do is to order his detention and return to York."

"He has escaped once, your worship," said Varley, deferentially, to the magistrate, "and may do so again, especially as he is well known to be leagued with highwaymen and housebreakers, and others of desperate character."

"Then a sufficient escort must be provided; those who have any connection with the York police in London must look to that part of the affair. I can only order him to be sent to York under their care, and I would advise you yourself, Mr. Varley, to go with them, since your evidence may be required when he reaches that place, to identify him anew, and then his execution will immediately follow."

Varley bowed and left the box, and Rowland Percy was removed from the bar. All had occurred in a very short space of time, and before many hours had passed over, a post-chaise and a strong escort was got ready, and the order for Rowland's removal, and the delivery of his body to the care of the York police, being produced, he was placed in it, securely handcuffed, and an officer on either side of him, while Bernard Varley and several mounted officers rode on either side of the carriage, all well armed.

The cavalcade, after a long and t resome jurney arrived safely at York; Rowland was once more consigned to the castle, and the unhappy Miranda made acquainted with all that had taken place.

The news of the apprehension of Rowland Percy spread with a most marvellous rapidity throughout York. His name was familiar to every one, and his history had so much of romantic interest attached to it, that scarcely any one in the county was so indifferent as not to have an ardent wish to see the man, concerning whose guilt or innocence there was such diversity of opinion, and who had, for so long a period, successfully resisted and set at nought a pursuit dictated by malice, revenge, passion, and stimulated by enormous rewards.

No wonder, that when the news spread from mouth to mouth, that the celebrated Rowland Percy was again arrested and brought to the original scene of his trial and condemnation, all who had leisure, or could call half an hour their own, should flock to the court to obtain a passing glance at the prisoner, and if possible, too,

Miranda, who, it was likewise known, had followed him through all his dangers and wanderings with a degree of faithfulness that had no parallel.

Hastily, and even rudely, Rowland was pushed into the presence of the assembled magistrates, and a very transient glance the crowd outside the court must have had of the prisoner; perchance, the violence and roughness with which Rowland Percy found himself treated by the York police, arose, in some measure, from a feeling among them, that they had, as Mr. Jones would have said, rather made a mess of the affair before, and let Percy escape from their hands a great deal easier than he should have been permitted to do.

Miranda had effected an entrance, with the assistance of Mr. Anderson, into the crowded court, over which she ran her eyes till they rested on the pale, jaded looking countenance of Rowland Percy, who seemed, by his expression, to have now given up all hope whatever.

He saw her at once, and a momentary light seemed to beam over his face; but it was like the pale glimpse of sunshine which for an instant will gleam forth on a wintry lanscape, reminding those who see it of the beauty and the brilliance of other days, and likewise the sadder for the comparison.

She would fain have reached the spot where he stood; but she was firmly repulsed by the officers, who said their orders were to allow no one whatever to speak to the prisoner, and that a particular direction had been given that she was to be prevented from holding the slightest communication with him.

The proceedings of the court were conducted with due judical form; the identity of the prisoner was sworn to, and he was handed over to the sheriff, that the law might take its course.

Mr. Anderson now addresed the sheriff saying, "I wish to know if the prisoner's friends can make an application to the secretary of state?"

The sheriff shook his head.

"I dare not delay," he said. "The execution must take place to-morrow morning."

A stifled cry burst from Miranda, and Mr. Anderson turned hastily to her, saying,—

"Hush! hush! For Heaven's sake, control your feelings. Be guided by me —say nothing."

With a low moan, Miranda sunk into a seat, and covered her face with her hands, while Rowland Percy appeared quite unconscious of all else, as he kept his eyes rivetted upon her with a painful interest.

"Mr. Sheriff, will you remove your prisoner?" said the magistrate.

"Ay, to death?" cried Varley.

"Miranda! Miranda!" said Rowland, and he stretched forth his arms over the bar at which he stood.

She sprang towards him, and no one hindered her.

"Rowland! Rowland! They yet dare not murder you. Heaven is merciful and just."

"Farewell, dearest—best ——"

Every one in the court was deeply affected, and for about two minutes no interruption was offered to the lovers. Then the sheriff nodded to the officers, and Rowland was taken away. With one piercing shriek, Miranda fainted on the floor of the court.

CHAPTER CLIV.

TWITTER'S WRITTEN CONFESSION.—THE ROBBERY.

WE must now return for a while to Twitter, whom we have lost sight of for some time. He no sooner got perfectly free from Bernard Varley, after his quarrel and fight in the street, and also of the mob, who for some distance continued to follow him, than he revolved over several circumstances in his mind, and he came to the resolution to put the plan he had long since formed into execution. Going to his hotel he gave orders for a chase to be instantly prepared to take him to Liverpool.

After he had arranged all for his immediate departure, so soon as the post-chaise should be announced, he called for writing materials, and after some hesitation he began to write. That writing was his confession of the murder, and other events that occured at the Grange.

Twitter carfully directed this paper to the Lord Mayor of the City of York, and sealed it up, though he had written the body of it in great haste and even perturbation of spirit, for every sound caused a start, and the recital of his own crimes brought bead-like drops of moisture upon his brow. At length he secured the packet carfully in his bosom, and as he extinguished the taper he had used to seal it, a waiter entered the room to say the carriage was ready.

"I am ready," exclaimed Twitter, as he rose, and pointing to a portmanteau and trunk, desired that they should be placed in it, and then following himself, he was soon safely shut in.

No sooner was he inside, than he hastily pulled up the blinds on either side, fearing of meeting by accident his arch enemy, Bernard Varley, and calling to the post-boy, he said—

No. 69

"Drive on fast as you can," and in another moment he was rattling over the stones at a rate that excited the attention of everybody who came in the road.

Often would he place his hands on different parts of his person where he had secreted his money, and congratulate himself on the success of all his plans, and glorify in the idea that he was a much better schemer than Bernard Varley after all, for his, Twitter's plans, would all succeed, while Bernard Varley's would lead him to destruction.

As the night closed around, the town of Liverpool came in sight, and, ere long the post-chaise rattled over the stones, and stopped at one of the first inns, not far from the docks, called the Royal George.

After some delay here a boat was obtained, with four stout seamen, and Twitter having settled his bill at the hotel, and requested the landlord to post his letter to the Mayor of York, put out into the Mersey, with the hope of discovering the Zephyr, the yacht which it may be remembered Varley had purchased, and had ordered to lie off for him.

The boatmen, in deference to Twitter's promises of good pay, stood out to sea a considerable distance, but without discovering any sign of the vessel he sought. At length the wind got up, with an evident approach of foul weather, and the men found all their exertions and endeavous to return to the Mersey were fruitless; they were in a dreadful position, in an open boat, and in a rough sea, and looking upon Twitter as the cause of their misfortune, they did not spare their oaths and abuse. Twitter himself was sunk in despair, and had he possessed sufficient courage, would have jumped overboard.

In this way they continued beating about till day began to break, and just as they were about to give up altogether, under the pressure of fatigue, they were discovered by a small sloop, which bore down to them; the boatmen appeared to be recognised by the crew of the vessel, and with Twitter were drawn up and placed in comparative safety on the sloop's deck.

Twitter soon began to perceive that he was in a smuggling craft, which did not tend to his comfort, especially when he found his boatmen in private talk with the commander of the sloop, who bent very sinister glances on Twitter. He was however, kindly invited into the smoky cabin, and thankfully received a glass of hot spirits and water, which in his wet condition was invaluable. It appeared, however, that something stronger—far stronger than spirits had been infused into the glass, for he shortly fell into a profound slumber, nor did he awaken for many hours. When he did awake, the sun was high in the heavens, and instead of being at sea, he was stretched by the side of a ditch, on a road towards the river side, not many miles from the town of Livepool. His exact position, however, was unknown to Twitter; but on examining his clothes, in which he had, as he thought, so securely hidden his money, he found that he was robbed of every farthing.

It would be in vain for us to attempt to describe the horror of the wretched man; we shall merely state then, that finding himself in that deplorable condition, with no resources to aid him in escaping from England, he determined not to remain anywhere near Liverpool, but to beg his way into some other part of the country, and wait in fear and trembling the course of events.

With this view he rose, and although stiff and faint with hunger, he made his way a few miles along the road, not daring to ask where he was, or where he was going, and seeking charity at wayside houses, from some of which he was turned with threats, while from others he received commiseration and assistance. At length he overtook a waggoner as night came on, and humbly solicited a ride, which the kind-hearted countryman after some hesitation allowed him.

When Samuel Twitter sunk down among the straw and litter that was in the waggon, he felt a sensation of relief, for he was wretchedly uneasy, and, moreover, beneath the ample canopy that was above his head, and nestled among the straw, he was secure from that curious observation with which he thought everybody regarded him.

His unpleasant thoughts did not prevent him from again sinking off to sleep, for the effects of the drug had not left him. And so he travelled on.

CHAPTER CLV.

THE HAPPY CONCLUSION.

WE now hasten to the conclusion of our tale. Twitter went on, not caring where eating what provision he had with him, and getting out occasionally for a draught of water, till he arrived at the waggon's destination, when to his intense surprise and horror he found himself in York, while he had secretly hoped he was nearing London! There was no help for it, however, and he was obliged to get out; it being an early hour when he arrived, he found great crowds in the streets, and soon ascertained that the morning of Rowland Percy's execution had arrived, but that it had been stayed, owing to the receipt of a communication by the mayor, and this the horror-stricken wretch felt convinced was the confession he had posted from Liverpool. He was ready to sink to the earth with agitation, which was if possible increased, when on turning a corner suddenly, he came in contact with his old tormentor, Jones, who had been let off by the London magistrates with a few days detention.

"What Sammy, my tulip," cried Jones; "you are just the very identical individual that was born to made my fortune. Why, money's bid for you, Sammy, and so you must do me the honour of taking a small walk with me, and inspecting the beauties of the castle of York, this morning. No, no denial," continued Jones, as Twitter would have shrunk from him, but had not strength to run, "I'm not proud, Sammy, and I don't mind walking as far with you; cos, why—there's five hundred golden reasons for it, my little man."

Mr. Jones thus enigmatically alluded to a reward of £500 which had been that morning offered for the apprehension of Samuel Twitter; and Twitter was not released from the iron grasp of Jones till he was safely given into custody, his tempter and fellow criminal, Varley, being already in durance. Varley, anxious to inculpate Twitter, admitted his own guilt, and insisted that Twitter was equally guilty.

A special mounted messenger was despatched to London, with an account from the sheriff of the whole affair, to the secretary of state, in order that Rowland Percy might be released in due form, although no bar was placed to his liberty in the meantime; and that very evening he supped with Mr. Anderson, where were guests, the mayor of York, the governor of the castle, the sheriff, and several respectable inhabitants of the city, who had all had a strong opinion of Rowland's innocence. And Miranda—was not she there, and happy? Yes, so happy, that her eyes, whenever they turned upon Rowland, would fill with tears, and she could scarcely believe herself so blessed. Before the party separated, a messenger came to the governor of the prison, to say that Varley was nearly raving mad, and that he had confessed to the will of Sir George Rankley, upon which he had taken possession of the Grange, being forged. This declaration put an end to all doubt on that subject.

* * * * * * *

Rowland and Miranda had nobody to consult but themselves about their marriage, and as that happened to be a point upon which they were quite unanimous, the ceremony took place within three days of that dreadful one on which it appeared almost impossible Rowland Percy could be saved from a dreadful and ignominious death.

The party were passing through the church, when a tall figure emerged from a pew, and coming up to Miranda, said,—

"Heaven bless you. May the joy of this day be only equalled by those that are to come. Farewell!"

"Witlet!" exclaimed Miranda and Rowland, both at once, and then the latter added, as he seized the hand of him who had done so much for both of them—

"My friend, I have made the greatest exertions to discover you. Where have you hidden yourself since I have been free myself to search for you? Remember that my house is your house, and that, do what I may, I never can wholly repay the great obligations I am under to you.'

"Nor I," said Miranda. "Witlet, but for you, I should not now feel the glow of happiness that irradiates my heart at this moment."

"Thank Heaven!" said Witlet, "you are happy, Miranda Rankley. Let my own fate be what it may, I—I——"

Emotion impeded his utterance, and waving his hand, he would have hurried away, but Rowland Percy detained him, saying—

"No, Witlet, you shall not go—stay with us. Leave not a gloom upon our hearts on your account on this most auspicious and happy day."

"You forget," whispered Witlet. "I am a highwayman. I am a hunted, persecuted man. I am a convict, and even now my liberty is at stake."

The sheriff, at this moment, entered the church, and advancing to Rowland, he said—

"Mr. Percy, the messenger from the secretary of state has just now arrived. Your own free pardon he brings, as well as a free pardon, which I and the mayor specially requested, for Edward Witlet and Jones, so that they are both free from this moment, and I have only to hope that they will try to lead a different life for the future, convinced as I am, that they are men possessed of sterling good qualities, if they will but make a proper use of them."

* * * * * * *

Both Twitter and Varley were arraigned for murder at the ensuing assizes, and declared guilty on their own confessions. They were executed amid the universal execrations of an immense assemblage of persons—the only circumstance worthy of record, being, that Varley, even on the scaffold, made an effort to strike Twitter, to whom he entertained so deadly a hatred.

Miranda sold the Grange estates, for they were too replete with painful recollections, to become the dwelling-place of her and her husband. They then bought a delightful property near Devon, where, in the course of a few years, several little Percys gambolled beneath the shadow of the majestic trees that adorned their father's estate.

Ned Witlet, after Miranda's marriage, rambled about a good deal; but at last he took a fancy to a farm, some two or three miles only from Percy's estate, and there he settled, married, and led the life he was well calculated to adorn—namely, that of an English country gentleman.

Jones, when Percy bought his new property, was duly installed as head gamekeeper and ranger, and everything else he chose to call himself, his principal duty consisting, when we last heard of him, in teaching Percy's eldest son running, climbing, shooting, fishing, and all sorts of miscellaneous mischief.

And Miranda, how sweetly and beautifully did her old smile come back to her. Need we say that all who had breathed a kind word to her or Percy during their affliction, had cause to bless her? Oh, no—our readers are too well acquainted wth the noble, tender, devoted heroic heart of Miranda, the Heiress of the Grange.